The Invincible
Miss Marple

THE INVINCIBLE MISS MARPLE

including
The Body in the Library
A Murder Is Announced
Murder with Mirrors

By AGATHA CHRISTIE

Garden City, New York

Contents

The Body
in the
Library

1

MRS. BANTRY was dreaming. Her sweet peas had just taken a First at the flower show. The vicar, dressed in cassock and surplice, was giving out the prizes in church. His wife wandered past, dressed in a bathing suit, but, as is the blessed habit of dreams, this fact did not arouse the disapproval of the parish in the way it would assuredly have done in real life. Mrs. Bantry was enjoying her dream a good deal. She usually did enjoy those early-morning dreams that were terminated by the arrival of early-morning tea. Somewhere in her inner consciousness was an awareness of the usual early-morning noises of the household. The rattle of the curtain rings on the stairs as the housemaid drew them, the noises of the second housemaid's dustpan and brush in the passage outside. In the distance the heavy noise of the front-door bolt being drawn back.

Another day was beginning. In the meantime she must extract as much pleasure as possible from the flower show, for already its dreamlike quality was becoming apparent.

Below her was the noise of the big wooden shutters in the drawing room being opened. She heard it, yet did not hear it. For quite half an hour longer the usual household noises would go on, discreet, subdued, not disturbing because they were so familiar. They would culminate in a swift, controlled sound of footsteps along the passage, the rustle of a print dress, the subdued chink of tea things as the tray was deposited on the table outside, then the soft knock and the entry of Mary to draw the curtains. In her sleep Mrs. Bantry frowned. Something disturbing was penetrating through the dream state, something out of its time. Footsteps along the passage, footsteps that were too hurried and too soon. Her ears listened unconsciously for the chink of china, but there was no chink of china. The knock came at the door. Automatically, from the depths of her dream, Mrs. Bantry said, "Come in." The door opened; now there would be the chink of curtain rings as the curtains were drawn back.

But there was no chink of curtain rings. Out of the dim green light Mary's voice came, breathless, hysterical. "Oh, ma'am, oh, ma'am, there's a body in the library!" And then, with a hysterical burst of sobs, she rushed out of the room again.

Mrs. Bantry sat up in bed. Either her dream had taken a very odd turn or else—or else Mary had really rushed into the room and had said—

incredibly fantastic!—that there was a body in the library. "Impossible," said Mrs. Bantry to herself. "I must have been dreaming." But even as she said it, she felt more and more certain that she had not been dreaming; that Mary, her superior self-controlled Mary, had actually uttered those fantastic words.

Mrs. Bantry reflected a minute and then applied an urgent conjugal elbow to her sleeping spouse. "Arthur, Arthur, wake up." Colonel Bantry grunted, muttered and rolled over on his side. "Wake up, Arthur. Did you hear what she said?"

"Very likely," said Colonel Bantry indistinctly. "I quite agree with you, Dolly," and promptly went to sleep again.

Mrs. Bantry shook him. "You've got to listen. Mary came in and said that there was a body in the library."

"Eh, what?"

"A body in the library."

"Who said so?"

"Mary."

Colonel Bantry collected his scattered faculties and proceeded to deal with the situation. He said, "Nonsense, old girl! You've been dreaming."

"No, I haven't. I thought so, too, at first. But I haven't. She really came in and said so."

"Mary came in and said there was a body in the library?"

"Yes."

"But there couldn't be," said Colonel Bantry.

"No—no, I suppose not," said Mrs. Bantry doubtfully. Rallying, she went on, "But then why did Mary say there was?"

"She can't have."

"She did."

"You must have imagined it."

"I didn't imagine it."

Colonel Bantry was by now thoroughly awake and prepared to deal with the situation on its merits. He said kindly, "You've been dreaming, Dolly. It's that detective story you were reading—*The Clue of the Broken Match.* You know, Lord Edgbaston finds a beautiful blonde dead on the library hearthrug. Bodies are always being found in libraries in books. I've never known a case in real life."

"Perhaps you will now," said Mrs. Bantry. "Anyway, Arthur, you've got to get up and see."

"But really, Dolly, it must have been a dream. Dreams often do seem wonderfully vivid when you first wake up. You feel quite sure they're true."

"I was having quite a different sort of dream—about a flower show and the vicar's wife in a bathing dress—something like that." Mrs. Bantry jumped out of bed and pulled back the curtains. The light of a fine autumn day flooded the room. "I did not dream it," said Mrs. Bantry firmly. "Get up at once, Arthur, and go downstairs and see about it."

"You want me to go downstairs and ask if there's a body in the library? I shall look a fool."

"You needn't ask anything," said Mrs. Bantry. "If there is a body—and of course it's just possible that Mary's gone mad and thinks she sees things that aren't there—well, somebody will tell you soon enough. You won't have to say a word."

Grumbling, Colonel Bantry wrapped himself in his dressing gown and left the room. He went along the passage and down the staircase. At the foot of it was a little knot of huddled servants; some of them were sobbing. The butler stepped forward impressively. "I'm glad you have come, sir. I have directed that nothing should be done until you came. Will it be in order for me to ring up the police, sir?"

"Ring 'em up about what?"

The butler cast a reproachful glance over his shoulder at the tall young woman who was weeping hysterically on the cook's shoulder. "I understood, sir, that Mary had already informed you. She said she had done so."

Mary gasped out, "I was so upset, I don't know what I said! It all came over me again and my legs gave way and my insides turned over! Finding it like that—Oh, oh, oh!"

She subsided again onto Mrs. Eccles, who said, "There, there, my dear," with some relish.

"Mary is naturally somewhat upset, sir, having been the one to make the gruesome discovery," explained the butler. "She went into the library, as usual, to draw the curtains, and—and almost stumbled over the body."

"Do you mean to tell me," demanded Colonel Bantry, "that there's a dead body in my library—my library?"

The butler coughed. "Perhaps, sir, you would like to see for yourself."

"Hullo, 'ullo, 'ullo. Police station here. Yes, who's speaking?" Police Constable Palk was buttoning up his tunic with one hand while the other held the telephone receiver. "Yes, yes, Gossington Hall. Yes? . . . Oh, good morning, sir." Police Constable Palk's tone underwent a slight modification. It became less impatiently official, recognizing the generous patron of the police sports and the principal magistrate of the district.

"Yes, sir? What can I do for you? . . . I'm sorry, sir, I didn't quite catch —A body, did you say? . . . Yes? . . . Yes, if you please, sir. . . . That's right, sir. . . . Young woman not known to you, you say? . . . Quite, sir. . . . Yes, you can leave it all to me."

Police Constable Palk replaced the receiver, uttered a long-drawn whistle and proceeded to dial his superior officer's number. Mrs. Palk looked in from the kitchen, whence proceeded an appetizing smell of frying bacon. "What is it?"

"Rummiest thing you ever heard of," replied her husband. "Body of a young woman found up at the Hall. In the colonel's library."

"Murdered?"

"Strangled, so he says."

"Who was she?"

"The colonel says he doesn't know her from Adam."

"Then what was she doing in 'is library?"

Police Constable Palk silenced her with a reproachful glance and spoke officially into the telephone. "Inspector Slack? Police Constable Palk here. A report has just come in that the body of a young woman was discovered this morning at seven-fifteen—"

Miss Marple's telephone rang when she was dressing. The sound of it flurried her a little. It was an unusual hour for her telephone to ring. So well ordered was her prim spinster's life that unforeseen telephone calls were a source of vivid conjecture. "Dear me," said Miss Marple, surveying the ringing instrument with perplexity. "I wonder who that can be?"

Nine o'clock to nine-thirty was the recognized time for the village to make friendly calls to neighbors. Plans for the day, invitations, and so on, were always issued then. The butcher had been known to ring up just before nine if some crisis in the meat trade had occurred. At intervals during the day spasmodic calls might occur, though it was considered bad form to ring up after nine-thirty at night.

It was true that Miss Marple's nephew, a writer, and therefore erratic, had been known to ring up at the most peculiar times; once as late as ten minutes to midnight. But whatever Raymond West's eccentricities, early rising was not one of them. Neither he nor anyone of Miss Marple's acquaintance would be likely to ring up before eight in the morning. Actually a quarter to eight. Too early even for a telegram, since the post office did not open until eight. "It must be," Miss Marple decided, "a wrong number." Having decided this, she advanced to the impatient instrument and quelled its clamor by picking up the receiver. "Yes?" she said.

"Is that you, Jane?"

Miss Marple was much surprised. "Yes, it's Jane. You're up very early, Dolly."

Mrs. Bantry's voice came, breathless and agitated, over the wire. "The most awful thing has happened."

"Oh, my dear!"

"We've just found a body in the library."

For a moment Miss Marple thought her friend had gone mad. "You've found a what?"

"I know. One doesn't believe it, does one? I mean I thought they only happened in books. I had to argue for hours with Arthur this morning before he'd even go down and see."

Miss Marple tried to collect herself. She demanded breathlessly, "But whose body is it?"

"It's a blonde."

"A what?"

"A blonde. A beautiful blonde—like books again. None of us have ever seen her before. She's just lying there in the library, dead. That's why you've got to come up at once."

"You want me to come up?"

"Yes, I'm sending the car down for you."

Miss Marple said doubtfully, "Of course, dear, if you think I can be of any comfort to you—"

"Oh, I don't want comfort. But you're so good at bodies."

"Oh, no, indeed. My little successes have been mostly theoretical."

"But you're very good at murders. She's been murdered, you see; strangled. What I feel is that if one has got to have a murder actually happening in one's house, one might as well enjoy it, if you know what I mean. That's why I want you to come and help me find out who did it and unravel the mystery, and all that. It really is rather thrilling, isn't it?"

"Well, of course, my dear, if I can be of any help."

"Splendid! Arthur's being rather difficult. He seems to think I shouldn't enjoy myself about it at all. Of course, I do know it's very sad and all that, but then I don't know the girl—and when you've seen her you'll understand what I mean when I say she doesn't look real at all."

A little breathless, Miss Marple alighted from the Bantrys' car, the door of which was held open for her by the chauffeur. Colonel Bantry came out on the steps and looked a little surprised. "Miss Marple? Er—very pleased to see you."

"Your wife telephoned to me," explained Miss Marple.

"Capital, capital. She ought to have someone with her. She'll crack up otherwise. She's putting a good face on things at the moment, but you know what it is—"

At this moment Mrs. Bantry appeared and exclaimed, "Do go back and eat your breakfast, Arthur. Your bacon will get cold."

"I thought it might be the inspector arriving," explained Colonel Bantry.

"He'll be here soon enough," said Mrs. Bantry. "That's why it's important to get your breakfast first. You need it."

"So do you. Much better come and eat something, Dolly."

"I'll come in a minute," said Mrs. Bantry. "Go on, Arthur." Colonel Bantry was shooed back into the dining room rather like a recalcitrant hen. "Now!" said Mrs. Bantry with an intonation of triumph. "Come on."

She led the way rapidly along the long corridor to the east of the house. Outside the library door Constable Palk stood on guard. He intercepted Mrs. Bantry with a show of authority. "I'm afraid nobody is allowed in, madam. Inspector's orders."

"Nonsense, Palk," said Mrs. Bantry. "You know Miss Marple perfectly well." Constable Palk admitted to knowing Miss Marple. "It's very important that she should see the body," said Mrs. Bantry. "Don't be stupid, Palk. After all, it's my library, isn't it?"

Constable Palk gave way. His habit of giving in to the gentry was lifelong. The inspector, he reflected, need never know it. "Nothing must be touched or handled in any way," he warned the ladies.

"Of course not," said Mrs. Bantry impatiently. "We know that. You can come in and watch, if you like." Constable Palk availed himself of this permission. It had been his intention anyway. Mrs. Bantry bore her friend triumphantly across the library to the big old-fashioned fireplace. She said, with a dramatic sense of climax, "There!"

Miss Marple understood then just what her friend had meant when she said the dead girl wasn't real. The library was a room very typical of its owners. It was large and shabby and untidy. It had big, sagging armchairs, and pipes and books and estate papers laid out on the big table. There were one or two good old family portraits on the walls, and some bad Victorian water colors, and some would-be-funny hunting scenes. There was a big vase of flowers in the corner. The whole room was dim and mellow and casual. It spoke of long occupation and familiar use and of links with tradition.

And across the old bearskin hearthrug there was sprawled something new and crude and melodramatic. The flamboyant figure of a girl. A girl with unnaturally fair hair dressed up off her face in elaborate curls and rings. Her thin body was dressed in a backless evening dress of white spangled satin; the face was heavily made up, the powder standing out grotesquely on its blue, swollen surface, the mascara of the lashes lying thickly on the distorted cheeks, the scarlet of the lips looking like a gash. The fingernails were enameled a deep blood red, and so were the toenails in their cheap silver sandal shoes. It was a cheap, tawdry, flamboyant figure, most incongruous in the solid, old-fashioned comfort of Colonel Bantry's library. Mrs. Bantry said in a low voice, "You see what I mean? It just isn't true?"

The old lady by her side nodded her head. She looked down long and thoughtfully at the huddled figure. She said at last in a gentle voice, "She's very young."

"Yes; yes, I suppose she is." Mrs. Bantry seemed almost surprised, like one making a discovery.

There was the sound of a car crunching on the gravel outside. Constable Palk said with urgency, "That'll be the inspector."

True to his ingrained belief that the gentry didn't let you down, Mrs. Bantry immediately moved to the door. Miss Marple followed her. Mrs. Bantry said, "That'll be all right, Palk." Constable Palk was immensely relieved.

Hastily downing the last fragments of toast and marmalade with a drink of coffee, Colonel Bantry hurried out into the hall and was relieved to see Colonel Melchett, the chief constable of the county, descending from a car, with Inspector Slack in attendance. Melchett was a friend of the colonel's; Slack he had never very much taken to—an energetic man who belied his name and who accompanied his bustling manner with a good deal of disregard for the feelings of anyone he did not consider important.

"Morning, Bantry," said the chief constable. "Thought I'd better come along myself. This seems an extraordinary business."

"It's—it's"—Colonel Bantry struggled to express himself—"it's incredible—fantastic!"

"No idea who the woman is?"

"Not in the slightest. Never set eyes on her in my life."

"Butler know anything?" asked Inspector Slack.

"Lorrimer is just as taken aback as I am."

"Ah," said Inspector Slack. "I wonder."

Colonel Bantry said, "There's breakfast in the dining room, Melchett, if you'd like anything."

"No, no, better get on with the job. Haydock ought to be here any minute now. . . . Ah, here he is." Another car drew up and big, broad-shouldered Doctor Haydock, who was also the police surgeon, got out. A second police car had disgorged two plain-clothes men, one with a camera.

"All set, eh?" said the chief constable. "Right. We'll go along. In the library, Slack tells me."

Colonel Bantry groaned. "It's incredible! You know, when my wife insisted this morning that the housemaid had come in and said there was a body in the library, I just wouldn't believe her."

"No, no, I can quite understand that. Hope your missus isn't too badly upset by it all."

"She's been wonderful—really wonderful. She's got old Miss Marple up here with her—from the village, you know."

"Miss Marple?" The chief constable stiffened. "Why did she send for her?"

"Oh, a woman wants another woman—don't you think so?"

Colonel Melchett said with a slight chuckle, "If you ask me, your wife's going to try her hand at a little amateur detecting. Miss Marple's quite the local sleuth. Put it over us properly once, didn't she, Slack?"

Inspector Slack said, "That was different."

"Different from what?"

"That was a local case, that was, sir. The old lady knows everything that goes on in the village, that's true enough. But she'll be out of her depth here."

Melchett said dryly, "You don't know very much about it yourself yet, Slack."

"Ah, you wait, sir. It won't take me long to get down to it."

In the dining room Mrs. Bantry and Miss Marple, in their turn, were partaking of breakfast. After waiting on her guest, Mrs. Bantry said urgently, "Well, Jane?" Miss Marple looked up at her slightly bewildered. Mrs. Bantry said hopefully, "Doesn't it remind you of anything?"

For Miss Marple had attained fame by her ability to link up trivial village happenings with graver problems in such a way as to throw light upon the latter.

"No," said Miss Marple thoughtfully. "I can't say that it does—not at the moment. I was reminded a little of Mrs. Chetty's youngest—Edie, you know—but I think that was just because this poor girl bit her nails and her front teeth stuck out a little. Nothing more than that. And of course," went on Miss Marple, pursuing the parallel further, "Edie was fond of what I call cheap finery too."

"You mean her dress?" said Mrs. Bantry.

"Yes, very tawdry satin, poor quality."

Mrs. Bantry said, "I know. One of those nasty little shops where everything is a guinea." She went on hopefully, "Let me see. What happened to Mrs. Chetty's Edie?"

"She's just gone into her second place, and doing very well, I believe," said Miss Marple.

Mrs. Bantry felt slightly disappointed. The village parallel didn't seem to be exactly hopeful.

"What I can't make out," said Mrs. Bantry, "is what she could possibly be doing in Arthur's study. The window was forced, Palk tells me. She might have come down here with a burglar, and then they quarreled —But that seems such nonsense, doesn't it?"

"She was hardly dressed for burglary," said Miss Marple thoughtfully.

"No, she was dressed for dancing or a party of some kind. But there's nothing of that kind down here or anywhere near."

"N-no," said Miss Marple doubtfully.

Mrs. Bantry pounced. "Something's in your mind, Jane."

"Well, I was just wondering—"

"Yes?"

"Basil Blake."

Mrs. Bantry cried impulsively, "Oh, no!" and added as though in explanation, "I know his mother."

The two women looked at each other. Miss Marple sighed and shook her head. "I quite understand how you feel about it."

"Selina Blake is the nicest woman imaginable. Her herbaceous borders are simply marvelous; they make me green with envy. And she's frightfully generous with cuttings."

Miss Marple passing over these claims to consideration on the part of Mrs. Blake, said, "All the same, you know, there has been a lot of talk."

"Oh, I know, I know. And of course Arthur goes simply livid when he hears him mentioned. He was really very rude to Arthur, and since then Arthur won't hear a good word for him. He's got that silly slighting way of talking that these boys have nowadays—sneering at people sticking up for their school or the Empire or that sort of thing. And then, of course, the clothes he wears! People say," continued Mrs. Bantry, "that it doesn't matter what you wear in the country. I never heard such nonsense. It's just in the country that everyone notices." She paused and added wistfully, "He was an adorable baby in his bath."

"There was a lovely picture of the Cheviot murderer as a baby in the paper last Sunday," said Miss Marple.

"Oh, but, Jane, you don't think he—"

"No, no, dear, I didn't mean that at all. That would indeed be jumping to conclusions. I was just trying to account for the young woman's presence down here. St. Mary Mead is such an unlikely place. And then it seemed to me that the only possible explanation was Basil Blake. He does have parties. People come down from London and from the studios—you remember last July? Shouting and singing—the most terrible noise—everyone very drunk, I'm afraid—and the mess and the broken glass next morning simply unbelievable—so old Mrs. Berry told me—and a young woman asleep in the bath with practically nothing on!"

Mrs. Bantry said indulgently, "I suppose they were film people."

"Very likely. And then—what I expect you've heard—several week ends lately he's brought down a young woman with him—a platinum blonde."

Mrs. Bantry exclaimed, "You don't think it's this one?"

"Well, I wondered. Of course, I've never seen her close to—only just getting in and out of the car, and once in the cottage garden when she was sun-bathing with just some shorts and a brassière. I never really saw her face. And all these girls, with their make-up and their hair and their nails, look so alike."

"Yes. Still, it might be. It's an idea, Jane."

2

IT WAS an idea that was being at that moment discussed by Colonel Melchett and Colonel Bantry. The chief constable, after viewing the body and seeing his subordinates set to work on their routine tasks, had adjourned with the master of the house to the study in the other wing. Colonel Melchett was an irascible-looking man with a habit of tugging at his short red mustache. He did so now, shooting a perplexed sideways glance at the other man. Finally he rapped out, "Look here, Bantry; got to get this off my chest. Is it a fact that you don't know from Adam who this woman is?"

The other's answer was explosive, but the chief constable interrupted him, "Yes, yes, old man, but look at it like this: Might be deuced awkward for you. Married man—fond of your missus and all that. But just between ourselves, if you were tied up with this girl in any way, better say so now. Quite natural to want to suppress the fact; should feel the same myself. But it won't do. Murder case. Facts bound to come out. Dash it all, I'm not suggesting you strangled the girl—not the sort of thing you'd do. I know that! But, after all, she came here—to this house. Put it, she broke in and was waiting to see you, and some bloke or other followed her down and did her in. Possible, you know. See what I mean?"

"I've never set eyes on that girl in my life! I'm not that sort of man!"

"That's all right then. Shouldn't blame you, you know. Man of the world. Still, if you say so—Question is, what was she doing down here? She doesn't come from these parts, that's quite certain."

"That whole thing's a nightmare," fumed the angry master of the house.

"The point is, old man, what was she doing in your library?"

"How should I know? I didn't ask her here."

"No, no. But she came here all the same. Looks as though she wanted to see you. You haven't had any odd letters or anything?"

"No, I haven't."

Colonel Melchett inquired delicately, "What were you doing yourself last night?"

"I went to the meeting of the Conservative Association. Nine o'clock, at Much Benham."

"And you got home when?"

"I left Much Benham just after ten. Had a bit of trouble on the way home, had to change a wheel. I got back at a quarter to twelve."

"You didn't go into the library?"

"No."

"Pity."

"I was tired. I went straight up to bed."

"Anyone waiting up for you?"

"No. I always take the latchkey. Lorrimer goes to bed at eleven, unless I give orders to the contrary."

"Who shuts up the library?"

"Lorrimer. Usually about seven-thirty this time of year."

"Would he go in there again during the evening?"

"Not with my being out. He left the tray with whisky and glasses in the hall."

"I see. What about your wife?"

"She was in bed when I got home, and fast asleep. She may have sat in the library yesterday evening, or in the drawing room. I didn't ask her."

"Oh, well, we shall soon know all the details. Of course it's possible one of the servants may be concerned, eh?"

Colonel Bantry shook his head. "I don't believe it. They're all a most respectable lot. We've had 'em for years."

Melchett agreed. "Yes, it doesn't seem likely that they're mixed up in it. Looks more as though the girl came down from town—perhaps with some young fellow. Though why they wanted to break into this house—"

Bantry interrupted. "London. That's more like it. We don't have goings on down here—at least—"

"Well, what is it?"

"Upon my word!" exploded Colonel Bantry. "Basil Blake!"

"Who's he?"

"Young fellow connected with the film industry. Poisonous young brute. My wife sticks up for him because she was at school with his mother, but of all the decadent useless young jackanapes—Wants his behind kicked. He's taken that cottage on the Lansham Road—you know, ghastly modern bit of building. He has parties there—shrieking, noisy crowds—and he has girls down for the week end."

"Girls?"

"Yes, there was one last week—one of these platinum blondes." The colonel's jaw dropped.

"A platinum blonde, eh?" said Melchett reflectively.

"Yes. I say, Melchett, you don't think—"

The chief constable said briskly, "It's a possibility. It accounts for a girl of this type being in St. Mary Mead. I think I'll run along and have a word with this young fellow Braid—Blake—what did you say his name was?"

"Blake. Basil Blake."

"Will he be at home, do you know?" asked Melchett.

"Let me see, what's today? Saturday? Usually gets here some time Saturday morning."

Melchett said grimly, "We'll see if we can find him."

Basil Blake's cottage, which consisted of all modern conveniences enclosed in a hideous shell of half timbering and sham Tudor, was known to the postal authorities and to William Booker, Builder, as "Chatsworth"; to Basil and his friends as "The Period Piece"; and to the village of St. Mary Mead at large as "Mr. Booker's new house." It was little more than a quarter of a mile from the village proper, being situated on a new building estate that had been bought by the enterprising Mr. Booker just beyond the Blue Boar, with frontage on what had been a particularly unspoiled country lane. Grossington Hall was about a mile farther on along the same road.

Lively interest had been aroused in St. Mary Mead when the news went round that "Mr. Booker's new house" had been bought by a film star. Eager watch was kept for the first appearance of the legendary creature in the village, and it may be said that as far as appearances went Basil Blake was all that could be asked for. Little by little, however, the real facts leaked out. Basil Blake was not a film star, not even a film actor. He was a very junior person, rejoicing in the position of about fifteenth in the list of those responsible for set decorations at Lenville Studios, headquarters of British New Era Films. The village maidens lost interest and the ruling class of censorious spinsters took exception to Basil Blake's way of life. Only the landlord of the Blue Boar continued to be enthusiastic about Basil and Basil's friends. The revenues of the Blue Boar had increased since the young man's arrival in the place.

The police car stopped outside the distorted rustic gate of Mr. Booker's fancy, and Colonel Melchett, with a glance of distaste at the excessive half timbering of Chatsworth, strode up to the front door and attacked it briskly with the knocker. It was opened much more promptly than he had expected. A young man with straight, somewhat long black hair, wearing orange corduroy trousers and a royal-blue shirt, snapped out, "Well, what do you want?"

"Are you Mr. Basil Blake?"

"Of course I am."

"I should be glad to have a few words with you if I may, Mr. Blake."

"Who are you?"

"I am Colonel Melchett, the chief constable of the county."

Mr. Blake said insolently, "You don't say so. How amusing."

And Colonel Melchett, following the other in, understood precisely what Colonel Bantry's reactions had been. The toe of his own boot itched. Containing himself, however, he said, with an attempt to speak pleasantly, "You're an early riser, Mr. Blake."

"Not at all. I haven't been to bed yet."

"Indeed?"

"But I don't suppose you've come here to inquire into my hours of bed-going, or if you have it's rather a waste of the county's time and money. What is it you want to speak to me about?"

Colonel Melchett cleared his throat. "I understand, Mr. Blake, that last week end you had a visitor—a—er—fair-haired young lady."

Basil Blake stared, threw back his head and roared with laughter. "Have the old cats been on to you from the village? About my morals? Damn it all, morals aren't a police matter. You know that."

"As you say," said Melchett dryly, "your morals are no concern of mine. I have come to you because the body of a fair-haired young woman of slightly—er—exotic appearance has been found—murdered."

" 'Struth!" Blake stared at him. "Where?"

"In the library at Gossington Hall."

"At Gossington? At old Bantry's? I say, that's pretty rich—old Bantry! The dirty old man!"

Colonel Melchett went very red in the face. He said sharply through the renewed mirth of the young man opposite him, "Kindly control your tongue, sir. I came to ask you if you can throw any light on this business."

"You've come round to ask me if I've missed a blonde? Is that it? Why should—Hullo, 'ullo, 'ullo! What's this?"

A car had drawn up outside with a scream of brakes. Out of it tumbled a young woman dressed in flapping black-and-white pajamas. She had scarlet lips, blackened eyelashes and a platinum-blond head. She strode up to the door, flung it open, and exclaimed angrily, "Why did you run out on me?"

Basil Blake had risen. "So there you are. Why shouldn't I leave you? I told you to clear out, and you wouldn't."

"Why should I because you told me to? I was enjoying myself."

"Yes, with that filthy brute, Rosenberg. You know what he's like."

"You were jealous, that's all."

"Don't flatter yourself. I hate to see a girl I like who can't hold her drink and lets a disgusting Central European paw her about."

"That's a lie. You were drinking pretty hard yourself and going on with the black-haired Spanish girl."

"If I take you to a party, I expect you to be able to behave yourself."

"And I refuse to be dictated to, and that's that. You said we'd go to the party and come on down here afterwards. I'm not going to leave a party before I'm ready to leave it."

"No, and that's why I left you flat. I was ready to come down here and I came. I don't hang round waiting for any fool of a woman."

"Sweet, polite person you are."

"You seem to have followed me down, all right."

"I wanted to tell you what I thought of you."

"If you think you can boss me, my girl, you're wrong."

"And if you think you can order me about, you can think again."

They glared at each other. It was at this moment that Colonel Melchett seized his opportunity and cleared his throat loudly. Basil Blake swung round on him. "Hullo, I forgot you were here. About time you took yourself off, isn't it? Let me introduce you—Dinah Lee—Colonel Blimp, of the county police. . . . And now, colonel, that you've seen that my blonde is alive and in good condition, perhaps you'll get on with the good work concerning old Bantry's little bit of fluff. Good morning!"

Colonel Melchett said, "I advise you to keep a civil tongue in your head, young man, or you'll let yourself in for trouble," and stumped out, his face red and wrathful.

3

In His office at Much Benham, Colonel Melchett received and scrutinized the reports of his subordinates. ". . . so it all seems clear enough, sir," Inspector Slack was concluding. "Mrs. Bantry sat in the library after dinner and went to bed just before ten. She turned out the lights when she left the room, and presumably no one entered the room afterward. The servants went to bed at half past ten, and Lorrimer, after putting the drinks in the hall, went to bed at a quarter to eleven. Nobody heard anything out of the usual, except the third housemaid, and she heard too much! Groans and a bloodcurdling yell and sinister footsteps and I don't know what. The second housemaid, who shares a room with her, says the other girl slept all night through without a sound. It's those ones that make up things that cause us all the trouble."

"What about the forced window?"

"Amateur job, Simmons says, done with a common chisel, ordinary pattern; wouldn't have made much noise. Ought to be a chisel about the house, but nobody can find it. Still, that's common enough where tools are concerned."

"Think any of the servants know anything?"

Rather unwillingly Inspector Slack replied, "No, sir. I don't think they do. They all seemed very shocked and upset. I had my suspicions of Lorrimer—reticent, he was, if you know what I mean—but I don't think there's anything in it."

Melchett nodded. He attached no importance to Lorrimer's reticence. The energetic Inspector Slack often produced that effect on the people he interrogated. The door opened and Doctor Haydock came in. "Thought I'd look in and give you the rough gist of things."

"Yes, yes, glad to see you. Well?"

"Nothing much. Just what you'd think. Death was due to strangulation. Satin waistband of her own dress, which was passed round the neck and crossed at the back. Quite easy and simple to do. Wouldn't have needed great strength—that is, if the girl was taken by surprise. There are no signs of a struggle."

"What about time of death?"

"Say between ten o'clock and midnight."

"You can't get nearer than that?"

Haydock shook his head with a slight grin. "I won't risk my professional reputation. Not earlier than ten and not later than midnight."

"And your own fancy inclines to which time?"

"Depends. There was a fire in the grate, the room was warm—all that would delay rigor and cadaveric stiffening."

"Anything more you can say about her?"

"Nothing much. She was young—about seventeen or eighteen, I should say. Rather immature in some ways but well developed muscularly. Quite a healthy specimen. She was *virgo intacta,* by the way." And with a nod of his head the doctor left the room.

Melchett said to the inspector, "You're quite sure she'd never been seen before at Gossington?"

"The servants are positive of that. Quite indignant about it. They'd have remembered if they'd ever seen her about in the neighborhood, they say."

"I expect they would," said Melchett. "Anyone of that type sticks out a mile round here. Look at that young woman of Blake's."

"Pity it wasn't her," said Slack. "Then we should be able to get on a bit."

"It seems to me this girl must have come down from London," said the chief constable thoughtfully. "Don't believe there will be any local leads. In that case, I suppose, we should do well to call in the Yard. It's a case for them, not for us."

"Something must have brought her down here, though," said Slack. He added tentatively, "Seems to me, Colonel and Mrs. Bantry must know something. Of course I know they're friends of yours, sir—"

Colonel Melchett treated him to a cold stare. He said stiffly, "You may rest assured that I'm taking every possibility into account. Every possibility." He went on, "You've looked through the list of persons reported missing, I suppose?"

Slack nodded. He produced a typed sheet. "Got 'em here. Mrs. Saunders, reported missing a week ago, dark-haired, blue-eyed, thirty-six. 'Tisn't her. And anyway, everyone knows, except her husband, that she's gone off with a fellow from Leeds—commercial. Mrs. Barnard—she's sixty-five. Pamela Reeves, sixteen, missing from her home last night, had attended Girl Guide rally, dark brown hair in pig-tails, five feet five—"

Melchett said irritably, "Don't go on reading idiotic details, Slack. This wasn't a schoolgirl. In my opinion—" He broke off as the telephone rang. "Hullo. . . . Yes, yes, Much Benham police headquarters. . . . What? . . . Just a minute." He listened and wrote rapidly. Then he spoke again, a new tone in his voice. "Ruby Keene, eighteen, occupation, professional dancer, five feet four inches, slender, platinum-blond hair, blue eyes, retroussé nose, believed to be wearing white diamanté evening dress, silver sandal shoes. Is that right? . . . What? . . . Yes, not a doubt of it, I should say. I'll send Slack over at once." He rang off and looked at his subordinate with rising excitement. "We've got it, I think. That was the Glenshire police." Glenshire was the adjoining county. "Girl reported missing from the Majestic Hotel, Danemouth."

"Danemouth," said Inspector Slack. "That's more like it." Danemouth was a large and fashionable watering place on the coast not far away.

"It's only a matter of eighteen miles or so from here," said the chief constable. "The girl was a dance hostess or something at the Majestic. Didn't come on to do her turn last night and the management was very fed up about it. When she was still missing this morning, one of the other girls got the wind up about her, or someone else did. It sounds a bit obscure. You'd better go over to Danemouth at once, Slack. Report there to Superintendent Harper and cooperate with him."

4

ACTIVITY was always to Inspector Slack's taste. To rush in a car, to silence rudely those people who were anxious to tell him things, to cut short conversations on the plea of urgent necessity—all this was the breath of life to Inspector Slack. In an incredibly short time, therefore, he had arrived at Danemouth, reported at police headquarters, had a brief interview with a distracted and apprehensive hotel manager, and, leaving the latter with the doubtful comfort of "Got to make sure it is the girl first, before we start raising the wind," was driving back to Much Benham in company with Ruby Keene's nearest relative. He had put through a short call to Much Benham before leaving Danemouth, so the chief constable was prepared for his arrival, though not perhaps for the brief introduction of "This is Josie, sir."

Colonel Melchett stared at his subordinate coldly. His feeling was that Slack had taken leave of his senses. The young woman who had just got out of the car came to the rescue. "That's what I'm known as professionally," she explained with a momentary flash of large, handsome white teeth. "Raymond and Josie, my partner and I call ourselves, and of course all the hotel know me as Josie. Josephine Turner's my real name."

Colonel Melchett adjusted himself to the situation and invited Miss Turner to sit down, meanwhile casting a swift professional glance over her. She was a good-looking young woman of perhaps nearer thirty than twenty; her looks depending more on skillful grooming than actual features. She looked competent and good-tempered, with plenty of common sense. She was not the type that would ever be described as glamorous, but she had, nevertheless, plenty of attraction. She was discreetly made up and wore a dark tailormade suit. She looked anxious and upset, but not, the colonel decided, particularly grief-stricken. As she sat down she said, "It seems too awful to be true. Do you really think it's Ruby?"

"That, I'm afraid, is what we've got to ask you to tell us. I'm afraid it may be rather unpleasant for you."

Miss Turner said apprehensively, "Does she—does she look very terrible?"

"Well, I'm afraid it may be rather a shock to you."

"Do—do you want me to look at her right away?"

"It would be best, I think, Miss Turner. You see, it's not much good asking you questions until we're sure. Best get it over, don't you think?"

"All right."

They drove down to the mortuary. When Josie came out after a brief visit she looked rather sick. "It's Ruby, all right," she said shakily. "Poor kid! Goodness, I do feel queer! There isn't"—she looked round wistfully —"any gin?"

Gin was not available, but brandy was and, after gulping a little down, Miss Turner regained her composure. She said frankly, "It gives you a turn, doesn't it, seeing anything like that? Poor little Ruby! What swine men are, aren't they?"

"You believe it was a man?"

Josie looked slightly taken aback. "Wasn't it? Well, I mean—I naturally thought—"

"Any special man you were thinking of?"

She shook her head vigorously. "No, not me. I haven't the least idea. Naturally, Ruby wouldn't have let on to me if—"

"If what?"

Josie hesitated. "Well, if she'd been—going about with anyone."

Melchett shot her a keen glance. He said no more until they were back at his office. Then he began, "Now, Miss Turner, I want all the information you can give me."

"Yes, of course. Where shall I begin?"

"I'd like the girl's full name and address, her relationship to you and all that you know about her."

Josephine Turner nodded. Melchett was confirmed in his opinion that she felt no particular grief. She was shocked and distressed, but no more. She spoke readily enough. "Her name was Ruby Keene—her professional name, that is. Her real name was Rosy Legge. Her mother was my mother's cousin. I've known her all my life, but not particularly well, if you know what I mean. I've got a lot of cousins; some in business, some on the stage. Ruby was more or less training for a dancer. She had some good engagements last year in panto and that sort of thing. Not really classy, but good provincial companies. Since then she's been engaged as one of the dancing partners at the Palais de Danse in Brixwell, South London. It's a nice, respectable place and they look after the girls well, but there isn't a great deal of money in it." She paused. Colonel Melchett nodded.

"Now this is where I come in. I've been dance and bridge hostess at the Majestic in Danemouth for three years. It's a good job, well paid and pleasant to do. You look after people when they arrive. Size them up, of course—some like to be left alone and others are lonely and want to get into the swing of things. You try and get the right people together for bridge and all that, and get the young people dancing with one another. It needs a bit of tact and experience."

Again Melchett nodded. He thought that this girl would be good at her job. She had a pleasant, friendly way with her and was, he thought, shrewd without being in the least intellectual.

"Besides that," continued Josie, "I do a couple of exhibition dances every evening with Raymond. Raymond Starr—he's the tennis and dancing pro. Well, as it happens, this summer I slipped on the rocks bathing one day and gave my ankle a nasty turn." Melchett had noticed that she walked with a slight limp.

"Naturally, that put the stop to dancing for a bit and it was rather awkward. I didn't want the hotel to get someone else in my place. There's always a danger"—for a minute her good-natured blue eyes were hard and sharp; she was the female fighting for existence—"that they may queer your pitch, you see. So I thought of Ruby and suggested to the manager that I should get her down. I'd carry on with the hostess business and the bridge and all that. Ruby would just take on the dancing. Keep it in the family, if you see what I mean." Melchett said he saw.

"Well, they agreed, and I wired to Ruby and she came down. Rather a chance for her. Much better class than anything she'd ever done before. That was about a month ago."

Colonel Melchett said, "I understand. And she was a success?"

"Oh, yes," Josie said carelessly. "She went down quite well. She doesn't dance as well as I do, but Raymond's clever and carried her through, and she was quite nice-looking, you know—slim and fair and baby-looking. Overdid the makeup a bit—I was always at her about that. But you know what girls are. She was only eighteen, and at that age they always go and overdo it. It doesn't do for a good-class place like the Majestic. I was always ticking her off about it and getting her to tone it down."

Melchett asked, "People liked her?"

"Oh, yes. Mind you, Ruby hadn't got much comeback. She was a bit dumb. She went down better with the older men than the young ones."

"Had she got any special friend?"

The girl's eyes met his with complete understanding. "Not in the way you mean. Or, at any rate, not that I knew about. But then, you see, she wouldn't tell me."

Just for a moment Melchett wondered why not. Josie did not give the impression of being a strict disciplinarian. But he only said, "Will you describe to me now when you last saw your cousin."

"Last night. She and Raymond do two exhibition dances. One at ten-thirty and the other at midnight. They finished the first one. After it, I noticed Ruby dancing with one of the young men staying at the hotel. I was playing bridge with some people in the lounge. There's a glass panel between the lounge and the ballroom. That's the last time I saw her. Just after midnight Raymond came up in a terrible taking; said where was Ruby; she hadn't turned up and it was time to begin. I was vexed, I can tell you! That's the sort of silly things girls do and get the management's back up, and then they get the sack! I went up with him to her room, but she wasn't there. I noticed that she'd changed; the dress she'd been dancing in—a sort of pink, foamy thing with full skirts—was lying over a chair. Usually she kept the same dress on, unless it was the special dance night—Wednesdays, that is.

"I'd no idea where she'd got to. We got the band to play one more fox trot. Still no Ruby, so I said to Raymond I'd do the exhibition dance with him. We chose one that was easy on my ankle and made it short, but it played up my ankle pretty badly all the same. It's all swollen this morning. Still Ruby didn't show up. We sat about waiting up for her until two o'clock. Furious with her, I was."

Her voice vibrated slightly. Melchett caught the note of real anger in it. Just for a moment, he wondered. He had a feeling of something deliberately left unsaid. He said, "And this morning, when Ruby Keene had not returned and her bed had not been slept in, you went to the police?" He knew, from Slack's brief telephone message from Danemouth, that that was not the case. But he wanted to hear what Josephine Turner would say.

She did not hesitate. She said, "No, I didn't."

"Why not, Miss Turner?"

Her eyes met his frankly. She said, "You wouldn't—in my place!"

"You think not?"

Josie said, "I've got my job to think about! The one thing a hotel doesn't want is scandal—especially anything that brings in the police. I didn't think anything had happened to Ruby. Not for a minute! I thought she'd just made a fool of herself about some young man. I thought she'd turn up all right, and I was going to give her a good dressing down when she did! Girls of eighteen are such fools."

Melchett pretended to glance through his notes. "Ah, yes, I see it was a Mr. Jefferson who went to the police. One of the guests staying at the hotel?"

Josephine Turner said shortly, "Yes."

Colonel Melchett asked, "What made this Mr. Jefferson do that?"

Josie was stroking the cuff of her jacket. There was a constraint in her manner. Again Colonel Melchett had a feeling that something was being withheld.

She said rather sullenly, "He's an invalid. He—he gets all het up rather easily. Being an invalid, I mean."

Melchett passed from that. He asked, "Who was the young man with whom you last saw your cousin dancing?"

"His name's Bartlett. He's been there about ten days."

"Were they on very friendly terms?"

"Not specially, I should say. Not that I knew, anyway." Again a curious note of anger in her voice.

"What does he have to say?"

"Said that after their dance Ruby went upstairs to powder her nose."

"That was when she changed her dress?"

"I suppose so."

"And that is the last thing you know? After that, she just—"

"Vanished," said Josie. "That's right."

"Did Miss Keene know anybody in St. Mary Mead? Or in this neighborhood?"

"I don't know. She may have. You see, quite a lot of young men come in to Danemouth to the Majestic, from all round about. I wouldn't know where they lived unless they happened to mention it."

"Did you ever hear your cousin mention Gossington?"

"Gossington?" Josie looked patently puzzled.

"Gossington Hall."

She shook her head. "Never heard of it." Her tone carried conviction. There was curiosity in it too.

"Gossington Hall," explained Colonel Melchett, "is where her body was found."

"Gossington Hall?" She stared. "How extraordinary!"

Melchett thought to himself, *Extraordinary's the word.* Aloud he said, "Do you know a Colonel or Mrs. Bantry?"

Again Josie shook her head.

"Or a Mr. Basil Blake?"

She frowned slightly. "I think I've heard that name. Yes, I'm sure I have, but I don't remember anything about him."

The diligent Inspector Slack slid across to his superior officer a page torn from his notebook. On it was penciled: "Col. Bantry dined at Majestic last week." Melchett looked up and met the inspector's eye. The chief constable flushed. Slack was an industrious and zealous officer and Melchett disliked him a good deal, but he could not disregard the challenge. The inspector was tacitly accusing him of favoring his own class—of shielding an "old school tie." He turned to Josie. "Miss Turner, I should like you, if you do not mind, to accompany me to Gossington Hall." Coldly, defiantly, almost ignoring Josie's murmur of assent, Melchett's eyes met Slack's.

5

ST. MARY MEAD was having the most exciting morning it had known for a long time. Miss Wetherby, a long-nosed, acidulated spinster, was the first to spread the intoxicating information. She dropped in upon her friend and neighbor, Miss Hartnell. "Forgive me coming so early, dear, but I thought perhaps you mightn't have heard the news."

"What news?" demanded Miss Hartnell. She had a deep bass voice and visited the poor indefatigably, however hard they tried to avoid her ministrations.

"About the body of a young woman that was found this morning in Colonel Bantry's library."

"In Colonel Bantry's library?"

"Yes. Isn't it terrible?"

"His poor wife!" Miss Hartnell tried to disguise her deep and ardent pleasure.

"Yes, indeed. I don't suppose she had any idea."

Miss Hartnell observed censoriously, "She thought too much about her garden and not enough about her husband. You've got to keep an eye on a man all the time—all the time," repeated Miss Hartnell fiercely.

"I know. I know. It's really too dreadful."

"I wonder what Jane Marple will say? Do you think she knew anything about it? She's so sharp about these things."

"Jane Marple has gone up to Gossington."

"What? This morning?"

"Very early. Before breakfast."

"But really! I do think—well, I mean, I think that is carrying things too far. We all know Jane likes to poke her nose into things, but I call this indecent!"

"Oh, but Mrs. Bantry sent for her."

"Mrs. Bantry sent for her?"

"Well, the car came. With Muswell driving it."

"Dear me. How very peculiar."

They were silent a minute or two, digesting the news. "Whose body?" demanded Miss Hartnell.

"You know that dreadful woman who comes down with Basil Blake?"

"That terrible peroxide blonde?" Miss Hartnell was slightly behind the times. She had not yet advanced from peroxide to platinum. "The one who lies about in the garden with practically nothing on?"

"Yes, my dear. There she was on the hearthrug, strangled!"

"But what do you mean—at Gossington?" Miss Wetherby nodded with infinite meaning. "Then Colonel Bantry too—" Again Miss Wetherby nodded. "Oh!"

There was a pause as the ladies savored this new addition to village scandal. "What a wicked woman!" trumpeted Miss Hartnell with righteous wrath.

"Quite, quite abandoned, I'm afraid!"

"And Colonel Bantry—such a nice quiet man—"

Miss Wetherby said zestfully, "Those quiet ones are often the worst. Jane Marple always says so."

Mrs. Price Ridley was among the last to hear the news. A rich and dictatorial widow, she lived in a large house next door to the vicarage. Her informant was her little maid, Clara. "A woman, you say, Clara? Found dead on Colonel Bantry's hearthrug?"

"Yes, mum. And they say, mum, as she hadn't anything on at all, mum —not a stitch!"

"That will do, Clara. It is not necessary to go into details."

"No, mum, and they say, mum, that at first they thought it was Mr. Blake's young lady what comes down for the weekends with 'im to Mr. Booker's new 'ouse. But now they say it's quite a different young lady. And the fishmonger's young man, he says he'd never have believed it of Colonel Bantry—not with him handing round the plate on Sundays and all."

"There is a lot of wickedness in the world, Clara," said Mrs. Price Ridley. "Let this be a warning to you."

"Yes, mum. Mother, she never will let me take a place where there's a gentleman in the 'ouse."

"That will do, Clara," said Mrs. Price Ridley.

It was only a step from Mrs. Price Ridley's house to the vicarage. Mrs. Price Ridley was fortunate enough to find the vicar in his study. The vicar, a gentle, middle-aged man, was always the last to hear anything.

"Such a terrible thing," said Mrs. Price Ridley, panting a little because she had come rather fast. "I felt I must have your advice, your counsel about it, dear vicar."

Mr. Clement looked mildly alarmed. He said, "Has anything happened?"

"Has anything happened!" Mrs. Price Ridley repeated the question dramatically. "The most terrible scandal! None of us had any idea of it. An abandoned woman, completely unclothed, strangled on Colonel Bantry's hearthrug."

The vicar stared. He said, "You—you are feeling quite well?"

"No wonder you can't believe it! I couldn't at first! The hypocrisy of the man! All these years."

"Please tell me exactly what all this is about."

Mrs. Price Ridley plunged into a full-swing narrative. When she had finished, the Reverend Mr. Clement said mildly, "But there is nothing, is there, to point to Colonel Bantry's being involved in this?"

"Oh, dear vicar, you are so unworldly! But I must tell you a little story. Last Thursday—or was it the Thursday before—well, it doesn't matter—I was going up to London by the cheap day train. Colonel Bantry was in the same carriage. He looked, I thought, very abstracted. And nearly the whole way he buried himself behind *The Times.* As though, you know, he didn't want to talk." The vicar nodded his head with complete comprehension and possible sympathy.

"At Paddington I said good-by. He had offered to get me a taxi, but I was taking the bus down to Oxford Street; but he got into one, and I distinctly heard him tell the driver to go to—Where do you think?" Mr. Clement looked inquiring.

"An address in St. John's Wood!" Mrs. Price Ridley paused triumphantly. The vicar remained completely unenlightened. "That, I consider, proves it," said Mrs. Price Ridley.

At Gossington, Mrs. Bantry and Miss Marple were sitting in the drawing room. "You know," said Mrs. Bantry, "I can't help feeling glad they've taken the body away. It's not nice to have a body in one's house."

Miss Marple nodded. "I know, dear. I know just how you feel."

"You can't," said Mrs. Bantry. "Not until you've had one. I know you had one next door once, but that's not the same thing. I only hope," she went on, "that Arthur won't take a dislike to the library. We sit there so much. What are you doing, Jane?" For Miss Marple, with a glance at her watch, was rising to her feet.

"Well, I was thinking I'd go home, if there's nothing more I can do for you."

"Don't go yet," said Mrs. Bantry. "The fingerprint men and the photographers and most of the police have gone, I know, but I still feel something might happen. You don't want to miss anything."

The telephone rang and she went off to answer. She returned with a beaming face. "I told you more things would happen. That was Colonel Melchett. He's bringing the poor girl's cousin along."

"I wonder why?" said Miss Marple.

"Oh, I suppose to see where it happened, and all that."

"More than that, I expect," said Miss Marple.

"What do you mean, Jane?"

"Well, I think, perhaps, he might want her to meet Colonel Bantry."

Mrs. Bantry said sharply, "To see if she recognizes him? I suppose—oh, yes, I suppose they're bound to suspect Arthur."

"I'm afraid so."

"As though Arthur could have anything to do with it!"

Miss Marple was silent. Mrs. Bantry turned on her accusingly. "And don't tell me about some frightful old man who kept his housemaid. Arthur isn't like that."

"No, no, of course not."

"No, but he really isn't. He's just, sometimes, a little bit silly about pretty girls who come to tennis. You know, rather fatuous and avuncular. There's no harm in it. And why shouldn't he? After all," finished Mrs. Bantry rather obscurely, "I've got the garden."

Miss Marple smiled. "You must not worry, Dolly," she said.

"No, I don't mean to. But all the same I do, a little. So does Arthur. It's upset him. All these policemen looking about. He's gone down to the farm. Looking at pigs and things always soothes him if he's been upset. . . . Hullo, here they are."

The chief constable's car drew up outside. Colonel Melchett came in, accompanied by a smartly dressed young woman. "This is Miss Turner, Mrs. Bantry. The cousin of the—er—victim."

"How do you do," said Mrs. Bantry, advancing with outstretched hand. "All this must be rather awful for you."

Josephine Turner said frankly, "Oh, it is. None of it seems real, somehow. It's like a bad dream."

Mrs. Bantry introduced Miss Marple. Melchett said casually, "Your good man about?"

"He had to go down to one of the farms. He'll be back soon."

"Oh." Melchett seemed rather at a loss.

Mrs. Bantry said to Josie, "Would you like to see where—where it happened? Or would you rather not?"

Josephine said, after a moment's pause, "I think I'd like to see."

Mrs. Bantry led her to the library, with Miss Marple and Melchett following behind. "She was there," said Mrs. Bantry, pointing dramatically. "On the hearthrug."

"Oh!" Josie shuddered. But she also looked perplexed. She said, her brow creased, "I just can't understand it! I can't!"

"Well, we certainly can't," said Mrs. Bantry.

Josie said slowly, "It isn't the sort of place—" and broke off.

Miss Marple nodded her head gently in agreement with the unfinished sentiment. "That," she murmured, "is what makes it so very interesting."

"Come now, Miss Marple," said Colonel Melchett good-humoredly, "haven't you got an explanation?"

"Oh, yes, I've got an explanation," said Miss Marple. "Quite a feasible one. But of course it's only my own idea. Tommy Bond," she continued, "and Mrs. Martin, our new schoolmistress. She went to wind up the clock and a frog jumped out."

Josephine Turner looked puzzled. As they all went out of the room she murmured to Mrs. Bantry, "Is the old lady a bit funny in the head?"

"Not at all," said Mrs. Bantry indignantly.

Josie said, "Sorry. I thought perhaps she thought she was a frog or something."

Colonel Bantry was just coming in through the side door. Melchett hailed him and watched Josephine Turner as he introduced them. But there was no sign of interest or recognition in her face. Melchett breathed a sigh of relief. Curse Slack and his insinuations. In answer to Mrs. Bantry's questions, Josie was pouring out the story of Ruby Keene's disappearance. "Frightfully worrying for you, my dear," said Mrs. Bantry.

"I was more angry than worried," said Josie. "You see, I didn't know then."

"And yet," said Miss Marple, "you went to the police. Wasn't that—excuse me—rather premature?"

Josie said eagerly, "Oh, but I didn't. That was Mr. Jefferson."

Mrs. Bantry said, "Jefferson?"

"Yes, he's an invalid."

"Not Conway Jefferson? But I know him well. He's an old friend of ours. . . . Arthur, listen. Conway Jefferson, he's staying at the Majestic, and it was he who notified the police! Isn't that a coincidence?"

Josephine Turner said, "Mr. Jefferson was there last summer too."

"Fancy! And we never knew. I haven't seen him for a long time." She turned to Josie. "How—how is he nowadays?"

Josie considered. "I think he's wonderful, really—quite wonderful. Considering, I mean. He's always cheerful—always got a joke."

"Are the family there with him?"

"Mr. Gaskell, you mean? And young Mrs. Jefferson? And Peter? Oh, yes."

There was something inhibiting in Josephine Turner's rather attractive frankness of manner. When she spoke of the Jeffersons there was something not quite natural in her voice. Mrs. Bantry said, "They're both very nice, aren't they? The young ones, I mean."

Josie said rather uncertainly, "Oh, yes; yes, they are. I—we—yes, they are really."

"And what," demanded Mrs. Bantry as she looked through the window at the retreating car of the chief constable, "did she mean by that? 'They are really.' Don't you think, Jane, that there's something—"

Miss Marple fell upon the words eagerly. "Oh, I do; indeed I do. It's quite unmistakable! Her manner changed at once when the Jeffersons were mentioned. She had seemed quite natural up to then."

"But what do you think it is, Jane?"

"Well, my dear, you know them. All I feel is that there is something, as you say, about them which is worrying that young woman. Another thing. Did you notice that when you asked her if she wasn't anxious about the girl being missing, she said that she was angry? And she looked angry—really angry! That strikes me as interesting, you know. I have a feeling—perhaps I'm wrong—that that's her main reaction to the fact of the girl's death. She didn't care for her, I'm sure. She's not grieving in any way. But I do think, very definitely, that the thought of that girl, Ruby Keene, makes her angry. And the interesting point is: Why?"

"We'll find out!" said Mrs. Bantry. "We'll go over to Danemouth and stay at the Majestic—yes, Jane, you too. I need a change for my nerves after what has happened here. A few days at the Majestic—that's what we need. And you'll meet Conway Jefferson. He's a dear—a perfect dear. It's the saddest story imaginable. He had a son and a daughter, both of whom he loved dearly. They were both married, but they still spent a lot of time at home. His wife, too, was the sweetest woman, and he was devoted to her. They were flying home one year from France and there was an accident. They were all killed. The pilot, Mrs. Jefferson, Rosamund and Frank. Conway had both legs so badly injured they had to be amputated. And he's been wonderful—his courage, his pluck. He was a very active man, and now he's a helpless cripple, but he never complains. His daughter-in-law lives with him; she was a widow when Frank Jefferson married her, and she had a son by her first marriage— Peter Carmody. They both live with Conway. And Mark Gaskell,

Rosamund's husband, is there, too, most of the time. The whole thing was the most awful tragedy."

"And now," said Miss Marple, "there's another tragedy."

Mrs. Bantry said, "Oh, yes, yes, but it's nothing to do with the Jeffersons."

"Isn't it?" said Miss Marple. "It was Mr. Jefferson who reported to the police."

"So he did. You know, Jane, that is curious."

6

COLONEL MELCHETT was facing a much annoyed hotel manager. With him was Superintendent Harper, of the Glenshire police, and the inevitable Inspector Slack—the latter rather disgruntled at the chief constable's willful usurpation of the case. Superintendent Harper was inclined to be soothing with the almost tearful Mr. Prestcott; Colonel Melchett tended toward a blunt brutality. "No good crying over spilt milk," he said sharply. "The girl's dead—strangled. You're lucky that she wasn't strangled in your hotel. This puts the inquiry in a different county and lets your establishment down extremely lightly. But certain inquiries have got to be made, and the sooner we get on with it the better. You can trust us to be discreet and tactful. So I suggest you cut the cackle and come to the horses. Just what, exactly, do you know about the girl?"

"I know nothing of her—nothing at all. Josie brought her here."

"Josie's been here some time?"

"Two years—no, three."

"And you like her?"

"Yes, Josie's a good girl—a nice girl. Competent. She gets on with people and smooths over differences. Bridge, you know, is a touchy sort of game." Colonel Melchett nodded feelingly. His wife was a keen but an extremely bad bridge player. Mr. Prestcott went on, "Josie was very good at calming down unpleasantness. She could handle people well—sort of bright and firm, if you know what I mean."

Again Melchett nodded. He knew now what it was that Miss Josephine Turner had reminded him of. In spite of the make-up and the smart turnout, there was a distinct touch of the nursery governess about her.

"I depend upon her," went on Mr. Prestcott. His manner became aggrieved. "What does she want to go playing about on slippery rocks in that damn-fool way for? We've got a nice beach here. Why couldn't she bathe from that? Slipping and falling and breaking her ankle! It wasn't fair to me! I pay her to dance and play bridge and keep people happy and amused, not to go bathing off rocks and breaking her ankle. Dancers ought to be careful of their ankles, not take risks! I was very annoyed about it. It wasn't fair to the hotel."

Melchett cut the recital short. "And then she suggested that this girl—her cousin—come down?"

Prestcott assented grudgingly. "That's right. It sounded quite a good idea. Mind you, I wasn't going to pay anything extra. The girl could have her keep, but as for salary, that would have to be fixed up between her and Josie. That's the way it was arranged. I didn't know anything about the girl."

"But she turned out all right?"

"Oh, yes, there wasn't anything wrong with her—not to look at, anyway. She was very young, of course; rather cheap in style, perhaps, for a place of this kind, but nice manners—quiet and well-behaved. Danced well. People liked her."

"Pretty?"

It had been a question hard to answer from a view of the blue, swollen face. Mr. Prestcott considered. "Fair to middling. Bit weaselly, if you know what I mean. Wouldn't have been much without make-up. As it was, she managed to look quite attractive."

"Many young men hanging about after her?"

"I know what you're trying to get at, sir." Mr. Prestcott became excited. "I never saw anything! Nothing special. One or two of the boys hung around a bit, but all in the day's work, so to speak. Nothing in the strangling line, I'd say. She got on well with the older people, too; had a kind of prattling way with her. Seemed quite a kid, if you know what I mean. It amused them."

Superintendent Harper said in a deep, melancholy voice, "Mr. Jefferson, for instance?"

The manager agreed. "Yes, Mr. Jefferson was the one I had in mind. She used to sit with him and his family a lot. He used to take her out for drives sometimes. Mr. Jefferson's very fond of young people and very good to them. I don't want to have any misunderstanding. Mr. Jefferson's a cripple. He can't get about much—only where his wheel chair will take him. But he's always keen on seeing young people enjoy themselves; watches the tennis and the bathing, and all that, and gives parties for young people here. He likes youth, and there's nothing bitter about him, as there well might be. A very popular gentleman and, I'd say, a very fine character."

Melchett asked, "And he took an interest in Ruby Keene?"

"Her talk amused him, I think."

"Did his family share his liking for her?"

"They were always very pleasant to her."

Harper said, "And it was he who reported the fact of her being missing to the police?"

He contrived to put into the words a significance and a reproach to which the manager instantly responded, "Put yourself in my place, Mr. Harper. I didn't dream for a minute anything was wrong. Mr. Jefferson came along to my office, storming and all worked up. The girl hadn't slept in her room. She hadn't appeared in her dance last night. She must have gone for a drive and had an accident, perhaps. The police must be informed at once. Inquiries made. In a state, he was, and quite high-handed. He rang up the police station then and there."

"Without consulting Miss Turner?"

"Josie didn't like it much. I could see that. She was very annoyed about the whole thing—annoyed with Ruby, I mean. But what could she say?"

"I think," said Melchett, "we'd better see Mr. Jefferson. . . . Eh, Harper?"

Superintendent Harper agreed. Mr. Prestcott went up with them to Conway Jefferson's suite. It was on the first floor, overlooking the sea. Melchett said carelessly, "Does himself pretty well, eh? Rich man?"

"Very well off indeed, I believe. Nothing's ever stinted when he comes here. Best rooms reserved, food usually à la carte, expensive wines—best of everything."

Melchett nodded. Mr. Prestcott tapped on the outer door and a woman's voice said, "Come in."

The manager entered, the others behind him. Mr. Prestcott's manner was apologetic as he spoke to the woman who turned her head, at their entrance, from her seat by the window. "I am so sorry to disturb you, Mrs. Jefferson, but these gentlemen are from the police. They are very anxious to have a word with Mr. Jefferson. Er—Colonel Melchett, Super-intendent Harper, Inspector—er—Slack, Mrs. Jefferson!" Mrs. Jefferson acknowledged the introduction by bending her head.

A plain woman, was Melchett's first impression. Then, as a slight smile came to her lips and she spoke, he changed his opinion. She had a singu-larly charming and sympathetic voice, and her eyes—clear hazel eyes— were beautiful. She was quietly but not unbecomingly dressed and was, he judged, about thirty-five years of age. She said, "My father-in-law is asleep. He is not strong at all, and this affair has been a terrible shock to him. We had to have the doctor, and the doctor gave him a sedative. As soon as he wakes he will, I know, want to see you. In the meantime, perhaps I can help you? Won't you sit down?"

Mr. Prestcott, anxious to escape, said to Colonel Melchett, "Well—er —if that's all I can do for you—" and thankfully received permission to depart.

With his closing of the door behind him, the atmosphere took on a mellow and more social quality. Adelaide Jefferson had the power of creating a restful atmosphere. She was a woman who never seemed to say anything remarkable, but who succeeded in stimulating other people to talk and in setting them at their ease. She struck, now, the right note when she said, "This business has shocked us all very much. We saw quite a lot of the poor girl, you know. It seems quite unbelievable. My father-in-law is terribly upset. He was very fond of Ruby."

Colonel Melchett said, "It was Mr. Jefferson, I understand, who reported her disappearance to the police."

He wanted to see exactly how she would react to that. There was a flicker—just a flicker—of—annoyance?—concern?—he could not say what exactly, but there was something, and it seemed to him that she had definitely to brace herself, as though to an unpleasant task, before going on. She said, "Yes, that is so. Being an invalid, he gets easily upset and worried. We tried to persuade him that it was all right, that there was some natural explanation, and that the girl herself would not like the police being notified. He insisted. Well"—she made a slight gesture—"he was right and we were wrong!"

Melchett asked, "Exactly how well did you know Ruby Keene, Mrs. Jefferson?"

She considered. "It's difficult to say. My father-in-law is very fond of young people and likes to have them round him. Ruby was a new type to him; he was amused and interested by her chatter. She sat with us a good deal in the hotel and my father-in-law took her out for drives in the car."

Her voice was quite noncommittal. Melchett thought: *She could say more if she chose.* He said, "Will you tell me what you can of the course of events last night?"

"Certainly, but there is very little that will be useful, I'm afraid. After dinner Ruby came and sat with us in the lounge. She remained even after the dancing had started. We had arranged to play bridge later, but we were waiting for Mark—that is, Mark Gaskell, my brother-in-law—he married Mr. Jefferson's daughter, you know—who had some important letters to write, and also for Josie. She was going to make a fourth with us."

"Did that often happen?"

"Quite frequently. She's a first-class player, of course, and very nice. My father-in-law is a keen bridge player and, whenever possible, liked to get hold of Josie to make the fourth, instead of an outsider. Naturally, as she has to arrange the fours, she can't always play with us, but she does whenever she can, and as"—her eyes smiled a little—"my father-in-law spends a lot of money in the hotel, the management is quite pleased for Josie to favor us."

Melchett asked, "You like Josie?"

"Yes, I do. She's always good-humored and cheerful, works hard and seems to enjoy her job. She's shrewd without being at all intellectual and —well, never pretends about anything. She's natural and unaffected."

"Please go on, Mrs. Jefferson."

"As I say, Josie had to get her bridge fours arranged and Mark was writing, so Ruby sat and talked with us a little longer than usual. Then Josie came along, and Ruby went off to do her first solo dance with Raymond—he's the dance and tennis professional. She came back to us afterward, just as Mark joined us. Then she went off to dance with a young man and we four started our bridge." She stopped and made a slight, significant gesture of helplessness. "And that's all I know! I just caught a glimpse of her once, dancing, but bridge is an absorbing game and I hardly glanced through the glass partition at the ballroom. Then, at midnight, Raymond came along to Josie very upset and asked where Ruby was. Josie, naturally, tried to shut him up, but—"

Superintendent Harper interrupted. He said in his quiet voice, "Why 'naturally,' Mrs. Jefferson?"

"Well—" She hesitated; looked, Melchett thought, a little put out. "Josie didn't want the girl's absence made too much of. She considered herself responsible for her in a way. She said Ruby was probably up in her bedroom, said the girl had talked about having a headache earlier. I don't think that was true, by the way; Josie said it by way of excuse. Raymond went off and telephoned up to Ruby's room, but apparently there was no answer, and he came back in rather a state—temperamental, you know. Josie went off with him and tried to soothe him down, and in the end she danced with him instead of Ruby. Rather plucky of her, because you could see afterward it had hurt her ankle. She came back to us when the dance was over and tried to calm down Mr. Jefferson. He had got worked up by then. We persuaded him, in the end, to go to bed; told him Ruby had probably gone for a spin in a car and that they'd had a puncture. He went to bed worried and this morning he began to agitate at once." She paused. "The rest you know."

"Thank you, Mrs. Jefferson. Now I'm going to ask you if you've any idea who could have done this thing?"

She said immediately, "No idea whatever. I'm afraid I can't help you in the slightest."

He pressed her. "The girl never said anything? Nothing about jealousy? About some man she was afraid of? Or intimate with?"

Adelaide Jefferson shook her head to each query. There seemed nothing more that she could tell them. The superintendent suggested that they should interview young George Bartlett and return to see Mr. Jefferson later. Colonel Melchett agreed and the three men went out, Mrs. Jefferson promising to send word as soon as Mr. Jefferson was awake.

"Nice woman," said the colonel, as they closed the door behind them.

"A very nice lady indeed," said Superintendent Harper.

7

GEORGE BARTLETT was a thin, lanky youth with a prominent Adam's apple and an immense difficulty in saying what he meant. He was in such a state of dither that it was hard to get a calm statement from him. "I say, it is awful, isn't it? Sort of thing one reads about in the Sunday papers, but one doesn't feel it really happens, don't you know?"

"Unfortunately there is no doubt about it, Mr. Bartlett," said the superintendent.

"No, no, of course not. But it seems so rum somehow. And miles from here and everything—in some country house, wasn't it? Awfully county and all that. Created a bit of a stir in the neighborhood, what?"

Colonel Melchett took charge. "How well did you know the dead girl, Mr. Bartlett?"

George Bartlett looked alarmed. "Oh, n-n-not well at all, s-s-sir. No, hardly, if you know what I mean. Danced with her once or twice, passed the time of day, bit of tennis—you know!"

"You were, I think, the last person to see her alive last night?"

"I suppose I was. Doesn't it sound awful? I mean she was perfectly all right when I saw her—absolutely."

"What time was that, Mr. Bartlett?"

"Well, you know, I never know about time. Wasn't very late, if you know what I mean."

"You danced with her?"

"Yes, as a matter of fact—well, yes, I did. Early on in the evening, though. Tell you what. It was just after her exhibition dance with the pro fellow. Must have been ten, half past, eleven—I don't know."

"Never mind the time. We can fix that. Please tell us exactly what happened."

"Well, we danced, don't you know. Not that I'm much of a dancer."

"How you dance is not really relevant, Mr. Bartlett."

George Bartlett cast an alarmed eye on the colonel and stammered, "No—er—n-n-no, I suppose it isn't. Well, as I say, we danced round and round, and I talked, but Ruby didn't say very much, and she yawned a bit. As I say, I don't dance awfully well, and so girls—well, inclined to give it a miss, if you know what I mean too. I know where I get off, so I said 'righty ho,' and that was that."

"What was the last you saw of her?"

"She went off upstairs."

"She said nothing about meeting anyone? Or going for a drive? Or—or having a date?" The colonel used the colloquial expression with a slight effort.

Bartlett shook his head. "Not to me." He looked rather mournful. "Just gave me the push."

"What was her manner? Did she seem anxious, abstracted, anything on her mind?"

George Bartlett considered. Then he shook his head. "Seemed a bit bored. Yawned, as I said. Nothing more."

Colonel Melchett said, "And what did you do, Mr. Bartlett?"

"Eh?"

"What did you do when Ruby Keene left you?"

George Bartlett gaped at him. "Let's see now. What did I do?"

"We're waiting for you to tell us."

"Yes, yes, of course. Jolly difficult, remembering things, what? Let me see. Shouldn't be surprised if I went into the bar and had a drink."

"Did you go into the bar and have a drink?"

"That's just it. I did have a drink. Don't think it was just then. Have an idea I wandered out, don't you know. Bit of air. Rather stuffy for September. Very nice outside. Yes, that's it. I strolled around a bit, then I came in and had a drink, and then I strolled back to the ballroom. Wasn't much doing. Noticed what's-er-name—Josie—was dancing again. With the tennis fellow. She'd been on the sick list—twisted ankle or something."

"That fixes the time of your return at midnight. Do you intend us to understand that you spent over an hour walking about outside?"

"Well, I had a drink, you know. I was—well, I was thinking of things."

This statement received more incredulity than any other. Colonel Melchett said sharply, "What were you thinking about?"

"Oh, I don't know. Things," said Mr. Bartlett vaguely.

"You have a car, Mr. Bartlett?"

"Oh, yes, I've got a car."

"Where was it—in the hotel garage?"

"No, it was in the courtyard, as a matter of fact. Thought I might go for a spin, you see."

"Perhaps you did go for a spin?"

"No, no, I didn't. Swear I didn't."

"You didn't, for instance, take Miss Keene for a spin?"

"Oh, I say, look here. What are you getting at? I didn't, I swear I didn't. Really, now."

"Thank you, Mr. Bartlett. I don't think there is anything more at the present. At present," repeated Colonel Melchett, with a good deal of emphasis on the words.

They left Mr. Bartlett looking after them with a ludicrous expression of alarm on his unintellectual face. "Brainless young ass," said Colonel Melchett. "Or isn't he?"

Superintendent Harper shook his head. "We've got a long way to go," he said.

8

NEITHER the night porter nor the barman proved helpful. The night porter remembered ringing up Miss Keene's room just after midnight and getting no reply. He had not noticed Mr. Bartlett leaving or entering the hotel. A lot of gentlemen and ladies were strolling in and out, the night being fine. And there were side doors off the corridor as well as the one in the main hall. He was fairly certain Miss Keene had not gone out by the main door, but if she had come down from her room, which was on the first floor, there was a staircase next to it and a door out at the end of the corridor leading onto the side terrace. She could have gone out of that, unseen, easily enough. It was not locked until the dancing was over at two o'clock.

The barman remembered Mr. Bartlett being in the bar the preceding evening, but could not say when. Somewhere about the middle of the evening, he thought. Mr. Bartlett had sat against the wall and was looking rather melancholy. He did not know how long he was in there. There were a lot of outside guests coming and going in the bar. He had noticed Mr. Bartlett, but he couldn't fix the time in any way.

As they left the bar they were accosted by a small boy about nine years old. He burst immediately into excited speech. "I say, are you the detectives? I'm Peter Carmody. It was my grandfather, Mr. Jefferson, who rang up the police about Ruby. Are you from Scotland Yard? You don't mind my speaking to you, do you?"

Colonel Melchett looked as though he were about to return a short answer, but Superintendent Harper intervened. He spoke benignly and heartily. "That's all right, my son. Naturally interests you, I expect?"

"You bet it does. Do you like detective stories? I do. I read them all and I've got autographs from Dorothy Sayers and Agatha Christie and Dickson Carr and H. C. Bailey. Will the murder be in the papers?"

"It'll be in the papers all right," said Superintendent Harper grimly.

"You see, I'm going back to school next week and I shall tell them all that I knew her—really knew her well."

"What did you think of her, eh?"

Peter considered. "Well, I didn't like her very much. I think she was rather a stupid sort of girl. Mum and Uncle Mark didn't like her much, either. Only grandfather. Grandfather wants to see you, by the way. Edwards is looking for you."

Superintendent Harper murmured encouragingly, "So your mother and your Uncle Mark didn't like Ruby Keene much? Why was that?"

"Oh, I don't know. She was always butting in. And they didn't like grandfather making such a fuss of her. I expect," said Peter cheerfully, "that they're glad she's dead."

Superintendent Harper looked at him thoughtfully. He said, "Did you hear them—er—say so?"

"Well, not exactly. Uncle Mark said, 'Well, it's one way out anyway,' and mum said, 'Yes, but such a horrible one,' and Uncle Mark said it was no good being hypocritical."

The men exchanged glances. At that moment a clean-shaven man neatly dressed in blue serge came up to them. "Excuse me, gentlemen. I am Mr. Jefferson's valet. He is awake now and sent me to find you, as he is very anxious to see you."

Once more they went up to Conway Jefferson's suite. In the sitting room Adelaide Jefferson was talking to a tall, restless man who was prowling nervously about the room. He swung around sharply to view the newcomers. "Oh, yes. Glad you've come. My father-in-law's been asking for you. He's awake now. Keep him as calm as you can, won't you? His health's not too good. It's a wonder, really, that this shock didn't do for him."

Harper said, "I'd no idea his health was as bad as that."

"He doesn't know it himself," said Mark Gaskell. "It's his heart, you see. The doctor warned Addie that he musn't be overexcited or startled. He more or less hinted that the end might come any time, didn't he, Addie?"

Mrs. Jefferson nodded. She said, "It's incredible that he's rallied the way he has."

Melchett said dryly, "Murder isn't exactly a soothing incident. We'll be as careful as we can." He was sizing up Mark Gaskell as he spoke. He didn't much care for the fellow. A bold, unscrupulous, hawklike face. One of those men who usually get their own way and whom women frequently admire. *But not the sort of fellow I'd trust,* the colonel thought to himself. Unscrupulous—that was the word for him. The sort of fellow who wouldn't stick at anything.

In the big bedroom overlooking the sea, Conway Jefferson was sitting in his wheeled chair by the window. No sooner were you in the room with him than you felt the power and magnetism of the man. It was as though the injuries which had left him a cripple had resulted in concentrating the vitality of his shattered body into a narrower and more intense focus. He had a fine head, the red of the hair slightly grizzled. The face was rugged and powerful, deeply sun-tanned, and the eyes were a startling blue. There was no sign of illness or feebleness about him. The deep lines on his face were the lines of suffering, not the lines of weakness. Here was a man who would never rail against fate, but accept it and pass on to victory. He said, "I'm glad you've come." His quick eyes took them in. He said to Melchett, "You're the chief constable of Radfordshire? Right. And you're Superintendent Harper? Sit down. Cigarettes on the table beside you."

They thanked him and sat down. Melchett said, "I understand, Mr. Jefferson, that you were interested in the dead girl?"

A quick, twisted smile flashed across the lined face. "Yes, they'll all have told you that! Well, it's no secret. How much has my family said to you?" He looked quickly from one to the other as he asked the question.

It was Melchett who answered. "Mrs. Jefferson told us very little beyond the fact that the girl's chatter amused you and that she was by way of being a protégée. We have only exchanged half a dozen words with Mr. Gaskell."

Conway Jefferson smiled. "Addie's a discreet creature, bless her. Mark would probably have been more outspoken. I think, Melchett, that I'd better tell you some facts rather fully. It's necessary, in order that you should understand my attitude. And, to begin with, it's necessary that I go back to the big tragedy of my life. Eight years ago I lost my wife, my son and my daughter in an aeroplane accident. Since then I've been like a man who's lost half himself—and I'm not speaking of my physical plight! I was a family man. My daughter-in-law and my son-in-law have been very good to me. They've done all they can to take the place of my flesh and blood. But I've realized—especially of late—that they have, after all, their own lives to live. So you must understand that, essentially, I'm a lonely man. I like young people. I enjoy them. Once or twice I've played with the idea of adopting some girl or boy. During this last month I got very friendly with the child who's been killed. She was absolutely natural —completely naïve. She chattered on about her life and her experiences —in pantomime, with touring companies, with mum and dad as a child in cheap lodgings. Such a different life from any I've known! Never complaining, never seeing it as sordid. Just a natural, uncomplaining, hardworking child, unspoilt and charming. Not a lady, perhaps, but thank God neither vulgar nor—abominable word—ladylike. I got more and more fond of Ruby. I decided, gentlemen, to adopt her legally. She would become, by law, my daughter. That, I hope, explains my concern for her and the steps I took when I heard of her unaccountable disappearance."

There was a pause. Then Superintendent Harper, his unemotional voice robbing the question of any offense, asked, "May I ask what your son-in-law and daughter-in-law said to that?"

Jefferson's answer came back quickly. "What could they say? They didn't, perhaps, like it very much. It's the sort of thing that arouses prejudice. But they behaved very well—yes, very well. It's not as though, you see, they were dependent on me. When my son Frank married, I turned over half my worldly goods to him then and there. I believe in that. Don't let your children wait until you're dead. They want the money when they're young, not when they're middle-aged. In the same way, when my daughter Rosamund insisted on marrying a poor man, I settled a big sum of money on her. That sum passed to him at her death. So, you see, that simplified the matter from the financial angle."

"I see, Mr. Jefferson," said Superintendent Harper.

But there was a certain reserve in his tone. Conway Jefferson pounced upon it. "But you don't agree, eh?"

"It's not for me to say, sir, but families, in my experience, don't always act reasonable."

"I dare say you're right, superintendent, but you must remember that Mr. Gaskell and Mrs. Jefferson aren't, strictly speaking, my family. They're not blood relations."

"That, of course, makes a difference," admitted the superintendent.

For a moment Conway Jefferson's eyes twinkled. He said, "That's not to say that they didn't think me an old fool! That would be the average person's reaction. But I wasn't being a fool! I know character. With education and polishing, Ruby Keene could have taken her place anywhere."

Melchett said, "I'm afraid we're being rather impertinent and inquisitive, but it's important that we should get at all the facts. You proposed to make full provision for the girl—that is, settle money upon her—but you hadn't already done so?"

Jefferson said, "I understand what you're driving at—the possibility of someone's benefiting by the girl's death. But nobody could. The necessary formalities for legal adoption were under way, but they hadn't yet been completed."

Melchett said slowly, "Then, if anything happened to you?" He left the sentence unfinished, as a query.

Conway Jefferson was quick to respond, "Nothing's likely to happen to me! I'm a cripple, but I'm not an invalid. Although doctors do like to pull long faces and give advice about not overdoing things. Not overdoing things! I'm as strong as a horse! Still, I'm quite aware of the fatalities of life. I've good reason to be! Sudden death comes to the strongest man—especially in these days of road casualties. But I'd provided for that. I made a new will about ten days ago."

"Yes?" Superintendent Harper leaned forward.

"I left the sum of fifty thousand pounds to be held in trust for Ruby Keene until she was twenty-five, when she would come into the principal."

Superintendent Harper's eyes opened. So did Colonel Melchett's. Harper said in an almost awed voice, "That's a very large sum of money, Mr. Jefferson."

"In these days, yes, it is."

"And you were leaving it to a girl you had only known a few weeks?"

Anger flashed into the vivid blue eyes. "Must I go on repeating the same thing over and over again? I've no flesh and blood of my own—no nieces or nephews or distant cousins, even! I might have left it to charity. I prefer to leave it to an individual." He laughed. "Cinderella turned into a princess overnight! A fairy godfather instead of a fairy godmother. Why not? It's my money. I made it."

Colonel Melchett asked, "Any other bequests?"

"A small legacy to Edwards, my valet, and the remainder to Mark and Addie in equal shares."

"Would—excuse me—the residue amount to a large sum?"

"Probably not. It's difficult to say exactly; investments fluctuate all the time. The sum involved, after death duties and expenses had been paid, would probably have come to something between five and ten thousand pounds net."

"I see."

"And you needn't think I was treating them shabbily. As I said, I divided up my estate at the time my children married. I left myself, actually, a very small sum. But after—after the tragedy I wanted something to occupy my mind. I flung myself into business. At my house in London I had a private line put in, connecting my bedroom with my office. I worked hard; it helped me not to think, and it made me feel that my—my mutilation had not vanquished me. I threw myself into work"—his voice took on a deeper note; he spoke more to himself than to his audience—"and by some subtle irony, everything I did prospered! My wildest speculations succeeded. If I gambled, I won. Everything I touched turned to gold. Fate's ironic way of righting the balance, I suppose."

The lines of suffering stood out on his face again. Recollecting himself, he smiled wryly at them.

"So, you see, the sum of money I left Ruby was indisputably mine, to do with as my fancy dictated."

Melchett said quickly, "Undoubtedly, my dear fellow. We are not questioning that for a moment."

Conway Jefferson said, "Good. Now I want to ask some questions in my turn, if I may. I want to hear more about this terrible business. All I know is that she—that little Ruby was found strangled in a house some twenty miles from here."

"That is correct. At Gossington Hall."

Jefferson frowned. "Gossington? But that's—"

"Colonel Bantry's house."

"Bantry! Arthur Bantry? But I know him. Know him and his wife! Met them abroad some years ago. I didn't realize they lived in this part of the world. Why, it's—" He broke off.

Superintendent Harper slipped in smoothly, "Colonel Bantry was dining in the hotel here Tuesday of last week. You didn't see him?"

"Tuesday? Tuesday? No, we were back late. Went over to Harden Head and had dinner on the way back."

Melchett said, "Ruby Keene never mentioned the Bantrys to you?"

Jefferson shook his head. "Never. Don't believe she knew them. Sure she didn't. She didn't know anybody but theatrical folk and that sort of thing." He paused, and then asked abruptly, "What's Bantry got to say about it?"

"He can't account for it in the least. He was out at a Conservative meeting last night. The body was discovered this morning. He says he's never seen the girl in his life."

Jefferson nodded. He said, "It certainly seems fantastic."

Superintendent Harper cleared his throat. He said, "Have you any idea at all, sir, who can have done this?"

"Good God, I wish I had!" The veins stood out on his forehead. "It's incredible, unimaginable! I'd say it couldn't have happened, if it hadn't happened!"

"There's no friend of hers from her past life, no man hanging about or threatening her?"

"I'm sure there isn't. She'd have told me if so. She's never had a regular boy friend. She told me so herself." Superintendent Harper thought, *Yes, I dare say that's what she told you. But that's as may be.* Conway Jefferson went on, "Josie would know better than anyone if there had been some man hanging about Ruby or pestering her. Can't she help?"

"She says not."

Jefferson said, frowning, "I can't help feeling it must be the work of some maniac—the brutality of the method, breaking into a country house, the whole thing so unconnected and senseless. There are men of that type, men outwardly sane, but who decoy girls, sometimes children, away and kill them."

Harper said, "Oh, yes, there are such cases, but we've no knowledge of anyone of that kind operating in this neighborhood."

Jefferson went on, "I've thought over all the various men I've seen with Ruby. Guests here and outsiders—men she'd danced with. They all seem harmless enough—the usual type. She had no special friend of any kind."

Superintendent Harper's face remained quite impassive, but, unseen by Conway Jefferson, there was still a speculative glint in his eye. It was quite possible, he thought, that Ruby Keene might have had a special friend, even though Conway Jefferson did not know about it. He said nothing, however.

The chief constable gave him a glance of inquiry and then rose to his feet. He said, "Thank you, Mr. Jefferson. That's all we need for the present."

Jefferson said, "You'll keep me informed of your progress?"

"Yes, yes, we'll keep in touch with you."

The two men went out. Conway Jefferson leaned back in his chair. His eyelids came down and veiled the fierce blue of his eyes. He looked, suddenly, a very tired man. Then, after a minute or two, the lids flickered. He called, "Edwards?"

From the next room the valet appeared promptly. Edwards knew his master as no one else did. Others, even his nearest, knew only his strength; Edwards knew his weakness. He had seen Conway Jefferson tired, discouraged, weary of life, momentarily defeated by infirmity and loneliness.

"Yes, sir?"

Jefferson said, "Get on to Sir Henry Clithering. He's at Melborne Abbas. Ask him, from me, to get here today if he can, instead of tomorrow. Tell him it's very urgent."

9

WHEN they were outside Jefferson's door, Superintendent Harper said, "Well, for what it's worth, we've got a motive, sir."

"H'm," said Melchett. "Fifty thousand pounds, eh?"

"Yes, sir. Murder's been done for a good deal less than that."

"Yes, but—"

Colonel Melchett left the sentence unfinished. Harper, however, understood him. "You don't think it's likely in this case? Well, I don't, either, as far as that goes. But it's got to be gone into, all the same."

"Oh, of course."

Harper went on, "If, as Mr. Jefferson says, Mr. Gaskell and Mrs. Jefferson are already well provided for and in receipt of a comfortable income, well, it's not likely they'd set out to do a brutal murder."

"Quite so. Their financial standing will have to be investigated, of course. Can't say I like the appearance of Gaskell much—looks a sharp, unscrupulous sort of fellow—but that's a long way from making him out a murderer."

"Oh, yes, sir, as I say, I don't think it's likely to be either of them, and from what Josie said I don't see how it would have been humanly possible. They were both playing bridge from twenty minutes to eleven until midnight. No, to my mind, there's another possibility much more likely."

Melchett said, "Boy friend of Ruby Keene's?"

"That's it, sir. Some disgruntled young fellow; not too strong in the head perhaps. Someone, I'd say, she knew before she came here. This adoption scheme, if he got wise to it, may just have put the lid on things. He saw himself losing her, saw her being removed to a different sphere of life altogether, and he went mad and blind with rage. He got her to come out and meet him last night, had a row with her over it, lost his head completely and did her in."

"And how did she come to be in Bantry's library?"

"I think that's feasible. They were out, say, in his car at the time. He came to himself, realized what he'd done, and his first thought was how to get rid of the body. Say they were near the gates of a big house at the time. The idea comes to him that if she's found there the hue and cry will center round the house and its occupants and will leave him comfortably out of it. She's a little bit of a thing. He could easily carry her. He's got a chisel in the car. He forces a window and plops her down on the hearthrug. Being a strangling case, there's no blood or mess to give him away in the car. See what I mean, sir?"

"Oh, yes, Harper, it's all perfectly possible. But there's still one thing to be done. *Cherchez l'homme.*"

"What? Oh, very good, sir." Superintendent Harper tactfully applauded Melchett's joke, although, owing to the excellence of the colonel's French accent, he almost missed the sense of the words.

"Oh—er—I say—er—c-c-could I speak to you a minute?" It was George Bartlett who thus waylaid the two men.

Colonel Melchett, who was not attracted to Mr. Bartlett, and who was eager to see how Slack had got on with the investigation of the girl's room and the questioning of the chambermaids, barked sharply, "Well, what is it—what is it?"

Young Mr. Bartlett retreated a step or two, opening and shutting his mouth and giving an unconscious imitation of a fish in a tank. "Well—er —probably isn't important, don't you know. Thought I ought to tell you. Matter of fact, can't find my car."

"What do you mean, can't find your car?" Stammering a good deal, Mr. Bartlett explained that what he meant was that he couldn't find his car.

Superintendent Harper said, "Do you mean it's been stolen?"

George Bartlett turned gratefully to the more placid voice. "Well, that's just it, you know. I mean, one can't tell, can one? I mean someone may just have buzzed off in it, not meaning any harm, if you know what I mean."

"When did you last see it, Mr. Bartlett?"

"Well, I was tryin' to remember. Funny how difficult it is to remember anything, isn't it?"

Colonel Melchett said coldly, "Not, I should think, to a normal intelligence. I understood you to say that it was in the courtyard of the hotel last night."

Mr. Bartlett was bold enough to interrupt. He said, "That's just it— was it?"

"What do you mean by 'was it'? You said it was."

"Well, I mean I thought it was. I mean—well, I didn't go out and look, don't you see?"

Colonel Melchett sighed. He summoned all his patience. He said, "Let's get this quite clear. When was the last time you saw—actually saw —your car? What make is it, by the way?"

"Minoan Fourteen."

"And you last saw it when?"

George Bartlett's Adam's apple jerked convulsively up and down. "Been trying to think. Had it before lunch yesterday. Was going for a spin in the afternoon. But somehow—you know how it is—went to sleep instead. Then, after tea, had a game of squash and all that, and a bath afterward."

"And the car was then in the courtyard of the hotel?"

"Suppose so. I mean, that's where I'd put it. Thought, you see, I'd take someone for a spin. After dinner, I mean. But it wasn't my lucky evening. Nothing doing. Never took the old bus out after all."

Harper said, "But as far as you knew, the car was still in the courtyard?"

"Well, naturally. I mean, I'd put it there, what?"

"Would you have noticed if it had not been there?"

Mr. Bartlett shook his head. "Don't think so, you know. Lot of cars going and coming and all that. Plenty of Minoans."

Superintendent Harper nodded. He had just cast a casual glance out of the window. There were at that moment no fewer than eight Minoan 14's in the courtyard—it was the popular cheap car of the year.

"Aren't you in the habit of putting your car away at night?" asked Colonel Melchett.

"Don't usually bother," said Mr. Bartlett. "Fine weather and all that, you know. Such a fag putting a car away in a garage."

Glancing at Colonel Melchett, Superintendent Harper said, "I'll join you upstairs, sir. I'll just get hold of Sergeant Higgins and he can take down particulars from Mr. Bartlett."

"Right, Harper."

Mr. Bartlett murmured wistfully, "Thought I ought to let you know, you know. Might be important, what?"

Mr. Prestcott had supplied his additional dancer with board and lodging. Whatever the board, the lodging was the poorest the hotel possessed. Josephine Turner and Ruby Keene had occupied rooms at the extreme end of a mean and dingy little corridor. The rooms were small, faced north onto a portion of the cliff that backed the hotel, and were furnished with the odds and end of suites that had once represented luxury and magnificence in the best suites. Now, when the hotel had been modernized and the bedrooms supplied with built-in receptacles for clothes, these large Victorian oak and mahogany wardrobes were relegated to those rooms occupied by the hotel's resident staff, or given to guests in the height of the season when all the rest of the hotel was full.

As Melchett and Harper saw at once, the position of Ruby Keene's room was ideal for the purpose of leaving the hotel without being observed, and was particularly unfortunate from the point of view of throwing light on the circumstances of that departure. At the end of the corridor was a small staircase which led down to an equally obscure corridor on the ground floor. Here there was a glass door which led out on the side terrace of the hotel, an unfrequented terrace with no view. You could go from it to the main terrace in front, or you could go down a winding path and come out in a lane that eventually rejoined the cliff road. Its surface being bad, it was seldom used.

Inspector Slack had been busy harrying chambermaids and examining Ruby's room for clues. They had been lucky enough to find the room exactly as it had been left the night before. Ruby Keene had not been in the habit of rising early. Her usual procedure, Slack discovered, was to sleep until about ten or half past and then ring for breakfast. Consequently, since Conway Jefferson had begun his representations to the manager very early, the police had taken charge of things before the chambermaids had touched the room. They had actually not been down that corridor at all. The other rooms there, at this season of the year, were opened and dusted only once a week. "That's all to the good, as far as it goes," Slack explained. "It means that if there were anything to find, we'd find it, but there isn't anything."

The Glenshire police had already been over the room for fingerprints, but there were none unaccounted for. Ruby's own, Josie's, and the two chambermaids'—one on the morning and one on the evening shift. There were also a couple of prints made by Raymond Starr, but these were accounted for by his story that he had come up with Josie to look for Ruby when she did not appear for the midnight exhibition dance.

There had been a heap of letters and general rubbish in the pigeonholes of the massive mahogany desk in the corner. Slack had just been carefully sorting through them, but he had found nothing of a suggestive nature. Bills, receipts, theater programs, cinema stubs, newspaper cuttings, beauty hints torn from magazines. Of the letters, there were some from Lil, apparently a friend from the Palais de Danse, recounting various affairs and gossip, saying they "missed Rube a lot. Mr. Findeison asked after you ever so often! Quite put out, he is! Young Reg has taken up with May now you've gone. Barney asks after you now and then. Things going much as usual. Old Grouser still as mean as ever with us girls. He ticked off Ada for going about with a fellow."

Slack had carefully noted all the names mentioned. Inquiries would be made, and it was possible some useful information might come to light. Otherwise the room had little to yield in the way of information.

Across a chair in the middle of the room was the foamy pink dance frock Ruby had worn early in the evening, with a pair of satin high-heeled shoes kicked off carelessly on the floor. Two sheer silk stockings were rolled into a ball and flung down. One had a ladder in it. Melchett recalled that the dead girl had had bare legs. This, Slack learned, was her custom. She used make-up on her legs instead of stockings, and only sometimes wore stockings for dancing; by this means saving expense. The wardrobe door was open and showed a variety of rather flashy evening dresses and a row of shoes below. There was some soiled underwear in the clothes basket; some nail parings, soiled face-cleaning tissue and bits of cotton wool stained with rouge and nail polish in the waste-paper basket—in fact, nothing out of the ordinary. The facts seemed plain to read. Ruby had hurried upstairs, changed her clothes and hurried off again—where?

Josephine Turner, who might be supposed to know most about Ruby's life and friends, had proved unable to help. But this, as Inspector Slack pointed out, might be natural. "If what you tell me is true, sir—about this adoption business, I mean—well, Josie would be all for Ruby breaking with any old friends she might have, and who might queer the pitch, so to speak. As I see it, this invalid gentleman gets all worked up about Ruby Keene being such a sweet, innocent, childish little piece of goods. Now supposing Ruby's got a tough boy friend—that won't go down so well with the old boy. So it's Ruby's business to keep that dark. Josie doesn't know much about the girl, anyway—not about her friends and all that. But one thing she wouldn't stand for—Ruby's messing up things by carrying on with some undesirable fellow. So it stands to reason that Ruby—who, as I see it, was a sly little piece!—would keep very dark about seeing any old friend. She wouldn't let on to Josie anything about it; otherwise Josie would say, 'No, you don't, my girl.' But you know what girls are—especially young ones—always ready to make a fool of themselves over a tough guy. Ruby wants to see him. He comes down here, cuts up rough about the whole business and wrings her neck."

"I expect you're right, Slack," said Colonel Melchett, disguising his usual repugnance for the unpleasant way Slack had of putting things. "If so, we ought to be able to discover this tough friend's identity fairly easily."

"You leave it to me, sir," said Slack with his usual confidence. "I'll get hold of this Lil girl at that Palais de Danse place and turn her right inside out. We'll soon get at the truth." Colonel Melchett wondered if they would. Slack's energy and activity always made him feel tired. "There's one other person you might be able to get a tip from, sir," went on Slack. "And that's the dance-and-tennis-pro fellow. He must have seen a lot of her, and he'd know more than Josie would. Likely enough she'd loosen her tongue a bit to him."

"I have already discussed that point with Superintendent Harper."

"Good, sir. I've done the chambermaids pretty thoroughly. They don't know a thing. Looked down on these two, as far as I can make out. Scamped the service as much as they dared. Chambermaid was in here last at seven o'clock last night, when she turned down the bed and drew the curtains and cleared up a bit. There's a bathroom next door, if you'd like to see it."

The bathroom was situated between Ruby's room and the slightly larger room occupied by Josie. It was unilluminating. Colonel Melchett silently marveled at the amount of aids to beauty that women could use. Rows of jars of face cream, cleansing cream, vanishing cream, skin-feeding cream. Boxes of different shades of powder. An untidy heap of every variety of lipstick. Hair lotions and brightening applications. Eyelash black, mascara, blue stain for under the eyes, at least twelve different shades of nail varnish, face tissues, bits of cotton wool, dirty powder puffs. Bottles of lotions—astringent, tonic, soothing, and so on. "Do you mean to say," he murmured feebly, "that women use all these things?"

Inspector Slack, who always knew everything, kindly enlightened him. "In private life, sir, so to speak, a lady keeps to one or two distinct shades —one for evening, one for day. They know what suits them and they keep to it. But these professional girls, they have to ring a change, so to speak. They do exhibition dances, and one night it's a tango, and the next a crinoline Victorian dance, and then a kind of Apache dance, and then just ordinary ballroom, and of course the make-up varies a good bit."

"Good Lord," said the colonel. "No wonder the people who turn out these creams and messes make a fortune."

"Easy money, that's what it is," said Slack. "Easy money. Got to spend a bit in advertisement, of course."

Colonel Melchett jerked his mind away from the fascinating and age-long problem of woman's adornments. He said, "There's still this dancing fellow. Your pigeon, superintendent."

"I suppose so, sir."

As they went downstairs Harper asked, "What did you think of Mr. Bartlett's story, sir?"

"About his car? I think, Harper, that that young man wants watching. It's a fishy story. Supposing that he did take Ruby Keene out in that car last night, after all?"

10

SUPERINTENDENT HARPER'S manner was slow and pleasant and absolutely noncommittal. These cases where the police of two counties had to collaborate were always difficult. He liked Colonel Melchett and considered him an able chief constable, but he was nevertheless glad to be tackling the present interview by himself. Never do too much at once, was Superintendent Harper's rule. Bare routine inquiry for the first time. That left the persons you were interviewing relieved, and predisposed them to be more unguarded in the next interview you had with them.

Harper already knew Raymond Starr by sight. A fine-looking specimen, tall, lithe and good-looking, with very white teeth in a deeply bronzed face. He was dark and graceful. He had a pleasant, friendly manner and was very popular in the hotel. "I'm afraid I can't help you much, superintendent. I knew Ruby quite well, of course. She'd been here over a month and we had practiced our dances together, and all that. But there's really very little to say. She was quite a pleasant and rather stupid girl."

"It's her friendships we're particularly anxious to know about. Her friendships with men."

"So I suppose. Well, I don't know anything. She'd got a few young men in tow in the hotel, but nothing special. You see, she was nearly always monopolized by the Jefferson family."

"Yes, the Jefferson family." Harper paused meditatively. He shot a shrewd glance at the young man. "What did you think of that business, Mr. Starr?"

Raymond Starr said coolly, "What business?"

Harper said, "Did you know that Mr. Jefferson was proposing to adopt Ruby Keene legally?"

This appeared to be news to Starr. He pursed up his lips and whistled. He said, "The clever little devil! Oh, well, there's no fool like an old fool.

"Well, what else can one say? If the old boy wanted to adopt someone, why didn't he pick upon a girl of his own class?"

"Ruby never mentioned the matter to you?"

"No, she didn't. I knew she was elated about something, but I didn't know what it was."

"And Josie?"

"Oh, I think Josie must have known what was in the wind. Probably she was the one who planned the whole thing. Josie's no fool. She's got a head on her, that girl."

Harper nodded. It was Josie who had sent for Ruby Keene. Josie, no doubt, who had encouraged the intimacy. No wonder she had been upset when Ruby had failed to show up for her dance that night and Conway Jefferson had begun to panic. She was envisaging her plans going awry. He asked, "Could Ruby keep a secret, do you think?"

"As well as most. She didn't talk about her own affairs much."

"Did she ever say anything—anything at all—about some friend of hers—someone from her former life—who was coming to see her here or whom she had had difficulty with? You know the sort of thing I mean, no doubt."

"I know perfectly. Well, as far as I'm aware, there was no one of the kind. Not by anything she ever said."

"Thank you. Now will you just tell me in your own words exactly what happened last night?"

"Certainly. Ruby and I did our ten-thirty dance together."

"No signs of anything unusual about her then?"

Raymond considered. "I don't think so. I didn't notice what happened afterward. I had my own partners to look after. I do remember noticing she was not in the ballroom. At midnight she hadn't turned up. I was very annoyed and went to Josie about it. Josie was playing bridge with the Jeffersons. She hadn't any idea where Ruby was, and I think she got a bit of a jolt. I noticed her shoot a quick, anxious glance at Mr. Jefferson. I persuaded the band to play another dance and I went to the office and got them to ring up Ruby's room. There wasn't any answer. I went back to Josie. She suggested that Ruby was perhaps asleep in her room. Idiotic suggestion really, but it was meant for the Jeffersons, of course! She came away with me and said we'd go up together."

"Yes, Mr. Starr. And what did she say when she was alone with you?"

"As far as I can remember, she looked very angry and said, 'Damned little fool. She can't do this sort of thing. It will ruin all her chances. Who's she with? Do you know?'

"I said that I hadn't the least idea. The last I'd seen of her was dancing with young Bartlett. Josie said, 'She wouldn't be with him. What can she be up to? She isn't with that film man, is she?' "

Harper said sharply, "Film man? Who was he?"

Raymond said, "I don't know his name. He's never stayed here. Rather an unusual-looking chap—black hair and theatrical-looking. He has something to do with the film industry, I believe—or so he told

Ruby. He came over to dine here once or twice and danced with Ruby afterward, but I don't think she knew him at all well. That's why I was surprised when Josie mentioned him. I said I didn't think he'd been here tonight. Josie said, 'Well, she must be out with someone. What on earth am I going to say to the Jeffersons?' I said what did it matter to the Jeffersons? And Josie said it did matter. And she said, too, that she'd never forgive Ruby if she went and messed things up.

"We'd got to Ruby's room by then. She wasn't there, of course, but she'd been there, because the dress she had been wearing was lying across a chair. Josie looked in the wardrobe and said she thought she'd put on her old white dress. Normally she'd have changed into a black velvet dress for our Spanish dance. I was pretty angry by this time at the way Ruby had let me down. Josie did her best to soothe me and said she'd dance herself, so that old Prestcott shouldn't get after us all. She went away and changed her dress, and we went down and did a tango— exaggerated style and quite showy, but not really too exhausting upon the ankles. Josie was very plucky about it, for it hurt her, I could see. After that, she asked me to help her soothe the Jeffersons down. She said it was important. So, of course, I did what I could."

Superintendent Harper nodded. He said, "Thank you, Mr. Starr." To himself he thought, *It was important all right. Fifty thousand pounds.* He watched Raymond Starr as the latter moved gracefully away. He went down the steps of the terrace, picking up a bag of tennis balls and a racket on the way. Mrs. Jefferson, also carrying a racket, joined him, and they went toward the tennis courts.

"Excuse me, sir." Sergeant Higgins, rather breathless, was standing at Superintendent Harper's side. The superintendent, jerked from the train of thought he was following, looked startled. "Message just come through for you from headquarters, sir. Laborer reported this morning saw glare as of fire. Half an hour ago they found a burnt-out car near a quarry—Venn's Quarry—about two miles from here. Traces of a charred body inside."

A flush came over Harper's heavy features. He said, "What's come to Glenshire? An epidemic of violence?" He asked, "Could they get the number of the car?"

"No, sir. But we'll be able to identify it, of course, by the engine number. A Minoan Fourteen, they think it is."

11

SIR HENRY CLITHERING, as he passed through the lounge of the Majestic, hardly glanced at its occupants. His mind was preoccupied. Nevertheless, as is the way of life, something registered in his subconscious. It waited its time patiently.

Sir Henry was wondering, as he went upstairs, just what had induced the sudden urgency of his friend's message. Conway Jefferson was not the type of man who sent urgent summonses to anyone. Something quite out of the usual must have occurred, decided Sir Henry.

Jefferson wasted no time in beating about the bush. He said, "Glad you've come. . . . Edwards, get Sir Henry a drink. . . . Sit down, man. You've not heard anything, I suppose? Nothing in the papers yet?"

Sir Henry shook his head, his curiosity aroused. "What's the matter?"

"Murder's the matter. I'm concerned in it, and so are your friends, the Bantrys."

"Arthur and Dolly Bantry?" Clithering sounded incredulous.

"Yes; you see, the body was found in their house."

Clearly and succinctly, Conway Jefferson ran through the facts. Sir Henry listened without interrupting. Both men were accustomed to grasping the gist of a matter. Sir Henry, during his term as commissioner of the Metropolitan Police, had been renowned for his quick grip on essentials. "It's an extraordinary business," he commented when the other had finished. "How do the Bantrys come into it, do you think?"

"That's what worries me. You see, Henry, it looks to me as though possibly the fact that I know them might have a bearing on the case. That's the only connection I can find. Neither of them, I gather, ever saw the girl before. That's what they say, and there's no reason to disbelieve them. It's most unlikely they should know her. Then isn't it possible that she was decoyed away and her body deliberately left in the house of friends of mine?"

Clithering said, "I think that's far-fetched."

"It's possible, though," persisted the other.

"Yes, but unlikely. What do you want me to do?"

Conway Jefferson said bitterly, "I'm an invalid. I disguise the fact—refuse to face it—but now it comes home to me. I can't go about as I'd like to, asking questions, looking into things. I've got to stay here meekly grateful for such scraps of information as the police are kind enough to dole out to me. Do you happen to know Melchett, by the way, the chief constable of Radfordshire?"

"Yes, I've met him." Something stirred in Sir Henry's brain. A face and figure noted unseeingly as he passed through the lounge. A straight-backed old lady whose face was familiar. It linked up with the last time he had seen Melchett. He said, "Do you mean you want me to be a kind of amateur sleuth? That's not my line."

Jefferson said, "You're not an amateur, that's just it."

"I'm not a professional any more. I'm on the retired list now."

Jefferson said, "That simplifies matters."

"You mean that if I were still at Scotland Yard I couldn't butt in? That's perfectly true."

"As it is," said Jefferson, "your experience qualifies you to take an interest in the case, and any co-operation you offer will be welcomed."

Clithering said slowly, "Etiquette permits, I agree. But what do you really want, Conway? To find out who killed this girl?"

"Just that."

"You've no idea yourself?"

"None whatever."

Sir Henry said slowly, "You probably won't believe me, but you've got an expert at solving mysteries sitting downstairs in the lounge at this minute. Someone who's better than I am at it, and who, in all probability, may have some local dope."

"What are you talking about?"

"Downstairs in the lounge, by the third pillar from the left, there sits an old lady with a sweet, placid, spinsterish face and a mind that has plumbed the depths of human iniquity and taken it as all in the day's work. Her name's Miss Marple. She comes from the village of St. Mary Mead, which is a mile and a half from Gossington; she's a friend of the Bantrys and, where crime is concerned, she's the goods, Conway."

Jefferson stared at him with thick puckered brows. He said heavily, "You're joking."

"No, I'm not. You spoke of Melchett just now. The last time I saw Melchett there was a village tragedy. Girl supposed to have drowned herself. Police, quite rightly, suspected that it wasn't suicide but murder. They thought they knew who did it. Along to me comes old Miss Marple, fluttering and dithering. She's afraid, she says, they'll hang the wrong person. She's got no evidence, but she knows who did do it. Hands me a piece of paper with a name written on it. And, Jefferson, she was right!"

Conway Jefferson's brows came down lower than ever. He grunted disbelievingly.

"Woman's intuition, I suppose," he said skeptically.

"No, she doesn't call it that. Specialized knowledge is her claim."

"And what does that mean?"

"Well, you know, Jefferson, we use it in police work. We get a burglary and we usually know pretty well who did it—of the regular crowd, that is. We know the sort of burglar who acts in a particular sort of way. Miss Marple has an interesting, though occasionally trivial, series of parallels from village life."

Jefferson said skeptically, "What is she likely to know about a girl who's been brought up in a theatrical millieu and probably never been in a village in her life?"

"I think," said Sir Henry Clithering firmly, "that she might have ideas."

Miss Marple flushed with pleasure as Sir Henry bore down upon her. "Oh, Sir Henry, this is indeed a great piece of luck, meeting you here."

Sir Henry was gallant. He said, "To me, it is a great pleasure."

Miss Marple murmured, flushing. "So kind of you."

"Are you staying here?"

"Well, as a matter of fact we are."

"We?"

"Mrs. Bantry's here too." She looked at him sharply. "Have you heard yet—Yes, I can see you have. It is terrible, is it not?"

"What's Dolly Bantry doing here? Is her husband here too?"

"No. Naturally, they both reacted quite differently. Colonel Bantry, poor man, just shuts himself up in his study or goes down to one of the farms when anything like this happens. Like tortoises, you know; they draw their heads in and hope nobody will notice them. Dolly, of course, is quite different."

"Dolly, in fact," said Sir Henry, who knew his old friend fairly well, "is almost enjoying herself, eh?"

"Well—er—yes. Poor dear."

"And she's brought you along to produce the rabbits out of the hat for her?"

Miss Marple said composedly, "Dolly thought that a change of scene would be a good thing and she didn't want to come alone." She met his eye and her own gently twinkled. "But of course your way of describing it is quite true. It's rather embarrassing for me because, of course, I am no use at all."

"No ideas? No village parallels?"

"I don't know much about it all yet."

"I can remedy that, I think. I'm going to call you into consultation, Miss Marple."

He gave a brief recital of the course of events. Miss Marple listened with keen interest. "Poor Mr. Jefferson," she said. "What a very sad story. These terrible accidents. To leave him alive, crippled, seems more cruel than if he had been killed too."

"Yes, indeed. That's why all his friends admire him so much for the resolute way he's gone on, conquering pain and grief and physical disabilities."

"Yes, it is splendid."

"The only thing I can't understand is this sudden outpouring of affection for this girl. She may, of course, have had some remarkable qualities."

"Probably not," said Miss Marple placidly.

"You don't think so?"

"I don't think her qualities entered into it."

Sir Henry said, "He isn't just a nasty old man, you know."

"Oh, no, no!" Miss Marple got quite pink. "I wasn't implying that for a minute. What I was trying to say was—very badly, I know—that he was just looking for a nice bright girl to take his dead daughter's place, and then this girl saw her opportunity and played it for all she was worth! That sounds rather uncharitable, I know, but I have seen so many cases of the kind. The young maidservant at Mr. Harbottle's, for instance. A very ordinary girl. but quiet, with nice manners. His sister was called away to nurse a dying relative, and when she got back she found the girl completely above herself, sitting down in the drawing room laughing and talking and not wearing her cap or apron. Miss Harbottle spoke to her very sharply, and the girl was impertinent, and then old Mr. Harbottle left her quite dumfounded by saying that he thought she had kept house for him long enough and that he was making other arrangements.

"Such a scandal as it created in the village, but poor Miss Harbottle had to go and live most uncomfortably in rooms in Eastbourne. People said things, of course, but I believe there was no familiarity of any kind. It was simply that the old man found it much pleasanter to have a young, cheerful girl telling him how clever and amusing he was than to have his sister continually pointing out his faults to him, even if she was a good, economical manager."

There was a moment's pause and then Miss Marple resumed, "And there was Mr. Badger, who had the chemist's shop. Made a lot of fuss over the young lady who worked in his cosmetics section. Told his wife they must look on her as a daughter and have her to live in the house. Mrs. Badger didn't see it that way at all."

Sir Henry said, "If she'd only been a girl in his own rank of life—a friend's child—"

Miss Marple interrupted him. "Oh, but that wouldn't have been nearly as satisfactory from his point of view. It's like King Cophetua and the beggar maid. If you're really rather a lonely tired old man, and if, perhaps, your own family have been neglecting you"—she paused for a second—"well, to befriend someone who will be overwhelmed with your magnificence—to put it rather melodramatically, but I hope you see what I mean—well, that's much more interesting. It makes you feel a much greater person—a beneficent monarch! The recipient is more likely to be dazzled, and that, of course, is a pleasant feeling for you." She paused and said, "Mr. Badger, you know, bought the girl in his shop some really fantastic presents—a diamond bracelet and a most expensive radiogramophone. Took out a lot of his savings to do it. However, Mrs. Badger, who was a much more astute woman than poor Miss Harbottle—marriage, of course, helps—took the trouble to find out a few things. And when Mr. Badger discovered that the girl was carrying on with a very undesirable young man connected with the race-courses, and had actually pawned the bracelet to give him money—well, he was completely disgusted and the affair passed over quite safely. And he gave Mrs. Badger a diamond ring the following Christmas."

Her pleasant, shrewd eyes met Sir Henry's. He wondered if what she had been saying was intended as a hint. He said, "Are you suggesting that if there had been a young man in Ruby Keene's life, my friend's attitude towards her might have altered?"

"It probably would, you know. I dare say in a year or two he might have liked to arrange for her marriage himself; though more likely he wouldn't—gentlemen are usually rather selfish. But I certainly think that if Ruby Keene had had a young man she'd have been careful to keep very quiet about it."

"And the young man might have resented that?"

"I suppose that is the most plausible solution. It struck me, you know, that her cousin, the young woman who was at Gossington this morning, looked definitely angry with the dead girl. What you've told me explains why. No doubt she was looking forward to doing very well out of the business."

"Rather a cold-blooded character, in fact?"

"That's too harsh a judgment, perhaps. The poor thing has had to earn her living, and you can't expect her to sentimentalize because a well-to-do man and woman—as you have described Mr. Gaskell and Mrs. Jefferson—are going to be done out of a further large sum of money to which they have really no particular moral right. I should say Miss Turner was a hardheaded, ambitious young woman with a good temper and considerable *joie de vivre.* A little," added Miss Marple, "like Jessie Golden, the baker's daughter."

"What happened to her?" asked Sir Henry.

"She trained as a nursery governess and married the son of the house, who was home on leave from India. Made him a very good wife, I believe."

Sir Henry pulled himself clear of these fascinating side issues. He said, "Is there any reason, do you think, why my friend Conway Jefferson should suddenly have developed this 'Cophetua complex,' if you like to call it that?"

"There might have been."

"In what way?"

Miss Marple said, hesitating a little, "I should think—it's only a suggestion, of course—that perhaps his son-in-law and daughter-in-law might have wanted to get married again."

"Surely he couldn't have objected to that?"

"Oh, no, not objected. But, you see, you must look at it from his point of view. He has a terrible shock and loss; so have they. The three bereaved people live together and the link between them is the loss they have all sustained. But Time, as my dear mother used to say, is a great healer. Mr. Gaskell and Mrs. Jefferson are young. Without knowing it themselves, they may have begun to feel restless, to resent the bonds that tied them to their past sorrow. And so, feeling like that, old Mr. Jefferson would have become conscious of a sudden lack of sympathy without knowing its cause. It's usually that. Gentlemen so easily feel neglected. With Mr. Harbottle it was Miss Harbottle going away. And with the Badgers it was Mrs. Badger taking such an interest in spiritualism and always going out to séances."

"I must say," said Sir Henry ruefully, "that I do dislike the way you reduce us all to a general common denominator."

Miss Marple shook her head sadly. "Human nature is very much the same anywhere, Sir Henry."

Sir Henry said distastefully, "Mr. Harbottle! Mr. Badger! And poor Conway! I hate to intrude the personal note, but have you any parallel for my humble self in your village?"

"Well, of course, there is Briggs."

"Who's Briggs?"

"He was the head gardener up at Old Hall. Quite the best man they ever had. Knew exactly when the under-gardeners were slacking off—quite uncanny it was! He managed with only three men and a boy, and the place was kept better than it had been with six. And took several Firsts with his sweet peas. He's retired now."

"Like me," said Sir Henry.

"But he still does a little jobbing, if he likes the people."

"Ah," said Sir Henry. "Again like me. That's what I'm doing now. Jobbing. To help an old friend."

"Two old friends."

"Two?" Sir Henry looked a little puzzled.

Miss Marple said, "I suppose you meant Mr. Jefferson. But I wasn't thinking of him. I was thinking of Colonel and Mrs. Bantry."

"Yes, yes, I see." He asked sharply, "Was that why you alluded to Dolly Bantry as 'poor dear' at the beginning of our conversation?"

"Yes. She hasn't begun to realize things yet. I know, because I've had more experience. You see, Sir Henry, it seems to me that there's a great possibility of this crime being the kind of crime that never does get solved. Like the Brighton trunk murders. But if that happens it will be absolutely disastrous for the Bantrys. Colonel Bantry, like nearly all retired military men, is really abnormally sensitive. He reacts very quickly to public opinion. He won't notice it for some time, and then it will begin to go home to him. A slight here, and a snub there, and invitations that are refused, and excuses that are made, and then, little by little, it will dawn upon him, and he'll retire into his shell and get terribly morbid and miserable."

"Let me be sure I understand you rightly, Miss Marple. You mean that, because the body was found in his house, people will think that he had something to do with it?"

"Of course they will! I've no doubt they're saying so already. They'll say so more and more. And people will cold-shoulder the Bantrys and avoid them. That's why the truth has got to be found out and why I was willing to come here with Mrs. Bantry. An open accusation is one thing and quite easy for a soldier to meet. He's indignant and he has a chance of fighting. But this other whispering business will break him—will break them both. So, you see, Sir Henry, we've got to find out the truth."

Sir Henry said, "Any ideas as to why the body should have been found in his house? There must be an explanation of that. Some connection."

"Oh, of course."

"The girl was last seen here about twenty minutes to eleven. By midnight, according to the medical evidence, she was dead. Gossington's about twenty miles from here. Good road for sixteen of those miles, until one turns off the main road. A powerful car could do it in well under half an hour. Practically any car could average thirty-five. But why anyone should either kill her here and take her body out to Gossington or should take her out to Gossington and strangle her there, I don't know."

"Of course you don't, because it didn't happen."

"Do you mean that she was strangled by some fellow who took her out in a car, and he then decided to push her into the first likely house in the neighborhood?"

"I don't think anything of the kind. I think there was a very careful plan made. What happened was that the plan went wrong."

Sir Henry stared at her. "Why did the plan go wrong?"

Miss Marple said rather apologetically, "Such curious things happen, don't they? If I were to say that this particular plan went wrong because human beings are so much more vulnerable and sensitive than anyone thinks, it wouldn't sound sensible, would it? But that's what I believe and —" She broke off. "Here's Mrs. Bantry now."

12

MRS. BANTRY was with Adelaide Jefferson. The former came up to Sir Henry and exclaimed, "You!"

"I, myself." He took both her hands and pressed them warmly. "I can't tell you how distressed I am at all this, Mrs. B."

Mrs. Bantry said mechanically, "Don't call me Mrs. B!" and went on, "Arthur isn't here. He's taking it all rather seriously. Miss Marple and I have come here to sleuth. Do you know Mrs. Jefferson?"

"Yes, of course."

He shook hands. Adelaide Jefferson said, "Have you seen my father-in-law?"

"Yes. I have."

"I'm glad. We're anxious about him. It was a terrible shock."

Mrs. Bantry said, "Let's go out on the terrace and have drinks and talk about it all." The four of them went out and joined Mark Gaskell, who was sitting at the extreme end of the terrace by himself. After a few desultory remarks and the arrival of the drinks, Mrs. Bantry plunged straight into the subject with her usual zest for direct action. "We can talk about it, can't we?" she said. "I mean we're all old friends—except Miss Marple, and she knows all about crime. And she wants to help."

Mark Gaskell looked at Miss Marple in a somewhat puzzled fashion. He said doubtfully, "Do you—er—write detective stories?" The most unlikely people, he knew, wrote detective stories. And Miss Marple, in her old-fashioned spinster's clothes, looked a singularly unlikely person.

"Oh, no, I'm not clever enough for that."

"She's wonderful," said Mrs. Bantry impatiently. "I can't explain now, but she is. . . . Now, Addie, I want to know all about things. What was she really like, this girl?"

"Well—" Adelaide Jefferson paused, glanced across at Mark and half laughed. She said, "You're so direct."

"Did you like her?"

"No, of course I didn't."

"What was she really like?" Mrs. Bantry shifted her inquiry to Mark Gaskell.

Mark said deliberately, "Common or garden gold digger. And she knew her stuff. She's got her hooks into Jeff all right." Both of them called their father-in-law "Jeff."

Sir Henry thought, looking disapprovingly at Mark, *Indiscreet fellow. Shouldn't be so outspoken.* He had always disapproved a little of Mark Gaskell. The man had charm, but he was unreliable—talked too much, was occasionally boastful—not quite to be trusted, Sir Henry thought. He had sometimes wondered if Conway Jefferson thought so too.

"But couldn't you do something about it?" demanded Mrs. Bantry.

Mark said dryly, "We might have, if we'd realized it in time."

He shot a glance at Adelaide and she colored faintly. There had been reproach in that glance.

She said, "Mark thinks I ought to have seen what was coming."

"You left the old boy alone too much, Addie. Tennis lessons and all the rest of it."

"Well, I had to have some exercise." She spoke apologetically. "Anyway, I never dreamed—"

"No," said Mark, "neither of us ever dreamed. Jeff has always been such a sensible, levelheaded old boy."

Miss Marple made a contribution to the conversation. "Gentlemen," she said with her old maid's way of referring to the opposite sex as though it were a species of wild animal, "are frequently not so levelheaded as they seem."

"I'll say you're right," said Mark. "Unfortunately, Miss Marple, we didn't realize that. We wondered what the old boy saw in that rather insipid and meretricious little bag of tricks. But we were pleased for him to be kept happy and amused. We thought there was no harm in her. No harm in her! I wish I'd wrung her neck."

"Mark," said Addie, "you really must be careful what you say."

He grinned at her engagingly. "I suppose I must. Otherwise people will think I actually did wring her neck. Oh, well, I suppose I'm under suspicion anyway. If anyone had an interest in seeing that girl dead, it was Addie and myself."

"Mark," cried Mrs. Jefferson, half laughing and half angry, "you really mustn't!"

"All right, all right," said Mark Gaskell pacifically. "But I do like speaking my mind. Fifty thousand pounds our esteemed father-in-law was proposing to settle upon that half-baked, nitwitted little slypuss."

"Mark, you mustn't! She's dead!"

"Yes, she's dead, poor little devil. And after all, why shouldn't she use the weapons that Nature gave her? Who am I to judge? Done plenty of rotten things myself in my life. No, let's say Ruby was entitled to plot and scheme, and we were mugs not to have tumbled to her game sooner."

Sir Henry said, "What did you say when Conway told you he proposed to adopt the girl?"

Mark thrust out his hands. "What could we say? Addie, always the little lady, retained her self-control admirably. Put a brave face upon it. I endeavored to follow her example."

"I should have made a fuss!" said Mrs. Bantry.

"Well, frankly speaking, we weren't entitled to make a fuss. It was Jeff's money. We weren't his flesh and blood. He'd always been damned good to us. There was nothing for it but to bite on the bullet." He added reflectively, "But we didn't love little Ruby."

Adelaide Jefferson said, "If only it had been some other kind of girl. Jeff had two godchildren, you know. If it had been one of them—well, one would have understood it." She added with a shade of resentment, "And Jeff's always seemed so fond of Peter."

"Of course," said Mrs. Bantry. "I always have known Peter was your first husband's child, but I'd quite forgotten it. I've always thought of him as Mr. Jefferson's grandson."

"So have I," said Adelaide. Her voice held a note that made Miss Marple turn in her chair and look at her.

"It was Josie's fault," said Mark. "Josie brought her here."

Adelaide said, "Oh, but surely you don't think it was deliberate, do you? Why, you've always liked Josie so much."

"Yes, I did like her. I thought she was a good sport."

"It was sheer accident, her bringing the girl down."

"Josie's got a good head on her shoulders, my girl."

"Yes, but she couldn't foresee—"

Mark said, "No, she couldn't. I admit it. I'm not really accusing her of planning the whole thing. But I've no doubt she saw which way the wind was blowing long before we did, and kept very quiet about it."

Adelaide said with a sigh, "I suppose one can't blame her for that."

Mark said, "Oh, we can't blame anyone for anything!"

Mrs. Bantry asked, "Was Ruby Keene very pretty?"

Mark stared at her. "I thought you'd seen—"

Mrs. Bantry said hastily, "Oh, yes, I saw her—her body. But she'd been strangled, you know, and one couldn't tell—" She shivered.

Mark said thoughtfully, "I don't think she was really pretty at all. She certainly wouldn't have been without any make-up. A thin ferrety little face, not much chin, teeth running down her throat, nondescript sort of nose—"

"It sounds revolting," said Mrs. Bantry.

"Oh, no, she wasn't. As I say, with make-up she managed to give quite an effect of good looks. . . . Don't you think so, Addie?"

"Yes, rather chocolate-box, pink-and-white business. She had nice blue eyes."

"Yes, innocent-baby stare, and the heavily blacked lashes brought out the blueness. Her hair was bleached, of course. It's true, when I come to think of it, that in coloring—artificial coloring, anyway—she had a kind of spurious resemblance to Rosamund—my wife, you know. I dare say that's what attracted the old man's attention to her." He sighed. "Well, it's a bad business. The awful thing is that Addie and I can't help being glad, really, that she's dead." He quelled a protest from his sister-in-law, "It's no good, Addie. I know what you feel. I feel the same. And I'm not going to pretend! But at the same time, if you know what I mean, I really am most awfully concerned for Jeff about the whole business. It's hit him very hard. I—" He stopped and stared toward the doors leading out of the lounge onto the terrace. "Well, well. See who's here. . . . What an unscrupulous woman you are, Addie."

Mrs. Jefferson looked over her shoulder, uttered an exclamation and got up, a slight color rising in her face. She walked quickly along the terrace and went up to a tall, middle-aged man with a thin brown face who was looking uncertainly about him.

Mrs. Bantry said, "Isn't that Hugo McLean?"

Mark Gaskell said, "Hugo McLean it is. Alias William Dobbin."

Mrs. Bantry murmured, "He's very faithful, isn't he?"

"Doglike devotion," said Mark. "Addie's only got to whistle and Hugo comes trotting along from any odd corner of the globe. Always hopes that someday she'll marry him. I dare say she will."

Miss Marple looked beamingly after them. She said, "I see. A romance?"

"One of the good old-fashioned kind," Mark assured her. "It's been going on for years. Addie's that kind of woman." He added meditatively, "I suppose Addie telephoned him this morning. She didn't tell me she had."

Edwards came discreetly along the terrace and paused at Mark's elbow. "Excuse me, sir. Mr. Jefferson would like you to come up."

"I'll come at once." Mark sprang up. He nodded to them, said, "See you later," and went off.

Sir Henry leaned forward to Miss Marple. He said, "Well, what do you think of the principal beneficiaries of the crime?"

Miss Marple said thoughtfully, looking at Adelaide Jefferson as she stood talking to her old friend, "I should think, you know, that she was a very devoted mother."

"Oh, she is," said Mrs. Bantry. "She's simply devoted to Peter."

"She's the kind of woman," said Miss Marple, "that everyone likes. The kind of woman that could go on getting married again and again. I don't mean a man's woman—that's quite different."

"I know what you mean," said Sir Henry.

"What you both mean," said Mrs. Bantry, "is that she's a good listener."

Sir Henry laughed. He said, "And Mark Gaskell?"

"Ah," said Miss Marple. "He's a downy fellow."

"Village parallel, please?"

"Mr. Cargill, the builder. He bluffed a lot of people into having things done to their houses they never meant to do. And how he charged them for it! But he could always explain his bill away plausibly. A downy fellow. He married money. So did Mr. Gaskell, I understand."

"You don't like him."

"Yes, I do. Most women would. But he can't take me in. He's a very attractive person, I think. But a little unwise, perhaps, to talk as much as he does."

" 'Unwise' is the word," said Sir Henry. "Mark will get himself into trouble if he doesn't look out." A tall dark young man in white flannels came up the steps to the terrace and paused just for a minute, watching Adelaide Jefferson and Hugo McLean. "And that," said Sir Henry obligingly, "is X, whom we might describe as an interested party. He is the tennis and dancing pro, Raymond Starr. Ruby Keene's partner."

Miss Marple looked at him with interest. She said, "He's very nice-looking, isn't he?"

"I suppose so."

"Don't be absurd, Sir Henry," said Mrs. Bantry. "There's no supposing about it. He is good-looking."

Miss Marple murmured, "Mrs. Jefferson has been taking tennis lessons, I think she said."

"Do you mean anything by that, Jane, or don't you?"

Miss Marple had no chance of replying to this down-right question. Young Peter Carmody came across the terrace and joined them. He addressed himself to Sir Henry. "I say, are you a detective too? I saw you talking to the superintendent—the fat one is a superintendent, isn't he?"

"Quite right, my son."

"And somebody told me you were a frightfully important detective from London. The head of Scotland Yard or something like that."

"The head of Scotland Yard is usually a complete dud in books, isn't he?"

"Oh, no; not nowadays. Making fun of the police is very old-fashioned. Do you know who did the murder yet?"

"Not yet, I'm afraid."

"Are you enjoying this very much, Peter?" asked Mrs. Bantry.

"Well, I am rather. It makes a change, doesn't it? I've been hunting round to see if I could find any clues, but I haven't been lucky. I've got a souvenir though. Would you like to see it? Fancy, mother wanted me to throw it away. I do think one's parents are rather trying sometimes." He produced from his pocket a small match box. Pushing it open, he disclosed the precious contents. "See, it's a fingernail. Her fingernail! I'm going to label it Fingernail of the Murdered Woman and take it back to school. It's a good souvenir, don't you think?"

"Where did you get it?" asked Miss Marple.

"Well, it was a bit of luck, really. Because of course I didn't know she was going to be murdered then. It was before dinner last night. Ruby caught her nail in Josie's shawl and it tore it. Mums cut it off for her and gave it to me and said put it in the wastepaper basket, and I meant to, but I put it in my pocket instead, and this morning I remembered and looked to see if it was still there, and it was, and now I've got it as a souvenir."

"Disgusting," said Mrs. Bantry.

Peter said politely, "Oh, do you think so?"

"Got any other souvenirs?" asked Sir Henry.

"Well, I don't know. I've got something that might be."

"Explain yourself, young man."

Peter looked at him thoughtfully. Then he pulled out an envelope. From the inside of it he extracted a piece of brown tape-like substance. "It's a bit of that chap George Bartlett's shoelace," he explained. "I saw his shoes outside the door this morning and I bagged a bit just in case."

"In case what?"

"In case he should be the murderer, of course. He was the last person to see her, and that's always frightfully suspicious, you know. . . . Is it nearly dinner-time, do you think? I'm frightfully hungry. It always seems such a long time between tea and dinner. . . . Hullo, there's Uncle Hugo. I didn't know mums had asked him to come down. I suppose she sent for him. She always does if she's in a jam. Here's Josie coming. . . . Hi, Josie!"

Josephine Turner, coming along the terrace, stopped and looked rather startled to see Mrs. Bantry and Miss Marple. Mrs. Bantry said pleasantly, "How d'you do, Miss Turner. We've come to do a bit of sleuthing."

Josie cast a guilty glance round. She said, lowering her voice, "It's awful. Nobody knows yet. I meant it isn't in the papers yet. I suppose everyone will be asking me questions, and it's so awkward. I don't know what I ought to say."

Her glance went rather wistfully toward Miss Marple, who said, "Yes, it will be a very difficult situation for you, I'm afraid."

Josie warmed to this sympathy. "You see, Mr. Prestcott said to me, 'Don't talk about it.' And that's all very well, but everyone is sure to ask me and you can't offend people, can you? Mr. Prestcott said he hoped I'd feel able to carry on as usual, and he wasn't very nice about it, so, of course, I want to do my best. And I really don't see why it should all be blamed on me."

Sir Henry said, "Do you mind me asking you a frank question?"

"Oh, do ask me anything you like," said Josie a little insincerely.

"Has there been any upleasantness between you and Mrs. Jefferson and Mr. Gaskell over all this?"

"Over the murder, do you mean?"

"No, I don't mean the murder."

Josie stood twisting her fingers together. She said rather sullenly, "Well, there has and there hasn't, if you know what I mean. Neither of them has said anything. But I think they blame it on me—Mr. Jefferson taking such a fancy to Ruby, I mean. It wasn't my fault, though, was it? These things happen, and I never dreamt of such a thing happening beforehand, not for a moment. I—I was quite dumfounded." Her words rang out with what seemed undeniable sincerity.

Sir Henry said kindly, "I'm sure you were. But once it had happened?"

Josie's chin went up. "Well, it was a piece of luck, wasn't it? Everyone's got the right to have a piece of luck sometimes." She looked from one to the other of them in a slightly defiant, questioning manner, and then went on across the terrace and into the hotel.

Peter said judicially, "I don't think she did it."

Miss Marple murmured, "It's interesting, that piece of fingernail. It had been worrying me, you know—how to account for her nails."

"Nails?" asked Sir Henry.

"The dead girl's nails," explained Mrs. Bantry. "They were quite short and, now that Jane says so, of course it was a little unlikely. A girl like that usually has absolute talons!"

Miss Marple said, "But of course if she tore one off, then she might clip the others close so as to match. Did they find nail parings in her room, I wonder?"

Sir Henry looked at her curiously. He said, "I'll ask Superintendent Harper when he gets back."

"Back from where?" asked Mrs. Bantry. "He hasn't gone over to Gossington, has he?"

Sir Henry said gravely, "No. There's been another tragedy. Blazing car in a quarry."

Miss Marple caught her breath. "Was there someone in the car?"

"I'm afraid so, yes."

Miss Marple said thoughtfully, "I expect that will be the Girl Guide who's missing—Patience—no, Pamela Reeves."

Sir Henry stared at her. "Now why on earth do you think that?"

Miss Marple got rather pink. "Well, it was given out on the wireless that she was missing from her home since last night. And her home was Daneleigh Vale—that's not very far from here—and she was last seen at the Girl Guide rally up on Danebury Downs. That's very close indeed. In fact, she'd have to pass through Danemouth to get home. So it does rather fit in, doesn't it? I mean it looks as though she might have seen— or perhaps heard—something that no one was supposed to see or hear. If so, of course, she'd be a source of danger to the murderer and she'd have to be removed. Two things like that must be connected, don't you think?"

Sir Henry said, his voice dripping a little, "You think a second murder?"

"Why not?" Her quiet, placid gaze met his. "When anyone has committed one murder he doesn't shrink from another, does he? Not even from a third."

"A third? You don't think there will be a third murder?"

"I think it's just possible. Yes, I think it's highly possible."

"Miss Marple," said Sir Henry, "you frighten me. Do you know who is going to be murdered?"

Miss Marple said, "I've a very good idea."

13

COLONEL MELCHETT and Superintendent Harper looked at each other. Harper had come over to Much Benham for a consultation. Melchett said gloomily, "Well, we know where we are—or rather where we aren't!"

"Where we aren't expresses it better, sir."

"We've got two deaths to take into account," said Melchett. "Two murders. Ruby Keene and the child, Pamela Reeves. Not much to identify her by, poor kid, but enough. One shoe escaped burning and has been identified as hers, and a button from her Girl Guide uniform. A fiendish business, superintendent."

Superintendent Harper said very quietly, "I'll say you're right, sir."

"I'm glad to say Haydock is quite certain she was dead before the car was set on fire. The way she was lying thrown across the seat shows that. Probably knocked on the head, poor kid."

"Or strangled, perhaps."

"You think so?"

"Well, sir, there are murderers like that."

"I know. I've seen the parents—the poor girl's mother's beside herself. Damned painful, the whole thing. The point for us to settle is: are the two murders connected?"

The superintendent ticked off the points on his fingers. "Attended rally of Girl Guides on Danebury Downs. Stated by companion to be normal and cheerful. Did not return with three companions by the bus to Medchester. Said to them that she was going to Danemouth to Woolworth's and would take the bus home from there. That's likely enough—Woolworth's in Danemouth is a big affair—the girl lived in the back country and didn't get many chances of going into town. The main road into Danemouth from the downs does a big round inland; Pamela Reeves took a short cut over two fields and a footpath and lane which would bring her into Danemouth near the Majestic Hotel. The lane, in fact, actually passes the hotel on the west side. It's possible, therefore, that she overheard or saw something—something concerning Ruby Keene—which would have proved dangerous to the murderer—say, for instance, that she heard him arranging to meet Ruby Keene at eleven that evening. He realizes that this schoolgirl has overheard and he has to silence her."

Colonel Melchett said, "That's presuming, Harper, that the Ruby Keene crime was premeditated, not spontaneous."

Superintendent Harper agreed. "I believe it was, sir. It looks as though it would be the other way—sudden violence, a fit of passion or jealousy—but I'm beginning to think that that's not so. I don't see, otherwise, how you can account for the death of the child. If she was a witness of the actual crime it would be late at night, round about eleven P.M., and what would she be doing round about the Majestic Hotel at that time of night? Why, at nine o'clock her parents were getting anxious because she hadn't returned."

"The alternative is that she went to meet someone in Danemouth unknown to her family and friends, and that her death is quite unconnected with the other death."

"Yes, sir, and I don't believe that's so. Look how even the old lady, old Miss Marple, tumbled to it at once that there was a connection. She asked at once if the body in the burnt car was the body of the Girl Guide. Very smart old lady, that. These old ladies are, sometimes. Shrewd, you know. Put their fingers on the vital spot."

"Miss Marple has done that more than once," said Colonel Melchett dryly.

"And besides, sir, there's the car. That seems to me to link up her death definitely with the Majestic Hotel. It was Mr. George Bartlett's car."

Again the eyes of the two men met. Melchett said, "George Bartlett? Could be! What do you think?"

Again Harper methodically recited various points. "Ruby Keene was last seen with George Bartlett. He says she went to her room—borne out by the dress she was wearing being found there—but did she go to her room and change in order to go out with him? Had they made a date to go out together earlier—discussed it, say, before dinner—and did Pamela Reeves happen to overhear?"

Colonel Melchett said, "He didn't report the loss of his car until the following morning, and he was extremely vague about it then; pretended that he couldn't remember exactly when he had last noticed it."

"That might be cleverness, sir. As I see it, he's either a very clever gentleman pretending to be a silly ass, or else—well, he is a silly ass."

"What we want," said Melchett, "is motive. As it stands, he had no motive whatever for killing Ruby Keene."

"Yes, that's where we're stuck every time. Motive. All the reports from —the Palais de Danse at Brixwell are negative, I understand."

"Absolutely! Ruby Keene had no special boy friend. Slack's been into the matter thoroughly. Give Slack his due; he is thorough."

"That's right, sir. 'Thorough' is the word."

"If there was anything to ferret out he'd have ferreted it out. But there's nothing there. He got a list of her most frequent dancing partners —all vetted and found correct. Harmless fellows, and all to produce alibis for that night."

"Ah," said Superintendent Harper. "Alibis. That's what we're up against."

Melchett looked at him sharply. "Think so? I've left that side of the investigation to you."

"Yes, sir. It's been gone into—very thoroughly. We applied to London for help over it."

"Well?"

"Mr. Conway Jefferson may think that Mr. Gaskell and young Mrs. Jefferson are comfortably off, but that is not the case. They're both extremely hard up."

"Is that true?"

"Quite true, sir. It's as Mr. Conway Jefferson said; he made over considerable sums of money to his son and daughter when they married. That was a number of years ago though. Mr. Frank Jefferson fancied himself as knowing good investments. He didn't invest in anything absolutely wildcat, but he was unlucky and showed poor judgment more than once. His holdings have gone steadily down. I should say that Mrs. Jefferson found it very difficult to make both ends meet and send her son to a good school."

"But she hasn't applied to her father-in-law for help?"

"No, sir. As far as I can make out she lives with him and, consequently, has no household expenses."

"And his health is such that he wasn't expected to live long?"

"That's right, sir. Now for Mr. Mark Gaskell. He's a gambler, pure and simple. Got through his wife's money very soon. Has got himself tangled up rather badly just at present. He needs money badly, and a good deal of it."

"Can't say I liked the looks of him much," said Colonel Melchett. "Wild-looking sort of fellow, what? And he's got a motive, all right. Twenty-five thousand pounds it meant to him, getting that girl out of the way. Yes, it's a motive all right."

"They both had a motive."

"I'm not considering Mrs. Jefferson."

"No, sir, I know you're not. And, anyway, the alibi holds for both of them. They couldn't have done it. Just that."

"You've got a detailed statement of their movements that evening?"

"Yes, I have. Take Mr. Gaskell first. He dined with his father-in-law and Mrs. Jefferson, had coffee with them afterward when Ruby Keene joined them. Then said he had to write letters and left them. Actually, he took his car and went for a spin down to the front. He told me quite frankly he couldn't stick playing bridge for a whole evening. The old boy's mad on it. So he made letters an excuse. Ruby Keene remained with the others. Mark Gaskell returned when she was dancing with Raymond. After the dance Ruby came and had a drink with them, then she went off with young Bartlett, and Gaskell and the others cut for partners and started their bridge. That was at twenty minutes to eleven, and he didn't leave the table until after midnight. That's quite certain, sir. Everyone says so—the family, the waiters, everyone. Therefore, he couldn't have done it. And Mrs. Jefferson's alibi is the same. She, too, didn't leave the table. They're out, both of them—out." Colonel Melchett leaned back, tapping the table with a paper cutter.

Superintendent Harper said, "That is, assuming the girl was killed before midnight."

"Haydock said she was. He's a very sound fellow in police work. If he says a thing, it's so."

"There might be reasons—health, physical idiosyncrasy or something."

"I'll put it to him." Melchett glanced at his watch, picked up the telephone receiver and asked for a number. He said, "Haydock ought to be in now. Now, assuming that she was killed after midnight—"

Harper said, "Then there might be a chance. There was some coming and going afterward. Let's assume that Gaskell had asked the girl to meet him outside somewhere—say at twenty past twelve. He slips away for a minute or two, strangles her, comes back, and disposes of the body later —in the early hours of the morning."

Melchett said, "Take her by car twenty miles to put her in Bantry's library? Dash it all, it's not a likely story."

"No, it isn't," the superintendent admitted at once.

The telephone rang. Melchett picked up the receiver. "Hello, Haydock, is that you? Ruby Keene. Would it be possible for her to have been killed after midnight?"

"I told you she was killed between ten and midnight."

"Yes, I know, but one could stretch it a bit, what?"

"No, you couldn't stretch it. When I say she was killed before midnight I mean before midnight, and don't try and tamper with the medical evidence."

"Yes, but couldn't there be some physiological what not? You know what I mean?"

"I know that you don't know what you're talking about. The girl was perfectly healthy and not abnormal in any way, and I'm not going to say she was just to help you fit a rope round the neck of some wretched fellow whom you police wallahs have got your knife into. Now, don't protest. I know your ways. And, by the way, the girl wasn't strangled willingly—that is to say, she was drugged first. Powerful narcotic. She died of strangulation, but she was drugged first." Haydock rang off.

Melchett said gloomily, "Well, that's that."

Harper said, "Thought I'd found another likely starter, but it petered out."

"What's that? Who?"

"Strictly speaking, he's your pigeon, sir. Name of Basil Blake. Lives near Gossington Hall."

"Impudent young jackanapes!" The colonel's brow darkened as he remembered Basil Blake's outrageous rudeness. "How's he mixed up in it?"

"Seems he knew Ruby Keene. Dined over at the Majestic quite often, danced with the girl. Do you remember what Josie said to Raymond when Ruby was discovered to be missing, 'She isn't with that film man, is she?' I've found out it was Blake she meant. He's employed with the Lenville Studios, you know. Josie has nothing to go upon except a belief that Ruby was rather keen on him."

"Very promising, Harper, very promising."

"Not so good as it sounds, sir. Basil Blake was at a party at the studios that night. You know the sort of thing. Starts at eight with cocktails and goes on and on until the air's too thick to see through and everyone passes out. According to Inspector Slack, who's questioned him, he left the show round about midnight. At midnight Ruby Keene was dead."

"Anyone bear out his statement?"

"Most of them, I gather, sir, were rather—er—far gone. The—er—young woman now at the bungalow, Miss Dinah Lee, says that statement is correct."

"Doesn't mean a thing."

"No, sir, probably not. Statements taken from other members of the party bear Mr. Blake's statement out, on the whole, though ideas as to time are somewhat vague."

"Where are these studios?"

Lenville, sir, thirty miles southwest of London."

"H'm—about the same distance from here?"

"Yes, sir."

Colonel Melchett rubbed his nose. He said in a rather dissatisfied tone, "Well, it looks as though we could wash him out."

"I think so, sir. There is no evidence that he was seriously attracted by Ruby Keene. In fact"—Superintendent Harper coughed primly—"he seems fully occupied with his own young lady."

Melchett said, "Well, we are left with X, an unknown murderer—so unknown Slack can't find a trace of him. Or Jefferson's son-in-law, who might have wanted to kill the girl, but didn't have a chance to do so. Daughter-in-law ditto. Or George Bartlett, who has an alibi, but, unfortunately, no motive either. Or with young Blake, who has an alibi and no motive. And that's the lot! No, stop. I suppose we ought to consider the dancing fellow, Raymond Starr. After all, he saw a lot of the girl."

Harper said slowly, "Can't believe he took much interest in her—or else he's a thundering good actor. And, for all practical purposes, he's got an alibi too. He was more or less in view from twenty minutes to eleven until midnight, dancing with various partners. I don't see that we can make a case against him."

"In fact," said Colonel Melchett, "we can't make a case against anybody."

"George Bartlett's our best hope," Harper said. "If we could only hit on a motive."

"You've had him looked up?"

"Yes, sir. Only child. Coddled by his mother. Came into a good deal of money on her death a year ago. Getting through it fast. Weak rather than vicious."

"May be mental," said Melchett hopefully.

Superintendent Harper nodded. He said, "Has it struck you, sir, that that may be the explanation of the whole case?"

"Criminal lunatic, you mean?"

"Yes, sir. One of those fellows who go about strangling young girls. Doctors have a long name for it."

"That would solve all our difficulties," said Melchett.

"There's only one thing I don't like about it," said Superintendent Harper.

"What?"

"It's too easy."

"H'm—yes, perhaps. So, as I said at the beginning, where are we?"

"Nowhere, sir," said Superintendent Harper.

14

CONWAY JEFFERSON stirred in his sleep and stretched. His arms were flung out, long, powerful arms into which all the strength of his body seemed to be concentrated since his accident. Through the curtains the morning light glowed softly. Conway Jefferson smiled to himself. Always, after a night of rest, he woke like this, happy, refreshed, his deep vitality renewed. Another day! So, for a minute, he lay. Then he pressed the special bell by his hand. And suddenly a wave of remembrance swept over him. Even as Edwards, deft and quiet-footed, entered the room a groan was wrung from his master. Edwards paused with his hand on the curtains. He said, "You're not in pain, sir?"

Conway Jefferson said harshly, "No. Go on, pull 'em." The clear light flooded the room. Edwards, understanding, did not glance at his master.

His face grim, Conway Jefferson lay remembering and thinking. Before his eyes he saw again the pretty, vapid face of Ruby. Only in his mind he did not use the adjective "vapid." Last night he would have said "innocent." A naïve, innocent child! And now? A great weariness came over Conway Jefferson. He closed his eyes. He murmured below his breath, "Margaret." It was the name of his dead wife.

"I like your friend," said Adelaide Jefferson to Mrs. Bantry. The two women were sitting on the terrace.

"Jane Marple's a very remarkable woman," said Mrs. Bantry.

"She's nice too," said Addie, smiling.

"People call her a scandalmonger," said Mrs. Bantry, "but she isn't really."

"Just a low opinion of human nature?"

"You could call it that."

"It's rather refreshing," said Adelaide Jefferson, "after having had too much of the other thing." Mrs. Bantry looked at her sharply. Addie explained herself. "So much high thinking—idealization of an unworthy object!"

"You mean Ruby Keene?"

Addie nodded. "I don't want to be horrid about her. There wasn't any harm in her. Poor little rat, she had to fight for what she wanted. She wasn't bad. Common and rather silly and quite good-natured, but a decided little gold digger. I don't think she schemed or planned. It was just that she was quick to take advantage of a possibility. And she knew how to appeal to an elderly man who was lonely."

"I suppose," said Mrs. Bantry thoughtfully, "that Conway was lonely."

Addie moved restlessly. She said, "He was this summer." She paused and then burst out, "Mark will have it that it was all my fault! Perhaps it was; I don't know." She was silent for a minute, then, impelled by some need to talk, she went on speaking in a difficult, almost reluctant way. "I —I've had such an odd sort of life. Mike Carmody, my first husband, died so soon after we were married it—it knocked me out. Peter, as you know, was born after his death. Frank Jefferson was Mike's great friend. So I came to see a lot of him. He was Peter's god-father—Mike had wanted that. I got very fond of him and—oh, sorry for him too."

"Sorry?" queried Mrs. Bantry with interest.

"Yes, just that. It sounds odd. Frank had always had everything he wanted. His father and mother couldn't have been nicer to him. And yet —how can I say it?—you see, old Mr. Jefferson's personality is so strong. If you live with it you can't somehow have a personality of your own. Frank felt that.

"When we were married he was very happy—wonderfully so. Mr. Jefferson was very generous. He settled a large sum of money on Frank; said he wanted his children to be independent and not have to wait for his death. It was so nice of him—so generous. But it was much too sudden. He ought really to have accustomed Frank to independence little by little.

"It went to Frank's head. He wanted to be as good a man as his father, as clever about money and business, as farseeing and successful. And of course he wasn't. He didn't exactly speculate with the money, but he invested in the wrong things at the wrong time. It's frightening, you know, how soon money goes if you're not clever about it. The more Frank dropped, the more eager he was to get it back by some clever deal. So things went from bad to worse."

"But, my dear," said Mrs. Bantry, "couldn't Conway have advised him?"

"He didn't want to be advised. The one thing he wanted was to do well on his own. That's why we never let Mr. Jefferson know. When Frank died there was very little left; only a tiny income for me. And I—I didn't let his father know either. You see"—she turned abruptly—"it would have seemed like betraying Frank to him. Frank would have hated it so. Mr. Jefferson was ill for a long time. When he got well he assumed that I was a very-well-off widow. I've never undeceived him. It's been a point of honor. He knows I'm very careful about money, but he just approves of that, thinks I'm a thrifty sort of woman. And of course Peter and I have lived with him practically ever since, and he's paid for all our living expenses. So I've never had to worry." She said slowly, "We've been like a family all these years, only—only, you see—or don't you see?—I've never been Frank's widow to him; I've been Frank's wife."

Mrs. Bantry grasped the implications. "You mean he's never accepted their deaths?"

"No. He's been wonderful. But he's conquered his own terrible tragedy by refusing to recognize death. Mark is Rosamund's husband and I'm Frank's wife, and though Frank and Rosamund aren't exactly here with us they are still existent."

Mrs. Bantry said softly, "It's a wonderful triumph of faith."

"I know. We've gone on, year after year. But suddenly, this summer, something went wrong in me. I felt—felt rebellious. It's an awful thing to say, but I didn't want to think of Frank any more! All that was over—my love and companionship with him, and my grief when he died. It was something that had been and wasn't any longer.

"It's awfully hard to describe. It's like wanting to wipe the slate clean and start again. I wanted to be me—Addie, still reasonably young and strong and able to play games and swim and dance—just a person. Even Hugo—you know Hugo McLean?—he's a dear and wants to marry me, but of course I've never really thought of it, but this summer I did begin to think of it—not seriously, only vaguely." She stopped and shook her head. "And so I suppose it's true. I neglected Jeff. I don't mean really neglected him, but my mind and thoughts weren't with him. When Ruby, as I saw, amused him, I was rather glad. It left me freer to go and do my own things. I never dreamed—of course I never dreamed—that he would be so—so infatuated with her!"

Mrs. Bantry asked, "And when did you find out?"

"I was dumfounded—absolutely dumfounded! And, I'm afraid, angry too."

"I'd have been angry," said Mrs. Bantry.

"There was Peter, you see. Peter's whole future depends on Jeff. Jeff practically looked on him as a grandson, or so I thought, but of course he wasn't a grandson. He was no relation at all. And to think that he was going to be disinherited!" Her firm, well-shaped hands shook a little where they lay in her lap. "For that's what it felt like. And for a vulgar golddigging little simpleton! Oh, I could have killed her!"

She stopped, stricken. Her beautiful hazel eyes met Mrs. Bantry's in a pleading horror. She said, "What an awful thing to say!"

Hugo McLean, coming quietly up behind them, asked, "What's an awful thing to say?"

"Sit down, Hugo. You know Mrs. Bantry, don't you?"

McLean had already greeted the older lady. He said, now, in a slow, persevering way, "What was an awful thing to say?"

Addie Jefferson said, "That I'd like to have killed Ruby Keene."

Hugo McLean reflected a minute or two. Then he said, "No, wouldn't say that if I were you. Might be misunderstood." His eyes, steady, reflective gray eyes, looked at her meaningly. He said, "You've got to watch your step, Addie." There was a warning in his voice.

When Miss Marple came out of the hotel and joined Mrs. Bantry a few minutes later, Hugo McLean and Adelaide Jefferson were walking down the path to the sea together. Seating herself, Miss Marple remarked, "He seems very devoted."

"He's been devoted for years! One of those men."

"I know. Like Major Bury. He hung round an Anglo-Indian widow for quite ten years. A joke among her friends! In the end she gave in, but, unfortunately, ten days before they were to have been married she ran away with the chauffeur. Such a nice woman, too, and usually so well balanced."

"People do do very odd things," agreed Mrs. Bantry. "I wish you'd been here just now, Jane. Addie Jefferson was telling me all about herself —how her husband went through all his money, but they never let Mr. Jefferson know. And then, this summer, things felt different to her—"

Miss Marple nodded. "Yes. She rebelled, I suppose, against being made to live in the past. After all, there's a time for everything. You can't sit in the house with the blinds down forever. I suppose Mrs. Jefferson just pulled them up and took off her widow's weeds, and her father-in-law, of course, didn't like it. Felt left out in the cold, though I don't suppose for a minute he realized who put her up to it. Still, he certainly wouldn't like it. And so, of course, like old Mr. Badger when his wife took up spiritualism, he was just ripe for what happened. Any fairly nice-looking young girl who listened prettily would have done."

"Do you think," said Mrs. Bantry, "that that cousin, Josie, got her down deliberately—that it was a family plot?"

Miss Marple shook her head. "No, I don't think so at all. I don't think Josie has the kind of mind that could foresee people's reactions. She's rather dense in that way. She's got one of those shrewd, limited, practical minds that never do foresee the future and are usually astonished by it."

"It seems to have taken everyone by surprise," said Mrs. Bantry. "Addie—and Mark Gaskell, too, apparently."

Miss Marple smiled. "I dare say he had his own fish to fry. A bold fellow with a roving eye! Not the man to go on being a sorrowing widower for years, no matter how fond he may have been of his wife. I should think they were both restless under old Mr. Jefferson's yoke of perpetual remembrance. Only," added Miss Marple cynically, "it's easier for gentlemen, of course."

At that very moment Mark was confirming this judgment on himself in a talk with Sir Henry Clithering. With characteristic candor Mark had gone straight to the heart of things. "It's just dawned on me," he said, "that I'm Favorite Suspect Number One to the police! They've been delving into my financial troubles. I'm broke, you know; or very nearly. If dear old Jeff dies according to schedule in a month or two, and Addie and I divide the dibs also according to schedule, all will be well. Matter of fact, I owe rather a lot. If the crash comes, it will be a big one! If I can stave it off, it will be the other way round; I shall come out on top and be very rich."

Sir Henry Clithering said, "You're a gambler, Mark."

"Always have been. Risk everything, that's my motto! Yes, it's a lucky thing for me that somebody strangled that poor kid. I didn't do it. I'm not a strangler. I don't really think I could ever murder anybody. I'm too easygoing. But I don't suppose I can ask the police to believe that! I must look to them like the answer to the criminal investigator's prayer! Motive, on the spot, not burdened with high moral scruples! I can't imagine why I'm not in the jug already. That superintendent's got a very nasty eye."

"You've got that useful thing, an alibi."

"An alibi is the fishiest thing on God's earth! No innocent person ever has an alibi! Besides, it all depends on the time of death, or something like that, and you may be sure if three doctors say the girl was killed at midnight, at least six will be found who will swear positively that she was killed at five in the morning—and where's my alibi then?"

"Well, you are able to joke about it."

"Damned bad taste, isn't it?" said Mark cheerfully. "Actually, I'm rather scared. One is, with murder! And don't think I'm not sorry for old Jeff. I am. But it's better this way—bad as the shock was—than if he'd found her out."

"What do you mean, found her out?"

Mark winked. "Where did she go off to last night? I'll lay you any odds you like she went to meet a man. Jeff wouldn't have liked that. He wouldn't have liked it at all. If he'd found she was deceiving him—that she wasn't the prattling little innocent she seemed—well, my father-in-law is an odd man. He's a man of great self-control, but the self-control can snap. And then, look out!"

Sir Henry glanced at him curiously. "Are you fond of him or not?"

"I'm very fond of him, and at the same time I resent him. I'll try and explain. Conway Jefferson is a man who likes to control his surroundings. He's a benevolent despot, kind, generous and affectionate, but his is the tune and the others dance to his piping."

Mark Gaskell paused.

"I loved my wife. I shall never feel the same for anyone else. Rosamund was sunshine and laughter and flowers, and when she was killed I felt just like a man in the ring who's had a knockout blow. But the referee's been counting a good long time now. I'm a man, after all. I like women. I don't want to marry again—not in the least. Well, that's all right. I've had to be discreet, but I've had my good times all right. Poor Addie hasn't. Addie's a really nice woman. She's the kind of woman men want to marry. Give her half a chance and she would marry again, and be happy and make the chap happy too.

"But old Jeff saw her always as Frank's wife and hypnotized her into seeing herself like that. He doesn't know it, but we've been in prison. I broke out, on the quiet, a long time ago. Addie broke out this summer, and it gave him a shock. It broke up his world. Result, Ruby Keene."

Irrepressibly he sang:

"But she is in her grave, and oh!
The difference to me!"

"Come and have a drink, Clithering."

It was hardly surprising, Sir Henry reflected, that Mark Gaskell should be an object of suspicion to the police.

DOCTOR METCALF was one of the best-known physicians in Danemouth. He had no aggressive bedside manner, but his presence in the sickroom had an invariably cheering effect. He was middle-aged, with a quiet pleasant voice. He listened carefully to Superintendent Harper and replied to his questions with gentle precision. Harper said, "Then I can take it, Doctor Metcalf, that what I was told by Mrs. Jefferson was substantially correct?"

"Yes, Mr. Jefferson's health is in a precarious state. For several years now the man has been driving himself ruthlessly. In his determination to live like other men he has lived at a far greater pace than the normal man of his age. He has refused to rest, to take things easy, to go slow, or any of the other phrases with which I and his other medical advisers have tendered our opinion. The result is that the man is an over-worked engine. Heart, lungs, blood pressure—they're all overstrained."

"You say Mr. Jefferson has resolutely refused to listen?"

"Yes. I don't know that I blame him. It's not what I say to my patients, superintendent, but a man may as well wear out as rust out. A lot of my colleagues do that, and take it from me, it's not a bad way. In a place like Danemouth one sees most of the other thing. Invalids clinging to life, terrified of overexerting themselves, terrified of a breath of drafty air, of a stray germ, of an injudicious meal."

"I expect that's true enough," said Superintendent Harper. "What it amounts to, then, is this: Conway Jefferson is strong enough, physically speaking—or I suppose I mean muscularly speaking. Just what can he do in the active line, by the way?"

"He has immense strength in his arms and shoulders. He was a very powerful man before his accident. He is extremely dexterous in his handling of his wheeled chair, and with the aid of crutches he can move himself about a room—from his bed to the chair, for instance."

"Isn't it possible for a man injured as Mr. Jefferson was to have artificial legs?"

"Not in his case. There was a spine injury."

"I see. Let me sum up again. Jefferson is strong and fit in the muscular sense. He feels well and all that?"

Metcalf nodded.

"But his heart is in a bad condition; any overstrain or exertion, or a shock or a sudden fright, and he might pop off. Is that it?"

"More or less. Overexertion is killing him slowly because he won't give in when he feels tired. That aggravates the cardiac condition. It is unlikely that exertion would kill him suddenly. But a sudden shock or fright might easily do so. That is why I expressly warned his family."

Superintendent Harper said slowly, "But in actual fact a shock didn't kill him. I mean, doctor, that there couldn't have been a much worse shock than this business, and he's still alive."

Doctor Metcalf shrugged his shoulders. "I know. But if you'd had my experience, superintendent, you'd know that case history shows the impossibility of prognosticating accurately. People who ought to die of shock and exposure don't die of shock and exposure, et cetera, et cetera. The human frame is tougher than one can imagine possible. Moreover, in my experience, a physical shock is more often fatal than a mental shock. In plain language, a door banging suddenly would be more likely to kill Mr. Jefferson than the discovery that a girl he was fond of had died in a particularly horrible manner."

"Why is that, I wonder?"

"The breaking of a piece of bad news nearly always sets up a defense reaction. It numbs the recipient. They are unable, at first, to take it in. Full realization takes a little time. But the banged door, someone jumping out of a cupboard, the sudden onslaught of a motor as you cross a road—all those things are immediate in their action. The heart gives a terrified leap—to put it in layman's language."

Superintendent Harper said slowly, "But as far as anyone would know, Mr. Jefferson's death might easily have been caused by the shock of the girl's death?"

"Oh, easily." The doctor looked curiously at the other. "You don't think—"

"I don't know what I think," said Superintendent Harper vexedly.

"But you'll admit, sir, that the two things would fit in very prettily together," he said a little later to Sir Henry Clithering. "Kill two birds with one stone. First the girl, and the fact of her death takes off Mr. Jefferson, too, before he's had any opportunity to altering his will."

"Do you think he will alter it?"

"You'd be more likely to know that, sir, than I would. What do you say?"

"I don't know. Before Ruby Keene came on the scene I happen to know that he had left his money between Mark Gaskell and Mrs. Jefferson. I don't see why he should now change his mind about that. But of course he might do so."

Superintendent Harper agreed.

"You never know what bee a man is going to get in his bonnet; especially when he doesn't feel there's any moral obligation in the disposal of his fortune. No blood relations in this case."

Sir Henry said, "He is fond of the boy—of young Peter."

"D'you think he regards him as a grandson? You'd know that better than I would, sir."

Sir Henry said slowly, "No, I don't think so."

"There's another thing I'd like to ask you, sir. It's a thing I can't judge for myself. But they're friends of yours, and so you'd know. I'd like very much to know just how fond Mr. Jefferson is of Mr. Gaskell and young Mrs. Jefferson. Nobody doubts that he was much attached to them both, but he was attached to them, as I see it, because they were, respectively, the husband and the wife of his daughter and his son. But supposing, for instance, one of them had married again?"

Sir Henry reflected. He said, "It's an interesting point you raise there. I don't know. I'm inclined to suspect—this is a mere opinion—that it would have altered his attitude a good deal. He would have wished them both well, borne no rancor, but I think—yes, I rather think that he would have taken very little more interest in them."

Superintendent Harper nodded. "In both cases, sir?"

"I think so, yes. In Mr. Gaskell's, almost certainly, and I rather think in Mrs. Jefferson's also, but that's not nearly so certain. I think he was fond of her for her own sake."

"Sex would have something to do with that," said Superintendent Harper sapiently. "Easier for him to look on her as a daughter than to look on Mr. Gaskell as a son. It works both ways. Women accept a son-in-law as one of the family easily enough, but there aren't many times when a woman looks on her son's wife as a daughter." Superintendent Harper went on, "Mind if we walk along this path, sir, to the tennis court? I see Miss Marple's sitting there. I want to ask her to do something for me. As a matter of fact, I want to rope you both in."

"In what way, superintendent?"

"To get at stuff that I can't get at myself. I want you to tackle Edwards for me, sir."

"Edwards? What do you want from him?"

"Everything you can think of. Everything he knows and what he thinks. About the relations between the various members of the family, his angle on the Ruby Keene business. Inside stuff. He knows better than anyone the state of affairs. And he wouldn't tell me. But he'll tell you. Because you're a gentleman and a friend of Mr. Jefferson's."

Sir Henry said grimly, "I've been sent for, urgently, to get at the truth. I mean to do my utmost." He added, "Where do you want Miss Marple to help you?"

"With some girls. Some of those Girl Guides. We've rounded up half a dozen or so—the ones who were most friendly with Pamela Reeves. It's possible that they may know something. You see, I've been thinking. It seems to me that if that girl was going to Woolworth's she would have tried to persuade one of the other girls to go with her. So I think it's possible that Woolworth's was only an excuse. If so, I'd like to know where the girl was really going. She may have let slip something. If so, I feel Miss Marple's the person to get it out of those girls. I'd say she knows a thing or two about girls."

"It sounds to me the kind of village domestic problem that is right up Miss Marple's street. She's very sharp, you know."

The superintendent smiled. He said, "I'll say you're right. Nothing much gets past her."

Miss Marple looked up at their approach and welcomed them eagerly. She listened to the superintendent's request and at once acquiesced. "I should like to help you very much, superintendent, and I think that perhaps I could be of some use. What with the Sunday school, you know, and Brownies and our Guides, and the orphanage quite near—I'm on the committee, you know, and often run in to have a little talk with the matron—and then servants—I usually have very young maids. Oh, yes, I've quite a lot of experience in when a girl is speaking the truth and when she's holding something back."

"In fact, you're an expert," said Sir Henry.

Miss Marple flashed him a reproachful glance and said, "Oh, please don't laugh at me, Sir Henry."

"I shouldn't dream of laughing at you. You've had the laugh on me too many times."

"One does see so much evil in a village," murmured Miss Marple in an explanatory voice.

"By the way," said Sir Henry, "I've cleared up one point you asked me about. The superintendent tells me that there were nail clippings in Ruby's wastepaper basket."

Miss Marple said thoughtfully, "There were? Then that's that—"

"Why did you want to know, Miss Marple?" asked the superintendent.

Miss Marple said, "It was one of the things that—well, that seemed wrong when I looked at the body. The hands were wrong somehow, and

I couldn't at first think why. Then I realized that girls who are very much made up, and all that, usually have long fingernails. Of course, I know that girls everywhere do bite their nails; it's one of those habits that are very hard to break oneself of. But vanity often does a lot to help. Still, I presumed this girl hadn't cured herself. And then the little boy—Peter, you know—he said something which showed that her nails had been long, only she caught one and broke it. So then, of course, she might have trimmed off the rest to make an even appearance, and I asked about clippings and Sir Henry said he'd find out."

Sir Henry remarked, "You said just now 'one of the things that seemed wrong when I looked at the body.' Was there something else?"

Miss Marple nodded vigorously. "Oh, yes!" she said. "There was the dress. The dress was all wrong."

Both men looked at her curiously. "Now, why?" said Sir Henry.

"Well, you see, it was an old dress. Josie said so, definitely, and I could see for myself that it was shabby and rather worn. Now, that's all wrong."

"I don't see why."

Miss Marple got a little pink. "Well, the idea is, isn't it, that Ruby Keene changed her dress and went off to meet someone on whom she presumably had what my young nephews call a 'crush'?"

The superintendent's eyes twinkled a little. "That's the theory. She'd got a date with someone—a boy friend, as the saying goes."

"Then why," demanded Miss Marple, "was she wearing an old dress?"

The superintendent scratched his head thoughtfully. He said, "I see your point. You think she'd wear a new one?"

"I think she'd wear her best dress. Girls do."

Sir Henry interposed, "Yes, but look here, Miss Marple. Suppose she was going outside to this rendezvous. Going in an open car, perhaps, or walking in some rough going. Then she'd not want to risk messing a new frock and she'd put on an old one."

"That would be the sensible thing to do," agreed the superintendent.

Miss Marple turned on him. She spoke with animation, "The sensible thing to do would be to change into trousers and a pullover, or into tweeds. That, of course—I don't want to be snobbish, but I'm afraid it's unavoidable—that's what a girl of—of our class would do."

"A well-bred girl," continued Miss Marple, warming to her subject, "is always very particular to wear the right clothes for the right occasion. I mean, however hot the day was, a well-bred girl would never turn up at a point-to-point in a silk flowered frock."

"And the correct wear to meet a lover?" demanded Sir Henry.

"If she were meeting him inside the hotel or somewhere where evening dress was worn, she'd wear her best evening frock, of course, but outside she'd feel she'd look ridiculous in evening dress and she'd wear her most attractive sports wear."

"Granted, Fashion Queen, but the girl Ruby—"

Miss Marple said, "Ruby, of course, wasn't—well, to put it bluntly, Ruby wasn't a lady. She belonged to the class that wear their best clothes, however unsuitable to the occasion. Last year, you know, we had a picnic outing at Scrantor Rocks. You'd be surprised at the unsuitable clothes the girls wore. Foulard dresses and patent-leather shoes and quite elaborate hats, some of them. For climbing about over rocks and in gorse and heather. And the young men in their best suits. Of course, hiking's different again. That's practically a uniform, and girls don't seem to realize that shorts are very unbecoming unless they are very slender."

The superintendent said slowly, "And you think that Ruby Keene—"

"I think that she'd have kept on the frock she was wearing—her best pink one. She'd only have changed it if she'd had something newer still."

Superintendent Harper said, "And what's your explanation, Miss Marple?"

Miss Marple said, "I haven't got one—yet. But I can't help feeling that it's important."

16

INSIDE the wire cage, the tennis lesson that Raymond Starr was giving had come to an end. A stout middle-aged woman uttered a few appreciative squeaks, picked up a sky-blue cardigan and went off toward the hotel. Raymond called out a few gay words after her. Then he turned toward the bench where the three onlookers were sitting. The balls dangled in a net in his hand, his racket was under one arm. The gay, laughing expression on his face was wiped off as though by a sponge from a slate. He looked tired and worried. Coming toward them he said, "That's over." Then the smile broke out again, that charming, boyish, expressive smile that went so harmoniously with his sun-tanned face and dark, lithe grace. Sir Henry found himself wondering how old the man was. Twenty-five, thirty, thirty-five? It was impossible to say. Raymond said, shaking his head a little, "She'll never be able to play, you know."

"All this must," said Miss Marple, "be very boring for you."

Raymond said simply, "It is sometimes. Especially at the end of the summer. For a time the thought of the pay buoys one up, but even that fails to stimulate imagination in the end."

Superintendent Harper got up. He said abruptly, "I'll call for you in half an hour's time, Miss Marple, if that will be all right?"

"Perfectly, thank you. I shall be ready."

Harper went off. Raymond stood looking after him. Then he said, "Mind if I sit for a bit?"

"Do," said Sir Henry. "Have a cigarette?" He offered his case, wondering as he did so why had had a slight feeling of prejudice against Raymond Starr. Was it simply because he was a professional tennis coach and dancer? If so, it wasn't the tennis, it was the dancing. The English, Sir Henry decided, had a distrust for any man who danced too well. This fellow moved with too much grace. Ramon—Raymond—which was his name? Abruptly, he asked the question.

The other seemed amused. "Ramon was my original professional name. Ramon and Josie—Spanish effect, you know. Then there was rather a prejudice against foreigners, so I became Raymond—very British."

Miss Marple said, "And is your real name something quite different?"

He smiled at her. "Actually my real name is Ramon. I had an Argentine grandmother, you see. *And that accounts for that swing from the hips,* thought Sir Henry parenthetically. "But my first name is Thomas. Painfully prosaic." He turned to Sir Henry. "You come from Devonshire, don't you, sir? From Stane? My people lived down that way. At Alsmonston."

Sir Henry's face lit up. "Are you one of the Alsmonston Starrs? I didn't realize that."

"No, I don't suppose you would." There was a slight bitterness in his voice.

Sir Henry said, "Bad luck—er—all that."

"The place being sold up after it had been in the family for three hundred years? Yes, it was rather! Still, our kind have to go, I suppose! We've outlived our usefulness. My elder brother went to New York. He's in publishing—doing well. The rest of us are scattered up and down the earth. I'll say it's hard to get a job nowadays when you've nothing to say for yourself except that you've had a public-school education. Sometimes, if you're lucky, you get taken on as a reception clerk at a hotel. The tie and the manner are an asset there. The only job I could get was showman in a plumbing establishment. Selling superb peach and lemon colored porcelain baths. Enormous showrooms, but as I never knew the price of the damned things or how soon we could deliver them, I got fired.

"The only things I could do were dance and play tennis. I got taken on at a hotel on the Riviera. Good pickings there. I suppose I was doing well. Then I overheard an old colonel—real old colonel, incredibly ancient, British to the backbone and always talking about Poona. He went up to the manager and said at the top of his voice: 'Where's the gigolo? I want to get hold of the gigolo. My wife and daughter want to dance, yer know. Where is the feller? What does he sting yer for? It's the gigolo I want.'" Raymond said, "Silly to mind. But I did. I chucked it. Came here. Less pay, but pleasanter. Mostly teaching tennis to rotund women who will never, never be able to play. That and dancing with the wallflower daughters of rich clients! Oh, well, it's life, I suppose. Excuse today's hard-luck story." He laughed. His teeth flashed out white, his eyes crinkled up at the corners. He looked suddenly healthy and happy and very much alive.

Sir Henry said, "I'm glad to have a chat with you. I've been wanting to talk with you."

"About Ruby Keene? I can't help you, you know. I don't know who killed her. I knew very little about her. She didn't confide in me."

Miss Marple said, "Did you like her?"

"Not particularly. I didn't dislike her." His voice was careless, uninterested.

Sir Henry said, "So you've no suggestions?"

"I'm afraid not. I'd have told Harper if I had. It just seems to me one of those things! Petty, sordid little crime, no clues, no motive."

"Two people had a motive," said Miss Marple.

Sir Henry looked at her sharply.

"Really?" Raymond looked surprised.

Miss Marple looked insistently at Sir Henry, and he said rather unwillingly, "Her death probably benefits Mrs. Jefferson and Mr. Gaskell to the amount of fifty thousand pounds."

"What?" Raymond looked really startled—more than startled, upset. "Oh, but that's absurd—absolutely absurd. Mrs. Jefferson—neither of them—could have had anything to do with it. It would be incredible to think of such a thing."

Miss Marple coughed. She said gently, "I'm afraid, you know, you're rather an idealist."

"I?" He laughed. "Not me! I'm a hard-boiled cynic."

"Money," said Miss Marple, "is a very powerful motive."

"Perhaps," Raymond said hotly. "But that either of those two would strangle a girl in cold blood—" He shook his head. Then he got up. "Here's Mrs. Jefferson now. Come for her lesson. She's late." His voice sounded amused. "Ten minutes late!"

Adelaide Jefferson and Hugo McLean were walking rapidly down the path toward them. With a smiling apology for her lateness, Addie Jefferson went onto the court. McLean sat down on the bench. After a polite inquiry whether Miss Marple minded a pipe, he lit it and puffed for some minutes in silence, watching critically the two white figures about the tennis court. He said at last, "Can't see what Addie wants to have lessons for. Have a game, yes. No one enjoys it better than I do. But why lessons?"

"Wants to improve her game," said Sir Henry.

"She's not a bad player," said Hugo. "Good enough, at all events. Dash it all, she isn't aiming to play at Wimbledon." He was silent for a minute or two. Then he said, "Who is this Raymond fellow? Where do they come from, these pros? Fellow looks like a Dago to me."

"He's one of the Devonshire Starrs," said Sir Henry.

"What? Not really?"

Sir Henry nodded. It was clear that this news was unpleasing to Hugo McLean. He scowled more than ever. He said, "Don't know why Addie sent for me. She seems not to have turned a hair over this business. Never looked better. Why send for me?"

Sir Henry asked with some curiosity, "When did she send for you?"

"Oh—er—when all this happened."

"How did you hear? Telephone or telegram?"

"Telegram."

"As a matter of curiosity, when was it sent off?"

"Well, I don't know exactly."

"What time did you receive it?"

"I didn't exactly receive it. It was telephoned on to me, as a matter of fact."

"Why, where were you?"

"Fact is, I'd left London the afternoon before. I was staying at Danebury Head."

"What? Quite near here?"

"Yes, rather funny, wasn't it? Got the message when I got in from a round of golf and came over here at once."

Miss Marple gazed at him thoughtfully. He looked hot and uncomfortable. She said, "I've heard it's very pleasant at Danebury Head and not very expensive."

"No, it's not expensive. I couldn't afford it if it was. It's a nice little place."

"We must drive over there one day," said Miss Marple.

"Eh? What? Oh—er—yes, I should." He got up. "Better take some exercise, get an appetite." He walked away stiffly.

"Women," said Sir Henry, "treat their devoted admirers very badly." Miss Marple smiled, but made no answer. "Does he strike you as rather a dull dog?" asked Sir Henry. "I'd be interested to know."

"A little limited in his ideas, perhaps," said Miss Marple. "But with possibilities, I think—oh, definitely possibilities."

Sir Henry, in his turn, got up. "It's time for me to go and do my stuff. I see Mrs. Bantry is on her way to keep you company."

Mrs. Bantry arrived breathless and sat down with a gasp. She said, "I've been talking to chambermaids. But it isn't any good. I haven't found out a thing more! Do you think that girl can really have been carrying on with someone without everybody in the hotel knowing all about it?"

"That's a very interesting point, dear. I should say definitely not. Somebody knows, depend upon it, if it's true. But she must have been very clever about it."

Mrs. Bantry's attention had strayed to the tennis court. She said approvingly, "Addie's tennis is coming on a lot. Attractive young man, that tennis pro. Addie's quite nice-looking. She's still an attractive woman. I shouldn't be at all surprised if she married again."

"She'll be quite a rich women, too, when Mr. Jefferson dies," said Miss Marple.

"Oh, don't always have such a nasty mind, Jane. Why haven't you solved this mystery yet? We don't seem to be getting on at all. I thought you'd know at once." Mrs. Bantry's tone held reproach.

"No, no, dear, I didn't know at once—not for some time."

Mrs. Bantry turned startled and incredulous eyes on her. "You mean you know now who killed Ruby Keene?"

"Oh, yes," said Miss Marple. "I know that!"

"But, Jane, who is it? Tell me at once."

Miss Marple shook her head very firmly and pursed up her lips. "I'm sorry, Dolly, but that wouldn't do at all."

"Why wouldn't it do?"

"Because you're so indiscreet. You would go round telling everyone—or if you didn't tell, you'd hint."

"No, indeed, I wouldn't. I wouldn't tell a soul."

"People who use that phrase are always the last to live up to it. It's no good, dear. There's a long way to go yet. A great many things that are quite obscure. You remember when I was so against letting Mrs. Partridge collect for the Red Cross and I couldn't say why. The reason was that her nose had twitched in just the same way that that maid of mine, Alice, twitched her nose when I sent her out to pay the accounts. Always paid them a shilling or so short and said it could go on to next week, which, of course, was exactly what Mrs. Partridge did, only on a much larger scale. Seventy-five pounds it was she embezzled."

"Never mind Mrs. Partridge," said Mrs. Bantry.

"But I had to explain to you. And if you care, I'll give you a hint. The trouble in this case is that everybody has been much too credulous and believing. You simply cannot afford to believe everything that people tell you. When there's anything fishy about, I never believe anyone at all. You see, I know human nature so well."

Mrs. Bantry was silent for a minute or two. Then she said in a different tone of voice, "I told you, didn't I, that I didn't see why I shouldn't enjoy myself over this case? A real murder in my own house! The sort of thing that will never happen again."

"I hope not," said Miss Marple.

"Well, so do I really. Once is enough. But it's my murder, Jane. I want to enjoy myself over it."

Miss Marple shot a glance at her. Mrs. Bantry said belligerently, "Don't you believe that?"

Miss Marple said sweetly, "Of course, Dolly, if you tell me so."

"Yes, but you never believe what people tell you, do you? You've just said so. Well, you're quite right." Mrs. Bantry's voice took on a sudden bitter note. She said, "I'm not altogether a fool. You may think, Jane, that I don't know what they're saying all over St. Mary Mead—all over the county! They're saying, one and all, that there's no smoke without fire; that if the girl was found in Arthur's library, then Arthur must know something about it. They're saying that the girl was Arthur's mistress; that she was his illegitimate daughter; that she was blackmailing him; they're saying anything that comes into their heads. And it will go on like that! Arthur won't realize it at first; he won't know what's wrong. He's such a dear old stupid that he'd never believe people would think things like that about him. He'll be cold-shouldered and looked at askance—whatever that means!—and it will dawn on him little by little, and suddenly he'll be horrified and cut to the soul, and he'll fasten up like a clam and just endure, day after day. It's because of all that's going to happen to him that I've come here to ferret out every single thing about it that I can! This murder's got to be solved! If it isn't, then Arthur's whole life will be wrecked, and I won't have that happen. I won't! I won't! I won't!" She paused for a minute and said, "I won't have the dear old boy go through hell for something he didn't do. That's the only reason I came to Danemouth and left him alone at home—to find the truth."

"I know, dear," said Miss Marple. "That's why I'm here too."

17

In A Quiet hotel room Edwards was listening deferentially to Sir Henry Clithering. "There are certain questions I would like to ask you, Edwards, but I want you first to understand quite clearly my position here. I was at one time commissioner of the police at Scotland Yard. I am now retired into private life. Your master sent for me when this tragedy occurred. He begged me to use my skill and experience in order to find out the truth." Sir Henry paused. Edwards, his pale, intelligent eyes on the other's face, inclined his head. He said, "Quite so, Sir Henry."

Clithering went on slowly and deliberately, "In all police cases there is necessarily a lot of information that is held back. It is held back for various reasons—because it touches on a family skeleton, because it is considered to have no bearing on the case, because it would entail awkwardness and embarrassment to the parties concerned."

Again Edwards said, "Quite so, Sir Henry."

"I expect, Edwards, that by now you appreciate quite clearly the main points of this business. The dead girl was on the point of becoming Mr. Jefferson's adopted daughter. Two people had a motive in seeing that this should not happen. Those two people are Mr. Gaskell and Mrs. Jefferson."

The valet's eyes displayed a momentary gleam. He said, "May I ask if they are under suspicion, sir."

"They are in no danger of arrest, if that is what you mean. But the police are bound to be suspicious of them and will continue to be so until the matter is cleared up."

"An unpleasant position for them, sir."

"Very unpleasant. Now to get at the truth, one must have all the facts of the case. A lot depends, must depend, on the reactions, the words and gestures, of Mr. Jefferson and his family. How did they feel, what did they show, what things were said? I am asking you, Edwards, for inside information—the kind of information that only you are likely to have. You know your master's moods. From observation of them you probably know what caused them. I am asking this, not as a policeman but as a friend of Mr. Jefferson's. That is to say, if anything you tell me is not, in my opinion relevant to the case, I shall not pass it on to the police." He paused.

Edwards said quietly, "I understand you, sir. You want me to speak quite frankly; to say things that, in the ordinary course of events, I should not say, and that—excuse me, sir—you wouldn't dream of listening to."

Sir Henry said, "You're a very intelligent fellow, Edwards. That's exactly what I do mean."

Edwards was silent for a minute or two, then he began to speak. "Of course I know Mr. Jefferson fairly well by now. I've been with him quite a number of years. And I see him in his 'off' moments, not only in his 'on' ones. Sometimes, sir, I've questioned in my own mind whether it's good for anyone to fight fate in the way Mr. Jefferson has fought. It's taken a terrible toll of him, sir. If, sometimes, he could have given way, been an unhappy, lonely, broken old man—well, it might have been better for him in the end. But he's too proud for that. He'll go down fighting—that's his motto. But that sort of thing leads, Sir Henry, to a lot of nervous reaction. He looks a good-tempered gentleman. I've seen him in violent rages when he could hardly speak for passion. And the one thing that roused him, sir, was deceit."

"Are you saying that for any particular reason, Edwards?"

"Yes, sir. I am. You asked me, sir, to speak quite frankly."

"That is the idea."

"Well, then, Sir Henry, in my opinion the young woman that Mr. Jefferson was so taken up with wasn't worth it. She was, to put it bluntly, a common little piece. And she didn't care a tuppence for Mr. Jefferson. All that play of affection and gratitude was so much poppycock. I don't say there was any harm in her, but she wasn't, by a long way, what Mr. Jefferson thought her. It was funny, that, sir, for Mr. Jefferson was a shrewd gentleman; he wasn't often deceived over people. But there, a gentleman isn't himself in his judgment when it comes to a young woman being in question. Young Mrs. Jefferson, you see, whom he'd always depended upon a lot for sympathy, had changed a good deal this summer. He noticed it and he felt it badly. He was fond of her, you see. Mr. Mark he never liked much."

Sir Henry interjected, "And yet he had him with him constantly?"

"Yes, but that was for Miss Rosamund's sake. Mrs. Gaskell, that was. She was the apple of his eye. He adored her. Mr. Mark was Miss Rosamund's husband. He always thought of him like that."

"Supposing Mr. Mark had married someone else?"

"Mr. Jefferson, sir, would have been furious."

Sir Henry raised his eyebrows. "As much as that?"

"He wouldn't have shown it, but that's what it would have been."

"And if Mrs. Jefferson had married again?"

"Mr. Jefferson wouldn't have liked that either, sir."

"Please go on, Edwards."

"I was saying, sir, that Mr. Jefferson fell for this young woman. I've often seen it happen with the gentlemen I've been with. Comes over them like a kind of disease. They want to protect the girl, and shield her, and shower benefits upon her, and nine times out of ten the girl is very well able to look after herself and has a good eye to the main chance."

"So you think Ruby Keene was a schemer?"

"Well, Sir Henry, she was quite inexperienced, being so young, but she had the makings of a very fine schemer indeed when she'd once got well into her swing, so to speak. In another five years she'd have been an expert at the game."

Sir Henry said, "I'm glad to have your opinion of her. It's valuable. Now, do you recall any incidents in which this matter was discussed between Mr. Jefferson and the members of his family?"

"There was very little discussion, sir. Mr. Jefferson announced what he had in mind and stifled any protests. That is, he shut up Mr. Mark, who was a bit outspoken. Mrs. Jefferson didn't say much—she's a quiet lady —only urged him not to do anything in a great hurry."

Sir Henry nodded. "Anything else? What was the girl's attitude?"

With marked distaste the valet said, "I should describe it, Sir Henry, as jubilant."

"Ah, jubilant, you say? You had no reason to believe, Edwards, that" —he sought about for a phrase suitable to Edwards—"that—er—her affections were engaged elsewhere?"

"Mr. Jefferson was not proposing marriage, sir. He was going to adopt her."

"Cut out the 'elsewhere' and let the question stand."

The valet said slowly, "There was one incident, sir. I happened to be a witness of it."

"That is gratifying. Tell me."

"There is probably nothing in it, sir. It was that one day, the young woman chancing to open her handbag, a small snapshot fell out. Mr. Jefferson pounced on it and said, 'Hullo, kitten, who's this, eh?'

"It was a snapshot, sir, of a young man, a dark young man with rather untidy hair, and his tie very badly arranged. Miss Keene pretended that she didn't know anything about it. She said, 'I've no idea, Jeffie. No idea at all. I don't know how it could have got into my bag. I didn't put it there.'

"Now, Mr. Jefferson, sir, wasn't quite a fool. That story wasn't good enough. He looked angry, his brows came down heavy, and his voice was gruff when he said, 'Now then, kitten, now then. You know who it is right enough.' She changed her tactics quick, sir. Looked frightened. She said, 'I do recognize him now. He comes here sometimes and I've danced with him. I don't know his name. The silly idiot must have stuffed his photo into my bag one day. These boys are too silly for anything!' She tossed her head and giggled and passed it off. But it wasn't a likely story, was it? And I don't think Mr. Jefferson quite believed it. He looked at her once or twice after that in a sharp way, and sometimes, if she'd been out, he asked her where she'd been."

Sir Henry said, "Have you ever seen the original of the photo about the hotel?"

"Not to my knowledge, sir. Of course I am not much downstairs in the public apartments."

Sir Henry nodded. He asked a few more questions, but Edwards could tell him nothing more.

In the police station at Danemouth Superintendent Harper was interviewing Jessie Davis, Florence Small, Beatrice Henniker, Mary Price and Lillian Ridgeway. They were girls much of an age, differing slightly in mentality. They ranged from "county" to farmers' and shopkeepers' daughters. One and all, they told the same story. Pamela Reeves had been just the same as usual; she had said nothing to any of them except that she was going to Woolworth's and would go home by a later bus.

In the corner of Superintendent Harper's office sat an elderly lady. The girls hardly noticed her. If they did they may have wondered who she was. She was certainly no police matron. Possibly they assumed that she, like them, was a witness to be questioned. The last girl was shown out. Superintendent Harper wiped his forehead and turned round to look at Miss Marple. His glance was inquiring, but not hopeful. Miss Marple, however, spoke crisply, "I'd like to speak to Florence Small."

The superintendent's eyebrows rose, but he nodded and touched a bell. A constable appeared. Harper said, "Florence Small."

The girl reappeared, ushered in by the constable. She was the daughter of a well-to-do farmer—a tall girl with fair hair, a rather foolish mouth and frightened brown eyes. She was twisting her hands and looked nervous. Superintendent Harper looked at Miss Marple, who nodded. The superintendent got up. He said, "This lady will ask you some questions." He went out, closing the door behind him.

Florence looked uneasily at Miss Marple. Her eyes looked rather like those of one of her father's calves.

Miss Marple said, "Sit down, Florence."

Florence Small sat down obediently. Unrecognized by herself, she felt suddenly more at home, less uneasy. The unfamiliar and terrorizing atmosphere of a police station was replaced by something more familiar—the accustomed tone of command of somebody whose business it was to give orders.

Miss Marple said, "You understand, Florence, that it's of the utmost importance that everything about poor Pamela's doings on the day of her death should be known?"

Florence murmured that she quite understood.

"And I'm sure you want to do your best to help?" Florence's eyes were wary as she said of course she did. "To keep back any piece of information is a very serious offense," said Miss Marple.

The girl's fingers twisted nervously in her lap. She swallowed once or twice. "I can make allowances," went on Miss Marple, "for the fact that you are naturally alarmed at being brought into contact with the police. You are afraid, too, that you may be blamed for not having spoken sooner. Possibly you are afraid that you may also be blamed for not stopping Pamela at the time. But you've got to be a brave girl and make a clean breast of things. If you refuse to tell what you know now, it will be a very serious matter indeed—very serious—practically perjury—and for that, as you know, you can be sent to prison."

"I—I don't—"

Miss Marple said sharply, "Now don't prevaricate, Florence! Tell me all about it at once! Pamela wasn't going to Woolworth's, was she?" Florence licked her lips with a dry tongue and gazed imploringly at Miss Marple, like a beast about to be slaughtered. "Something to do with the films, wasn't it?" asked Miss Marple.

A look of intense relief mingled with awe passed over Florence's face. Her inhibitions left her. She gasped, "Oh, yes!"

"I thought so," said Miss Marple. "Now I want you to tell me all the details, please."

Words poured from Florence in a gush. "Oh, I've been ever so worried. I promised Pam, you see, I'd never say a word to a soul. And then, when she was found, all burned up in that car—oh, it was horrible and I thought I should die—I felt it was all my fault. I ought to have stopped her. Only I never thought, not for a minute, that it wasn't all right. And then I was asked if she'd been quite as usual that day and I said 'Yes' before I'd had time to think. And not having said anything then, I didn't see how I could say anything later. And after all, I didn't know anything—not really—only what Pam told me."

"What did Pam tell you?"

"It was as we were walking up the lane to the bus on the way to the rally. She asked me if I could keep a secret, and I said yes, and she made me swear not to tell. She was going into Danemouth for a film test after the rally! She'd met a film producer—just back from Hollywood, he was. He wanted a certain type, and he told Pam she was just what he was looking for. He warned her, though, not to build on it. You couldn't tell, he said, not until you saw how a person photographed. It might be no good at all. It was a kind of Bergner part, he said. You had to have someone quite young for it. A schoolgirl, it was, who changes places with a revue artist and has a wonderful career. Pam's acted in plays at school and she's awfully good. He said he could see she could act, but she'd have to have some intensive training. It wouldn't be all beer and skittles, he told her; it would be hard work. Did she think she could stick it?"

Florence Small stopped for breath. Miss Marple felt rather sick as she listened to the glib rehash of countless novels and screen stories. Pamela Reeves, like most other girls, would have been warned against talking to strangers, but the glamour of films would have obliterated all that.

"He was absolutely businesslike about it all," continued Florence. "Said if the test was successful she'd have a contract, and he said that as she was young and inexperienced she ought to let a lawyer look at it before she signed it. But she wasn't to pass on that he'd said that. He asked her if she'd have trouble with her parents, and Pam said she probably would, and he said, 'Well, of course that's always a difficulty with anyone as young as you are, but I think if it was put to them that this was a wonderful chance that wouldn't happen once in a million times, they'd see reason.' But anyway, he said, it wasn't any good going into that until they knew the result of the test. She mustn't be disappointed if it failed. He told her about Hollywood and about Vivien Leigh—how she'd suddenly taken London by storm, and how these sensational leaps into fame did happen. He himself had come back from America to work with the Lenville Studios and put some pep into the English film companies."

Miss Marple nodded.

Florence went on, "So it was all arranged. Pam was to go into Danemouth after the rally and meet him at his hotel and he'd take her along to the studios—they'd got a small testing studio in Danemouth, he told her. She'd have her test and she could catch the bus home afterward. She could say she'd been shopping, and he'd let her know the results of the test in a few days, and if it was favorable Mr. Harmsteiter, the boss, would come along and talk to her parents.

"Well, of course, it sounded too wonderful! I was green with envy! Pam got through the rally without turning a hair—we always call her a regular poker face. Then, when she said that she was going into Danemouth to Woolworth's, she just winked at me.

"I saw her start off down the footpath." Florence began to cry. "I ought to have stopped her! I ought to have stopped her! I ought to have known a thing like that couldn't be true! I ought to have told someone. Oh, dear, I wish I was dead!"

"There, there." Miss Marple patted her on the shoulder. "It's quite all right. No one will blame you, Florence. You've done the right thing in telling me."

She devoted some minutes to cheering the child up.

Five minutes later she was telling the girl's story to Superintendent Harper. The latter looked very grim. "The clever devil!" he said. "I'll cook his goose for him! This puts rather a different aspect on things."

"Yes, it does."

Harper looked at her sideways. "It doesn't surprise you?"

"I expected something of the kind," Miss Marple said.

Superintendent Harper said curiously, "What put you on to this particular girl? They all looked scared to death and there wasn't a pin to choose between them, as far as I could see."

Miss Marple said gently, "You haven't had as much experience with girls telling lies as I have. Florence looked at you very straight, if you remember, and stood very rigid and just fidgeted with her feet like the others. But you didn't watch her as she went out of the door. I knew at once then that she'd got something to hide. They nearly always relax too soon. My little maid Janet always did. She'd explain quite convincingly that the mice had eaten the end of a cake and give herself away by smirking as she left the room."

"I'm very grateful to you," said Harper. He added thoughtfully, "Lenville Studios, eh?"

Miss Marple said nothing. She rose to her feet.

"I'm afraid," she said, "I must hurry away. So glad to have been able to help you."

"Are you going back to the hotel?"

"Yes, to pack up. I must go back to St. Mary Mead as soon as possible. There's a lot for me to do there."

18

MISS MARPLE passed out through the French windows of her drawing room, tripped down her neat garden path, through a garden gate, in through the vicarage garden gate, across the vicarage garden and up to the drawing-room window, where she tapped gently on the pane. The vicar was busy in his study composing his Sunday sermon, but the vicar's wife, who was young and pretty, was admiring the progress of her off-spring across the hearthrug. "Can I come in, Griselda?"

"Oh, do, Miss Marple. Just look at David! He gets so angry because he can only crawl in reverse. He wants to get to something, and the more he tries the more he goes backwards into the coalbox!"

"He's looking very bonny, Griselda."

"He's not bad, is he?" said the young mother, endeavoring to assume an indifferent manner. "Of course I didn't bother with him much. All the books say a child should be left alone as much as possible."

"Very wise, dear," said Miss Marple. "Ahem—I came to ask if there was anything special you are collecting for at the moment?"

The vicar's wife turned somewhat astonished eyes upon her. "Oh, heaps of things," she said cheerfully. "There always are." She ticked them off on her fingers. "There's the Nave Restoration Fund, and St. Giles' Mission, and our Sale of Work next Wednesday, and the Unmarried Mothers, and a Boy Scouts Outing, and the Needlework Guild, and the Bishop's Appeal for Deep-Sea Fishermen."

"Any of them will do," said Miss Marple. "I thought I might make a little round—with a book, you know—if you would authorize me to do so."

"Are you up to something? I believe you are. Of course I authorize you. Make it the Sale of Work; it would be lovely to get some real money instead of those awful sachets and comic penwipers and depressing children's frocks and dusters all done up to look like dolls. . . . I suppose," continued Griselda, accompanying her guest to the window, "that you wouldn't like to tell me what it's all about?"

"Later, my dear," said Miss Marple, hurrying off.

With a sigh the young mother returned to the hearthrug and, by way of carrying out her principles of stern neglect, butted her son three times in the stomach, so that he caught hold of her hair and pulled it with gleeful yells. They then rolled over and over in a grand rough and tumble until the door opened and the vicarage maid announced to the most influential parishioner, who didn't like children, "Missus is in here."

Whereupon Griselda sat up and tried to look dignified and more what a vicar's wife should be.

Miss Marple, clasping a small black book with penciled entries in it, walked briskly along the village street until she came to the crossroads. Here she turned to the left and walked past the Blue Boar until she came to Chatsworth, alias "Mr. Booker's new house." She turned in at the gate, walked up to the front door and knocked on it briskly. The door was opened by the blond young woman named Dinah Lee. She was less carefully made up than usual and, in fact, looked slightly dirty. She was wearing gray slacks and an emerald jumper.

"Good morning," said Miss Marple briskly and cheerfully. "May I just come in for a minute?" She pressed forward as she spoke, so that Dinah Lee, who was somewhat taken aback at the call, had no time to make up her mind. "Thank you so much," said Miss Marple, beaming amiably at her and sitting down rather gingerly on a period bamboo chair. "Quite warm for the time of year, is it not?" went on Miss Marple, still exuding geniality.

"Yes, rather. Oh, quite," said Miss Lee. At a loss how to deal with the situation, she opened a box and offered it to her guest. "Er—have a cigarette?"

"Thank you so much, but I don't smoke. I just called, you know, to see if I could enlist your help for our Sale of Work next week."

"Sale of Work?" said Dinah Lee, as one who repeats a phrase in a foreign language.

"At the vicarage," said Miss Marple. "Next Wednesday."

"Oh!" Miss Lee's mouth fell open. "I'm afraid I couldn't—"

"Not even a small subscription—half a crown perhaps?" Miss Marple exhibited her little book.

"Oh—er—well, yes. I dare say I could manage that." The girl looked relieved and turned to hunt in her handbag.

Miss Marple's sharp eyes were looking round the room. She said, "I see you've no hearthrug in front of the fire." Dinah Lee turned round and stared at her. She could not but be aware of the very keen scrutiny the old lady was giving her, but it aroused in her no other emotion than slight annoyance. Miss Marple recognized that. She said, "It's rather dangerous, you know. Sparks fly out and mark the carpet."

Funny old tabby, thought Dinah, but she said quite amiably, if somewhat vaguely, "There used to be one. I don't know where it's got to."

"I suppose," said Miss Marple, "it was the fluffy wooly kind?"

"Sheep," said Dinah. "That's what it looked like." She was amused now. An eccentric old bean, this. She held out a half crown. "Here you are," she said.

"Oh, thank you, my dear." Miss Marple took it and opened the little book. "Er—what name shall I write down?"

Dinah's eyes grew suddenly hard and contemptuous. *Nosy old cat,* she thought. *That's all she came for—prying around for scandal.* She said clearly and with malicious pleasure, "Miss Dinah Lee."

Miss Marple looked at her steadily. She said, "This is Mr. Basil Blake's cottage, isn't it?"

"Yes, and I'm Miss Dinah Lee!" Her voice rang out challengingly, her head went back, her blue eyes flashed.

Very steadily Miss Marple looked at her. She said, "Will you allow me to give you some advice, even though you may consider it impertinent?"

"I shall consider it impertinent. You had better say nothing."

"Nevertheless," said Miss Marple, "I am going to speak. I want to advise you, very strongly, not to continue using your maiden name in the village."

Dinah stared at her. She said, "What—what do you mean?"

Miss Marple said earnestly, "In a very short time you may need all the sympathy and good will you can find. It will be important to your husband, too, that he shall be thought well of. There is a prejudice in old-fashioned country districts against people living together who are not married. It has amused you both, I dare say, to pretend that that is what you are doing. It kept people away, so that you weren't bothered with what I expect you would call 'old frumps.' Nevertheless, old frumps have their uses."

Dinah demanded, "How did you know we are married?"

Miss Marple smiled a deprecating smile. "Oh, my dear," she said.

Dinah persisted, "No, but how did you know? You didn't—you didn't go to Somerset House?"

A momentary flicker showed in Miss Marple's eyes. "Somerset House? Oh, no. But it was quite easy to guess. Everything, you know, gets round in a village. The—er—the kind of quarrels you have—typical of early days of marriage. Quite—quite unlike an illicit relationship. It has been said, you know—and I think quite truly—that you can only really get under anybody's skin if you are married to them. When there is no—no legal bond, people are much more careful; they have to keep assuring themselves how happy and halcyon everything is. They have, you see, to justify themselves. They dare not quarrel! Married people, I have noticed, quite enjoy their battles and the—er—appropriate reconciliations." She paused, twinkling benignly.

"Well, I—" Dinah stopped and laughed. She sat down and lit a cigarette. "You're absolutely marvelous!" she said. Then she went on, "But why do you want us to own up and admit to respectability?"

Miss Marple's face was grave now. She said, "Because any minute now your husband may be arrested for murder."

19

FOR AN interval Dinah stared at Miss Marple. Then she said incredulously, "Basil? Murder? Are you joking?"

"No, indeed. Haven't you seen the papers?"

Dinah caught her breath. "You mean that girl at the Majestic Hotel. Do you mean they suspect Basil of killing her?"

"Yes."

"But it's nonsense!"

There was the whir of a car outside, the bang of a gate. Basil Blake flung open the door and came in, carrying some bottles. He said, "Got the gin and the vermouth. Did you—" He stopped and turned incredulous eyes on the prim, erect visitor.

Dinah burst out breathlessly, "Is she mad? She says you're going to be arrested for the murder of that girl Ruby Keene."

"Oh, God!" said Basil Blake. The bottles dropped from his arms onto the sofa. He reeled to a chair and dropped down in it and buried his face in his hands. He repeated, "Oh, my God! Oh, my God!"

Dinah darted over to him. She caught his shoulders. "Basil, look at me! It isn't true! I know it isn't true! I don't believe it for a moment!"

His hand went up and gripped hers. "Bless you, darling."

"But why should they think—You didn't even know her, did you?"

"Oh, yes, he knew her," said Miss Marple.

Basil said fiercely, "Be quiet, you old hag! . . . Listen, Dinah, darling. I hardly knew her at all. Just ran across her once or twice at the Majestic. That's all—I swear that's all!"

Dinah said, bewildered, "I don't understand. Why should anyone suspect you, then?"

Basil groaned. He put his hands over his eyes and rocked to and fro. Miss Marple said, "What did you do with the hearthrug?"

His reply came mechanically, "I put it in the dustbin."

Miss Marple clucked her tongue vexedly. "That was stupid—very stupid. People don't put good hearthrugs in dustbins. It had spangles in it from her dress, I suppose?"

"Yes, I couldn't get them out."

Dinah cried, "What are you talking about?"

Basil said sullenly, "Ask her. She seems to know all about it."

"I'll tell you what I think happened, if you like," said Miss Marple. "You can correct me, Mr. Blake, if I go wrong. I think that after having a violent quarrel with your wife at a party and after having had, perhaps, rather too much—er—to drink, you drove down here. I don't know what time you arrived."

Basil Blake said sullenly, "About two in the morning. I meant to go up to town first; then, when I got to the suburbs, I changed my mind. I thought Dinah might come down here after me. So I drove down here. The place was all dark. I opened the door and turned on the light and I saw—and I saw—" He gulped and stopped.

Miss Marple went on, "You saw a girl lying on the hearthrug. A girl in a white evening dress, strangled. I don't know whether you recognized her then—"

Basil Blake shook his head violently. "I couldn't look at her after the first glance; her face was all blue, swollen; she'd been dead some time and she was there—in my living room!" He shuddered.

Miss Marple said gently, "You weren't, of course, quite yourself. You were in a fuddled state and your nerves are not good. You were, I think, panic-stricken. You didn't know what to do—"

"I thought Dinah might turn up any minute. And she'd find me there with a dead body—a girl's dead body—and she'd think I'd killed her. Then I got an idea. It seemed—I don't know why—a good idea at the time. I thought: 'I'll put her in old Bantry's library. Damned pompous old stick, always looking down his nose, sneering at me as artistic and effeminate. Serve the pompous brute right,' I thought. 'He'll look a fool when a dead lovely is found on his hearthrug.' " He added with a pathetic eagerness to explain, "I was a bit drunk, you know, at the time. It really seemed positively amusing to me. Old Bantry with a dead blonde."

"Yes, yes," said Miss Marple. "Little Tommy Bond had very much the same idea. Rather a sensitive boy, with an inferiority complex, he said teacher was always picking on him. He put a frog in the clock and it jumped out at her. You were just the same," went on Miss Marple, "only, of course, bodies are more serious matters than frogs."

Basil groaned again. "By the morning I'd sobered up. I realized what I'd done. I was scared stiff. And then the police came here—another damned pompous ass of a chief constable. I was scared of him, and the only way I could hide it was by being abominably rude. In the middle of it all, Dinah drove up."

Dinah looked out of the window. She said, "There's a car driving up now. There are men in it."

"The police, I think," said Miss Marple.

Basil Blake got up. Suddenly he became quite calm and resolute. He even smiled. He said, "So I'm in for it, am I? All right, Dinah, sweet, keep your head. Get onto old Sims—he's the family lawyer—and go to mother and tell her about our marriage. She won't bite. And don't worry. I didn't do it. So it's bound to be all right, see, sweetheart?"

There was a tap on the cottage door. Basil called, "Come in."

Inspector Slack entered with another man. He said, "Mr. Basil Blake?"

"Yes."

"I have a warrant here for your arrest on the charge of murdering Ruby Keene on the night of September twentieth last. I warn you that anything you say may be used at your trial. You will please accompany me now. Full facilities will be given you for communicating with your solicitor."

Basil nodded. He looked at Dinah, but did not touch her. He said, "So long, Dinah."

Cool customer, thought Inspector Slack. He acknowledged the presence of Miss Marple with a half bow and a "Good morning," and thought to himself, *Smart old pussy; she's on to it. Good job we've got that hearthrug. That and finding out from the car-park man at the studio that he left that party at eleven instead of midnight. Don't think those friends of his meant to commit perjury. They were bottled, and Blake told 'em firmly the next day it was twelve o'clock when he left, and they believed him. Well, his goose is cooked good and proper. Mental, I expect. Broadmoor, not hanging. First the Reeves kid, probably strangled her, drove her out to the quarry, walked back into Danemouth, picked up his own car in some side lane, drove to this party, then back to Danemouth, brought Ruby Keene out here, strangled her, put her in old Bantry's library, then probably got the wind up about the car in the quarry, drove there, set it on fire and got back here. Mad—sex and blood lust—lucky this girl's escaped. What they call recurring mania, I expect.*

Alone with Miss Marple, Dinah Blake turned to her. She said, "I don't know who you are, but you've got to understand this: Basil didn't do it."

Miss Marple said, "I know he didn't. I know who did do it. But it's not going to be easy to prove. I've an idea that something you said just now may help. It gave me an idea—the connection I'd been trying to find. Now, what was it?"

20

"I'M HOME, Arthur!" declared Mrs. Bantry, announcing the fact like a royal proclamation as she flung open the study door.

Colonel Bantry immediately jumped up, kissed his wife and declared heartily, "Well, well, that's splendid!"

The colonel's words were unimpeachable, the manner very well done, but an affectionate wife of as many years' standing as Mrs. Bantry was not deceived. She said immediately, "Is anything the matter?"

"No, of course not, Dolly. What should be the matter?"

"Oh, I don't know," said Mrs. Bantry vaguely. "Things are so queer, aren't they?"

She threw off her coat as she spoke, and Colonel Bantry picked it up carefully and laid it across the back of the sofa. All exactly as usual, yet not as usual. Her husband, Mrs. Bantry thought, seemed to have shrunk. He looked thinner, stooped more, there were pouches under his eyes, and those eyes were not ready to meet hers. He went on to say, still with that affection of cheerfulness, "Well, how did you enjoy your time at Danemouth?"

"Oh, it was great fun. You ought to have come, Arthur."

"Couldn't get away, my dear. Lot of things to attend to here."

"Still, I think the change would have done you good. And you like the Jeffersons?"

"Yes, yes, poor fellow. Nice chap. All very sad."

"What have you been doing with yourself since I've been away?"

"Oh, nothing much; been over the farms, you know. Agreed that Anderson shall have a new roof. Can't patch it up any longer."

"How did the Radfordshire Council meeting go?"

"I—well, as a matter of fact, I didn't go."

"Didn't go? But you were taking the chair."

"Well, as a matter of fact, Dolly, seems there was some mistake about that. Asked me if I'd mind if Thompson took it instead."

"I see," said Mrs. Bantry. She peeled off a glove and threw it deliberately into the wastepaper basket. Her husband went to retrieve it and she stopped him, saying sharply, "Leave it. I hate gloves." Colonel Bantry glanced at her uneasily. Mrs. Bantry said sternly, "Did you go to dinner with the Duffs on Thursday?"

"Oh, that? It was put off. Their cook was ill."

"Stupid people," said Mrs. Bantry. She went on, "Did you go to the Naylors' yesterday?"

"I rang up and said I didn't feel up to it; hoped they'd excuse me. They quite understood."

"They did, did they?" said Mrs. Bantry grimly. She sat down by the desk and absent-mindedly picked up a pair of gardening scissors. With them she cut off the fingers, one by one, of her second glove.

"What are you doing, Dolly?"

"Feeling destructive," said Mrs. Bantry. She got up. "Where shall we sit after dinner, Arthur? In the library?"

"Well—er—I don't think so—eh? Very nice in here—or the drawing room."

"I think," said Mrs. Bantry, "that we'll sit in the library."

Her steady eyes met his. Colonel Bantry drew himself up to his full height. A sparkle came into his eye. He said, "You're right, my dear. We'll sit in the library!"

Mrs. Bantry put down the telephone receiver with a sigh of annoyance. She had rung up twice, and each time the answer had been the same. Miss Marple was out. Of a naturally impatient nature, Mrs. Bantry was never one to acquiesce in defeat. She rang up, in rapid succession, the vicarage, Mrs. Price Ridley, Miss Hartnell, Miss Wetherby and, as a last resort, the fishmonger, who, by reason of his advantageous geographical position, usually knew where everybody was in the village. The fishmonger was sorry, but he had not seen Miss Marple at all in the village tnat morning. She had not been on her usual round. "Where can the woman be?" demanded Mrs. Bantry impatiently, aloud.

There was a deferential cough behind her. The discreet Lorrimer murmured, "You were requiring Miss Marple, madam? I have just observed her approaching the house."

Mrs. Bantry rushed to the front door, flung it open and greeted Miss Marple breathlessly, "I've been trying to get you everywhere. Where have you been?" She glanced over her shoulder. Lorrimer had discreetly vanished. "Everything's too awful! People are beginning to cold-shoulder Arthur! He looks years older. We must do something, Jane. You must do something!"

Miss Marple said, "You needn't worry, Dolly," in a rather peculiar voice.

Colonel Bantry appeared from the study door. "Ah, Miss Marple.

Good morning. Glad you've come. My wife's been ringing you up like a lunatic."

"I thought I'd better bring you the news," said Miss Marple as she followed Mrs. Bantry into the study.

"News?"

"Basil Blake has just been arrested for the murder of Ruby Keene."

"Basil Blake?" cried the colonel.

"But he didn't do it," said Miss Marple.

Colonel Bantry took no notice of this statement. It is doubtful if he even heard it. "Do you mean to say he strangled that girl and then brought her along and put her in my library?"

"He put her in your library," said Miss Marple, "but he didn't kill her."

"Nonsense. If he put her in my library, of course he killed her! The two things go together!"

"Not necessarily. He found her dead in his own cottage."

"A likely story," said the colonel derisively. "If you find a body—why, you ring up the police, naturally, if you're an honest man."

"Ah," said Miss Marple, "but we haven't all got such iron nerves as you have, Colonel Bantry. You belong to the old school. The younger generation is different."

"Got no stamina," said the colonel, repeating a well-worn opinion of his.

"Some of them," said Miss Marple, "have been through a bad time. I've heard a good deal about Basil. He did ARP work, you know, when he was only eighteen. He went into a burning house and brought out four children, one after another. He went back for a dog, although they told him it wasn't safe. The building fell in on him. They got him out, but his chest was badly crushed and he had to lie in plaster for a long time after that. That's when he got interested in designing."

"Oh!" The colonel coughed and blew his nose. "I—er—never knew that."

"He doesn't talk about it," said Miss Marple.

"Er—quite right. Proper spirit. Must be more in the young chap than I thought. Shows you ought to be careful in jumping to conclusions." Colonel Bantry looked ashamed. "But all the same"—his indignation revived—"what did he mean, trying to fasten a murder on me?"

"I don't think he saw it like that," said Miss Marple. "He thought of it more as a—as a joke. You see, he was rather under the influence of alcohol at the time."

"Bottled, was he?" said Colonel Bantry, with an Englishman's sympathy for alcoholic excess. "Oh, well, can't judge a fellow by what he does when he's drunk. When I was at Cambridge, I remember I put a certain utensil—well—well, never mind. Deuce of a row there was about it." He chuckled, then checked himself sternly. He looked at Miss Marple with eyes that were shrewd and appraising. He said, "You don't think he did the murder, eh?"

"I'm sure he didn't."

"And you think you know who did?"

Miss Marple nodded.

Mrs. Bantry, like an ecstatic Greek chorus, said, "Isn't she wonderful?" to an unhearing world.

"Well, who was it?"

Miss Marple said, "I was going to ask you to help me. I think if we went up to Somerset House we should have a very good idea."

21

SIR HENRY'S face was very grave. He said, "I don't like it."

"I am aware," said Miss Marple, "that it isn't what you call orthodox. But it is so important, isn't it, to be quite sure—to 'make assurance doubly sure,' as Shakespeare has it? I think, if Mr. Jefferson would agree—"

"What about Harper? Is he to be in on this?"

"It might be awkward for him to know too much. But there might be a hint from you. To watch certain persons—have them trailed, you know."

Sir Henry said slowly, "Yes, that would meet the case."

Superintendent Harper looked piercingly at Sir Henry Clithering. "Let's get this quite clear, sir. You're giving me a hint?"

Sir Henry said, "I'm informing you of what my friend has just informed me—he didn't tell me in confidence—that he purposes to visit a solicitor in Danemouth tomorrow for the purpose of making a new will."

The superintendent's bushy eyebrows drew downward over his steady eyes. He said, "Does Mr. Conway Jefferson propose to inform his son-in-law and daughter-in-law of that fact?"

"He intends to tell them about it this evening."

"I see." The superintendent tapped his desk with a penholder. He repeated again, "I see." Then the piercing eyes bored once more into the eyes of the other man. Harper said, "So you're not satisfied with the case against Basil Blake?"

"Are you?"

The superintendent's mustaches quivered. He said, "Is Miss Marple?" The two men looked at each other. Then Harper said, "You can leave it to me. I'll have men detailed. There will be no funny business, I can promise you that."

Sir Henry said, "There is one more thing. You'd better see this." He unfolded a slip of paper and pushed it across the table.

This time the superintendent's calm deserted him. He whistled. "So that's it, is it? That puts an entirely different complexion on the matter. How did you come to dig up this?"

"Women," said Sir Henry, "are eternally interested in marriages."

"Especially," said the superintendent, "elderly single women."

*   *   *

Conway Jefferson looked up as his friend entered. His grim face relaxed into a smile. He said, "Well, I told 'em. They took it very well."

"What did you say?"

"Told 'em that, as Ruby was dead, I felt that fifty thousand I'd originally left her should go to something that I could associate with her memory. It was to endow a hostel for young girls working as professional dancers in London. Damned silly way to leave your money—surprised they swallowed it—as though I'd do a thing like that." He added meditatively, "You know, I made a fool of myself over that girl. Must be turning into a silly old man. I can see it now. She was a pretty kid, but most of what I saw in her I put there myself. I pretended she was another Rosamund. Same coloring, you know. But not the same heart or mind. Hand me that paper; rather an interesting bridge problem."

Sir Henry went downstairs. He asked a question of the porter.

"Mr. Gaskell, sir? He's just gone off in his car. Had to go to London."

"Oh, I see. Is Mrs. Jefferson about?"

"Mrs. Jefferson, sir, has just gone up to bed."

Sir Henry looked into the lounge and through to the ballroom. In the lounge Hugo McLean was doing a crossword puzzle and frowning a good deal over it. In the ballroom, Josie was smiling valiantly into the face of a stout, perspiring man as her nimble feet avoided his destructive tread. The stout man was clearly enjoying his dance. Raymond, graceful and weary, was dancing with an anemic-looking girl with adenoids, dull brown hair and an expensive and exceedingly unbecoming dress. Sir Henry said under his breath, "And so to bed," and went upstairs.

It was three o'clock. The wind had fallen, the moon was shining over the quiet sea. In Conway Jefferson's room there was no sound except his own heavy breathing as he lay half propped up on pillows. There was no breeze to stir the curtains at the window, but they stirred. For a moment they parted and a figure was silhouetted against the moonlight. Then they fell back into place. Everything was quiet again, but there was someone else inside the room. Nearer and nearer to the bed the intruder stole. The deep breathing on the pillow did not relax. There was no sound, or hardly any sound. A finger and thumb were ready to pick up a fold of skin; in the other hand the hypodermic was ready. And then, suddenly, out of the shadows a hand came and closed over the hand that held the needle; the other arm held the figure in an iron grasp. An unemotional voice, the voice of the law, said, "No, you don't! I want that needle!" The light switched on, and from his pillows Conway Jefferson looked grimly at the murderer of Ruby Keene.

22

Sir Henry Clithering said, "Speaking as Watson, I want to know your methods, Miss Marple."

Superintendent Harper said, "I'd like to know what put you on to it first."

Colonel Melchett said, "You've done it again, by Jove, Miss Marple. I want to hear all about it from the beginning."

Miss Marple smoothed the pure silk of her best evening gown. She flushed and smiled and looked very self-conscious. She said, "I'm afraid you'll think my 'methods,' as Sir Henry calls them, are terribly amateurish. The truth is, you see, that most people—and I don't exclude policemen—are far too trusting for this wicked world. They believe what is told them. I never do. I'm afraid I always like to prove a thing for myself."

"That is the scientific attitude," said Sir Henry.

"In this case," continued Miss Marple, "certain things were taken for granted from the first, instead of just confining oneself to the facts. The facts, as I noted them, were that the victim was quite young and that she bit her nails and that her teeth stuck out a little—as young girls' so often do if not corrected in time with a plate—and children are very naughty about their plates and take them out when their elders aren't looking.

"But that is wandering from the point. Where was I? Oh, yes, looking down at the dead girl and feeling sorry, because it is always sad to see a young life cut short, and thinking that whoever had done it was a very wicked person. Of course it was all very confusing, her being found in Colonel Bantry's library, altogether too like a book to be true. In fact, it made the wrong pattern. It wasn't, you see, meant, which confused us a lot. The real idea had been to plant the body on poor young Basil Blake —a much more likely person—and his action in putting it in the colonel's library delayed things considerably and must have been a source of great annoyance to the real murderer. Originally, you see, Mr. Blake would have been the first object of suspicion. They'd have made inquiries at Danemouth, found he knew the girl, then found he had tied himself up with another girl, and they'd have assumed that Ruby came to blackmail him or something like that, and that he'd strangled her in a fit of rage. Just an ordinary, sordid, what I call night-club type of crime!"

"But that, of course, all went wrong, and interest became focused much too soon on the Jefferson family—to the great annoyance of a certain person.

"As I've told you, I've got a very suspicious mind. My nephew Raymond tells me, in fun, of course—that I have a mind like a sink. He says that most Victorians have. All I can say is that the Victorians knew a good deal about human nature. As I say, having this rather insanitary—or surely sanitary?—mind, I looked at once at the money angle of it. Two people stood to benefit by this girl's death—you couldn't get away from that. Fifty thousand pounds is a lot of money; especially when you are in financial difficulties, as both these people were. Of course they both seemed very nice, agreeable people; they didn't seem likely people, but one never can tell, can one?

"Mrs. Jefferson, for instance—everyone liked her. But it did seem clear that she had become very restless that summer and that she was tired of the life she led, completely dependent on her father-in-law. She knew, because the doctor had told her, that he couldn't live long, so that was all right—to put it callously—or it would have been all right if Ruby Keene hadn't come along. Mrs. Jefferson was passionately devoted to her son, and some women have a curious idea that crimes committed for the sake of their offspring are almost morally justified. I have come across that attitude once or twice in the village. 'Well, 'twas all for Daisy, you see, miss,' they say, and seem to think that that makes doubtful conduct quite all right. Very lax thinking.

"Mr. Mark Gaskell, of course, was a much more likely starter, if I may use such a sporting expression. He was a gambler and had not, I fancied, a very high moral code. But for certain reasons I was of the opinion that a woman was concerned in this crime.

"As I say, with my eye on motive the money angle seemed very suggestive. It was annoying, therefore, to find that both these two people had alibis for the time when Ruby Keene, according to the medical evidence, had met her death. But soon afterward there came the discovery of the burnt-out car with Pamela Reeves' body in it, and then the whole thing leaped to the eye. The alibis, of course, were worthless.

"I now had two halves of the case, and both quite convincing, but they did not fit. There must be a connection, but I could not find it. The one person whom I knew to be concerned in the crime hadn't got a motive. It was stupid of me," said Miss Marple meditatively. "If it hadn't been for Dinah Lee I shouldn't have thought of it—the most obvious thing in the world. Somerset House! Marriage! It wasn't a question of only Mr. Gaskell or Mrs. Jefferson; there was the further possibility of marriage. If either of those two was married, or even was likely to marry, then the other party to the marriage contract was involved too. Raymond, for instance, might think he had a pretty good chance of marrying a rich wife. He had been very assiduous to Mrs. Jefferson, and it was his charm, I think, that awoke her from her long widowhood. She had been quite content just being a daughter to Mr. Jefferson. Like Ruth and Naomi—only Naomi, if you remember, took a lot of trouble to arrange a suitable marriage for Ruth.

"Besides Raymond, there was Mr. McLean. She liked him very much, and it seemed highly possible that she would marry him in the end. He wasn't well off and he was not far from Danemouth on the night in question. So, it seemed, didn't it," said Miss Marple, "as though anyone might have done it? But, of course, really, in my own mind, I knew. You couldn't get away, could you, from those bitten nails?"

"Nails?" said Sir Henry. "But she tore her nail and cut the others."

"Nonsense," said Miss Marple. "Bitten nails and closecut nails are quite different! Nobody could mistake them who knew anything about girls' nails—very ugly, bitten nails, as I always tell the girls in my class. Those nails, you see, were a fact. And they could only mean one thing. The body in Colonel Bantry's library wasn't Ruby Keene at all.

"And that brings you straight to the one person who must be concerned. Josie! Josie identified the body. She knew—she must have known—that it wasn't Ruby Keene's body. She said it was. She was puzzled—completely puzzled—at finding that body where it was. She practically betrayed that fact. Why? Because she knew—none better—where it ought to have been found! In Basil Blake's cottage. Who directed our attention to Basil? Josie, by saying to Raymond that Ruby might have been with the film man. And before that, by slipping a snapshot of him into Ruby's handbag. Josie! Josie, who was shrewd, practical, hard as nails and all out for money.

"Since the body wasn't the body of Ruby Keene, it must be the body of someone else. Of whom? Of the other girl who was also missing. Pamela Reeves! Ruby was eighteen, Pamela sixteen. They were both healthy, rather immature, but muscular girls. But why, I asked myself, all this hocus-pocus? There could be only one reason—to give certain persons an alibi. Who had alibis for the supposed time of Ruby Keene's death? Mark Gaskell, Mrs. Jefferson and Josie.

"It was really quite interesting, you know, tracing out the course of events, seeing exactly how the plan had worked out. Complicated and yet simple. First of all, the selection of the poor child, Pamela; the approach to her from the film angle. A screen test; of course the poor child couldn't resist it. Not when it was put up to her as plausibly as Mark Gaskell put it. She comes to the hotel, he is waiting for her, he takes her in by the side door and introduces her to Josie—one of their make-up experts! That poor child—it makes me quite sick to think of it! Sitting in Josie's bathroom while Josie bleaches her hair and makes up her face and varnishes her fingernails and toenails. During all this the drug was given. In an ice-cream soda, very likely. She goes off into a coma. I imagine that they put her into one of the empty rooms opposite. They were only cleaned once a week, remember.

"After dinner Mark Gaskell went out in his car—to the sea front, he said. That is when he took Pamela's body to the cottage, arranged it, dressed in one of Ruby's old dresses, on the hearthrug. She was still unconscious, but not dead, when he strangled her with the belt of the frock. Not nice, no, but I hope and pray she knew nothing about it. Really, I feel quite pleased to think of him hanging. . . . That must have been just after ten o'clock. Then back at top speed and into the lounge where Ruby Keene, still alive, was dancing her exhibition dance with Raymond. I should imagine that Josie had given Ruby instructions beforehand. Ruby was accustomed to doing what Josie told her. She was to change, go into Josie's room and wait. She, too, was drugged; probably in the after-dinner coffee. She was yawning, remember, when she talked to young Bartlett.

"Josie came up later with Raymond to 'look for her,' but nobody but Josie went into Josie's room. She probably finished the girl off then—with an injection, perhaps, or a blow on the back of the head. She went down, danced with Raymond, debated with the Jeffersons where Ruby could be and finally went up to bed. In the early hours of the morning she dressed the girl in Pamela's clothes, carried the body down the side stairs and out—she was a strong, muscular young woman—fetched George Bartlett's car, drove two miles to the quarry, poured petrol over the car and set it alight. Then she walked back to the hotel, probably timing her arrival there for eight or nine o'clock—up early in her anxiety about Ruby!"

"An intricate plot," said Colonel Melchett.

"Not more intricate than the steps of a dance," said Miss Marple.

"I suppose not."

"She was very thorough," said Miss Marple. "She even foresaw the discrepancy of the nails. That's why she managed to break one of Ruby's nails on her shawl. It made an excuse for pretending that Ruby had clipped her nails close."

Harper said, "Yes, she thought of everything. And the only real proof you had was a schoolgirl's bitten nails."

"More than that," said Miss Marple. "People will talk too much. Mark Gaskell talked too much. He was speaking of Ruby and he said, 'her teeth ran down her throat.' But the dead girl in Colonel Bantry's library had teeth that stuck out."

Conway Jefferson said rather grimly, "And was the last dramatic finale your idea, Miss Marple?"

"Well, it was, as a matter of fact. It's so nice to be sure, isn't it?"

"Sure is the word," said Conway Jefferson grimly.

"You see," said Miss Marple, "once those two knew that you were going to make a new will, they'd have to do something. They'd already committed two murders on account of the money. So they might as well commit a third. Mark, of course, must be absolutely clear, so he went off to London and established an alibi by dining at a restaurant with friends and going on to a night club. Josie was to do the work. They still wanted Ruby's death to be put down to Basil's account, so Mr. Jefferson's death must be thought due to his heart failing. There was digitalis, so the superintendent tells me, in the syringe. Any doctor would think death from heart trouble quite natural in the circumstances. Josie had loosened one of the stone balls on the balcony and she was going to let it crash down afterward. His death would be put down to the shock of the noise."

Melchett said, "Ingenious devil."

Sir Henry said, "So the third death you spoke of was to be Conway Jefferson?"

Miss Marple shook her head. "Oh, no, I meant Basil Blake. They'd have got him hanged if they could."

"Or shut up in Broadmoor," said Sir Henry.

Through the doorway floated Adelaide Jefferson. Hugo McLean followed her. The latter said, "I seem to have missed most of this! Haven't got the hang of it yet. What was Josie to Mark Gaskell?"

Miss Marple said, "His wife. They were married a year ago. They were keeping it dark until Mr. Jefferson died."

Conway Jefferson grunted. He said, "Always knew Rosamund had married a rotter. Tried not to admit it to myself. She was fond of him. Fond of a murderer! Well, he'll hang, as well as the woman. I'm glad he went to pieces and gave the show away."

Miss Marple said, "She was always the strong character. It was her plan throughout. The irony of it is that she got the girl down here by herself, never dreaming that she would take Mr. Jefferson's fancy and ruin all her own prospects."

Jefferson said, "Poor lass. Poor little Ruby."

Adelaide laid her hand on his shoulder and pressed it gently. She looked almost beautiful tonight. She said, with a little catch in her breath, "I want to tell you something, Jeff. At once. I'm going to marry Hugo."

Conway Jefferson looked up at her for a moment. He said gruffly, "About time you married again. Congratulations to you both. By the way, Addie, I'm making out a new will tomorrow."

She nodded. "Oh, yes. I know."

Jefferson said, "No, you don't. I'm settling ten thousand pounds on you. Everything else goes to Peter when I die. How does that suit you, my girl?"

"Oh, Jeff!" Her voice broke. "You're wonderful!"

"He's a nice lad. I'd like to see a good deal of him in—in the time I've got left."

"Oh, you shall!"

"Got a great feeling for crime, Peter has," said Conway Jefferson meditatively. "Not only has he got the fingernail of the murdered girl—one of the murdered girls, anyway—but he was lucky enough to have a bit of Josie's shawl caught in with the nail. So he's got a souvenir of the murderess too! That makes him very happy!"

Hugo and Adelaide passed by the ballroom. Raymond came up to them. Adelaide said rather quickly, "I must tell you my news. We're going to be married."

The smile on Raymond's face was perfect—a brave, pensive smile. "I hope," he said, ignoring Hugo and gazing into her eyes, "that you will be very, very happy."

They passed on and Raymond stood looking after them. "A nice woman," he said to himself. "A very nice woman. And she would have had money too. The trouble I took to mug up that bit about the Devonshire Starrs. Oh, well, my luck's out. Dance, dance, little gentleman!"

And Raymond returned to the ballroom.

A
Murder
Is
Announced

To
RALPH & ANNE NEWMAN
at whose house I first tasted
"DELICIOUS DEATH!"

Contents

1. *"A Murder Is Announced"*

BETWEEN 7:30 and 8:30 every morning except Sundays, Johnnie Butt made the round of the village of Chipping Cleghorn on his bicycle, whistling vociferously through his teeth and alighting at each house or cottage to shove through the letter box such morning papers as had been ordered by the occupants of the house in question from Mr. Totman, stationer, of the High Street. Thus at Colonel and Mrs. Easterbrook's he delivered *The Times* and the *Daily Graphic;* at Mrs. Swettenham's he left *The Times* and the *Daily Worker;* at Miss Hinchliffe and Miss Murgatroyd's he left the *Daily Telegraph* and the *News Chronicle;* at Miss Blacklock's he left the *Telegraph, The Times* and the *Daily Mail.*

At all these houses, and indeed at practically every house in Chipping Cleghorn, he delivered every Friday a copy of the *North Benham News and Chipping Cleghorn Gazette,* known locally simply as the *Gazette.*

Thus, on Friday mornings, after a hurried glance at the headlines in the daily paper (INTERNATIONAL SITUATION CRITICAL! U.N. MEETS TODAY! BLOODHOUNDS SEEK BLOND TYPIST'S KILLER! THREE COLLIERIES IDLE. TWENTY-THREE DIE OF FOOD POISONING IN SEASIDE HOTEL, *etc.),* most of the inhabitants of Chipping Cleghorn eagerly opened the *Gazette* and plunged into the local news. After a cursory glance at CORRESPONDENCE (in which the passionate hates and feuds of rural life found full play), nine out of ten subscribers then turned to the PERSONAL column. Here were grouped together higgledy-piggledy articles for sale or wanted, frenzied appeals for domestic help, innumerable insertions regarding dogs, announcements concerning poultry and garden equipment; and various other items of an interesting nature to those living in the small community of Chipping Cleghorn.

This particular Friday, October 29th—was no exception to the rule. . . .

II

Mrs. Swettenham, pushing back the pretty little gray curls from her forehead, opened *The Times,* looked with a lackluster eye at the left-hand center page, decided that, as usual, if there *was* any exciting news, *The Times* had succeeded in camouflaging it in an impeccable manner; took a look at the BIRTHS, MARRIAGES and DEATHS, particularly the latter; then, her duty done, she put aside *The Times* and eagerly seized the Chipping Cleghorn *Gazette.*

When her son Edmund entered the room a moment later, she was already deep in the PERSONAL column.

"Good morning, dear," said Mrs. Swettenham. "The Smedleys are selling their Daimler. A 1935—that's rather a long time ago, isn't it?"

Her son grunted, poured himself a cup of coffee, helped himself to a couple of kippers, sat down at the table and opened the *Daily Worker* which he propped up against the toast rack.

"Bull mastiff puppies," read out Mrs. Swettenham. "I really don't know how people manage to feed big dogs nowadays—I really don't. . . . H'm, Selina Lawrence is advertising for a cook again. I could tell her it's just a waste of time advertising in these days. She hasn't put her address, only a box number—that's quite fatal—I could have told her so —servants simply insist on knowing where they are going. They like a good address. . . . False teeth—I can't think why false teeth are so popular. Best prices paid. . . . Beautiful bulbs. Our special selection. They sound rather cheap. . . . Here's a girl wants an Interesting post—would travel. I daresay! Who wouldn't? Dachshunds . . . I've never really cared for dachshunds myself—I don't mean because they're German, because we've got over all that—I just don't care for them, that's all. Yes, Mrs. Finch?"

The door had opened to admit the head and torso of a grim-looking female in an aged velvet beret.

"Good morning, mum," said Mrs. Finch. "Can I clear?"

"Not yet. We haven't finished," said Mrs. Swettenham. "Not quite finished," she added ingratiatingly.

Casting a look at Edmund and his paper, Mrs. Finch sniffed and withdrew.

"I've only just begun," said Edmund, just as his mother remarked:

"I do wish you wouldn't read that horrid paper, Edmund. Mrs. Finch doesn't like it at all."

"I don't see what my political views have to do with Mrs. Finch."

"And it isn't," pursued Mrs. Swettenham, "as though you were a worker. You don't do any work at all."

"That's not in the least true," said Edmund indignantly. "I'm writing a book."

"I meant real work," said Mrs. Swettenham. "And Mrs. Finch does matter. If she takes a dislike to us and won't come, who else could we get?"

"Advertise in the *Gazette*," said Edmund grinning.

"I've just told you that's no use. Oh, dear me, nowadays unless one has an old Nannie in the family, who will go into the kitchen and do everything, one is simply sunk."

"Well, why haven't we an old Nannie? How remiss of you not to have provided me with one! What were you thinking about?"

"You had an ayah, dear."

"No foresight," murmured Edmund.

Mrs. Swettenham was once more deep in the PERSONAL column.

"Second-hand motor-mower for sale. Now I wonder—Goodness, what a price! . . . More dachshunds. . . . Do write or communicate, desperate, Woggles. What silly nicknames people have. . . . Cocker Spaniels . . . do you remember darling Susie, Edmund? She really was human. Understood every word you said to her. . . . Sheraton sideboard for sale. Genuine family antique. Mrs. Lucas, Dayas Hall. What a liar that woman is! Sheraton indeed!"

Mrs. Swettenham sniffed and then continued her reading:

"All a mistake, darling. Undying love. Friday as usual. J. I suppose they've had a lovers' quarrel—or do you think it's a code for burglars? More dachshunds! Really, I do think people have gone a little crazy about breeding dachshunds. I mean, there are other dogs. Your uncle Simon used to breed Manchester terriers. Such graceful little things. I do like dogs with legs. . . . Lady going abroad will sell her navy two-piece suiting . . . no measurements or price given. A marriage is announced —no, a *murder* . . . *what?* Well, I never! Edmund, *Edmund*, listen to this: *A murder is announced and will take place on Friday, October 29th, at Little Paddocks, at 6:30 P.M. Friends please accept this, the only intimation.* What an extraordinary thing! *Edmund!*"

"What's that?" Edmund looked up from his newspaper.

"Friday, October 29th—why, that's today."

"Let me see." Her son took the paper from her.

"But what does it mean?" Mrs. Swettenham asked with lively curiosity.

Edmund Swettenham rubbed his nose doubtfully.

"Some sort of party, I suppose. The Murder Game—that kind of thing."

"Oh," said Mrs. Swettenham doubtfully. "It seems a very odd way of doing it. Just sticking it in the advertisements like that. Not at all like Letitia Blacklock, who always seems to me such a sensible woman."

"Probably got up by the bright young things she has in the house."

"It's very short notice. Today. Do you think we're just supposed to go?"

"It says, 'Friends please accept this, the only intimation,'" her son pointed out.

"Well. I think these new-fangled ways of giving invitations are very tiresome," said Mrs. Swettenham decidedly.

"All right, Mother, you needn't go."

"No," agreed Mrs. Swettenham.

There was a pause.

"Do you really want that last piece of toast, Edmund?"

"I should have thought my being properly nourished mattered more than letting that old hag clear the table."

"Sh, dear, she'll hear you . . . Edmund, what happens at a Murder Game?"

"I don't know exactly. They pin pieces of paper upon you, or something—no, I think you draw them out of a hat. And somebody's the victim and somebody else is a detective—and then they turn the lights out and somebody taps you on the shoulder and then you scream and lie down and sham dead."

"It sounds quite exciting."

"Probably a beastly bore. I'm not going."

"Nonsense, Edmund," said Mrs. Swettenham resolutely. "I'm going and you're coming with me. That's settled!"

III

"Archie," said Mrs. Easterbrook to her husband, "listen to this."

Colonel Easterbrook paid no attention, because he was already snorting with impatience over an article in *The Times*.

"Trouble with these fellows is," he said, "that none of them know the first thing about India! Not the first thing!"

"I know, dear, I know."

"If they did, they wouldn't write such piffle."

"Yes, I know. Archie do listen. *A murder is announced and will take place on Friday, October 29th* (that's today), *at Little Paddocks, at 6:30 P.M. Friends please accept this, the only intimation.*"

She paused triumphantly. Colonel Easterbrook looked at her indulgently but without much interest.

"Murder Game," he said.

"Oh."

"That's all it is. Mind you," he unbent a little, "it can be very good fun if it's well done. But it needs good organizing by someone who knows the ropes. You draw lots. One person's the murderer, nobody knows who. Lights out. Murderer chooses his victim. The victim has to count twenty before he screams. Then the person who's chosen to be the detective takes charge. Questions everybody. Where they were, what they were doing, tries to trip the real fellow up. Yes, it's a good game—if the detective—er—knows something about police work."

"Like you, Archie. You had all those interesting cases to try in your district."

Colonel Easterbrook smiled indulgently and gave his mustache a complacent twirl.

"Yes, Laura," he said. "I daresay I could give them a hint or two." And he straightened his shoulders.

"Miss Blacklock ought to have asked you to help her in getting the thing up."

The colonel snorted.

"Oh, well, she's got that young cub staying with her. Expect this is his idea. Nephew or something. Funny idea, though, sticking it in the paper."

"It was in the PERSONAL column. We might never have seen it. I suppose it is an invitation, Archie?"

"Funny kind of invitation. I can tell you one thing. They can count me out."

"Oh, Archie," Mrs. Easterbrook's voice rose in a shrill wail.

"Short notice. For all they know I might be busy."

"But you are not, are you, darling?" Mrs. Easterbrook lowered her voice persuasively. "And I do think, Archie, that you really ought to go —just to help poor Miss Blacklock out. I'm sure she's counting on you to make the thing a success. I mean, you know so much about police work and procedure. The whole thing will fall flat if you don't go and help to make it a success. After all, one must be neighborly."

Mrs. Easterbrook put her synthetic blond head on one side and opened her blue eyes very wide.

"Of course, if you put it like that, Laura . . ." Colonel Easterbrook twirled his gray mustache again importantly, and looked with indulgence on his fluffy little wife. Mrs. Easterbrook was at least thirty years younger than her husband.

"If you put it like that, Laura," he said.

"I really do think it's your duty, Archie," said Mrs. Easterbrook solemnly.

IV

The Chipping Cleghhorn *Gazette* had also been delivered at Boulders, the picturesque three cottages knocked into one, inhabited by Miss Hinchliffe and Miss Murgatroyd.

"Hinch?"

"What is it, Murgatroyd?"

"Where are you?"

"Henhouse."

"Oh."

Paddling gingerly through the long wet grass, Miss Amy Murgatroyd approached her friend. The latter, attired in corduroy slacks and battle-dress tunic, was conscientiously stirring in handfuls of balancer meal to a repellently steaming basin full of cooked potato peelings and cabbage stumps.

She turned her head with its short manlike crop and weatherbeaten countenance towards her friend.

Miss Murgatroyd, who was fat and amiable, wore a checked tweed skirt and a shapeless pullover of brilliant royal blue. Her curly bird's-nest of gray hair was in a good deal of disorder and she was slightly out of breath.

"In the *Gazette*," she panted. "Just listen—what can it mean? *A murder is announced and will take place on Friday, October 29th, at Little Paddocks, at 6:30 P.M. Friends please accept this, the only intimation.*"

She paused, breathless, as she finished reading, and awaited some authoritative pronouncement.

"Daft," said Miss Hinchliffe.

"Yes, but what do you think it means?"

"Means a drink, anyway," said Miss Hinchliffe.

"You think it's a sort of invitation?"

"We'll find out what it means when we get there," said Miss Hinchliffe. "Bad sherry, I expect. You'd better get off the grass, Murgatroyd. You've got your bedroom slippers on still. They're soaked."

"Oh, dear." Miss Murgatroyd looked down ruefully at her feet. "How many eggs today?"

"Seven. That damned hen's still broody. I must get her into the coop."

"It's a funny way of putting it, don't you think?" Amy Murgatroyd asked, reverting to the notice in the *Gazette*. Her voice was slightly wistful.

But her friend was made of sterner and more single-minded stuff. She was intent on dealing with recalcitrant poultry and no announcement in a paper, however enigmatic, could deflect her.

She squelched heavily through the mud and pounced upon a speckled hen. There was a loud and indignant squawking.

"Give me ducks every time," said Miss Hinchliffe. "Far less trouble."

V

"Oo, scrumptious!" said Mrs. Harmon across the breakfast table to her husband, the Rev. Julian Harmon. "There's going to be a murder at Miss Blacklock's."

"A murder?" said her husband, slightly surprised. "When?"

"This afternoon . . . at least this evening. Six-thirty. Oh, bad luck, darling; you've got your preparations for confirmation then. It is a shame. And you do so love murders!"

"I don't really know what you're talking about, Bunch."

Mrs. Harmon, the roundness of whose form and face had early led to the sobriquet of "Bunch" being substituted for her baptismal name of Diana, handed the *Gazette* across the table.

"There. All among the second-hand pianos and the old teeth."

"What a very extraordinary announcement."

"Isn't it?" said Bunch happily. "You wouldn't think that Miss Blacklock cared about murders and games and things, would you? I suppose it's the young Simmonses put her up to it—though I should have thought Julia Simmons would find murders rather crude. Still, there it is, and I do think, darling, it's a shame you can't be there. Anyway, I'll go and tell you all about it, though it's rather wasted on me, because I don't really like games that happen in the dark. They frighten me, and I do hope I shan't have to be the one who's murdered. If someone suddenly puts a hand on my shoulder and whispers, 'You're dead,' I know my heart will give such a big thump that perhaps it really might kill me! Do you think that's likely?"

"No, Bunch. I think you're going to live to be an old, old woman—with me."

"And die on the same day and be buried in the same grave. That would be lovely."

Bunch beamed from ear to ear at this agreeable prospect.

"You seem very happy, Bunch," said her husband, smiling.

"Who'd not be happy if they were me?" demanded Bunch rather confusedly. "With you and Susan and Edward, and all of you fond of me and not caring if I'm stupid— And the sun shining! And this lovely big house to live in!"

The Rev. Julian Harmon looked round the big bare dining room and assented doubtfully.

"Some people would think it was the last straw to have to live in this great rambling draughty place."

"Well, I like big rooms. All the nice smells from outside can get in and stay there. And you can be untidy and leave things about and they don't clutter you."

"No labor-saving devices or central heating. It means a lot of work for you, Bunch."

"Oh, Julian, it doesn't. I get up at half past six and light the boiler and rush round like a steam-engine, and by eight it's all done. And I keep it nice, don't I, with beeswax and polish and big jars of autumn leaves? It's not really harder to keep a big house clean than a small one. You go round with mops and things much quicker, because your behind isn't always bumping into things like it is in a small room. And I like sleeping in a big cold room—it's so cosy to snuggle down with just the tip of your nose telling you what it's like up above. And whatever size house you live in, you peel the same amount of potatoes and wash up the same amount of plates and all that. Think how nice it is for Edward and Susan to have a big empty room to play in where they can have railways and dolls' tea parties all over the floor and never have to put them away. And then it's nice to have extra bits of the house that you can let people have to live in. Jimmy Symes and Johnnie Finch—they'd have had to live with their in-laws otherwise. And you know, Julian, it isn't nice living with your in-laws. You're devoted to mother, but you wouldn't really have liked to start our married life living with her and father. And I shouldn't have liked it either. I'd have gone on feeling like a little girl."

Julian smiled at her.

"You're rather like a little girl still, Bunch."

Julian Harmon himself had clearly been a model designed by nature for the age of sixty. He was still about twenty-five years short of achieving Nature's purpose.

"I know I'm stupid—"

"You're not stupid, Bunch. You're very clever."

"No, I'm not. I'm not a bit intellectual. Though I do try . . . and I really love it when you talk to me about books and history and things. I think perhaps it wasn't an awfully good idea to read Gibbon aloud to me in the evenings, because if it's been a cold wind out, and it's nice and hot by the fire, there's something about Gibbon that does rather make me go to sleep."

Julian laughed.

"But I do love listening to you, Julian. Tell me the story again about the old vicar who preached about Ahasuerus."

"You know that by heart, Bunch."

"Just tell it to me again. Please."

Her husband complied.

"It was old Scrymgour. Somebody looked into his church one day. He was leaning out of the pulpit and preaching fervently to a couple of old charwomen. He was shaking his finger at them and saying, 'Aha! I know what you are thinking. You think that the Great Ahasuerus of the First Lesson was Artaxerxes the Second. But he wasn't!' And then with enormous triumph, 'He was Artaxerxes the Third!'"

It had never struck Julian Harmon as a particularly funny story, but it never failed to amuse Bunch.

Her clear laugh floated out.

"The old pet!" she exclaimed. "I think you'll be exactly like that some day, Julian."

Julian looked rather uneasy.

"I know," he said with humility. "I do feel very strongly that I can't always get the proper simple approach."

"I shouldn't worry," said Bunch, rising and beginning to pile the breakfast plates on a tray. "Mrs. Butt told me yesterday that Butt, who never went to church and used to be practically the local atheist, comes every Sunday now on purpose to hear you preach."

She went on, with a very fair imitation of Mrs. Butt's super refined voice:

" 'And Butt was saying only the other day, Madam, to Mr. Timkins from Little Worsdale, that we'd got real culture here in Chipping Cleghorn. Not like Mr. Goss, at Little Worsdale, who talks to the congregation as though they were children who hadn't had any education. Real culture, Butt said, that's what we've got. Our vicar's a highly educated gentleman—Oxford, not Milchester—and he gives us the full benefit of his education. All about the Romans and the Greeks he knows, and the Babylonians and the Assyrians, too. And even the vicarage cat, Butt says, is called after an Assyrian king!' So there's glory for you," finished Bunch triumphantly. "Goodness, I must get on with things or I shall never get done. Come along, Tiglath-Pileser, you shall have the herring bones."

Opening the door and holding it dexterously ajar with her foot, she shot through with the loaded tray, singing in a loud and not particularly tuneful voice, her own version of a sporting song:

> *"It's a fine murdering day" (sang Bunch),*
> *"And as balmy as May,*
> *And the sleuths from the village are gone,"*

A rattle of crockery being dumped in the sink drowned the next lines, but as the Rev. Julian Harmon left the house, he heard the final triumphant assertion:

> *"And we'll all go a'murdering today!"*

2. *Breakfast at Little Paddocks*

AT LITTLE PADDOCKS also breakfast was in progress.

Miss Blacklock, a woman of sixty-odd, the owner of the house, sat at the head of the table. She wore country tweeds—and with them, rather incongruously, a choker necklace of large false pearls. She was reading Lane Norcott in the *Daily Mail*. Julia Simmons was languidly glancing through the *Telegraph*. Patrick Simmons was checking up on the crossword in *The Times*. Miss Dora Bunner was giving her attention wholeheartedly to the local weekly paper.

Miss Blacklock gave a subdued chuckle, Patrick muttered, "Adherent —not adhesive—that's where I went wrong."

Suddenly a loud cluck, like a startled hen, came from Miss Bunner.

"Letty—Letty—have you seen this? Whatever can it mean?"

"What's the matter, Dora?"

"The most extraordinary advertisement. It says Little Paddocks quite distinctly. But whatever can it mean?"

"If you'd let me see, Dora dear—"

Miss Bunner obediently surrendered the paper into Miss Blacklock's outstretched hand, pointing to the item with a tremulous forefinger.

"Just look, Letty."

Miss Blacklock looked. Her eyebrows went up. She threw a quick scrutinizing glance round the table. Then she read the advertisement out loud.

"A murder is announced and will take place on Friday, October 29th, at Little Paddocks, at 6:30 P.M. Friends please accept this, the only intimation."

Then she said sharply:

"Patrick, is this your idea?"

Her eyes rested searchingly on the handsome devil-may-care face of the young man at the other end of the table.

Patrick Simmons' disclaimer came quickly.

"No, indeed, Aunt Letty. Whatever put that idea into your head? Why should I know anything about it?"

"I wouldn't put it past you," said Miss Blacklock grimly. "I thought it might be your idea of a joke."

"A joke? Nothing of the kind."

"And you, Julia?"

Julia, looking bored, said: "Of course not."

Miss Bunner murmured: "Do you think Mrs. Haymes—" and looked at an empty place where someone had breakfasted earlier.

"Oh, I don't think our Phillipa would try and be funny," said Patrick. "She's a serious girl, she is."

"But what's the idea, anyway?" said Julia, yawning. "What does it mean?"

Miss Blacklock said slowly, "I suppose—it's some silly sort of hoax."

"But why?" Dora Bunner exclaimed. "What's the point of it? It seems a very stupid sort of joke. And in very bad taste."

Her flabby cheeks quivered indignantly, and her short-sighted eyes sparkled with indignation.

Miss Blacklock smiled at her.

"Don't work yourself up over it, Bunny," she said. "It's just somebody's idea of humor, but I wish I knew whose."

"It says today," pointed out Miss Bunner. "Today at 6:30 P.M. What do you thing is going to happen?"

"Death!" said Patrick in sepulchral tones. "Delicious Death."

"Be quiet, Patrick," said Miss Blacklock as Miss Bunner gave a little yelp.

"I only meant the special cake that Mitzi makes," said Patrick apologetically. "You know we always call it Delicious Death."

Miss Blacklock smiled a little absent-mindedly.

Miss Bunner persisted, "But, Letty, what do you really think—"

Her friend cut across the words with reassuring cheerfulness.

"I know one thing that will happen at 6:30," she said dryly. "We'll have half the village up here, agog with curiosity. I'd better make sure we've got some sherry in the house."

II

"You are worried, aren't you, Letty?"

Miss Blacklock started. She had been sitting at her writing table, absent-mindedly drawing little fishes on the blotting paper. She looked up into the anxious face of her old friend.

She was not quite sure what to say to Dora Bunner. Bunny, she knew, mustn't be worried or upset. She was silent for a moment or two, thinking.

She and Dora Bunner had been at school together. Dora then had been a pretty, fair-haired, blue-eyed, rather stupid girl. Her being stupid hadn't mattered, because her gaiety and high spirits and her prettiness had made her an agreeable companion. She ought, her friend thought, to have married some nice Army officer, or a country solicitor. She had so many good qualities—affection, devotion, loyalty. But life had been unkind to Dora Bunner. She had had to earn her living. She had been painstaking but never competent at anything she undertook.

The two friends had lost sight of each other. But six months ago a letter had come to Miss Blacklock, a rambling, pathetic letter. Dora's health had given way. She was living in one room, trying to subsist on her old-age pension. She endeavored to do needlework, but her fingers were stiff with rheumatism. She mentioned their schooldays—since then life had driven them apart—but could—possibly—her old friend help?

Miss Blacklock had responded impulsively. Poor Dora, poor, pretty, silly, fluffy Dora. She had swooped down upon Dora, had carried her off, had installed her at Little Paddocks with the comforting fiction that "the housework is getting too much for me. I need someone to help me run the house." It was not for long—the doctor had told her that—but sometimes she found poor old Dora a sad trial. She muddled everything, upset the temperamental foreign "help," miscounted the laundry, lost bills and letters—and sometimes reduced the competent Miss Blacklock to an agony of exasperation. Poor old muddle-headed Dora, so loyal, so anxious to help, so pleased and proud to think she was of assistance—and, alas, so completely unreliable.

Miss Blacklock said sharply:

"Don't, Dora. You know I asked you—"

"Oh." Miss Bunner looked guilty. "I know. I forgot. But—but you are, aren't you?"

"Worried? No. At least," she added truthfully, "not exactly. You mean about that silly notice in the *Gazette?*"

"Yes—even if it's a joke, it seems to me it's a—a spiteful sort of joke."

"Spiteful?"

"Yes. It seems to me there's spite there somewhere. I mean—it's not a nice kind of joke."

Miss Blacklock looked at her friend. The mild eyes, the long obstinate mouth, the slightly upturned nose. Poor Dora, so maddening, so muddle-headed, so devoted and such a problem. A dear fussy old idiot and yet, in a queer way, with an instinctive sense of values.

"I think you're right, Dora," said Miss Blacklock. "It's not a nice joke."

"I don't like it at all," said Dora Bunner with unsuspected vigor. "It frightens me." She added suddenly: "And it frightens you, Letitia."

"Nonsense," said Miss Blacklock with spirit.

"It's dangerous. I'm sure it is. Like those people who send you bombs done up in parcels."

"My dear, it's just some silly idiot trying to be funny."

"But it isn't funny."

It wasn't really very funny . . . Miss Blacklock's face betrayed her thoughts, and Dora cried triumphantly, "You see. You think so, too!"

"But, Dora, my dear—"

She broke off. Through the door there surged a tempestuous young woman with a well-developed bosom heaving under a tight jersey. She had on a dirndl skirt of a bright color and had greasy dark braids wound round and round her head. Her eyes were dark and flashing.

She said gustily: "I can speak to you, yes, please, no?"

Miss Blacklock sighed.

"Of course, Mitzi, what is it?"

Sometimes she thought it would be preferable to do the entire work of the house as well as the cooking rather than be bothered with the eternal nerve storms of her refugee "lady help."

"I tell you at once—it is in order, I hope? I give you my notices and I go—I go at once!"

"For what reason? Has somebody upset you?"

"Yes, I am upset," said Mitzi dramatically. "I do not wish to die! Already in Europe I escape. My family they all die—they are all killed—my mother, my little brother, my so sweet little niece—all, all they are killed. But me I run away—I hide. I get to England. I work. I do work that never—never would I do in my own country—I—"

"I know all that," said Miss Blacklock crisply. It was, indeed, a constant refrain of Mitzi's lips. "But why do you want to leave now?"

"Because again they come to kill me!"

"Who do?"

"My enemies. The Nazis! Or perhaps this time it is the Bolsheviks. They find out I am here. They come to kill me. I have read it—yes—it is in the newspaper!"

"Oh, you mean in the *Gazette?*"

"Here, it is written here." Mitzi produced the *Gazette* from where she had been holding it behind her back. "See—here it says murder. At Little

Paddocks. That is here, is it not? This evening at six-thirty. Ah! I do not wait to be murdered—no."

"But why should this apply to you? It's—we think it is a joke."

"A joke? It is not a joke to murder someone."

"No, of course not. But, my dear child, if anyone wanted to murder you, they wouldn't advertise the fact in the paper, would they?"

"You do not think they would?" Mitzi seemed a little shaken. "You think, perhaps, they do not mean to murder anyone at all? Perhaps it is you they mean to murder, Miss Blacklock."

"I certainly can't believe anyone wants to murder me," said Miss Blacklock lightly. "And, really, Mitzi, I don't see why anyone should want to murder you. After all, why should they?"

"Because they are bad peoples . . . very bad peoples. I tell you, my mother, my little brother, my so sweet niece . . ."

"Yes, yes," Miss Blacklock stemmed the flow adroitly. "But I cannot really believe anyone wants to murder you, Mitzi. Of course, if you want to go off like this at a moment's notice, I cannot possibly stop you. But I think you will be very silly if you do."

She added firmly, as Mitzi looked doubtful:

"We'll have that beef the butcher sent stewed for lunch. It looks very tough."

"I make you a goulash, a special goulash."

"If you prefer to call it that, certainly. And perhaps you could use up that rather hard bit of cheese in making some cheese straws. I think some people may come in this evening for drinks."

"This evening? What do you mean, this evening?"

"At half past six."

"But that is the time in the paper? Who should come then? Why should they come?"

"They're coming to the funeral," said Miss Blacklock with a twinkle. "That'll do now, Mitzi. I'm busy. Shut the door after you," she added firmly.

"And that's settled her for the moment," she said as the door closed behind a puzzled-looking Mitzi.

"You are so efficient, Letty," said Miss Bunner admiringly.

3. *At 6:30 P.M.*

"WELL, here we are, all set," said Miss Blacklock. She looked round the double drawing-room with an appraising eye. The rose-patterned chintzes—the two bowls of bronze chrysanthemums, the small vase of violets and the silver cigarette box on a table by the wall, the tray of drinks on the center table.

Little Paddocks was a medium-sized house built in the early Victorian style. It had a long shallow veranda and green-shuttered windows. The long narrow drawing-room, which lost a good deal of light owing to the veranda roof, had originally had double doors at one end, leading into a small room with a bay window. A former generation had removed the double doors and replaced them with portières of velvet. Miss Blacklock had dispensed with the portières so that the two rooms had become definitely one. There was a fireplace at each end, but neither fire was lit, although a gentle warmth pervaded the room.

"You've had the central heating lit," said Patrick.

Miss Blacklock nodded.

"It's been so misty and damp lately. The whole house felt clammy. I got Evans to light it before he went."

"The precious, precious coke?" said Patrick, mockingly.

"As you say, the precious coke. But otherwise there would have been the even more precious coal. You know the Fuel Office won't even let us have the little bit that's due us each week—not unless we can say definitely that we haven't any other means of cooking."

"I suppose once there were heaps of coke and coal for everybody?" said Julia, with the interest of one hearing about an unknown country.

"Yes, and cheap, too."

"And anyone could go and buy as much as they wanted, without filling in anything, and there wasn't any shortage? There was lots of it then?"

"All kinds and qualities—and not all stones and slates like what we get nowadays."

"It must have been a wonderful world," said Julia with awe in her voice.

Miss Blacklock smiled. "Looking back on it, I certainly think so. But then I'm an old woman. It's natural for me to prefer my own times. But you young things oughtn't to think so."

"I needn't have had a job then," said Julia. "I could just have stayed at home and done the flowers, and written notes . . . why did one write notes and who were they to?"

"All the people that you now ring up on the telephone," said Miss Blacklock with a twinkle. "I don't believe you even know how to write, Julia."

"Not in the style of that delicious *Complete Letter Writer* I found the other day. Heavenly! It told you the correct way of refusing a proposal of marriage from a widower."

"I doubt if you would have enjoyed staying at home as much as you think," said Miss Blacklock. "There were duties, you know." Her voice was dry. "However, I don't really know much about it. Bunny and I," she smiled affectionately at Dora Bunner, "went into the labor market early."

"Oh, we did, we did indeed," agreed Miss Bunner. "Those naughty, naughty children. I'll never forget them. Of course Letty was clever. She was a business woman, secretary to a big financier."

The door opened and Phillipa Haymes came in. She was tall and fair and placid-looking. She looked round the room in surprise.

"Hullo," she said. "Is it a party? Nobody told me."

"Of course," cried Patrick. "Our Phillipa doesn't know. The only woman in Chipping Cleghorn who doesn't, I bet."

Phillipa looked at him inquiringly.

"Here you behold," said Patrick dramatically, waving a hand, "the scene of a murder!"

Phillipa Haymes looked faintly puzzled.

"Here," Patrick indicated the two big bowls of chrysanthemums, "are the funeral wreaths and these dishes of cheese straws and olives represent the funeral baked meats."

Phillipa looked inquiringly at Miss Blacklock.

"Is it a joke?" she asked. "I'm always terribly stupid at seeing jokes."

"It's a very nasty joke," said Dora Bunner with energy. "I don't like it at all."

"Show her the advertisement," said Miss Blacklock. "I must go and shut up the ducks. It's dark. They'll be in by now."

"Let me do it," said Phillipa.

"Certainly not, my dear. You've finished your day's work."

"I'll do it, Aunt Letty," offered Patrick.

"No, you won't," said Miss Blacklock with energy. "Last time you didn't latch the door properly."

"I'll do it, Letty dear," cried Miss Bunner. "Indeed, I should love to. I'll just slip on my galoshes—and now where did I put my cardigan?"

But Miss Blacklock, with a smile, had already left the room.

"It's no good, Bunny," said Patrick. "Aunt Letty's so efficient that she can never bear anybody else to do things for her. She really much prefers to do everything herself."

"She loves it," said Julia.

"I didn't notice you making any offers of assistance," said her brother.

Julia smiled lazily.

"You've just said Aunt Letty likes to do things herself," she pointed out. "Besides," she held out a well-shaped leg in a sheer stocking, "I've got my best stockings on."

"Death in silk stockings!" declaimed Patrick.

"Not silk; nylons, you idiot."

"That's not nearly such a good title."

"Won't somebody please tell me," cried Phillipa plaintively, "why there is all this insistence on death?"

Everybody tried to tell her at once—nobody could find the *Gazette* to show her because Mitzi had taken it into the kitchen.

Miss Blacklock returned a few minutes later.

"There," she said briskly, "that's done." She glanced at the clock. "Twenty past six. Somebody ought to be here soon—unless I'm entirely wrong in my estimate of my neighbors."

"I don't see why anybody should come," said Phillipa, looking bewildered.

"Don't you, dear? I daresay you wouldn't. But most people are rather more inquisitive than you are."

"Phillipa's attitude to life is that she just isn't interested," said Julia, rather nastily.

Phillipa did not reply.

Miss Blacklock was glancing round the room. Mitzi had put the sherry and three dishes containing olives, cheese straws and some little fancy pastries on the table in the middle of the room.

"You might move that tray—or the whole table if you like—round the corner into the bay window in the other room, Patrick, if you don't mind. After all, I am not giving a party! I haven't asked anyone. And I don't intend to make it obvious that I expect people to turn up."

"You wish, Aunt Letty, to disguise your intelligent anticipation?"

"Very nicely put, Patrick. Thank you, my dear boy."

"Now we can all give a lovely performance of a quiet evening at home," said Julia, "and be quite surprised when somebody drops in."

Miss Blacklock had picked up the sherry bottle. She stood holding it uncertainly in her hand.

Patrick reassured her.

"There's quite half a bottle there. It ought to be enough."

"Oh, yes—yes . . ." She hesitated. Then, with a slight flush, she said, "Patrick, would you mind . . . there's a new bottle in the cupboard in the pantry . . . bring it and a corkscrew. I—we—might as well have a new bottle. This—this has been opened some time."

Patrick went on his errand without a word. He returned with the new bottle and drew the cork. He looked up curiously at Miss Blacklock as he placed it on the tray.

"Taking things seriously, aren't you, darling?" he asked gently.

"Oh," cried Dora Bunner shocked. "Surely, Letty, you can't imagine—"

"Hush," said Miss Blacklock quickly. "That's the bell. You see, my intelligent anticipation is being justified."

II

Mitzi opened the door of the drawing-room and admitted Colonel and Mrs. Easterbrook. She had her own methods of announcing people.

"Here is Colonel and Mrs. Easterbrook to see you," she said conversationally.

Colonel Easterbrook was very bluff and breezy to cover some slight embarrassment.

"Hope you don't mind us dropping in," he said. (A subdued gurgle came from Julia.) "Happened to be passing this way—eh, what? Quite a mild evening. Notice you've got your central heating on. We haven't started ours yet."

"Aren't your chrysanthemums lovely?" gushed Mrs. Easterbrook. "Such beauties!"

"They're rather scraggy really," said Julia.

Mrs. Easterbrook greeted Phillipa Haymes with a little extra cordiality to show that she quite understood that Phillipa was not really an agricultural laborer.

"How is Mrs. Lucas's garden getting on?" she asked. "Do you think it will ever be straight again? Completely neglected all through the war—and then only that dreadful old man Ashe who simply did nothing but sweep up a few leaves and put in a few cabbage plants."

"It's yielding to treatment," said Phillipa. "But it will take a little time."

Mitzi opened the door again and said, "Here are the ladies from Boulders."

"Evening," said Miss Hinchliffe, striding over and taking Miss Blacklock's hand in her formidable grip. "I said to Murgatroyd: 'Let's just drop in at Little Paddocks!' I wanted to ask you how your ducks are laying."

"The evenings do draw in so quickly now, don't they?" said Miss Murgatroyd to Patrick in a rather fluttery way. "What lovely chrysanthemums!"

"Scraggy!" said Julia.

"Why can't you be co-operative?" murmured Patrick to her in a reproachful aside.

"You've got your central heating on," said Miss Hinchliffe. She said it accusingly. "Very early."

"The house gets so damp this time of year," said Miss Blacklock.

Patrick signaled with his eyebrows: "Sherry yet?" and Miss Blacklock signaled back: "Not yet."

She said to Colonel Easterbrook:

"Are you getting any bulbs from Holland this year?"

The door again opened and Mrs. Swettenham came in rather guiltily, followed by a scowling and uncomfortable Edmund.

"Here we are!" said Mrs. Swettenham, gaily, gazing round her with frank curiosity. Then, feeling suddenly uncomfortable, she went on: "I just thought I'd pop in and ask you if by any chance you wanted a kitten, Miss Blacklock? Our cat is just—"

"About to be brought to bed of the progeny of a ginger tom," said Edmund. "The result will, I think, be frightful. Don't say you haven't been warned!"

"She's a very good mouser," said Mrs. Swettenham hastily. And added: "What lovely chrysanthemums!"

"You've got your central heating on, haven't you?" asked Edmund with an air of originality.

"Aren't people just like gramophone records?" murmured Julia.

"I don't like the news," said Colonel Easterbrook to Patrick, buttonholing him fiercely. "I don't like it at all. If you ask me, war's inevitable —absolutely inevitable."

"I never pay any attention to news," said Patrick.

Once more the door opened and Mrs. Harmon came in.

Her battered felt hat was stuck on the back of her head in a vague attempt to be fashionable and she had put on a rather limp frilly blouse instead of her usual pullover.

"Hullo, Miss Blacklock," she exclaimed, beaming all over her round face. "I'm not too late, am I? When does the murder begin?"

III

There was an audible series of gasps. Julia gave an approving little giggle, Patrick crinkled up his face and Miss Blacklock smiled at her latest guest.

"Julian is just frantic with rage that he can't be here," said Mrs. Harmon. "He adores murders. That's really why he preached such a good sermon last Sunday—I suppose I oughtn't to say it was a good sermon as he's my husband—but it really was good, didn't you think? So much better than his usual sermons. But as I was saying it was all because of *Death Does the Hat Trick*. Have you read it? The girl at Boots kept it for me specially. It's simply baffling. You keep thinking you know—and then the whole thing switches round—and there are a lovely lot of murders, four or five of them. Well, I left it in the study when Julian was shutting himself up there to do his sermon, and he just picked it up and simply could not put it down! And consequently he had to write his sermon in a frightful hurry and had to just put down what he wanted to say very simply—without any scholarly twists and bits and learned references—and naturally it was heaps better. Oh, dear, I'm talking too much. But do tell me, when is the murder going to begin?"

Miss Blacklock looked at the clock on the mantelpiece.

"If it's going to begin," she said cheerfully, "it ought to begin soon. It's just a minute to the half hour. In the meantime, have a glass of sherry."

Patrick moved with alacrity through the archway. Miss Blacklock went to the table by the archway where the cigarette box was.

"I'd love some sherry," said Mrs. Harmon. "But what do you mean by if?"

"Well," said Miss Blacklock. "I'm as much in the dark as you are. I don't know what—"

She stopped and turned her head as the little clock on the mantelpiece began to chime. It had a sweet, silvery, bell-like tone. Everybody was silent and nobody moved. They all stared at the clock.

It chimed a quarter—and then the half. As the last note died away all the lights went out.

IV

Delighted gasps and feminine squeaks of appreciation were heard in the darkness. "It's beginning," cried Mrs. Harmon in an ecstasy. Dora Bunner's voice cried out plaintively, "Oh, I don't like it!" Other voices said, "How terribly, terribly frightening!" "It gives me the creeps." "Archie, where are you?" "What do I have to do?" "Oh dear—did I step on your foot? I'm so sorry."

Then, with a crash, the door swung open. A powerful flashlight played rapidly round the room. A man's hoarse nasal voice, reminiscent to all of pleasant afternoons at the movies, directed the company crisply to:

"Stick 'em up! Stick 'em up, I tell you!" the voice barked.

Delightedly, hands were raised willingly above heads.

"Isn't it wonderful?" breathed a female voice. "I'm so thrilled."

And then, unexpectedly, a revolver spoke. It spoke twice. The ping of two bullets shattered the complacency of the room. Suddenly the game was no longer a game. Somebody screamed . . .

The figure in the doorway whirled suddenly around, it seemed to hesitate, a third shot rang out, it crumpled and then it crashed to the ground. The flashlight dropped and went out. There was darkness once again. And gently, with a little Victorian protesting moan, the drawing-room door, as was its habit when not propped open, swung gently to and latched with a click.

V

Inside the drawing-room there was pandemonium. Various voices spoke at once. "Lights!" "Can't you find the switch?" "Who's got a lighter?" "Oh, I don't like it, I don't like it." "But those shots were real!" "It was a real revolver he had." "Was it a burglar?" "Oh, Archie, I want to get out of here." "Please, has somebody got a lighter?"

And then, almost at the same moment, two lighters clicked and burned with small steady flames.

Everybody blinked and peered at each other. Startled face looked into startled face. Against the wall by the archway Miss Blacklock stood with her hand up to her face. The light was too dim to show more than that something dark was trickling over her fingers.

Colonel Easterbrook cleared his throat and rose to the occasion.

"Try the switches, Swettenham," he ordered.

Edmund, near the door, obediently jerked the switch up and down.

"Off at the main, or a fuse," said the colonel. "Who's making that awful row?"

A female voice had been screaming steadily from somewhere beyond the closed door. It rose now in pitch and with it came the sound of fists hammering on a door.

Dora Bunner, who had been sobbing quietly, called out, "It's Mitzi. Somebody's murdering Mitzi . . ."

Patrick muttered: "No such luck."

Miss Blacklock said: "We must get candles. Patrick, will you—"

The colonel was already opening the door. He and Edmund, their lighters flickering, stepped into the hall. They almost stumbled over a recumbent figure there.

"Seems to have knocked him out," said the colonel. "Where's that woman making that hellish noise?"

"In the dining-room," said Edmund.

The dining-room was just across the hall. Someone was beating on the panels and howling and screaming.

"She's locked in," said Edmund, stooping down. He turned the key and Mitzi came out like a bounding tiger.

The dining-room light was still on. Silhouetted against it, Mitzi presented a picture of insane terror and continued to scream. A touch of comedy was introduced by the fact that she had been engaged in cleaning silver and was still holding a chamois leather and a large fish slice.

"Be quiet, Mitzi," said Miss Blacklock.

"Stop it," said Edmund, and as Mitzi showed no disposition to stop screaming, he leaned forward and gave her a sharp slap on the cheek. Mitzi gasped and hiccuped into silence.

"Get some candles," said Miss Blacklock. "In the kitchen cupboard. Patrick, you know where the fuse-box is?"

"The passage behind the scullery? Right, I'll see what I can do."

Miss Blacklock had moved forward into the light thrown from the dining-room and Dora Bunner gave a sobbing gasp. Mitzi let out another full-blooded scream.

"The blood, the blood!" she gasped. "You are shot—Miss Blacklock, you bleed to death."

"Don't be so stupid," snapped Miss Blacklock. "I'm hardly hurt at all. It just grazed my ear."

"But, Aunt Letty," said Julia, "the blood."

And indeed Miss Blacklock's white blouse and pearls and her hand were a horrifyingly gory sight.

"Ears always bleed," said Miss Blacklock. "I remember fainting in the hairdresser's when I was a child. The man had only just snipped my ear. There seemed to be a basin of blood at once. But we must have some light."

"I get the candles," said Mitzi.

Julia went with her and they returned with several candles stuck into saucers.

"Now let's have a look at our malefactor," said the colonel. "Hold the candles down low, will you, Swettenham? As many as you can."

"I'll come the other side," said Phillipa.

With a steady hand she took a couple of saucers. Colonel Easterbrook knelt down.

The recumbent figure was draped in a roughly made black cloak with a hood to it. There was a black mask over the face and he wore black cotton gloves. The hood had slipped back disclosing a ruffled fair head.

Colonel Easterbrook turned him over, felt the pulse, the heart . . . then drew away his fingers with an exclamation of distaste, looking down on them. They were sticky and red.

"Shot himself," he said.

"Is he badly hurt?" asked Miss Blacklock.

"H'm. I'm afraid he's dead. May have been suicide—or he may have tripped himself up with that cloak thing and the revolver went off as he fell. If I could see better—"

At that moment, as though by magic, the lights came on again.

With a queer feeling of unreality those inhabitants of Chipping Cleghorn who stood in the hall of Little Paddocks realized that they stood in the presence of violent and sudden death. Colonel Easterbrook's hand was stained red. Blood was still trickling down Miss Blacklock's neck over her blouse and skirt, and the grotesquely sprawled figure of the intruder lay at their feet.

Patrick, coming from the dining-room, said, "It seemed to be just one fuse gone . . ." He stopped.

Colonel Easterbrook tugged at the small black mask.

"Better see who the fellow is," he said. "Though I don't suppose it's anyone we know."

He detached the mask. Necks were craned forward. Mitzi hiccuped and gasped, but the others were very quiet.

"He's quite young," said Mrs. Harmon with a note of pity in her voice.

And suddenly Dora Bunner cried out excitedly:

"Letty, Letty, it's the young man from the Spa Hotel in Medenham Wells. The one who came out here and wanted you to give him money to get back to Switzerland and you refused. I suppose the whole thing was just a pretext—to spy out the house. . . . Oh, dear—he might easily have killed you."

Miss Blacklock, in command of the situation, said incisively, "Phillipa, take Bunny into the dining-room and give her a half glass of brandy. Julia dear, just run up to the bathroom and bring me the sticking plaster out of the bathroom cupboard—it's so messy bleeding like a pig. Patrick, will you ring up the police at once?"

4. *The Royal Spa Hotel*

GEORGE RYDESDALE, Chief Constable of Middleshire, was a quiet man. Of medium height, with shrewd eyes under rather bushy brows, he was in the habit of listening rather than talking. Then, in his unemotional voice, he would give a brief order—and the order was obeyed.

He was listening now to Detective Inspector Dermot Craddock. Craddock was now officially in charge of the case. Rydesdale had recalled him last night from Liverpool where he had been sent to make certain inquiries in connection with another case. Rydesdale had a good opinion of Craddock. He not only had brains and imagination, he had also, which Rydesdale appreciated even more, the self-discipline to go slow, to check and examine each fact and to keep an open mind until the very end of a case.

"Constable Legg took the call, sir," Craddock was saying. "He seems to have acted very well, with promptitude and presence of mind. And it can't have been easy. About a dozen people all trying to talk at once, including one of those Mittel Europas who go off the deep end at the mere sight of a policeman. Made sure she was going to be locked up, and fairly screamed the place down."

"Deceased has been identified?"

"Yes, sir. Rudi Scherz. Swiss nationality. Employed at the Royal Spa Hotel, Medenham Wells, as a receptionist. If you agree, sir, I thought I'd take the Royal Spa Hotel first, and go out to Chipping Cleghorn afterwards. Sergeant Fletcher is out there now. He'll see the bus people and then go on to the house."

Rydesdale nodded approval.

The door opened and the Chief Constable looked up.

"Come in, Henry," he said. "We've got something here that's a little out of the ordinary."

Sir Henry Clithering, ex-Commissioner of Scotland Yard, came in with slightly raised eyebrows. He was a tall, distinguished-looking, elderly man.

"It may appeal to even your blasé palate," went on Rydesdale.

"I was never blasé," said Sir Henry indignantly.

"The latest idea," said Rydesdale, "is to advertise one's murders beforehand. Show Sir Henry that advertisement, Craddock."

"The *North Benham News and Chipping Cleghorn Gazette*," said Sir Henry. "Quite a mouthful." He read the half inch of print indicated by Craddock's finger. "Hm, yes, somewhat unusual."

"Any line on who inserted this advertisement?" asked Rydesdale.

"By the description, sir, it was handed in by Rudi Scherz himself—on Wednesday."

"Nobody questioned it? The person who accepted it didn't think it odd?"

"The adenoidal blonde who receives the advertisements is quite incapable of thinking, I should say, sir. She just counted the words and took the money."

"What was the idea?" asked Sir Henry.

"Get a lot of the locals curious," suggested Rydesdale. "Get them all together at a particular place at a particular time, then hold them up and relieve them of their spare cash and valuables. As an idea, it's not without originality."

"What sort of a place is Chipping Cleghorn?" asked Sir Henry.

"A large, sprawling, picturesque village. Butcher, baker, grocer, quite a good antique shop—two tea shops. Self-consciously a beauty spot. Caters to the motoring tourist. Also highly residential. Cottages formerly lived in by agricultural laborers now converted and lived in by elderly spinsters and retired couples. A certain amount of building done around about in Victorian times."

"I know," said Sir Henry. "Nice old pussies and retired colonels. Yes, if they noticed that advertisement they'd all come sniffing round at 6:30 to see what was up. Lord, I wish I had my own particular old pussy here. Wouldn't she like to get her nice ladylike teeth into this? Right up her street it would be."

"Who's your own particular pussy, Henry? An aunt?"

"No." Sir Henry sighed. "She's no relation." He said reverently: "She's just the finest detective God ever made. Natural genius cultivated in a suitable soil."

He turned upon Craddock.

"Don't you despise the old pussies in this village of yours, my boy," he said. "In case this turns out to be a high-powered mystery, which I don't suppose for a moment it will, remember that an elderly unmarried woman who knits and gardens is streets ahead of any detective sergeant. She can tell you what might have happened and what ought to have happened and even what actually did happen! And she can tell you why it happened!"

"I'll bear that in mind, sir," said Detective Inspector Craddock in his most formal manner, and nobody would have guessed that Dermot Eric Craddock was actually Sir Henry's godson and was on easy and intimate terms with his godfather.

Rydesdale gave a quick outline of the case to his friend.

"They'd all turn up at 6:30, I grant you that," he said. "But would that Swiss fellow know they would? And another thing, would they be likely to have much loot on them to be worth the taking?"

"A couple of old-fashioned brooches, a string of seed pearls—a little loose change, perhaps a note or two—not more," said Sir Henry thoughtfully. "Did this Miss Blacklock keep much money in the house?"

"She says not, sir. Five pounds odd, I understand."

"Mere chicken feed," said Rydesdale.

"What you're getting at," said Sir Henry, "is that this fellow liked to play-act—it wasn't the loot, it was the fun of playing and acting the holdup. Movie stuff, eh? It's quite possible. How did he manage to shoot himself?"

Rydesdale drew a paper towards him.

"Preliminary medical report. The revolver was discharged at close range—singeing . . . h'm . . . nothing to show whether accident or suicide. Could have been done deliberately, or he could have tripped and fallen and the revolver which he was holding close to him could have gone off. Probably the latter." He looked at Craddock. "You'll have to question the witnesses very carefully and make them say exactly what they saw."

Detective Inspector Craddock said sadly, "They'll all have seen something different."

"It's always interested me," said Sir Henry, "what people do see at a moment of intense excitement and nervous strain. What they do see and, even more interesting, what they don't see."

"Where's the report on the revolver?"

"Foreign make—fairly common on the Continent—Scherz did not hold a permit for it—and did not declare it on coming into England."

"Bad lad," said Sir Henry.

"Unsatisfactory character all round. Well, Craddock, go and see what you can find out about him at the Royal Spa Hotel."

II

At the Royal Spa Hotel Inspector Craddock was taken straight to the manager's office.

The manager, Mr. Rowlandson, a tall florid man with a hearty manner, greeted Inspector Craddock with expansive geniality.

"Glad to help you in any way we can, Inspector," he said. "Really, a most surprising business. I'd never have credited it—never. Scherz seemed a very ordinary, pleasant young chap—not at all my idea of a holdup man."

"How long has he been with you, Mr. Rowlandson?"

"I was looking that up before you came. A little over three months. Quite good credentials, the usual permits, etc."

"And you found him satisfactory?"

Without seeming to do so, Craddock marked the infinitesimal pause before Rowlandson replied.

"Quite satisfactory."

Craddock made use of a technique he had found efficacious before now.

"No, no, Mr. Rowlandson," he said, gently shaking his head. "That's not really quite the case, is it?"

"We-ll—" The manager seemed slightly taken aback.

"Come now, there was something wrong. What was it?"

"That's just it. I don't know."

"But you thought there was something wrong?"

"Well—yes—I did . . . but I've nothing really to go upon. I shouldn't like my conjectures to be written down and quoted against me."

Craddock smiled pleasantly.

"I know just what you mean. You needn't worry. But I've got to get some idea of what this fellow Scherz was like. You suspected him of—what?"

Rowlandson said, rather reluctantly, "Well, there was trouble, once or twice, about the bills. Items charged that oughtn't to have been there."

"You mean you suspected that he charged up certain items which didn't appear in the hotel records, and that he pocketed the difference when the bill was paid?"

"Something like that. Put it at the best, there was gross carelessness on his part. Once or twice quite a big sum was involved. Frankly, I got our accountant to go over his books, suspecting that he was—well, a wrong 'un; but though there were various mistakes and a good deal of slipshod method, the actual cash was quite correct. So I came to the conclusion that I must be mistaken."

"Supposing you hadn't been wrong? Supposing Scherz had been helping himself to various small sums here and there, he could have covered himself, I suppose, by making good the money?"

"Yes, if he had the money. But people who help themselves to 'small sums' as you put it—are usually hard up for those sums and spend them offhand."

"So if he wanted money to replace missing sums, he would have had to get money—by a holdup or other means?"

"Yes. I wonder if this is his first attempt."

"Might be. It was certainly a very amateurish one. Is there anyone else he could have got money from? Any woman in his life?"

"One of the waitresses in the Grill. Her name's Myrna Harris."

"I'd better have a talk with her."

III

Myrna Harris was a pretty girl with a glorious head of red hair and a pert nose.

She was alarmed and wary, and deeply conscious of the indignity of being interviewed by the police.

"I don't know a thing about it, sir. Not a thing," she protested. "If I'd known what he was like I'd never have gone out with Rudi at all. Naturally, seeing as he worked as receptionist here, I thought he was all right. Naturally I did. What I say is, the hotel ought to be more careful when they employ people—especially foreigners. Because you never know where you are with foreigners. I suppose he might have been in with one of these gangs you read about."

"We think," said Craddock, "that he was working quite on his own."

"Fancy—and him so quiet and respectable. You'd never think. Though there have been things missed—now I come to think of it. A diamond brooch—and a little gold locket, I believe. But I never dreamed that it could have been Rudi."

"I'm sure you didn't," said Craddock. "Anyone might have been taken in. You knew him fairly well?"

"I don't know that I'd say well."

"But you were friendly?"

"Oh, we were friendly—that's all, just friendly. Nothing serious at all. I'm always on my guard with foreigners, anyway. They've often got a way with them, but you never know do you? Some of those Poles during the war! And even some of the Americans! Never let on they're married men until it's too late. Rudi talked big and all that—but I always took it with a grain of salt."

Craddock seized on the phrase.

"Talked big, did he? That's very interesting, Miss Harris. I can see you're going to be a lot of help to us. In what way did he talk big?"

"Well, about how rich his people were in Switzerland—and how important. But that didn't go with his being as short of money as he was. He always said that because of the money regulation he couldn't get money from Switzerland over here. That might be, I suppose, but his things weren't expensive. His clothes, I mean. They weren't really class. I think, too, that a lot of the stories he used to tell me were so much hot air. About climbing in the Alps, and saving people's lives on the edge of a glacier. Why, he turned quite giddy just going along the edge of Boulter's Gorge. Alps, indeed!"

"You went out with him a good deal?"

"Yes—well—yes, I did. He had awfully good manners and he knew how to—to look after a girl. The best seats at the pictures, always. And even flowers he'd buy me sometimes. And he was just a lovely dancer—lovely."

"Did he mention this Miss Blacklock to you at all?"

"She comes in and lunches here sometimes, doesn't she? And she's stayed here once. No, I don't think Rudi ever mentioned her. I didn't know he knew her."

"Did he mention Chipping Cleghorn?"

He thought a faintly wary look came into Myrna Harris's eyes but he couldn't be sure.

"I don't think so . . . I think he did once ask about buses—what time they went—but I can't remember if that was Chipping Cleghorn or somewhere else. It wasn't just lately."

He couldn't get more out of her. Rudi Scherz had seemed just as usual. She hadn't seen him the evening before. She'd had no idea—no idea at all—she stressed the point, that Rudi Scherz was a crook.

And probably, Craddock thought, that was quite true.

5. *Miss Blacklock and Miss Bunner*

LITTLE PADDOCKS was very much as Detective Inspector Craddock had imagined it to be. He noted ducks and chickens, and what had been until lately an attractive herbaceous border and in which a few late Michael- mas daisies showed a last dying splash of purple beauty. The lawn and the paths showed signs of neglect.

Summing up, Detective Inspector Craddock thought: Probably not much money to spend on gardeners—fond of flowers and a good eye for planning and massing a border. House needs painting. Most houses do nowadays. Pleasant little property.

As Craddock's car stopped before the front door, Sergeant Fletcher came round the side of the house. With an erect military bearing, Ser- geant Fletcher looked like a guardsman, and was able to impart several different meanings to the one monosyllable: "Sir."

"So there you are, Fletcher."

"Sir," said Sergeant Fletcher.

"Anything to report?"

"We've finished going over the house, sir. Scherz doesn't seem to have left any fingerprints anywhere. He wore gloves, of course. No signs of any of the doors or windows being forced to effect an entrance. He seems to have come out from Medenham on the bus, arriving here at six o'clock. Side door of the house was locked at 5:30, I understand. Looks as though he must have walked in through the front door. Miss Blacklock states that that door isn't usually locked until the house is shut up for the night. The maid, on the other hand, states that the front door was locked all the afternoon—but she'd say anything. Very temperamental you'll find her. Mittel Europa refugee of some kind."

"Difficult, is she?"

"Sir!" said Sergeant Fletcher, with intense feeling.

Craddock smiled.

Fletcher resumed his report.

"Lighting system is quite in order everywhere. We haven't spotted yet how he operated the lights. It was just the one circuit went. Drawing- room and hall. Of course, nowadays, the wall brackets and lamps wouldn't all be on one fuse—but this is old-fashioned installation and wiring. Don't see how he could have tampered with the fuse box because it's out by the scullery and he'd have had to go through the kitchen, so the maid would have seen him."

"Unless she was in it with him?"

"That's very possible. Both foreigners—and I wouldn't trust her a yard —not a yard."

Craddock noticed two enormous frightened black eyes peering out of a window by the front door. The face, flattened against the pane, was hardly visible.

"That her there?"

"That's right, sir."

The face disappeared.

Craddock rang the front doorbell.

After a long wait the door was opened by a good-looking young woman with chestnut hair and a bored expression.

"Detective Inspector Craddock," said Craddock.

The young woman gave him a cool stare out of very attractive hazel eyes and said, "Come in. Miss Blacklock is expecting you."

The hall, Craddock noted, was long and narrow and seemed almost incredibly full of doors.

The young woman threw open one on the left, and said: "Inspector Craddock, Aunt Letty. Mitzi wouldn't go to the door. She's shut herself up in the kitchen and she's making the most marvelous moaning noises. I shouldn't think we'd get any lunch."

She added in an explanatory manner to Craddock, "She doesn't like the police," and withdrew, shutting the door behind her.

Craddock advanced to meet the owner of Little Paddocks.

He saw a tall active-looking woman of about sixty. Her gray hair had a slight natural wave and made a distinguished setting for an intelligent resolute face. She had keen gray eyes and a square determined chin. There was a surgical dressing on her left ear. She wore no make-up and was plainly dressed in a well-cut tweed coat and skirt and pullover. Round the neck of the latter she wore, rather unexpectedly, a set of old-fashioned cameos—a Victorian touch which seemed to hint at a sentimental streak not otherwise apparent.

Close beside her, with an eager round face and untidy hair escaping from a hairnet, was a woman of about the same age whom Craddock had no difficulty in recognizing as the "Dora Bunner—companion" of Constable Legg's notes—to which the latter had added an off-the-record commentary of "Scatty!"

Miss Blacklock spoke in a pleasant well-bred voice.

"Good morning, Inspector Craddock. This is my friend, Miss Bunner, who helps me run the house. Won't you sit down? You won't smoke, I suppose?"

"Not on duty, I'm afraid, Miss Blacklock."

"What a shame!"

Craddock's eyes took in the room with a quick, practiced glance. Typical Victorian double drawing-room. Two long windows in this room, built-out bay window in the other . . . chairs . . . sofa . . . center table with a big bowl of chrysanthemums—another bowl in the window—all fresh and pleasant without much originality. The only incongruous note was a small silver vase with dead violets in it on a table near the archway into the further room. Since he could not imagine Miss Blacklock tolerating dead flowers in a room, he imagined it to be the only indication that something out of the way had occurred to distract the routine of a well-run household.

He said, "I take it, Miss Blacklock, that this is the room in which the —incident occurred?"

"Yes."

"And you should have seen it last night," Miss Bunner exclaimed. "Such a mess. Two little tables knocked over, and the leg off one—people barging about in the dark—and someone put down a lighted cigarette and burnt one of the best bits of furniture. People—young people especially—are so careless about these things . . . Luckily none of the china got broken—"

Miss Blacklock interrupted gently but firmly, "Dora, all these things, vexatious as they may be, are only trifles. It will be best, I think, if we just answer Inspector Craddock's questions."

"Thank you, Miss Blacklock. I shall come to what happened last night presently. First of all, I want you to tell me when you first saw the dead man—Rudi Scherz."

"Rudi Scherz?" Miss Blacklock looked slightly surprised. "Is that his name? Somehow, I thought—Oh, well, it doesn't matter. My first encounter with him was when I was in Medenham Spa for a day's shopping about—let me see—about three weeks ago. We—Miss Bunner and I—were having lunch at the Royal Spa Hotel. As we were just leaving after lunch, I heard my name spoken. It was this young man. He said: 'It is Miss Blacklock, is it not?' And went on to say that perhaps I did not remember him, but that he was the son of the proprietor of the Hôtel des Alpes at Montreux, where my sister and I had stayed for nearly a year during the war."

"The Hôtel des Alpes, Montreux," noted Craddock. "And did you remember him, Miss Blacklock?"

"No, I didn't. Actually, I had no recollection of ever having seen him before. These boys at hotel reception desks all look exactly alike. We had had a very pleasant time at Montreux and the proprietor there had been extremely obliging, so I tried to be as civil as possible and said I hoped he was enjoying being in England, and he said, yes, that his father had sent him over for six months to learn the hotel business. It all seemed quite natural."

"And your next encounter?"

"About—yes, it must have been ten days ago, he suddenly turned up here. I was very surprised to see him. He apologized for troubling me, but said I was the only person he knew in England. He told me that he urgently needed money to return to Switzerland as his mother was dangerously ill."

"But Letty didn't give it to him," Miss Bunner put in breathlessly.

"It was a thoroughly fishy story," said Miss Blacklock with vigor. "I made up my mind that he was definitely a wrong 'un. That story about wanting the money to return to Switzerland was nonsense. His father could easily have wired for arrangements to have been made in this country. These hotel people are all in with each other. I suspected that he'd been embezzling money or something of that kind." She paused and said dryly, "In case you think I'm hardhearted, I was secretary for many years to a big financier and one becomes wary about appeals for money. I know simply all the hard luck stories there are.

"The only thing that did surprise me," she added thoughtfully, "was that he gave in so easily. He went away at once without any more argument. It's as though he had never expected to get the money."

"Do you think now, looking back on it, that his coming was really by way of a pretext to spy out the land?"

Miss Blacklock nodded her head vigorously.

"That's exactly what I do think—now. He made certain remarks as I let him out—about the rooms. He said, 'You have a very nice dining-room' (which, of course, it isn't—it's a horrid dark little room), just as an excuse to look inside. And then he sprang forward and unfastened the front door; he said, 'Let me.' I think now he wanted to have a look at the fastening. Actually, like most people round here, we never lock the front door until it gets dark. Anyone could walk in."

"And the side door? There is a side door to the garden, I understand?"

"Yes. I went out through it to shut up the ducks not long before the people arrived."

"Was it locked when you went out?"

Miss Blacklock frowned.

"I can't remember . . . I think so. I certainly locked it when I came in."

"That would be about quarter past six?"

"Somewhere about then."

"And the front door?"

"That's not usually locked until later."

"Then Scherz could have walked in quite easily that way. Or he could have slipped in whilst you were out shutting up the ducks. He'd already spied out the lay of the land and had probably noted various places of concealment—cupboards, etc. Yes, that all seems quite clear."

"I beg your pardon, it isn't at all clear," said Miss Blacklock. "Why on earth should anyone take all that elaborate trouble to come and burgle this house and stage that silly sort of holdup?"

"Do you keep money in the house, Miss Blacklock?"

"About five pounds in that desk there, and perhaps a pound or two in my purse."

"Jewelry?"

"A couple of rings and brooches and the cameos I'm wearing. You must agree with me, Inspector, that the whole thing's absurd."

"It wasn't burglary at all," cried Miss Bunner. "I've told you so, Letty, all along. It was revenge! Because you wouldn't give him that money! He deliberately shot at you—twice."

"Ah," said Craddock. "We'll come now to last night. What happened exactly, Miss Blacklock? Tell me in your own words as nearly as you can remember."

Miss Blacklock reflected a moment.

"The clock struck," she said. "The one on the mantelpiece. I remember saying that if anything were going to happen it would have to happen soon. And then the clock struck. We all listened to it without saying anything. It chimes, you know. It chimed the two quarters and then, quite suddenly, the lights went out."

"What lights were on?"

"The wall brackets in here and in the further room. The standard lamp and the two small reading lamps weren't on."

"Was there a flash first, or a noise when the lights went out?"

"I don't think so."

"I'm sure there was a flash," said Dora Bunner. "And a crackling noise. Dangerous!"

"And then, Miss Blacklock?"

"The door opened—"

"Which door? There are two in the room."

"Oh, this door in here. The one in the other room doesn't open. It's a dummy. The door opened and there he was, a masked man with a revolver. It just seemed too fantastic for words, but, of course, at the time I just thought it was a silly joke. He said something—I forget what—"

"Hands up or I shoot!" supplied Miss Bunner dramatically.

"Something like that," said Miss Blacklock, rather doubtfully.

"And you all put your hands up?"

"Oh yes," said Miss Bunner. "We all did. I mean it was part of it."

"I didn't," said Miss Blacklock crisply. "It seemed so utterly silly. And I was annoyed by the whole thing."

"And then?"

"The flashlight was right in my eyes. It dazzled me. And then, quite incredibly, I heard a bullet whiz past me and hit the wall by my head. Somebody shrieked and then I felt a burning pain in my ear and heard the second report."

"It was terrifying," put in Miss Bunner.

"And what happened next, Miss Blacklock?"

"It's difficult to say—I was so staggered by the pain and the surprise. The—the figure turned away and seemed to stumble and then there was another shot and his flashlight went out and everybody began pushing and calling out. All banging into each other."

"Where were you standing, Miss Blacklock?"

"She was over by the table. She'd got the vase of violets in her hand," said Miss Bunner breathlessly.

"I was over here." Miss Blacklock went over to the small table by the archway. "Actually, it was the cigarette box I'd got in my hand."

Inspector Craddock examined the wall behind her. The two bullet holes showed plainly. The bullets themselves had been extracted and had been sent for comparison with the revolver.

He said quietly, "You had a very near escape, Miss Blacklock."

"He did shoot at her," said Miss Bunner. "Deliberately at her! I saw him. He turned the flash round on everybody until he found her and then he held it right at her and just fired at her. He meant to kill you, Letty."

"Dora dear, you've just got that into your head from mulling the whole thing over and over."

"He shot at you," repeated Dora stubbornly. "He meant to shoot you and when he'd missed, he shot himself. I'm certain that's the way it was!"

"I don't think he meant to shoot himself for a minute," said Miss Blacklock. "He wasn't the kind of man who shoots himself."

"You tell me, Miss Blacklock, that until the revolver was fired you thought the whole business was a joke?"

"Naturally. What else could I think it was?"

"Who did you think was the author of this joke?"

"You thought Patrick had done it at first," Dora Bunner reminded her.

"Patrick?" asked the Inspector, sharply.

"My young cousin, Patrick Simmons," Miss Blacklock continued sharply, annoyed with her friend. "It did occur to me when I saw this advertisement that it might be some attempt at humor on his part, but he denied it absolutely."

"And then you were worried, Letty," said Miss Bunner. "You were worried, although you pretended not to be. And you were quite right to be worried. It said a murder is announced—and it was announced—your murder! And if the man hadn't missed, you would have been murdered. And then where should we all be?"

Dora Bunner was trembling as she spoke. Her face was puckered up and she looked as though she were going to cry.

Miss Blacklock patted her on the shoulder.

"It's all right, Dora dear—don't get excited. It's so bad for you. Everything's quite all right. We've had a nasty experience, but it's over now." She added, "You must pull yourself together for my sake, Dora. I rely on you, you know, to keep the house going. Isn't it the day for the laundry to come?"

"Oh, dear me, Letty, how fortunate you reminded me! I wonder if they'll return that missing pillowcase. I must make a note in the book about it. I'll go and see to it at once."

"And take these violets away," said Miss Blacklock. "There's nothing I hate more than dead flowers."

"What a pity. I picked them fresh yesterday. They haven't lasted at all —Oh, dear, I must have forgotten to put any water in the vase. Fancy that! I'm always forgetting things. Now I must go and see about the laundry. They might be here any moment."

She bustled away, looking quite happy again.

"She's not very strong," said Miss Blacklock, "and excitements are bad for her. Is there anything more you want to know, Inspector?"

"I just want to know exactly how many people make up your household here and something about them."

"Yes, well in addition to myself and Dora Bunner, I have two young cousins living here at present, Patrick and Julia Simmons."

"Cousins? Not a nephew and niece?"

"No, they call me Aunt Letty, but actually they are distant cousins. Their mother was my second cousin."

"Have they always made their home with you?"

"Oh, dear, no; only for the last two months. They lived in the South of France before the war. Patrick went into the Navy and Julia, I believe, was in one of the Ministries. She was at Llandudno. When the war was over their mother wrote and asked me if they could possibly come to me as paying guests—Julia is training as a dispenser in Milchester General Hospital, Patrick is studying for an engineering degree at Milchester University. Milchester, as you know, is only fifty minutes by bus, and I was very glad to have them here. This house is really too large for me. They pay a small sum for board and lodging and it all works out very well." She added with a smile, "I like having somebody young about the place."

"Then there is a Mrs. Haymes, I believe?"

"Yes. She works as an assistant gardener at Dayas Hall, Mrs. Lucas's place. The cottage there is occupied by the old gardener and his wife and Mrs. Lucas asked if I could billet her here. She's a very nice girl. Her husband was killed in Italy, and she has a boy of eight who is at a prep school and whom I have arranged to have here in the holidays."

"And by way of domestic help?"

"A Mrs. Huggins from the village comes up five mornings a week and I have a foreign refugee with a most unpronounceable name as a kind of lady cook help. You will find Mitzi rather difficult, I'm afraid. She has a kind of persecution mania."

Craddock nodded. He was conscious in his own mind of yet another of Constable Legg's invaluable commentaries. Having appended the word "Scatty" to Dora Bunner, and "All right" to Letitia Blacklock, he had embellished Mitzi's record with the one word, "Liar."

As though she had read his mind Miss Blacklock said, "Please don't be too prejudiced against the poor thing because she's a liar. I do really believe that, like so many liars, there is a real substratum of truth behind her lies. I mean that though, to take an instance, her atrocity stories have grown and grown until every kind of unpleasant story that has ever appeared in print has happened to her or her relatives personally; she did have a bad shock initially and did see one, at least, of her relatives killed. I think a lot of these displaced persons feel, perhaps justly, that their claim to our notice and sympathy lies in their atrocity value and so they exaggerate and invent."

She added, "Quite frankly, Mitzi is a maddening person. She exasperates and infuriates us all, she is suspicious and sulky, is perpetually having 'feelings' and thinking herself insulted. But in spite of it all, I really am sorry for her." She smiled. "And, also, when she wants to, she can cook very nicely."

"I'll try not to ruffle her more than I can help," said Craddock soothingly. "Was that Miss Julia Simmons who opened the door to me?"

"Yes. Would you like to see her now? Patrick has gone out. Phillipa Haymes you will find working at Dayas Hall."

"Thank you, Miss Blacklock. I'd like to see Miss Simmons now if I may."

6. *Julia, Mitzi and Patrick*

JULIA, when she came into the room and sat down in the chair vacated by Letitia Blacklock, had an air of composure that Craddock, for some reason, found annoying. She fixed a limpid gaze on him and waited for his questions.

Miss Blacklock had tactfully left the room.

"Please tell me about last night, Miss Simmons."

"Last night?" murmured Julia with a blank stare. "Oh, we all slept like logs. Reaction, I suppose."

"I mean last night from six o'clock onwards."

"Oh, I see. Well, a lot of tiresome people came—"

"They were?"

She gave him another limpid stare.

"Don't you know all this already?"

"I'm asking the questions, Miss Simmons," said Craddock pleasantly.

"My mistake. I always find repetitions so dready. Apparently you don't . . . Well, there were Colonel and Mrs. Easterbrook, Miss Hinchliffe and Miss Murgatroyd, Mrs. Swettenham and Edmund Swettenham, and Mrs. Harmon, the vicar's wife. They arrived in that order. And if you want to know what they said—they all said the same things in turn. 'I see you've got your central heating on' and 'What lovely chrysanthemums!' "

Craddock bit his lip. The mimicry was good.

"The exception was Mrs. Harmon. She's rather a pet. She came in with her hat falling off and her shoelaces untied and she asked straight out when the murder was going to happen. It embarrassed everybody because they'd all been pretending they'd dropped in by chance. Aunt Letty said in her dry way that it was due to happen quite soon. And then that clock chimed and just as it finished the lights went out, the door was flung open and a masked figure said, 'Stick 'em up, guys,' or something like that. It was exactly like a bad film. Really, quite ridiculous. And then he fired two shots at Aunt Letty and suddenly it wasn't ridiculous any more."

"Where was everybody when this happened?"

"When the light went out? Well, just standing about, you know. Mrs.

Harmon was sitting on the sofa—Hinch (that's Miss Hinchliffe) had taken up a manly stance in front of the fireplace."

"You were all in this room, or the far room?"

"Mostly, I think, in this room. Patrick had gone into the other to get the sherry. I think Colonel Easterbrook went after him, but I don't really know. We were—well—as I said, just standing about."

"Where were you, yourself?"

"I think I was over by the window. Aunt Letty went to get the cigarettes."

"On that table by the archway?"

"Yes—and then the lights went out and the bad film started."

"The man had a powerful flashlight. What did he do with it?"

"Well, he shone it on us. Horribly dazzling. It just made you blink."

"I want you to answer this very carefully, Miss Simmons. Did he hold it steady or did he move it about?"

Julia considered. Her manner was now definitely less weary.

"He moved it," she said slowly. "Like a spotlight in a dance hall. It was full in my eyes and then it went on round the room and then the shots came. Two shots."

"And then?"

"He whirled round—and Mitzi began to scream like a siren from somewhere and his flashlight went out and there was another shot. And then the door closed (it does, you know, slowly, with a whining noise—quite uncanny) and there we were all in the dark, not knowing what to do, and poor Bunny squealing like a pig and Mitzi going all out across the hall."

"Would it be your opinion that the man shot himself deliberately, or do you think he stumbled and the revolver went off accidentally?"

"I haven't the faintest idea. The whole thing was so stagy. Actually, I thought it was still some silly joke—until I saw the blood from Aunt Letty's ear. But even if you were actually going to fire a revolver to make the thing more real, you'd be careful to fire it well above someone's head, wouldn't you?"

"You would indeed. Do you think he could see clearly who he was firing at? I mean, was Miss Blacklock clearly outlined in the light of the torch?"

"I've no idea. I wasn't looking at her. I was looking at the man."

"What I'm getting at is—do you think the man was deliberately aiming at her—at her in particular, I mean?"

Julia seemed a little startled by the idea.

"You mean deliberately picking on Aunt Letty? Oh, I shouldn't think so . . . After all, if he wanted to take a pot shot at Aunt Letty, there would be heaps of more suitable opportunities. There would be no point in collecting all the friends and neighbors just to make it more difficult. He could have shot her from behind a hedge in the good old Irish fashion any day of the week, and probably got away with it."

And that, thought Craddock, was a very complete reply to Dora Bunner's suggestion of a deliberate attack on Letitia Blacklock.

He said, with a sigh, "Thank you, Miss Simmons. I'd better go and see Mitzi now."

"Mind her fingernails," warned Julia. "She's a tartar!"

II

Craddock, with Fletcher in attendance, found Mitzi in the kitchen. She was rolling pastry and looked up suspiciously as they entered.

Her black hair hung over her eyes; she looked sullen and the purple jumper and brilliant green skirt she wore were not becoming to her pasty complexion.

"What do you come in my kitchen for, Mr. Policeman? You are police, yes? Always, always there is persecution—ah! I should be used to it by now. They say it is different here in England, but no, it is just the same. You come to torture me, yes, to make me say things, but I shall say nothing. You will tear off my fingernails, and put lighted matches on my skin—oh, yes, and worse than that. But I will not speak, do you hear? I shall say nothing—nothing at all. And you will send me away to a concentration camp, and I shall not care."

Craddock looked at her thoughtfully, selecting what was likely to be the best method of attack. Finally he sighed and said, "O.K. then; get your hat and coat."

"What is that you say?" Mitzi looked startled.

"Get your hat and coat and come along. I haven't got my nail-pulling apparatus and the rest of the bag of tricks with me. We keep all that down at the station. Got the handcuffs handy, Fletcher?"

"Sir!" said Sergeant Fletcher, with appreciation.

"But I do not want to come!" screeched Mitzi, backing away from him.

"Then you'll answer civil questions civilly. If you like, you can have a solicitor present."

"A lawyer? I do not like a lawyer. I do not want a lawyer."

She put the rolling-pin down, dusted her hands on a cloth and sat down.

"What do you want to know?" she asked sulkily.

"I want your account of what happened here last night."

"You know very well what happened."

"I want your account of it."

"I tried to go away. Did she tell you that? When I saw that in the paper saying about murder, I wanted to go away. She would not let me. She is very hard—not at all sympathetic. She made me stay. But I knew—I knew what would happen. I knew I should be murdered."

"Well, you weren't murdered, were you?"

"No," admitted Mitzi grudgingly.

"Come now, tell me what happened."

"I was nervous. Oh, I was nervous. All that evening. I hear things. People moving about. Once I think someone is in the hall moving stealthily—but it is only that Mrs. Haymes coming through the side door so as not to dirty the front steps, she says. Much she cares! She is a Nazi herself, that one, with her fair hair and her blue eyes, so superior and looking at me and thinking that I—I am only dirt—"

"Never mind Mrs. Haymes."

"Who does she think she is? Has she had expensive university education like I have? Has she a degree in Economics? No, she is just a paid laborer. She digs and mows grass and is paid so much every Saturday. Who is she to call herself a lady?"

"Never mind Mrs. Haymes, I said. Go on."

"I take the sherry and the glasses, and the little pastries that I have made so nice into the drawing-room. Then the bell rings and I answer the door. Again and again and again I answer the door. It is degrading—but I do it. And then I go back into the pantry and I start to polish the silver, and I think it will be very handy, that, because if someone comes to kill me, I have there close at hand the big carving knife, all sharp."

"Very foresighted of you."

"And then, suddenly—I hear shots. I think: It has come—it is happening. I run through the dining-room (the other door—it will not open). I stand a moment to listen and then there comes another shot and a big thud, out there in the hall, and I turn the door handle, but it is locked outside. I am shut in there like a rat in a trap. And I go mad with fear. I scream and I scream and I beat upon the door. And at last—at last—they turn the key and let me out. And then I bring candles, many, many candles—and the lights go on, and I see blood—blood! Ah, *Gott in Himmel,* the blood! It is not the first time I have seen blood. My little brother

—I see him killed before my eyes—I see the blood in the street—people shot, dying—I—"

"Yes," said Inspector Craddock. "Thank you very much."

"And now," said Mitzi dramatically, "you can arrest me and take me to prison!"

"Not today," said Inspector Craddock.

III

As Craddock and Fletcher went through the hall to the front door, it was flung open and a tall, handsome young man almost collided with them.

"Sleuths, as I live!" cried the young man.

"Mr. Patrick Simmons?"

"Quite right, Inspector. You're the Inspector, aren't you, and the other's the Sergeant?"

"You are quite right, Mr. Simmons. Can I have a word with you, please?"

"I am innocent, Inspector. I swear I am innocent."

"Now then, Mr. Simmons, don't play the fool. I've a good many other people to see and I don't want to waste time. What's this room? Can we go in here?"

"It's the so-called study—but nobody studies."

"I was told that you were studying," said Craddock.

"I found I couldn't concentrate on mathematics, so I came home."

In a businesslike manner Inspector Craddock demanded full name, age, details of war service.

"And now, Mr. Simmons, will you describe what happened last night?"

"We killed the fatted calf, Inspector. That is, Mitzi set her hand to making savory pastries, Aunt Letty opened a new bottle of sherry—"

Craddock interrupted.

"A new bottle? Was there an old one?"

"Yes, half full. But Aunt Letty didn't seem to fancy it."

"Was she nervous then?"

"Oh, not really. She's extremely sensible. It was old Bunny, I think, who had put the wind up—prophesying disaster all day."

"Miss Bunner was definitely apprehensive then?"

"Oh, yes, she enjoyed herself thoroughly."

"She took the advertisement seriously?"

"It scared her into fits."

"Miss Blacklock seems to have thought, when she first read that advetisement, that you had had something to do with it. Why was that?"

"Ah, sure, I get blamed for everything round here!"

"You didn't have anything to do with it, did you, Mr. Simmons?"

"Me? Never in the world."

"Had you ever seen or spoken to this Rudi Scherz?"

"Never saw him in my life."

"It was the kind of joke you might have played, though?"

"Who's been telling you that? Just because I once made Bunny an apple pie bed—and sent Mitzi a postcard saying the Gestapo was on her track—"

"Just give me your account of what happened."

"I'd just gone into the small drawing-room to fetch the drinks when, hey, presto, the lights went out. I turned round and there's a fellow standing in the doorway saying, 'Stick your hands up,' and everybody gasping and squealing. And just when I'm wondering if I can rush him, he starts firing a revolver and then crash down he goes and his flashlight goes out and we're in the dark again, and Colonel Easterbrook starts shouting orders in his barrack-room voice. 'Lights!' he says, and will my lighter go on? No, it won't, as is the way of those cussed inventions."

"Did it seem to you that the intruder was definitely aiming at Miss Blacklock?"

"Ah, how could I tell? I should say he just loosed off his revolver for the fun of the thing—and then found, maybe, he'd gone too far."

"And shot himself?"

"It could be. When I saw the face of him, he looked like the kind of little pasty thief who might easily lose his nerve."

"And you're sure you had never seen him before?"

"Never."

"Thank you, Mr. Simmons. I shall want to interview the other people who were here last night. What would be the best order in which to take them?"

"Well, our Phillipa—Mrs. Haymes—works at Dayas Hall. The gates of it are nearly opposite this gate. After that, the Swettenhams are the nearest. Anyone will tell you."

7. *Among Those Present*

DAYAS HALL had certainly suffered during the war years. Couch grass grew enthusiastically over what had once been an asparagus bed, as evidenced by a few waving tufts of asparagus foliage. Groundsel, bindweed and other garden pests showed every sign of vigorous growth.

A portion of the kitchen garden bore evidence of having been reduced to discipline and here Craddock found a sour-looking old man leaning pensively on a spade.

"It's Mrs. 'Aymes you want? I couldn't say where you'd find 'er. 'As 'er own ideas, she 'as, about what she'll do. Not one to take advice. I could show'er—show 'er willing—but what's the good? Won't listen, these young ladies won't! Think they know everything because they've put on breeches and gone for a ride on a tractor. But it's gardening that's needed here. And that isn't learned in a day. Gardening, that what this place needs."

"It looks as though it does," said Craddock.

The old man chose to take this remark as an aspersion.

"Now, look here, mister, what do you suppose I can do with a place this size? Three men and a boy, that's what it used to 'ave. And that's what it wants. There's not many men could put in the work on it that I do. 'Ere sometimes, I am, till eight o'clock at night. Eight o'clock."

"What do you work by? An oil lamp?"

"Naterally I don't mean this time o' year. Naterally. Summer evenings I'm talking about."

"Oh," said Craddock. "I'd better go and look for Mrs. Haymes."

The rustic displayed some interest.

"What are you wanting 'er for? Police, aren't you? She been in trouble, or is it the do there was up to Little Paddocks? Masked man bursting in and holding up a roomful of people with a revolver. Ah! That sort of thing wouldn't 'ave 'appened afore the war. Deserters, that's what it is. Desperate men roaming the countryside. Why don't the military round 'em up?"

"I've no idea," said Craddock. "I suppose this holdup caused a lot of talk?"

"That it did. What's us coming to? That's what Ned Barker said. Comes of going to the pictures so much, he said. But Tom Riley, he says it comes of letting these furriners run about loose. And depend on it, he says, that girl as cooks up there for Miss Blacklock and 'as such a nasty temper—she's in it, he said. She's a Communist or worse, he says, and we don't like that sort 'ere. And Marlene, who's behind the bar, you understand, she will 'ave it that there must be something very valuable up at Miss Blacklock's. Not that you'd think it, she says, for I'm sure Miss Blacklock goes about as plain as plain, except for them great rows of false pearls she wears. And, then she says—supposin' as them pearls is real; and Florrie (that's old Bellamy's daughter), she says, 'Nonsense,' she says—'noovo art—that's what they are—costume jewelry,' she says. Costume jewelry—that's a fine way of labeling a string of false pearls. Roman pearls, the gentry used to call 'em once—and Parisian diamonds—my wife was a lady's maid and I know. But what does it all mean—just glass! I suppose it's costume jewelry that young Miss Simmons wears—gold ivy leaves and dogs and such like. 'Tisn't often you see a real bit of gold nowadays—even wedding rings they make of this gray plattinghum stuff. Shabby, I call it—for all that it costs the earth."

Old Ashe paused for breath and then continued, " 'Miss Blacklock don't keep much money in the 'ouse, that I do know,' says Jim Huggins, speaking up. He should know, for it's his wife as goes up and does for 'em at Little Paddocks, and she's a woman as knows most of what's going on. Nosy, if you get me."

"Did he say what Mrs. Huggins's view was?"

"That Mitzi's mixed up in it, that's what she thinks. Awful temper she 'as, and the airs she gives herself! Called Mrs. Huggins a working woman to her face the other morning."

Craddock stood a moment, checking over in his orderly mind the substance of the old gardener's remarks. It gave him a good cross section of rural opinion in Chipping Cleghorn, but he didn't think there was anything to help him in his task. He turned away and the old man called after him grudgingly:

"Maybe you'd find her in the apple orchard. She's younger than I am for getting the apples down."

And sure enough, in the apple orchard Craddock found Phillipa Haymes. His first view was a pair of nice legs encased in breeches, sliding easily down the trunk of a tree. Then Phillipa, her face flushed, her hair ruffled by the branches, stood looking at him in a startled fashion.

Make a good Rosalind, Craddock thought automatically, for Detective Inspector Craddock was a Shakespeare enthusiast and had played the part of the melancholy Jaques with great success in a performance of *As You Like It* for the Police Orphanage.

A moment later he amended his view. Phillipa Haymes was too wooden for Rosalind, her fairness and her impassivity were intensely English, but English of the twentieth rather than of the sixteenth century. Well-bred, unemotional English, without a sparkle of mischief.

"Good morning, Mrs. Haymes. I'm sorry if I startled you. I'm Detective Inspector Craddock of the Middleshire Police. I wanted to have a word with you."

"About last night?"

"Yes."

"Will it take long? Shall we—"

She looked about her rather doubtfully.

Craddock indicated a fallen tree trunk.

"Rather informal," he said pleasantly, "but I don't want to interrupt your work longer than necessary."

"Thank you."

"It's just for the record. You came in from work at what time last night?"

"At about half past five. I'd stayed about twenty minutes later in order to finish some watering in the greenhouse."

"You came in by which door?"

"The side door. One cuts across by the ducks and the hen-house from the drive. It saves going round and, besides, it avoids dirtying up the front porch. I'm in rather a mucky state sometimes."

"You always come in that way?"

"Yes."

"The door was unlocked?"

"Yes. During the summer it's usually wide open. This time of the year it's shut but not locked. We all go out and in that way a good deal. I locked it when I came in."

"Do you always do that?"

"I've been doing it for the last week. You see, it gets dark at six. Miss Blacklock goes out to shut up the ducks and the hens sometimes in the evening, but she very often goes out through the kitchen door."

"And you are quite sure you did lock the side door this time?"

"I really am quite sure about that."

"Quite so, Mrs. Haymes. And what did you do when you came in?"

"Kicked off my muddy footwear and went upstairs, had a bath and changed. Then I came down and found that a kind of party was in progress. I hadn't known anything about this funny advertisement until then."

"Now please describe just what occurred when the holdup happened."

"Well, the lights went out suddenly—"

"Where were you?"

"By the mantelpiece. I was searching for my lighter which I thought I had put down there. The lights went out—and everybody giggled. Then the door was flung open and this man shone a flashlight on us and flourished a revolver and told us to put our hands up."

"Which you proceeded to do?"

"Well, I didn't actually. I thought it was just fun, and I was tired and didn't think I really needed to put them up."

"In fact, you were bored by the whole thing?"

"I was, rather. And then the revolver went off. The shots sounded deafening and I was really frightened. The flashlight went whirling round and dropped and went out, and then Mitzi started screaming. It was just like a pig being killed."

"Did you find the flashlight very dazzling?"

"No, not particularly. It was quite a strong one, though. It lit up Miss Bunner for a moment and she looked quite like a turnip ghost—you know, all white and staring with her mouth open and her eyes starting out of her head."

"The man moved the flashlight?"

"Oh, yes, he played it all round the room."

"As though he were looking for someone?"

"Not particularly, I should say."

"And after that, Mrs. Haymes?"

Phillipa Haymes frowned.

"Oh, it was all a terrible muddle and confusion. Edmund Swettenham and Patrick Simmons switched on their lighters and they went out into the hall and we followed, and someone opened the dining-room door— the lights hadn't gone out there—and Edmund Swettenham gave Mitzi a terrific slap on the cheek and brought her out of her screaming fit, and after that it wasn't so bad."

"You saw the body of the dead man?"

"Yes."

"Was he known to you? Had you ever seen him before?"

"Never."

"Have you any opinion as to whether his death was accidental, or do you think he shot himself deliberately?"

"I haven't the faintest idea."

"You didn't see him when he came to the house previously?"

"No. I believe it was in the middle of the morning and I wouldn't have been there."

"Thank you, Mrs. Haymes. One thing more. You haven't any valuable jewelry? Rings, bracelets, anything of that kind?"

Phillipa shook her head.

"My engagement ring—a couple of brooches."

"And, as far as you know, there was nothing of particular value in the house?"

"No. I mean there is some quite nice silver—but nothing out of the ordinary."

"Thank you, Mrs. Haymes."

II

As Craddock retraced his steps through the kitchen garden he came face to face with a large, red-faced lady, carefully corseted.

"Good morning," she said belligerently. "What do you want here?"

"Mrs. Lucas? I am Detective Inspector Craddock."

"Oh, that's who you are. I beg your pardon. I don't like strangers forcing their way into my garden, wasting the gardener's time. But I quite understand you have to do your duty."

"Quite so."

"May I ask if we are to expect a repetition of that outrage last night at Miss Blacklock's? Is it a gang?"

"We are satisfied, Mrs. Lucas, that it was not the work of a gang."

"There are far too many robberies nowadays. The police are getting slack." Craddock did not reply. "I suppose you've been talking to Phillipa Haymes?"

"I wanted her account as an eyewitness."

"You couldn't have waited until one o'clock, I suppose? After all, it would be fairer to question her in her time, rather than in mine."

"I'm anxious to get back to headquarters."

"Not that one expects consideration nowadays. Or a decent day's work. On duty late, half an hour's pottering. A break for relief at ten o'clock. No work done at all the moment the rain starts. When you want the lawn mowed there's always something wrong with the mower. And off duty five or ten minutes before the proper time."

"I understand from Mrs. Haymes that she left here at twenty minutes past five yesterday instead of five o'clock."

"Oh, I daresay she did. Give her her due, Mrs. Haymes is quite keen on her work, though there have been days when I have come out here and not been able to find her anywhere. She is a lady by birth, of course, and one feels it one's duty to do something for these poor young war widows. Not that it isn't very inconvenient. Those long school holidays, and the arrangement is that she has extra time off then. I told her that there are really excellent camps nowadays where children can be sent and where they have a delightful time and enjoy it far more than wandering about with their parents. They need practically not come home at all in the summer holidays."

"But Mrs. Haymes didn't take kindly to that idea?"

"She's as obstinate as a mule, that girl. Just the time of year when I want the tennis court mowed and marked nearly every day. Old Ashe gets the lines crooked. But my convenience is never considered!"

"I presume Mrs. Haymes takes a smaller salary than is usual."

"Naturally. What else could she expect?"

"Nothing, I'm sure," said Craddock. "Good morning, Mrs. Lucas."

III

"It was dreadful," said Mrs. Swettenham happily. "Quite—quite—dreadful, and what I say is that they ought to be far more careful what advertisements they accept at the *Gazette* office. At the time, when I read it, I thought it was very, very odd. I said so, didn't I, Edmund?"

"Do you remember just what you were doing when the lights went out, Mrs. Swettenham?" asked the Inspector.

"How that reminds me of my old Nannie! *Where was Moses when the light went out?* The answer, of course, was 'in the dark.' Just like us yesterday evening. All standing about and wondering what was going to happen. And then, you know, the thrill when it suddenly went pitch black. And the door opening—just a dim figure standing there with a revolver and that blinding light and a menacing voice saying, 'Your money or your life!' Oh, I've never enjoyed anything so much. And then, a minute later, of course, it was all dreadful. Real bullets, just whistling past our ears! It must have been just like the commandos in the war."

"Whereabouts were you standing or sitting at the time, Mrs. Swettenham?"

"Now, let me see, where was I? Who was I talking to, Edmund?"

"I really haven't the least idea, Mother."

"Was it Miss Hinchliffe I was asking about giving the hens cod-liver oil in the cold weather? Or was it Mrs. Harmon—no, she'd only just arrived. I think I was just saying to Colonel Easterbrook that I thought it was really very dangerous to have an atom research station in England. It ought to be on some lonely island in case the radioactivity gets loose."

"You don't remember if you were sitting or standing?"

"Does it really matter, Inspector? I was somewhere over by the window or near the mantelpiece, because I know I was quite near the clock when it struck. Such a thrilling moment! Waiting to see if anything might be going to happen."

"You describe the light from the flashlight as blinding. Was it turned full on you?"

"It was right in my eyes. I couldn't see a thing."

"Did the man hold it still, or did he move it about, from person to person?"

"Oh, I don't really know. Which did he do, Edmund?"

"It moved rather slowly over us all, so as to see what we were all doing, I suppose, in case we should try and rush him."

"And where exactly in the room were you, Mr. Swettenham?"

"I'd been talking to Julia Simmons. We were both standing up in the middle of the room—the long room."

"Was everyone in that room, or was there someone in the far room?"

"Phillipa Haymes had moved in there, I think. She was over by that far mantelpiece. I think she was looking for something."

"Have you any idea as to whether the third shot was suicide or an accident?"

"I've no idea at all. The man seemed to swerve round very suddenly and then crumple up and fall—but it was all very confused. You must realize that you couldn't really see anything. And then that refugee girl started yelling the place down."

"I understand it was you who unlocked the dining-room door and let her out?"

"Yes."

"The door was definitely locked on the outside?"

Edmund looked at him curiously.

"Certainly it was. Why, you don't imagine—"

"I just like to get my facts quite clear. Thank you, Mr. Swettenham."

IV

Inspector Craddock was forced to spend quite a long time with Colonel and Mrs. Easterbrook. He had to listen to a long disquisition on the psychological aspect of the case.

"The psychological approach—that's the only thing nowadays," the colonel told him. "You've got to understand your criminal. Now, the whole setup here is plain as plain to a man who's had the wide experience that I have. Why does this fellow put that ad in? Psychology. He wants to advertise himself—to focus attention on himself. He's been passed over, perhaps despised as a foreigner by the other employees at the Spa Hotel. A girl has turned him down, perhaps. He wants to rivet her attention on him. Who is the idol of the movies nowadays—the gangster—the tough guy? Very well, he will be a tough guy. Robbery with violence. A mask? A revolver? But he wants an audience—he must have an audience. So he arranges for an audience. And then, at the supreme moment, his part runs away with him—he's more than a burglar. He's a killer. He shoots —blindly—"

Inspector Craddock caught gladly at a word.

"You say 'blindly,' Colonel Easterbrook. You didn't think that he was firing deliberately at one particular person—at Miss Blacklock, that is to say?"

"No, no. He just loosed off, as I say, blindly. And that's what brought him to himself. The bullet hit someone—actually, it was only a graze, but he doesn't know that. He comes to himself with a bang. All this—this make-believe he's been indulging in—is real. He's shot at someone— perhaps killed someone. . . . It's all up with him. And so, in blind panic, he turns the revolver on himself."

Colonel Easterbrook paused, cleared his throat appreciatively and said, in a satisfied voice. "Plain as a pikestaff, that's what it is; plain as a pikestaff."

"It really is wonderful," said Mrs. Easterbrook, "the way you know exactly what happened, Archie."

Her voice was warm with admiration.

Inspector Craddock thought it was wonderful, too, but he was not quite so warmly appreciative.

"Exactly where were you in the room, Colonel Easterbrook, when the actual shooting business took place?"

"I was standing with my wife—near a center table with some flowers on it."

"I caught hold of your arm, didn't I, Archie, when it happened? I was simply scared to death. I just had to hold on to you."

"Poor little kitten," said the colonel playfully.

V

The Inspector ran Miss Hinchliffe to earth beside a pigsty.

"Nice creatures, pigs," said Miss Hinchliffe, scratching a wrinkled pink back. "Coming on well, isn't he? Good bacon round about Christmas time. Well, what do you want to see me about? I told your people last night I hadn't the least idea who the man was. Never saw him anywhere in the neighborhood snooping about or anything of that sort. Our Mrs. Mopp says he came from one of the big hotels in Medenham Wells. Why didn't he hold up someone there if he wanted to? Get a much better haul."

That was undeniable—Craddock proceeded with his inquiries.

"Where were you exactly when the incident took place?"

"Incident! Reminds me of my A.R.P. days. Saw some incidents then, I can tell you. Where was I when the shooting started? That what you want to know?"

"Yes."

"Leaning up against the mantelpiece, hoping to God someone would offer me a drink soon," replied Miss Hinchliffe promptly.

"Do you think that the shots were fired blindly, or aimed carefully at one particular person?"

"You mean aimed at Letty Blacklock? How the devil should I know? Damned hard to sort out what your impressions really were or what really happened, after it's all over. All I know is the lights went out, and that flashlight went whirling round, dazzling us all, and then the shots were fired and I thought to myself, If that damned young fool Patrick Simmons is playing his jokes with a loaded revolver, somebody will get hurt."

"You thought it was Patrick Simmons."

"Well, it seemed likely. Edmund Swettenham is intellectual and writes books and doesn't care for horseplay, and old Colonel Easterbrook wouldn't think that sort of thing funny. But Patrick's a wild boy. However, I apologize to him for the idea."

"Did your friend think it might be Patrick Simmons?"

"Murgatroyd? You'd better talk to her yourself. Not that you'll get any sense out of her. She's down in the orchard. I'll yell for her if you like."

Miss Hinchliffe raised her stentorian voice in a powerful bellow:

"Hi-youp, Murgatroyd!"

"Coming—" floated back a thin cry.

"Hurry up—poleece!" bellowed Miss Hinchliffe.

Miss Murgatroyd arrived at a brisk trot, very much out of breath. Her skirt was down at the hem and her hair was escaping from an inadequate hairnet. Her round good-natured face beamed.

"Is it Scotland Yard?" she asked breathlessly. "I'd no idea, or I wouldn't have left the house."

"We haven't called in Scotland Yard yet, Miss Murgatroyd. I'm Inspector Craddock from Milchester."

"Well, that's very nice, I'm sure," said Miss Murgatroyd vaguely. "Have you found any clues?"

"Where were you at the time of the crime, that's what he wants to know, Murgatroyd," said Miss Hinchliffe. She winked at Craddock.

"Oh, dear," gasped Miss Murgatroyd. "Of course. I ought to have been prepared. Alibis, of course. Now, let me see, I was just with everybody else."

"You weren't with me," said Miss Hinchliffe.

"Oh, dear, Hinch, wasn't I? No, of course, I'd been admiring the chrysanthemums. Very poor specimens really. And then it all happened —only I didn't really know it had happened—I mean I didn't know that anything like that had happened. I didn't imagine for a moment it was a real revolver—and all so awkward in the dark, and that dreadful screaming. I got it all wrong, you know. I thought she was being murdered—I mean the refugee girl. I thought she was having her throat cut across the hall somewhere. I didn't know it was him—I mean I didn't even know there was a man. It was really just a voice, you know, saying, 'Put them up, please!' "

" 'Stick 'em up!' " Miss Hinchliffe corrected. "And no suggestion of 'please' about it."

"It's so terrible to think that until that girl started screaming I was actually enjoying myself. Only being in the dark was very awkward and I got a knock on my corn. Agony, it was. Is there anything more you want to know, Inspector?"

"No," said Inspector Craddock, eyeing Miss Murgatroyd speculatively. "I don't really think there is."

Her friend gave a short bark of laughter.

"He's got you taped, Murgatroyd."

"I'm sure, Hinch," said Miss Murgatroyd, "that I'm only too willing to say anything I can."

"He doesn't want that," said Miss Hinchliffe.

She looked at the Inspector. "If you're doing this geographically, I suppose you'll go to the vicarage next. You might get something there.

Mrs. Harmon looks as vague as they make them—but I sometimes think she's got brains. Anyway, she's got something."

As they watched the Inspector and Sergeant Fletcher stalk away, Amy Murgatroyd said breathlessly, "Oh, Hinch, was I very awful? I do get so flustered!"

"Not at all." Miss Hinchliffe smiled. "On the whole, I should say you did very well."

VI

Inspector Craddock looked round the big shabby room with a sense of pleasure. It reminded him a little of his own Cumberland home. Faded chintz, big shabby chairs, flowers and books strewn about and a spaniel in a basket. Mrs. Harmon, too, with her distraught air, her general disarray and her eager face he found sympathetic.

But she said at once, frankly, "I shan't be any help to you, because I shut my eyes. I hate being dazzled. And then there were shots and I screwed them up tighter than ever. And I did wish, oh, I did wish, that it had been a quiet murder. I don't like bangs."

"So you didn't see anything." The Inspector smiled at her. "But you heard—"

"Oh, my goodness, yes, there was plenty to hear. Doors opening and shutting, and people saying silly things and gasping and old Mitzi screaming like a steam-engine—and poor Bunny squealing like a trapped pig. And everyone pushing and falling over everyone else. However, when there really didn't seem to be any more bangs coming, I opened my eyes. Everyone was out in the hall then, with candles. And then the lights came on and suddenly it was all as usual—I don't mean really as usual, but we were ourselves again, not just—people in the dark. People in the dark are quite different, aren't they?"

"I think I know what you mean, Mrs. Harmon."

Mrs. Harmon smiled at him.

"And there he was," she said. "A rather weasely looking foreigner—all pink and surprised-looking—lying there dead—with a revolver beside him. It didn't—oh, it didn't seem to make sense somehow."

It did not make sense to the Inspector either. . . .

The whole business worried him.

8. *Enter Miss Marple*

CRADDOCK laid the typed transcript of the various interviews before the Chief Constable. The latter had just finished reading the wire received from the Swiss police.

"So he had a police record all right," said Rydesdale. "Hm—very much as one thought."

"Yes, sir."

"Jewelry . . . hm, yes . . . falsified entries . . . yes . . . check. Definitely a dishonest fellow."

"Yes, sir—in a small way."

"Quite so. And small things lead to large things."

"I wonder, sir."

The Chief Constable looked up.

"Worried, Craddock?"

"Yes, sir."

"Why? It's a straightforward story. Or isn't it? Let's see what all these people you've been talking to have to say."

He drew the report towards him and read it through rapidly.

"The usual thing—plenty of inconsistencies and contradictions. Different people's accounts of a few moments of stress never agree. But the main picture seems clear enough."

"I know, sir—but it's an unsatisfactory picture. If you know what I mean—it's the wrong picture."

"Well, let's take the facts. Rudi Scherz took the 5:20 bus from Medenham to Chipping Cleghorn, arriving there at six o'clock. Evidence of conductor and two passengers. From the bus stop he walked away in the direction of Little Paddocks. He got into the house with no particular difficulty—probably through the front door. He held up the company with a revolver, he fired two shots, one of which slightly wounded Miss Blacklock; he then killed himself with a third shot, whether accidentally or deliberately there is not sufficient evidence to show. The reasons why he did all this are profoundly unsatisfactory, I agree. But why isn't really a question we are called upon to answer. A coroner's jury may bring it in suicide—or accidental death. Whichever verdict it is, it's the same as far as we're concerned. We can write finis."

"You mean we can always fall back upon Colonel Easterbrook's psychology," said Craddock gloomily.

Rydesdale smiled.

"After all, the colonel's probably had a good deal of experience," he said. "I'm pretty sick of the psychological jargon that's used so glibly about everything nowadays—but we can't really rule it out."

"I still feel the picture's all wrong, sir."

"Any reason to believe that somebody in the setup at Chipping Cleghorn is lying to you?"

Craddock hesitated.

"I think the foreign girl knows more than she lets on. But that may be just prejudice on my part."

"You think she might possibly have been in it with this fellow? Let him into the house? Put him up to it?"

"Something of the kind. I wouldn't put it past her. But that surely indicates that there really was something valuable, money or jewelry, in the house, and that doesn't seem to have been the case. Miss Blacklock negatived it quite decidedly. So did the others. That leaves us with the proposition that there was something valuable in the house that nobody knew about—"

"Quite a best-seller plot."

"I agree it's ridiculous, sir. The only other point is Miss Bunner's certainty that it was a definite attempt by Scherz to murder Miss Blacklock."

"Well, from what you say—and from her statement—this Miss Bunner—"

"Oh, I agree, sir," Craddock put in quickly, "she's an utterly unreliable witness. Highly suggestible. Anyone could put a thing into her head —but the interesting thing is that this is quite her own theory—no one has suggested it to her. Everybody else negatives it. For once she's not swimming with the tide. It definitely is her own impression."

"And why should Rudi Scherz want to kill Miss Blacklock?"

"There you are, sir. I don't know. Miss Blacklock doesn't know— unless she's a much better liar than I think she is. Nobody knows. So presumably it isn't true."

He sighed.

"Cheer up, Craddock," said the Chief Constable. "I'm taking you off to lunch with Sir Henry and myself. The best that the Royal Spa Hotel in Medenham Wells can provide."

"Thank you, sir." Craddock looked slightly surprised.

"You see, we received a letter—" He broke off as Sir Henry Clithering entered the room. "Ah, there you are, Henry."

Sir Henry, informal this time, said, "Morning, Dermot."

"I've got something for you, Henry," said the Chief Constable.

"What's that?"

"Authentic letter from an old pussy. Staying at the Royal Spa Hotel. Something she thinks we might like to know in connection with this Chipping Cleghorn business."

"The old pussies," said Sir Henry triumphantly. "What did I tell you? They hear everything. They see everything. And, unlike the famous adage, they speak all evil. What's this particular one got hold of?"

Rydesdale consulted the letter.

"Writes just like my old grandmother," he complained. "Spiky. Like a spider in the ink bottle, and all underlined. A good deal about how she hopes it won't be taking up our valuable time, but might possibly be of some slight assistance etc., etc. What's her name? Jane—something—Murple—no, Marple, Jane Marple."

"Ye gods and little fishes," said Sir Henry, "can it be? George, it's my own particular, one and only, four-starred pussy. The super-pussy of all old pussies. And she has managed somehow to be at Medenham Wells, instead of peacefully at home in St. Mary Mead, just at the right time to be mixed up in a murder. Once more a murder is announced—for the benefit and enjoyment of Miss Marple."

"Well, Henry," said Rydesdale sardonically. "I'll be glad to see your paragon. Come on! We'll lunch at the Royal Spa and we'll interview the lady. Craddock, here, is looking highly skeptical."

"Not at all, sir," said Craddock politely.

He thought to himself that sometimes his godfather carried things a bit far.

II

Miss Jane Marple was very nearly, if not quite, as Craddock had pictured her. She was far more benignant then he had imagined and a good deal older. Indeed she seemed very old. She had snow-white hair and a pink, crinkled face and very soft, innocent blue eyes, and she was heavily enmeshed in fleecy wool. Wool round her shoulders in the form of a lacy cape and wool that she was knitting and which turned out to be a baby's shawl.

She was all incoherent delight and pleasure at seeing Sir Henry, and became quite flustered when introduced to the Chief Constable and Detective Inspector Craddock.

"But really, Sir Henry, how fortunate . . . how very fortunate. So long since I have seen you . . . Yes, my rheumatism. Very bad of late. Of course, I couldn't have afforded this hotel (really fantastic what they charge nowadays), but Raymond—my nephew, Raymond West, you may remember him—"

"Everyone knows his name."

"Yes, the dear boy has been so successful with his clever books. The last one was the Book Society choice—quite the worst one he has written, actually, but I do think that is so often the case, don't you? The dear boy insisted on paying all my expenses. And his dear wife is making a name for herself, too, as an artist. Mostly jugs of dying flowers and broken combs on windowsills. I never dare tell her, but I still admire Blair Leighton and Alma-Tadema. Oh, but I'm chattering. And the Chief Constable himself—indeed I never expected—so afraid I shall be taking up his time—"

Completely ga-ga, thought the disgusted Detective Inspector Craddock.

"Come into the manager's private room," said Rydesdale. "We can talk better there."

When Miss Marple had been disentangled from her wool and her spare knitting-pins collected, she accompanied them, fluttering and protesting, to Mr. Rowlandson's comfortable sitting room.

"Now, Miss Marple, let's hear what you have to tell us," said the Chief Constable.

Miss Marple came to the point with unexpected brevity.

"It was a check," she said. "He altered it."

"He?"

"The young man at the desk here, the one who is supposed to have staged that holdup and shot himself."

"He altered a check, you say?"

Miss Marple nodded.

"Yes. I have it here." She extracted it from her bag and laid it on the table. "It came this morning with my others from the bank. You can see, it was for seven pounds, and he altered it to seventeen. A stroke in front of the seven, and *teen* added after the word seven with a nice artistic little blot just blurring the whole word. Really, very nicely done. A certain amount of practice, I should say. It's the same ink, because I wrote the check actually at the desk. I should think he'd done it quite often before, wouldn't you?"

"He picked the wrong person to do it to, this time," remarked Sir Henry.

Miss Marple nodded agreement.

"Yes. I'm afraid he would never have gone very far in crime. I was quite the wrong person. Some busy young married woman, or some girl having a love affair—that's the kind who write checks for all sorts of different sums and don't really look through their passbooks carefully. But an old woman who has to be careful of the pennies, and who has formed habits—that's quite the wrong person to choose. Seventeen pounds is a sum I never write a check for. Twenty pounds, a round sum, for the monthly wages and books. And for my personal expenditure I usually cash seven—it used to be five, but everything has gone up so."

"And perhaps he reminded you of someone?" prompted Sir Henry, mischief in his eye.

Miss Marple smiled and shook her head at him.

"You are very naughty, Sir Henry. As a matter of fact he did. Fred Tyler, at the fish shop. Always slipped an extra one in the shillings column. Eating so much fish as we do nowadays, it made a long bill, and lots of people never added it up. Just ten shillings in his pocket every time; not much but enough to get himself a few neckties and take Jessie Spragg (the girl in the draper's) to the pictures. Cut a splash, that's what these young fellows want to do. Well, the very first week I was here, there was a mistake in my bill. I pointed it out to the young man and he apologized very nicely and looked very much upset; but I thought to myself then, You've got a shifty eye, young man.

"What I mean by a shifty eye," continued Miss Marple, "is the kind that looks very straight at you and never looks away nor blinks."

Craddock gave a sudden movement of appreciation. He thought to himself, Jim Kelly to the life, remembering a notorious swindler he had helped to put behind bars not long ago.

"Rudi Scherz was a thoroughly unsatisfactory character," said Rydesdale. "He's got a police record in Switzerland, we find."

"Made the place too hot for him, I suppose, and came over here with forged papers?" said Miss Marple.

"Exactly," said Rydesdale.

"He was going about with the little red-haired waitress from the dining-room," said Miss Marple. "Fortunately I don't think her heart's affected at all. She just liked to have someone a bit different, and he used to give her flowers and chocolates, which the English boys don't do much. Has she told you all she knows?" she asked, turning suddenly to Craddock. "Or not quite all yet?"

"I'm not absolutely sure," said Craddock cautiously.

"I think there's a little to come," said Miss Marple. "She's looking very worried. Brought me kippers instead of herrings this morning, and forgot the milk jug. Usually she's an excellent waitress. Yes, she's worried. Afraid she might have to give evidence or something like that. But I expect"—her candid blue eyes swept over the manly proportions and handsome face of Detective Inspector Craddock with truly feminine Victorian appreciation—"that you will be able to persuade her to tell you all she knows."

Detective Inspector Craddock blushed and Sir Henry chuckled.

"It might be important," said Miss Marple. "He may have told her who it was."

Rydesdale stared at her.

"Who what was?"

"I express myself so badly. Who it was who put him up to it, I mean."

"So you think someone put him up to it?"

Miss Marple's eyes widened in surprise.

"Oh, but surely—I mean—Here's a personable young man—who filches a little bit here and a little bit there—alters a small check, perhaps helps himself to a small piece of jewelry if it's left lying around or takes a little money from the till—all sorts of small, petty thefts. Keeps himself going in ready money so that he can dress well and take a girl about—all that sort of thing. And then, suddenly, he goes off with a revolver, holds up a roomful of people and shoots at someone. He'd never have done a thing like that—not for a moment! He wasn't that kind of person. It doesn't make sense."

Craddock drew in his breath sharply. That was what Letitia Blacklock had said. What the vicar's wife had said. What he himself felt with increasing force. *It didn't make sense.* And now Sir Henry's old pussy was saying it, too, with complete certainty in her fluting old lady's voice.

"Perhaps you'll tell us, Miss Marple," he said, and his voice was suddenly aggressive, "what did happen, then?"

She turned on him in surprise.

"But how should I know what happened? There was an account in the paper—but it says so little. One can make conjectures, of course, but one has no accurate information."

"George," said Sir Henry, "would it be very unorthodox if Miss Marple were allowed to read the notes of the interviews Craddock had with these people at Chipping Cleghorn?"

"It may be unorthodox," said Rydesdale, "but I've not got where I am by being orthodox. She can read them. I'd be curious to hear what she has to say."

Miss Marple was all embarrassment.

"I'm afraid you've been listening to Sir Henry. Sir Henry is always too kind. He thinks too much of any little observations I may have made in the past. Really, I have no gifts—no gifts at all—except perhaps a certain knowledge of human nature. People, I find, are apt to be far too trustful. I'm afraid that I have a tendency always to believe the worst. Not a nice trait, but so often justified by subsequent events."

"Read these," said Rydesdale, thrusting the typewritten sheets upon her. "They won't take you long. After all, these people are your kind—you must know a lot of people like them. You may be able to spot something that we haven't. The case is just going to be closed. Let's have an amateur's opinion on it before we shut up the files. I don't mind telling you that Craddock here isn't satisfied. He says, like you, that it doesn't make sense."

There was silence whilst Miss Marple read. She put the typewritten sheets down at last.

"It's very interesting," she said with a sigh. "All the different things that people say—and think. The things they see—or think that they see. And all so complex, nearly all so trivial and if one thing isn't trivial, it's so hard to spot which one—like a needle in a haystack."

Craddock felt a twinge of disappointment. Just for a moment or two, he had wondered if Sir Henry might be right about this funny old lady. She might have put her finger on something—old people were often very sharp. He'd never, for instance, been able to conceal anything from his own great aunt Emma. She had finally told him that his nose twitched when he was about to tell a lie.

But just a few fluffy generalities, that was all that Sir Henry's famous Miss Marple could produce. He felt annoyed with her and said rather curtly, "The truth of the matter is that the facts are indisputable. Whatever conflicting details these people give, they all saw one thing. They saw a masked man with a revolver and a flashlight open the door and hold them up, and whether they think he said, 'Stick 'em up,' or 'Your money or your life,' or whatever phrase is associated with a holdup in their minds, they saw him."

"But surely," said Miss Marple gently. "They couldn't—actually—have seen anything at all . . ."

Craddock caught his breath. She'd got it! She was sharp, after all. He was testing her by that speech of his, but she hadn't fallen for it. It didn't actually make any difference to the facts, or to what happened, but she'd realized, as he had, that those people who had seen a masked man holding them up couldn't really have seen him at all.

"If I understand rightly," Miss Marple had a pink flush on her cheeks, her eyes were bright and pleased as a child's, "there wasn't any light in the hall outside—and not on the landing upstairs either?"

"That's right," said Craddock.

"And so, if a man stood in the doorway and flashed a powerful light in the room, *nobody could see anything but that light,* could they?"

"No, they couldn't. I tried it out."

"And so when some of them say they saw a masked man, et cetera, they are really, though they don't realize it, recapitulating from what they saw afterwards—when the lights came on. So it all fits in very well, doesn't it, on the assumption that Rudi Scherz was the—I think 'fall guy' is the expression I mean?"

Rydesdale stared at her in such surprise that she grew pinker still.

"I may have got the term wrong," she murmured. "I am not very clever about Americanisms—and I understand they change very quickly. I got it from one of Mr. Dashiell Hammett's stories. (I understand from my nephew Raymond that he is considered at the top of the tree in what is called the tough style of literature.) A 'fall guy,' if I understand it rightly, means someone who will be blamed for a crime really committed by someone else. This Rudi Scherz seems to me exactly the right type for that. Rather stupid really, you know, but full of cupidity and probably extremely credulous."

Rydesdale said, smiling tolerantly, "Are you suggesting that he was persuaded by someone to go out and take pot shots at a roomful of people? Rather a tall order."

"I think he was told that it was a joke," said Miss Marple. "He was paid for doing it, of course. Paid, that is, to put an advertisement in the newspaper, to go out and spy out the household premises and then, on the night in question, he was to go there, assume a mask and a black cloak and throw open a door, brandish a flashlight and cry, 'Hands up!' "

"And fire off a revolver?"

"No, no," said Miss Marple. "He never had a revolver."

"But everyone says—" began Rydesdale, and stopped.

"Exactly," said Miss Marple. "Nobody could possibly have seen a revolver even if he had one. And I don't think he had. I think that after he'd called, 'Hands up,' somebody came up quietly behind him in the darkness and fired those two shots over his shoulder. It frightened him to death. He swung around and as he did so, that other person shot him and then let the revolver drop beside him . . . ."

The three men looked at her. Sir Henry said softly, "It's a possible theory."

"But who is Mr. X who came up in the darkness?" asked the Chief Constable.

Miss Marple coughed.

"You'll have to find out from Miss Blacklock who wanted to kill her."

Good for old Dora Bunner, thought Craddock. Instinct against intelligence every time.

"So you think it was a deliberate attempt on Miss Blacklock's life?" asked Rydesdale.

"It certainly has that appearance," said Miss Marple. "Though there are one or two difficulties. But what I was really wondering about was whether there mightn't be a short cut. I've no doubt that whoever arranged this with Rudi Scherz took pains to tell him to keep his mouth shut about it, and perhaps he did keep his mouth shut; but if he talked to anybody it would probably be to that girl, Myrna Harris. And he may—he just may—have dropped some hint as to the kind of person who'd suggested the whole thing."

"I'll see her now," said Craddock, rising.

Miss Marple nodded.

"Yes, do Inspector Craddock. I'll feel happier when you have. Because once she's told you anything she knows she'll be much safer."

"Safer? Yes, I see."

He left the room. The Chief Constable said doubtfully, but tactfully, "Well, Miss Marple, you've certainly given us something to think about."

III

"I'm sorry about it, I am really," said Myrna Harris. "It's ever so nice of you not to be ratty about it. But you see Mum's the sort of person who fusses like anything. And it did look as though I'd—what's the phrase—been an accessory before the fact." (The words ran glibly off her tongue.) "I mean, I was afraid you'd never take my word for it that I only thought it was just a bit of fun."

Inspector Craddock repeated the reassuring phrases with which he had broken down Myrna's resistance.

"I will. I'll tell you all about it. But you will keep me out of it if you can because of Mum? It all started with Rudi breaking a date with me. We were going to the pictures that evening and then he said he wouldn't be able to come and I was a bit standoffish with him about it—because, after all, it had been his idea and I don't fancy being stood up by a foreigner. And he said it wasn't his fault, and I said that was a likely story, and then he said he'd got a bit of a lark on that night—and that he wasn't going to be out of pocket by it and how would I fancy a wristwatch? So I said what did he mean by a lark? And he said not to tell anyone, but there was to be a party somewhere and he was to stage a sham holdup. Then he showed me the advertisement he'd put in and I had to laugh. He was a bit scornful about it all. Said it was kids' stuff really—but that was just like the English. They never really grew up— and of course I said what did he mean by talking like that about us—and we had a bit of an argument, but we made it up. Only you can understand, can't you, sir, that when I read all about it, and it hadn't been a joke at all and Rudi had shot someone and then shot himself—why, I didn't know what to do. I thought if I said I knew about it beforehand, it would look as though I were in on the whole thing. But it really did seem like a joke when he told me about it. I'd have sworn he meant it that way. I didn't even know he'd got a revolver. He never said anything about taking a revolver with him."

Craddock comforted her and then asked the most important question.

"Who did he say it was who had arranged this party?"

But there he drew a blank.

"He never said who it was that was getting him to do it. I suppose nobody was, really. It was all his own doing."

"He didn't mention a name? Did he say he—or she?"

"He didn't say anything except that it was going to be a scream. 'I shall laugh to see all their faces.' That's what he said."

He hadn't had long to laugh, Craddock thought.

IV

"It is only a theory," said Rydesdale as they drove back to Medenham. "Nothing to support it, nothing at all. Put it down as old maid's vaporings and let it go, eh?"

"I'd rather not do that, sir."

"It's all very improbable. A mysterious X appearing suddenly in the darkness behind our Swiss friend. Where did he come from? Who was he? Where had he been?"

"He could have come in through the side door," said Craddock, "just as Scherz came. Or," he added slowly, "he could have come from the kitchen."

"She could have come from the kitchen, you mean?"

"Yes, sir, it's a possibility. I've not been satisfied about that girl all along. She strikes me as a nasty bit of goods. All that screaming and hysterics—it could have been put on. She could have worked on this young fellow, let him in at the right moment, rigged the whole thing, shot him, bolted back into the dining-room, caught up her bit of silver and her chamois and started her screaming act."

"Against that we have the fact that—er—What's-his-name—oh, yes, Edmund Swettenham, definitely says the key was turned on the outside of the door, and that he turned it to release her. Any other door into that part of the house?"

"Yes, there's a door to the back stairs and kitchen just under the stairs, but it seems the handle came off three weeks ago and nobody's come to put it on yet. In the meantime, you can't open the door. I'm bound to say that story seems correct. The spindle and the two handles were on a shelf outside the door in the hall and they were thickly coated with dust, but, of course, a professional would have ways of opening that door all right."

"Better look up the girl's record. See if her papers are in order. But it seems to me the whole thing is very theoretical."

Again the Chief Constable looked inquiringly at his subordinate. Craddock replied quietly, "I know, sir, and, of course, if you think the case ought to be closed, it must be. But I'd appreciate it if I could work on it for just a little longer."

Rather to his surprise the Chief Constable said quietly and approvingly, "Good lad."

"There's the revolver to work on. If this theory is correct, it wasn't Scherz's revolver and certainly nobody so far has been able to say that Scherz ever had a revolver."

"It's a German make."

"I know, sir. But this country's absolutely full of continental makes of guns. All the Americans brought them back and so did our chaps. You can't go by that."

"True enough. Any other lines of inquiry?"

"There's got to be a motive. If there's anything in this theory at all, it means that last Friday's business wasn't a mere joke and wasn't an ordinary holdup; it was a cold-blooded attempt at murder. Somebody tried to murder Miss Blacklock. Now why? It seems to me that if anyone knows the answer to that, it must be Miss Blacklock herself."

"I understand she rather poured cold water on that idea?"

"She poured cold water on the idea that Rudi Scherz wanted to murder her. And she was quite right. And there's another thing, sir."

"Yes?"

"Somebody might try again."

"That would certainly prove the truth of the theory," said the Chief Constable dryly. "By the way, look after Miss Marple, won't you?"

"Miss Marple? Why?"

"I gather she is taking up residence at the vicarage in Chipping Cleghorn and coming into Medenham Wells twice a week for her treatments. It seems that Mrs. What's-her-name is the daughter of an old friend of Miss Marple's. Good sporting instincts, that old bean. Oh, well, I suppose she hasn't much excitement in her life and sniffing round after possible murderers gives her a kick."

"I wish she wasn't coming," said Craddock seriously.

"Going to get under your feet?"

"Not that, sir, but she's a nice old thing. I shouldn't like anything to happen to her . . . always supposing, I mean, that there's anything in this theory."

9. *Concerning a Door*

"I'M SORRY to bother you again, Miss Blacklock—"

"Oh, it doesn't matter. I suppose, as the inquest was adjourned for a week, you're hoping to get more evidence?"

Detective Inspector Craddock nodded.

"To begin with, Miss Blacklock, Rudi Scherz was not the son of the proprietor of the Hôtel des Alpes at Montreux. He seems to have started his career as an orderly in a hospital at Berne. A good many of the patients missed small pieces of jewelry. Under another name he was a waiter at one of the small winter sports places. His specialty there was making out duplicate bills in the restaurant with items on one that didn't appear on the other. The difference, of course, went into his pocket. After that he was in a department store in Zürich. Their losses from shoplifting were rather above the average while he was with them. It seems likely that the shoplifting wasn't entirely due to customers."

"He was a picker-up of unconsidered trifles, in fact?" said Miss Blacklock dryly. "Then I was right in thinking that I had not seen him before?"

"You were quite right. No doubt you were pointed out to him at the Royal Spa Hotel and he pretended to recognize you. The Swiss police had begun to make his own country rather too hot for him, and he came over here with a very nice set of forged papers and took a job at the Royal Spa."

"Quite a good hunting ground," said Miss Blacklock dryly. "It's extremely expensive and very well off people stay there. Some of them are careless about their bills, I expect."

"Yes," said Craddock. "There were prospects of a satisfactory harvest."

Miss Blacklock was frowning.

"I see all that," she said. "But why come to Chipping Cleghorn? What does he think we've got here that could possibly be better than the rich Royal Spa Hotel?"

"You stick to your statement that there's nothing of especial value in the house?"

"Of course there isn't. I should know. I can assure you, Inspector, we've not got an unrecognized Rembrandt or anything like that."

"Then it looks, doesn't it, as though your friend Miss Bunner were right? He came here to attack you."

("There, Letty, what did I tell you!" "Oh, nonsense, Bunny.")

"But is it nonsense?" said Craddock. "I think, you know, that it's true."

Miss Blacklock stared very hard at him.

"Now let's get this straight. You really believe that this young man came out here—having previously arranged by means of an advertisement that half the village would turn up agog—at that particular time—"

"But he mayn't have meant that to happen," interrupted Miss Bunner eagerly. "It may have been just a horrid sort of warning—to you, Letty— that's how I read it at the time. 'A murder is announced.' I felt in my bones that it was sinister—if it had all gone as planned he would have shot you and got away—and how would anyone have ever known who it was?"

"That's true enough," said Miss Blacklock. "But—"

"I knew that advertisement wasn't a joke, Letty. I said so. And look at Mitzi—she was frightened, too!"

"Ah," said Craddock, "Mitzi. I'd like to know rather more about that young woman."

"Her permit and papers are quite in order."

"I don't doubt that," said Craddock dryly. "Scherz's papers appeared to be quite correct, too."

"But why should this Rudi Scherz want to murder me? That's what you don't attempt to explain, Inspector Craddock."

"There may have been someone behind Scherz," said Craddock slowly. "Have you thought of that?"

He used the words metaphorically though it flashed across his mind that if Miss Marple's theory was correct, the words would also be true in a literal sense. In any case, they made little impression on Miss Blacklock who still looked skeptical.

"The point remains the same," she said. "Why on earth should anyone want to murder me?"

"It's the answer to that that I want you to give me, Miss Blacklock."

"Well, I can't! That's flat. I've no enemies. As far as I'm aware I've always lived on perfectly good terms with my neighbors. I don't know any guilty secrets about anyone. The whole idea is ridiculous! And if what you're hinting is that Mitzi has something to do with this, that's absurd, too. As Miss Bunner has just told you, she was frightened to death when she saw that advertisement in the *Gazette*. She actually wanted to pack up and leave the house then and there."

"That may have been a clever move on her part. She may have known you'd press her to stay."

"Of course, if you've made up your mind about it, you'll find an answer to everything. But I can assure you that if Mitzi had taken an unreasoning dislike to me, she might conceivably poison my food, but I'm sure she wouldn't go in for all this elaborate rigmarole.

"The whole idea's absurd. I believe you police have got an anti-foreigner complex. Mitzi may be a liar but she's not a cold-blooded murderer. Go and bully her if you must. But when she's departed in a whirl of indignation, or shut herself up howling in her room, I've a good mind to make you cook the dinner. Mrs. Harmon is bringing some old lady who is staying with her to tea this afternoon and I wanted Mitzi to make some little cakes—but I suppose you'll upset her completely. Can't you possibly go and suspect somebody else?"

II

Craddock went out to the kitchen. He asked Mitzi questions that he had asked her before and received the same answers.

Yes, she had locked the front door soon after four o'clock. No, she did not always do so, but that afternoon she had been nervous because of "that dreadful advertisement." It was no good locking the side door because Miss Blacklock and Miss Bunner went out that way to shut up the ducks and feed the chickens and Mrs. Haymes usually came in that way from work.

"Mrs. Haymes says she locked the door when she came in at 5:30."

"Ah, and you believe her—oh, yes, you believe her—"

"Do you think we shouldn't believe her?"

"What does it matter what I think? You will not believe me."

"Supposing you give us a chance. You think Mrs. Haymes didn't lock that door?"

"I think she was very careful not to lock it."

"What do you mean by that?" asked Craddock.

"That young man, he does not work alone. No, he knows where to come, he knows that when he comes a door will be left open for him—oh, very conveniently open!"

"What are you trying to say?"

"What is the use of what I say? You will not listen. You say I am a poor refugee girl who tell lies. You say that a fair-haired English lady, oh, no, she does not tell lies—she is so British—so honest. So you believe her and not me. But I could tell you. Oh, yes, I could tell you!"

She banged down a saucepan on the stove.

Craddock was in two minds whether to take notice of what might be only a stream of spite.

"We note everything we are told," he said.

"I shall not tell you anything at all. Why should I? You are all alike. You persecute and despise poor refugees. If I say to you that when, a week before, that young man comes to ask Miss Blacklock for money and she sends him away, as you say, with a flea in the ear—if I tell you that after that I hear him talking with Mrs. Haymes—yes, out there in the summer-house—all you say is that I make it up!"

And so you probably are making it up, thought Craddock. But he said aloud, "You couldn't hear what was said out in the summer-house."

"There you are wrong," screamed Mitzi triumphantly. "I go out to get nettles—it makes very nice vegetables, nettles. They do not think so, but I cook it and not tell them. And I hear them talking in there. He say to her, 'But where can I hide?' And she say, 'I will show you'—and then she say, 'At a quarter past six,' and I think, *Ach,* so that is how you behave, my fine lady! After you come back from work, you go out to meet a man. You bring him into the house. Miss Blacklock, I think, she will not like that. She will turn you out. I will watch, I think, and listen and then I will tell Miss Blacklock. But I understand now I was wrong. It was not love she planned with him, it was to rob and to murder. But you will say I make all this up. Wicked Mitzi, you will say. I will take her to prison."

Craddock wondered. She might be making it up. But possibly she might not. He asked cautiously, "You are sure it was this Rudi Scherz she was talking to?"

"Of course I am sure. He just leave and I see him go from the drive across to the summer-house. And presently," said Mitzi defiantly, "I go out to see if there are any nice young green nettles."

Would there, the Inspector wondered, be any nice young green nettles in October? But he appreciated that Mitzi had had to produce a hurried reason for what had undoubtedly been nothing more than plain snooping.

"You didn't hear any more than what you have told me?"

Mitzi looked aggrieved.

"That Miss Bunner, the one with the long nose, she call and call me. 'Mitzi! Mitzi!' So I have to go. Oh, she is irritating. Always interfering. Says she will teach me to cook. Her cooking! It tastes, yes, everything does, of water, water, water!"

"Why didn't you tell me this the other day?" asked Craddock sternly.

"Because I did not remember—I did not think . . . Only afterwards do I say to myself, it was planned then—planned with her."

"You are quite sure it was Mrs. Haymes?"

"Oh, yes, I am sure. Oh, yes, I am very sure. She is a thief, that Mrs. Haymes. A thief and the associate of thieves. What she gets for working in the garden, it is not enough for such a fine lady, no. She has to rob Miss Blacklock who has been kind to her. Oh, she is bad, bad, bad, that one!"

"Supposing," said the Inspector, watching her closely, "that someone was to say that you had been seen talking to Rudi Scherz?"

The suggestion had less effect than he had hoped for. Mitzi merely snorted and tossed her head.

"If anyone they see me talking to him, that is lies, lies, lies, lies," she said contemptuously. "To tell lies about anyone, that is easy, but in England you have to prove them true. Miss Blacklock tell me that, and it is true, is it not? I do not speak with murderers and thieves. And no English policeman shall say I do. And how can I do cooking for lunch if you are here, talk, talk, talk? Go out of my kitchens, please. I want now to make a very careful sauce."

Craddock went obediently. He was a little shaken in his suspicions of Mitzi. Her story about Phillipa Haymes had been told with great conviction. Mitzi might be a liar (he thought she was), but he fancied that there might be some substratum of truth in this particular tale. He resolved to speak to Phillipa on the subject. She had seemed to him, when he questioned her, a quiet, well-bred young woman. He had had no suspicion of her.

Crossing the hall, in his abstraction he tried to open the wrong door. Miss Bunner, descending the staircase, hastily put him right.

"Not that door," she said. "It doesn't open. The next one to the left. Very confusing, isn't it? So many doors."

"There are a good many," said Craddock, looking up and down the narrow hall.

Miss Bunner amiably enumerated them for him.

"First, the door to the cloakroom, and then the cloaks cupboard door and then the dining-room—that's on that side. And on this side, the dummy door that you were trying to get through and then there's the drawing-room door proper, and then the china cupboard door and the door of the little flower room and at the end the side door. Most confusing. Especially these two being so near together. I've often tried the wrong one by mistake. We used to have the hall table against it, as a matter of fact, but then we moved it along against the wall there."

Craddock had noted, almost mechanically, a thin line horizontally across the panels of the door he had been trying to open. He realized now it was the mark where the table had been. Something stirred vaguely in his mind as he asked, "Moved? How long ago?"

In questioning Dora Bunner there was fortunately no need to give a reason for any questions. Any query on any subject seemed perfectly natural to the garrulous Miss Bunner, who delighted in the giving of information however trivial.

"Now let me see, really quite recently—ten days or a fortnight ago."

"Why was it moved?"

"I really can't remember. Something to do with the flowers. I think Phillipa did a big vase—she arranges flowers quite beautifully—all Autumn coloring and twigs and branches, and it was so big it caught your hair as you went past, and so Phillipa said, 'Why not move the table along and anyway the flowers would look much better against the bare wall than against the panels of the door.' Only we had to take down Wellington at Waterloo. Not a print I'm really very fond of. We put it under the stairs."

"It's not really a dummy, then?" Craddock asked, looking at the door.

"Oh, no, it's a real door, if that's what you mean. It's the door of the small drawing-room, but when the rooms were thrown into one, one didn't need two doors, so this one was fastened up."

"Fastened up?" Craddock tried it again gently. "You mean it's nailed up? Or just locked?"

"Oh, locked, I think, and bolted, too."

He saw the bolt at the top and tried it. The bolt slid back easily—too easily . . .

"When was it last opened?" he asked Miss Bunner.

"Oh, years and years ago, I imagine. It's never been opened since I've been here, I know that."

"You don't know where the key is?"

"There are a lot of keys in the hall table drawer. It's probably among those."

Craddock followed her and looked at a rusty assortment of old keys pushed far back in the drawer. He scanned them and selected one that looked different from the rest and went back to the door. The key fitted and turned easily. He pushed and the door slid open noiselessly.

"Oh, do be careful," cried Miss Bunner. "There may be something resting against it inside. We never open it."

"Don't you?" said the Inspector.

His face now was grim. He said with emphasis:

"This door's been opened quite recently, Miss Bunner. The lock's been oiled and the hinges."

She stared at him, her foolish face agape.

"But who could have done that?" she asked.

"That's what I mean to find out," said Craddock grimly. He thought—X from outside? No—X was here—in this house—X was in the drawing-room that night.

10. *Pip and Emma*

MISS BLACKLOCK listened to him this time with more attention. She was an intelligent woman, as he had known, and she grasped the implications of what he had to tell her.

"Yes," she said quietly, "that does alter things . . . No one had any right to meddle with that door. Nobody has meddled with it to my knowledge."

"You see what it means," the Inspector urged. "When the lights went out, anybody in this room the other night could have slipped out of that door, come up behind Rudi Scherz and fired at you."

"Without being seen or heard or noticed?"

"Without being seen or heard or noticed. Remember, when the lights went out people moved, exclaimed, bumped into each other. And after that all that could be seen was the blinding light of the flashlight."

Miss Blacklock said slowly, "And you believe that one of those people —one of my nice commonplace neighbors—slipped out and tried to murder me? Me? But why? For goodness' sake, why?"

"I've a feeling that you must know the answer to that question, Miss Blacklock."

"But I don't, Inspector. I can assure you I don't."

"Well, let's make a start. Who gets your money if you were to die?"

Miss Blacklock said rather reluctantly, "Patrick and Julia. I've left the furniture in this house and a small annuity to Bunny. Really I've not much to leave. I had holdings in German and Italian securities which became worthless, and what with taxation and the lower percentages that are now paid on invested capital, I can assure you I'm not worth murdering—I put most of my money into an annuity about a year ago."

"Still, you have some income, Miss Blacklock, and your nephew and niece would come into it."

"And so Patrick and Julia would plan to murder me? I simply don't believe it. They're not desperately hard up or anything like that."

"Do you know that for a fact?"

"No. I suppose I only know it from what they've told me . . . But I really refuse to suspect them. Some day I might be worth murdering, but not now."

"What do you mean by some day you might be worth murdering, Miss Blacklock?" Inspector Craddock pounced on the statement.

"Simply that one day—possibly quite soon—I may be a very rich woman."

"That sounds interesting. Will you explain?"

"Certainly. You may not know it, but for more than twenty years I was secretary to, and closely associated with, Randall Goedler."

Craddock was interested. Randall Goedler had been a big name in the world of finance. His daring speculations and the rather theatrical publicity with which he surrounded himself had made him a personality not quickly forgotten. He had died, if Craddock remembered rightly, in 1937 or 1938.

"He's rather before your time, I expect," said Miss Blacklock. "But you've probably heard of him."

"Oh, yes. He was a millionaire, wasn't he?"

"Oh, several times over—though his finances fluctuated. He always risked most of what he made on some new *coup.*"

She spoke with a certain animation, her eyes brightened by memory.

"Anyway, he died a very rich man. He had no children. He left his fortune in trust for his wife during her lifetime and after her death to me absolutely."

A vague memory stirred in the Inspector's mind.

IMMENSE FORTUNE TO COME TO FAITHFUL SECRETARY— something of that kind.

"For the last twelve years or so," said Miss Blacklock with a slight twinkle, "I've had an excellent motive for murdering Mrs. Goedler—but that doesn't help you, does it?"

"Did—excuse me for asking this—did Mrs. Goedler resent her husband's disposition of his fortune?"

Miss Blacklock was now looking frankly amused.

"You needn't be so very discreet. What you really mean is, was I Randall Goedler's mistress? No, I wasn't. I don't think Randall ever gave me a sentimental thought, and I certainly didn't give him one. He was in love with Belle (his wife), and remained in love with her until he died. I think in all probability it was gratitude on his part that prompted his making his will. You see, Inspector, in the very early days, when Randall was still on an insecure footing, he came very near to disaster. It was a question of just a few thousand of actual cash. It was a big *coup,* and a very exciting one; daring, as all his schemes were; but he just hadn't got that little bit of cash to tide him over. I came to the rescue. I had a little money of my own. I believed in Randall. I sold out every penny I had and gave it to him. It did the trick. A week later he was an immensely wealthy man.

"After that, he treated me more or less as a junior partner. Oh, they were exciting days!" She sighed. "I enjoyed it all thoroughly. Then my father died, and my only sister was left a hopeless invalid. I had to give it all up and go and look after her. Randall died a couple of years later. I had made quite a lot of money during our association and I didn't really expect him to leave me anything, but I was very touched, yes, and very proud, to find that if Belle predeceased me (and she was one of those delicate creatures whom everyone always says won't live long), I was to inherit his entire fortune. I really think the poor man didn't know who to leave it to. Belle's a dear, and she was delighted about it. She's really a very sweet person. She lives up in Scotland. I haven't seen her for years— we just write at Christmas. I went with my sister to a sanatorium in Switzerland just before the war. She died of consumption out there."

She was silent for a moment or two, then said, "I only came back to England just over a year ago."

"You said you might be a rich woman very soon. How soon?"

"I heard from the nurse attendant who looks after Belle Goedler that Belle is sinking rapidly. It may be—only a few weeks."

She added sadly, "The money won't mean much to me now. I've got quite enough still for my rather simple needs. Once I should have enjoyed playing the markets again—but now . . . Oh, well, one grows old. Still, you do see, Inspector, don't you, that if Patrick and Julia wanted to kill me for a financial reason they'd be crazy not to wait for another few weeks."

"Yes, Miss Blacklock, but what happens if you should predecease Mrs. Goedler? Who does the money go to then?"

"D'you know, I've never really thought. Pip and Emma, I suppose . . ."

Craddock stared and Miss Blacklock smiled.

"Does that sound rather crazy? I believe, if I predecease Belle, the money would go to the legal offspring—or whatever the term is—of Randall's only sister, Sonia. Randall had quarreled with his sister. She married a man whom he considered a crook and worse."

"And was he a crook?"

"Oh, definitely, I should say. But I believe a very attractive person to women. He was a Greek or a Romanian or something—what was his name now?—Stamfordis, Dmitri Stamfordis."

"Randall Goedler cut his sister out of his will when she married this man?"

"Oh, no! Sonia was a very wealthy woman in her own right. Randall had already settled packets of money on her, as far as possible in a way so that her husband couldn't touch it. But I believe that when the lawyers urged him to put in someone in case I predeceased Belle, he reluctantly put down Sonia's offspring, simply because he couldn't think of anyone else and he wasn't the sort of man to leave money to charities."

"And there were children of the marriage?"

"Well, there are Pip and Emma." She laughed. "I know it sounds ridiculous. All I know is that Sonia wrote once to Belle after her marriage, telling her to tell Randall that she was extremely happy and that she had just had twins and was calling them Pip and Emma. As far as I know she never wrote again. But Belle, of course, may be able to tell you more."

Miss Blacklock had been amused by her own recital. The Inspector did not look amused.

"It comes to this," he said. "If you had been killed the other night, there are presumably at least two people in the world who would have come into a very large fortune. You were wrong, Miss Blacklock, when you say that there is no one who had a motive for desiring your death. There are two people, at least, who are vitally interested. How old would this brother and sister be?"

Miss Blacklock frowned.

"Let me see . . . 1922 . . . no—it's difficult to remember . . . I suppose about twenty-five or twenty-six." Her face had sobered. "But you surely don't think—"

"I think somebody shot at you with the intent to kill you. I think it possible that that same person or persons might try again. I would like you, if you will, to be very, very careful, Miss Blacklock. One murder has been arranged and did not come off. I think it possible that another murder may be arranged very soon."

II

Phillipa Haymes straightened her back and pushed back a tendril of hair from her damp forehead. She was cleaning a flower border.

"Yes, Inspector?"

She looked at him inquiringly. In return he gave her a rather closer scrutiny than he had done before. Yes, a good-looking girl, a very English type with her pale ash-blond hair and her rather long face. An obstinate chin and mouth. Something of repression—of tautness about her. The eyes were blue, very steady in their glance, and told you nothing at all. The sort of girl, he thought, who would keep a secret well.

"I'm sorry always to bother you when you're at work, Mrs. Haymes," he said, "but I didn't want to wait until you came back for lunch. Besides, I thought it might be easier to talk to you here, away from Little Paddocks."

"Yes, Inspector?"

No emotion and little interest in the voice. But was there a note of wariness—or did he imagine it?

"A certain statement has been made to me this morning. This statement concerns you."

Phillipa raised her eyebrows very slightly.

"You told me, Mrs. Haymes, that this man Rudi Scherz was quite unknown to you?"

"Yes."

"That when you saw him there, dead, it was the first time you had set eyes on him. Is that so?"

"Certainly. I had never seen him before."

"You did not, for instance, have a conversation with him in the summer-house of Little Paddocks?"

"In the summer-house?"

He was almost sure he caught a note of fear in her voice.

"Yes, Mrs. Haymes."

"Who says so?"

"I am told that you had a conversation with this man Rudi Scherz, and that he asked you where he could hide and you replied you would show him, and that a time, a quarter past six, was definitely mentioned. It would be a quarter past six, roughly, when Scherz would get here from the bus stop on the evening of the holdup."

There was a moment's silence. Then Phillipa gave a short scornful laugh. She looked amused.

"I don't know who told you that," she said. "At least I can guess. It's a very silly clumsy story—spiteful, of course. For some reason Mitzi dislikes me even more than she dislikes the rest of us."

"You deny it?"

"Of course it's not true . . . I never met or saw Rudi Scherz in my life, and I was nowhere near the house that morning. I was over here working."

Inspector Craddock said very gently,

"Which morning?"

There was a momentary pause. Her eyelids flickered.

"Every morning. I'm here every morning. I don't get away until one o'clock."

She added scornfully, "It's no good listening to what Mitzi tells you. She tells lies all the time."

"And that's that," said Craddock, when he was walking away with Sergeant Fletcher. "Two young women whose stories flatly contradict each other. Which one am I to believe?"

"Everyone seems to agree that this foreign girl tells whoppers," said Fletcher. "It's been my experience in dealing with aliens that lying comes more easy than truth-telling. Seems to be clear she's got a spite against this Mrs. Haymes."

"So if you were me, you'd believe Mrs. Haymes?"

"Unless you've got reason to think otherwise, sir."

And Craddock hadn't, not really—only the remembrance of a pair of over-steady blue eyes and the glib enunciation of the words "that morning." For to the best of his recollection he hadn't said whether the interview in the summer-house had taken place in the morning or the afternoon.

Still, Miss Blacklock, or if not Miss Blacklock, certainly Miss Bunner, might have mentioned the visit of the young foreigner who had come to cadge his fare back to Switzerland. And Phillipa Haymes might have therefore assumed that the conversation was supposed to have taken place on that particular morning.

But Craddock still thought that there had been a note of fear in her voice as she asked, "In the summer-house?"

He decided to keep an open mind on the subject.

III

It was very pleasant in the vicarage garden. One of those sudden spells of Autumn warmth had descended upon England. Inspector Craddock could never remember if it was St. Martin's or St. Luke's Summer, but he knew that it was very pleasant—and also very enervating. He sat in a deck chair provided for him by an energetic Bunch, just on her way to a Mothers' Meeting, and, well protected with shawls and a large rug round her knees, Miss Marple sat knitting beside him. The sunshine, the peace, the steady click of Miss Marple's knitting-needles, all combined to produce a soporific feeling in the Inspector. And yet, at the same time, there was a nightmarish feeling at the back of his mind. It was like the familiar dream where an undertone of menace grows and finally turns ease into terror . . .

He said abruptly, "You oughtn't to be here."

Miss Marple's needles stopped clicking for a moment. Her placid china-blue eyes regarded him thoughtfully.

She said, "I know what you mean. You're a very conscientious boy. But it's perfectly all right. Bunch's father (he was rector of our parish, a very fine scholar) and her mother (who is a most remarkable woman—real spiritual power) are very old friends of mine. It's the most natural thing in the world that when I'm at Medenham I should come on here to stay with Bunch for a little."

"Oh, perhaps," said Craddock. "But—but don't snoop around . . . I've a feeling—I have really—that it isn't safe."

Miss Marple smiled a little.

"But I'm afraid," she said, "that we old women always do snoop. It would be very odd and much more noticeable if I didn't. Questions about mutual friends in different parts of the world and whether they remember so and so, and do they remember who it was that Lady Somebody's daughter married? All that helps, doesn't it?"

"Helps?" said the Inspector rather stupidly.

"Helps to find out if people are who they say they are," said Miss Marple.

She went on:

"Because that's what's worrying you, isn't it? And that's really the particular way the world has changed since the war. Take this place, Chipping Cleghorn, for instance. It's very much like St. Mary Mead where I live. Fifteen years ago one knew who everybody was. The Bantrys in the big house—and the Hartnels and the Price Ridleys and the Weatherbys . . . They were people whose fathers and mothers and grandfathers and grandmothers, or whose aunts and uncles, had lived there before them. If somebody new came to live there, they brought letters of introduction, or they'd been in the same regiment or served on the same ship as someone already there. If anybody new—really new—really a stranger—came, well, they stuck out—everybody wondered about them and didn't rest till they found out."

She nodded her head gently.

"But it's not like that any more. Every village and small country place is full of people who've just come and settled there without any ties to bring them. The big houses have been sold, and the cottages have been converted and changed. And people just come—and all you know about them is what they say of themselves. They've come, you see, from all over the world. People from India and Hong Kong and China, and people who used to live in France and Italy in little cheap places and odd islands. And people who've made a little money and can afford to retire. But nobody knows any more who anyone is. You can have Benares brassware in your house and talk about tiffin and *chota Hazri*—and you can have pictures of Taormina and talk about the English church and the library—like Miss Hinchliffe and Miss Murgatroyd. You can come from the South of France, or have spent your life in the East. People take you at your own valuation. They don't wait to call until they've had a letter from a friend saying that the So-and-So's are delightful people and she's known them all their lives."

And that, thought Craddock, was exactly what was oppressing him. He didn't know. There were just faces and personalities and they were backed up by ration books and identity cards—nice neat identity cards with numbers on them, without photographs or fingerprints. Anybody who took the trouble could have a suitable identity card—and partly because of that, the subtler links that had held English social rural life together had fallen apart. In a town nobody expected to know his neighbor. In the country now nobody knew his neighbor either, though possibly he still thought he did . . .

Because of the oiled door, Craddock knew that there had been somebody in Letitia Blacklock's drawing-room who was not the pleasant friendly country neighbor he or she pretended to be . . .

And because of that he was afraid for Miss Marple who was frail and old and who noticed things . . .

He said: "We can, to a certain extent, check up on these people . . ." But he knew that that wasn't so easy. India and China and Hong Kong and the South of France . . . It wasn't as easy as it would have been fifteen years ago. There were people, as he knew only too well, who were going about the country with borrowed identities—borrowed from people who had met sudden death by "incidents" in the cities. There were organizations who bought up identities, who faked identity cards and ration books—there were a hundred small rackets springing into being. You could check up—but it would take time—and time was what he hadn't got, because Randall Goedler's widow was very near death.

It was then that, worried and tired, lulled by the sunshine, he told Miss Marple about Randall Goedler and Pip and Emma.

"Just a couple of names," he said. "Nicknames at that! They mayn't exist. They may be respectable citizens living in Europe somewhere. On the other hand, one, or both, of them may be here in Chipping Cleghorn . . ."

Twenty-five years old approximately—who filled that description? He said, thinking aloud:

"That nephew and niece of hers—or cousins, or whatever they are . . . I wonder when she saw them last—"

Miss Marple said gently, "I'll find out for you, shall I?"

"Now, please, Miss Marple, don't—"

"It will be quite simple, Inspector; you really need not worry. And it won't be noticeable if I do it, because, you see, it won't be official. If there is anything wrong you don't want to put them on their guard."

Pip and Emma, thought Craddock, Pip and Emma? He was getting obsessed by Pip and Emma. That attractive dare-devil young man, the good-looking girl with the cool stare . . .

He said: "I may find out more about them in the next forty-eight hours. I'm going up to Scotland. Mrs. Goedler, if she's able to talk, may know a good deal more about them."

"I think that's a very wise move." Miss Marple hesitated. "I hope," she murmured, "that you have warned Miss Blacklock to be careful?"

"I've warned her, yes. And I shall leave a man here to keep an unobtrusive eye on things."

He avoided Miss Marple's eye which said plainly enough that a policeman keeping an eye on things would be little good if the danger was in the family circle . . .

"And remember," said Craddock, looking squarely at her, "I've warned you."

"I assure you, Inspector," said Miss Marple, "that I can take care of myself."

11. *Miss Marple Comes to Tea*

IF LETITIA BLACKLOCK seemed slightly absent-minded when Mrs. Harmon came to tea and brought a guest who was staying with her, Miss Marple, the guest in question, was hardly likely to notice the fact since it was the first time she had met her hostess.

The old lady was very charming in her gentle gossipy fashion. She revealed herself almost at once to be one of those old ladies who have a constant preoccupation with burglars.

"They can get in anywhere, my dear," she assured her hostess, "absolutely anywhere nowadays. So many new American methods. I myself pin my faith to a very old-fashioned device. A cabin hook and eye. They can pick locks and draw back bolts but a brass hook and eye defeats them. Have you ever tried that?"

"I'm afraid we're not very good at bolts and bars," said Miss Blacklock cheerfully. "There's really nothing much to burgle."

"A chain on the front door," Miss Marple advised. "Then the maid need only open it a crack and see who is there and they can't force their way in."

"I expect Mitzi, our Mittel European, would love that."

"The holdup you had must have been very, very frightening," said Miss Marple. "Bunch has been telling me all about it."

"I was scared stiff," said Bunch.

"It was an alarming experience," admitted Miss Blacklock.

"It really seems like Providence that the man tripped himself up and shot himself. These burglars are so violent nowadays. How did he get in?"

"Well, I'm afraid we don't lock our doors much."

"Oh, Letty," exclaimed Miss Bunner. "I forgot to tell you the Inspector was most peculiar this morning. He insisted on opening the second door—you know, the one that's never been opened—the one over there. He hunted for the key and everything and said the door had been oiled. But I can't see why because—"

Too late she got Miss Blacklock's signal to be quiet, and paused open-mouthed.

"Oh, Letty, I'm so—sorry—I mean, I do beg your pardon, Letty—Oh, dear, how stupid I am."

"It doesn't matter," said Miss Blacklock, but she was annoyed. "Only I don't think Inspector Craddock wants that talked about. I didn't know you had been there when he was experimenting, Dora. You do understand, don't you, Mrs. Harmon?"

"Oh, yes," said Bunch. "We won't breathe a word, will we, Aunt Jane? But I wonder why he—"

She relapsed into thought. Miss Bunner fidgeted and looked miserable, bursting out at last: "I always say the wrong thing. Oh, dear, I'm nothing but a trial to you, Letty."

Miss Blacklock said quickly, "You're my great comfort, Dora. And, anyway, in a small place like Chipping Cleghorn, there aren't really any secrets."

"Now that is very true," said Miss Marple. "I'm afraid, you know, that things do get round in the most extraordinary way. Servants, of course, and yet it can't only be that, because one has so few servants nowadays. Still, there are the daily women and perhaps they are worse, because they go to everybody in turn and pass the news round."

"Oh," said Bunch Harmon suddenly. "I've got it! Of course, if that door could open, too, someone might have gone out of here in the dark and done the holdup—only, of course, they didn't—because it was the man from the Royal Spa Hotel. Or wasn't it? . . . No, I don't see after all . . ." she frowned.

"Did it all happen in this room then?" asked Miss Marple, adding apologetically, "I'm afraid you must think me sadly curious, Miss Blacklock—but it really is so very exciting—like something one reads about in the paper—and actually to have happened to someone one knows . . . I'm just longing to hear all about it and to picture it all, if you know what I mean—"

Immediately Miss Marple received a confused and voluble account from Bunch and Miss Bunner—with occasional emendations and corrections from Miss Blacklock.

In the midde of it Patrick came in and good-naturedly entered into the spirit of the recital—going so far as to enact himself the part of Rudi Scherz.

"And Aunt Letty was there—in the corner by the archway—Go and stand there, Aunt Letty."

Miss Blacklock obeyed, and then Miss Marple was shown the actual bullet holes.

"What a marvelous—what a providential escape," she gasped.

"I was just going to offer my guests cigarettes—" Miss Blacklock indicated the big silver box on the table.

"People are so careless when they smoke," said Miss Bunner disapprovingly. "Nobody really respects good furniture as they used to do. Look at the horrid burn somebody made on this beautiful table by putting a cigarette down on it. Disgraceful."

Miss Blacklock sighed.

"Sometimes, I'm afraid, one thinks too much of one's possessions."

"But it's such a lovely table, Letty."

Miss Bunner loved her friend's possessions with as much fervor as though they had been her own. Bunch Harmon had always thought it was a very endearing trait in her. She showed no sign of envy.

"It is a lovely table," said Miss Marple politely. "And what a very pretty china lamp on it."

Again it was Miss Bunner who accepted the compliment as though she and not Miss Blacklock was the owner of the lamp.

"Isn't it delightful? Dresden. There is a pair of them. The other's in the spare room, I think."

"You know where everything in this house is, Dora—or you think you do," said Miss Blacklock good-humoredly. "You care far more about my things than I do."

Miss Bunner flushed.

"I do like nice things," she said. Her voice was half defiant—half wistful.

"I must confess," said Miss Marple, "that my own few possessions are very dear to me, too—so many memories, you know. It's the same with photographs. People nowadays have so few photographs about. Now I like to keep all the pictures of my nephews and nieces as babies—and then as children—and so on."

"You've got a horrible one of me, aged three," said Bunch. "Holding a fox terrier and squinting."

"I expect your aunt has many photographs of you," said Miss Marple, turning to Patrick.

"Oh, we're only distant cousins," said Patrick.

"I believe Elinor did send me one of you as a baby, Pat," said Miss Blacklock. "But I'm afraid I didn't keep it. I'd really forgotten how many children she had or what their names were until she wrote me about you two being over here."

"Another sign of the times," said Miss Marple. "Nowadays one so often doesn't know one's younger relations at all. In the old days, with all the big family reunions, that would have been impossible."

"I last saw Pat's and Julia's mother at a wedding thirty years ago," said Miss Blacklock. "She was a very pretty girl."

"That's why she has such handsome children," said Patrick with a grin.

"You've got a marvelous old album," said Julia. "Do you remember, Aunt Letty, we looked through it the other day. The hats!"

"And how smart we thought ourselves," said Miss Blacklock with a sigh.

"Never mind, Aunt Letty," said Patrick. "Julia will come across a snapshot of herself in about thirty years' time—and won't she think she looks a guy!"

"Did you do that on purpose?" said Bunch, as she and Miss Marple were walking home. "Talk about photographs I mean?"

"Well, my dear, it is interesting to know that Miss Blacklock didn't know either of her two young relatives by sight. Yes—I think Inspector Craddock will be interested to hear that."

12. *Morning Activities in Chipping Cleghorn*

EDMUND SWETTENHAM sat down rather precariously on a garden roller.

"Good morning, Phillipa," he said.

"Hullo."

"Are you very busy?"

"Moderately."

"What are you doing?"

"Can't you see?"

"No. I'm not a gardener. You seem to be playing with earth in some fashion."

"I'm pricking out winter lettuce."

"Pricking out? What a curious term! Like pinking. Do you know what pinking is? I only learned the other day. I always thought it was a term for professional dueling."

"Do you want anything particular?" asked Phillipa coldly.

"Yes. I want to see you."

Phillipa gave him a quick glance.

"I wish you wouldn't come here like this. Mrs. Lucas won't like it."

"Doesn't she allow you to have followers?"

"Don't be absurd."

"Followers. That's another nice word. It describes my attitude perfectly. Respectful—at a distance—but firmly pursuing."

"Please go away, Edmund. You've no business to come here."

"You're wrong," said Edmund triumphantly. "I have business here. Mrs. Lucas rang up my mama this morning and said she had a good many vegetable marrows."

"Masses of them."

"And would we like to exchange a pot of honey for a vegetable marrow or so?"

"That's not a fair exchange at all! Vegetable marrows are quite unsalable at the moment—everybody has such a lot."

"Naturally. That's why Mrs. Lucas rang up. Last time, if I remember rightly, the exchange suggested was some skim milk—skim milk, mark you—in exchange for some lettuces. It was then very early in the season for lettuces. They were about a shilling each."

Phillipa did not speak.

Edmund tugged at his pocket and extracted a pot of honey.

"So here," he said, "is my alibi. Used in a loose and quite indefensible meaning of the term. If Mrs. Lucas pops her bust round the door of the potting shed, I'm here in quest of vegetable marrows. There is absolutely no question of dalliance."

"I see."

"Do you ever read Tennyson?" inquired Edmund conversationally.

"Not very often."

"You should. Tennyson is shortly going to make a comeback in a big way. When you turn on your radio in the evening it will be the *Idylls of the King* you will hear and not interminable Trollope. I always thought the Trollope pose was the most unbearable affectation. Perhaps a little of Trollope, but not to drown in him. But speaking of Tennyson, have you read *Maud?*"

"Once, long ago."

"It's got some points about it." He quoted softly. " 'Faultily faultless, icily regular, splendidly null.' That's you, Phillipa."

"Hardly a compliment!"

"No, it wasn't meant to be. I gather Maud got under the poor fellow's skin just like you've got under mine."

"Don't be absurd, Edmund."

"Oh, hell, Phillipa, why are you like you are? What goes on behind your splendidly regular features? What do you think? What do you feel? Are you happy, or miserable, or frightened or what? There must be something."

Phillipa said quietly, "What I feel is my own business."

"It's mine, too. I want to make you talk. I want to know what goes on in that quiet head of yours. I've a right to know. I have really. I didn't want to fall in love with you. I wanted to sit quietly and write my book. Such a nice book, all about how miserable the world is. It's frightfully easy to be clever about how miserable everybody is. And it's all a habit, really. Yes, I've suddenly become convinced of that. After reading a life of Burne-Jones."

Phillipa had stopped pricking out. She was staring at him with a puzzled frown.

"What has Burne-Jones got to do with it?"

"Everything. When you've read all about the Pre-Raphaelites you realize just what fashion is. They were all terrifically hearty and slangy and jolly, and laughed and joked, and everything was fine and wonderful. That was fashion, too. They weren't any happier or heartier than we are. And we're not any more miserable than they were. It's all fashion, I tell you. After the last war, we went in for sex. Now it's all frustration. None of it matters. Why are we talking about all this? I started out to talk about us. Only I got cold feet and shied off. Because you won't help me."

"What do you want me to do?"

"Talk! Tell me things. Is it your husband? Did you adore him and he's dead and so you've shut up like a clam? Is that it? All right, you adored him, and he's dead. Well, other girls' husbands are dead—lots of them—and some of the girls loved their husbands. They tell you so in bars, and cry a bit when they're drunk enough, and then want to go to bed with you so that they'll feel better. It's one way of getting over it, I suppose. You've got to get over it, Phillipa. You're young—and you're extremely lovely—and I love you like hell. Talk about your damned husband, tell me about him."

"There's nothing to tell. We met and got married."

"You must have been very young."

"Too young."

"Then you weren't happy with him? Go on, Phillipa."

"There's nothing to go on about. We were married. We were as happy as most people are, I suppose. Harry was born. Ronald went overseas. He —he was killed in Italy."

"And now there's Harry?"

"And now there's Harry."

"I like Harry. He's a really nice kid. He likes me. We'd get on. What about it, Phillipa? Shall we get married? You can go on gardening and I can go on writing my book and in the holidays we'll leave off working and enjoy ourselves. We can manage, with tact, not to have to live with mother. She can fork out a bit to support her adored son. I sponge, I write tripey books. I have defective eyesight and I talk too much. That's the worst. Will you try it?"

Phillipa looked at him. She saw a tall, rather solemn young man with an anxious face and large spectacles. His sandy head was rumpled and he was regarding her with a reassuring friendliness.

"No," said Phillipa.

"Definitely no?"

"Definitely no."

"Why?"

"You don't know anything about me."

"Is that all?"

"No, you don't know anything about anything."

Edmund considered.

"Perhaps not," he admitted. "But who does? Phillipa, my adored one—" He broke off.

A shrill and prolonged yapping was rapidly approaching.

"Pekes in the high hall garden," said Edmund
"When twilight was falling (only it's eleven A.M.);
Phil, Phil, Phil, Phil,
They were crying and calling . . .

"Your name doesn't lend itself to the rhythm, does it? Sounds like an Ode to a Fountain Pen. Have you got another name?"

"Joan. Please go away. That's Mrs. Lucas."

"Joan, Joan, Joan, Joan. Better, but still not good. *When greasy Joan the pot doth keel*—that's not a nice picture of married life, either."

"Mrs. Lucas is—"

"Oh, hell," said Edmund. "Get me a blasted vegetable marrow."

II

Sergeant Fletcher had the house at Little Paddocks to himself.

It was Mitzi's day off. She always went by the eleven o'clock bus into Medenham Wells. By arrangement with Miss Blacklock, Sergeant Fletcher had the run of the house. She and Dora Bunner had gone down to the village.

Fletcher worked fast. Someone in the house had oiled and prepared that door, and whoever had done it, had done it in order to be able to leave the drawing-room unnoticed as soon as the lights went out. That ruled out Mitzi who wouldn't have needed to use the door.

Who was left? The neighbors, Fletcher thought, might also be ruled out. He didn't see how they could have found an opportunity to oil and prepare the door. That left Patrick and Julia Simmons, Phillipa Haymes and possibly Dora Bunner. The young Simmonses were in Milchester. Phillipa Haymes was at work. Sergeant Fletcher was free to search out any secrets he could. But the house was disappointingly innocent. Fletcher, who was an expert on electricity, could find nothing suggestive in the wiring or appurtenances of the electric fixtures to show how the lights had been turned off. Making a rapid survey of the household bedrooms, he found an irritating normality. In Phillipa Haymes' room were photographs of a small boy with serious eyes, an earlier photo of the same child, a pile of schoolboy letters, a theater program or two. In Julia's room there was a drawer full of snapshots of the south of France. Bathing photos, a village set amidst mimosa. Patrick's held some souvenirs of Naval days. Dora Bunner's held few personal possessions and they seemed innocent enough.

And yet, thought Fletcher, someone in the house must have oiled that door.

His thoughts broke off at a sound below stairs. He went quickly to the top of the staircase and looked down.

Mrs. Swettenham was crossing the hall. She had a basket on her arm. She looked into the drawing-room, crossed the hall and went into the dining-room. She came out again without the basket.

Some faint sound that Fletcher made, a board that creaked unexpectedly under his feet, made her turn her head. She called up, "Is that you, Miss Blacklock?"

"No, Mrs. Swettenham, it's me," said Fletcher.

Mrs. Swettenham gave a faint scream.

"Oh! How you startled me. I thought it might be another burglar."

Fletcher came down the stairs.

"This house doesn't seem very well protected against burglars," he said. "Can anybody always walk in and out just as they like?"

"I just brought up some of my quinces," explained Mrs. Swettenham. "Miss Blacklock wants to make quince jelly and she hasn't got a quince tree here. I left them in the dining-room."

Then she smiled.

"Oh, I see, you mean how did I get in? Well, I just came in through the side door. We all walk in and out of each other's houses, Sergeant. Nobody dreams of locking a door until it's dark. I mean it would be so awkward, wouldn't it, if you brought things and couldn't get in to leave them? It's not like the old days when you rang a bell and a servant always came to answer it." Mrs. Swettenham sighed. "In India, I remember," she said mournfully, "we had eighteen servants—eighteen. Not counting the ayah. Just as a matter of course. And at home, when I was a girl, we always had three—although mother always felt it was terribly poverty stricken not to be able to afford a kitchen maid. I must say that I find life very odd nowadays, Sergeant, though I know one mustn't complain. So much worse for the miners always getting psittacosis (or is that parrot disease?) and having to come out of the mines and try to be gardeners though they don't know weeds from spinach."

She added, as she tripped towards the door, "I mustn't keep you. I expect you're very busy. Nothing else is going to happen, is it?"

"Why should it, Mrs. Swettenham?"

"I just wondered, seeing you here. I thought it might be a gang. You'll tell Miss Blacklock about the quinces, won't you?"

Mrs. Swettenham departed. Fletcher felt like a man who has received an unexpected jolt. He had been assuming—erroneously, he now perceived—that it must have been someone in the house who had done the oiling of the door. He saw now that he was wrong. An outsider had only to wait until Mitzi had departed by bus and Letitia Blacklock and Dora Bunner were both out of the house. Such an opportunity must have been simplicity itself. That meant that he couldn't rule out anybody who had been in the drawing-room that night.

III

"Murgatroyd."

"Yes, Hinch?"

"I've been doing a bit of thinking."

"Have you, Hinch?"

"Yes, the great brain has been working. You know, Murgatroyd, the whole setup the other evening was decidedly fishy."

"Fishy?"

"Yes. Tuck your hair up, Murgatroyd, and take this trowel. Pretend it's a revolver."

"Oh," said Miss Murgatroyd nervously.

"All right. It won't bite you. Now come along to the kitchen door. You're going to be the burglar. You stand here. Now you're going into the kitchen to hold up a lot of nitwits. Take the flashlight. Switch it on."

"But it's broad daylight!"

"Use your imagination, Murgatroyd. Switch it on."

Miss Murgatroyd did so, rather clumsily, shifting the trowel under one arm while she did so.

"Now then," said Miss Hinchliffe, "off you go. Remember the time you played Hermia in *A Midsummer Night's Dream* at the Women's Institute? Act. Give it all you've got. 'Stick 'em up!' Those are your lines —and don't ruin them by saying 'Please.' "

Obediently, Miss Murgatroyd raised her flashlight, flourished the trowel and advanced on the kitchen door.

Transferring the torch to her right hand, she swiftly turned the handle and stepped forward, resuming the flashlight in her left hand.

"Stick 'em up!" she fluted, adding vexedly: "Dear me, this is very difficult, Hinch."

"Why?"

"The door. It's a swing door, it keeps coming back and I've got both hands full."

"Exactly," boomed Miss Hinchliffe. "And the drawing-room door at Little Paddocks always swings too. It isn't a swing door like this, but it won't stay open. That's why Letty Blacklock bought that absolutely delectable heavy glass doorstop from Elliot's in the High Street. I don't mind saying I've never forgiven her for getting in ahead of me there. I was beating the old brute down most successfully. He'd come down from eight guineas to six pound ten, and then Blacklock comes along and buys the damned thing. I'd never seen as attractive a doorstop; you don't often get those glass bubbles in that big size."

"Perhaps the burglar put the doorstop against the door to keep it open," suggested Miss Murgatroyd.

"Use your common sense, Murgatroyd. What does he do? Throw the door open, say, 'Excuse me a moment,' stoop and put the stop into position and then resume business by saying, 'Hands up'? Try holding the door with your shoulder."

"It's still very awkward," complained Miss Murgatroyd.

"Exactly," said Miss Hinchliffe. "A revolver, a flashlight and a door to hold open—a bit too much, isn't it? So what's the answer?"

Miss Murgatroyd did not attempt to supply an answer. She looked inquiringly and admiringly at her masterful friend and waited to be enlightened.

"We know he'd got a revolver, because he fired it," said Miss Hinchliffe. "And we know he had a flashlight because we all saw it—that is, unless we're all the victims of mass hypnotism, like explanations of the Indian rope trick—(what a bore that old Easterbrook is with his Indian stories)—so the question is, did someone hold that door open for him?"

"But who could have done that?"

"Well, you could have for one, Murgatroyd. As far as I remember, you were standing directly behind it when the lights went out." Miss Hinchliffe laughed heartily. "Highly suspicious character, aren't you, Murgatroyd? But who'd think it to look at you? Here, give me that trowel—thank heavens it isn't really a revolver. You'd have shot yourself by now!"

IV

"It's a most extraordinary thing," muttered Colonel Easterbrook. "Most extraordinary. Laura."

"Yes, darling?"

"Come into my dressing room a moment."

"What is it, darling?"

Mrs. Easterbrook appeared through the open door.

"Remember my showing you that revolver of mine?"

"Oh, yes, Archie, a nasty horrid black thing."

"Yes. Hun souvenir. Was in this drawer, wasn't it?"

"Yes, it was."

"Well, it's not there now."

"Archie, how extraordinary!"

"You haven't moved it or anything?"

"Oh, no, I'd never dare to touch the horrid thing."

"Think old Mother What's-her-name did?"

"Oh, I shouldn't think so, for a minute. Mrs. Butt would never do a thing like that. Shall I ask her?"

"No—no, better not. Don't want to start a lot of talk. Tell me, do you remember when it was I showed it to you?"

"Oh, about a week ago. You were grumbling about your collars and the laundry and you opened this drawer wide and there it was at the back and I asked you what it was."

"Yes, that's right. About a week ago. You don't remember the date?"

Mrs. Easterbrook considered, eyelids down over her eyes, a shrewd brain working.

"Of course," she said. "It was Saturday. The day we were to have gone in to the pictures, but we didn't."

"Hm—sure it wasn't before that? Wednesday? Thursday, or even the week before that?"

"No, dear," said Mrs. Easterbrook. "I remember quite distinctly. It was Saturday, the 30th. It just seems a long time because of all the trouble there's been. And I can tell you how I remember. It's because it was the day after the holdup at Miss Blacklock's. Because when I saw your revolver it reminded me of the shooting the night before."

"Ah," said Colonel Easterbrook, "then that's a great load off my mind."

"Oh, Archie, why?"

"Just because if that revolver had disappeared before the shooting—well, it might possibly have been my revolver that was pinched by that Swiss fellow."

"But how would he have known you had one?"

"These gangs have a most extraordinary communication service. They get to know everything about a place and who lives there."

"What a lot you do know, Archie."

"Ha! Yes. Seen a thing or two in my time. Still, as you definitely remember seeing my revolver after the holdup—well, that settles it. The revolver that Swiss fellow used can't have been mine, can it?"

"Of course it can't."

"A great relief. I should have had to go to the police about it. And they ask a lot of awkward questions. Bound to. As a matter of fact, I never took out a license for it. Somehow, after a war, one forgets these peace-time regulations. I looked on it as a war souvenir, not as a firearm."

"Yes, I see. Of course."

"But all the same—where on earth can the damned thing be?"

"Perhaps Mrs. Butt took it. She's always seemed quite honest but perhaps she felt nervous after the holdup and thought she'd like to—to have a revolver in the house. Of course, she'll never admit doing that. I shan't even ask her. She might get offended. And what should we do then? This is such a big house—I simply couldn't."

"Quite so," said Colonel Easterbrook. "Better not say anything."

13. *Morning Activities in Chipping Cleghorn (Continued)*

MISS MARPLE came out of the vicarage gate and walked down the little lane that led into the main street.

She walked fairly briskly with the aid of the Rev. Julian Harmon's stout ashplant stick.

She passed the Red Cow and the butcher's and stopped for a brief moment to look into the window of Mr. Elliot's antique shop. This was cunningly situated next door to the Bluebird Tea Room and Café so that rich motorists, after stopping for a nice cup of tea and the somewhat euphemistically named "Home made Cakes" of a bright saffron color, could be tempted by Mr. Elliot's judiciously planned shop window.

In this antique bow frame, Mr. Elliot catered for all tastes. Two pieces of Waterford glass reposed on an impeccable wine cooler. A walnut bureau, made up of various bits and pieces proclaimed itself a genuine bargain and on a table, in the window itself, was a nice assortment of cheap doorknockers and quaint pixies, a few chipped bits of Dresden, a couple of sad-looking bead necklaces, a mug with "A Present from Tunbridge Wells" on it and some tidbits of Victorian silver.

Miss Marple gave the window her rapt attention, and Mr. Elliot, an elderly obese spider, peeped out of his web to appraise the possibilities of this new fly.

But just as he decided that the charms of the "Present from Tunbridge Wells" were about to be too much for the lady who was staying at the vicarage (for, of course, Mr. Elliot, like everybody else, knew exactly who she was), Miss Marple saw out of the corner of her eye Miss Dora Bunner entering the Bluebird Café, and immediately decided that what she needed to counteract the cold wind was a nice cup of morning coffee.

Four or five ladies were already engaged in sweetening their morning shopping by a pause for refreshments. Miss Marple, blinking a little in the gloom of the interior of the Bluebird, and hovering artistically, was greeted by the voice of Dora Bunner at her elbow.

"Oh, good morning, Miss Marple. Do sit down here. I'm all alone."

"Thank you."

Miss Marple subsided gratefully onto the rather angular little blue painted armchair which the Bluebird affected.

"Such a sharp wind," she complained. "And I can't walk very fast because of my rheumatic leg."

"Oh, I know. I had sciatica one year—and really most of the time I was in agony."

The two ladies talked rheumatism, sciatica and neuritis for some moments with avidity. A sulky-looking girl in a pink overall with a flight of bluebirds down the front of it took their order for coffee and cakes with a yawn and an air of weary patience.

"The cakes," Miss Bunner said in a conspiratorial whisper, "are really quite good here."

"I was so interested in that very pretty girl I met as we were coming away from Miss Blacklock's the other day," said Miss Marple. "I think she said she does gardening. Or is she on the land? Hynes—was that her name?"

"Oh, yes, Phillipa Haymes. Our Lodger, as we call her." Miss Bunner laughed at her own humor. "Such a nice quiet girl. A lady, if you know what I mean."

"I wonder now. I knew a Colonel Haymes—in the Indian cavalry. Her father perhaps?"

"She's Mrs. Haymes. A widow. Her husband was killed in Sicily or Italy. Of course it might have been his father."

"I wondered, perhaps, if there might be a little romance on the way," Miss Marple suggested roguishly. "With that tall young man?"

"With Patrick, do you mean? Oh, I don't—"

"No, I meant a young man with spectacles. I've seen him about."

"Oh, of course, Edmund Swettenham. Sh! That's his mother, Mrs. Swettenham, over in the corner. I don't know, I'm sure. You think he admires her? He's such an odd young man—says the most disturbing things sometimes. He's supposed to be clever, you know," said Miss Bunner with frank disapproval.

"Cleverness isn't everything," said Miss Marple, shaking her head. "Ah, here is our coffee."

The sulky girl deposited it with a clatter. Miss Marple and Miss Bunner pressed cakes on each other.

"I was so interested to hear you were at school with Miss Blacklock. Yours is indeed an old friendship."

"Yes, indeed." Miss Bunner sighed. "Very few people would be as loyal to their old friends as dear Miss Blacklock is. Oh, dear, those days seem a long time ago. Such a pretty girl and enjoyed life so much. It all seemed so sad."

Miss Marple, though with no idea of what had seemed so sad, sighed and shook her head.

"Life is indeed hard," she murmured.

"'And sad affliction bravely borne,'" murmured Miss Bunner, her eyes suffusing with tears. "I always think of that verse. True patience, true resignation. Such courage and patience ought to be rewarded, that is what I say. What I feel is that nothing is too good for dear Miss Blacklock, and whatever good things come to her, she truly deserves them."

"Money," said Miss Marple, "can do a lot to ease one's path in life."

She felt herself safe in this observation since she judged that it must be Miss Blacklock's prospects of future affluence to which her friend referred.

The remark, however, started Miss Bunner on another train of thought.

"Money!" she exclaimed with bitterness. "I don't believe, you know, that until one has really experienced it, one can know what money, or rather the lack of it, means."

Miss Marple nodded her white head sympathetically.

Miss Bunner went on rapidly, working herself up, and speaking with a flushed face.

"I've heard people say so often, 'I'd rather have flowers on the table, than a meal without them.' But how many meals have those people ever missed? They don't know what it is—nobody knows who hasn't been through it—to be really hungry. Bread, you know, and a jar of meat paste, and a scrape of margarine. Day after day and how one longs for a good plate of meat and two vegetables. And the shabbiness. Darning one's clothes and hoping it won't show. And applying for jobs and always being told you're too old. And then perhaps getting a job and after all one isn't strong enough. One faints. And you're back again. It's the rent—always the rent—that's got to be paid—otherwise you're out in the street. And in these days it leaves so little over. One's old-age pension doesn't go far—indeed it doesn't."

"I know," said Miss Marple gently. She looked with compassion at Miss Bunner's twitching face.

"I wrote to Letty. I just happened to see her name in the paper. It was a luncheon in aid of Milchester Hospital. There it was in black and white, Miss Letitia Blacklock. It brought the past back to me. I hadn't heard of her for years and years. She's been secretary, you know, to that very rich man, Goedler. She was always a clever girl—the kind that gets on in the world. Not so much looks as character. I thought—well, I thought—

perhaps she'll remember me—and she's one of the people I could ask for a little help. I mean someone you've known as a girl—been at school with —well, they do know about you—they know you're not just a—a begging letter writer—"

Tears came into Dora Bunner's eyes.

"And then Letty came and took me away—said she neeeded someone to help her. Of course, I was very surprised—very surprised—but then newspapers do get things wrong. How kind she was—and how sympathetic. And remembering all the old days so well . . . I'd do anything for her—I really would. And I try very hard, but I'm afraid sometimes I muddle things—my head's not what it was. I make mistakes. And I forget and say foolish things. She's very patient. What's so nice about her is that she always pretends that I am useful to her. That's real kindness, isn't it?"

Miss Marple said gently, "Yes, that's real kindness."

"I used to worry, you know, even after I came to Little Paddocks— about what would become of me if—if anything were to happen to Miss Blacklock. After all, there are so many accidents—these motors dashing about—one never knows, does one? But naturally I never said anything —but she must have guessed. Suddenly one day she told me that she'd left me a small annuity in her will—and—what I value far more—all her beautiful furniture. I was quite overcome— But she said nobody else would value it as I should—and that is quite true—I can't bear to see some lovely piece of china smashed—or wet glasses put down on a table and leaving a mark. I do really look after her things. Some people—some people especially, are so terribly careless—and sometimes worse than careless!

"I'm not really as stupid as I look," Miss Bunner continued with simplicity. "I can see, you know, when Letty's being imposed upon. Some people—I won't name names—but they take advantage. Dear Miss Blacklock is, perhaps, just a shade too trusting."

Miss Marple shook her head.

"That's a mistake."

"Yes, it is. You and I, Miss Marple, know the world. Dear Miss Blacklock—" she shook her head.

Miss Marple thought that as the secretary of a big financier Miss Blacklock might be presumed to know the world, too. But probably what Dora Bunner meant was that Letty Blacklock had always been comfortably off, and that the comfortably off do not know the deeper abysses of human nature.

"That Patrick!" said Miss Bunner with a suddenness and an asperity that made Miss Marple jump. "Twice, at least, to my knowledge, he's got money out of her. Pretending he's hard up. Run into debt. All that sort of thing. She's far too generous. All she said to me was when I remonstrated with her, 'The boy's young, Dora. Youth is the time to have your fling.' "

"Well, that's true enough," said Miss Marple. "Such a handsome young man, too."

"Handsome is as handsome does," said Dora Bunner. "Much too fond of poking fun at people. And a lot of goings on with girls, I expect. I'm just a figure of fun to him—that's all. He doesn't seem to realize that people have their feelings."

"Young people are rather careless that way," said Miss Marple.

Miss Bunner leaned forward suddenly with a mysterious air.

"You won't breathe a word, will you, my dear?" she demanded. "But I can't help feeling that he was mixed up in this dreadful business. I think he knew that young man—or else Julia did. I daren't hint at such a thing to dear Miss Blacklock—at least I did, and she just snapped my head off. And, of course, it's awkward—because he's her nephew—or at any rate her cousin—and if the Swiss young man shot himself Patrick might be held morally responsible, mightn't he? If he'd put him up to it, I mean. I'm really terribly confused about the whole thing. Everyone making such a fuss about that other door into the drawing-room. That's another thing that worries me—the detective saying it had been oiled. Because you see, I saw—"

She came to an abrupt stop.

Miss Marple paused to select a phrase.

"Most difficult for you," she said sympathetically. "Naturally you wouldn't want anything to get round to the police."

"That's just it," Dora Bunner cried. "I lie awake at nights and worry . . . because, you see, I came upon Patrick in the shrubbery the other day. I was looking for eggs—one hen hides out—and there he was holding a feather and a cup—an oily cup. And he jumped most guiltily when he saw me and he said: 'I was just wondering what this was doing here.' Well, of course, he's a quick thinker. I should say he thought that up quickly when I startled him. And how did he come to find a thing like that in the shrubbery unless he was looking for it, knowing perfectly well it was there? Of course, I didn't say anything."

"No, no, of course not."

"But I gave him a look, if you know what I mean."

Dora Bunner stretched out her hand and bit abstractedly into a lurid salmon-colored cake.

"And then another day I happened to overhear him having a very curious conversation with Julia. They seemed to be having a kind of quarrel. He was saying, 'If I thought you had anything to do with a thing like that!' And Julia (she's always so calm, you know) said: 'Well, little brother, what would you do about it?' And then, most unfortunately, I trod on that board that always squeaks, and they saw me. So I said, quite gaily: 'You two having a quarrel?' And Patrick said, 'I'm warning Julia not to go in for these black market clothes coupons deals.' Oh, it was all very slick, but I don't believe they were talking about anything of the sort! And, if you ask me, I believe Patrick had tampered with that lamp in the drawing-room—to make the lights go out, because I remember distinctly that it was the shepherdess—not the shepherd. And the next day—"

She stopped and her face grew pink. Miss Marple turned her head to see Miss Blacklock standing behind them—she must have just come in.

"Coffee and gossip, Bunny?" said Miss Blacklock with quite a shade of reproach in her voice. "Good morning, Miss Marple. Cold, isn't it?"

"We were just talking about clothes coupons," said Miss Bunner hurriedly. "They really don't give us enough, do they? A little better now shoes have come off. But fifteen still for a winter coat is too much."

The doors flew open with a clang and Bunch Harmon came into the Bluebird with a rush.

"Hullo," she said, "am I too late for coffee?"

"No, dear," said Miss Marple. "Sit down and have a cup."

"We must get home," said Miss Blacklock. "Done your shopping, Bunny?"

Her tone was indulgent once more, but her eyes still held a slight reproach.

"Yes—yes, thank you, Letty. I must just pop into the chemist's in passing and get some aspirin and some corn plasters."

As the door of the Bluebird swung to behind them, Bunch asked, "What were you talking about?"

Miss Marple did not reply at once. She waited whilst Bunch gave the order, then she said, "Family solidarity is a very strong thing. Very strong. Do you remember some famous case—I really can't remember what it was. They said the husband poisoned his wife. In a glass of wine. Then, at the trial, the daughter said she'd drunk half her mother's glass —so that knocked the case against her father to pieces. They do say— but it may be just rumor—that she never spoke to her father or lived with him again. Of course, a father is one thing—and a nephew or a distant cousin is another. But, still, there it is—no one wants a member of their own family hanged, do they?"

"No," said Bunch considering. "I shouldn't think they would."

Miss Marple leaned back in her chair. She murmured under her breath, "People are really very alike, everywhere."

"Who am I like?"

"Well, really, dear, you are very much like yourself. I don't know that you remind me of anyone in particular. Except perhaps—"

"Here it comes," said Bunch.

"I was just thinking of a parlormaid of mine, dear."

"A parlormaid? I should make a terrible parlormaid."

"Yes, dear, so did she. She was no good at all at waiting at table. Put everything on the table crooked, mixed up the kitchen knives with the dining room ones and her cap (this was a long time ago, dear)—her cap was never straight."

Bunch adjusted her hat automatically.

"Anything else?" she demanded anxiously.

"I kept her because she was so pleasant to have about the house—and because she used to make me laugh. I liked the way she said things straight out. Came to me one day, 'Of course I don't know, m'am,' she says, 'but Florrie, the way she sits down, it's just like a married woman.' And sure enough poor Florrie was in trouble—the gentlemanly assistant at the hairdresser's. Fortunately it was in good time, and I was able to have a little talk with him, and they had a very nice wedding and settled down quite happily. She was a good girl, Florrie, but inclined to be taken in by a gentlemanly appearance."

"She didn't do a murder, did she?" asked Bunch. "The parlormaid, I mean."

"No, indeed," said Miss Marple. "She married a Baptist minister and they had a family of five."

"Just like me," said Bunch. "Though I've only got as far as Edward and Susan up to date."

She added after a minute or two, "Who are you thinking about now, Aunt Jane?"

"Quite a lot of people, dear, quite a lot of people," said Miss Marple vaguely.

"In St. Mary Mead?"

"Mostly . . . I was really thinking about Nurse Ellerton—really an excellent, kindly woman. Took care of that old lady, seemed really fond of her. Then the old lady died. And another came and she died. Morphia. It all came out. Done in the kindest way, and the shocking thing was that the woman herself really couldn't see that she'd done anything wrong.

They hadn't long to live in any case, she said, and one of them had cancer and quite a lot of pain."

"You mean—it was a mercy killing?"

"No, no. They signed their money away to her. She liked money, you know . . .

"And then there was that young man on the liner—Mrs. Pusey at the paper shop, her nephew. Brought stuff home he'd stolen and got her to dispose of it. Said it was things that he'd bought abroad. She was quite taken in. And then when the police came round and started asking questions, he tried to bash her on the head, so that she shouldn't be able to give him away. . . . Not a nice young man—but very good-looking. Had two girls in love with him. He spent a lot of money on one of them."

"The nastiest one, I suppose," said Bunch.

"Yes, dear. And there was Mrs. Cray at the wool shop. Devoted to her son, spoilt him, of course. He got in with a very queer lot. Do you remember Joan Croft, Bunch?"

"N—no, I don't think so."

"I thought you might have seen her when you were with me on a visit. Used to stalk about smoking a cigar or a pipe. We had a bank holdup once, and Joan Croft was in the bank at the time. She knocked the man down and took his revolver away from him. She was congratulated on her courage by the Bench."

Bunch listened attentively. She seemed to be learning by heart.

"And—" she prompted.

"That girl at St. Jean des Collines that summer. Such a quiet girl—not so much quiet as silent. Everybody liked her, but they never got to know her much better. . . . We heard afterwards that her husband was a forger. It made her feel cut off from people. It made her, in the end, a little queer. Brooding does, you know."

"Any Anglo-Indian colonels in your reminiscences, darling?"

"Naturally, dear. There was Major Vaughan at The Larches and Colonel Wright at Simla Lodge. Nothing wrong with either of them. But I do remember Mr. Hodgson, the bank manager who went on a cruise and married a woman young enough to be his daughter. No idea of where she came from—except what she told him, of course."

"And that wasn't true?"

"No, dear, it definitely wasn't."

"Not bad," said Bunch nodding, and ticking people off of her fingers. "We've had devoted Dora, and handsome Patrick, and Mrs. Swettenham and Edmund, and Phillipa Haymes, and Colonel Easterbrook and Mrs. Easterbrook—and, if you ask me, I should say you're absolutely right about her. But there wouldn't be any reason for her murdering Letty Blacklock."

"Miss Blacklock, of course, might know something about her that she didn't want known."

"Oh, darling, that old Tanqueray stuff? Surely that's dead as the hills."

"It might not be. You see, Bunch, you are not the kind that minds much about what people think of you."

"I see what you mean," said Bunch suddenly. "If you'd been up against it, and then, rather like a shivering stray cat, you'd found a home and cream and a warm stroking hand and you were called Pretty Pussy and somebody thought the world of you . . . You'd do a lot to keep that . . . Well, I must say, you've presented me with a very complete gallery of people."

"You didn't get them all right, you know," said Miss Marple mildly.

"Didn't I? Where did I slip up? Julia, *pretty Juliar is peculiar.*"

"Three and sixpence," said the sulky waitress, materializing out of the gloom.

"And," she added, her bosom heaving beneath the bluebirds, "I'd like to know, Mrs. Harmon, why you call me peculiar. I had an aunt who joined the Peculiar People, but I've always been good Church of England myself, as the late Rev. Hopkinson can tell you."

"I'm terribly sorry," said Bunch. "I was just quoting a song. I didn't mean you at all. I didn't know your name was Julia."

"Quite a coincidence," said the sulky waitress cheering up. "No offense, I'm sure, but hearing my name, as I thought—well, naturally, if you think someone's talking about you, it's only human nature to listen. Thank you."

She departed with her tip.

"Aunt Jane," said Bunch, "don't look so upset. What is it?"

"But surely," murmured Miss Marple. "That couldn't be so. There's no reason—"

"Aunt Jane!"

Miss Marple sighed and then smiled brightly.

"It's nothing, dear," she said.

"Did you think you knew who did the murder?" asked Bunch. "Who was it?"

"I don't know at all," said Miss Marple. "I got an idea for a moment—but it's gone. I wish I did know. Time's so short. So terribly short."

"What do you mean short?"

"That old lady up in Scotland may die any moment."

Bunch said staring, "Then you really do believe in Pip and Emma. You think it was them—and that they'll try again?"

"Of course they'll try again," said Miss Marple almost absent-mindedly. "If they tried once, they'll try again. If you've made up your mind to murder someone, you don't stop because it didn't come off the first time. Especially if you're fairly sure you're not suspected."

"But if it's Pip and Emma," said Bunch, "there are only two people it could be. It must be Patrick and Julia. They're brother and sister and they're the only ones who are the right age."

"My dear, it isn't nearly as simple as that. There are all sorts of ramifications and combinations. There's Pip's wife if he's married, or Emma's husband. There's their mother—she's an interested party even if she doesn't inherit direct. If Letty Blacklock hasn't seen her for thirty years, she'd probably not recognize her now. One elderly woman is very like another. You remember Mrs. Wotherspoon drew her own and Mrs. Bartlett's old-age pension although Mrs. Bartlett had been dead for years. Anyway, Miss Blacklock's shortsighted. Haven't you noticed how she peers at people? And then there's the father. Apparently he was a real bad lot."

"Yes, but he's a foreigner."

"By birth. But there's no reason to believe he speaks broken English and gesticulates with his hands. I daresay he could play the part of—of an Anglo-Indian colonel as well as anybody else."

"Is that what you think?"

"No, I don't. I don't indeed, dear. I just think that there's a great deal of money at stake, a great deal of money. And I'm afraid I know only too well the really terrible things that people will do to lay their hands on a lot of money."

"I suppose they will," said Bunch. "It doesn't really do them any good, does it? Not in the end?"

"No—but they don't usually know that."

"I can understand it." Bunch smiled suddenly, her sweet rather crooked smile. "One feels it would be different for oneself . . . Even I feel that." She considered, You pretend to yourself that you'd do a lot of good with all that money. Schemes. . . . Homes for unwanted children. . . . Tired mothers. . . . A lovely rest abroad somewhere for elderly women who have worked too hard. . . .

Her face grew somber. Her eyes were suddenly dark and tragic.

"I know what you're thinking." she said to Miss Marple. "You're thinking that I'd be the worst kind. Because I'd kid myself. If you just wanted the money for selfish reasons you'd at any rate see what you were like. But once you began to pretend about doing good with it, you'd be able to persuade yourself, perhaps, that it wouldn't very much matter killing someone."

Then her eyes cleared.

"But I shouldn't," she said. "I shouldn't really kill anyone. Not even if they were old, or ill or doing a lot of harm in the world. Not even if they were blackmailers or—or absolute beasts." She fished a fly carefully out of the dregs of the coffee and arranged it on the table to dry. "Because people like living, don't they? So do flies. Even if you're old and in pain and can just crawl out in the sun. Julian says those people like living even more than strong young people do. It's harder, he says, for them to die, the struggle's greater. I like living myself—not just being happy and enjoying myself and having a good time. I mean living—waking up and feeling, all over me, that I'm there—tickling over."

She blew on the fly gently; it waved its legs and flew rather drunkenly away.

"Cheer up, darling Aunt Jane," said Bunch. "I'd never kill anybody."

14. *Excursion into the Past*

AFTER a night in the train Inspector Craddock alighted at a small station in the Highlands.

It struck him for a moment as strange that the wealthy Mrs. Goedler —an invalid—with a choice of a London house in a fashionable Square, an estate in Hampshire and a villa in the South of France, should have selected this remote Scottish home as her residence. Surely she was cut off here from many friends and distractions. It must be a lonely life—or was she too ill to notice or care about her surroundings?

A car was waiting to meet him. A big old-fashioned Daimler with an elderly chauffeur driving it. It was a sunny morning and the Inspector enjoyed the twenty-mile drive, though he marveled anew at this preference for isolation. A tentative remark to the chauffeur brought partial enlightenment.

"It's her own home as a girl. Ay, she's the last of the family. And she and Mr. Goedler were always happier here than anywhere, though it wasn't often he could get away from London. But when he did they enjoyed themselves like a couple of bairns."

When the gray walls of the old keep came in sight, Craddock felt that time was slipping backwards. An elderly butler received him, and after a wash and a shave he was shown into a room with a huge fire burning in the grate, and breakfast was served to him.

After breakfast, a tall middle-aged woman in nurse's dress, with a pleasant and competent manner, came in and introduced herself as Sister McClelland.

"I have my patient all ready for you, Mr. Craddock. She is, indeed, looking forward to seeing you."

"I'll do my best not to excite her," Craddock promised.

"I had better warn you of what will happen. You will find Mrs. Goedler apparently quite normal. She will talk and enjoy talking and then—quite suddenly—her powers will fail. Come away at once, then, and send for me. She is, you see, kept almost entirely under the influence of morphia. She drowses most of the time. In preparation for your visit, I have given her a strong stimulant. As soon as the effect of the stimulant wears off, she will relapse into semiconsciousness."

"I quite understand, Miss McClelland. Would it be in order for you to tell me exactly what the state of Mrs. Goedler's health is?"

"Well, Mr. Craddock, she is a dying woman. Her life cannot be prolonged for more than a few weeks. To say that she should have been dead years ago would strike you as odd, yet it is the truth. What has kept Mrs. Goedler alive is her intense enjoyment and love of being alive. That sounds, perhaps, an odd thing to say of someone who has lived the life of an invalid for many years and has not left her home here for fifteen years, but it is true. Mrs. Goedler has never been a strong woman—but she has retained to an astonishing degree the will to live." She added with a smile, "She is a very charming woman, too, as you will find."

Craddock was shown into a large bedroom where a fire was burning and where an old lady lay in a large canopied bed. Though she was only about seven or eight years older than Letitia Blacklock, her fragility made her seem older than her years.

Her white hair was carefully arranged, a froth of pale blue wool enveloped her neck and shoulders. There were lines of pain on the face, but lines of sweetness, too. And there was, strangely enough, what Craddock could only describe as a roguish twinkle in her faded blue eyes.

"Well, this is interesting," she said. "It's not often I receive a visit from the police. I hear Letitia Blacklock wasn't much hurt by this attempt on her? How is my dear Blackie?"

"She's very well, Mrs. Goedler. She sent you her love."

"It's a long time since I've seen her . . . For many years now, it's been just a card at Christmas. I asked her to come up here when she came back to England after Charlotte's death, but she said it would be painful after so long and perhaps she was right . . . Blackie always had a lot of sense. I had an old school friend to see me about a year ago and, Lor' "— she smiled—"we bored each other to death. After we'd finished all the 'Do you remembers?' there wasn't anything to say. Most embarrassing."

Craddock was content to let her talk before pressing his questions. He wanted, as it were, to get back into the past, to get the feel of the Goedler-Blacklock ménage.

"I suppose," said Belle shrewdly, "that you want to ask about the money? Randall left it all to go to Blackie after my death. Really, of course, Randall never dreamed that I'd outlive him. He was a big strong man, never a day's illness, and I was always a mass of aches and pains and complaints and doctors coming and pulling long faces over me."

"I don't think complaints would be the right word, Mrs. Goedler."

The old lady chuckled.

"I didn't mean it in the complaining sense. I've never been too sorry for myself. But it was always taken for granted that I, being the weakly one, would go first. It didn't work out that way. No—it didn't work out that way . . ."

"Why, exactly, did your husband leave his money the way he did?"

"You mean, why did he leave it to Blackie? Not for the reason you've probably been thinking." The roguish twinkle was very apparent. "What minds you policemen have! Randall was never in the least in love with her and she wasn't with him. Letitia, you know, has really got a man's mind. She hasn't any feminine feelings or weaknesses. I don't believe she was ever in love with any man. She used a little make-up in deference to prevailing custom, but not to make herself look prettier." There was pity in the old voice as she went on: "She never knew any of the fun of being a woman."

Craddock looked with interest at the frail little figure in the big bed. Belle Goedler, he realized, had enjoyed—still enjoyed—being a woman. She twinkled at him.

"I've always thought," she said, "it must be terribly dull to be a man."

Then she said thoughtfully, "I think Randall looked on Blackie very much as a kind of younger brother. He relied on her judgment which was always excellent. She kept him out of trouble more than once, you know."

"She told me that she came to his rescue once with money."

"That, yes, but I meant more than that. One can speak the truth after all these years. Randall couldn't really distinguish between what was crooked and what wasn't. His conscience wasn't sensitive. The poor dear really didn't know what was just smart—and what was dishonest. Blackie kept him straight. That's one thing about Letitia Blacklock, she's absolutely dead straight. She would never do anything that was dishonest. She's a very fine character, you know. I've always admired her. They had a terrible girlhood, those girls. The father was an old country doctor —terrifically pigheaded and narrow-minded—the complete family tyrant. Letitia broke away, came to London and trained herself as a chartered accountant. The other sister was an invalid, there was a deformity of kinds and she never saw people or went out. That's why, when the old man died, Letitia gave up everything to go home and look after her sister. Randall was wild with her—but it made no difference. If Letitia thought a thing was her duty, she'd do it. And you couldn't move her."

"How long was that before your husband died?"

"A couple of years, I think. Randall made his will before she left the firm, and he didn't alter it. He said to me: 'We've no one of our own.' (Our little boy died, you know, when he was two years old.) 'After you and I are gone, Blackie had better have the money. She'll play the markets and make 'em sit up.'

"You see," Belle went on, "Randall enjoyed the whole money-making game so much—it wasn't just the money—it was the adventure, the risks, the excitement of it all. And Blackie liked it, too. She had the same adventurous spirit and the same judgment. Poor darling, she'd never had any of the usual fun—being in love, and leading men on and teasing them —and having a home and children and all the real fun of life."

Craddock thought it was odd, the real pity and indulgent contempt felt by this woman, a woman whose life had been hampered by illness, whose only child had died, whose husband had died, leaving her to a lonely widowhood, and who had been a hopeless invalid for years.

She nodded her head at him.

"I know what you're thinking. But I've had all the things that make life worth while—they may have been taken from me—but I have had them. I was pretty and gay as a girl, I married the man I loved, and he never stopped loving me. My child died, but I had him for two precious years. I've had a lot of physical pain—but if you have pain, you know how to enjoy the exquisite pleasure of the times when pain stops. And everyone's been kind to me, always . . . I'm a lucky woman, really."

Craddock seized upon an opening in her former remarks.

"You said just now, Mrs. Goedler, that your husband left his fortune to Miss Blacklock because he had no one else to leave it to. But that's not strictly true, is it? He had a sister."

"Oh, Sonia. But they'd quarreled years ago and made a clean break of it."

"He disapproved of her marriage?"

"Yes, she married a man called—now what was his name—?"

"Stamfordis."

"That's it. Dmitri Stamfordis. Randall always said he was a crook. The two men didn't like each other from the first. But Sonia was wildly in love with him and quite determined to marry him. And I really never saw why she shouldn't. Men have such odd ideas about these things. Sonia wasn't a mere girl—she was twenty-five, and she knew exactly what she was doing. He was a crook, I daresay—I mean really a crook, I believe he had a criminal record—and Randall always suspected the name he was passing under wasn't his own. Sonia knew all that. The point was, which, of course, Randall couldn't appreciate, that Dmitri was really a wildly attractive person to women. And he was just as much in love with Sonia as she was with him. Randall insisted that he was just marrying her for her money—but that wasn't true. Sonia was very handsome, you know.

And she had plenty of spirit. If the marriage had turned out badly, if Dmitri had been unkind to her or unfaithful to her, she would just have cut her losses and walked out on him. She was a rich woman and could do as she chose with her life."

"The quarrel was never made up?"

"No. Randall and Sonia never had got on very well. She resented his trying to prevent the marriage. She said, 'Very well. You're quite impossible! This is the last you hear of me!' "

"But it was not the last you heard of her?"

Belle smiled.

"No, I got a letter from her about eighteen months afterwards. She wrote from Budapest, I remember, but she didn't give an address. She told me to tell Randall that she was extremely happy and that she'd just had twins."

"And she told you their names?"

Again Belle smiled. "She said they were born just after midday and she intended to call them Pip and Emma. That may have been just a joke, of course."

"Didn't you hear from her again?"

"No. She said she and her husband and the babies were going to America on a short stay. I never heard any more . . ."

"You don't happen, I suppose, to have kept that letter?"

"No, I'm afraid not . . . I read it to Randall and he just grunted: 'She'll regret marrying that fellow one of these days.' That's all he ever said about it. We really forgot about her. She went right out of our lives. . . ."

"Nevertheless, Mr. Goedler left his estate to her children in the event of Miss Blacklock predeceasing you?"

"Oh, that was my doing. I said to him, when he told me about the will, 'And suppose Blackie dies before I do?' He was quite surprised. I said, 'Oh, I know Blackie is as strong as a horse and I'm a delicate creature—but there's such a thing as accidents, you know, and there's such a thing as creaking gates . . .' And he said, 'There's no one—absolutely no one.' I said, 'There's Sonia.' And he said at once, 'And let that fellow get hold of my money? No—indeed!' I said, 'Well, her children then. Pip and Emma, and there may be lots more by now'—and so he grumbled, but he did put it in."

"And from that day to this," Craddock said slowly, "you've heard nothing of your sister-in-law or her children?"

"Nothing—They may be dead—they may be—anywhere."

They may be in Chipping Cleghorn, thought Craddock.

As though she read his thoughts, a look of alarm came into Belle Goedler's eyes. She said, "Don't let them hurt Blackie. Blackie's good—really good—you mustn't let harm come to—"

Her voice trailed off suddenly. Craddock saw the sudden gray shadows round her mouth and eyes.

"You're tired," he said. "I'll go."

She nodded.

"Send Mac to me," she whispered. "Yes, tired . . ." She made a feeble motion of her hand. "Look after Blackie . . . nothing must happen to Blackie . . . look after her . . ."

"I'll do my very best, Mrs. Goedler." He rose and went to the door. Her voice, a thin thread of sound, followed him.

"Not long now—until I'm dead—dangerous for her—take care . . ."

Sister McClelland passed him as he went out. He said uneasily, "I hope I haven't done her harm."

"Oh, I don't think so, Mr. Craddock. I told you she would tire quite suddenly."

Later, he asked the nurse, "The only thing I hadn't time to ask Mrs. Goedler was whether she had any old photographs. If so, I wonder—"

She interrupted him.

"I'm afraid there's nothing of that kind. All her personal papers and things were stored with their furniture from the London house at the beginning of the war. Mrs. Goedler was desperately ill at the time. Then the storage depository was blitzed. Mrs. Goedler was very upset at losing so many personal souvenirs and family papers. I'm afraid there's nothing of that kind."

So that was that, Craddock thought.

Yet he felt his journey had not been in vain. Pip and Emma, those twin wraiths, were not quite wraiths.

Craddock thought, Here's a brother and sister brought up somewhere in Europe. Sonia Goedler was a rich woman at the time of her marriage, but money in Europe hasn't remained money. Queer things have happened to money during these war years. And so there are two young people, the son and daughter of a man who had a criminal record. Suppose they came to England, more or less penniless? What would they do? Find out about any rich relatives. Their uncle, a man of vast fortune, is dead. Possibly the first thing they'd do would be to look up that uncle's will. See if by any chance money had been left to them or to their mother. So they go to Somerset House and learn the contents of his will, and then, perhaps, they learn of the existence of Miss Letitia Blacklock. Then they make inquiries about Randall Goedler's widow. She's an invalid, living up in Scotland, and they find out she hasn't long to live. If this Letitia Blacklock dies before her, they will come into a vast fortune. What then?

Craddock thought, they wouldn't go to Scotland. They'd find out where Letitia Blacklock is living now. And they'd go there—but not as themselves . . . They'd go together—or separately? Emma . . . I wonder . . . Pip and Emma. . . . I'll eat my hat if Pip, or Emma, or both of them, aren't in Chipping Cleghorn now.

15. *Delicious Death*

IN THE kitchen at Little Paddocks, Miss Blacklock was giving instructions to Mitzi.

"Sardine sandwiches as well as the tomato ones. And some of those little scones you make so nicely. And I'd like you to make that special cake of yours."

"It is a party, then, that you want all these things?"

"It's Miss Bunner's birthday, and some people will be coming to tea."

"At her age one does not have birthdays. It is better to forget."

"Well, she doesn't want to forget. Several people are bringing her presents—and it will be nice to make a little party of it."

"That is what you say last time—and see what happened!"

Miss Blacklock controlled her temper.

"Well, it won't happen this time."

"How do you know what may happen in this house? All day long I shiver and at night I lock my door and I look in the wardrobe to see no one is hidden there."

"That ought to keep you nice and safe," said Miss Blacklock coldly.

"The cake that you want me to make, it is the—" Mitzi uttered a sound that to Miss Blacklock's English ear sounded like *Schwitzebzr*, or, alternatively, like cats spitting at each other.

"That's the one. The rich one."

"Yes. It is rich. For it I have nothing! Impossible to make such a cake. I need for it chocolate and much butter, and sugar and raisins."

"You can use this tin of butter that was sent us from America. And some of the raisins we were keeping for Christmas, and here is a slab of chocolate and a pound of sugar."

Mitzi's face suddenly burst into radiant smiles.

"So, I make him for you good—good!" she cried, in an ecstasy. "It will be rich, rich, of a melting richness! And on top I will put the icing—chocolate icing—I make him so nice—and write on it *Good Wishes*. These English people with their cakes that taste of sand, never, never will they have tasted such a cake. Delicious, they will say—delicious—"

Her face clouded again.

"Mr. Patrick. He called it Delicious Death. My cake! I will not have my cake called that!"

"It was a compliment really," said Miss Blacklock. "He meant it was worth dying to eat such a cake."

Mitzi looked at her doubtfully.

"Well, I do not like that word—death. They are not dying because they eat my cake, no, they feel much much better."

"I'm sure we all shall."

Miss Blacklock turned away and left the kitchen with a sigh of relief at the successful ending of the interview. With Mitzi one never knew.

She ran into Dora Bunner outside.

"Oh, Letty, shall I run in and tell Mitzi just how to cut the sandwiches?"

"No," said Miss Blacklock, steering her friend firmly into the hall. "She's in a good mood now and I don't want her disturbed."

"But I could just show her—"

"Please don't show her anything, Dora. These central Europeans don't like being shown. They hate it."

Dora looked at her doubtfully. Then she suddenly broke into smiles.

"Edmund Swettenham just rang up. He wished me many happy returns of the day and said he was bringing me a pot of honey as a present this afternoon. Isn't it kind? I can't imagine how he knew it was my birthday."

"Everybody seems to know. You must have been talking about it, Dora."

"Well, I did just happen to mention that today I should be fifty-nine—"

"You're sixty-four," said Miss Blacklock with a twinkle.

"And Miss Hinchliffe said, 'You don't look it. What age do you think I am?' Which was rather awkward because Miss Hinchliffe always looks so peculiar that she might be any age. She said she was bringing me some eggs, by the way. I said our hens hadn't been laying very well lately."

"We're not doing so badly out of your birthday," said Miss Blacklock. "Honey, eggs—a magnificent box of chocolates from Julia—"

"I don't know where she gets such things."

"Better not ask. Her methods are probably strictly illegal."

"And your lovely brooch." Miss Bunner looked down proudly at her bosom on which was pinned a small diamond leaf.

"Do you like it? I'm glad. I never cared for jewelry."

"I love it."

"Good. Let's go and feed the ducks."

II

"Ha!" cried Patrick dramatically, as the party took their places round the dining room table. "What do I see before me? Delicious Death."

"Hush," said Miss Blacklock. "Don't let Mitzi hear you. She objects to your name for her cake very much."

"Nevertheless, Delicious Death it is! Is it Bunny's birthday cake?"

"Yes, it is," said Miss Bunner. "I really am having the most wonderful birthday."

Her cheeks were flushed with excitement and had been ever since Colonel Easterbrook had handed her a small box of sweets and declaimed with a bow, "Sweets to the Sweet!"

Julia had turned her head away hurriedly, and had been frowned at by Miss Blacklock.

Full justice was done to the good things on the tea table and they rose from their seats after a round of crackers.

"I feel slightly sick," said Julia. "It's that cake. I remember I felt just the same last time."

"It's worth it," said Patrick.

"These foreigners certainly understand confectionery," said Miss Hinchliffe. "What they can't make is a plain boiled pudding."

Everybody was respectfully silent, though it seemed to be hovering on Patrick's lips to ask if anyone really wanted a plain boiled pudding.

"Got a new gardener?" asked Miss Hinchliffe of Miss Blacklock as they returned to the drawing-room.

"No, why?"

"Saw a man snooping round the henhouse. Quite a decent looking Army type."

"Oh that," said Julia. "That's our detective."

Mrs. Easterbrook dropped her handbag.

"Detective?" she exclaimed. "But—but—why?"

"I don't know," said Julia. "He prowls about and keeps an eye on the house. He's protecting Aunt Letty, I suppose."

"Absolute nonsense," said Miss Blacklock. "I can protect myself, thank you."

"But surely it's all over now," cried Mrs. Easterbrook. "Though I meant to ask you, why did they adjourn the inquest?"

"Police aren't satisfied," said her husband. "That's what that means."

"But aren't satisfied of what?"

Colonel Easterbrook shook his head with the air of a man who could say a good deal more if he chose. Edmund Swettenham, who disliked the colonel, said, "The truth of it is, we're all under suspicion."

"But suspicion of what?" repeated Mrs. Easterbrook.

"Loitering with intent," said Edmund. "The intent being to commit murder upon the first opportunity."

"Oh, don't, please don't, Mr. Swettenham." Dora Bunner began to cry. "I'm sure nobody here could possibly want to kill dear, dear Letty."

There was a moment of horrible embarrassment. Edmund turned scarlet, murmured, "Just a joke." Phillipa suggested in a high clear voice that they might listen to the six o'clock news and the suggestion was received with enthusiastic assent.

Patrick murmured to Julia: "We need Mrs. Harmon here. She'd be sure to say in that high clear voice of hers, 'But I suppose somebody is still waiting for a good chance to murder you, Miss Blacklock?'"

"I'm glad she and that old Miss Marple couldn't come," said Julia. "That old woman is the prying kind. And a mind like a sink, I should think. Real Victorian type."

Listening to the news led easily into a pleasant discussion on the horrors of atomic warfare. Colonel Easterbrook said that the real menace to civilization was undoubtedly Russia, and Edmund said that he had several charming Russian friends—which announcement was coldly received.

The party broke up with renewed thanks to the hostess.

"Enjoy yourself, Bunny?" asked Miss Blacklock, as the last guest was sped.

"Oh, I did. But I've got a terrible headache. It's the excitement, I think."

"It's the cake," said Patrick. "I feel a bit livery myself. And you've been nibbling chocolates all the morning."

"I'll go and lie down, I think," said Miss Bunner. "I'll take a couple of aspirin and try and have a nice sleep."

"That would be a very good plan," said Miss Blacklock.

Miss Bunner departed upstairs.

"Shall I shut up the ducks for you, Aunt Letty?"

Miss Blacklock looked at Patrick severely.

"If you'll be sure to latch that door properly."

"I will. I swear I will."

"Have a glass of sherry, Aunt Letty," said Julia. "As my old nurse used to say, 'It will settle your stomach.' A revolting phrase—but curiously apposite at this moment."

"Well, I daresay it might be a good thing. The truth is, one isn't used to rich things. Oh, Bunny, how you made me jump. What is it?"

"I can't find my aspirin," said Miss Bunner disconsolately.

"Well, take some of mine, dear; they're by my bed."

"There's a bottle on my dressing table," said Phillipa.

"Thank you—thank you very much. If I can't find mine—but I know I've got it somewhere. A new bottle. Now where could I have put it?"

"There's heaps in the bathroom," said Julia impatiently. "This house is chock full of aspirin."

"It vexes me to be so careless and mislay things," replied Miss Bunner, retreating up the stairs again.

"Poor old Bunny," said Julia, holding up her glass. "Do you think we ought to have given her some sherry?"

"Better not, I think," said Miss Blacklock. "She's had a lot of excitement today, and it isn't really good for her. I'm afraid she'll be the worse for it tomorrow. Still, I really do think she has enjoyed herself!"

"She's loved it," said Phillipa.

"Let's give Mitzi a glass of sherry," suggested Julia. "Hi, Pat," she called as she heard him entering the side door, "fetch Mitzi."

So Mitzi was brought in and Julia poured her out a glass of sherry.

"Here's to the best cook in the world," said Patrick raising his glass.

Mitzi was gratified—but felt nevertheless that a protest was due.

"That is not so. I am not really a cook. In my country I do intellectual work."

"Then you're wasted," said Patrick. "What's intellectual work compared to a chef-d'oeuvre like Delicious Death?"

"Oo—I say to you I do not like—"

"Never mind what you like, my girl," said Patrick. "That's my name for it and here's to it. Let's all drink to Delicious Death and to hell with the aftereffects."

III

"Phillipa, my dear, I want to talk to you."

"Yes, Miss Blacklock?"

Phillipa Haymes looked up in slight surprise.

"You're not worrying about anything, are you?"

"Worrying?"

"I've noticed that you've looked worried lately. There isn't anything wrong, is there?"

"Oh, no, Miss Blacklock. What should there be?"

"Well—I wondered. I thought, perhaps that you and Patrick—"

"Patrick?" Phillipa looked really surprised.

"It's not so, then. Please forgive me if I've been impertinent. But you've been thrown together a lot—and although Patrick is a relation, I don't think he's the type to make a satisfactory husband. Not for some time to come, at all events."

Phillipa's face had frozen into a hard immobility.

"I shan't marry again," she said.

"Oh, yes, you will some day, my child. You're young. But we needn't discuss that. There's no other trouble? You're not worried about—money, for instance?"

"No, I'm quite all right."

"I know you get anxious sometimes about your boy's education. That's why I want to tell you something. I drove into Milchester this afternoon to see Mr. Beddingfeld, my lawyer. Things haven't been very settled lately and I thought I would like to make a new will—in view of certain eventualities. Apart from Bunny's legacy, everything goes to you, Phillipa."

"What?" Phillipa spun round. Her eyes stared. She looked dismayed, almost frightened.

"But I don't want it—really, I don't . . . Oh I'd rather not . . . And anyway, why? Why to me?"

"Perhaps," said Miss Blacklock in a peculiar voice, "because there's no one else."

"But there's Patrick and Julia."

"Yes, there's Patrick and Julia." The odd note in Miss Blacklock's voice was still there.

"They are your relations."

"Very distant ones. They have no claim on me."

"But I—I haven't either—I don't know what you think—Oh, I don't want it."

Her gaze held more hostility than gratitude. There was something almost like fear in her manner.

"I know what I'm doing, Phillipa. I've become fond of you—and there's the boy . . . You won't get very much if I should die now—but in a few weeks' time it might be different."

Her eyes met Phillipa's steadily.

"But you're not going to die!" Phillipa protested.

"Not if I can avoid it by taking due precautions."

"Precautions?"

"Yes. Think it over . . . And don't worry any more."

She left the room abruptly. Phillipa heard her speaking to Julia in the hall.

Julia entered the drawing-room a few moments later. There was a slightly steely glitter in her eyes.

"Played your cards rather well, haven't you, Phillipa? I see you're one of those quiet ones . . . a dark horse . . ."

"So you heard—"

"Yes, I heard. I rather think I was meant to hear."

"What do you mean?"

"Our Letty's no fool . . . Well, anyway, you're all right, Phillipa. Sitting pretty, aren't you?"

"Oh, Julia—I didn't mean—I never meant—"

"Didn't you? Of course you did. You're fairly up against things, aren't you? Hard up for money. But just remember this—if anyone bumps off Aunt Letty now, you'll be suspect Number 1."

"But I shan't be. It would be idiotic if I killed her now when—if I waited—"

"So you do know about old Mrs. What's-her-name dying up in Scotland? I wondered . . . Phillipa, I'm beginning to believe you're a very dark horse indeed."

"I don't want to do you and Patrick out of anything."

"Don't you, my dear? I'm sorry—but I don't believe you."

16. *Inspector Craddock Returns*

INSPECTOR CRADDOCK had had a bad night on his journey home. His dreams had been less dreams than nightmares. Again and again he was racing through the gray corridors of an old-world castle in a desperate attempt to get somewhere, or to prevent something in time. Finally, he dreamed that he awoke. An enormous relief surged over him. Then the door of his compartment slid slowly open, and Letitia Blacklock looked in at him with blood running down her face, and said reproachfully: "Why didn't you save me? You could have if you'd tried."

This time he really awoke.

Altogether, the Inspector was thankful finally to reach Milchester. He went straight away to make his report to Rydesdale who listened carefully.

"It doesn't take us much further," he said. "But it confirms what Miss Blacklock told you. Pip and Emma—hm, I wonder."

"Patrick and Julia Simmons are the right age, sir. If we could establish that Miss Blacklock hadn't seen them since they were children—"

With a very faint chuckle, Rydesdale said: "Our ally, Miss Marple, has established that for us. Actually, Miss Blacklock had never seen either of them at all until two months ago."

"Then surely, sir—"

"It's not so easy as all that, Craddock. We've been checking up. On what we've got, Patrick and Julia seem definitely to be out of it. His Naval record is genuine—quite a good record barring a tendency to 'insuborination.' We've checked with Cannes, and an indignant Mrs. Simmons says of course her son and daughter are at Chipping Cleghorn with her cousin Letitia Blacklock. So that's that!"

"And Mrs. Simmons *is* Mrs. Simmons?"

"She's been Mrs. Simmons for a very long time, that's all I can say," said Rydesdale dryly.

"That seems clear enough. Only—those two fitted. Right age. Not known to Miss Blacklock personally. If we wanted a Pip and Emma—well, there they were."

The Chief Constable nodded thoughtfully, then he pushed a paper across to Craddock.

"Here's a little something we've dug up on Mrs. Easterbrook."

The Inspector read with lifted eyebrows.

"Very interesting," he remarked. "Hoodwinked that old ass pretty well, hasn't she? It doesn't tie in with this business though, as far as I can see."

"Apparently not."

"And here's an item that concerns Mrs. Haymes."

Again Craddock's eyebrows rose.

"I think I'll have to have another talk with the lady," he said.

"You think this information might be relevant?"

"I think it might be. It would be a long shot, of course . . ."

The two men were silent for a moment or two.

"How has Fletcher got on, sir?"

"Fletcher has been exceedingly active. He's made a routine search of the house by agreement with Miss Blacklock—but he didn't find anything significant. Then he's been checking up on who could have had the opportunity of oiling that door. Checking who was up at the house on the days that that foreign girl was out. A little more complicated than we thought, because it appears she goes for a walk most afternoons. Usually down to the village where she has a cup of coffee at the Bluebird. So that when Miss Blacklock and Miss Bunner are out—which is most afternoons—they go blackberrying —the coast is clear."

"And the doors are always left unlocked?"

"They used to be. I don't suppose they are now."

"What are Fletcher's results? Who's known to have been in the house when it was left empty?"

"Practically the whole lot of them."

Rydesdale consulted a page in front of him.

"Miss Murgatroyd was there with a hen to sit on some eggs. (Sounds complicated but that's what she says.) Very flustered about it all and contradicts herself, but Fletcher thinks that's temperamental and not a sign of guilt."

"Might be," Craddock admitted. "She flaps."

"Then Mrs. Swettenham came up to fetch some horse meat that Miss Blacklock had left for her on the kitchen table because Miss Blacklock had been in to Milchester in the car that day and always gets Mrs. Swettenham's horse meat for her. That makes sense to you?"

Craddock considered.

"Why didn't Miss Blacklock leave the horse meat when she passed Mrs. Swettenham's house on her way back from Milchester?"

"I don't know, but she didn't. Mrs. Swettenham says she (Miss B.)

always leaves it on the kitchen table, and she (Mrs. S.) likes to fetch it when Mitzi isn't there because Mitzi is sometimes so rude."

"Hangs together quite well. And the next?"

"Miss Hinchliffe. Says she wasn't there at all lately. But she was. Because Mitzi saw her coming out of the side door one day and so did a Mrs. Butt (she's one of the locals). Miss H. then admitted she might have been there but had forgotten. Can't remember what she went for. Says she probably just dropped in."

"That's rather odd."

"So was her manner, apparently. Then there's Mrs. Easterbrook. She was exercising the dear dogs out that way and she just popped in to see if Miss Blacklock would lend her a knitting pattern but Miss Blacklock wasn't in. She says she waited a little."

"Just so. Might be snooping round. Or might be oiling a door. And the Colonel?"

"Went there one day with a book on India that Miss Blacklock had expressed a desire to read."

"Had she?"

"Her account is that she tried to get out of having to read it, but it was no use."

"And that's fair enough," sighed Craddock. "If anyone is really determined to lend you a book, you never can get out of it!"

"We don't know if Edmund Swettenham was up there. He's extremely vague. Said he did drop in occasionally on errands for his mother, but thinks not lately."

"In fact, it's all inconclusive."

"Yes."

Rydesdale said, with a slight grin, "Miss Marple has also been active. Fletcher reports she had morning coffee at the Bluebird. She's been to sherry at Boulders and to tea at Little Paddocks. She's admired Mrs. Swettenham's garden—and dropped in to see Colonel Easterbrook's Indian curios."

"She may be able to tell us if Colonel Easterbrook's a pukka colonel or not."

"She'd know, I agree—he seems all right. We'd have to check with the Far East authorities to get certain identification."

"And in the meantime—" Craddock broke off. "Do you think Miss Blacklock would consent to go away?"

"Go away from Chipping Cleghorn?"

"Yes. Take the faithful Bunner with her, perhaps, and leave for an unknown destination. Why shouldn't she go up to Scotland and stay with Belle Goedler? It's a pretty un-get-at-able place."

"Stop there and wait for her to die? I don't think she'd do that. I don't think any nice-natured woman would like that suggestion."

"It it's a matter of saving her life—"

"Come now, Craddock, it isn't quite so easy to bump someone off as you seem to think."

"Isn't it, sir?"

"Well—in one way—it's easy enough, I agree. Plenty of methods. Weed-killer. A bash on the head when she's out shutting up the poultry, a pot shot from behind a hedge. All quite simple. But to bump someone off and not be suspected of bumping them off—that's not quite so easy. And they must realize by now that they're all under observation. The original carefully planned scheme failed. Our unknown murderer has got to think up something else."

"I know that, sir. But there's the time element to consider. Mrs. Goedler's a dying woman—she might pop off any minute. That means that our murderer can't afford to wait."

"True."

"And another thing, sir. He—or she—must know that we're checking up on everybody."

"And that takes time," said Rydesdale with a sigh. "It means checking with the East, with India. Yes, it's a long, tedious business."

"So that's another reason for—hurry. I'm sure, sir, that the danger is very real. It's a very large sum that's at stake. If Belle Goedler dies—"

He broke off as a constable entered.

"Constable Legg on the line from Chipping Cleghorn, sir."

"Put him through here."

Inspector Craddock, watching the Chief Constable, saw his features harden and stiffen.

"Very good," barked Rydesdale. "Detective Inspector Craddock will be coming out immediately."

He put the receiver down.

"Is it—" Craddock broke off.

Rydesdale shook his head.

"No," he said. "It's Dora Bunner. She wanted some aspirin. Apparently she took some from a bottle beside Letitia Blacklock's bed. There were only a few tablets left in the bottle. She took two and left one. The doctor's got that one and is sending it to be analyzed. He says it's definitely not aspirin."

"She's dead?"

"Yes, found dead in her bed this morning. Died in her sleep. Doctor says he doesn't think it was natural, though her health was in a bad state. Narcotic poisoning, that's his guess. Autopsy's fixed for tonight."

"Aspirin tablets by Letitia Blacklock's bed. The clever, clever devil. Patrick told me Miss Blacklock threw away a half bottle of sherry—opened a new one. I don't suppose she'd have thought of doing that with an open bottle of aspirin. Who had been in the house this time—within the last day or two? The tablets can't have been there long."

Rydesdale looked at him.

"All our lot were there yesterday," he said. "Birthday party for Miss Bunner. Any of them could have nipped upstairs and done a neat little substitution. Or, of course, anyone living in the house could have done it any time."

17. *The Album*

STANDING by the vicarage gate, well wrapped up, Miss Marple took the note from Bunch's hand.

"Tell Miss Blacklock," said Bunch, "that Julian is terribly sorry he can't come up himself. He's got a parishioner dying out at Locke Hamlet. He'll come up after lunch if Miss Blacklock would like to see him. The note's about the arrangements for the funeral. He suggests Wednesday if the inquest's on Tuesday. Poor old Bunny. It's so typical of her, somehow, to get hold of poisoned aspirin meant for someone else. Good-by, darling. I hope the walk won't be too much for you. But I've simply got to get that child to hospital at once."

Miss Marple said the walk wouldn't be too much for her, and Bunch rushed off.

Whilst waiting for Miss Blacklock, Miss Marple looked round the drawing-room, and wondered just exactly what Dora Bunner had meant that morning in the Bluebird by saying that she believed Patrick had "tampered with the lamp" to "make the lights go out." What lamp? And how had he "tampered" with it?

She must, Miss Marple decided, have meant the small lamp that stood on the table by the archway. She had said something about a shepherdess or a shepherd—and this was actually a delicate piece of Dresden china, a shepherd in a blue coat and pink breeches, holding what had originally been a candlestick and had now been adapted to electricity. The shade was a plain vellum and a little too big so that it almost masked the figure. What else was it that Dora Bunner had said? "I remember distinctly that it was the shepherdess. And the next day—" Certainly it was a shepherd now.

Miss Marple remembered that when she and Bunch had come to tea, Dora Bunner had said something about the lamp being one of a pair. Of course—a shepherd and shepherdess. And it had been the shepherdess on the day of the holdup—and the next morning it had been the other lamp —the lamp that was here now, the shepherd. The lamps had been changed over during the night. And Dora Bunner had had reason to believe (or had believed without reason) that it was Patrick who had changed them.

Why? Because, if the original lamp were examined, it would show just how Patrick had managed to "make the lights go out." How had he managed? Miss Marple looked earnestly at the lamp in front of her. The cord ran along the table over the edge and was plugged into the wall. There was a small pear-shaped switch halfway along the cord. None of it suggested anything to Miss Marple because she knew very little about electricity.

Where was the shepherdess lamp, she wondered. In the "spare room" or thrown away, or—where was it Dora Bunner had come upon Patrick Simmons with a feather and an oily cup? In the shrubbery? Miss Marple made up her mind to put all these points to Inspector Craddock.

At the very beginning Miss Blacklock had leaped to the conclusion that her nephew Patrick had been behind the insertion of that advertisement. That kind of instinctive belief was often justified, or so Miss Marple believed. Because, if you knew people fairly well, you knew the kind of things they thought of . . .

Patrick Simmons . . .

A handsome young man. An engaging young man. A young man whom women liked, both young women and old women. The kind of man, perhaps, that Randall Goedler's sister had married. Could Patrick Simmons be Pip? But he'd been in the Navy during the war. The police could soon check up on that.

Only—sometimes—the most amazing impersonations did happen.

You could get away with a great deal if you had enough audacity . . .

The door opened and Miss Blacklock came in. She looked, Miss Marple thought, many years older. All the life and energy had gone out of her.

"I'm very sorry, disturbing you like this," said Miss Marple. "But the vicar had a dying parishioner and Bunch had to rush a sick child to hospital. The vicar wrote you a note."

She held it out and Miss Blacklock took it and opened it.

"Do sit down, Miss Marple," she said. "It's very kind of you to have brought this."

She read the note through.

"The vicar's a very understanding man," she said quietly. "He doesn't offer one fatuous consolations . . . Tell him that these arrangements will do very well. Her—her favorite hymn was *Lead, Kindly Light.*"

Her voice broke suddenly.

Miss Marple said gently, "I am only a stranger, but I am so very, very sorry."

And suddenly, uncontrollably, Letitia Blacklock wept. It was a piteous, overmastering grief, with a kind of hopelessness about it. Miss Marple sat quite still.

Miss Blacklock sat up at last. Her face was swollen and blotched with tears.

"I'm sorry," she said. "It—it just came over me. What I've lost. She—she was the only link with the past, you see. The only one who—remembered. Now that she's gone I'm quite alone."

"I know what you mean," said Miss Marple. "One is alone when the last one who remembers is gone. I have nephews and nieces and kind friends—but there's no one who knew me as a young girl—no one who belongs to the old days. I've been alone for quite a long time now."

Both women sat silent for some moments.

"You understand very well," said Letitia Blacklock. She rose and went over to her desk. "I must write a few words to the vicar." She held the pen rather awkwardly and wrote slowly.

"Arthritic," she explained. "Sometimes I can hardly write at all."

She sealed up the envelope and addressed it.

"If you wouldn't mind taking it, it would be very kind."

Hearing a man's voice in the hall, she said quickly, "That's Inspector Craddock."

She went to the mirror over the fireplace and applied a small powder puff to her face.

Craddock came in with a grim angry face.

He looked at Miss Marple with disapprobation.

"Oh," he said. "So you're here."

Miss Blacklock turned from the mantelpiece.

"Miss Marple kindly came up with a note from the vicar."

Miss Marple said in a flurried manner, "I am going at once—at once. Please don't let me hamper you in any way."

"Were you at the tea party here yesterday afternoon?"

Miss Marple said, nervously, "No—no, I wasn't. Bunch drove me over to call on some friends."

"Then there's nothing you can tell me." Craddock held the door open in a pointed manner, and Miss Marple scuttled out in a somewhat abashed fashion.

"Nosy Parkers, these old women," said Craddock.

"I think you're being unfair to her," said Miss Blacklock. "She really did come with a note from the vicar."

"I bet she did."

"I don't think it was idle curiosity."

"Well, perhaps, you're right, Miss Blacklock, but my own diagnosis would be a severe attack of Nosy Parkeritis . . ."

"She's a very harmless old creature," said Miss Blacklock.

Dangerous as a rattlesnake if you only knew, the Inspector thought grimly. But he had no intention of taking anyone into his confidence unnecessarily. Now that he knew definitely there was a killer at large, he felt that the less said the better. He didn't want the next person bumped off to be Jane Marple.

Somewhere—a killer . . . Where?

"I won't waste time offering sympathy, Miss Blacklock," he said. "As a matter of fact, I feel pretty bad about Miss Bunner's death. We ought to have been able to prevent it."

"I don't see what you could have done."

"No—well, it wouldn't have been easy. But now we've got to work fast. Who's doing this, Miss Blacklock? Who's had two shots at killing you, and will probably, if we don't work fast enough, soon have another?"

Letitia Blacklock shivered. "I don't know, Inspector—I don't know at all!"

"I've checked up with Mrs. Goedler. She's given me all the help she can. It wasn't very much. There are just a few people who would definitely profit by your death. First: Pip and Emma. Patrick and Julia Simmons are the right age, but their background seems clear enough. Anyway, we can't concentrate on those two alone. Tell me, Miss Blacklock, would you recognize Sonia Goedler if you saw her?"

"Recognize Sonia? Why, of course—" She stopped suddenly. "No," she said slowly, "I don't know that I would. It's a long time. Thirty years . . . She'd be an elderly woman now."

"What was she like as you remember her?"

"Sonia?" Miss Blacklock considered for some moments. "She was rather small, dark . . ."

"Any special peculiarities? Mannerisms?"

"No—no, I don't think so. She was gay—very gay."

"She mayn't be so gay now," said the Inspector. "Have you got a photograph of her?"

"Of Sonia? Let me see—not a proper photograph. I've got some old snapshots—in an album somewhere—at least I think there's one of her."

"Ah. Can I have a look at it?"

"Yes, of course. Now where did I put that album?"

"Tell me, Miss Blacklock, do you consider it remotely possible that Mrs. Swettenham might be Sonia Goedler?"

"Mrs. Swettenham?" Miss Blacklock looked at him in lively astonishment. "But her husband was in the Government Service—in India first, I think, and then in Hong Kong."

"What you mean is, that that's the story she's told you. You don't, as we say in the Courts, know it of your own knowledge, do you?"

"No," said Miss Blacklock slowly. "When you put it like that, I don't . . . But Mrs. Swettenham? Oh, it's absurd!"

"Did Sonia Goedler ever do any acting? Amateur theatricals?"

"Oh, yes. She was good."

"There you are! Another thing, Mrs. Swettenham wears a wig. At least," the Inspector corrected himself, "Mrs. Harmon says she does."

"Yes—yes, I suppose it might be a wig. All those little gray curls. But I still think it's absurd. She's really very nice and exceedingly funny sometimes."

"Then there's Miss Hinchliffe and Miss Murgatroyd. Could either of them be Sonia Goedler?"

"Miss Hinchliffe is too tall. She's as tall as a man."

"Miss Murgatroyd then?"

"Oh, but—oh, no, I'm sure Miss Murgatroyd couldn't be Sonia."

"You don't see very well, do you, Miss Blacklock?"

"I'm nearsighted; is that what you mean?"

"Yes. What I'd like to see is a snapshot of this Sonia Goedler, even if it's a long time ago and not a good likeness. We're trained, you know, to pick out resemblances, in a way no amateur can ever do."

"I'll try and find it for you."

"Now."

"What, at once?"

"I'd prefer it."

"Very well. Now, let me see. I saw that album when we were tidying a lot of books out of the cupboard. Julia was helping me. She laughed, I remember, at the clothes we used to wear in those days . . . The books we put in the shelf in the drawing-room. Where did we put the albums and the big bound volumes of the *Art Journal?* What a wretched memory I have! Perhaps Julia will remember. She's at home today."

"I'll find her."

The Inspector departed on his quest. He did not find Julia in any of the downstairs rooms. Mitzi, asked where Miss Simmons was, said crossly that it was not her affair.

"Me! I stay in my kitchen and concern myself with the lunch. And nothing do I eat that I have not cooked myself. Nothing, do you hear?"

The Inspector called up the stairs, "Miss Simmons," and getting no response, went up.

He met Julia face to face just as he turned the corner of the landing. She had just emerged from a door that showed behind it a small twisty staircase.

"I was up in the attic," she explained. "What is it?"

Inspector Craddock explained.

"Those old photograph albums? Yes, I remember them quite well. We put them in the big cupboard in the study, I think. I'll find them for you."

She led the way downstairs and pushed open the study door. Near the window there was a large cupboard. Julia pulled it open and disclosed a heterogeneous mass of objects.

"Junk," said Julia. "All junk. But elderly people simply will not throw things away."

The Inspector knelt down and took a couple of old-fashioned albums from the bottom shelf.

"Are these they?"

"Yes."

Miss Blacklock came in and joined them.

"Oh, so that's where we put them. I couldn't remember."

Craddock had the books on the table and was turning the pages.

Women in large cartwheel hats, women with dresses tapering down to their feet so that they could hardly walk. The photos had captions neatly printed underneath them, but the ink was old and faded.

"It would be in this one," said Miss Blacklock. "On about the second or third page. The other book is after Sonia had married and gone away." She turned a page. "It ought to be here." She stopped.

There were several empty spaces on the page. Craddock bent down and deciphered the faded writing: "Sonia . . . Self . . . R.G." A little further along, "Sonia and Belle on beach." And again on the opposite page, "Picnic at Skeyne." He turned over another page: "Charlotte, Self, Sonia, R.G."

Craddock stood up. His lips were grim.

"Somebody has removed these photographs—not long ago, I should say."

"There weren't any blank spaces when we looked at them the other day. Were there, Julia?"

"I didn't look very closely—only at some of the dresses. But no, you're right, Aunt Letty, there weren't any blank spaces."

Craddock looked grimmer still.

"Somebody," he said, "has removed every photo of Sonia Goedler from this album."

18. *The Letters*

"SORRY to worry you again, Mrs. Haymes."

"It doesn't matter," said Phillipa coldly.

"Shall we go into this room here?"

"The study? Yes, if you like, Inspector. It's very cold. There's no fire."

"It doesn't matter. It's not for long. And we're not so likely to be overheard here."

"Does that matter?"

"Not to me, Mrs. Haymes. It might to you."

"What do you mean?"

"I think you told me, Mrs. Haymes, that your husband was killed fighting in Italy?"

"Well?"

"Wouldn't it have been simpler to have told me the truth—that he was a deserter from his regiment."

He saw her face grow white, and her hands close and unclose themselves.

She said bitterly, "Do you have to rake up everything?"

Craddock said dryly, "We expect people to tell us the truth about themselves."

She was silent. Then she said, "Well?"

"What do you mean by 'Well,' Mrs. Haymes?"

"I mean, what are you going to do about it? Tell everybody? Is that necessary—or fair—or kind?"

"Does nobody know?"

"Nobody here. Harry—" Her voice changed. "My son, he doesn't know. I don't want him to know. I don't want him to know—ever."

"Then let me tell you that you're taking a very big risk, Mrs. Haymes. When the boy is old enough to understand, tell him the truth. If he finds out by himself some day—it won't be good for him. If you go on stuffing him up with tales of his father dying like a hero—"

"I don't do that. I'm not completely dishonest. I just don't talk about it. His father was—killed in the war. After all, that's what it amounts to —for us."

"But your husband is still alive?"

"Perhaps. How should I know?"

"When did you see him last, Mrs. Haymes?"

Phillipa said quickly, "I haven't seen him for years."

"Are you quite sure that's true? You didn't, for instance, see him about a fortnight ago?"

"What are you suggesting?"

"It never seemed to me very likely that you met Rudi Scherz in the summer-house here. But Mitzi's story was very emphatic. I suggest, Mrs. Haymes, that the man you came back from work to meet that morning was your husband."

"I didn't meet anybody in the summer-house."

"He was hard up for money, perhaps, and you supplied him with some?"

"I've not seen him, I tell you. I didn't meet anybody in the summer-house."

"Deserters are often rather desperate men. They often take part in robberies, you know. Holdups. Things of that kind. And they have foreign revolvers very often that they've brought back from abroad."

"I don't know where my husband is. I haven't seen him for years."

"Is that your last word, Mrs. Haymes?"

"I've nothing else to say."

II

Craddock came away from his interview with Phillipa Haymes feeling angry and baffled.

"Obstinate as a mule," he said to himself angrily.

He was fairly sure that Phillipa was lying, but he hadn't succeeded in breaking down her obstinate denials.

He wished he knew a little more about ex-Captain Haymes. His information was meager. An unsatisfactory Army record, but nothing to suggest that Haymes was likely to turn criminal.

And, anyway, Haymes didn't fit in with the oiled door.

Someone in the house had done that, or someone with easy access to it.

He stood looking up the staircase, and suddenly he wondered what Julia had been doing up in the attic. An attic, he thought, was an unlikely place for the fastidious Julia to visit.

What had she been doing up there?

He ran lightly up to the first floor. There was no one about. He opened the door out of which Julia had come and went up the narrow stairs to the attic.

There were trunks there, old suitcases, various broken articles of furniture, a chair with a leg off, a broken china lamp, part of an old dinner service.

He turned to the trunks and opened the lid of one.

Clothes. Old-fashioned, quite good quality women's clothes. Clothes belonging, he supposed, to Miss Blacklock, or to her sister who had died.

He opened another trunk.

Curtains.

He passed to a small attaché case. It had papers in it and letters. Very old letters, yellowed with time.

He looked at the outside of the case which had the initials CLB on it. He deduced correctly that it had belonged to Letitia's sister Charlotte. He unfolded one of the letters. It began, *Dearest Charlotte: Yesterday Belle felt well enough to go for a picnic. R. G. also took a day off. The Asvogel flotation has gone splendidly; R. G. is terribly pleased about it. The preference shares are at a premium.*

He skipped the rest and looked at the signature:

Your loving sister, Letitia.

He picked up another.

Darling Charlotte: I wish you would sometimes make up your mind to see people. You do exaggerate, you know. It isn't nearly as bad as you think. And people really don't mind things like that. It's not the disfigurement you think it is.

He nodded his head. He remembered Belle Goedler saying that Charlotte Blacklock had a disfigurement or deformity of some kind. Letitia had, in the end, resigned her job to go and look after her sister. These letters all breathed the anxious spirit of her affection and love for an invalid. She had written her sister, apparently, long accounts of everyday happenings, of any little detail that she thought might interest the sick girl. And Charlotte had kept these letters. Occasionally odd snapshots had been enclosed.

Excitement suddenly flooded Craddock's mind. Here, it might be, he would find a clue. In these letters there would be written down things that Letitia Blacklock herself had long forgotten. Here was a faithful picture of the past and somewhere amongst it there might be a clue that would help him to identify the unknown. Photographs, too. There might, just possibly, be a photograph of Sonia Goedler here that the person who had taken the other photos out of the album did not know about.

Inspector Craddock packed the letters up again carefully, closed the case and started down the stairs.

Letitia Blacklock, standing on the landing below, looked at him in amazement.

"Was that you up in the attic? I heard footsteps. I couldn't imagine who—"

"Miss Blacklock, I have found some letters here, written by you to your sister Charlotte many years ago. Will you allow me to take them away and read them?"

She flushed angrily.

"Must you do a thing like that? Why? What good can they be to you?"

"They might give me a picture of Sonia Goedler, of her character— there may be some allusion—some incident—that will help."

"They are private letters, Inspector."

"I know."

"I suppose you will take them anyway . . . You have the power to do so, I suppose, or you can easily get it. Take them—take them! But you'll find very little about Sonia. She married and went away only a year or two after I began to work for Randall Goedler."

Craddock said obstinately, "There may be something." He added, "We've got to try everything. I assure you the danger is very real."

She said, biting her lips:

"I know. Bunny is dead—from taking an aspirin tablet that was meant for me. It may be Patrick, or Julia, or Phillipa or Mitzi next—somebody young with their life in front of them. Somebody who drinks a glass of wine that is poured out for me, or eats a chocolate that is sent to me. Oh, take the letters—take them away. And afterwards burn them. They don't mean anything to anyone but me and Charlotte. It's all over—gone— past. Nobody remembers now . . ."

Her hand went up to the choker of false pearls she was wearing. Craddock thought how incongruous it looked with her tweed coat and skirt.

She said again, "Take the letters."

III

It was the following afternoon that the Inspector called at the vicarage. It was a dark gusty day.

Miss Marple had her chair pulled close to the fire and was knitting. Bunch was on hands and knees, crawling about the floor, cutting out material to a pattern.

She sat back and pushed a mop of hair out of her eyes, looking up expectantly at Craddock.

"I don't know if it's a breach of confidence," said the Inspector, addressing himself to Miss Marple, "but I'd like you to look at this letter."

He explained the circumstances of his discovery in the attic.

"It's rather a touching collection of letters," he said. "Miss Blacklock poured out everything in the hopes of sustaining her sister's interest in life and keeping her health good. There's a very clear picture of an old father in the background—old Dr. Blacklock. A real old pigheaded bully, absolutely set in his ways, and convinced that everything he thought and said was right. Probably killed thousands of patients through obstinacy. He wouldn't stand for any new ideas or methods."

"I don't really know that I blame him there," said Miss Marple. "I always feel that the young doctors are only too anxious to experiment. After they've whipped out all our teeth, and administered quantities of very peculiar glands, and removed bits of our insides, they then confess that nothing can be done for us. I really prefer the old-fashioned remedy of big black bottles of medicine. After all, one can always pour those down the sink."

She took the letter that Craddock handed her.

He said:

"I want you to read it because I think that that generation is more easily understood by you than by me. I don't know really quite how these people's minds worked."

Miss Marple unfolded the fragile paper.

Dearest Charlotte,

I've not written for two days because we've been having the most terrible domestic complications. Randall's sister Sonia—(you remember her? She came to take you out in the car that day? How I wish you would go out more)—Sonia has declared her intention of marrying one Dmitri Stamfordis. I've only seen him once. Very attractive—not to be trusted, I should say. R.G. raves against him and says he is a crook and a swindler. Belle, bless her, just smiles and lies on her sofa. Sonia, who though she looks so impassive has really a terrific temper, is simply wild with R.G. I really thought yesterday she was going to murder him!

I've done my best. I've talked to Sonia and I've talked to R.G. and I've got them both in a more reasonable frame of mind and then they come together and it all starts over again! You've no idea how *tiring* it is. R.G. has been making enquiries—and it does really seem as though this Stamfordis man is thoroughly undesirable.

In the meantime, business is being neglected. I carry on at the office and in a way it's rather fun because R.G. gives me a free hand. He said to me yesterday: "Thank heaven, there's one sane person in the world. You're never likely to fall in love with a crook, Blackie, are you?" I said I didn't think I was likely to fall in love with anybody. R.G. said: "Let's start a few new hares in the city." He's really rather a mischievous devil sometimes and he sails terribly near the wind. "You're quite determined to keep me on the straight and narrow path, aren't you, Blackie?" he said the other day. And I shall, too! I can't understand how people can't *see* when a thing's dishonest—but R.G. really and truly *doesn't.* He only knows what is actually against the law.

Belle only laughs at all this. She thinks the fuss about Sonia is all nonsense. "Sonia has her own money," she said. "Why shouldn't she marry this man if she wants to?" I said it might turn out to be a terrible mistake and Belle said, "It's never a mistake to marry a man you want to marry—even if you regret it." And then she said, "I suppose Sonia doesn't want to break with Randall because of money. Sonia's very fond of money."

No more now. How is Father? I won't say give him my love. But you can if you think it's better to do so. Have you seen more people? You really must not be morbid, darling.

Sonia asks to be remembered to you. She has just come in and is closing and unclosing her hands like an angry cat sharpening its claws. I think she and R.G. have had another row. Of course Sonia can be very irritating. She stares you down with that cool stare of hers.

Lots of love, darling, and buck up. This iodine treatment may make a lot of difference. I've been enquiring about it and it really does seem to have good results.

Your loving sister,
Letitia

Miss Marple folded the letter and handed it back. She looked abstracted.

"Well, what do you think about her?" Craddock urged. "What picture do you get of her?"

"Of Sonia? It's difficult, you know, to see anyone through another person's mind . . . Determined to get her own way—that, definitely, I think. And wanting the best of two worlds . . ."

"Closing and unclosing her hands like an angry cat," murmured Craddock. "You know, that reminds me of someone . . ."

He frowned.

"Making enquiries . . ." murmured Miss Marple.

"If we could get hold of the result of those enquiries—" said Craddock.

"Does that letter remind you of anything in St. Mary Mead?" asked Bunch, rather indistinctly since her mouth was full of pins.

"I really can't say it does, dear . . . Dr. Blacklock was, perhaps, a little like Mr. Curtiss the Wesleyan minister. He wouln't let his child wear a plate on her teeth. Said it was the Lord's will if her teeth stuck out. 'After all,' I said to him, 'you do trim your beard and cut your hair. It might be the Lord's will that your hair should grow out.' He said that was quite different. So like a man. But that doesn't help us with our present problem."

"We've never traced that revolver, you know. It wasn't Rudi Scherz's. If I knew who had had a revolver in Chipping Cleghorn."

"Colonel Easterbrook has one," said Bunch. "He keeps it in his collar drawer."

"How do you know, Mrs. Harmon?"

"Mrs. Butt told me. She's my daily. Or rather, my twice weekly. Being a military gentleman, she said, he'd naturally have a revolver and very handy it would be if burglars were to come along."

"When did she tell you this?"

"Ages ago. About six months ago, I should think."

"Colonel Easterbrook?" murmured Craddock.

"It's like those pointer things at fairs, isn't it?" said Bunch, still speaking through a mouthful of pins. "Go round and round and stop at something different every time."

"You're telling me!" said Craddock and groaned.

"Colonel Easterbrook was up at Little Paddocks to leave a book there one day. He could have oiled that door then. He was quite straightforward about being there, though. Not like Miss Hinchliffe."

Miss Marple coughed gently.

"You must make allowances for the times we live in, Inspector," she said. Craddock looked at her uncomprehendingly.

"After all," said Miss Marple, "you *are* the police, aren't you? People can't say everything they'd like to say to the police, can they?"

"I don't see why not," said Craddock. "Unless they've got some criminal matter to conceal."

"She means butter," said Bunch, crawling actively round a table leg to anchor a floating bit of paper. "Butter and corn for hens and sometimes cream—and sometimes even a side of bacon."

"Show him that note from Miss Blacklock," said Miss Marple. "It's some time ago now, but it reads like a first-class mystery story."

"What have I done with it? Is this the one you mean, Aunt Jane?" Miss Marple took it and looked at it.

"Yes," she said with satisfaction. "That's the one."

She handed it to the Inspector.

I have made inquiries—Thursday is the day, Miss Blacklock had written. *Any time after three. If there is any for me leave it in the usual place.*

Bunch spat out her pins and laughed. Miss Marple was watching the Inspector's face.

The vicar's wife took upon herself to explain.

"Thursday is the day one of the farms round here makes butter. They let anybody they like have a bit. It's usually Miss Hinchliffe who collects it. She's very much in with all the farmers—because of her pigs, I think. But it's all a bit hush-hush, you know; a kind of local scheme of barter. One person gets butter and sends along cucumbers, or something like that—and a little something when a pig's killed. And now and then an animal has an 'accident' and has to be destroyed. Oh, you know the sort of thing. Only one can't very well say it right out to the police. Because I suppose quite a lot of this barter is illegal—only nobody really knows because it's all so complicated. But I expect Hinch had slipped into Little Paddocks with a pound of butter or something and had put it in the 'usual place.' That's a flour bin under the cupboard, by the way. It doesn't have flour in it."

Craddock sighed.

"I'm glad I came here to you ladies," he said.

"There are clothing coupons, too," said Bunch. "Not usually bought—that's not considered honest. No money passes. But people like Mrs. Butt or Mrs. Finch or Mrs. Huggins like a nice woolen dress or a winter coat that hasn't seen too much wear and they pay for it with coupons instead of money."

"You'd better not tell me any more," said Craddock. "It's all against the law."

"Then there oughtn't to be such silly laws," said Bunch, filling her mouth up with pins again. "I don't do it, of course, because Julian doesn't like me to, so I don't. But I know what's going on, of course."

A kind of despair was coming over the Inspector.

"It all sounds so pleasant and ordinary," he said. "Funny and petty and simple. And yet one woman and a man have been killed, and another woman may be killed before I can get anything definite to go on. I've left off worrying about Pip and Emma for the moment. I'm concentrating on

Sonia. I wish I knew what she looked like. There was a snapshot or two in with these letters, but not one that could have been her."

"How do you know it couldn't have been her? Do you know what she looked like?"

"She was small and dark, Miss Blacklock said."

"Really," said Miss Marple, "that's very interesting."

"There was one snap that reminded me vaguely of someone. A tall fair girl with her hair all done up on top of her head. I don't know who she could have been. Anyway, it can't have been Sonia. Do you think Mrs. Swettenham could have been dark when she was a girl?"

"Not very dark," said Bunch. "She's got blue eyes."

"I hoped there might be a photo of Dmitri Stamfordis—but I suppose that was too much to hope for—Well"—he took up the letter—"I'm sorry this doesn't suggest anything to you, Miss Marple."

"Oh, but it does," said Miss Marple. "It suggests a good deal—Just read it through again, Inspector—especially where it says that Randall Goedler was making inquiries about Dmitri Stamfordis."

Craddock stared at her.

The telephone rang.

Bunch got up from the floor and went out into the hall where, in accordance with the best Victorian traditions, the telephone had originally been placed and where it still was.

She re-entered the room to say to Craddock, "It's for you."

Slightly surprised, the Inspector went out to the instrument—carefully shutting the door of the living room behind him.

"Craddock? Rydesdale here."

"Yes, sir."

"I've been looking through your report. In the interview you had with Phillipa Haymes I see she states positively that she hasn't seen her husband since his desertion from the Army."

"That's right, sir—she was most emphatic. But in my opinion she wasn't speaking the truth."

"I agree with you. Do you remember a case about ten days ago—man run over by a lorry—taken to Milchester General with concussion and a fractured pelvis?"

"The fellow who snatched a child practically from under the wheels of a lorry, and got run down himself?"

"That's the one. No papers of any kind on him and nobody came forward to identify him. Looked as though he might be on the run. He died last night without regaining consciousness. But he's been identified

—deserter from the Army—Ronald Haymes, ex-Captain in the South Loamshires."

"Phillipa Haymes' husband?"

"Yes. He had an old Chipping Cleghorn bus ticket on him, by the way —and quite a reasonable amount of money."

"So he did get money from his wife? I always thought he was the man Mitzi overhead talking to her in the summer-house. She denied it flatly, of course. But surely, sir, that lorry accident was before—"

Rydesdale took the words out of his mouth.

"Yes, he was taken to Milchester General on the 28th. The holdup at Little Paddocks was on the 29th. That lets him out of any possible connection with it. But his wife, of course, knew nothing about the accident. She may have been thinking all along that he was concerned in it. She'd hold her tongue—naturally—after all he was her husband."

"It was a fairly gallant bit of work, wasn't it, sir?" said Craddock slowly.

"Rescuing that child from the lorry? Yes. Plucky. Don't suppose it was cowardice that made Haymes desert. Well, all that's past history. For a man who'd blotted his copybook, it was a good death."

"I'm glad for her sake," said the Inspector. "And for that boy of theirs."

"Yes, he needn't be too ashamed of his father. And the young woman will be able to marry again now."

Craddock said slowly, "I was thinking of that, sir . . . It opens up— possibilities."

"You'd better break the news to her since you're on the spot."

"I will, sir. I'll push along there now. Or perhaps I'd better wait until she's back at Little Paddocks. It may be rather a shock—and there's someone else I rather want to have a word with first."

19. *Reconstruction of the Crime*

"I'LL PUT on a lamp by you before I go," said Bunch. "It's so dark in here. There's going to be a storm, I think."

She lifted the small reading lamp to the other side of the table where it would throw light on Miss Marple's knitting as she sat in a wide high-backed chair.

As the cord pulled across the table, Tiglath-Pileser, the cat, leapt upon it and bit and clawed it violently.

"No, Tiglath-Pileser, you mustn't. He really is awful. Look, he's nearly bitten it through—it's all frayed. Don't you understand, you idiotic puss, that you may get a nasty electric shock if you do that?"

"Thank you, dear," said Miss Marple, and put out a hand to turn on the lamp.

"It doesn't turn on there. You have to press that silly little switch halfway along the cord. Wait a minute. I'll take these flowers out of the way."

She lifted a bowl of Christmas roses across the table. Tiglath-Pileser, his tail switching, put out a mischievous paw and clawed Bunch's arm. She spilled some of the water out of the vase. It fell on the frayed area of cord and on Tiglath-Pileser himself, who leapt to the floor with an indignant hiss.

Miss Marple pressed the small pear-shaped switch. Where the water had soaked the frayed cord there was a flash and a crackle.

"Oh, dear," said Bunch. "It's blown out. Now I suppose all the lights in here are off." She tried them. "Yes, they are. So stupid being all on the same thingumabob. And it's made a burn on the table, too. Naughty Tiglath-Pileser—it's all his fault. Aunt Jane—what's the matter? Did it startle you?"

"It's nothing, dear. Just something I saw quite suddenly which I ought to have seen before. . . ."

"I'll go and fix the fuse and get the lamp from Julian's study."

"No, dear, don't bother. You'll miss your bus. I don't want any more light. I just want to sit quietly and—think about something. Hurry, dear, or you won't catch your bus."

When Bunch had gone, Miss Marple sat quite still for about two minutes. The air of the room was heavy and menacing with the gathering storm outside.

Miss Marple drew a sheet of paper towards her.

She wrote first: *Lamp?* and underlined it heavily.

After a moment or two, she wrote another word.

Her pencil traveled down the paper, making brief monosyllabic notes. . . .

II

In the rather dark living room of Boulders with its low ceiling and latticed windowpanes, Miss Hinchliffe and Miss Murgatroyd were having an argument.

"The trouble with you, Murgatroyd," said Miss Hinchliffe, "is that you won't try."

"But I tell you, Hinch, I can't remember a thing."

"Now look here, Amy Murgatroyd, we're going to do some constructive thinking. So far we haven't shone on the detective angle. I was quite wrong over that door business. You didn't hold the door open for the murderer after all. You're cleared, Murgatroyd!"

Miss Murgatroyd gave a rather watery smile.

"It's just our luck to have the only silent cleaning woman in Chipping Cleghorn," continued Miss Hinchliffe. "Usually I'm thankful for it, but this time it means we've got off to a bad start. Everybody else in the place knows about that second door in the drawing-room being used—and we only heard about it yesterday—"

"I still don't quite understand how—"

"It's perfectly simple. Our original premises were quite right. You can't hold open a door, wave a flashlight and shoot with a revolver all at the same time. We kept in the revolver and the flashlight and cut out the door. Well, we were wrong. It was the revolver we ought to have cut out."

"But he did have a revolver," said Miss Murgatroyd. "I saw it. It was there on the floor beside him."

"When he was dead, yes. It's all quite clear. He didn't fire that revolver—"

"Then who did?"

"That's what we're going to find out. But whoever did it, the same person put a couple of poisoned aspirin tablets by Letty Blacklock's bed —and thereby bumped off poor Dora Bunner. And that couldn't have been Rudi Scherz, because he's as dead as a doornail. It was someone who was in the room that night of the holdup and probably someone who was at the birthday party, too. And the only person that lets out is Mrs. Harmon."

"You think someone put those aspirins there the day of the birthday party?"

"Why not?"

"But how could they?"

"Well, we all went to the loo, didn't we?" said Miss Hinchliffe coarsely. "And I washed my hands in the bathroom because of that sticky cake. And little Sweetie Easterbrook powdered her grubby little face in Blacklock's bedroom, didn't she?"

"Hinch! Do you think she—"

"I don't know yet. Rather obvious, if she did. I don't think, if you were going to plant some tablets, that you'd want to be seen in the bedroom at all. Oh, yes there were plenty of opportunities."

"The men didn't go upstairs."

"There are back stairs. After all, if a man leaves the room, you don't follow him to see if he really is going where you think he is going. It wouldn't be delicate! Anyway, don't argue, Murgatroyd. I want to get back to the original attempt on Letty Blacklock. Now, to begin with, get the facts firmly into your head, because it's all going to depend upon you."

Miss Murgatroyd looked alarmed.

"Oh, dear, Hinch, you know what a muddle I get into!"

"It's not a question of your brains, or the gray fluff that passes for brains with you. It's a question of eyes. It's a question of what you saw."

"But I didn't see anything."

"The trouble with you is, Murgatroyd, as I said just now, that you won't try. Now pay attention. This is what happened: Whoever it is that's got it in for Letty Blacklock was there in that room that evening. He (I say he because it's easier, but there's no reason why it should be a man more than a woman except, of course, that men are dirty dogs), well, he has previously oiled that second door that leads out of the drawing-room and which is supposed to be nailed up or something. Don't ask me when he did it, because that confuses things. Actually, by choosing my time, I could walk into any house in Chipping Cleghorn and do anything I liked there for half an hour or so with no one being the wiser. It's just a question of working out where the daily women are and when the occupiers are out and exactly where they've gone and how long they'll be. Just good staff work. Now to continue: He's oiled that second door. It will open without a sound. Here's the setup: Lights go out, door A (the front door) opens with a flourish. Business with flashlight and holdup lines. In the meantime, while we're all goggling, X (that's the best term to use) slips quietly out by door B into the dark hall, comes up behind that Swiss idiot, takes a couple of shots at Letty Blacklock and then shoots the Swiss. Drops the revolver, where lazy thinkers like you will assume it's evidence that the Swiss did the shooting, and nips back into the room again by the time that someone gets a lighter going. Got it?"

"Yes—ye-es, but who was it?"

"Well, if you don't know, Murgatroyd, nobody does!"

"Me?" Miss Murgatroyd fairly twittered in alarm. "But I don't know anything at all. I don't really, Hinch!"

"Use that fluff of yours you call a brain. To begin with, where was everybody when the lights went out?"

"I don't know."

"Yes, you do. You're maddening, Murgatroyd. You know where you were, don't you? You were behind the door."

"Yes—yes, I was. It knocked against my corn when it flew open."

"Why don't you go to a proper chiropodist instead of messing about yourself with your feet? You'll give yourself blood poisoning one of these days. Come on now—you're behind the door. I'm standing against the mantelpiece with my tongue hanging out for a drink. Letty Blacklock is by the table near the archway, getting the cigarettes. Patrick Simmons has gone through the archway into the small room where Letty Blacklock has had the drinks put. Agreed?"

"Yes, yes, I remember all that."

"Good; now somebody else followed Patrick into that room or was just starting to follow him. One of the men. The annoying thing is that I can't remember whether it was Easterbrook or Edmund Swettenham. Do you remember?"

"No, I don't."

"You wouldn't! And there was someone else who went through to the small room: Phillipa Haymes. I remember that distinctly because I remember noticing what a nice flat back she has, and I thought to myself that girl would look well on a horse. I was watching her and thinking just that. She went over to the mantelpiece in the other room. I don't know what it was she wanted there, because at that moment the lights went out.

"So that's the position. In the far drawing-room are Patrick Simmons, Phillipa Haymes and either Colonel Easterbrook or Edmund Swettenham—we don't know which. Now, Murgatroyd, pay attention. The most probable thing is that it was one of those three who did it. If anyone wanted to get out of that far door, they'd naturally take care to put themselves in a convenient place when the lights went out. So, as I say, in all probability, it's one of those three. And in that case, Murgatroyd, there's not a thing you can do about it!"

Miss Murgatroyd brightened perceptibly.

"On the other hand," continued Miss Hinchliffe, "there's the possibility that it wasn't one of those three. And that's where you come in, Murgatroyd."

"But how should I know anything about it?"

"As I said before, if you don't nobody does."

"But I don't! I really don't! I couldn't see anything at all!"

"Oh, yes, you could. You're the only person who could see. You were standing behind the door. You couldn't look at the flashlight—because the door was between you and it. You were facing the other way, the same way as the flashlight was pointing. The rest of us were just dazzled. But you weren't dazzled."

"No—no, perhaps not, but I didn't see anything, the flashlight went round and round—"

"Showing you what? It rested on faces, didn't it? And on tables? And on chairs?"

"Yes—yes, it did . . . Miss Bunner, her mouth wide open and her eyes popping out of her head, staring and blinking."

"That's the stuff!" Miss Hinchliffe gave a sigh of relief. "The difficulty there is in making you use that gray fluff of yours! Now then, keep it up."

"But I didn't see any more. I didn't really."

"You mean you saw an empty room? Nobody standing about? Nobody sitting down?"

"No, of course not that. Mrs. Harmon was sitting on the arm of a chair. She had her eyes tight shut and her knuckles all doubled up to her face—like a child."

"Good, that's Mrs. Harmon and Miss Bunner. Don't you see yet what I'm getting at? The difficulty is that I don't want to put ideas into your head. But when we've eliminated who you did see—we can get on to the important point which is, was there anyone you didn't see? Got it? Besides the tables and the chairs and the chrysanthemums and the rest of it, there were certain people: Julia Simmons, Mrs. Swettenham, Mrs. Easterbrook—either Colonel Easterbrook or Edmund Swettenham—Dora Bunner and Bunch Harmon. All right, you saw Bunch Harmon and Dora Bunner. Cross them off. Now think, Murgatroyd, *think*, was there one of those people who definitely *wasn't* there?"

Miss Murgatroyd jumped slightly as a branch knocked against the open window. She shut her eyes. She murmured to herself . . .

"The flowers . . . on the table . . . the big armchair . . . the flashlight didn't come round as far as you, Hinch—Mrs. Harmon, yes. . . ."

The telephone rang sharply. Miss Hinchliffe went to it.

"Hullo, yes? The station?"

The obedient Miss Murgatroyd, her eyes closed, was reliving the night of the 29th. The flashlight sweeping slowly round . . . a group of people . . . the windows . . . the sofa . . . Dora Bunner . . . the wall . . . the table with the lamp . . . the archway . . . the sudden spat of the revolver . . .

". . . but that's extraordinary!" said Miss Murgatroyd.

"What?" Miss Hinchliffe was barking angrily into the telephone. "Been there since this morning? What time? Damn and blast you, and you only ring me up now? I'll set the S.P.C.A. after you. An oversight? Is that all you've got to say?"

She banged down the receiver.

"It's that dog," she said. "The red setter. Been at the station since this morning—since this morning at eight o'clock! Without a drop of water! And the idiots only ring me up now. I'm going to get her right away."

She plunged out of the room, Miss Murgatroyd squeaking shrilly in her wake.

"But listen, Hinch, a most extraordinary thing . . . I don't understand it . . ."

Miss Hinchliffe had dashed out of the door and across to the shed which served as a garage.

"We'll go on with it when I come back," she called. "I can't wait for you to come with me. You've got your bedroom slippers on as usual."

She pressed the starter of the car and backed out of the garage with a jerk. Miss Murgatroyd skipped nimbly sideways.

"But listen, Hinch, I must tell you—"

"When I come back . . ."

The car jerked and shot forwards. Miss Murgatroyd's voice came faintly after it on a high excited note:

"But, Hinch, she wasn't there . . ."

III

Overhead, the clouds had been gathering thick and dark. Miss Murgatroyd plunged across to a line of string on which she had, some hours previously, hung out a couple of jumpers and a pair of woolen combinations to dry.

She was murmuring under her breath:

"Really most extraordinary . . . Oh, dear, I shall never get these down in time . . . and they were nearly dry. . . ."

She struggled with a recalcitrant clothespeg, then turned her head, as she heard someone approaching.

Then she smiled a pleased welcome.

"Hullo—do go inside; you'll get wet."

"Let me help you."

"Oh, if you don't mind . . . so annoying if they all get soaked again. I really ought to let down the line, but I think I can just reach."

"Here's your scarf. Shall I put it round your neck?"

"Oh, thank you . . . Yes, perhaps . . . If I could just reach this peg. . . ."

The woolen scarf was slipped round her neck and then, suddenly, pulled tight . . .

Miss Murgatroyd's mouth opened, but no sound came except a small choking gurgle.

And the scarf was pulled tighter still . . .

IV

On her way back from the station, Miss Hinchliffe stopped the car to pick up Miss Marple who was hurrying along the street.

"Hullo," she shouted. "You'll get very wet. Come and have tea with us. I saw Bunch waiting for the bus. You'll be all alone at the vicarage. Come and join us. Murgatroyd and I are doing a bit of reconstruction of the crime. I rather think we're just getting somewhere. Mind the dog. She's rather nervous."

"What a beauty."

"Yes, lovely bitch, isn't she? Those fools kept her at the station since this morning without letting me know. I told them off, the lazy devils. Oh! Excuse my language, I was brought up by grooms at home in Ireland."

The little car turned with a jerk into the small back yard of Boulders.

A crowd of eager ducks and fowls encircled the two ladies as they descended.

"Curse Murgatroyd," said Miss Hinchliffe, "she hasn't given 'em their corn."

"Is it difficult to get corn?" Miss Marple inquired.

Miss Hinchliffe winked.

"I'm in with most of the farmers," she said.

Shooing away the hens, she escorted Miss Marple towards the cottage.

"Hope you're not too wet?"

"No, this is a very good mackintosh."

"I'll light the fire if Murgatroyd hasn't lit it. Hiyah, Murgatroyd? Where is the woman? Murgatroyd! Where's that dog? She's disappeared now."

A slow dismal howl came from outside.

"Curse the silly bitch." Miss Hinchliffe tramped to the door and called:

"Hyoup, Cutie—Cutie! Damn silly name but that's what they called her apparently. We must find her another name. Hiyah, Cutie!"

The red setter was sniffing at something lying below the taut line where a row of garments swirled in the wind.

"Murgatroyd's not even had the sense to bring the washing in. Where is she?"

Again the red setter nosed at what seemed to be a pile of clothes, and raised her nose high in the air and howled again.

"What's the matter with the dog?"

Miss Hinchliffe strode across the grass.

And quickly, apprehensively, Miss Marple ran after her. They stood there, side by side, the rain beating down on them and the older woman's arm went round the younger one's shoulders.

She felt the muscles go stiff and taut as Miss Hinchliffe stood looking down on the thing lying there, with the blue congested face and the protruding tongue.

"I'll kill whoever did this," said Miss Hinchliffe in a low quite voice, "if I once get my hands on her. . . ."

Miss Marple said questioningly:

"Her?"

Miss Hinchliffe turned a ravaged face towards her.

"Yes. I know who it is—near enough . . . That is, it's one of three possibles."

She stood for another moment, looking down at her dead friend, and then turned towards the house. Her voice was dry and hard.

"We must ring up the police," she said. "And while we're waiting for them, I'll tell you. My fault, in a way, that Murgatroyd's lying out there. I made a game of it . . . Murder isn't a game . . ."

"No," said Miss Marple. "Murder isn't a game."

"You know something about it, don't you?" said Miss Hinchliffe as she lifted the receiver and dialed.

She made a brief report and hung up.

"They'll be here in a few minutes . . . Yes, I heard that you'd been mixed up in this sort of business before . . . I think it was Edmund Swettenham told me so . . . Do you want to hear what we were doing, Murgatroyd and I?"

Succinctly she described the conversation held before her departure for the station.

"She called after me, you know, just as I was leaving . . . That's how I know it's a woman and nòt a man . . . If I'd waited—if I'd only listened! God dammit, the dog could have stopped where she was for another quarter of an hour."

"Don't blame yourself, my dear. That does no good. One can't foresee."

"No, one can't . . . Something tapped against the window, I remember. Perhaps she was outside there then—yes, of course, she must have been . . . coming to the house . . . and there were Murgatroyd and I shouting at each other. Top of our voices . . . She heard . . . She heard it all . . ."

"You haven't told me yet what your friend said."

"Just one sentence! *She wasn't there.*'"

She paused. "You see? There were three women we hadn't eliminated. Mrs. Swettenham, Mrs. Easterbrook, Julia Simmons. And one of those three—*wasn't there* . . . She wasn't there in the drawing-room because she had slipped out through the other door and was out in the hall."

"Yes," said Miss Marple, "I see."

"It's one of those three women. I don't know which. But I'll find out!"

"Excuse me," said Miss Marple. "But did she—did Miss Murgatroyd, I mean—say it exactly as you said it?"

"How d'you mean—as I said it?"

"Oh, dear, how can I explain? You said it like this. *She wasn't there.* An equal emphasis on every word. You see, there are three ways you could say it. You could say, '*She* wasn't there.' Very personal. Or again, 'She *wasn't* there.' Confirming some suspicion already held. Or else you could say (and this is nearer to the way you said it just now), 'She wasn't *there.*' Quite blankly—with the emphasis, if there was emphasis—on the *there.*"

"I don't know." Miss Hinchliffe shook her head. "I can't remember . . . How the hell can I remember? I think, yes, surely she'd say, '*She* wasn't there.' That would be the natural way, I should think. But I simply don't know. Does it make any difference?"

"Yes," said Miss Marple thoughtfully. "I think so. It's a very *slight* indication, of course, but I think it *is* an indication. Yes, I should think it makes a lot of difference."

20. *Miss Marple Is Missing*

THE POSTMAN, rather to his disgust, had lately been given orders to make an afternoon delivery of letters in Chipping Cleghorn as well as a morning one.

On this particular afternoon he left three letters at Little Paddocks at exactly ten minutes to five.

One was addressed to Phillipa Haymes in a schoolboy's hand; the other two were for Miss Blacklock. She opened them as she and Phillipa sat down at the tea table. The torrential rain had enabled Phillipa to leave Dayas Hall early today, since once she had shut up the greenhouses there was nothing more to do.

Miss Blacklock tore open her first letter which was a bill for repairing the kitchen boiler. She snorted angrily.

"Dymond's prices are preposterous—quite preposterous. Still, I suppose all the other people are just as bad."

She opened the second letter which was in a handwriting quite unknown to her.

> *Dear Cousin Letty (it said),*
> *I hope it will be all right for me to come to you on Tuesday? I wrote to Patrick two days ago but he hasn't answered. So I presume it's all right. Mother is coming to England next month and hopes to see you then.*
> *My train arrives at Chipping Cleghorn at 6:15 if that's convenient?*
> > *Yours affectionately,*
> > *Julia Simmons*

Miss Blacklock read the letter once with astonishment pure and simple, and then again with a certain grimness. She looked up at Phillipa who was smiling over her son's letter.

"Are Julia and Patrick back, do you know?"

Phillipa looked up.

"Yes, they came in just after I did. They went upstairs to change. They were wet."

"Perhaps you'd not mind going and calling them."

"Of course I will."

"Wait a moment—I'd like you to read this."

She handed Phillipa the letter she had received.

Phillipa read it and frowned. "I don't understand . . ."

"Nor do I, quite . . . I think it's about time I did. Call Patrick and Julia, Phillipa."

Phillipa called from the bottom of the stairs, "Patrick! Julia! Miss Blacklock wants you."

Patrick came running down the stairs and entered the room.

"Don't go, Phillipa," said Miss Blacklock.

"Hullo, Aunt Letty," said Patrick cheerfully. "Want me?"

"Yes, I do. Perhaps you'll give me an explanation of this?"

Patrick's face showed an almost comical dismay as he read.

"I meant to telegraph her! What an ass I am!"

"This letter, I presume, is from your sister Julia?"

"Yes—Yes, it is."

Miss Blacklock said grimly, *"Then who, may I ask, is the young woman whom you brought here as Julia Simmons,* and who I was given to understand was your sister and my cousin?"

"Well—you see—Aunt Letty—the fact of the matter is—I can explain it all—I know I oughtn't to have done it—but it really seemed more of a lark than anything else. If you'll just let me explain—"

"I am waiting for you to explain. *Who is this young woman?"*

"Well, I met her at a cocktail party soon after I got demobbed. We got talking and I said I was coming here and then—well, we thought it might be rather a good wheeze if I brought her along . . . You see Julia, the real Julia, was mad to go on the stage and mother had seven fits at the idea—however, Julia got a chance to join a jolly good repertory company up in Perth or somewhere and she thought she'd give it a try—but she thought she'd keep Mum calm by letting Mum think that she was here with me, studying to be a dispenser like a good little girl."

"I still want to know who this other young woman is."

Patrick turned with relief as Julia, cool and aloof, came into the room.

"The balloon's gone up," he said.

Julia raised her eyebrows. Then, still cool, she came forward and sat down.

"O.K." she said. "That's that. I suppose you're very angry?" She studied Miss Blacklock's face with almost dispassionate interest. "I should be if I were you."

"Who are you?"

Julia sighed.

"I think the moment's come when I make a clean breast of things.

Here we go. I'm one-half of the Pip and Emma combination. To be exact, my christened name is Emma Jocelyn Stamfordis—only father soon dropped the Stamfordis. I think he called himself De Courcy next.

"My father and mother, let me tell you, split up about three years after Pip and I were born. Each of them went their own way. And they split us up. I was father's part of the loot. He was a bad parent on the whole, though quite a charming one. I had various desert spells of being educated in convents—when father hadn't any money, or was preparing to engage in some particularly nefarious deal. He used to pay the first term with every sign of affluence and then depart and leave me on the nuns' hands for a year or two. In the intervals, he and I had some very good times together, moving in cosmopolitan society. However, the war separated us completely. I've no idea of what's happened to him. I had a few adventures myself. I was with the French Resistance for a time. Quite exciting. To cut a long story short, I landed up in London and began to think about my future. I knew that mother's brother with whom she'd had a frightful row, had died a very rich man. I looked up his will to see if there was anything for me. There wasn't—not directly, that is to say. I made a few inquiries about his widow—it seemed she was quite gaga and kept under drugs and was dying by inches. Frankly, it looked as though *you* were my best bet. You were going to come into a hell of a lot of money and from all I could find out, you didn't seem to have anyone much to spend it on. I'll be quite frank. It occurred to me that if I could get to know you in a friendly kind of way, and if you took a fancy to me —well, after all, conditions have changed a bit, haven't they, since Uncle Randall died? I mean, any money we ever had has been swept away in the cataclysm of Europe. I thought you might pity a poor orphan girl, all alone in the world, and make her, perhaps, a small allowance."

"Oh, you did, did you?" said Miss Blacklock grimly.

"Yes. Of course, I hadn't seen you then . . . I visualized a kind of sob stuff approach . . . Then, by a marvelous stroke of luck, I met Patrick here—and he turned out to be your nephew or your cousin, or something. Well, that struck me as a marvelous chance. I went bullheaded for Patrick and he fell for me in a most gratifying way. The real Julia was all wet about this acting stuff and I soon persuaded her it was her duty to Art to go and fix herself up in some uncomfortable lodgings in Perth and train to be the new Sarah Bernhardt.

"You mustn't blame Patrick too much. He felt awfully sorry for me, all alone in the world—and he soon thought it would be a really marvelous idea for me to come here as his sister and do my stuff."

"And he also approved of your continuing to tell a tissue of lies to the police?"

"Have a heart, Letty. Don't you see that when that ridiculous holdup business happened—or rather after it happened—I began to feel I was in a bit of a spot? Let's face it; I've got a perfectly good motive for putting you out of the way. You've only got my word for it now that I wasn't the one who tried to do it. You can't expect me deliberately to go and incriminate myself. Even Patrick got nasty ideas about me from time to time, and if even *he* could think things like that, what on earth would the police think? That Detective Inspector struck me as a man of singularly skeptical mind. No; I figured out the only thing for me to do was to sit tight as Julia and just fade away when term came to an end.

"How was I to know that fool Julia, the real Julia, would go and have a row with the producer, and fling the whole thing up in a fit of temperament? She writes to Patrick and asks if she can come here, and instead of wiring to her 'Keep away,' he goes and forgets to do anything at all!" She cast an angry glance at Patrick. "Of all the utter idiots!"

She sighed.

"You don't know the straits I've been put to in Milchester! Of course, I haven't been to the hospital at all. But I had to go somewhere. Hours and hours I've spent in the pictures, seeing the most frightful films over and over again."

"Pip and Emma," murmured Miss Blacklock. "I never believed, somehow, in spite of what the Inspector said, that they were real—"

She looked searchingly at Julia.

"You're Emma," she said. "Where's Pip?"

Julia's eyes, limpid and innocent, met hers.

"I don't know," she said. "I haven't the least idea."

"I think you're lying, Julia. When did you see him last?"

Was there a momentary hesitation before Julia spoke?

She said clearly and deliberately, "I haven't seen him since we were both three years old—when my mother took him away. I haven't seen either him or my mother. I don't know where they are."

"And that's all you have to say?"

Julia sighed.

"I could say I was sorry. But it wouldn't really be true; because actually I'd do the same thing again—though not if I'd known about this murder business, of course."

"Julia," said Miss Blacklock, "I call you that because I'm used to it. You were with the French Resistance, you say?"

"Yes. For eighteen months."

"Then I suppose you learned to shoot?"

Again those cool blue eyes met hers.

"I can shoot all right. I'm a first-class shot. I didn't shoot at you, Letitia Blacklock, though you've only got my word for that. But I can tell you this, that if *I* had shot at you, I wouldn't have been likely to miss."

II

The sound of a car driving up to the door broke through the tenseness of the moment.

"Who can that be?" asked Miss Blacklock.

Mitzi put a tousled head in. She was showing the whites of her eyes.

"It is the police come again," she said. "This, it is persecution! Why will they not leave us alone? I will not bear it. I will write to the Prime Minister. I will write to your King."

Craddock's hand put her firmly and not too kindly aside. He came in with such a grim set to his lips that they all looked at him apprehensively. This was a new Inspector Craddock.

He said sternly, "Miss Murgatroyd has been murdered. She was strangled—not more than an hour ago." His eyes singled out Julia. "You—Miss Simmons—where have you been all day?"

Julia said warily, "In Milchester. I've just got in."

"And you?" The eyes went on to Patrick.

"Yes."

"Did you both come back here together?"

"Yes—yes, we did," said Patrick.

"No," said Julia. "It's no good, Patrick. That's the kind of lie that will be found out at once. The bus people know us well. I came back on the earlier bus, Inspector—the one that gets here at four o'clock."

"And what did you do then?"

"I went for a walk."

"In the direction of Boulders?"

"No, I went across the fields."

He stared at her. Julia, her face pale, her lips tense, stared back.

Before anyone could speak, the telephone rang.

Miss Blacklock, with an inquiring glance at Craddock, picked up the receiver.

"Yes, Who? Oh, Bunch. What? No. No, she hasn't. I've no idea . . . Yes, he's here now."

She lowered the instrument and said:

"Mrs. Harmon would like to speak to you, Inspector. Miss Marple has not come back to the vicarage and Mrs. Harmon is worried about her."

Craddock took two strides forward and gripped the telephone.

"Craddock speaking."

"I'm worried, Inspector." Bunch's voice came through with a childish tremor in it. "Aunt Jane's out somewhere—and I don't know where. And they say that Miss Murgatroyd's been killed. Is it true?"

"Yes, it's true, Mrs. Harmon. Miss Marple was there, with Miss Hinchliffe, when they found the body."

"Oh, so that's where she is." Bunch sounded relieved.

"No—no, I'm afraid she isn't. Not now. She left there about—let me see—half an hour ago. She hasn't got home?"

"No—she hasn't. It's only ten minutes' walk. Where can she be?"

"Perhaps she's called in on one of your neighbors?"

"I've rung them up—all of them. She's not there. I'm frightened, Inspector."

So am I, thought Craddock.

He said quickly, "I'll come around to you—at once."

"Oh, do—there's a piece of paper. She was writing on it before she went out. I don't know if it means anything . . . It just seems gibberish to me."

Craddock replaced the receiver.

Miss Blacklock said anxiously, "Has something happened to Miss Marple? Oh, I hope not."

"I hope not, too." His mouth was grim.

"She's so old—and frail."

"I know."

Miss Blacklock, standing with her hand pulling at the choker of pearls round her neck, said in a hoarse voice, "It's getting worse and worse. Whoever's doing these things must be mad, Inspector—quite mad . . ."

"I wonder."

The choker of pearls round Miss Blacklock's neck broke under the clutch of her nervous fingers. The smooth white globules rolled all over the room.

Letitia cried out in an anguished tone, "My pearls—my *pearls*—" The agony in her voice was so acute that they all looked at her in astonishment. She turned, her hand to her throat, and rushed sobbing out of the room.

Phillipa began picking up the pearls.

"I've never seen her so upset over anything," she said. "Of course—she always wears them. Do you think, perhaps, that someone special gave them to her? Randall Goedler, perhaps?"

"It's possible," said the Inspector slowly.

"They're not—they couldn't be—real by any chance?" Phillipa asked from where, on her knees, she was still collecting the shining white globes.

Taking one in his hand, Craddock was just about to reply contemptuously. "Real? Of course not!" when he suddenly stifled the words.

After all, *could* the pearls be real?

They were so large, so even, so white that their falseness seemed palpable, but Craddock remembered suddenly a police case where a string of real pearls had been bought for a few shillings in a pawnbroker's shop.

Letitia Blacklock had assured him that there was no jewelry of value in the house. If these pearls were, by any chance, genuine, they must be worth a fabulous sum. And if Randall Goedler had given them to her—then they might be worth any sum you cared to name.

They looked false—they *must* be false, but—if they were real?

Why not? She might herself be unaware of their value. Or she might choose to protect her treasure by treating it as though it were a cheap ornament worth a couple of guineas at most. What would they be worth if real? A fabulous sum . . . Worth doing murder for—*if anybody knew about them . . .*

With a start, the Inspector wrenched himself away from his speculations. Miss Marple was missing. He must go to the vicarage.

III

He found Bunch and her husband waiting for him, their faces anxious and drawn.

"She hasn't come back," said Bunch.

"Did she say she was coming back here when she left Boulders?" asked Julian.

"She didn't actually say so," said Craddock slowly, throwing his mind back to the last time he had seen Jane Marple.

He remembered the grimness of her lips and the severe frosty light in those usually gentle blue eyes.

Grimness, an inexorable determination . . . to do what? To go where?

"She was talking to Sergeant Fletcher when I last saw her," he said. "Just by the gate. And then she went through it and out. I took it she was going straight home to the vicarage. I would have sent her in the car—but there was so much to attend to, and she slipped away very quietly. Fletcher may know something! Where's Fletcher?"

But Sergeant Fletcher, it seemed, as Craddock learned when he rang up Boulders, was neither to be found there nor had he left any message where he had gone. There was some idea that he had returned to Milchester for some reason.

The Inspector rang up headquarters in Milchester, but no news of Fletcher was to be found there.

Then Craddock turned to Bunch as he remembered what she had told him over the telephone.

"Where's that paper? You said she'd been writing something on a bit of paper."

Bunch brought it to him. He spread it out on the table and looked down on it. Bunch leant over his shoulder and spelled it out as he read. The writing was shaky and not easy to read:

Lamp.

Then came the word *Violets.*

Then, after a space:

Where is bottle of aspirin?

The next item in this curious list was more difficult to make out. "Delicious Death," Bunch read. "That's Mitzi's cake."

"Making enquiries," read Craddock.

"Inquiries? What about, I wonder? What's this? *Severe affliction bravely borne . . .* What on earth—!"

"Iodine," read the Inspector. "Pearls. Ah, pearls."

"And then *Lotty*— no, *Letty.* Her *e's* look like *o's.* And then *Berne.* And what's this? *Old-Age Pension . . .*"

They looked at each other in bewilderment.

Craddock recapitulated swiftly.

"Lamp. Violets. Where is bottle of aspirin? Delicious Death. Making enquiries. Severe affliction bravely borne. Iodine. Pearls. Letty. Berne. Old-Age Pension."

Bunch asked: "Does it mean anything? Anything at all? I can't see any connection."

Craddock said slowly: "I've just a glimmer—but I don't see. It's odd that she should have put that down about pearls."

"What about pearls? What does it mean?"

"Does Miss Blacklock always wear that three-tier choker of pearls?"

"Yes, she does. We laugh about it sometimes. They're so dreadfully pale-looking, aren't they. But I suppose she thinks it's fashionable."

"There might be another reason," said Craddock slowly.

"You don't mean that they're *real?* Oh, they *couldn't* be!"

"How often have you had an opportunity of seeing real pearls of that size, Mrs. Harmon?"

"But they're so glassy."

Craddock shrugged his shoulders.

"Anyway, they don't matter now. It's Miss Marple that matters. We've got to find her."

They'd got to find her before it was too late—but perhaps it was already too late? Those penciled words showed that she was on the track . . . But that was dangerous—horribly dangerous. And where the hell was Fletcher?

Craddock strode out of the vicarage to where he'd left his car. Search —that was all he could do—search.

A voice spoke to him out of the dripping laurels, "Sir!" said Sergeant Fletcher urgently. *"Sir . . ."*

21. *Three Women*

DINNER was over at Little Paddocks. It had been a silent and uncomfortable meal.

Patrick, uneasily aware of having fallen from grace, only made spasmodic attempts at conversation—and such as he did make were not well received. Phillipa Haymes was sunk in abstraction. Miss Blacklock herself had abandoned the effort to behave with her normal cheerfulness. She had changed for dinner and had come down wearing her necklace of cameos but for the first time fear showed from her darkly circled eyes, and betrayed itself by her twitching hands.

Julia alone had maintained her air of cynical detachment throughout the evening.

"I'm sorry, Letty," she said, "that I can't pack my bag and go. But I presume the police wouldn't allow it. I don't suppose I'll darken your roof—or whatever the expression is—for long. I should imagine that Inspector Craddock will be round with a warrant and the handcuffs any moment. In fact, I can't imagine why something of the kind hasn't happened already."

"He's looking for the old lady—for Miss Marple," said Miss Blacklock.

"Do you think she's been murdered, too?" Patrick asked with scientific curiosity. "But why? What could she know?"

"I don't know," said Miss Blacklock dully. "Perhaps Miss Murgatroyd told her something."

"If she's been murdered, too," said Patrick, "there seems to be logically only one person who could have done it."

"Who?"

"Hinchliffe, of course," said Patrick triumphantly. "That's where she was last seen alive—at Boulders. My solution would be that she never left Boulders."

"My head aches," said Miss Blacklock in a dull voice. She pressed her fingers to her forehead. "Why should Hinch murder Miss Marple? It doesn't make sense."

"It would if Hinch had really murdered Murgatroyd," said Patrick triumphantly.

Phillipa came out of her apathy to say, "Hinch wouldn't murder Murgatroyd."

Patrick was in an argumentative mood.

"She might have if Murgatroyd had blundered on something to show that she—Hinch—was the criminal."

"Anyway, Hinch was at the station when Murgatroyd was killed."

"She could have murdered Murgatroyd before she left."

Startling them all, Letitia Blacklock suddenly screamed out, "Murder, murder, *murder*—! Can't you talk *anything* else? I'm frightened, don't you understand? I'm frightened. I wasn't before. I thought I could take care of myself . . . But what can you do against a murderer who's waiting—and watching—and biding his time! Oh, God!"

She droppped her head forward on her hands. A moment later she looked up and apologized stiffly.

"I'm sorry. I—I lost control."

"That's all right, Aunt Letty," said Patrick affectionately. "I'll look after you."

"You?" was all Letitia Blacklock said, but the disillusionment behind the word was almost an accusation.

That had been shortly before dinner, and Mitzi had then created a diversion by coming and declaring that she was not going to cook the dinner.

"I do not do anything more in this house. I go to my room. I lock myself in. I stay there until it is daylight. I am afraid—people are being killed—that Miss Murgatroyd with her stupid English face—who would want to kill her? Only a maniac! Then it is a maniac that is about! And a maniac does not care who he kills. But me, I do not want to be killed! There are shadows in that kitchen—and I hear noises—I think there is someone out in the yard, and then I think I see a shadow by the larder door and then it is footsteps I hear. So I go now to my room and I lock the door and perhaps even I put the chest of drawers against it. And in the morning I tell that cruel hard policeman that I go away from here. And if he will not let me, I say: 'I scream and I scream and I scream until you have to let me go!' "

Everybody, with a vivid recollection of what Mitzi could do in the screaming line, shuddered at the threat.

"So I go to my room," said Mitzi, repeating the statement once more to make her intention quite clear. With a symbolic action, she cast off the cretonne apron she had been wearing. "Good night, Miss Blacklock. Perhaps, in the morning, you may not be alive. So, in case that is so, I say good-by."

She departed abruptly and the door, with its usual gentle whine, closed softly after her.

Julia got up.

"I'll see to dinner," she said in a matter-of-fact way. "Rather a good arrangement—less embarrassing for you all than having me sit down at table with you. Patrick (since he's constituted himself your protector, Aunt Letty) had better taste every dish first. I don't want to be accused of poisoning you on top of everything else."

So Julia had cooked and served a really excellent meal.

Phillipa had come out to the kitchen with an offer of assistance but Julia had said firmly that she didn't want any help.

"Julia, there's something I want to say—"

"This is no time for girlish confidences," said Julia firmly. "Go on back in the dining-room, Phillipa."

Now dinner was over and they were in the drawing-room with coffee on the small table by the fire—and nobody seemed to have anything to say. They were waiting—that was all.

At 8:30 Inspector Craddock rang up.

"I shall be with you in about a quarter of an hour's time," he announced. "I'm bringing Colonel and Mrs. Easterbrook and Mrs. Swettenham and her son with me."

"But, really, Inspector . . . I can't cope with people tonight—"

Miss Blacklock's voice sounded as though she were at the end of her tether.

"I know how you feel, Miss Blacklock. I'm sorry. But this is urgent."

"Have you—found Miss Marple?"

"No," said the Inspector and rang off.

Julia took the coffee tray out to the kichen where, to her surprise, she found Mitzi contemplating the piled-up dishes and plates by the sink.

Mitzi burst into a torrent of words:

"See what you do in my so nice kitchen! That frying pan—only, *only* for omlettes do I use it! And you, what have you used it for?"

"Frying onions."

"Ruined—*ruined!* It will have now to be *washed* and never—*never*—do I wash my omlette pan. I rub it carefully with a greasy newspaper, that is all. And this saucepan here that you have used—that one, I use him only for milk—"

"Well, I don't know what pans you use for what," said Julia crossly. "You chose to go to bed and why on earth you've chosen to get up again, I can't imagine. Go away again and leave me to wash up in peace."

"No, I will not let you use my kitchen."

"Oh, Mitzi, you *are* impossible!"

Julia stalked angrily out of the kitchen and at that moment the door-bell rang.

"I do not go to the door," Mitzi called from the kitchen. Julia muttered an impolite Continental expression under her breath and stalked to the front door.

It was Miss Hinchliffe.

"Evening," she said in her gruff voice. "Sorry to barge in. Inspector's rung up, I expect?"

"He didn't tell us you were coming," said Julia, leading the way to the drawing-room.

"He said I needn't come unless I liked," said Miss Hinchliffe. "But I do like."

Nobody offered Miss Hinchliffe sympathy or mentioned Miss Murgatroyd's death. The ravaged face of the tall vigorous woman told its own tale, and would have made any expression of sympathy an impertinence.

"Turn all the lights on," said Miss Blacklock. "And put more coal on the fire. I'm cold—horribly cold. Come and sit here by the fire, Miss Hinchliffe. The Inspector said he would be here in a quarter of an hour. It must be nearly that now."

"Mitzi's come down again," said Julia.

"Has she? Sometimes I think that girl's mad—quite mad. But then perhaps we're all mad."

"I've no patience with this saying that all people who commit crimes are mad," barked Miss Hinchliffe. "Horribly and intelligently sane—that's what I think a criminal is!"

The sound of a car was heard outside and presently Craddock came in with Colonel and Mrs. Easterbrook and Edmund and Mrs. Swettenham.

They were all curiously subdued.

Colonel Easterbrook said in a voice that was like an echo of his usual tones. "Ha! A good fire."

Mrs. Easterbrook wouldn't take off her fur coat and sat down close to her husband. Her face, usually pretty and rather vapid, was like a little pinched weasel face. Edmund was in one of his furious moods and scowled at everybody. Mrs. Swettenham made what was evidently a great effort, and which resulted in a kind of parody of herself.

"It's awful—isn't it?" she said conversationally. "Everything, I mean. And, really, the less one says, the better. Because one doesn't know *who next*— like the plague. Dear Miss Blacklock, don't you think you ought to have a little brandy? Just half a wineglass even? I always think there's nothing like brandy—such a wonderful stimulant. I—it seems so terrible of us—forcing our way in here like this, but Inspector Craddock made us come. And it seems so terrible—she hasn't been found, you know. That poor old thing from the vicarage, I mean. Bunch Harmon is nearly frantic. Nobody knows where she went instead of going home. She didn't come to us. I've not even seen her today. And I should know if she had come to the house because I was in the drawing-room—at the back, you know, and Edmund was in his study writing—and that's at the front—so if she'd come either way we should have seen. And, oh, I do hope and pray that nothing has happened to that dear sweet old thing—all her faculties still and *everything.*"

"Mother," said Edmund in a voice of acute suffering, "can't you shut up?"

"I'm sure, dear, I don't want to say a *word,*" said Mrs. Swettenham, and sat down on the sofa by Julia.

Inspector Craddock stood near the door. Facing him, almost in a row, were the three women. Julia and Mrs. Swettenham on the sofa. Mrs. Easterbrook on the arm of her husband's chair. He had not brought about this arrangement, but it suited him very well.

Miss Blacklock and Miss Hinchliffe were crouching over the fire. Edmund stood near them. Phillipa was far back in the shadows.

Craddock began without preamble.

"You all know that Miss Murgatroyd's been killed," he began. "We've reason to believe that the person who killed her was a woman. And for certain other reasons we can narrow it down still more. I'm about to ask certain ladies here to account for what they were doing between the hours of 4:00 and 4:20 this afternoon. I have already had an account of her movements from—from the young lady who has been calling herself Miss Simmons. I will ask her to repeat that statement. At the same time, Miss Simmons, I must caution you that you need not answer if you think your answers may incriminate you, and anything you say will be taken down by Constable Edwards and may be used as evidence in court."

"You have to say that, don't you?" said Julia. She was rather pale, but still composed. "I repeat that between 4:00 and 4:20 I was walking along the field leading down to the brook by Compton Farm. I came back to the road by that field with three poplars in it. I didn't meet anyone as far as I can remember. I did not go near Boulders."

"Mrs. Swettenham?"

Edmund said, "Are you cautioning all of us?"

The Inspector turned to him.

"No. At the moment only Miss Simmons. I have no reason to believe that any other statement made will be incriminating, but anyone, of course, is entitled to have a solicitor present and to refuse to answer questions unless one *is* present."

"Oh, but that would be very silly and a complete waste of time," cried Mrs. Swettenham. "I'm sure I can tell you at once exactly what I was doing. That's what you want, isn't it? Shall I begin now?"

"Yes, please, Mrs. Swettenham."

"Now let me see." Mrs. Swettenham closed her eyes, opened them again. "Of course, I had nothing *at all* to do with killing Miss Murgatroyd. I'm sure *everybody* here knows *that*. But I'm a woman of the world, I know quite well that the police have to ask all the most unnecessary questions and write the answers down very carefully, because it's all for what they call 'the record.' That's it, isn't it?" Mrs. Swettenham flashed the question at the diligent Constable Edwards and added graciously, "I'm not going too fast for you, I hope?"

Constable Edwards, a good shorthand writer, but with little social *savoir faire,* turned red to the ears and replied, "It's quite all right, madam. Well, perhaps a *little* slower would be better."

Mrs. Swettenham resumed her discourse with emphatic pauses where she considered a comma or a full stop might be appropriate.

"Well, of course, it's difficult to say—exactly—because I've not got, really, a very good sense of time. And ever since the war quite half our clocks haven't gone at all, and the ones that do go are often either fast or slow or stop because we haven't wound them up." Mrs. Swettenham paused to let this picture of confused time sink in and then went on earnestly, "What I *think* I was doing at four o'clock was turning the heel of my sock (and for some extraordinary reason I was going round the wrong way—in purl, you know, not plain), but if I *wasn't* doing that, I must have been outside, snipping off the dead chrysanthemums—no, that was earlier—before the rain."

"The rain," said the Inspector, "started at 4:10 exactly."

"Did it now? That helps a lot. Of course, I was upstairs putting a wash basin in the passage where the rain always comes through. And it was coming through so fast that I guessed at once that the gutter was stopped up again. So I came down and got my mackintosh and rubber boots. I called Edmund, but he didn't answer, so I thought perhaps he'd got to a very important place in his novel and I wouldn't disturb him, and I've done it quite often myself before. With the broom handle, you know, tied onto that long thing you push up windows with."

"You mean," said Craddock, noting bewilderment on his subordinate's face, "that you were cleaning out the gutter?"

"Yes, it was all choked up with leaves. It took a long time and I got rather wet, but I got it clear at last. And then I went in and got changed and washed—so *smelly,* dead leaves—And then I went into the kitchen and put the kettle on. It was 6:15 by the kitchen clock."

Constable Edwards blinked.

"Which means," finished Mrs. Swettenham triumphantly, "that it was exactly twenty minutes to five. Or near enough," she added.

"Did anybody see what you were doing whilst you were out cleaning the gutter?"

"No, indeed," said Mrs. Swettenham. "I'd soon have roped them in to help if they had! It's a most difficult thing to do single-handed."

"So, by your own statement, you were outside, in a mackintosh and boots, at the time when the rain was coming down, and, according to you, you were employed during that time in cleaning out a gutter, but you have no one who can substantiate that statement?"

"You can look at the gutter," said Mrs. Swettenham. "It's beautifully clear."

"Did you hear your mother call to you, Mr. Swettenham?"

"No," said Edmund. "I was fast asleep."

"Edmund," said his mother reproachfully, "I thought you were writing."

Inspector Craddock turned to Mrs. Easterbrook.

"Now, Mrs. Easterbrook?"

"I was sitting with Archie in his study," said Mrs. Easterbrook, fixing wide innocent eyes on him. "We were listening to the radio together, weren't we, Archie?"

There was a pause. Colonel Easterbrook was very red in the face. He took his wife's hand in his.

"You don't understand these things, kitten," he said. "I—well, I must say, Inspector, you've rather sprung this business on us. My wife, you know, had been terribly upset by all this. She's nervous and highly strung and doesn't appreciate the importance of—of taking due consideration before she makes a statement."

"Archie," cried Mrs. Easterbrook reproachfully, "are you going to say you weren't with me?"

"Well, I wasn't, was I, my dear? I mean, one's got to stick to the facts. Very important in this sort of inquiry. I was talking to Lampson, the farmer at Croft End, about some chicken netting. That was about a quarter to four. I didn't get home until after the rain had stopped. Just before tea. A quarter to five. Laura was toasting the scones."

"And had *you* been out also, Mrs. Easterbrook?"

The pretty face looked more like a weasel's than ever. Her eyes had a trapped look.

"No—no, I just sat listening to the radio. I didn't go out. Not then. I'd been out earlier. About—about half past three. Just for a little walk. Not far."

She looked as though she expected more questions, but Craddock said quietly, "That's all, Mrs. Easterbrook."

He went on: "These statements will be typed out. You can read them and sign them if they are substantially correct."

Mrs. Easterbrook looked at him with sudden venom.

"Why don't you ask the others where they were? That Haymes woman? And Edmund Swettenham? How do you know he *was* asleep indoors? Nobody saw him."

Inspector Craddock said quietly, "Miss Murgatroyd, before she died, made a certain statement. On the night of the holdup here, *someone* was absent from the room. Someone who was supposed to have been in the room all the time. Miss Murgatroyd told her friend the names of the people she *did* see. By a process of elimination, she made the discovery that there was someone she did *not* see."

"Nobody could see anything," said Julia.

"Murgatroyd could," said Miss Hinchliffe, speaking suddenly in her deep voice. "She was over there behind the door, where Inspector Craddock is now. She was the only person who could see anything of what was happening."

"Aha! That is what you think, is it?" demanded Mitzi.

She had made one of her dramatic entrances, flinging open the door and almost knocking Craddock sideways. She was in a frenzy of excitement.

"Ah, you do not ask Mitzi to come in here with the others, do you, you stiff policeman? I am only Mitzi! Mitzi in the kitchen! Let her stay in the kitchen where she belongs! But I tell you that Mitzi, as well as anyone else, perhaps better, yes, better, can see things. Yes, I see things. I see something the night of the burglary. I see something and I do not quite believe it, and I hold my tongue till now. I think to myself I will not tell what it is I have seen, not yet. I will wait."

"And when everything had calmed down, you meant to ask for a little money from a certain person, eh?" said Craddock.

Mitzi turned on him like an angry cat.

"And why not? Why look down your nose? Why should I not be paid for it if I have been so generous as to keep silence? Especially if some day there will be money—much, *much* money. Oh! I have heard things—I know what goes on. I know this Pippemmer—this secret society of which *she*"—she flung a dramatic finger towards Julia—"is an agent. Yes, I would have waited and asked for money—but now I am afraid. I would rather be *safe*. For soon, perhaps, someone will kill *me*. So I will tell what I know."

"All right then," said the Inspector skeptically. "What do you know?"

"I tell you." Mitzi spoke solemnly. "On that night I am *not* in the pantry cleaning silver as I say—I am already in the dining-room when I hear the gun go off. I look through the keyhole. The hall it is black, but the gun go off again and the flashlight it falls—and it swings round as it falls—and I see *her*. I see *her* there close to him, with the gun in her hand. I see Miss Blacklock."

"Me?" Miss Blacklock sat up in astonishment. "You must be mad!"

"But that's impossible!" cried Edmund. "Mitzi couldn't have seen Miss Blacklock—"

Craddock cut in and his voice had the corrosive quality of a deadly acid.

"Couldn't she, Mr. Swettenham? And why not? Because it *wasn't* Miss Blacklock who was standing there with the gun? It was *you*, wasn't it?"

"I? Of course not—what the *hell!*"

"You took Colonel Easterbrook's revolver. *You* fixed up the business with Rudi Scherz—as a good joke. You had followed Patrick Simmons into the far room and when the lights went out, you slipped out through the carefully oiled door. You shot at Miss Blacklock and then you killed Rudi Scherz. A few seconds later you were back in the drawing-room, clicking your lighter."

For a moment Edmund seemed at a loss for words, then he spluttered out, "The whole idea is *monstrous*. Why *me?* What earthly motive had I got?"

"If Miss Blacklock dies before Mrs. Goedler, two people inherit—remember? The two we know of as Pip and Emma. Julia Simmons has turned out to be Emma—"

"And you think I'm Pip?" Edmund laughed. "Fantastic—absolutely *fantastic!* I'm about the right age—nothing else. And I can prove to you, you damned fool, that I *am* Edmund Swettenham. Birth certificate, schools university—everything."

"He isn't Pip." The voice came from the shadows in the corner. Phillippa Haymes came forward, her face pale. *"I'm Pip,* Inspector."

"You, Mrs. Haymes?"

"Yes. Everybody seems to have assumed that Pip was a boy—Julia knew, of course, that her twin was another girl—I don't know why she didn't say so this afternoon—"

"Family solidarity," said Julia. "I suddenly realized who you were. I'd had no idea till that moment."

"I'd had the same idea as Julia did," said Phillipa, her voice trembling a little. "After I—lost my husband and the war was over, I wondered what I was going to do. My mother died many years ago. I found out where Miss Blacklock lived and I—I came here. I took a job with Mrs. Lucas. I hoped that, since this Miss Blacklock was an elderly woman without relatives, she might, perhaps, be willing to help. Not me, because I could work, but help with Harry's education. After all, it *was* Goedler money and she'd no one particular of her own to spend it on.

"And then—" Phillipa spoke faster; it was as though now her long reserve had broken down, she couldn't get the words out fast enough— "that holdup happened and I began to be frightened. Because it seemed to me that the only possible person with a motive for killing Miss Blacklock was *me*. I hadn't the least idea who Julia was—we weren't identical twins and we're not much alike to look at. No, it seemed as though I was the only one bound to be suspected."

She stopped and pushed her fair hair back from her face, and Craddock suddenly realized that a faded snapshot in the box of letters must have been a photograph of Phillipa's mother. The likeness was undeniable. He knew too why that mention of closing and unclosing hands had seemed familiar—Phillipa was doing it now.

"Miss Blacklock has been good to me. Very, *very* good to me—I didn't try to kill her. I never thought of killing her. But all the same, I'm Pip." She added, "You see, you needn't suspect Edmund any more."

"Needn't I?" said Craddock. Again there was that acid biting tone in his voice. "Edmund Swettenham's a young man who's fond of money. A young man, perhaps, who would like to marry a rich wife. But she wouldn't be a rich wife *unless Miss Blacklock died before Mrs. Goedler.* And since it seemed almost certain that Mrs. Goedler would die before Miss Blacklock, well—he had to do something about it—*didn't you, Mr. Swettenham?*"

"It's a damned lie!" Edmund shouted.

And then, suddenly, a sound rose on the air. It came from the kitchen —a long unearthly shriek of terror.

"That isn't Mitzi!" cried Julia.

"No," said Inspector Craddock, "it's someone who's murdered three people . . ."

22. *The Truth*

WHEN the Inspector turned on Edmund Swettenham, Mitzi had crept quietly out of the room and back to the kitchen. She was running water into the sink when Miss Blacklock entered.

Mitzi gave her a shame-faced sideways look.

"What a liar you are, Mitzi," said Miss Blacklock pleasantly. "Here—that isn't the way to wash up. The silver first, and fill the sink right up. You can't wash up in about two inches of water."

Mitzi turned the taps on obediently.

"You are not angry at what I say, Miss Blacklock?" she asked.

"If I were to be angry at all the lies you tell, I should never be out of a temper," said Miss Blacklock.

"I will go and say to the Inspector that I make it all up, shall I?" asked Mitzi.

"He knows that already," said Miss Blacklock pleasantly.

Mitzi turned off the taps and as she did so two hands came up behind her head and with one swift movement forced it down into the water-filled sink.

"Only *I* know that you're telling the truth for once," said Miss Blacklock viciously.

Mitzi thrashed and struggled but Miss Blacklock was strong and her hands held the girl's head firmly under water.

Then, from somewhere quite close behind her, Dora Bunner's voice rose piteously on the air:

"Oh, Lotty—Lotty—don't do it . . . Lotty!"

Miss Blacklock screamed. Her hands flew up in the air, and Mitzi, released, came up choking and spluttering.

Miss Blacklock screamed again and again. For there was no one there in the kitchen with her—

"Dora, Dora, forgive me. I had to . . . I had to—"

She rushed distractedly towards the scullery door—and the bulk of Sergeant Fletcher barred her way, just as Miss Marple stepped, flushed and triumphant, out of the broom cupboard.

"I could always mimic people's voices," said Miss Marple.

"You'll have to come with me, madam," said Sergeant Fletcher. "I was a witness of your attempt to drown this girl. And there will be other charges. I must warn you, Letitia Blacklock—"

"Charlotte Blacklock," corrected Miss Marple. "That's who she is, you know. Under that choker of pearls she always wears you'll find the scar of the operation."

"Operation?"

"Operation for goiter."

Miss Blacklock, quite calm now, looked at Miss Marple.

"So you know all about it?" she said.

"Yes, I've known for some time."

Charlotte Blacklock sat down by the table and began to cry.

"You shouldn't have done that," she said. "Not made Dora's voice come. I loved Dora. I really loved Dora.

Inspector Craddock and the others had crowded in the doorway.

Constable Edwards, who added a knowledge of first aid and artificial respiration to his other accomplishments, was busy with Mitzi. As soon as Mitzi could speak she was lyrical with self-praise.

"I do that good, do I not? I am clever! And I am brave! Oh, I am brave! Very, very nearly was *I* murdered, too. But I am so brave I risk *everything*."

With a rush Miss Hinchliffe thrust aside the others and leaped upon the weeping figure of Charlotte Blacklock by the table.

It took all Sergeant Fletcher's strength to hold her off.

"Now then—" he said. "Now then—No, no, Miss Hinchliffe—"

Between clenched teeth Miss Hinchliffe was muttering, "Let me get at her. Just let me get at her. It was she who killed Amy Murgatroyd."

Charlotte Blacklock looked up and sniffed.

"I didn't want to kill her. I didn't want to kill anybody—I had to—But it's Dora I mind about—after Dora was dead, I was all alone—ever since she died—I've been alone—oh, Dora—Dora—"

And once again she dropped her head on her hands and wept.

23. *Evening at the Vicarage*

MISS MARPLE sat in the tall armchair. Bunch was on the floor in front of the fire with her arms round her knees.

The Reverend Julian Harmon was leaning forward and was for once looking more like a schoolboy than a man foreshadowing his own maturity. And Inspector Craddock was smoking his pipe and drinking a whisky and soda and was clearly very much off duty. An outer circle was composed of Julia, Patrick, Edmund and Phillipa.

"I think it's your story, Miss Marple," said Craddock.

"Oh, no, my dear boy. I only just helped a little, here and there. *You* were in charge of the whole thing, and conducted it all, and you know so much that I don't."

"Well, tell it together," said Bunch impatiently. "Bits each. Only let Aunt Jane start because I like the muddly way her mind works. When did you first think that the whole thing was a put-up job by the Blacklock?"

"Well, my dear Bunch, it's hard to say. Of course, right at the very beginning, it did seem as though the ideal person—or rather the *obvious* person, I should say—to have arranged the holdup *was* Miss Blacklock herself. She was the only person who was known to have been in contact with Rudi Scherz, and how much easier to arrange something like that when it's your own house. The central heating for instance. No fire— because that would have meant light in the room. But the only person who could have arranged *not* to have a fire was the mistress of the house herself.

"Not that I thought of all that at the time—it just seemed to me that it was a pity it *couldn't* be as simple as that! Oh no, I was taken in like everyone else. I thought that someone really did want to kill Letitia Blacklock."

"I think I'd like to get clear first on what really happened," said Bunch. "Did this Swiss boy recognize her?"

"Yes. He'd worked in—"

She hesitated and looked at Craddock.

"In Dr. Adolf Koch's clinic in Berne," said Craddock. "Koch was a world-famous specialist on operations for goiter. Charlotte Blacklock went there to have her goiter removed and Rudi Scherz was one of the orderlies. When he came to England he recognized in the hotel a lady who had been a patient and on the spur of the moment he spoke to her. I daresay he mightn't have done that if he'd paused to think, because he left the place under a cloud, but that was sometime after Charlotte had been there, so she wouldn't know anything about it."

"So he never said anything to her about Montreux and his father being a hotel proprietor?"

"Oh, no, she made that up to account for his having spoken to her."

"It must have been a great shock to her," said Miss Marple thoughtfully. "She felt reasonably safe—and then—the almost impossible mischance of somebody turning up who had known her—not as one of the two Miss Blacklocks—she was prepared for *that*— but definitely as *Charlotte* Blacklock, a patient who'd been operated on for goiter.

"But you wanted to go through it all from the beginning. Well, the beginning, I think—if Inspector Craddock agrees with me—was when Charlotte Blacklock, a pretty, lighthearted, affectionate girl, developed that enlargement of the thyroid gland that's called a goiter. It ruined her life, because she was a very sensitive girl. A girl, too, who had always set a lot of stress on her personal appearance. And girls just at that age in their teens, are particularly sensitive about themselves. If she'd had a mother, or a reasonable father, I don't think she would have got into the morbid state she undoubtedly did get into. She had no one, you see, to take her out of herself and force her to see people and lead a normal life and not think too much about her infirmity. And, of course, in a different household, she might have been sent for an operation many years earlier.

"But Dr. Blacklock, I think, was an old-fashioned, narrow-minded, tyrannical and obstinate man. He didn't believe in these operations. Charlotte must take it from him that nothing could be done—apart from dosage with iodine and other drugs. Charlotte *did* take it from him, and I think her sister also placed more faith in Dr. Blacklock's powers as a physician than he deserved.

"Charlotte was devoted to her father in a rather weak and soppy way. She thought, definitely, that her father knew best. But she shut herself up more and more as the goiter became larger and more unsightly, and refused to see people. She was actually a kindly affectionate creature."

"That's an odd description of a murderess," said Edmund.

"I don't know that it is," said Miss Marple. "Weak and kindly people are often very treacherous. And if they've got a grudge against life it saps the little moral strength that they may possess.

"*Letitia* Blacklock, of course, had quite a different personality. Inspector Craddock told me that Belle Goedler described her as really *good*—

and I think Letitia *was* good. She was a woman of great integrity who found—as she put it herself—a great difficulty in understanding how people couldn't see what was dishonest. Letitia Blacklock, however tempted, would never have contemplated any kind of fraud for a moment.

"Letitia was devoted to her sister. She wrote her long accounts of everything that happened in an effort to keep her sister in touch with life. She was worried by the morbid state Charlotte was getting into.

"Finally, Dr. Blacklock died. Letitia, without hesitation, threw up her position with Randall Goedler and devoted herself to Charlotte. She took her to Switzerland to consult authorities there on the possibility of operating. It had been left until very late—but, as we know, the operation was successful. The deformity was gone—and the scar this operation had left was easily hidden by a choker of pearls or beads.

"The war had broken out. A return to England was difficult and the two sisters stayed in Switzerland, doing various Red Cross and other work. That's right, isn't it, Inspector?"

"Yes, Miss Marple."

"They got occasional news from England—amongst other things, I expect, they heard that Belle Goedler could not live long. I'm sure it would be only human nature for them both to have planned and talked together of the days ahead when a big fortune would be theirs to spend. One has got to realize, I think, that this prospect meant much more to *Charlotte* than it did to Letitia. For the first time in her life, Charlotte could go about feeling herself a normal woman, a woman at whom no one looked with either repulsion or pity. She was free at last to enjoy life —and she had a whole lifetime, as it were, to crowd into her remaining years. To travel, to have a house and beautiful grounds—to have clothes and jewels, and go to plays and concerts, to gratify every whim—it was all a kind of fairy tale come true to Charlotte.

"And then Letitia, the strong healthy Letitia, got flu which turned to pneumonia and she died within the space of a week! Not only had Charlotte lost her sister, but the whole dream existence she had planned for herself was canceled. I think, you know, that she may have felt almost resentful towards Letitia. Why need Letitia have died, just then, when they had just had a letter saying Belle Goedler could not last long? Just one more month, perhaps, and the money would have been Letitia's— and hers when Letitia died . . .

"Now this is where I think the difference between the two came in. Charlotte didn't really feel that what she suddenly thought of doing was wrong—not really wrong. The money was meant to come to Letitia—it *would* have come to Letitia in the course of a few months—and she regarded herself and Letitia as one.

"Perhaps the idea didn't occur to her until the doctor or someone asked her sister's Christian name—and then she realized how to nearly everyone they had appeared as the two Miss Blacklocks—elderly, well-bred Englishwomen, dressed much the same, with a strong family resemblance—(and, as I pointed out to Bunch, one elderly woman is *so* like another). Why shouldn't it be *Charlotte* who had died and *Letitia* who was alive?

"It was an impulse, perhaps, more than a plan. Letitia was buried under Charlotte's name. 'Charlotte' was dead, 'Letitia' came to England. All the natural initiative and energy, dormant for so many years, were now in the ascendant. As Charlotte, she had played second fiddle. She now assumed the airs of command, the feeling of command that had been Letitia's. They were not really so unlike in mentality—though there was, I think, a big difference *morally.*

"Charlotte had, of course, to take one or two obvious precautions. She bought a house in a part of England quite unknown to her. The only people she had to avoid were a few people in her own native town in Cumberland (where, in any case, she'd lived as a recluse) and, of course, Belle Goedler, who had known Letitia so well that any impersonation would have been out of the question. Handwriting difficulties were got over by the arithritic condition of her hands. It was really very easy because so few people had ever really known Charlotte."

"But supposing she'd met people who'd known Letitia?" asked Bunch. "There must have been plenty of those."

"They wouldn't matter in the same way. Someone might say: 'I came across Letitia Blacklock the other day. She's changed so much I really wouldn't have known her.' But there still wouldn't have been any suspicion in their minds that she wasn't Letitia. People *do* change in the course of ten years. *Her* failure to recognize *them* could always be put down to her near-sightedness: and you must remember that she knew every detail of Letitia's life in London—the people she met—the places she went. She'd got Letitia's letters to refer to, and she could quickly have disarmed any suspicion by mention of some incident, or an inquiry after a mutual friend. No, it was recognition as *Charlotte* that was the only thing she had to fear.

"She settled down at Little Paddocks, got to know her neighbors and, when she got a letter asking dear Letitia to be kind, she accepted with pleasure the visit of two young cousins she had never seen. Their acceptance of her as Aunt Letty increased her security.

"The whole thing was going splendidly. And then—she made her big mistake. It was a mistake that arose solely from her kindness of heart and her naturally affectionate nature. She got a letter from an old school friend who had fallen on evil days, and she hurried to the rescue. Perhaps it may have been partly because she was, in spite of everything, lonely. Her secret kept her in a way apart from people. And she had been genuinely fond of Dora Bunner and remembered her as a symbol of her own gay carefree days at school. Anyway, on an impulse, she answered Dora's letter in person. And very surprised Dora must have been! She'd written to *Letitia* and the sister who turned up in answer to her letter was *Charlotte*. There was never any question of pretending to be Letitia to Dora. Dora was one of the few old friends who had been admitted to see Charlotte in her lonely and unhappy days.

"And because she knew that Dora would look at the matter in exactly the same way as she did herself, she told Dora what she had done. Dora approved wholeheartedly. In her confused muddle-headed mind it seemed only right that dear Lotty should not be done out of her inheritance by Letty's untimely death. Lotty *deserved* a reward for all the patient suffering she had borne so bravely. It would have been most unfair if all that money should have gone to someone nobody had ever heard of.

"She quite understood that nothing must be allowed to get out. It was like an extra pound of butter. You couldn't talk about it but there was nothing wrong about having it. So Dora came to Little Paddocks—and very soon Charlotte began to understand that she had made a terrible mistake. It was not merely the fact that Dora Bunner, with her muddles and her mistakes and her bungling, was quite maddening to live with. Charlotte could have put up with that—because she really cared for Dora, and, anyway, knew from the doctor that Dora hadn't a very long time to live. But Dora very soon became a real danger. Though Charlotte and Letitia had called each other by their full names, Dora was the kind of person who always used abbreviations. To her the sisters had always been Letty and Lotty. And though she schooled her tongue resolutely to call her friend Letty—the old name often slipped out. Memories of the past, too, were rather apt to come to her tongue—forgetful allusions. It began to get on her nerves.

"Still, nobody was likely to pay much attention to Dora's inconsistencies. The real blow to Charlotte's security came, as I say, when she was recognized and spoken to by Rudi Scherz at the Royal Spa Hotel.

"I think that the money Rudi Scherz used to replace his earlier defalcations at the hotel may have come from Charlotte Blacklock. Inspector

Craddock doesn't believe—and I don't either—that Rudi Scherz applied to her for money with any idea of blackmail in his head."

"He hadn't the faintest idea he knew anything to blackmail her about," said Inspector Craddock. "He knew that he was quite a personable young man—and he was aware by experience that personable young men sometimes can get money out of elderly ladies if they tell a hard luck story convincingly enough.

"But she may have seen it differently. She may have thought that it *was* a form of insidious blackmail, that perhaps he suspected something—and that later, if there was publicity in the papers, as there might be after Belle Goedler's death, he would realize that in her he had found a gold mine.

"And she was committed to the fraud now. She'd established herself as Letitia Blacklock. With the bank. With Mrs. Goedler. The only snag was this rather dubious Swiss hotel clerk, an unreliable character and possibly a blackmailer. If only he were out of the way—she'd be safe.

"Perhaps she made it all up as a kind of fantasy first. She'd been starved of emotion and drama in her life. She pleased herself by working out the details. How would she go about getting rid of him?

"She made her plan. And at last she decided to act on it. She told her story of a sham holdup at a party to Rudi Scherz, explained that she wanted a stranger to act the part of the 'gangster,' and offered him a generous sum for his co-operation.

"And the fact that he agreed without any suspicion is what makes me quite certain that Scherz had no idea that he had any kind of hold over her. To him she was just a rather foolish old woman, very ready to part with money.

"She gave him the advertisement to insert, arranged for him to pay a visit to Little Paddocks to study the geography of the house and showed him the spot where she would meet him and let him into the house on the night in question. Dora Bunner, of course, knew nothing about all this.

"The day came—" He paused.

Miss Marple took up the tale in her gentle voice.

"She must have spent a very miserable day. You see, it still wasn't too late to draw back. . . . Dora Bunner told us that Letty was frightened that day and she must have been frightened. Frightened of what she was going to do, frightened of the plan going wrong—but not frightened enough to draw back.

"It had been fun, perhaps, getting the revolver out of Colonel Easterbrook's collar drawer. Taking along eggs, or jam—slipping upstairs in the empty house. It had been fun getting the second door in the drawing-room oiled, so that it would open and shut noiselessly. Fun suggesting the moving of the table outside the door so that Phillipa's flower arrangements would show to better advantage. It may have all seemed like a game. But what was going to happen next definitely wasn't a game any longer. Oh, yes, she was frightened . . . Dora Bunner was right about that."

"All the same, she went through with it," said Craddock. "And it all went according to plan. She went out just after six to 'shut up the ducks,' and she let Scherz in then and gave him the mask and cloak and gloves and the flashlight. Then, at 6:30, when the clock begins to strike, she's ready by that table near the archway with her hand on the cigarette box. It's all so natural. Patrick, acting as host, has gone for the drinks. She, the hostess, is fetching the cigarettes. She's judged, quite correctly, that when the clock begins to strike, everyone will look at the clock. They did. Only one person, the devoted Dora, kept her eyes fixed on her friend. And she told us, in her very first statement, exactly what Miss Blacklock did. She said that Miss Blacklock had picked up the vase of violets."

"She'd previously frayed the cord of the lamp so that the wires were nearly bare. The whole thing only took a second. The cigarette box, the vase and the little switch were all close together. She picked up the violets, spilt the water on the frayed place and switched on the lamp. Water's a good conductor of electricity. The wires burned out."

"Just like the other afternoon at the vicarage," said Bunch. "That's what startled you so, wasn't it, Aunt Jane?"

"Yes, my dear. I'd been puzzling about those lights. I'd realized that there were two lamps, a pair, and that one had been changed for the other—probably during the night."

"That's right," said Craddock. "When Fletcher examined that lamp the next morning it was, like all the others, perfectly in order, no frayed cord or burned out wires."

"I'd understood what Dora Bunner meant by saying it had been the *shepherdess* the night before," said Miss Marple, "but I fell into the error of thinking, as she thought, that *Patrick* had been responsible. The interesting thing about Dora Bunner was that she was quite unreliable in repeating things she had heard—she always used her imagination to exaggerate or distort them, and she was usually wrong in what she *thought* —but she was quite accurate about the things she *saw*. She saw Letitia pick up the violets—"

"And of course, when dear Bunch split the water from the Christmas roses onto the lamp wire—I realized at once that only Miss Blacklock herself could have put out the lights because only she was near that table."

"I could kick myself," said Craddock. "Dora Bunner even prattled about a burn on the table where someone had 'put their cigarette down' —but nobody had even lit a cigarette . . . And the violets were dead because there was no water in the vase—a slip on Letitia's part—she ought to have filled it up again. But I suppose she thought nobody would notice and, as a matter of fact, Miss Bunner was quite ready to believe that she herself had put no water in the vase to begin with."

He went on:

"She was highly suggestible, of course. And Miss Blacklock took advantage of that more than once. Bunny's suspicions of Patrick were, I think, induced by her."

"Why pick on me?" demanded Patrick in an aggrieved tone.

"It was not, I think, a serious suggestion—but it would keep Bunny distracted from any suspicion that Miss Blacklock might be stage managing the business. Well, we know what happened next. As soon as the lights went and everyone was exclaiming, she slipped out through the previously oiled door and up behind Rudi Scherz who was turning his flashlight round the room and playing his part with gusto. I don't suppose he realized for a moment she was there behind him with her gardening gloves pulled on and the revolver in her hand. She waits till the light reaches the spot she must aim for—the wall near which she is supposed to be standing. Then she fires rapidly twice and as he swings round startled, she holds the revolver close to his body and fires again. She lets the revolver fall by his body, throws her gloves carelessly on the hall table, then back through the other door and across to where she had been standing when the light went out. She nicked her ear—I don't quite know how—"

"Nail scissors, I expect," said Miss Marple. "Just a snip on the lobe of the ear lets out a lot of blood. That was very good psychology, of course. The actual blood running down over her white blouse made it seem certain that she *had* been shot at, and that it had been a near miss."

"It ought to have gone off quite all right," said Craddock. "Dora Bunner's insistence that Scherz had definitely aimed at Miss Blacklock had its uses. Without meaning it, Dora Bunner conveyed the impression that she'd actually seen her friend wounded. It might have been brought in suicide or accidental death. And the case would have been closed. That it was kept open is due to Miss Marple here."

"Oh, no, no." Miss Marple shook her head energetically. "Any little efforts on my part were quite incidental. It was you who weren't satisfied, Mr. Craddock. It was *you* who wouldn't let the case be closed."

"I wasn't happy about it," said Craddock. "I knew it was all wrong somewhere. But I didn't see *where* it was wrong, till you showed me. And after that Miss Blacklock had a real piece of bad luck. I discovered that that second door had been tampered with. Until that moment, whatever we agreed *might* have happened—we'd nothing to go upon but a pretty theory. But that oiled door was *evidence*. And I hit upon it by pure chance—by catching hold of a handle by mistake."

"I think you were *led* to it, Inspector," said Miss Marple. "But then I'm old-fashioned."

"So the hunt was up again," said Craddock. "But this time with a difference. We were looking now for someone with a motive to kill Letitia Blacklock."

"And there *was* someone with a motive, and Miss Blacklock knew it," said Miss Marple. "I think she recognized Phillipa almost at once. Because Sonia Goedler seems to have been one of the very few people who had been admitted to Charlotte's privacy. And when one is old (you wouldn't know this yet, Mr. Craddock) one has a much better memory for a face you've seen when you were young than you have for anyone you've only met a year or two ago. Phillipa must have been just about the same age as her mother was as Charlotte remembered her, and she was very like her mother. The odd thing is that I think Charlotte was very pleased to recognize Phillipa. She became very fond of Phillipa and I think, unconsciously, it helped to stifle any qualms of conscience she may have had. She told herself that when she inherited the money, she was going to look after Phillipa. She would treat her as a daughter. Phillipa and Harry should live with her. She felt quite happy and beneficent about it. But once the Inspector began asking questions and finding out about 'Pip and Emma,' Charlotte became very uneasy. She didn't want to make a scapegoat of Phillipa. Her whole idea had been to make the business look like a holdup by a young criminal and his accidental death. But now, with the discovery of the oiled door, the whole viewpoint was changed. And, except for Phillipa, there wasn't (as far as *she* knew, for she had absolutely no idea of Julia's identity) anyone with the least possible motive for wishing to kill her. She did her best to shield Phillipa's identity. She was quick-witted enough to tell you when you asked her, that Sonia was small and dark and she took the old snapshots out of the album so that you shouldn't notice any resemblance at the same time that she removed snapshots of Letitia herself."

"And to think I suspected Mrs. Swettenham of being Sonia Goedler," said Craddock disgustedly.

"My poor mama," murmured Edmund. "A woman of blameless life—or so I have always believed."

"But, of course," Miss Marple went on, "it was Dora Bunner who was the real danger. Every day Dora got more forgetful and more talkative. I remember the way Miss Blacklock looked at her the day we went to tea there. Do you know why? Dora had just called her Lotty again. It seemed to us a mere harmless slip of the tongue. But it frightened Charlotte. And so it went on. Poor Dora could not stop herself talking. That day we had coffee together in the Bluebird, I had the oddest impression that Dora was talking about *two* people, not one—and so, of course, she was. At one moment she spoke of her friend as not pretty but having so much character—but almost at the same moment she described her as a pretty, lighthearted girl. She'd talk of Letty as so clever and so successful —and then say what a sad life she'd had, and then there was that quotation about stern affliction bravely borne—which really didn't seem to fit Letitia's life at all. Charlotte must, I think, have overheard a good deal that morning she came into the cafe. She certainly must have heard Dora mention about the lamp having been changed—about its being the shepherd and not the shepherdess. And she realized then what a very real danger to her security poor devoted Dora Bunner was.

"I'm afraid that that conversation with me in the café really sealed Dora's fate—if you'll excuse such a melodramatic expression. But I think it would have come to the same in the end . . . Because life couldn't be safe for Charlotte while Dora Bunner was alive. She loved Dora—she didn't want to kill Dora—but she couldn't see any other way. And, I expect (like Nurse Ellerton that I was telling you about, Bunch) she persuaded herself that it was really almost a *kindness*. Poor Bunny—not long to live anyway and perhaps a painful end. The queer thing is that she did her best to make Bunny's last day a happy day. The birthday party—and the special cake . . ."

"Delicious Death," said Phillipa with a shudder.

"Yes—yes, it was rather like that . . . she tried to give her friend a delicious death . . . The party, and all the things she liked to eat, and trying to stop people saying things to upset her. And then the tablets, whatever they were, in the aspirin bottle by her own bed so that Bunny, when she couldn't find the new bottle of aspirin she'd just bought, would go there to get some. And it would look, as it did look, that the tablets had been meant for *Letitia* . . .

"And so Bunny died in her sleep, quite happily, and Charlotte felt safe again. But she missed Dora Bunner—she missed her affection and her loyalty, she missed being able to talk to her about the old days . . . She cried bitterly the day I came up with that note from Julian—and her grief was quite genuine. She'd killed her own dear friend . . ."

"That's horrible," said Bunch. "Horrible."

"But it's very human," said Julian Harmon. "One forgets how human murderers are."

"I know," said Miss Marple. "Human. And often very much to be pitied. But very dangerous, too. Especially a weak kindly murderer like Charlotte Blacklock. Because, once a weak person gets *really* frightened, they get quite savage with terror and they've no self-control at all."

"Murgatroyd?" said Julian.

"Yes, poor Miss Murgatroyd. Charlotte must have come up to the cottage and heard them rehearsing the murder. The window was open and she listened. It had never occurred to her until that moment that there was anyone else who could be a danger to her. Miss Hinchliffe was urging her friend to remember what she'd seen and until that moment Charlotte hadn't realized that anyone could have seen anything at all. She'd assumed that everybody would automatically be looking at Rudi Scherz. She must have held her breath outside the window and listened. Was it going to be all right? And then, just as Miss Hinchliffe rushed off to the station, Miss Murgatroyd got to a point which showed that she had stumbled on the truth. She called after Miss Hinchliffe: 'She wasn't *there* . . .'

"I asked Miss Hinchliffe, you know, if that was the way she said it . . . Because if she'd said '*She* wasn't there,' it wouldn't have meant the same thing."

"Now that's too subtle a point for me," said Craddock.

Miss Marple turned her eager pink and white face to him.

"Just think what's going on in Miss Murgatroyd's mind . . . One does see things, you know, and not know one sees them. In a railway accident once, I remember noticing a large blister of paint at the side of the carriage. I could have *drawn* it for you afterward. And once, when there was a fly bomb in London—splinters of glass everywhere—and the shock —but what I remember best is a woman standing in front of me who had a big hole halfway up the leg of her stocking and the stockings didn't match. So when Miss Murgatroyd stopped thinking and just tried to remember what she *saw,* she remembered a good deal.

"She started, I think, near the mantelpiece, where the torch must have hit first—then it went along the two windows and there were people in between the windows and her. Mrs. Harmon with her knuckles screwed into her eyes for instance. She went on in her mind, following the torch past Miss Bunner with her mouth open and her eyes staring—past a blank wall and a table with a lamp and a cigarette box. And then came the shots—and quite suddenly she remembered a most incredible thing. She'd seen the wall where Letitia Blacklock had been standing when she was shot, and at the moment when the revolver went off and Letty was shot, *Letty hadn't been there* . . .

"You see what I mean now? She'd been thinking of the three women Miss Hinchliffe had told her to think about. If one of them hadn't been there, it would have been the *personality* she'd have fastened upon. She'd have said—in effect—'*That's* the one! *She* wasn't there!' But it was a *place* that was in her mind—a place where someone should have been—but the place wasn't filled—there wasn't anybody there. The place was there—but the person wasn't. And she couldn't take it in all at once. 'How extraordinary. Hinch,' she said. 'She wasn't *there*' . . . So that could only mean Letitia Blacklock . . ."

"But you knew before that, didn't you?" said Bunch. "When the lamp went out. When you wrote down those things on the paper."

"Yes, my dear. It all came together then, you see—all the various isolated bits—and made a coherent pattern."

Bunch quoted softly, *"Lamp?* Yes. *Violet?* Yes. *Bottle of aspirin.* You mean that Bunny had been going to buy a new bottle that day, and so she ought not to have needed to take Letitia's?"

"Not unless her own bottle had been taken or hidden. It had to appear as though Letitia Blacklock was the one meant to be killed."

"Yes, I see. And then 'Delicious Death.' The cake—but more than the cake. The whole party setup. A happy day for Bunny before she died. Treating her rather like a dog you were going to destroy. That's what I find the most horrible thing of all—the sort of—of spurious kindness."

"She *was* quite a kindly woman. What she said at the last in the kitchen was quite true. 'I didn't want to kill anybody.' What she wanted was a great deal of money that didn't belong to her! And before that desire—(and it had become a kind of obsession—the money was to pay her back for all the suffering life had inflicted on her)—everything else went to the wall. People with a grudge against the world are always dangerous. They seem to think life owes them something. I've known many an invalid who has suffered far worse and been cut off from life much more than Charlotte Blacklock—and they've managed to lead happy contented lives. It's what's in *yourself* that makes you happy or unhappy. But, oh, dear, I'm afraid I'm straying away from what we were talking about. Where were we?"

"Going over your list," said Bunch. "What did you mean by 'Making enquiries'? Inquiries about what?"

Miss Marple shook her head playfully at Inspector Craddock.

"You ought to have seen that, Inspector Craddock. You showed me that letter from Letitia Blacklock to her sister. It had the word 'enquiries' in it twice—each time spelt with an *e*. But in the note I asked Bunch to show you, Miss Blacklock had written 'inquiries' with an *i*. People don't usually alter their spelling as they get older. It seemed to me very significant."

"Yes," Craddock agreed. "I ought to have spotted that."

Bunch was continuing: *"Severe affliction bravely borne.* That's what Bunny said to you in the café and, of course, Letitia hadn't had any affliction. *Iodine.* That put you on the track of goiter?"

"Yes, dear. Switzerland, you know, and Miss Blacklock giving the impression that her sister had died of consumption. But I remembered then that the greatest authorities on goiter and the most skillful surgeons operating on it are Swiss. And it linked up with those really rather preposterous pearls that Letitia Blacklock always wore. Not really her *style* —but just right for concealing the scar."

"I understand now her agitation the night the string broke," said Craddock. "It seemed at the time quite disproportionate."

"And after that, it was Lotty you wrote, not Letty as we thought," said Bunch.

"Yes, I remembered that the sister's name was Charlotte, and that Dora Bunner had called Miss Blacklock Lotty once or twice—and that each time she did so, she had been very upset afterwards."

"And what about Berne and Old-Age Pension?"

"Rudi Scherz had been an orderly in a hospital in Berne."

"And Old-Age Pension?"

"Oh, my dear Bunch, I mentioned that to you in the Bluebird though I didn't really see the application then. How Mrs. Wotherspoon drew Mrs. Bartlett's Old-Age Pension as well as her own—though Mrs. Bartlett had been dead for years—simply because one old woman is so like another old woman—Yes, it all made a pattern and I felt so worked up I went out to cool my head a little and think what could be done about proving all this. Then Miss Hinchliffe picked me up and we found Miss Murgatroyd . . ."

Miss Marple's voice dropped. It was no longer excited and pleased. It was quiet and remorseless.

"I knew then something had *got* to be done. Quickly! But there still wasn't any *proof.* I thought out a possible plan and I talked to Sergeant Fletcher."

"And have I had Fletcher on the carpet for it!" said Craddock. "He'd no business to go agreeing to your plans without reporting first to me."

"He didn't like it, but I talked him into it," said Miss Marple. "We went up to Little Paddocks and I got hold of Mitzi."

Julia drew a deep breath and said, "I can't imagine how you ever got her to do it."

"I worked on her, my dear," said Miss Marple. "She thinks far too much about herself anyway, and it will be good for her to have done something for others. I flattered her up, of course, and said I was sure if she'd been in her own country she'd have been in the Resistance movement, and she said, 'Yes, indeed.' And I said I could see she had got just the temperament for that sort of work. She was brave, didn't mind taking risks and could act a part. I told her stories of deeds done by girls in the Resistance movements, some of them true, and some of them, I'm afraid, invented. She got tremendously worked up!"

"Marvelous," said Patrick.

"And then I got her to agree to do her part. I rehearsed her till she was word perfect. Then I told her to go upstairs to her room and not come down until Inspector Craddock came. The worst of these excitable people is that they're apt to go off half-cocked and start the whole thing before the time."

"She did it very well," said Julia.

"I don't quite see the point," said Bunch. "Of course, I wasn't there—" she added apologetically.

"The point? It was a little complicated—and rather touch and go. The idea was that Mitzi, whilst admitting, as though casually, that blackmail *had* been in her mind, was now so worked up and terrified that she was willing to come out with the truth. She'd seen, through the keyhole of the dining-room, Miss Blacklock in the hall with a revolver behind Rudi Scherz. She'd seen, that is, *what had actually taken place.* Now the only danger was that Charlotte Blacklock might have realized that, as the key was in the keyhole, Mitzi couldn't possibly have seen anything at all. But I banked on the fact that you don't think of things like that when you've just had a bad shock. All she could take in was that Mitzi had seen her."

Craddock took over the story.

"But—and this was essential—I pretended to receive this with skepticism, and I made an immediate attack, as though unmasking my batteries at last, upon someone who had not been previously suspected. I accused Edmund—"

"And very nicely *I* played *my* part," said Edmund. "Hot denial. All according to plan. What wasn't according to plan, Phillipa, my love, was you throwing in your little chirp and coming out into the open as 'Pip.' Neither the Inspector nor I had any idea you were Pip. I was going to be Pip! It threw us off our stride for the moment, but the Inspector made a masterly comeback and made some perfectly filthy insinuations about my wanting a rich wife which will probably stick in your subconscious and make irreparable trouble between us one day."

"I don't see why that was necessary."

"Don't you? It meant that, *from Charlotte Blacklock's point of view,* the only person who suspected or knew the truth, was *Mitzi.* The suspicions of the police were elsewhere. They had treated Mitzi for the moment as a liar. But if Mitzi were to persist, they might listen to her and take her seriously. So Mitzi had got to be silenced.

"Mitzi went straight out of the room and back to the kitchen—just like I had told her," said Miss Marple. "Miss Blacklock came out after her almost immediately. Mitzi was apparently alone in the kitchen. Sergeant Fletcher was behind the scullery door. And I was in the broom cupboard in the kitchen. Luckily I'm very thin."

Bunch looked at Miss Marple.

"What did you expect to happen, Aunt Jane?"

"One of two things. Either Charlotte would offer Mitzi money to hold her tongue—and Sergeant Fletcher would be a witness to that offer, or else—or else I thought she'd try to kill Mitzi."

"But she couldn't hope to get away with *that?* She'd have been suspected at once."

"Oh, my dear, she was past reasoning. She was just a snapping, terrified, cornered rat. Think what had happened that day. The scene between Miss Hinchliffe and Miss Murgatroyd. Miss Hinchliffe driving off to the station. As soon as she comes back Miss Murgatroyd will explain that Letitia Blacklock wasn't in the room that night. That's just a few minutes in which to make sure Miss Murgatroyd can't tell anything. No time to make a plan or set a stage. Just crude murder. She greets the poor woman and strangles her. Then a quick rush home, to change, to be sitting by the fire when the others come in, as though she'd never been out.

"And then came the revelation of Julia's identity. She breaks her pearls and is terrified they may notice her scar. Later, the Inspector telephones that he's bringing everyone there. No time to think, to rest. Up to her neck in murder now, no mercy killing—or undesirable young man to be put out of the way. Crude plain murder. Is she safe? Yes, so far. And then comes Mitzi yet *another* danger. Kill Mitzi, stop her tongue! She's beside herself with fear. Not human any longer. Just a dangerous animal."

"But why were you in the broom cupboard, Aunt Jane?" asked Bunch. "Couldn't you have left it to Sergeant Fletcher?"

"It was safer with two of us, my dear. And, besides, I knew I could mimic Dora Bunner's voice. If anything could break Charlotte Blacklock down, that would."

"And it did . . . !"

"Yes . . . she went to pieces."

There was a long silence as memory laid hold of them and then, speaking with determined lightness, to ease the strain, Julia said, "It's made a wonderful difference to Mitzi. She told me yesterday that she was taking a post near Southampton. And she said" (Julia produced a very good imitation of Mitzi's accent). " 'I go there and if they say to me you have to register with the police—you are an alien, I say to them, "Yes, I will register! The police, they know me well. I assist the police! Without me the police never would they have made the arrest of a very dangerous criminal. I risked my life because I am brave—brave like a lion—I do not care about risks." "Mitzi," they say to me, "you are a *heroine,* you are superb." "Ach! it is nothing," I say.' "

Julia stopped.

"And a great deal more," she added.

"I think," said Edmund thoughtfully, "that soon Mitzi will have assisted the police in not one but hundreds of cases!"

"She's softened toward me," said Phillipa. "She actually presented me with the recipe for Delicious Death as a kind of wedding present. She added that I was on no account to divulge the secret to Julia, because Julia had ruined her omelette pan."

"Mrs. Lucas," said Edmund, "is all over Phillipa now that since Belle Goedler's death, Phillipa and Julia have inherited the Goedler millions. She sent us some silver asparagus tongs as a wedding present. I shall have enormous pleasure in *not* asking her to the wedding!"

"And so they lived happily ever after," said Patrick. "Edmund and Phillipa—And Julia and Patrick?" he added tentatively.

"Not with me, you won't live happily ever after," said Julia. "The remarks that Inspector Craddock improvised to address to Edmund apply far more aptly to you. You *are* the sort of soft young man who would like a rich wife. Nothing doing!"

"There's gratitude for you," said Patrick. "After all I did for that girl."

"Nearly landed me in prison on a murder charge—that's what your forgetfulness nearly did for me," said Julia. "I shall never forget that evening when your sister's letter came. I really thought I was in for it. I couldn't see any way out. As it is," she added musingly, "I think I shall go on the stage."

"What? You, too?" groaned Patrick.

"Yes. I might go to Perth. See if I can get your Julia's place in the Rep there. Then, when I've learned my job, I shall go into theater management—and put on Edmund's plays, perhaps."

"I thought you wrote novels," said Julian Harmon.

"Well, so did I," said Edmund. "I began writing a novel. Rather good it was. Pages about an unshaven man getting out of bed and what he smelt like, and the gray streets, and a horrible old woman with dropsy and a vicious young tart who dribbled down her chin—and they all talked interminably about the state of the world and wondered what they were alive for. And suddenly I began to wonder, too . . . And then a rather comic idea occurred to me . . . and I jotted it down—and then I worked up rather a good little scene . . . All very obvious stuff. But, somehow, I got interested . . . and before I knew what I was doing I'd finished a roaring farce in three acts."

"What's it called?" asked Patrick. *"What the Butler Saw?"*

"Well, it easily might be . . . As a matter of fact I've called it *Elephants Do Forget.* What's more, it's been accepted and it's going to be produced!"

"Elephants Do Forget," murmured Bunch. "I thought they didn't?"

The Rev. Julian Harmon gave a guilty start.

"My goodness! I've been so interested. My *sermon* . . ."

"Detective stories again," said Bunch. "Real life ones this time."

"You might preach on *Thou Shalt Do No Murder,"* suggested Patrick.

"No," said Julian Harmon quietly, "I shan't take that as my text."

"No," said Bunch. "You're quite right, Julian. I know a much nicer text, a happy text." She quoted in her fresh voice, " 'For lo, the Spring is here and the Voice of the Turtle is heard in the Land'—I haven't got it quite right—but you know the one I mean. Though why a *turtle* I can't think. I shouldn't think turtles have got nice voices at all."

"The word turtle," explained the Rev. Julian Harmon, "is not very happily translated. It doesn't mean a reptile but the turtle dove. The Hebrew word in the original is—"

Bunch interrupted him by giving him a hug and saying:

"I know one thing—*You* think that the Ahasuerus of the Bible is Artaxerxes the Second, but between you and me it was Artaxerxes the Third."

As always, Julian Harmon wondered why his wife should think that story so particularly funny. . . .

"Tiglath-Pileser wants to go and help you," said Bunch. "He ought to be a very proud cat. *He* showed us how the lights went out."

Epilogue

"WE OUGHT to order some papers," said Edmund to Phillipa upon the day of their return to Chipping Cleghorn after the honeymoon. "Let's go along to Totman's."

Mr. Totman, a heavy-breathing, slow-moving man, received them with affability.

"Glad to see you back, sir. *And* madam."

"We want to order some papers."

"Certainly, sir. And your mother is keeping well, I hope? Quite settled down at Bournemouth?"

"She loves it," said Edmund who had not the faintest idea whether this was so or not, but like most sons, preferred to believe that all was well with those loved, but frequently irritating beings, parents.

"Yes, sir. Very agreeable place. Went there for my holiday last year. Mrs. Totman enjoyed it very much."

"I'm glad. About papers, we'd like—"

"And I hear you have a play on in London, sir. Very amusing so they tell me."

"Yes, it's doing very well."

"Called *Elephants Do Forget,* so I hear. You'll excuse me, sir, asking you, but I always thought that they *didn't*—forget, I mean."

"Yes—yes, exactly—I've begun to think it was a mistake calling it that. So many people have said just what you say."

"A kind of natural history fact, I've always understood."

"Yes—yes. Like earwigs making good mothers."

"Do they indeed, sir? Now that's a fact I *didn't* know."

"About the papers—"

"*The Times,* sir, I think it was?" Mr. Totman paused with pencil uplifted.

"*The Daily Worker,*" said Edmund firmly, "And the *Daily Telegraph,*" said Phillipa. "And the *New Statesman,*" said Edmund. "The *Radio Times,*" said Phillipa. "The *Spectator,*" said Edmund. "The *Gardener's Chronicle,*" said Phillipa.

They both paused to take breath.

"Thank you, sir," said Mr. Totman. "*And* the *Gazette,* I suppose?"

"No," said Edmund.

"No," said Phillipa.

"Excuse me, you *do* want the *Gazette?*"

"No, we don't."

"Certainly not."

"You don't want the *North Benham News and Chipping Cleghorn Gazette?*"

"No."

"You don't want me to send it along to you every week?"

"No." Edmund added: "Is that quite clear now?"

"Oh, yes, sir—yes."

Edmund and Phillipa went out, and Mr. Totman padded into his back parlor.

"Got a pencil, Mother?" he said. "My pen's run out."

"Here you are," said Mrs. Totman, seizing the order book. "I'll do it. What do they want?"

"Daily Worker, Daily Telegraph—Radio Times, New Statesman Spectator—let me see—Gardener's Chronicle."

"Gardener's Chronicle," repeated Mrs. Totman, writing busily. "And the *Gazette.*"

"They don't want the *Gazette.*"

"What?"

"They don't want the *Gazette.* They said so."

"Nonsense," said Mrs. Totman. "You don't hear properly. Of course they want the *Gazette!* Everybody has the *Gazette.* How else would they know what's going on round here?"

*Murder
with
Mirrors*

1

MRS. VAN RYDOCK moved a little back from the mirror and sighed.

"Well, that'll have to do," she murmured.

"Think it's all right, Jane?"

Miss Marple eyed the Lanvanelli creation appraisingly.

"It seems to me a very beautiful gown," she said.

"The gown's all right," said Mrs. Van Rydock and sighed.

"Take it off, Stephanie," she said.

The elderly maid with the grey hair and the small pinched mouth, eased the gown carefully up over Mrs. Van Rydock's upstretched arms.

Mrs. Van Rydock stood in front of the glass in her peach satin slip. She was exquisitely corseted. Her still shapely legs were encased in fine nylon stockings. Her face, beneath a layer of cosmetics and constantly toned up by massage, appeared almost girlish at a slight distance. Her hair was less grey than tending to hydrangea blue and was perfectly set. It was practically impossible when looking at Mrs. Van Rydock, to imagine what she would be like in a natural state. Everything that money could do had been done for her—reinforced by diet, massage, and constant exercises.

Ruth Van Rydock looked humorously at her friend.

"Do you think most people would guess, Jane, that you and I are practically the same age?"

Miss Marple responded loyally.

"Not for a moment, I'm sure," she said reassuringly. "I'm afraid, you know, that *I* look every minute of *my* age!"

Miss Marple was white-haired, with a soft pink and white wrinkled face and innocent china blue eyes. She looked a very sweet old lady. Nobody would have called Mrs. Van Rydock a sweet old lady.

"I guess you do, Jane," said Mrs. Van Rydock. She grinned suddenly, "And so do I. Only not in the same way. 'Wonderful how that old hag keeps her figure.' That's what they say of me. But they know I'm an old hag all right! And, my God, do I feel like one!"

She dropped heavily onto the satin quilted chair.

"That's all right, Stephanie," she said. "You can go."

Stephanie gathered up the dress and went out.

"Good old Stephanie," said Ruth Van Rydock. "She's been with me for over thirty years now. She's the only woman who knows what I really look like! Jane, I want to talk to you."

Miss Marple leant forward a little. Her face took on a receptive expression. She looked, somehow, an incongruous figure in the ornate bedroom of the expensive Hotel suite. She was dressed in rather dowdy black, carried a large shopping bag and looked every inch a lady.

"I'm worried, Jane. About Carrie Louise."

"Carrie Louise?" Miss Marple repeated the name musingly. The sound of it took her a long way back.

The *pensionnat* in Florence. Herself, the pink and white English girl from a Cathedral Close. The two Martin girls, Americans, exciting to the English girl because of their quaint ways of speech and their forthright manner and vitality. Ruth, tall, eager, on top of the world, Carrie Louise small, dainty, wistful.

"When did you see her last, Jane?"

"Oh! not for many many years. It must be twenty-five at least. Of course we still send cards at Christmas."

Such an odd thing, friendship! She, young Jane Marple, and the two Americans. Their ways diverging almost at once, and yet the old affection persisting; occasional letters, remembrances at Christmas. Strange that Ruth whose home—or rather homes—had been in America should be the sister whom she had seen the more often of the two. No, perhaps not strange. Like most Americans of her class, Ruth had been cosmopolitan, every year or two she had come over to Europe, rushing from London to Paris, on to the Riviera, and back again, and always keen to snatch a few moments wherever she was, with her old friends. There had been many meetings like this one. In Claridge's, or the Savoy, or the Berkeley, or the Dorchester. A *recherché* meal, affectionate reminiscences, and a hurried and affectionate goodbye. Ruth had never had time to visit St. Mary Mead. Miss Marple had not, indeed, ever expected it. Everyone's life has a *tempo*. Ruth's was Presto whereas Miss Marple's was content to be Adagio.

So it was American Ruth whom she had seen most of, whereas Carrrie Louise who lived in England, she had not now seen for over twenty years. Odd, but quite natural, because when one lives in the same country there is no need to arrange meetings with old friends. One assumes that, sooner or later, one will see them without contrivance. Only, if you move in different spheres, that does not happen. The paths of Jane Marple and Carrie Louise did not cross. It was as simple as that.

"Why are you worried about Carrie Louise, Ruth?" asked Miss Marple.

"In a way that's what worries me most! I just don't know."

"She's not ill?"

"She's very delicate—always has been. I wouldn't say she'd been any worse than usual—considering that she's getting on just as we all are."

"Unhappy?"

"Oh *no.*"

No, it wouldn't be that, thought Miss Marple. It would be difficult to imagine Carrie Louise unhappy—and yet there were times in her life when she must have been. Only—the picture did not come clearly. Bewildered—yes—incredulous—yes—but violent grief—no.

Mrs. Van Rydock's words came appositely.

"Carrie Louise," she said, "has always lived right out of this world. She doesn't know what it's like. Maybe it's *that* that worries me."

"Her circumstances," began Miss Marple, then stopped, shaking her head. "No," she said.

"No, it's she herself," said Ruth van Rydock. "Carrie Louise was always the one of us who had ideals. Of course it was the fashion when we were young to have ideals—we all had them, it was the proper thing for young girls. You were going to nurse lepers, Jane, and I was going to be a nun. One gets over all that nonsense. Marriage, I suppose one might say, knocks it out of one. Still, take it by and large, I haven't done badly out of marriage."

Miss Marple thought that Ruth was expressing it mildly. Ruth had been married three times, each time to an extremely wealthy man, and the resultant divorces had increased her bank balance without in the least souring her disposition.

"Of course," said Mrs. Van Rydock, "I've always been tough. Things don't get me down. I've not expected too much of life and certainly not expected too much of men—and I've done very well out of it—and no hard feelings. Tommy and I are still excellent friends, and Julius often asks me my opinion about the market." Her face darkened. "I believe that's what worries me about Carrie Louise—she's always had a tendency, you know, to marry *cranks.*"

"Cranks?"

"People with ideals. Carrie Louise was always a push-over for ideals. There she was, as pretty as they make them, just seventeen and listening with her eyes as big as saucers to old Gulbrandsen holding forth about his plans for the human race. Over fifty, and she married him, a widower with a family of grown-up children—all because of his philantropic ideas. She used to sit listening to him spellbound. Just like Desdemona and Othello. Only fortunately there was no Iago about to mess things up—

and anyway Gulbrandsen wasn't coloured. He was a Swede or a Norwegian or something."

Miss Marple nodded thoughtfully. The name of Gulbrandsen had an International significance. A man who with shrewd business acumen and perfect honesty had built up a fortune so colossal that really philanthropy had been the only solution to the disposal of it. The name still held significance. The Gulbrandsen Trust, the Gulbrandsen Research Fellowships, the Gulbrandsen Administrative Almshouses, and best known of all the vast educational College for the sons of working men.

"She didn't marry him for his money, you know," said Ruth, "*I* should have if I'd married him at all. But not Carrie Louise. I don't know what would have happened if he hadn't died when she was thirty-two. Thirty-two's a very nice age for a widow. She's got experience, but she's still adaptable."

The spinster listening to her, nodded gently whilst her mind reviewed, tentatively, widows she had known in the village of St. Mary Mead.

"I was really happiest about Carrie Louise when she was married to Johnnie Restarick. Of course *he* married her for her money—or if not exactly that, at any rate he wouldn't have married her if she hadn't had any. Johnnie was a selfish pleasure loving lazy hound, but that's so much safer than a crank. All Johnnie wanted was to live soft. He wanted Carrie Louise to go to the best dressmakers and have yachts and cars and enjoy herself with him. That kind of man is so very *safe*. Give him comfort and luxury and he'll purr like a cat and be absolutely charming to you. I never took that scene designing and theatrical stuff of his very seriously. But Carrie Louise was thrilled by it—saw it all as Art with a capital A. and really forced him back into those surroundings and then that dreadful Yugoslavian woman got hold of him and just swept him off with her. He didn't really want to go. If Carrie Louise had waited and been sensible, he would have come back to her."

"Did she care very much?" asked Miss Marple.

"That's the funny thing. I don't really believe she did. She was absolutely sweet about it all—but then she would be. She *is* sweet. Quite anxious to divorce him so that he and that creature could get married. And offering to give those two boys of his by his first marriage a home with her because it would be more settled for them. So there poor Johnnie was—he *had* to marry the woman and she led him an awful six months and then drove him over a precipice in a car in a fit of rage. They *said* it was an accident, but *I* think it was just temper!"

Mrs. Van Rydock paused, took up a mirror and gazed at her face searchingly. She picked up her eyebrow tweezers and pulled out a hair.

"And what does Carrie Louise do next but marry this man Lewis Serrocold. Another crank! Another man with ideals! Oh I don't say he isn't devoted to her—I think he is—but he's bitten by that same bug of wanting to improve everbody's lives for them. And really, you know, nobody can do that but yourself."

"I wonder," said Miss Marple.

"Only, of course, there's a fashion in these things, just like there is in clothes. (My dear, have you seen what Christian Dior is trying to make us wear in the way of skirts?) Where was I? Oh, yes, Fashion. Well, there's a fashion in philanthropy too. It used to be education in Gulbrandsen's day. But that's out of date now. The State has stepped in. Everyone expects education as a matter of right—and doesn't think much of it when they get it! Juvenile Delinquency—that's what is the rage nowadays. All these young criminals and potential criminals. Everyone's mad about them. You should see Lewis Serrocold's eyes sparkle behind those thick glasses of his. Crazy with enthusiasm! One of those men of enormous will power who like living on a banana and a piece of toast and put all their energies into a Cause. And Carrie Louise eats it up —just as she always did. But I don't like it, Jane. They've had meetings of the Trustees and the whole place has been turned over to this new idea. It's a training establishment now for these juvenile criminals, complete with psychiatrists and psychologists and all the rest of it. There Lewis and Carrie Louise are, living there, surrounded by these boys—who aren't perhaps quite normal. And the place stiff with occupational therapists and teachers and enthusiasts, half of *them* quite mad. Cranks, all the lot of them, and my little Carrie Louise in the middle of it all!"

She paused—and stared helplessly at Miss Marple.

Miss Marple said in a faintly puzzled voice:

"But you haven't told me yet, Ruth, what you are really afraid of."

"I tell you, I don't *know!* And *that's* what worries me. I've just been down there—for a flying visit. And I felt all along that there was something wrong. In the atmosphere—in the house—I know I'm not mistaken. I'm sensitive to atmosphere, always have been. Did I ever tell you how I urged Julius to sell out of Amalgamated Cereals before the crash came? And wasn't I right? Yes, something is *wrong* down there. But I don't know why or what—if it's these dreadful young jailbirds—or if it's nearer home. I can't say what it is. There's Lewis just living for his ideas and not noticing anything else, and Carrie Louise, bless her, never seeing or hearing or thinking anything except what's a lovely sight, or a lovely sound, or a lovely thought. It's sweet but it isn't *practical.* There *is* such a thing as evil—and I want you, Jane, to go down there right away and find out just exactly what's the matter."

"*Me?*" exclaimed Miss Marple. "Why me?"

"Because you've got a nose for that sort of thing. You always had. You've always been a sweet innocent looking creature, Jane, and all the time underneath nothing has ever surprised you, you always believe the worst."

"The worst is so often true," murmured Miss Marple.

"Why you have such a poor idea of human nature, I can't think—living in that sweet peaceful village of yours, so old world and pure."

"You have never lived in a village, Ruth. The things that go on in a pure peaceful village would probably surprise you."

"Oh I daresay. My point is that they don't surprise *you.* So you *will* go down to Stonygates and find out what's wrong, won't you?"

"But Ruth dear, that would be a most difficult thing to do."

"No, it wouldn't be. I've thought it all out. If you won't be absolutely mad at me, I've prepared the ground already."

Mrs. Van Rydock paused, eyed Miss Marple rather uneasily, lighted a cigarette, and plunged rather nervously into explanation.

"You'll admit, I'm sure, that things have been difficult in this country since the war, for people with small fixed incomes—for people like you, that is to say, Jane."

"Oh yes, indeed. But for the kindness, the really great kindness of my nephew Raymond, I don't know really where I should be."

"Never mind your nephew," said Mrs. Van Rydock. "Carrie Louise knows nothing about your nephew—or if she does, she knows him as a writer and has no idea that he's your nephew. The point, as I put it to Carrie Louise, is that it's just too bad about dear Jane. Really sometimes hardly enough to eat, and of course far too proud ever to appeal to old friends. One couldn't, I said, suggest *money*—but a nice long rest in lovely surroundings, with an old friend and with plenty of nourishing food, and no cares or worries—" Ruth Van Rydock paused and then added defiantly, "Now go on—be mad at me if you want to be."

Miss Marple opened her china blue eyes in gentle surprise.

"But why should I be mad at you, Ruth? A very ingenious and plausible approach. I'm sure Carrie Louise responded."

"She's writing to you. You'll find the letter when you get back. Honestly, Jane, you don't feel that I've taken an unpardonable liberty? You won't mind—"

She hesitated and Miss Marple put her thoughts deftly into words.

"Going to Stonygates as an object of charity—more or less under false pretences? Not in the least—if it is *necessary.* You think it is necessary—and I am inclined to agree with you."

Mrs. Van Rydock stared at her.

"But why? What have you heard?"

"I haven't heard anything. It's just your conviction. You're not a fanciful woman, Ruth."

"No, but I haven't anything definite to go upon."

"I remember," said Miss Marple thoughtfully, "one Sunday morning at church—it was the second Sunday in Advent—sitting behind Grace Lamble and feeling more and more worried about her. Quite sure, you know, that something was wrong—badly wrong—yet being quite unable to say why. A most disturbing feeling and very very definite."

"And was there something wrong?"

"Oh yes. Her father, the old Admiral, had been *very* peculiar for some time, and the very next day he went for her with the coal hammer, roaring out that she was Antichrist masquerading as his daughter. He nearly killed her. They took him away to the asylum and she eventually recovered after months in Hospital—but it was a very near thing."

"And you'd actually had a premonition that day in church?"

"I wouldn't call it a premonition. It was founded on *fact*— these things usually are, though one doesn't always recognise it at the time. She was wearing her Sunday hat the wrong way round. Very significant, really, because Grace Lamble was a most precise woman, not at all vague or absent-minded—and the circumstances under which she would not notice which way her hat was put on to go to church were really extremely limited. Her father, you see, had thrown a marble paperweight at her and it had shattered the looking glass. She had caught up her hat, put it on, and hurried out of the house. Anxious to keep up appearances and for the servants not to hear anything. She put down these actions, you see, to 'dear Papa's Naval temper,' she didn't realise that his mind was definitely unhinged. Though she ought to have realised it clearly enough. He was always complaining to her of being spied upon and of enemies—all the usual symptoms, in fact."

Mrs. Van Rydock gazed respectfully at her friend.

"Maybe, Jane," she said, "that St. Mary Mead of yours isn't quite the idyllic retreat that I've always imagined it."

"Human nature, dear, is very much the same everywhere. It is more difficult to observe it closely in a city, that is all."

"And you'll go to Stonygates?"

"I'll go to Stonygates. A little unfair, perhaps, on my nephew Raymond. To let it be thought that he does not assist me, I mean. Still the dear boy is in Mexico for six months. And by that time it should all be over."

"What should all be over?"

"Carrie Louise's invitation will hardly be for an indefinite stay. Three weeks, perhaps—a month. That should be ample."

"For you to find out what is wrong?"

"For me to find out what is wrong."

"My, Jane," said Mrs. Van Rydock, "you've got a lot of confidence in yourself, haven't you?"

Miss Marple looked faintly reproachful.

"*You* have confidence in me, Ruth. Or so you say . . . I can only assure you that I shall endeavour to justify your confidence."

2

BEFORE catching her train back to St. Mary Mead (Wednesday special cheap day return) Miss Marple, in a precise and businesslike fashion, collected certain data.

"Carrie Louise and I have corresponded after a fashion, but it has largely been a matter of Christmas cards or calendars. It's just the facts I should like, Ruth dear—and also some idea as to whom exactly I shall encounter in the household at Stonygates."

"Well, you know about Carrie Louise's marriage to Gulbrandsen. There were no children and Carrie Louise took that very much to heart. Gulbrandsen was a widower, and had three grown-up sons. Eventually they adopted a child. Pippa, they called her—a lovely little creature. She was just two years old when they got her."

"Where did she come from? What was her background?"

"Really, now, Jane, I can't remember—if I ever heard, that is. An Adoption Society, maybe? Or some unwanted child that Gulbrandsen had heard about. Why? Do you think it's important?"

"Well, one always likes to know the background, so to speak. But please go on."

"The next thing that happened was that Carrie Louise found that she was going to have a baby after all. I understand from doctors that that quite often happens."

Miss Marple nodded.

"I believe so."

"Anyway, it did happen, and in a funny kind of way, Carrie Louise was almost disconcerted, if you can understand what I mean. Earlier, of course, she'd have been wild with joy. As it was, she'd given such a devoted love to Pippa that she felt quite apologetic to Pippa for putting her nose out of joint, so to speak. And then Mildred, when she arrived, was really a very unattractive child. Took after the Gulbrandsens—who were solid and worthy—but definitely homely. Carrie Louise was always so anxious to make no difference between the adopted child and her own child that I think she rather tended to overindulge Pippa and pass over Mildred. Sometimes I think that Mildred resented it. However I didn't see them often. Pippa grew up a very beautiful girl and Mildred grew up a plain one. Eric Gulbrandsen died when Mildred was fifteen and Pippa eighteen. At twenty Pippa married an Italian, the Marchese di San Severiano—oh quite a genuine Marchese—not an adventurer, or anything like that. She was by way of being an heiress (naturally, or San Severiano wouldn't have married her—you know what Italians are!). Gulbrandsen left an equal sum in trust for both his own and his adopted daughter. Mildred married a Canon Strete—a nice man but given to colds in the head. About ten or fifteen years older than she was. Quite a happy marriage, I believe.

"He died a year ago and Mildred has come back to Stonygates to live with her mother. But that's getting on too fast, I've skipped a marriage or two. I'll go back to them. Pippa married her Italian. Carrie Louise was quite pleased about the marriage. Guido had beautiful manners and was very handsome, and he was a fine sportsman. A year later Pippa had a daughter and died in childbirth. It was a terrible tragedy and Guido San Severiano was very cut up. Carrie Louise went to and fro between Italy and England a good deal and it was in Rome that she met Johnnie Restarick and married him. The Marchese married again and he was quite willing for his little daughter to be brought up in England by her exceedingly wealthy grandmother. So they all settled down at Stonygates, Johnnie Restarick and Carrie Louise, and Johnnie's two boys, Alexis and Stephen (Johnnie's first wife was a Russian), and the baby Gina. Mildred married her Canon soon afterwards. Then came all this business of Johnnie and the Yugoslavian woman and the divorce. The boys still came to Stonygates for their holidays and were devoted to Carrie Louise and then in 1938, I think it was, Carrie Louise married Lewis."

Mrs. Van Rydock paused for breath.

"You've not met Lewis?"

Miss Marple shook her head.

"No, I think I last saw Carrie Louise in 1928. She very sweetly took me to Covent Garden—to the Opera."

"Oh yes. Well, Lewis was a very suitable person for her to marry. He was the head of a very celebrated firm of Chartered Accountants. I think he met her first over some question of the finance of the Gulbrandsen Trust and the College. He was well off, just about her own age and a man of absolutely upright life. But he *was* a crank. He was absolutely rabid on the subject of the redemption of young criminals."

Ruth Van Rydock sighed.

"As I said just now, Jane, there are fashions in philanthropy. In Gulbrandsen's time it was Education. Before that it was soup kitchens—"

Miss Marple nodded.

"Yes, indeed. Port wine jelly and calf's head broth taken to the sick. My mother used to do it."

"That's right. Feeding the body gave way to feeding the mind. Everyone went mad on educating the lower classes. Well, that's passed. Soon, I expect, the fashionable thing to do will be not to educate your children, preserve their illiteracy carefully until they're eighteen. Anyway the Gulbrandsen Trust and Education Fund was in some difficulties because the State was taking over its functions. Then Lewis came along with his passionate enthusiasm about constructive training for juvenile delinquents. His attention had been drawn to the subject first in the course of his profession—auditing accounts where ingenious young men had perpetrated frauds. He was more and more convinced that juvenile delinquents were not subnormal—that they had excellent brains and abilities and only needed the right direction."

"There is something in that," said Miss Marple. "But it is not entirely true. I remember—"

She broke off and glanced at her watch.

"Oh, dear—I mustn't miss the 6.30."

Ruth Van Rydock said urgently:

"And you will go to Stonygates?"

Gathering up her shopping bag and her umbrella Miss Marple said:

"If Carrie Louise asks me—"

"She will ask you. You'll go? Promise, Jane?"

Jane Marple promised.

3

MISS MARPLE got out of the train at Market Kimble station. A kindly fellow passenger handed out her suitcase after her, and Miss Marple, clutching a string bag, a faded leather handbag and some miscellaneous wraps, uttered appreciative twitters of thanks.

"So kind of you, I'm sure . . . So difficult nowadays—not many porters. I get so flustered when I travel."

The twitters were drowned by the booming noise of the station announcer saying loudly but indistinctly that the 3.18 was standing at Platform 1 and was about to proceed to various unidentifiable stations.

Market Kimble was a large empty windswept station with hardly any passengers or railway staff to be seen on it. Its claim to distinction lay in having six platforms and a bay where a very small train of one carriage was puffing importantly.

Miss Marple, rather more shabbily dressed than was her custom (so lucky that she hadn't given away the old speckledy), was peering around her uncertainly when a young man came up to her.

"Miss Marple?" he said. His voice had an unexpectedly dramatic quality about it, as though the utterance of her name were the first words of a part he was playing in amateur theatricals. "I've come to meet you—from Stonygates."

Miss Marple looked gratefully at him, a charming helpless looking old lady with, if he had chanced to notice it, very shrewd blue eyes. The personality of the young man did not quite match his voice. It was less important, one might almost say insignificant. His eyelids had a trick of fluttering nervously.

"Oh thank you," said Miss Marple. "There's just this suitcase."

She noticed that the young man did not pick up her suitcase himself. He flipped a finger at a porter who was trundling some packing cases past on a trolley.

"Bring it out, please," he said, and added importantly, "For Stonygates."

The porter said cheerfully:

"Rightyho. Shan't be long."

Miss Marple fancied that her new acquaintance was not too pleased about this. It was as if Buckingham Palace had been dismissed as no more important than 3 Laburnum Road.

He said, "The railways get more impossible every day!"

Guiding Miss Marple towards the exit, he said: "I'm Edgar Lawson. Mrs. Serrocold asked me to meet you. I help Mr. Serrocold in his work."

There was again the faint insinuation that a busy and important man had, very charmingly, put important affairs on one side out of chivalry to his employer's wife.

And again the impression was not wholly convincing—it had a theatrical flavour.

Miss Marple began to wonder about Edgar Lawson.

They came out of the station and Edgar guided the old lady to where a rather elderly Ford V8 was standing.

He was just saying "Will you come in front with me, or would you prefer the back?" when there was a diversion.

A new gleaming two seater Rolls Bentley came purring into the station yard and drew up in front of the Ford. A very beautiful young woman jumped out of it and came across to them. The fact that she wore dirty corduroy slacks and a simple aertex shirt open at the neck seemed somehow to enhance the fact that she was not only beautiful but expensive.

"There you are, Edgar. I thought I wouldn't make it in time. I see you've got Miss Marple. I came to meet her." She smiled dazzlingly at Miss Marple showing a row of lovely teeth in a sunburnt southern face. "I'm Gina," she said. "Carrie Louise's granddaughter. What was your journey like? Simply foul? What a nice string bag. I *love* string bags. I'll take it and the coats and then you can get in better."

Edgar's face flushed. He protested.

"Look here, Gina, I came to meet Miss Marple. It was all arranged . . ."

Again the teeth flashed in that wide lazy smile.

"Oh I know, Edgar, but I suddenly thought it would be nice if I came along. I'll take her with me and you can wait and bring her cases up."

She slammed the door on Miss Marple, ran round to the other side, jumped in the driving seat, and they purred swiftly out of the station.

Looking back, Miss Marple noticed Edgar Lawson's face.

"I don't think, my dear," she said, "that Mr. Lawson is very pleased."

Gina laughed.

"Edgar's a frightful idiot," she said. "Always so pompous about things. You'd really think he *mattered!*"

Miss Marple asked, "Doesn't he *matter?*"

"Edgar?" There was an unconscious note of cruelty in Gina's scornful laugh. "Oh, he's bats anyway."

"Bats?"

"They're all bats at Stonygates," said Gina. "I don't mean Lewis and Grandam and me and the boys—and not Miss Bellever, of course. But the others. Sometimes I feel *I'm* going a bit bats myself living there. Even Aunt Mildred goes out on walks and mutters to herself all the time—and you don't expect a Canon's widow to do that, do you?"

They swung out of the station approach and accelerated up the smooth surfaced empty road. Gina shot a swift sideways glance at her companion.

"You were at school with Grandam, weren't you? It seems so queer."

Miss Marple knew perfectly what she meant. To youth it seems very odd to think that age was once young and pigtailed and struggled with decimals and English literature.

"It must," said Gina with awe in her voice, and obviously not meaning to be rude, "have been a *very* long time ago."

"Yes, indeed," said Miss Marple. "You feel that more with me than you do with your grandmother, I expect?"

Gina nodded. "It's cute of you saying that. Grandam, you know, gives one a curiously ageless feeling."

"It is a long time since I've seen her. I wonder if I shall find her much changed."

"Her hair's grey, of course," said Gina vaguely. "And she walks with a stick because of her arthritis. It's got much worse lately. I suppose that—" she broke off, and then asked: "Have you been to Stonygates before?"

"No, never. I've heard a great deal about it, of course."

"It's pretty ghastly really," said Gina cheerfully. "A sort of Gothic monstrosity. What Steve calls Best Victorian Lavatory period. But it's fun, too, in a way. Only of course everything's madly earnest and you tumble over psychiatrists everywhere underfoot. Enjoying themselves madly. Rather like Scout masters, only worse. The young criminals are rather pets, some of them. One showed me how to diddle locks with a bit of wire and one angelic faced boy gave me a lot of points about coshing people."

Miss Marple considered this information thoughtfully.

"It's the thugs I like best," said Gina. "I don't fancy the queers so much. Of course Lewis and Dr. Maverick think they're *all* queers—I mean they think it's repressed desires and disordered home life and their mother getting off with soldiers and all that. I don't really see it myself because some people have had awful home lives and yet have managed to turn out quite all right."

"I'm sure it is all a very difficult problem," said Miss Marple.

Gina laughed, again showing her magnificent teeth.

"It doesn't worry me much. I suppose some people have these sorts of urges to make the world a better place. Lewis is quite dippy about it all—he's going to Aberdeen next week because there's a case coming up in the police court—a boy with five previous convictions."

"The young man who met me at the station? Mr. Lawson. He helps Mr. Serrocold, he told me. Is he his secretary?"

"Oh Edgar hasn't brains enough to be a secretary. He's a *case* really. He used to stay at hotels and pretend he was a V.C. or a fighter pilot and borrow money and then do a flit. I think he's just a rotter. But Lewis goes through a routine with them all. Makes them feel one of the family and gives them jobs to do and all that to encourage their sense of responsibility. I daresay we shall be murdered by one of them one of these days." Gina laughed heartily.

Miss Marple did not laugh.

They turned in through some imposing gates where a Commissionaire was standing on duty in a military manner and drove up a drive flanked with rhododendrons. The drive was badly kept and the grounds seemed neglected.

Interpreting her companion's glance, Gina said, "No gardeners during the war, and since we haven't bothered. But it does look rather terrible."

They came round a curve and Stonygates appeared in its full glory. It was, as Gina had said, a vast edifice of Victorian Gothic—a kind of temple to Plutocracy. Philanthropy had added to it in various wings and outbuildings which, while not positively dissimilar in style, had robbed the structure as a whole of any cohesion or purpose.

"Hideous, isn't it?" said Gina affectionately. "There's Grandam on the terrace. I'll stop here and you can go and meet her."

Miss Marple advanced along the terrace towards her old friend.

From a distance, the slim little figure looked curiously girlish in spite of the stick on which she leaned and her slow and obviously rather painful progress. It was as though a young girl was giving an exaggerated imitation of old age.

"Jane," said Mrs. Serrocold.

"Dear Carrie Louise."

Yes, unmistakably Carrie Louise. Strangely unchanged, strangely youthful still, although, unlike her sister, she used no cosmetics or artificial aids to youth. Her hair was grey, but it had always been of a silvery fairness and the colour had changed very little. Her skin had still a rose leaf pink and white appearance, though now it was a crumpled rose leaf. Her eyes had still their starry innocent glance. She had the slender youthful figure of a girl and her head kept its eager birdlike tilt.

"I do blame myself," said Carrie Louise in her sweet voice, "for letting it be so long. *Years* since I saw you, Jane dear. It's just lovely that you've come at last to pay us a visit here."

From the end of the terrace Gina called:

"You ought to come in, Grandam. It's getting cold—and Jolly will be furious."

Carrie Louise gave her little silvery laugh.

"They all fuss about me so," she said. "They rub it in that I'm an old woman."

"And you don't feel like one."

"No, I don't, Jane. In spite of all my aches and pains—and I've got plenty. Inside I go on feeling just a chit like Gina. Perhaps everyone does. The glass shows them how old they are and they just don't believe it. It seems only a few months ago that we were at Florence. Do you remember Fräulein Schweich and her boots?"

The two elderly women laughed together at events that had happened nearly half a century ago.

They walked together to a side door. In the doorway a gaunt elderly lady met them. She had an arrogant nose, a short haircut and wore stout well cut tweeds.

She said fiercely:

"It's absolutely crazy of you, Cara, to stay out so late. You're absolutely incapable of taking care of yourself. What will Mr. Serrocold say?"

"Don't scold me, Jolly," said Carrie Louise pleadingly. She introduced Miss Bellever to Miss Marple.

"This is Miss Bellever who is simply everything to me. Nurse, dragon, watchdog, secretary, housekeeper and very faithful friend."

Juliet Bellever sniffed, and the end of her big nose turned rather pink, a sign of emotion.

"I do what I can," she said gruffly. "This is a crazy household. You simply can't arrange any kind of planned routine."

"Darling Jolly, of course you can't. I wonder why you ever try. Where are you putting Miss Marple?"

"In the Blue Room. Shall I take her up?" asked Miss Bellever.

"Yes, please do, Jolly. And then bring her down to tea. It's in the library to-day, I think."

The Blue Room had heavy curtains of a rich faded blue brocade that must have been, Miss Marple thought, about fifty years old. The furniture was mahogany, big and solid, and the bed was a vast mahogany fourposter. Miss Bellever opened a door into a connecting bathroom. This was unexpectedly modern, orchid in colouring and with much dazzling chromium.

She observed grimly:

"John Restarick had ten bathrooms put into the house when he married Cara. The plumbing is about the only thing that's ever been modernized. He wouldn't hear of the rest being altered—said the whole place was a perfect Period Piece. Did you ever know him at all?"

"No, I never met him. Mrs. Serrocold and I have met very seldom though we have always corresponded."

"He was an agreeable fellow," said Miss Bellever. "No good, of course! A complete rotter. But pleasant to have about the house. Great charm. Women liked him far too much. That was his undoing in the end. Not really Cara's type."

She added with a brusque resumption of her practical manner:

"The housemaid will unpack for you. Do you want a wash before tea?"

Receiving an affirmative answer, she said that Miss Marple would find her waiting at the top of the stairs.

Miss Marple went into the bathroom and washed her hands and dried them a little nervously on a very beautiful orchid coloured face towel. Then she removed her hat and patted her soft white hair into place.

Opening her door she found Miss Bellever waiting for her and was conducted down the big gloomy staircase and across a vast dark hall and into a room where bookshelves went up to the ceiling and a big window looked out over an artificial lake.

Carrie Louise was standing by the window and Miss Marple joined her.

"What a very imposing house this is," said Miss Marple. "I feel quite lost in it."

"Yes, I know. It's ridiculous, really. It was built by a prosperous iron master—or something of that kind. He went bankrupt not long after. I don't wonder really. There were about fourteen living rooms—all enormous. I've never seen what people *can* want with more than one sitting room. And all those huge bedrooms. Such a lot of unnecessary space. Mine is terribly overpowering—and quite a long way to walk from the bed to the dressing table. And great heavy dark crimson curtains."

"You haven't had it modernized and redecorated?"

Carrie Louise looked vaguely surprised.

"No. On the whole it's very much as it was when I first lived here with

Eric. It's been repainted, of course, but they always do it the same colour. Those things don't really matter, do they? I mean I shouldn't have felt justified in spending a lot of money on that kind of thing when there are so many things that are so much more important."

"Have there been no changes at all in the house?"

"Oh yes—heaps of them. We've just kept a kind of block in the middle of the house as it was—the Great Hall and the rooms off and over. They're the best ones and Johnnie—my second husband—was lyrical over them and said they should never be touched or altered—and of course he was an artist and a designer and he knew about these things. But the East and West wings have been completely remodelled. All the rooms partitioned off and divided up, so that we have offices, and bed-rooms for the teaching staff, and all that. The boys are all in the College building—you can see it from here."

Miss Marple looked out towards where large red brick buildings showed through a belt of sheltering trees. Then her eyes fell on something nearer at hand, and she smiled a little.

"What a very beautiful girl Gina is," she said.

Carrie Louise's face lit up.

"Yes, isn't she?" she said softly. "It's so lovely to have her back here again. I sent her to America at the beginning of the war—to Ruth. Did Ruth talk about her at all?"

"No. At least she did just mention her."

Carrie Louise sighed.

"Poor Ruth! She was frightfully upset over Gina's marriage. But I've told her again and again that I don't blame her in the least. Ruth doesn't realise, as I do, that the old barriers and class shibboleths are gone—or at any rate are going.

"Gina was doing war work—and she met this young man. He was a Marine and had a very good war record. And a week later they were married. It was all far too quick, of course, no time to find out if they were really suited to each other—but that's the way of things nowadays. Young people belong to their generation. We may think they're unwise in many of their doings, but we have to accept their decisions. Ruth, though, was terribly upset."

"She didn't consider the young man suitable?"

"She kept saying that one didn't know anything about him. He came from the Middle West and he hadn't any money—and naturally no pro-fession. There are hundreds of boys like that everywhere—but it wasn't Ruth's idea of what was right for Gina. However, the thing was done. I was so glad when Gina accepted my invitation to come over here with her husband. There's so much going on here—jobs of every kind, and if Walter wants to specialise in medicine or get a degree or anything he could do it in this country. After all, this is Gina's home. It's delightful to have her back, to have someone so warm and gay and alive in the house."

Miss Marple nodded and looked out of the window again at the two young people standing near the lake.

"They're a remarkably handsome couple, too," she said. "I don't wonder Gina fell in love with him!"

"Oh, but that—that isn't Wally." There was, quite suddenly, a touch of embarrassment, or restraint, in Mrs. Serrocold's voice. "That's Steve—the younger of Johnnie Restarick's two boys. When Johnnie—when he went away, he'd no place for the boys in the holidays, so I always had them here. They look on this as their home. And Steve's here permanently now. He runs our dramatic branch. We have a theatre, you know, and plays—we encourage all the artistic instincts. Lewis says that so much of this juvenile crime is due to exhibitionism, most of the boys have had such a thwarted unhappy home life, and these hold ups and burglaries make them feel heroes. We urge them to write their own plays and act in them and design and paint their own scenery. Steve is in charge of the theatre. He's so keen and enthusiastic. It's wonderful what life he's put into the whole thing."

"I see," said Miss Marple slowly.

Her long distance sight was good (as many of her neighbours knew to their cost in the village of St. Mary Mead) and she saw very clearly the dark handsome face of Stephen Restarick as he stood facing Gina, talking eagerly. Gina's face she could not see, since the girl had her back to them, but there was no mistaking the expression in Stephen Restarick's face.

"It isn't any business of mine," said Miss Marple, "but I suppose you realise, Carrie Louise, that he's in love with her."

"Oh no—" Carrie Louise looked troubled. "Oh no, I do hope not."

"You were always up in the clouds, Carrie Louise. There's not the least doubt about it."

4

BEFORE Mrs. Serrocold could say anything, her husband came in from the hall carrying some open letters in his hand.

Lewis Serrocold was a short man, not particularly impressive in appearance, but with a personality that immediately marked him out. Ruth had once said of him that he was more like a dynamo than a human being. He usually concentrated entirely on what was immediately occupying his attention and paid no attention to the objects or persons who were surrounding them.

"A bad blow, dearest," he said. "That boy, Jackie Flint. Back at his tricks again. And I really did think he meant to go straight this time if he got a proper chance. He was most earnest about it. You know we found he'd always been keen on railways—and both Maverick and I thought that if he got a job on the railways he'd stick to it and make good. But it's the same story. Petty thieving from the parcels office. Not even stuff he could want or sell. That shows that it *must* be psychological. We haven't really got to the root of the trouble. But I'm not giving up."

"Lewis—this is my old friend, Jane Marple."

"Oh how d'you do," said Mr. Serrocold absently. "So glad—they'll prosecute, of course. A nice lad, too, not too many brains but a really nice boy. Unspeakable home he came from. I—"

He suddenly broke off, and the dynamo was switched onto the guest.

"Why, Miss Marple, I'm so delighted you've come to stay with us for a while. It will make such a great difference to Caroline to have a friend of old days with whom she can exchange memories. She has in many ways a grim time here—so much sadness in the stories of these poor children. We do hope you'll stay with us a very long time."

Miss Marple felt the magnetism and realised how attractive it would have been to her friend. That Lewis Serrocold was a man who would always put causes before people she did not doubt for a moment. It might have irritated some women, but not Carrie Louise.

Lewis Serrocold sorted out another letter.

"At any rate we've *some* good news. This is from the Wiltshire and Somerset Bank. Young Morris is doing extremely well. They're thoroughly satisfied with him and in fact are promoting him next month. I always knew that all he needed was responsibility—that, and a thorough grasp of the handling of money and what it means."

He turned to Miss Marple.

"Half these boys don't *know* what money is. It represents to them going to the Pictures or to the Dogs, or buying cigarettes—and they're clever with figures and find it exciting to juggle them round. Well, I believe in—what shall I say?—rubbing their noses in the stuff—train them in accountancy, in figures—show them the whole inner romance of money, so to speak. Give them skill and then responsibility—let them handle it officially. Our greatest successes have been that way—only two out of thirty-eight have let us down. One's head cashier in a firm of druggists—a really responsible position—"

He broke off to say: "Tea's in, dearest," to his wife.

"I thought we were having it here. I told Jolly."

"No, it's in the Hall. The others are there."

"I thought they were all going to be out."

Carrie Louise linked her arm through Miss Marple's and they went into the Great Hall. Tea seemed a rather incongruous meal in its surroundings. The tea things were piled haphazard on a tray—while utility cups mixed with the remnants of what had been Rockingham and Spode teaservices. There was a loaf of bread, two pots of jam, and some cheap and unwholesome-looking cakes.

A plump middle-aged woman with grey hair sat behind the tea table and Mrs. Serrocold said:

"This is Mildred, Jane. My daughter Mildred. You haven't seen her since she was a tiny girl."

Mildred Strete was the person most in tune with the house that Miss Marple had so far seen. She looked prosperous and dignified. She had married late in her thirties a Canon of the Church of England and was now a widow. She looked exactly like a Canon's widow, respectable and slightly dull. She was a plain woman with a large unexpressive face and dull eyes. She had been, Miss Marple reflected, a very plain little girl.

"And this is Wally Hudd—Gina's husband."

Wally was a big young man, with hair brushed up on his head and a sulky expression. He nodded awkwardly and went on cramming cake into his mouth.

Presently Gina came in with Stephen Restarick. They were both very animated.

"Gina's got a wonderful idea for that backcloth," said Stephen. "You know, Gina, you've got a very definite flair for theatrical designing."

Gina laughed and looked pleased. Edgar Lawson came in and sat down by Lewis Serrocold. When Gina spoke to him, he made a pretence of not answering.

Miss Marple found it all a little bewildering and was glad to go to her room and lie down after tea.

There were more people still at dinner, a young Doctor Maverick who was either a psychiatrist or a psychologist—Miss Marple was rather hazy about the difference—and whose conversation, dealing almost entirely with the jargon of his trade, was practically unintelligible to her. There were also two spectacled young men who held posts on the teaching side and a Mr. Baumgarten who was an occupational therapist and three intensely bashful youths who were doing their "house guest" week. One of them, a fairhaired lad with very blue eyes was, Gina informed her in a whisper, the expert with the "cosh."

The meal was not a particularly appetizing one. It was indifferently cooked and indifferently served. A variety of costumes was worn. Miss Bellever wore a high black dress, Mildred Strete wore evening dress and a woollen cardigan over it. Carrie Louise had on a short dress of grey wool —Gina was resplendent in a kind of peasant get-up. Wally had not changed, nor had Stephen Restarick, Edgar Lawson had on a neat dark blue suit. Lewis Serrocold wore the conventional dinner jacket. He ate very little and hardly seemed to notice what was on his plate.

After dinner Lewis Serrocold and Dr. Maverick went away to the latter's office. The occupational therapist and the schoolmasters went away to some lair of their own. The three "cases" went back to the college. Gina and Stephen went to the theatre to discuss Gina's idea for a set. Mildred knitted an indeterminate garment and Miss Bellever darned socks. Wally sat in a chair gently tilted backwards and stared into space. Carrie Louise and Miss Marple talked about old days. The conversation seemed strangely unreal.

Edgar Lawson alone seemed unable to find a niche. He sat down and then got up restlessly.

"I wonder if I ought to go to Mr. Serrocold," he said rather loudly. "He may need me."

Carrie Louise said gently, "Oh I don't think so. He was going to talk over one or two points with Dr. Maverick this evening."

"Then I certainly won't butt in! I shouldn't dream of going where I wasn't wanted. I've already wasted time today going down to the station when Mrs. Hudd meant to go herself."

"She ought to have told you," said Carrie Louise. "But I think she just decided at the last moment."

"You do realise, Mrs. Serrocold, that she made me look a complete fool! A complete fool!"

"No, no," said Carrie Louise, smiling, "You mustn't have these ideas."

"I know I'm not needed or wanted . . . I'm perfectly aware of *that*. If things had been different—if I'd had my proper place in life it would be very different. Very different indeed. It's no fault of mine that I haven't got my proper place in life."

"Now, Edgar," said Carrie Louise. "Don't work yourself up about nothing. Jane thinks it was very kind of you to meet her. Gina always has these sudden impulses—she didn't mean to upset you."

"Oh yes, she did. It was done on purpose—to humiliate me—"

"Oh Edgar—"

"You don't know half of what's going on, Mrs. Serrocold. Well, I won't say any more now except good night."

Edgar went out shutting the door with a slam behind him.

Miss Bellever snorted:

"Atrocious manners."

"He's so sensitive," said Carrie Louise vaguely.

Mildred Strete clicked her needles and said sharply:

"He really is a most odious young man. You shouldn't put up with such behaviour, Mother."

"Lewis says he can't help it."

Mildred said sharply:

"Everyone can help behaving rudely. Of course I blame Gina very much. She's so completely scatterbrained in everything she undertakes. She does nothing but make trouble. One day she encourages the young man and the next day she snubs him. What can you expect?"

Wally Hudd spoke for the first time that evening.

He said:

"That guy's crackers. That's all there is to it! Crackers!"

2

In her bedroom that night Miss Marple tried to review the pattern of Stonygates, but it was as yet too confused. There were currents and cross currents here—but whether they could account for Ruth Van Rydock's uneasiness it was impossible to tell. It did not seem to Miss Marple that Carrie Louise was affected in any way by what was going on round her. Stephen was in love with Gina. Gina might or might not be in love with Stephen. Walter Hudd was clearly not enjoying himself. These were inci-

dents that might and did occur in all places and at most times. There
was, unfortunately, nothing exceptional about them. They ended in the
divorce court and everybody hopefully started again—when fresh tangles
were created. Mildred Strete was clearly jealous of Gina and disliked her.
That, Miss Marple thought, was very natural.

She thought over what Ruth Van Rydock had told her. Carrie Louise's
disappointment at not having a child—the adoption of little Pippa—and
then the discovery that, after all, a child was on the way.

"Often happens like that," Miss Marple's doctor had told her. "Relief
of tension, maybe, and then Nature can do its work."

He had added that it was usually hard lines on the adopted child.

But that had not been so in this case. Both Gulbrandsen and his wife
had adored little Pippa. She had made her place too firmly in their hearts
to be lightly set aside. Gulbrandsen was already a father. Paternity meant
nothing new to him. Carrie Louise's maternal yearnings had been as-
suaged by Pippa. Her pregnancy had been uncomfortable and the actual
birth difficult and prolonged. Possibly Carrie Louise, who had never
cared for reality, did not enjoy her first brush with it.

There remained two little girls growing up, one pretty and amusing,
the other plain and dull. Which again, Miss Marple thought, was quite
natural. For when people adopt a baby girl, they choose a pretty one.
And though Mildred might have been lucky and taken after the Martins
who had produced handsome Ruth and dainty Carrie Louise, Nature
elected that she should take after the Gulbrandsens who were large and
stolid and uncompromisingly plain.

Moreover Carrie Louise was determined that the adopted child should
never feel her position and in making sure of this she was over-indulgent
to Pippa and sometimes less than fair to Mildred.

Pippa had married and gone away to Italy, and Mildred for a time had
been the only daugher of the house. But then Pippa had died and Carrie
Louise had brought Pippa's baby back to Stonygates and once more
Mildred had been out of it. There had been the new marriage—the
Restarick boys. In 1934 Mildred had married Canon Strete, a scholarly
Antiquarian about ten or fifteen years older and had gone away to live in
the South of England. Presumably she had been happy—but one did not
really know. There had been no children. And now here she was, back
again in the same house where she had been brought up. And once again,
Miss Marple thought, not particularly happy in it.

Gina, Stephen, Wally, Mildred, Miss Bellever who liked an ordered
routine and was unable to enforce it. Lewis Serrocold who was clearly
blissfully and wholeheartedly happy; an idealist able to translate his

ideals into practical measures. In none of these personalities did Miss
Marple find what Ruth's words had led her to believe she might find.
Carrie Louise seemed secure, remote at the heart of the whirlpool—as
she had been all her life. What then, in that atmosphere, had Ruth felt to
be wrong . . . ? Did she, Jane Marple, feel it also?

What of the outer personalities of the whirlpool—the occupational
therapists, the schoolmasters, earnest, harmless young men, confident
young Dr. Maverick, the three pink-faced innocent-eyed young delinquents—Edgar Lawson. . . .

And here, just before she fell asleep, Miss Marple's thoughts stopped
and revolved speculatively round the figure of Edgar Lawson. Edgar
Lawson reminded her of someone or something. There *was* something a
little wrong about Edgar Lawson—perhaps more than a little. Edgar
Lawson was maladjusted—that was the phrase, wasn't it? But surely that
didn't, and couldn't, touch Carrie Louise?

Mentally, Miss Marple shook her head.

What worried her was something more than that.

5

GENTLY eluding her hostess the next morning, Miss Marple went out into the gardens. Their condition distressed her. They had once been an ambitiously set out achievement. Clumps of rhododendrons, smooth slopes of lawn, massed borders of herbaceous plants, clipped box-hedges surrounding a formal rose garden. Now all was largely derelict, the lawns raggedly mown, the borders full of weeds with tangled flowers struggling through them, the paths moss-covered and neglected. The kitchen gardens on the other hand, enclosed by red brick walls, were prosperous and well stocked. That, presumably, was because they had a utility value. So, also, a large portion of what had once been lawn and flower garden, was now fenced off and laid out in tennis courts and a bowling green.

Surveying the herbaceous border, Miss Marple clicked her tongue vexedly and pulled up a flourishing plant of groundsel.

As she stood with it in her hand, Edgar Lawson came into view. Seeing Miss Marple, he stopped and hesitated. Miss Marple had no mind to let him escape. She called him briskly. When he came she asked him if he knew where any gardening tools were kept.

Edgar said vaguely that there was a gardener somewhere who would know.

"It's such a pity to see this border so neglected," twittered Miss Marple. "I'm so fond of gardens." And since it was not her intention that Edgar should go in search of any necessary implement she went on quickly:

"It's about all an old and useless woman can find to do. Now I don't suppose *you* ever bother your head about gardens, Mr. Lawson. You have so much real and important work to do. Being in a responsible position here, with Mr. Serrocold. You must find it all most interesting."

He answered quickly, almost eagerly:

"Yes—yes—it is interesting."

"And you must be of the greatest assistance to Mr. Serrocold."

His face darkened.

"I don't know. I can't be sure. It's what's *behind* it all—"

He broke off. Miss Marple watched him thoughtfully. A pathetic undersized young man, in a neat dark suit. A young man that few people would look at twice, or remember if they did look . . .

There was a garden seat nearby and Miss Marple drifted towards it and sat. Edgar stood frowning in front of her.

"I'm sure," said Miss Marple brightly, "that Mr. Serrocold relies on you a *great* deal."

"I don't know," said Edgar. "I really don't know." He frowned and almost absently sat down beside her. "I'm in a very difficult position."

"Yes?" said Miss Marple.

The young man Edgar sat staring in front of him.

"This is all highly confidential," he said suddenly.

"Of course," said Miss Marple.

"If I had my rights—"

"Yes?"

"I might as well tell you . . . You won't let it go any further I'm sure?"

"Oh no." She noticed he did not wait for her disclaimer.

"My father—actually, my father is a very important man."

This time there was no need to say anything. She had only to listen.

"Nobody knows except Mr. Serrocold. You see, it might prejudice my father's position if the story got out." He turned to her. He smiled. A sad dignified smile. "You see, *I'm Winston Churchill's son.*"

"Oh," said Miss Marple. "I *see.*"

And she did see. She remembered a rather sad story in St. Mary Mead —and the way it had gone.

Edgar Lawson went on, and what he said had the familiarity of a stage scene.

"There were reasons. My mother wasn't free. Her own husband was in an asylum—there could be no divorce—no question of marriage. I don't really blame them. At least, I think I don't . . . He's done, always, everything he could. Discreetly, of course. And that's where the trouble has arisen. He's got enemies—and they're against me, too. They've managed to keep us apart. They watch me. Wherever I go, they spy on me. And they make things go wrong for me."

Miss Marple shook her head.

"Dear, dear," she said.

"In London I was studying to be a doctor. They tampered with my exams—they altered the answers. They *wanted* me to fail. They followed me about the streets. They told things about me to my landlady. They hound me wherever I go."

"Oh, but you can't be sure of that," said Miss Marple soothingly.

"I tell you I *know!* Oh they're very cunning. I never get a glimpse of them or find out who they are. But I shall find out . . . Mr. Serrocold took me away from London and brought me down here. He was kind—very kind. But even here, you know, I'm not *safe*. They're here, too. Working against me. Making the others dislike me. Mr. Serrocold says that isn't true—but Mr. Serrocold doesn't know. Or else—I wonder—sometimes I've thought—"

He broke off. He got up.

"This is all confidential," he said. "You do understand that, don't you? But if you notice anyone *following* me—*spying*, I mean—you might let me know *who it is!*"

He went away, then—neat, pathetic, insignificant. Miss Marple watched him and wondered. . . .

A voice spoke.

"Nuts," it said. "Just nuts."

Walter Hudd was standing beside her. His hands were thrust deep in his pockets and he was frowning as he stared after Edgar's retreating figure.

"What kind of a joint is this, anyway?" he said. "They're all bughouse, the whole lot of them."

Miss Marple said nothing and Walter went on.

"That Edgar guy—what do you make of him? Says his father's really Lord Montgomery. Doesn't seem likely to me! Not *Monty!* Not from all I've heard about him."

"No," said Miss Marple. "It doesn't seem very likely."

"He told Gina something quite different—some bunk about being really the heir to the Russian throne—said he was some Grand Duke's son or other. Hell, doesn't the chap know who his father really was?"

"I should imagine not," said Miss Marple. "That is probably just the trouble."

Walter sat down beside her, dropping his body onto the seat with a slack movement. He repeated his former statement.

"They're all bughouse here."

"You don't like being at Stonygates?"

The young man frowned.

"I simply don't *get* it—that's all! I don't get it. Take this place—the house—the whole setup. They're rich, these people. They don't need dough—they've got it. And look at the way they live. Cracked antique china and cheap plain stuff all mixed up. No proper upper class servants —just some casual hired help. Tapestries and drapes and chair-covers all satin and brocade and stuff—and it's falling to pieces! Big silver tea urns and what do you know—all yellow and tarnished for want of cleaning. Mrs. Serrocold just doesn't care. Look at that dress she had on last night.

Darned under the arms, nearly worn out—and yet she could go to a store and order what she liked. Bond Street or whatever it is. Dough? They're rolling in dough."

He paused and sat, deliberating.

"I understand being poor. There's nothing much wrong with it. If you're young and strong and ready to work. I never had much money, but I was all set to get where I wanted. I was going to open a garage. I'd got a bit of money put by. I talked to Gina about it. She listened. She seemed to understand. I didn't know much about her. All those girls in uniform, they look about the same. I mean you can't tell from looking at them who's got dough and who hasn't. I thought she was a cut above me, perhaps, education and all that. But it didn't seem to matter. We fell for each other. We got married. I'd got my bit put by and Gina had some too, she told me. We were going to set up a gas station back home—Gina was willing. Just a couple of crazy kids we were—mad about each other. Then that snooty Aunt of Gina's started making trouble . . . And Gina wanted to come here to England to see her grandmother. Well, that seemed fair enough. It was her home, and I was curious about England anyway. I'd heard a lot about it. So we came. Just a visit—that's what I thought."

The frown became a scowl.

"But it hasn't turned out like that. We're caught up in this crazy business. Why don't we stay here—make our home here—that's what they say. Plenty of jobs for me. Jobs! I don't want a job feeding candy to gangster kids and helping them play at kids' games . . . what's the sense of it all? This place could be swell—*really* swell— Don't people who've got money understand their luck? Don't they understand that most of the world can't have a swell place like this and that they've got one? Isn't it plain crazy to kick your luck when you've got it? I don't mind working if I've got to. But I'll work the way I like and at what I like —and I'll work to get somewhere. This place makes me feel I'm tangled up in a spider's web. And Gina—I can't make Gina out. She's not the same girl I married over in the States. I can't—dang it all—I can't even *talk* to her now. Oh hell!"

Miss Marple said gently:

"I quite see your point of view."

Wally shot a swift glance at her.

"You're the only one I've shot my mouth off to so far. Most of the time I shut up like a clam. Don't know what it is about you—you're English right enough, really English—but in the durndest way you remind me of my aunt Betsy back home."

"Now that's very nice."

"A lot of sense she had," Wally continued reflectively. "Looked as frail as though you could snap her in two, but actually she was tough—yes, sir, I'll say she was tough."

He got up.

"Sorry talking to you this way," he apologised. For the first time, Miss Marple saw him smile. It was a very attractive smile and Wally Hudd was suddenly transfigured from an awkward sulky boy into a handsome and appealing young man. "Had to get things off my chest, I suppose. But too bad picking on you."

"Not at all, my dear boy," said Miss Marple. "I have a nephew of my own—only, of course, a great deal older than you are."

Her mind dwelt for a moment on the sophisticated modern writer Raymond West. A greater contrast to Walter Hudd could not have been imagined.

"You've got other company coming," said Walter Hudd. "That dame doesn't like me. So I'll quit. So long, ma'am. Thanks for the talk."

He strode away and Miss Marple watched Mildred Strete coming across the lawn to join her.

2

"I see you've been victimised by the terrible young man," said Mrs. Strete, rather breathlessly, as she sank down on the seat. "What a tragedy that is."

"A tragedy?"

"Gina's marriage. It all came about from sending her off to America. I told Mother at the time it was most unwise. After all, this is quite a quiet district. We had hardly any raids here. I do so dislike the way many people gave way to panic about their families—and themselves, too, very often."

"It must have been difficult to decide what was right to do," said Miss Marple thoughtfully. "Where children were concerned, I mean. With the prospect of possible invasion, it might have meant their being brought up under a German regime—as well as the danger of bombs."

"All nonsense," said Mrs. Strete. "I never had the least doubt that we should win. But Mother has always been quite unreasonable where Gina is concerned. The child was always spoilt and indulged in every way. There was absolutely no need to take her away from Italy in the first place."

"Her father raised no objection, I understand?"

"Oh San Severiano! You know what Italians are. Nothing matters to them but money. He married Pippa for her money, of course."

"Dear me. I always understood he was very devoted to her and was quite inconsolable at her death."

"He pretended to be, no doubt. Why Mother ever countenanced her marrying a foreigner, I can't imagine. Just the usual American pleasure in a title, I suppose."

Miss Marple said mildly:

"I have always thought that dear Carrie Louise was almost too unworldly in her attitude to life."

"Oh I know. I've no patience with it. Mother's fads and whims and idealistic projects. You've no idea, Aunt Jane, of all that it has meant. I can speak with knowledge, of course. I was brought up in the middle of it all."

It was with a very faint shock that Miss Marple heard herself addressed as Aunt Jane. And yet that had been the convention of those times. Her Christmas presents to Carrie Louise's children were always labelled "With love from Aunt Jane" and as "Aunt Jane" they thought of her, when they thought of her at all. Which was not, Miss Marple supposed, very often.

She looked thoughtfully at the middle-aged woman sitting beside her. At the pursed tight mouth, the deep lines from the nose down, the hands tightly pressed together.

She said gently:

"You must have had—a difficult childhood."

Mildred Strete turned eager grateful eyes to her.

"Oh I'm so glad that somebody appreciates that. People don't really know what children go through. Pippa, you see, was the pretty one. She was older than I was, too. It was always she who got all the attention. Both Father and Mother encouraged her to push herself forward—not that she needed any encouragement—to show off. I was always the quiet one. I was shy—Pippa didn't know what shyness was. A child can suffer a great deal, Aunt Jane."

"I know that," said Miss Marple.

" 'Mildred's so stupid'—that's what Pippa used to say. But I was younger than she was. Naturally I couldn't be expected to keep up with her in lessons. And it's very unfair on a child when her sister is always put in front of her.

" 'What a lovely little girl,' people used to say to Mamma. They never noticed *me*. And it was Pippa that Papa used to joke and play with.

Someone ought to have seen how hard it was on *me*. All the notice and attention going to her. I wasn't old enough to realise that it's *character* that matters."

Her lips trembled, then hardened again.

"And it was unfair—really unfair—I was their own child. Pippa was only adopted. *I* was the daughter of the house. She was—nobody."

"Probably they were extra indulgent to her on that account," said Miss Marple.

"They liked her best," said Mildred Strete. And added: "A child whose own parents didn't want her—or more probably illegitimate."

She went on:

"It's come out in Gina. There's bad blood there. Blood will tell. Lewis can have what theories he likes about environment. Bad blood does tell. Look at Gina."

"Gina is a very lovely girl," said Miss Marple.

"Hardly in behaviour," said Mrs. Strete. "Everyone but Mother notices how she is carrying on with Stephen Restarick. Quite disgusting, I call it. Admittedly she made a very unfortunate marriage but marriage is marriage and one should be prepared to abide by it. After all, she chose to marry that dreadful young man."

"Is he so dreadful?"

"Oh dear Aunt Jane! He really looks to me quite like a gangster. And so surly and rude. He hardly opens his mouth. And he always looks so dirty and uncouth."

"He is unhappy, I think," said Miss Marple mildly.

"I really don't know why he should be—apart from Gina's behaviour, I mean. Everything has been done for him here. Lewis has suggested several ways in which he could try to make himself useful—but he prefers to skulk about doing nothing." She burst out: "Oh this whole place is impossible—quite impossible. Lewis thinks of nothing but these horrible young criminals. And Mother thinks of nothing but him. Everything Lewis does is right. Look at the state of the garden—the weeds—the overgrowth. And the house—nothing properly done. Oh I know a domestic staff is difficult nowadays, but it can be got. It's not as though there were any shortage of money. It's just that nobody *cares*. If it were *my* house—"

She stopped.

"I'm afraid," said Miss Marple, "that we have all to face the fact that conditions are different. These large establishments are a great problem. It must be sad for you, in a way, to come back here and find everything so different. Do you really prefer living here to—well—somewhere of your own?"

Mildred Strete flushed.

"After all, it's my home," she said. "It was my father's house. Nothing can alter that. I've a right to be here if I choose. And I do choose. If only Mother were not so impossible! She won't even buy herself proper clothes. It worries Jolly a lot."

"I was going to ask you about Miss Bellever."

"Such a comfort having her here. She adores Mother. She's been with her a long time now—she came in John Restarick's time. And was wonderful, I believe, during the whole sad business. I expect you heard that he ran away with a dreadful Yugoslavian woman—a most abandoned creature. She's had any amount of lovers, I believe. Mother was very fine and dignified about it all. Divorced him as quietly as possible. Even went so far as to have the Restarick boys for their holidays—quite unnecessary, really, other arrangements could have been made. It would have been unthinkable, of course, to have let them go to their father and that woman. Anyway, Mother had them here . . . And Miss Bellever stood by all through things and was a tower of strength. I sometimes think she makes Mother even more vague than she need be, by doing all the practical things herself. But I really don't know what Mother would do without her."

She paused and then remarked in a tone of surprise,

"Here is Lewis. How odd. He seldom comes out in the garden."

Mr. Serrocold came towards them in the same single-minded way that he did everything. He appeared not to notice Mildred, because it was only Miss Marple who was in his mind.

"I'm so sorry," he said. "I wanted to take you round our institution and show you everything. Caroline asked me to. Unfortunately I have to go off to Liverpool. The case of the boy and the railways parcels office. But Maverick will take you. He'll be here in a few minutes. I shan't be back until the day after tomorrow. It will be splendid if we can get them not to prosecute."

Mildred Strete got up and walked away. Lewis Serrocold did not notice her go. His earnest eyes gazed at Miss Marple through thick glasses.

"You see," he said, "the Magistrates nearly always take the wrong view. Sometimes they're too severe, but sometimes they're too lenient. If these boys get a sentence of a few months it's no deterrent—they get a kind of a kick out of it, even. Boast about it to their girl friends. But a severe sentence often sobers them. They realise that the game isn't worth it. Or else it's better not to serve a prison sentence at all. Corrective training—constructional training like we have here."

Miss Marple burst firmly into speech.

"Mr. Serrocold," she said. "Are you quite satisfied about young Mr. Lawson? Is he—is he quite normal?"

A disturbed expression appeared on Lewis Serrocold's face.

"I do hope he's not relapsing. What has he been saying?"

"He told me that he was Winston Churchill's son—"

"Of course—of course. The usual statements. He's illegitimate, as you've probably guessed, poor lad, and of very humble beginnings. He was a case recommended to me by a Society in London. He'd assaulted a man in the street who he said was spying on him. All very typical—Dr. Maverick will tell you. I went into his case history. Mother was a poor class but a respectable family in Plymouth. Father a sailor—she didn't even know his name . . . Child brought up in difficult circumstances. Started romancing about his father and later about himself. Wore uniform and decorations he wasn't entitled to—all quite typical. But Maverick considers the prognosis hopeful. If we can give him confidence in himself. I've given him responsibility here, tried to make him appreciate that it's not a man's birth that matters, but what he *is.* I've tried to give him confidence in his own ability. The improvement was marked. I was very happy about him. And now you say—"

He shook his head.

"Mightn't he be dangerous, Mr. Serrocold?"

"Dangerous? I don't think he has shown any suicidal tendencies."

"I wasn't thinking of suicide. He talked to me of enemies—of persecution. Isn't that, forgive me—a dangerous sign?"

"I don't really think it has reached such a pitch. But I'll speak to Maverick. So far, he has been hopeful—very hopeful."

He looked at his watch.

"I must go. Ah, here is our dear Jolly. She will take charge of you."

Miss Bellever, arriving briskly, said, "The car is at the door, Mr. Serrocold. Dr. Maverick rang through from the Institute. I said I would bring Miss Marple over. He will meet us at the gates."

"Thank you. I must go. My brief case?"

"In the car, Mr. Serrocold."

Lewis Serrocold hurried away. Looking after him, Miss Bellever said:

"Someday that man will drop down dead in his tracks. It's against human nature never to relax or rest. He only sleeps four hours a night."

"He is very devoted to this cause," said Miss Marple.

"Never thinks of anything else," said Miss Bellever grimly. "Never dreams of looking after his wife or considering her in any way. She's a sweet creature, as you know, Miss Marple, and she ought to have love and attention. But nothing's thought of or considered here except a lot of whining boys and young men who want to live easily and dishonestly and don't care about the idea of doing a little hard work. What about the decent boys from decent homes? Why isn't something done for them? Honesty just isn't interesting to cranks like Mr. Serrocold and Dr. Maverick and all the bunch of half-baked sentimentalists we've got here. I and my brothers were brought up the hard way, Miss Marple, and we weren't encouraged to whine. Soft, that's what the world is nowadays!"

They had crossed the garden and passed through a palisaded gate and had come to the entrance gate which Eric Gulbrandsen had erected as an entrance to his College, a sturdily built, hideous, red brick building.

Dr. Maverick, looking, Miss Marple decided, distinctly abnormal himself came out to meet them.

"Thank you, Miss Bellever," he said. "Now, Miss—er—oh yes, Miss Marple—I'm sure you're going to be interested in what we're doing here. In our splendid approach to this great problem. Mr. Serrocold is a man of great insight—great vision. And we've got Sir John Stillwell behind us —my old chief. He was at the Home Office until he retired and his influence turned the scales in getting this started. It's a *medical* problem —that's what we've got to get the legal authorities to understand. Psychiatry came into its own in the war. The one positive good that did come out of it—Now first of all I want you to see our initial approach to the problem. Look up—"

Miss Marple looked up at the words carved over the large arched doorway.

RECOVER HOPE
ALL YE WHO ENTER HERE

"Isn't that splendid? Isn't that just the right note to strike? You don't want to scold these lads—or punish them. That's what they're hankering after half the time, punishment. We want to make them feel what fine fellows they are."

"Like Edgar Lawson?" said Miss Marple.

"Interesting case, that. Have you been talking to him?"

"He has been talking to me," said Miss Marple. She added apologetically, "I wondered if, perhaps, he isn't a little *mad?*"

Dr. Maverick laughed cheerfully.

"We're all mad, dear lady," he said as he ushered her in through the door. "That's the secret of existence. We're all a little mad."

6

ON THE WHOLE it was rather an exhausting day. Enthusiasm in itself can be extremely wearing, Miss Marple thought. She felt vaguely dissatisfied with herself and her own reactions. There was a pattern here—perhaps several patterns, and yet she herself could obtain no clear glimpse of it or them. Any vague disquietude she felt centered round the pathetic but inconspicuous personality of Edgar Lawson. If she could only find in her memory the right parallel.

Painstakingly she rejected the curious behaviour of Mr. Selkirk's delivery van—the absent-minded postman—the gardener who worked on Whitmonday—and that very curious affair of the summer weight combinations.

Something that she could not quite put her finger on was wrong about Edgar Lawson—something that went beyond the observed and admitted facts. But for the life of her, Miss Marple did not see how that wrongness, whatever it was, affected her friend Carrie Louise. In the confused patterns of life at Stonygates people's troubles and desires impinged on each other. But none of them (again as far as she could see), impinged on Carrie Louise.

Carrie Louise . . . Suddenly Miss Marple realised that it was she alone, except for the absent Ruth, who used that name. To her husband, she was Caroline. To Miss Bellever, Cara. Stephen Restarick usually addressed her as Madonna. To Wally she was formally Mrs. Serrocold, and Gina elected to address her as Grandam—a mixture, she had explained, of Grande Dame and Grandmamma.

Was there some significance, perhaps, in the various names that were found for Caroline Louise Serrocold? Was she to all of them a symbol and not quite a real person?

When on the following morning Carrie Louise, dragging her feet a little as she walked, came and sat down on the garden seat beside her friend and asked her what she was thinking about, Miss Marple replied promptly:

"You, Carrie Louise."

"What about me?"

"Tell me honestly—is there anything here that worries you?"

"Worries me?" The other woman raised wondering clear blue eyes. "But Jane, what should worry me?"

"Well, most of us have worries." Miss Marple's eyes twinkled a little. "I have. Slugs, you know—and the difficulty of getting linen properly darned—and not being able to get sugar candy for making my damson gin. Oh, lots of little things—it seems unnatural that you shouldn't have any worries at all."

"I suppose I must have really," said Mrs. Serrocold vaguely. "Lewis works too hard, and Stephen forgets his meals slaving at the theatre and Gina is very jumpy—but I've never been able to alter people—I don't see how you can. So it wouldn't be any good worrying, would it?"

"Mildred's not very happy, either, is she?"

"Oh no," said Carrie Louise. "Mildred never is happy. She wasn't as a child. Quite unlike Pippa who was always radiant."

"Perhaps," suggested Miss Marple, "Mildred has cause not to be happy?"

Carrie Louise said quietly:

"Because of being jealous? Yes, I daresay. But people don't really need a cause for feeling what they do feel. They're just made that way. Don't you think so, Jane?"

Miss Marple thought briefly of Miss Moncrieff, a slave to a tyrannical invalid mother. Poor Miss Moncrieff who longed for travel and to see the world. And of how St. Mary Mead in a decorous way had rejoiced when Mrs. Moncrieff was laid in the churchyard and Miss Moncrieff, with a nice little income, was free at last. And of how Miss Moncrieff, starting on her travels, had got no further than Hyères where, calling to see one of "mother's oldest friends," she had been so moved by the plight of an elderly hypochondriac that she had cancelled her travel reservations and taken up her abode in the villa to be bullied, overworked, and to long, wistfully, once more, for the joys of a wider horizon.

Miss Marple said:

"I expect you're right, Carrie Louise."

"Of course my being so free from cares is partly due to Jolly. Dear Jolly. She came to me when Johnnie and I were just married and was wonderful from the first. She takes care of me as though I were a baby and quite helpless. She'd do anything for me. I feel quite ashamed sometimes. I really believe Jolly would murder someone for me, Jane. Isn't that an awful thing to say?"

"She's certainly very devoted," agreed Miss Marple.

"She gets so indignant." Mrs. Serrocold's silvery laugh rang out. "She'd like me to be always ordering wonderful clothes, and surrounding myself with luxuries, and she thinks everybody ought to put me first and to dance attendance on me. She's the one person who's absolutely unimpressed by Lewis's enthusiasm. All our poor boys are in her view pampered young criminals and not worth taking trouble over. She thinks this place is damp and bad for my rheumatism, and that I ought to go to Egypt or somewhere warm and dry."

"Do you suffer much from rheumatism?"

"It's got much worse lately. I find it difficult to walk. Horrid cramps in my legs. Oh well—" again there came that bewitching elfin smile, "age must tell."

Miss Bellever came out of the French windows and hurried across to them.

"A telegram, Cara, just come over the telephone. *Arriving this afternoon, Christian Gulbrandsen.*"

"Christian?" Carrie Louise looked very surprised. "I'd no idea he was in England."

"The Oak Suite, I suppose?"

"Yes, please, Jolly. Then there will be no stairs."

Miss Bellever nodded and turned back to the house.

"Christian Gulbrandsen is my stepson," said Carrie Louise. "Eric's eldest son. Actually he's two years older than I am. He's one of the trustees of the Institute—the principal trustee. How very annoying that Lewis is away. Christian hardly ever stays longer than one night. He's an immensely busy man. And there are sure to be so many things they would want to discuss."

Christian Gulbrandsen arrived that afternoon in time for tea. He was a big heavy featured man, with a slow methodical way of talking. He greeted Carrie Louise with every sign of affection.

"And how is our little Carrie Louise? You do not look a day older. Not a day."

His hands on her shoulders—he stood smiling down at her. A hand tugged his sleeve.

"Christian!"

"Ah," he turned— "it is Mildred? How are you, Mildred?"

"I've not really been at all well lately."

"That is bad. That is bad."

There was a strong resemblance between Christian Gulbrandsen and his half sister Mildred. There was nearly thirty years of difference in age and they might easily have been taken for father and daughter. Mildred herself seemed particularly pleased by his arrival. She was flushed and talkative, and had talked repeatedly during the day of "my brother," "my brother Christian," "my brother, Mr. Gulbrandsen."

"And how is little Gina?" said Gulbrandsen, turning to that young woman. "You and your husband are still here, then?"

"Yes. We've quite settled down, haven't we, Wally?"

"Looks like it," said Wally.

Gulbrandsen's small shrewd eyes seemed to sum up Wally quickly. Wally, as usual, looked sullen and unfriendly.

"So here I am with all the family again," said Gulbrandsen.

His voice displayed a rather determined geniality—but in actual fact, Miss Marple thought, he was not feeling particularly genial. There was a grim set to his lips and a certain preoccupation in his manner.

Introduced to Miss Marple he swept a keen look over her as though measuring and appraising this newcomer.

"We'd no idea you were in England, Christian," said Mrs. Serrocold.

"No, I came over rather unexpectedly."

"It is too bad that Lewis is away. How long can you stay?"

"I meant to go tomorrow. When will Lewis be back?"

"Tomorrow afternoon or evening."

"It seems then that I must stay another night."

"If you'd only let us know—"

"My dear Carrie Louise, my arrangements, they were made very suddenly."

"You will stay to see Lewis?"

"Yes, it is necessary that I see Lewis."

Miss Bellever said to Miss Marple: "Mr. Gulbrandsen and Mr. Serrocold are both trustees of the Gulbrandsen Institute. The others are the Bishop of Cromer and Mr. Gilfoy."

Presumably, then, it was on business concerned with the Gulbrandsen Institute that Christian Gulbrandsen had come to Stonygates. It seemed to be assumed so by Miss Bellever and everyone else. And yet Miss Marple wondered.

Once or twice the old man cast a thoughtful puzzled look at Carrie Louise when she was not aware of it—a look that puzzled Carrie Louise's watching friend. From Carrie Louise he shifted his gaze to the others, examining them one and all with a kind of covert appraisal that seemed distinctly odd.

After tea Miss Marple withdrew tactfully from the others to the library, but rather to her surprise when she had settled herself with her knitting, Christian Gulbrandsen came in and sat down beside her.

"You are a very old friend, I think, of our dear Carrie Louise?" he said.

"We were at school together in Italy, Mr. Gulbrandsen. Many many years ago."

"Ah yes. And you are fond of her?"

"Yes, indeed," said Miss Marple warmly.

"So, I think, is everyone. Yes, I truly think that. It should be so. For she is a very dear and enchanting person. Always, since my father married her, I and my brothers have loved her very much. She has been to us like a very dear sister. She was a faithful wife to my father and loyal to all his ideas. She has never thought of herself, but put the welfare of others first."

"She has always been an idealist," said Miss Marple.

"An idealist? Yes. Yes, that is so. And therefore it may be that she does not truly appreciate the evil that there is in the world."

Miss Marple looked at him, surprised. His face was very stern.

"Tell me," he said. "How is her health?"

Again Miss Marple felt surprised.

"She seems to me very well—apart from arthritis—or rheumatism."

"Rheumatism? Yes. And her heart? Her heart is good?"

"As far as I know." Miss Marple was still more surprised. "But until yesterday I had not seen her for many years. If you want to know the state of her health, you should ask somebody in the house here. Miss Bellever, for instance."

"Miss Bellever— Yes, Miss Bellever. Or Mildred?"

"Or, as you say, Mildred."

Miss Marple was faintly embarrassed.

Christian Gulbrandsen was staring at her very hard.

"There is not between the mother and daughter, a very great sympathy, would you say?"

"No, I don't think there is."

"I agree. It is a pity—her only child, but there it is. Now this Miss Bellever, you think, is really attached to her?"

"Very much so."

"And Carrie Louise leans on this Miss Bellever?"

"I think so."

Christian Gulbrandsen was frowning. He spoke as though more to himself than to Miss Marple.

"There is the little Gina—but she is so young. It is difficult—" He broke off. "Sometimes," he said simply, "it is hard to know what is best to be done. I wish very much to act for the best. I am particularly anxious that no harm and no unhappiness should come to that dear lady. But it is not easy—not easy at all."

Mrs. Strete came into the room at that moment.

"Oh there you are, Christian. We were wondering where you were. Dr. Maverick wants to know if you would like to go over anything with him."

"That is the new young doctor here? No—no, I will wait until Lewis returns."

"He's waiting in Lewis's study. Shall I tell him—"

"I will have a word with him myself."

Gulbrandsen hurried out. Mildred Strete stared after him and then stared at Miss Marple.

"I wonder if anything is wrong. Christian is very unlike himself . . . Did he say anything—"

"He only asked me about your mother's health."

"Her health? Why should he ask you about that?"

Mildred spoke sharply, her large square face flushing unbecomingly.

"I really don't know."

"Mother's health is perfectly good. Surprisingly so for a woman of her age. Much better than mine as far as that goes." She paused a moment before saying: "I hope you told him so?"

"I don't really know anything about it," said Miss Marple. "He asked me about her heart."

"Her *heart?*"

"Yes."

"There's nothing wrong with Mother's heart. Nothing at all!"

"I'm delighted to hear you say so, my dear."

"What on earth put all these queer ideas into Christian's head?"

"I've no idea," said Miss Marple.

7

THE NEXT DAY passed uneventfully to all appearances, yet to Miss Marple it seemed that there were signs of an inner tension. Christian Gulbrandsen spent his morning with Dr. Maverick in going round the Institute and in discussing the general results of the Institute's policy. In the early afternoon Gina took him for a drive and after that Miss Marple noticed that he induced Miss Bellever to show him something in the gardens. It seemed to her that it was a pretext for ensuring a tête-à-tête with that grim woman. And yet, if Christian Gulbrandsen's unexpected visit had only to do with business matters, why this wish for Miss Bellever's company, since the latter dealt only with the domestic side of matters?

But in all this, Miss Marple could tell herself that she was being fanciful. The only really disturbing incident of the day happened about four o'clock. She had rolled up her knitting and had gone out in the garden to take a little stroll before tea. Rounding a straggling rhododendron she came upon Edgar Lawson who was striding along muttering to himself and who nearly ran into her.

He said, "I beg your pardon," hastily, but Miss Marple was startled by the queer staring expression of his eyes.

"Aren't you feeling well, Mr. Lawson?"

"Well? How should I be feeling well? I've had a shock—a terrible shock."

"What kind of a shock?"

The young man gave a swift glance past her, and then a sharp uneasy glance to either side. His doing so gave Miss Marple a nervous feeling.

"Shall I tell you?" He looked at her doubtfully. "I don't know. I don't really *know* I've been so spied upon."

Miss Marple made up her mind. She took him firmly by the arm.

"If we walk down this path . . . There, now, there are no trees or bushes near. Nobody can overhear."

"No—no, you're right." He drew a deep breath, bent his head and almost whispered his next words. "I've made a discovery. A terrible discovery."

"What kind of a discovery?"

Edgar Lawson began to shake all over. He was almost weeping.

"To have trusted someone! To have believed . . . and it was lies—all lies. Lies to keep me from finding out the truth. I can't bear it. It's too wicked. You see, he was the one person I trusted, and now to find out that all the time he's been at the bottom of it all. It's *he* who's been my enemy! It's *he* who has been having me followed about and spied upon. But he can't get away with it any more. I shall speak out. I shall tell him I know what he has been doing."

"Who is *'he'?*" demanded Miss Marple.

Edgar Lawson drew himself up to his full height. He might have looked pathetic and dignified. But actually he only looked ridiculous.

"I'm speaking of my father."

"Viscount Montgomery—or do you mean Winston Churchill?"

Edgar threw her a glance of scorn.

"They let me think that—just to keep me from guessing the truth. But I know now. I've got a friend—a real friend. A friend who tells me the truth and lets me know just how I've been deceived. Well, my father will have to reckon with *me*. I'll throw his lies in his face! I'll challenge him with the truth. We'll see what he's got to say to that."

And suddenly breaking away, Edgar went off at a run and disappeared in the Park.

Her face grave, Miss Marple went back to the house.

"We're all a little mad, dear lady," Dr. Maverick had said.

But it seemed to her that in Edgar's case it went rather further than that.

2

Lewis Serrocold arrived back at six thirty. He stopped the car at the gates and walked to the house through the park. Looking out of her window, Miss Marple saw Christian Gulbrandsen go out to meet him and the two men, having greeted one another, turned and paced to and fro up and down the terrace.

Miss Marple had been careful to bring her bird glasses with her. At this moment she brought them into action. Was there, or was there not, a flight of siskins by that far clump of trees?

She noted as the glasses swept down before rising that both men were looking seriously disturbed. Miss Marple leant out a little further. Scraps of conversation floated up to her now and then. If either of the men should look up, it would be quite clear that an enraptured bird watcher had her attention fixed on a point far removed from their conversation.

"—how to spare Carrie Louise the knowledge—" Gulbrandsen was saying.

The next time they passed below, Lewis Serrocold was speaking.

"—if it *can* be kept from her. I agree that it is she who must be considered . . ."

Other faint snatches came to the listener.

"—Really serious—" "—not justified—" "too big a responsibility to take—" "we should, perhaps, take outside advice—"

Finally Miss Marple heard Christian Gulbrandsen say:

"Ach, it grows cold. We must go inside."

Miss Marple drew her head in through the window with a puzzled expression. What she had heard was too fragmentary to be easily pieced together—but it served to confirm that vague apprehension that had been gradually growing upon her and about which Ruth Van Rydock had been so positive.

Whatever was wrong at Stonygates, it definitely affected Carrie Louise.

3

Dinner that evening was a somewhat constrained meal. Both Gulbrandsen and Lewis were absentminded and absorbed in their own thoughts. Walter Hudd glowered even more than usual and for once Gina and Stephen seemed to have little to say either to each other or to the company at large. Conversation was mostly sustained by Dr. Maverick who had a lengthy technical discussion with Mr. Baumgarten, the Occupational Therapist.

When they moved into the Hall after dinner, Christian Gulbrandsen excused himself almost at once. He said he had an important letter to write.

"So if you will forgive me, dear Carrie Louise, I will go now to my room."

"You have all you want there? Jolly?"

"Yes, yes. Everything. A typewriter, I asked, and one has been put there. Miss Bellever has been most kind and attentive."

He left the Great Hall by the door on the left which led past the foot of the main staircase and along a corridor, at the end of which was a suite of bedroom and bathroom.

When he had gone out Carrie Louise said,

"Not going down to the theatre tonight, Gina?"

The girl shook her head. She went over and sat by the window overlooking the front drive and the court.

Stephen glanced at her, then strolled over to the big grand piano. He sat down at it and strummed very softly—a queer melancholy little tune. The two Occupational Therapists, Mr. Baumgarten and Mr. Lacy and Dr. Maverick, said goodnight and left. Walter turned the switch of a reading lamp and with a crackling noise half the lights in the Hall went out.

He growled.

"That darned switch is always faulty. I'll go and put a new fuse in."

He left the Hall and Carrie Louise murmured, "Wally's so clever with electrical gadgets and things like that. You remember how he fixed that toaster?"

"It seems to be all he does do here," said Mildred Strete. "Mother, have you taken your tonic?"

Miss Bellever looked annoyed.

"I declare I completely forgot tonight." She jumped up and went into the dining room, returning presently with a small glass containing a little rose coloured fluid.

Smiling a little, Carrie Louise held out an obedient hand.

"Such horrid stuff and nobody lets me forget it," she said, making a wry face.

And then, rather unexpectedly, Lewis Serrocold said: "I don't think I should take it tonight, my dear. I'm not sure it really agrees with you."

Quietly, but with that controlled energy always so apparent in him, he took the glass from Miss Bellever and put it down on the big oak Welsh dresser.

Miss Bellever said sharply,

"Really, Mr. Serrocold, I can't agree with you there. Mrs. Serrocold had been very much better since—"

She broke off and turned sharply.

The front door was pushed violently open and allowed to swing to with a crash. Edgar Lawson came into the big dim Hall with the air of a star performer making a triumphal entry.

He stood in the middle of the floor and struck an attitude.

It was almost ridiculous—but not quite ridiculous.

Edgar said theatrically:

"So I have found you, O mine enemy!"

He said it to Lewis Serrocold.

Mr. Serrocold looked mildly astonished.

"Why Edgar, what is the matter?"

"You can say that to me—you! You know what's the matter. You've been deceiving me, spying on me, working with my enemies against me."

Lewis took him by the arm.

"Now, now, my dear lad, don't excite yourself. Tell me all about it quietly. Come into my office."

He led him across the Hall and through a door on the right closing it behind him. After he had done so, there was another sound, the sharp sound of a key being turned in the lock.

Miss Bellever looked at Miss Marple, the same idea in both their minds. *It was not Lewis Serrocold who had turned the key.*

Miss Bellever said sharply: "That young man is just about to go off his head in my opinion. It isn't safe."

Mildred said: "He's a most unbalanced young man—and absolutely ungrateful for everything that's been done for him— You ought to put your foot down, Mother."

With a faint sigh Carrie Louise murmured:

"There's no harm in him really. He's fond of Lewis. He's very fond of him."

Miss Marple looked at her curiously. There had been no fondness in the expression that Edgar had turned on Lewis Serrocold a few moments previously, very far from it. She wondered, as she had wondered before, if Carrie Louise deliberately turned her back on reality.

Gina said sharply:

"He had something in his pocket. Edgar, I mean. Playing with it."

Stephen murmured as he took his hands from the keys:

"In a film it would certainly have been a revolver."

Miss Marple coughed.

"I think, you know," she said apologetically, "it *was* a revolver."

From behind the closed doors of Lewis's office the sound of voices had been plainly discernible. Now, suddenly, they became clearly audible. Edgar Lawson shouted whilst Lewis Serrocold's voice kept its even reasonable note.

"Lies—lies—lies, all lies. *You're* my father. I'm *your* son. You've deprived me of my rights. *I* ought to own this place. You hate me—you want to get rid of me!"

There was a soothing murmur from Lewis and then the hysterical voice rose still higher. It screamed out foul epithets. Edgar seemed rapidly losing control of himself. Occasional words came from Lewis— "calm—just be calm—you know none of this is true—" But they seemed not to soothe, but on the contrary to enrage the young man still further.

Insensibly everyone in the hall was silent, listening intently to what went on behind the locked door of Lewis's study.

"I'll make you listen to me," yelled Edgar. "I'll take that supercilious expression off your face. I'll have revenge, I tell you. Revenge for all you've made me suffer."

The other voice came curtly, unlike Lewis's usual unemotional tones.

"Put that revolver down!"

Gina cried sharply:

"Edgar will kill him. He's crazy. Can't we get the police or something?"

Carrie Louise, still unmoved, said softly:

"There's no need to worry, Gina. Edgar loves Lewis. He's just dramatising himself, that's all."

Edgar's voice sounded through the door in a laugh that Miss Marple had to admit sounded definitely insane.

"Yes, I've got a revolver—and it's loaded. No, don't speak, don't move. You're going to hear me out. It's you who started this conspiracy against me and now you're going to pay for it."

What sounded like the report of a firearm made them all start, but Carrie Louise said:

"It's all right, it's outside—in the Park somewhere."

Behind the locked door, Edgar was raving in a high screaming voice.

"You sit there looking at me—looking at me—pretending to be unmoved. Why don't you get down on your knees and beg for mercy? I'm going to shoot, I tell you. I'm going to shoot you dead! I'm your son—your unacknowledged despised son—you wanted me hidden away, out of the world altogether, perhaps. You set your spies to follow me—to hound me down—you plotted against me. You, my father! My father. I'm only a bastard, aren't I? Only a bastard. You went on filling me up with lies. Pretending to be kind to me, and all the time—all the time . . . You're not fit to live. I won't let you live."

Again there came a stream of obscene profanity. Somewhere during the scene Miss Marple was conscious of Miss Bellever saying:

"We must *do* something," and leaving the Hall.

Edgar seemed to pause for breath and then he shouted out,

"You're going to die—to *die*. You're going to die *now*. Take *that*, you devil, and *that!*"

Two sharp cracks rang out—not in the Park this time, but definitely behind the locked door.

Somebody, Miss Marple thought it was Mildred, cried out:

"Oh God, what shall we do?"

There was a thud from inside the room and then a sound, almost more terrible than what had gone before, the sound of slow heavy sobbing.

Somebody strode past Miss Marple and started shaking and rattling the door.

It was Stephen Restarick.

"Open the door. Open the door," he shouted.

Miss Bellever came back into the Hall. In her hand she held an assortment of keys.

"Try some of these," she said breathlessly.

At that moment the fused lights came on again. The Hall sprang into life again after its eerie dimness.

Stephen Restarick began trying the keys.

They heard the inside key fall out as he did so.

Inside that wild desperate sobbing went on.

Walter Hudd, coming lazily back into the Hall, stopped dead and demanded:

"Say, what's going on round here?"

Mildred said tearfully,

"That awful crazy young man has shot Mr. Serrocold."

"Please." It was Carrie Louise who spoke. She got up and came across to the study door. Very gently she pushed Stephen Restarick aside. "Let me speak to him."

She called—very softly— "Edgar . . . Edgar . . . let me in, will you? Please, Edgar."

They heard the key fitted into the lock. It turned and the door was slowly opened.

But it was not Edgar who opened it. It was Lewis Serrocold. He was breathing hard as though he had been running, but otherwise he was unmoved.

"It's all right, dearest," he said. "Dearest, it's quite all right."

"We thought you'd been shot," said Miss Bellever gruffly.

Lewis Serrocold frowned. He said with a trifle of asperity:

"Of course I haven't been shot."

They could see into the study by now. Edgar Lawson had collapsed by the desk. He was sobbing and gasping. The revolver lay on the floor where it had dropped from his hand.

"But we heard the shots," said Mildred.

"Oh yes, he fired twice."

"And he missed you?"

"Of course he missed me," snapped Lewis.

Miss Marple did not consider that there was any of course about it. The shots must have been fired at fairly close range.

Lewis Serrocold said irritably:

"Where's Maverick? It's Maverick we need."

Miss Bellever said:

"I'll get him. Shall I ring up the police as well?"

"Police? Certainly not."

"Of course we must ring up the police," said Mildred. "He's dangerous."

"Nonsense," said Lewis Serrocold. "Poor lad. Does he look dangerous?"

At the moment he did not look dangerous. He looked young and pathetic and rather repulsive.

His voice had lost its carefully acquired accent.

"I didn't mean to do it," he groaned. "I dunno what came over me—talking all that stuff—I must have been mad."

Mildred sniffed.

"I really must have been mad. I didn't mean to. Please, Mr. Serrocold, I really didn't mean to."

Lewis Serrocold patted him on the shoulder.

"That's all right, my boy. No damage done."

"I might have killed you, Mr. Serrocold."

Walter Hudd walked across the room and peered at the wall behind the desk.

"The bullets went in here," he said. His eye dropped to the desk and the chair behind it. "Must have been a near miss," he said grimly.

"I lost my head. I didn't rightly know what I was doing. I thought he'd done me out of my rights. I thought—"

Miss Marple put in the question she had been wanting to ask for some time.

"Who told you," she asked, "that Mr. Serrocold was your father?"

Just for a second a sly expression peeped out of Edgar's distracted face. It was there and gone in a flash.

"Nobody," he said. "I just got it into my head."

Walter Hudd was staring down at the revolver where it lay on the floor.

"Where the Hell did you get that gun?" he demanded.

"Gun?" Edgar stared down at it.

"Looks mighty like my gun," said Walter. He stooped down and picked it up. "By heck, it *is!* You took it out of my room, you creeping louse you."

Lewis Serrocold interposed between the cringing Edgar and the menacing American.

"All this can be gone into later," he said. "Ah, here's Maverick. Take a look at him, will you, Maverick?"

Dr. Maverick advanced upon Edgar with a kind of professional zest. "This won't do, Edgar," he said. "This won't do, you know."

"He's a dangerous lunatic," said Mildred sharply. "He's been shooting off a revolver and raving. He only just missed my step-father."

Edgar gave a little yelp and Dr. Maverick said reprovingly:

"Careful, please, Mrs. Strete."

"I'm sick of all this. Sick of the way you all go on here! I tell you this man's a lunatic."

With a bound Edgar wrenched himself away from Dr. Maverick and fell to the floor at Serrocold's feet.

"Help me. Help me. Don't let them take me away and shut me up. Don't let them . . ."

An unpleasing scene, Miss Marple thought.

Mildred said angrily, "I tell you he's—"

Her mother said soothingly,

"Please, Mildred. Not now. He's suffering."

Walter muttered:

"Suffering cripes! They're all cuckoo round here."

"I'll take charge of him," said Dr. Maverick. "You come with me, Edgar. Bed and a sedative—and we'll talk everything over in the morning. Now you trust me, don't you?"

Rising to his feet and trembling a little, Edgar looked doubtfully at the young doctor and then at Mildred Strete.

"She said—I was a lunatic."

"No, no, you're not a lunatic."

Miss Bellever's footsteps rang purposefully across the Hall. She came in with her lips pursed together and a flushed face.

"I've telephoned the police," she said grimly. "They will be here in a few minutes."

Carrie Louise said, "Jolly!" in tones of dismay.

Edgar uttered a wail.

Lewis Serrocold frowned angrily.

"I told you, Jolly, I did *not* want the police summoned. This is a medical matter."

"That's as may be," said Miss Bellever. "I've my own opinion. But I had to call the police. Mr. Gulbrandsen's been shot dead."

8

IT WAS a moment or two before anyone took in what she was saying.

Carrie Louise said incredulously:

"Christian shot? Dead? Oh, surely, that's impossible."

"If you don't believe me," said Miss Bellever, pursing her lips, and addressing not so much Carrie Louise, as the assembled company, "go and look for yourselves."

She was angry. And her anger sounded in the crisp sharpness of her voice.

Slowly, unbelievingly, Carrie Louise took a step towards the door. Lewis Serrocold put a hand on her shoulder.

"No, dearest, let me go."

He went out through the doorway. Dr. Maverick, with a doubtful glance at Edgar, followed him. Miss Bellever went with them.

Miss Marple gently urged Carrie Louise into a chair. She sat down, her eyes looking hurt and stricken.

"Christian—shot?" she said again.

It was the bewildered hurt tone of a child.

Walter Hudd remained close by Edgar Lawson, glowering down at him. In his hand he held the gun that he had picked up from the floor.

Mrs. Serrocold said in a wondering voice:

"But who could possibly want to shoot *Christian?*"

It was not a question that demanded an answer.

Walter muttered under his breath:

"Nuts! The whole lot of them."

Stephen had moved protectively closer to Gina. Her young startled face was the most vivid thing in the room.

Suddenly the front door opened and a rush of cold air together with a man in a big overcoat came in.

The heartiness of his greeting seemed incredibly shocking.

"Hullo, everybody, what's going on tonight? A lot of fog on the road. I had to go dead slow."

For a startled moment, Miss Marple thought that she was seeing double. Surely the same man could not be standing by Gina and coming in by the door. Then she realised that it was only a likeness and not, when you looked closely, such a very strong likeness. The two men were clearly brothers with a strong family resemblance, but no more.

Where Stephen Restarick was thin to the point of emaciation the newcomer was sleek. The big coat with the astrakhan collar fitted the sleekness of body snugly. A handsome young man and one who bore upon him the authority and good humour of success.

But Miss Marple noted one thing about him. His eyes, as he entered the Hall, looked immediately at Gina.

He said, a little doubtfully:

"You *did* expect me? You got my wire?"

He was speaking now to Carrie Louise. He came towards her.

Almost mechanically, she put up her hand to him. He took it and kissed it gently. It was an affectionate act of homage, not a mere theatrical courtesy.

She murmured:

"Of course, Alex dear—of course. Only, you see—things have been happening—"

"Happening?"

Mildred gave the information, gave it with a kind of grim relish that Miss Marple found distasteful.

"Christian Gulbrandsen," she said. "My brother Christian Gulbrandsen has been found shot dead."

"Good God," Alex registered a more than life-size dismay. "Suicide, do you mean?"

Carrie Louise moved swiftly.

"Oh no," she said. "It couldn't be suicide. Not *Christian!* Oh no."

"Uncle Christian would never shoot himself, I'm sure," said Gina.

Alex Restarick looked from one person to the other. From his brother Stephen he received a short confirmative nod. Walter Hudd stared back at him with faint resentment. Alex's eyes rested on Miss Marple with a sudden frown. It was as though he had found some unwanted prop on a stage set.

He looked as though he would like her explained. But nobody explained her, and Miss Marple continued to look an old, fluffy and sweetly bewildered old lady.

"When?" asked Alex. "When did this happen, I mean?"

"Just before you arrived," said Gina. "About—oh three or four minutes ago, I suppose. Why, of course, we actually heard the shot. Only we didn't notice it—not really."

"Didn't notice it? Why not?"

"Well, you see, there were other things going on . . ." Gina spoke rather hesitantly.

"Sure were," said Walter with emphasis.

Juliet Bellever came into the Hall by the door from the library.

"Mr. Serrocold suggests that we should all wait in the library. It would be convenient for the police. Except for Mrs. Serrocold. You've had a shock, Cara. I've ordered some hot bottles to be put in your bed. I'll take you up and—"

Rising to her feet, Carrie Louise shook her head.

"I must see Christian first," she said.

"Oh no, dear. Don't upset yourself—"

Carrie Louise put her very gently to one side.

"Dear Jolly—you don't understand." She looked round and said, "Jane?"

Miss Marple had already moved towards her.

"Come with me, will you, Jane?"

They moved together towards the door. Dr. Maverick, coming in, almost collided with them.

Miss Bellever exclaimed:

"Dr. Maverick. Do stop her. So foolish."

Carrie Louise looked calmly at the young doctor. She even gave a tiny smile.

Dr. Maverick said: "You want to go and—see him?"

"I must."

"I see." He stood aside. "If you feel you must, Mrs. Serrocold. But afterwards, please go and lie down and let Miss Bellever look after you. At the moment you do not feel the shock, but I assure you that you will do so."

"Yes. I expect you are quite right. I will be quite sensible. Come, Jane."

The two women moved out through the door, past the foot of the main staircase and along the corridor, past the dining room on the right and the double door leading to the kitchen quarters on the left, past the side door to the terrace and on to the door that gave admission to the Oak Suite that had been allotted to Christian Gulbrandsen. It was a room furnished as a sitting room more than a bedroom, with a bed in an alcove to one side and a door leading into a dressing room and bathroom.

Carrie Louise stopped on the threshold. Christian Gulbrandsen had been sitting at the big mahogany desk with a small portable typewriter open in front of him. He sat there now, but slumped sideways in the chair. The high arms of the chair prevented him from slipping to the floor.

Lewis Serrocold was standing by the window. He had pulled the curtain a little aside and was gazing out into the night.

He looked round and frowned.

"My dearest, you shouldn't have come."

He came towards her and she stretched out a hand to him. Miss Marple retreated a step or two.

"Oh yes, Lewis. I had to—see him. One has to know just exactly how things are."

She walked slowly towards the desk.

Lewis said warningly:

"You mustn't touch anything. The police must have things left exactly as he found them."

"Of course. He was shot deliberately by someone, then?"

"Oh yes." Lewis Serrocold looked a little surprised that the question had even been asked. "I thought—you knew that?"

"I did really. Christian would not commit suicide, and he was such a competent person that it could not possibly have been an accident. That only leaves"—she hesitated a moment—"murder."

She walked up behind the desk and stood looking down at the dead man. There was sorrow and affection in her face.

"Dear Christian," she said. "He was always good to me."

Softly, she touched the top of his head with her fingers.

"Bless you and thank you, dear Christian," she said.

Lewis Serrocold said with something more like emotion than Miss Marple had ever seen in him before:

"I wish to God I could have spared you this, Caroline."

His wife shook her head gently.

"You can't really spare anyone anything," she said. "Things always have to be faced sooner or later. And therefore it had better be sooner. I'll go and lie down now. I suppose you'll stay here, Lewis, until the police come?"

"Yes."

Carrie Louise turned away and Miss Marple slipped an arm round her.

9

INSPECTOR CURRY and his entourage found Miss Bellever alone in the Great Hall when they arrived.

She came forward efficiently.

"I am Juliet Bellever, companion and secretary to Mrs. Serrocold."

"It was you who found the body and telephoned to us?"

"Yes. Most of the household are in the library—through that door there. Mr. Serrocold remained in Mr. Gulbrandsen's room to see that nothing was disturbed. Dr. Maverick who first examined the body will be here very shortly. He had to take a—case over to the other wing. Shall I lead the way?"

"If you please."

"Competent woman," thought the Inspector to himself. "Seems to have got the whole thing taped."

He followed her along the corridor.

For the next twenty minutes the routine of police procedure was duly set in motion. The photographer took the necessary pictures. The police surgeon arrived and was joined by Dr. Maverick. Half an hour later, the ambulance had taken away the mortal remains of Christian Gulbrandsen, and Inspector Curry started his official interrogation.

Lewis Serrocold took him into the library and he glanced keenly round the assembled people making brief notes in his mind. An old lady with white hair, a middle-aged lady, the good-looking girl he'd seen driving her car round the countryside, that odd looking American husband of hers. A couple of young men who were mixed up in the outfit somewhere or other and the capable woman, Miss Bellever, who'd phoned him and met him on arrival.

Inspector Curry had already thought out a little speech and he now delivered it as planned.

"I'm afraid this is all very upsetting to you," he said, "and I hope not to keep you too long this evening. We can go into things more thoroughly tomorrow. It was Miss Bellever who found Mr. Gulbrandsen dead and I'll ask Miss Bellever to give me an outline of the general situation as that will save too much repetition. Mr. Serrocold, if you want to go up to your wife, please do and when I have finished with Miss Bellever, I should like to talk to you. Is that all quite clear? Perhaps there is some small room where—"

Lewis Serrocold said:

"My office, Jolly?"

Miss Bellever nodded, and said: "I was just going to suggest it."

She led the way across the Great Hall and Inspector Curry and his attendant Sergeant followed her.

Miss Bellever arranged them and herself suitably. It might have been she and not Inspector Curry who was in charge of the investigation.

The moment had come, however, when the initiative passed to him. Inspector Curry had a pleasant voice and manner. He looked quiet and serious and just a little apologetic. Some people made the mistake of underrating him. Actually he was as competent in his way as Miss Bellever was in hers. But he preferred not to make a parade of the fact.

He cleared his throat.

"I've had the main facts from Mr. Serrocold. Mr. Christian Gulbrandsen was the eldest son of the late Eric Gulbrandsen, the founder of the Gulbrandsen Trust and Fellowship . . . and all the rest of it. He was one of the trustees of this place and he arrived here unexpectedly yesterday. That is correct?"

"Yes."

Inspector Curry was pleased by her conciseness. He went on.

"Mr. Serrocold was away in Liverpool. He returned this evening by the 6.30 train."

"Yes."

"After dinner this evening, Mr. Gulbrandsen announced his intention of working in his own room and left the rest of the party here after coffee had been served. Correct?"

"Yes."

"Now, Miss Bellever, please tell me in your own words how you came to discover him dead."

"There was a rather unpleasant incident this evening. A young man, a psychopathic case, became very unbalanced and threatened Mr. Serrocold with a revolver. They were locked in this room. The young man eventually fired the revolver—you can see the bullet holes in the wall there. Fortunately Mr. Serrocold was unhurt. After firing the shots, this young man went completely to pieces. Mr. Serrocold sent me to find Dr. Maverick. I got through on the house phone but he was not in his room. I found him with one of his colleagues and gave him the message and he came here at once. On my own way back I went to Mr. Gulbrandsen's room. I wanted to ask him if there was anything he would like—hot

milk, or whisky before settling for the night. I knocked, but there was no
response, so I opened the door. I saw that Mr. Gulbrandsen was dead. I
then rang you up."

"What entrances and exits are there to the house? And how are they
secured? Could anyone have come in from outside without being heard
or seen?"

"Anyone could have come in by the side door to the terrace. That is
not locked until we all go to bed, as people come in and out that way to
go to the College buildings."

"And you have, I believe, between two hundred and two hundred and
fifty juvenile delinquents in the College?"

"Yes. But the College buildings are well secured and patrolled. I
should say it was most unlikely that anyone could leave the College
unsponsored."

"We shall have to check up on that, of course. Had Mr. Gulbrandsen
given any cause for—shall we say, rancour? Any unpopular decisions as
to policy?"

Miss Bellever shook her head.

"Oh no, Mr. Gulbrandsen had nothing whatever to do with the running of the College, or with administrative matters."

"What was the purpose of his visit?"

"I have no idea."

"But he was annoyed to find Mr. Serrocold absent, and immediately
decided to wait until he returned?"

"Yes."

"So his business here was definitely with Mr. Serrocold?"

"Yes. But it would be—because it would be almost certainly business
to do with the Institute."

"Yes, presumably that is so. Did he have a conference with Mr. Serrocold?"

"No, there was no time. Mr. Serrocold only arrived just before dinner
this evening."

"But after dinner, Mr. Gulbrandsen said he had important letters to
write and went away to do so. He didn't suggest a session with Mr.
Serrocold?"

Miss Bellever hesitated.

"No. No, he didn't."

"Surely that was rather odd—if he had waited on at inconvenience to
himself to see Mr. Serrocold?"

"Yes, it was odd."

The oddness of it seemed to strike Miss Bellever for the first time.

"Mr. Serrocold did not accompany him to his room?"

"No. Mr. Serrocold remained in the Hall."

"And you have no idea at what time Mr. Gulbrandsen was killed?"

"I think it is possible that we heard the shot. If so, it was at twenty-three minutes past nine."

"You heard a shot? And it did not alarm you?"

"The circumstances were peculiar."

She explained in rather more detail the scene between Lewis Serrocold and Edgar Lawson which had been in progress.

"So it occurred to no one that the shot might actually have come from within the house?"

"No. No, I certainly don't think so. We were all so relieved, you know, that the shot didn't come from in here."

Miss Bellever added rather grimly:

"You don't expect murder and attempted murder in the same house on the same night."

Inspector Curry acknowledged the truth of that.

"All the same," said Miss Bellever, suddenly, "you know I believe that's what made me go along to Mr. Gulbrandsen's room later. I did mean to ask him if he would like anything, but it was a kind of excuse to reassure myself that everything was all right."

Inspector Curry stared at her for a moment.

"What made you think it mightn't be all right?"

"I don't know. I think it was the shot outside. It hadn't meant anything at the time. But afterwards it came back into my mind. I told myself that it was only a backfire from Mr. Restarick's car—"

"Mr. Restarick's car?"

"Yes. Alex Restarick. He arrived by car this evening—he arrived just after all this happened."

"I see. When you discovered Mr. Gulbrandsen's body, did you touch anything in the room?"

"Of course not." Miss Bellever sounded reproachful. "Naturally I knew that nothing must be touched or moved."

"And just now, when you took us into the room, everything was exactly as it had been when you found the body?"

Miss Bellever considered. She sat back screwing up her eyes. She had, Inspector Curry thought, one of those photographic memories.

"One thing was different," she said. "There was nothing in the type-writer."

"You mean," said Inspector Curry, "that when you first went in Mr.

Gulbrandsen had been writing a letter on the typewriter, and that that letter had since been removed?"

"Yes, I'm almost sure that I saw the white edge of the paper sticking up."

"Thank you, Miss Bellever. Who else went into that room before we arrived?"

"Mr. Serrocold, of course. He remained there when I came to meet you. And Mrs. Serrocold and Miss Marple went there. Mrs. Serrocold insisted."

"Mrs. Serrocold and Miss Marple," said Inspector Curry. "Which is Miss Marple?"

"The old lady with white hair. She was a schoolfriend of Mrs. Serrocold's. She came on a visit about four days ago."

"Well, thank you, Miss Bellever. All that you have told us is quite clear. I'll go into things with Mr. Serrocold now. Ah, but perhaps—Miss Marple's an old lady, isn't she? I'll just have a word with her first and then she can go off to bed. Rather cruel to keep an old lady like that up," said Inspector Curry virtuously. "This must have been a shock to her."

"I'll tell her, shall I?"

"If you please."

Miss Bellever went out. Inspector Curry looked at the ceiling.

"Gulbrandsen?" he said. "Why Gulbrandsen? Two hundred odd maladjusted youngsters on the premises. No reason any of them shouldn't have done it. Probably one of them did. But why Gulbrandsen? The stranger within the gates."

Sergeant Lake said: "Of course we don't know everything yet."

Inspector Curry said:

"So far, we don't know anything at all."

He jumped up and was gallant when Miss Marple came in. She seemed a little flustered and he hurried to put her at her ease.

"Now don't upset yourself, M'am." The old ones like M'am, he thought. To them, police officers were definitely of the lower classes and should show respect to their betters. "This is all very distressing, I know. But we've just got to get the facts clear. Get it all clear."

"Oh yes, I know," said Miss Marple. "So difficult, isn't it? To be clear about anything, I mean. Because if you're looking at one thing, you can't be looking at another. And one so often looks at the wrong thing, though whether because one happens to do so or because you're meant to, it's very hard to say. Misdirection, the conjurers call it. So clever, aren't they? And I never *have* known how they manage with a bowl of goldfish —because really that cannot fold up small, can it?"

Inspector Curry blinked a little and said soothingly:

"Quite so. Now, M'am, I've had an account of this evening's events from Miss Bellever. A most anxious time for all of you, I'm sure."

"Yes, indeed. It was all so *dramatic,* you know."

"First this to do between Mr. Serrocold and"—he looked down at a note he had made—"this Edgar Lawson."

"A very odd young man," said Miss Marple. "I have felt all along that there was something wrong about him."

"I'm sure you have," said Inspector Curry. "And then, after that excitement was over, there came Mr. Gulbrandsen's death. I understand that you went with Mrs. Serrocold to see the—er—the body."

"Yes, I did. She asked me to come with her. We are very old friends."

"Quite so. And you went along to Mr. Gulbrandsen's room. Did you touch anything while you were in the room, either of you?"

"Oh no. Mr. Serrocold warned us not to."

"Did you happen to notice, M'am, whether there was a letter or a piece of paper, say, in the typewriter?"

"There wasn't," said Miss Marple promptly. "I noticed that at once because it seemed to me odd. Mr. Gulbrandsen was sitting there at the typewriter so he must have been typing something. Yes, I thought it very odd."

Inspector Curry looked at her sharply. He said:

"Did you have much conversation with Mr. Gulbrandsen while he was here?"

"Very little."

"There is nothing especial—or significant that you can remember?"

Miss Marple considered.

"He asked me about Mrs. Serrocold's health. In particular, about her heart."

"Her heart? Is there something wrong with her heart?"

"Nothing whatever, I understand."

Inspector Curry was silent for a moment or two, then he said:

"You heard a shot this evening during the quarrel between Mr. Serrocold and Edgar Lawson?"

"I didn't actually hear it myself. I am a little deaf, you know. But Mrs. Serrocold mentioned it as being outside in the Park."

"Mr. Gulbrandsen left the party immediately after dinner, I understand?"

"Yes, he said he had letters to write."

"He didn't show any wish for a business conference with Mr. Serrocold?"

"No."

Miss Marple added:

"You see, they'd already had one little talk."

"They had? When? I understood that Mr. Serrocold only returned home just before dinner."

"That's quite true, but he walked up through the Park, and Mr. Gulbrandsen went out to meet him and they walked up and down the terrace together."

"Who else knows this?"

"I shouldn't think anybody else," said Miss Marple. "Unless, of course, Mr. Serrocold told Mrs. Serrocold. I just happened to be looking out of my window—at some birds."

"Birds?"

"Birds." Miss Marple added after a moment or two: "I thought, perhaps, they might be siskins."

Inspector Curry was uninterested in siskins.

"You didn't," he said delicately, "happen to—er—overhear anything of what they said?"

Innocent china blue eyes met his.

"Only fragments, I'm afraid," said Miss Marple gently.

"And those fragments?"

Miss Marple was silent a moment, then she said:

"I do not know the actual subject of their conversation, but their immediate concern was to keep whatever it was from the knowledge of Mrs. Serrocold. To spare her—that was how Mr. Gulbrandsen put it, and Mr. Serrocold said, 'I agree that it is she who must be considered.' They also mentioned a 'big responsibility' and that they should, perhaps, 'take outside advice.' "

She paused.

"I think, you know, you had better ask Mr. Serrocold himself about all this."

"We shall do so. M'am. Now there is nothing else that struck you as unusual this evening?"

Miss Marple considered.

"It was all so unusual if you know what I mean—"

"Quite so. Quite so."

Something flickered into Miss Marple's memory.

"There was one rather unusual incident. Mr. Serrocold stopped Mrs. Serrocold from taking her medicine. Miss Bellever was quite put out about it."

She smiled in a deprecating fashion.

"But that, of course, is such a little thing . . ."

"Yes, of course. Well, thank you, Miss Marple."

As Miss Marple went out of the room, Sergeant Lake said:

"She's old but she's sharp . . ."

10

LEWIS SERROCOLD came into the office and immediately the whole focus of the room shifted. He turned to close the door behind him, and in doing so he created an atmosphere of privacy. He walked over and sat down not in the chair Miss Marple had just vacated but in his own chair behind the desk. Miss Bellever had settled Inspector Curry in a chair drawn up to one side of the desk, as though unconsciously she had reserved Lewis Serrocold's chair against his coming.

When he had sat down, Lewis Serrocold looked at the two police officers thoughtfully. His face looked drawn and tired. It was the face of a man who was passing through a severe ordeal, and it surprised Inspector Curry a little because, though Christian Gulbrandsen's death must undeniably have been a shock to Lewis Serrocold, yet Gulbrandsen had not been a close friend or relation, only a rather remote connection by marriage.

In an odd way, the tables seemed to have been turned. It did not seem as though Lewis Serrocold had come into the room to answer police questioning. It seemed rather that Lewis Serrocold had arrived to preside over a court of inquiry. It irritated Inspector Curry a little.

He said briskly:

"Now, Mr. Serrocold—"

Lewis Serrocold still seemed lost in thought. He said with a sigh: "How difficult it is to know the right thing to do."

Inspector Curry said:

"I think *we* will be the judges as to that, Mr. Serrocold. Now about Mr. Gulbrandsen, he arrived unexpectedly, I understand?"

"Quite unexpectedly."

"You did not know he was coming?"

"I had not the least idea of it."

"And you have no idea of why he came?"

Lewis Serrocold said quietly,

"Oh yes, I know why he came. He told me."

"When?"

"I walked up from the station. He was watching from the house and came out to meet me. It was then that he explained what had brought him here."

"Business connected with the Gulbrandsen Institute, I suppose?"

"Oh no, it was nothing to do with the Gulbrandsen Institute."

"Miss Bellever seemed to think it was."

"Naturally. That would be the assumption. Gulbrandsen did nothing to correct that impression. Neither did I."

"Why, Mr. Serrocold?"

Lewis Serrocold said slowly:

"Because it seemed to both of us important that no hint should arise as to the real purpose of his visit."

"What was the real purpose?"

Lewis Serrocold was silent for a minute or two. He sighed.

"Gulbrandsen came over here regularly twice a year for meetings of the trustees. The last meeting was only a month ago. Consequently he was not due to come over again for another five months. I think, therefore, that anyone might realise that the business that brought him must definitely be urgent business, but I still think that the normal assumption would be that it *was* a business visit, and that the matter, however urgent —would be a Trust matter. As far as I know, Gulbrandsen did nothing to contradict that impression—or thought he didn't. Yes, perhaps that is nearer the truth—he thought he didn't."

"I'm afraid, Mr. Serrocold, that I don't quite follow you."

Lewis Serrocold did not answer at once. Then he said gravely,

"I fully realise that with Gulbrandsen's death—which was murder, undeniably murder, I have got to put all the facts before you. But frankly, I am concerned for my wife's happiness and peace of mind. It is not for me to dictate to you, Inspector, but if you can see your way to keeping certain things from her as far as possible I shall be grateful. You see, Inspector Curry, Christian Gulbrandsen came here expressly to tell me that he believed my wife was being slowly and cold-bloodedly poisoned."

"What?"

Curry leaned forward incredulously.

Serrocold nodded.

"Yes, it was, as you can imagine, a tremendous shock to me. I had had no suspicion of such a thing myself, but as soon as Christian told me, I realised that certain symptoms my wife had complained of lately, were quite compatible with that belief. What she took to be rheumatism, leg cramps, pain, and occasional sickness. All that fits in very well *with the symptoms of arsenical poisoning.*"

"Miss Marple told us that Christian Gulbrandsen asked her about the condition of Mrs. Serrocold's heart?"

"Did he now? That is interesting. I suppose he thought that a heart poison would be used since it paved the way to a sudden death without undue suspicion. But I think myself that arsenic is more likely."

"You definitely think, then, that Christian Gulbrandsen's suspicions were well founded?"

"Oh yes, I think so. For one thing, Gulbrandsen would hardly come to me with such a suggestion unless he was fairly sure of his facts. He was a cautious and hardheaded man, difficult to convince, but very shrewd."

"What was his evidence?"

"We had no time to go into that. Our interview was a hurried one. It served only the purpose of explaining his visit, and a mutual agreement that nothing whatever should be said to my wife about the matter until we were sure of our facts."

"And whom did he suspect of administering poison?"

"He did not say, and actually I don't think he knew. He *may* have suspected. I think now that he probably did suspect—otherwise why should he be killed?"

"But he mentioned no name to you?"

"He mentioned no name. We agreed that we must investigate the matter thoroughly, and he suggested inviting the advice and co-operation of Dr. Galbraith, the Bishop of Cromer. Dr. Galbraith is a very old friend of the Gulbrandsens and is one of the trustees of the Institute. He is a man of great wisdom and experience and would be of great help and comfort to my wife if—if it was necessary to tell her of our suspicions. We meant to rely on his advice as to whether or not to consult the police."

"Quite extraordinary," said Curry.

"Gulbrandsen left us after dinner to write to Dr. Galbraith. He was actually in the act of typing a letter to him when he was shot."

"How do you know?"

Lewis said calmly, "Because I took the letter out of the typewriter. I have it here."

From his breast pocket, he drew out a folded typewritten sheet of paper and handed it to Curry.

The latter said sharply,

"You shouldn't have taken this, or touched anything in the room."

"I touched nothing else. I know that I committed an unpardonable offence in your eyes in moving this, but I had a very strong reason. I felt certain that my wife would insist on coming into the room and I was afraid that she might read something of what is written here. I admit myself in the wrong, but I am afraid I would do the same again. I would do anything—*anything*—to save my wife unhappiness."

Inspector Curry said no more for the moment. He read the typewritten sheet.

Dear Dr. Galbraith. If it is at all possible, I beg that you will come to Stonygates as soon as you receive this. A crisis of extraordinary gravity has arisen and I am at a loss how to deal with it. I know how deep your affection is for our dear Carrie Louise, and how grave your concern will be for anything that affects her. How much has she got to know? How much can we keep from her? Those are the questions that I find so difficult to answer.

Not to beat about the bush, I have reason to believe that that sweet and innocent lady is being slowly poisoned. I first suspected this when—

Here the letter broke off abruptly.

Curry said:

"And when he had reached this point Christian Gulbrandsen was shot?"

"Yes."

"But why on earth was this letter left in the typewriter?"

"I can only conceive of two reasons—one that the murderer had no idea to whom Gulbrandsen was writing and what was the subject of the letter. Secondly—he may not have had time. He may have heard someone coming and only had just time to escape unobserved."

"And Gulbrandsen gave you no hint as to who he suspected—if he did suspect anyone?"

There was, perhaps, a very slight pause before Lewis answered. "None whatever."

He added, rather obscurely:

"Christian was a very fair man."

"How do you think this poison, arsenic or whatever it may be—was or is being administered?"

"I thought over that whilst I was changing for dinner and it seemed to me that the most likely vehicle was some medicine, a tonic, that my wife was taking. As regards food we all partook of the same dishes and my wife has nothing specially prepared for her. But anyone could add arsenic to the medicine bottle."

"We must take the medicine and have it analysed."

Lewis said quietly,

"I already have a sample of it. I took it this evening before dinner."

From a drawer in the desk, he took out a small corked bottle with a red fluid in it.

Inspector Curry said with a curious glance,

"You think of everything, Mr. Serrocold."

"I believe in acting promptly. To-night, I stopped my wife from taking her usual dose. It is still in a glass on the oak dresser in the Hall—the bottle of tonic itself is in the drawing room."

Curry leaned forward across the desk. He lowered his voice and spoke confidentially and without officialdom.

"You'll excuse me, Mr. Serrocold, but just *why* are you so anxious to keep this from your wife? Are you afraid she'd panic? Surely, for her own sake, it would be as well if she were warned."

"Yes—yes, that may well be so. But I don't think you quite understand. Without knowing my wife Caroline, it would be difficult. My wife, Inspector Curry, is an idealist, a completely trustful person. Of her it may truly be said that she sees no evil, hears no evil, and speaks no evil. It would be inconceivable to her that anyone could wish to kill her. But we have to go farther than that. It is not just 'anyone.' It is a case—surely you see that—of somebody possibly very near and dear to her. . . ."

"So that's what you think?"

"We have got to face facts. Close at hand we have a couple of hundred warped and stunted personalities who have expressed themselves often enough by crude and senseless violence. But by the very nature of things, none of *them* can be suspect in this case. A slow poisoner is someone living in the intimacy of family life. Think of the people who are here in this house; her husband, her daughter, her granddaughter, her granddaughter's husband, her stepson whom she regards as her own son, Miss Bellever, her devoted companion and friend of many years. All very near and dear to her—and yet the suspicion must arise—is it one of them?"

Curry said slowly,

"There *are* outsiders—"

"Yes, in a sense. There is Dr. Maverick, one or two of the staff are often with us, there are the servants—but frankly, what possible motive could they have?"

Inspector Curry said,

"And there's young—what is his name again—Edgar Lawson?"

"Yes. But he has only been down here as a casual visitor just lately. He has no possible motive. Besides, he is deeply attached to Caroline—just as everyone is."

"But he's unbalanced. What about this attack on you tonight?"

Serrocold waved it aside impatiently.

"Sheer childishness. He had no intention of harming me."

"Not with these two bullet holes in the wall? He shot at you, didn't he?"

"He didn't mean to hit me. It was playacting, no more."

"Rather a dangerous form of playacting, Mr. Serrocold."

"You don't understand. You must talk to our psychiatrist, Dr. Maverick. Edgar is an illegitimate child. He has consoled himself for his lack of a father and a humble origin by pretending to himself that he is the son of a celebrated man. It's a well-known phenomenon, I assure you. He was improving, improving very much. Then, for some reason, he had a setback. He identified me as his 'father' and made a melodramatic attack, waving a revolver and uttering threats. I was not in the least alarmed. When he had actually fired the revolver, he broke down and sobbed and Dr. Maverick took him away and gave him a sedative. He'll probably be quite normal tomorrow morning."

"You don't wish to bring a charge against him?"

"That would be the worst thing possible—for him, I mean."

"Frankly, Mr. Serrocold, it seems to me he ought to be under restraint. People who go about firing off revolvers to bolster up their egos—! One has to think of the community, you know."

"Talk to Dr. Maverick on the subject," urged Lewis. "He'll give you the professional point of view. In any case," he added, "poor Edgar certainly did not shoot Gulbrandsen. He was in here threatening to shoot *me.*"

"That's the point I was coming to, Mr. Serrocold. We've covered the outside. Anyone, it seems, could have come in from *outside,* and shot Mr. Gulbrandsen, since the terrace door was unlocked. But there is a narrower field *inside* the house, and in view of what you have been telling me, it seems to me that very close attention must be paid to that. It seems possible that, with the exception of old Miss—er—yes, Marple who happened to be looking out of her bedroom window, no one was aware that you and Christian Gulbrandsen had already had a private interview. If so, Gulbrandsen may have been shot to prevent him communicating his suspicions to you. Of course it is too early to say as yet what other motives may exist. Mr. Gulbrandsen was a wealthy man, I presume?"

"Yes, he was a very wealthy man. He has sons and daughters and grandchildren—all of whom will probably benefit by his death. But I do not think that any of his family are in this country, and they are all solid and highly respectable people. As far as I know, there are no black sheep amongst them."

"Had he any enemies?"

"I should think it most unlikely. He was—really, he was not that type of man."

"So it boils down, doesn't it, to this house and the people in it? Who from *inside* the house could have killed him?"

Lewis Serrocold said slowly,

"That is difficult for me to say. There are the servants and the members of my household and our guests. They are, from your point of view, all possibilities, I suppose. I can only tell you that, as far as I know, everyone except the servants was in the Great Hall when Christian left it and whilst I was there, nobody left it."

"Nobody at all?"

"I think—" Lewis frowned in an effort of remembrance—"oh yes. Some of the lights fused—Mr. Walter Hudd went to see to it."

"That's the American gentleman?"

"Yes—of course I don't know what took place after Edgar and I came here."

"And you can't give me anything nearer than that, Mr. Serrocold?"

Lewis Serrocold shook his head.

"No, I'm afraid I can't help you. It's—it's all quite inconceivable."

Inspector Curry sighed. He said:

"You can tell the party that they can all go to bed. I'll talk to them tomorrow."

When Serrocold had left the room, Inspector Curry said to Lake:

"Well—what do you think?"

"Knows—or thinks he knows, who did it," said Lake.

"Yes. I agree with you. And he doesn't like it a bit. . . ."

11

GINA greeted Miss Marple with a rush as the latter came down to breakfast the next morning.

"The police are here again," she said. "They're in the library this time. Wally is absolutely fascinated by them. He can't understand their being so quiet and so remote. I think he's really quite thrilled by the whole thing. I'm not. I hate it. I think it's horrible. Why do you think I'm so upset? Because I'm half Italian?"

"Very possibly. At least perhaps it explains why you don't mind showing what you feel."

Miss Marple smiled just a little as she said this.

"Jolly's frightfully cross," said Gina, hanging on Miss Marple's arm and propelling her into the dining room. "I think really because the police are in charge and she can't exactly 'run' them like she runs everybody else.

"Alex and Stephen," continued Gina severely, as they came into the dining room where the two brothers were finishing their breakfast, "just don't care."

"Gina dearest," said Alex, "you are most unkind. Good morning, Miss Marple. I care intensely. Except for the fact that I hardly knew your uncle Christian, I'm far and away the best suspect. You do realise that, I hope."

"Why?"

"Well, I was driving up to the house at about the right time, it seems. And they've been checking up on times and it seems that I took too much time between the lodge and the house—time enough, the implication is, to leave the car, run round the house, go in through the side door, shoot Christian and rush out and back to the car again."

"And what were you really doing?"

"I thought little girls were taught quite young not to ask indelicate questions. Like an idiot, I stood for several minutes taking in the fog effect in the headlights and thinking what I'd use to get that effect on a stage. For my new 'Limehouse' ballet."

"But you can tell them that!"

"Naturally. But you know what policemen are like. They say 'thank you' very civilly and write it all down, and you've no idea *what* they are thinking except that one does feel they have rather sceptical minds."

"It would amuse me to see you in a spot, Alex," said Stephen with his thin rather cruel smile. "Now *I'm* quite all right! I never left the Hall last night."

Gina cried, "But they couldn't possibly think it was one of *us!*"

Her dark eyes were round and dismayed.

"Don't say it must have been a tramp, dear," said Alex, helping himself lavishly to marmalade. "It's so hackneyed."

Miss Bellever looked in at the door and said:

"Miss Marple, when you have finished your breakfast, will you go to the library?"

"You again," said Gina. "Before any of us."

She seemed a little injured.

"Hi, what was that?" asked Alex.

"Didn't hear anything," said Stephen.

"It was a pistol shot."

"They've been firing shots in the room where Uncle Christian was killed," said Gina. "I don't know why. And outside too."

The door opened again and Mildred Strete came in. She was wearing black with some onyx beads.

She murmured good morning without looking at anyone and sat down.

In a hushed voice she said:

"Some tea, please, Gina. Nothing much to eat—just some toast."

She touched her nose and eyes delicately with the handkerchief she held in one hand. Then she raised her eyes and looked in an unseeing way at the two brothers. Stephen and Alex became uncomfortable. Their voices dropped to almost a whisper and presently they got up and left.

Mildred Strete said, whether to the Universe or Miss Marple was not quite certain, "Not even a black tie!"

"I don't suppose," said Miss Marple apologetically, "that they knew beforehand that a murder was going to happen."

Gina made a smothered sound and Mildred Strete looked sharply at her.

"Where's Walter this morning?" she asked.

Gina flushed.

"I don't know. I haven't seen him."

She sat there uneasily like a guilty child.

Miss Marple got up.

"I'll go to the library now," she said.

2

Lewis Serrocold was standing by the window in the library.

There was no one else in the room.

He turned as Miss Marple came in and came forward to meet her, taking her hand in his.

"I hope," he said, "that you are not feeling the worse for the shock. To be at close quarters with what is undoubtedly murder must be a great strain on anyone who has not come in contact with such a thing before."

Modesty forbade Miss Marple to reply that she was, by now, quite at home with murder. She merely said that life in St. Mary Mead was not quite so sheltered as outside people believed.

"Very nasty things go on in a village, I assure you," she said. "One has an opportunity of studying things there that one would never have in a town."

Lewis Serrocold listened indulgently, but with only half an ear.

He said very simply: "I want your help."

"But of course, Mr. Serrocold."

"It is a matter that affects my wife—affects Caroline. I think that you are really attached to her?"

"Yes, indeed. Everyone is."

"That is what I believed. It seems that I am wrong. With the permission of Inspector Curry, I am going to tell you something that no one else as yet knows. Or perhaps I should say what only one person knows."

Briefly, he told her what he had told Inspector Curry the night before.

Miss Marple looked horrified.

"I can't believe it, Mr. Serrocold. I really can't believe it."

"That is what I felt when Christian Gulbrandsen told me."

"I should have said that dear Carrie Louise had not got an enemy in the world."

"It seems incredible that she should have. But you see the implication? Poisoning—slow poisoning—is an intimate family matter. It must be one of our closely knit little household—"

"If it is *true*. Are you sure that Mr. Gulbrandsen was not mistaken?"

"Christian was not mistaken. He is too cautious a man to make such a statement without foundation. Besides, the police took away Caroline's medicine bottle and a separate sample of its contents. There was arsenic in both of them—and arsenic was not prescribed. The actual quantitative tests will take longer—but the actual fact of arsenic being present is established."

"Then her rheumatism—the difficulty in walking—all that—"

"Yes, leg cramps are typical, I understand. Also, before you came, Caroline has had one or two severe attacks of a gastric nature—I never dreamed until Christian came—"

He broke off. Miss Marple said softly: "So Ruth was right!"

"Ruth?"

Lewis Serrocold sounded surprised. Miss Marple flushed.

"There is something I have not told you. My coming here was not entirely fortuitous. If you will let me explain—I'm afraid I tell things so badly. Please have patience."

Lewis Serrocold listened whilst Miss Marple told him of Ruth's unease and urgency.

"Extraordinary," he commented. "I had no idea of this."

"It was all so vague," said Miss Marple. "Ruth herself didn't know why she had this feeling. There must be a reason—in my experience there always is—but 'something wrong' was as near as she could get."

Lewis Serrocold said grimly:

"Well, it seems that she was right. Now, Miss Marple, you see how I am placed. Am I to tell Caroline of this?"

Miss Marple said quickly, "Oh no," in a distressed voice, and then flushed and stared doubtfully at Lewis. He nodded.

"So you feel as I do? As Christian Gulbrandsen did. Should we feel like that with an ordinary woman?"

"Carrie Louise is *not* an ordinary woman. She lives by her trust, by her belief in human nature—oh dear, I am expressing myself very badly. But I do feel that until we know who—"

"Yes, that is the crux. But you do see, Miss Marple, that there is a risk in saying nothing—"

"And so you want me to—how shall I put it?—watch over her?"

"You see, you are the only person whom I can trust," said Lewis Serrocold simply. "Everyone here *seems* devoted. But are they? Now your attachment goes back many years."

"And also I only arrived a few days ago," said Miss Marple pertinently.

Lewis Serrocold smiled.

"Exactly."

"It is a very mercenary question," said Miss Marple apologetically. "But who exactly would benefit if dear Carrie Louise were to die?"

"Money!" said Lewis bitterly. "It always boils down to money, does it?"

"Well, I really think it must in this case. Because Carrie Louise is a very sweet person with a great deal of charm, and one cannot really imagine anyone disliking her. She couldn't, I mean, have an *enemy*. So then it does boil down, as you put it, to a question of money, because as you don't need me to tell you, Mr. Serrocold, people will quite often do anything for money."

"I suppose so, yes."

He went on: "Naturally Inspector Curry has already taken up that point. Mr. Gilfoy is coming down from London today and can give detailed information. Gilfoy, Gilfoy, Jaimes and Gilfoy are a very eminent firm of lawyers. This Gilfoy's father was one of the original trustees and they drew up both Caroline's will and the original will of Eric Gulbrandsen. I will put it in simple terms for you—"

"Thank you," said Miss Marple gratefully. "So mystifying the law, I always think."

"Eric Gulbrandsen after endowment of the College and his various fellowships and trusts and other charitable bequests, and having settled an equal sum on his daughter Mildred and on his adopted daughter Pippa (Gina's mother), left the remainder of his vast fortune in trust, the income from it to be paid to Caroline for her lifetime."

"And after her death?"

"After her death it was to be divided equally between Mildred and Pippa—or their children if they themselves had predeceased Caroline."

"So that in fact it goes to Mrs. Strete and to Gina."

"Yes. Caroline has also quite a considerable fortune of her own—though not in the Gulbrandsen class. Half of this she made over to me four years ago. Of the remaining amount, she left ten thousand pounds to Juliet Bellever, and the rest equally divided between Alex and Stephen Restarick, her two stepsons."

"Oh dear," said Miss Marple. "That's bad. That's very bad."

"You mean?"

"It means everyone in the house had a financial motive."

"Yes. And yet, you know, I can't believe that any of these people would do murder. I simply can't . . . Mildred is her daughter—and already quite well provided for. Gina is devoted to her grandmother. She is generous and extravagant, but has no acquisitive feelings. Jolly Bellever is fanatically devoted to Caroline. The two Restaricks care for Caroline as though she were really their mother. They have no money of their own to speak of, but quite a lot of Caroline's income has gone towards financing their enterprises—especially so with Alex. I simply can't believe either of those two would deliberately poison her for the sake of inheriting money at her death. I just can't believe any of it, Miss Marple."

"There's Gina's husband, isn't there?"

"Yes," said Lewis gravely. "There is Gina's husband."

"You don't really know much about him. And one can't help seeing that he's a very unhappy young man."

Lewis sighed.

"He hasn't fitted in here—no. He's no interest in or sympathy for what we're trying to do. But after all, why should he? He's young, crude, and he comes from a country where a man is esteemed by the success he makes of life."

"Whilst here we are so very fond of failures," said Miss Marple.

Lewis Serrocold looked at her sharply and suspiciously.

She flushed a little and murmured rather incoherently:

"I think sometimes, you know, one can overdo things the other way . . . I mean the young people with a good heredity, and brought up wisely in a good home—and with grit and pluck and the ability to get on in life—well, they are really, when one comes down to it—the sort of people a country *needs.*"

Lewis frowned and Miss Marple hurried on, getting pinker and pinker and more and more incoherent.

"Not that I don't appreciate—I do indeed—you and Carrie Louise—a really noble work—real compassion—and one should have compassion because after all it's what people *are* that counts—good and bad luck—and much more expected (and rightly) of the lucky ones. But I do think sometimes one's sense of proportion—Oh I don't mean *you,* Mr. Serrocold. Really I don't know *what* I mean—but the English *are* rather odd that way. Even in war, so much prouder of their defeats and their retreats than of their victories. Foreigners never can understand why we're so proud of Dunkerque. It's the sort of thing they'd prefer not to mention themselves. But we always seem to be almost embarrassed by a victory—and treat it as though it weren't quite nice to boast about it. And look at all our poets! The Charge of the Light Brigade. And the little Revenge went down in the Spanish Main. It's really a very odd characteristic when you come to think of it!"

Miss Marple drew a fresh breath.

"What I really mean is that everything here must seem rather peculiar to young Walter Hudd."

"Yes," Lewis allowed. "I see your point. And Walter has certainly a fine war record. There's no doubt about his bravery."

"Not that that helps," said Miss Marple candidly. "Because war is one thing, and everyday life is quite another. And actually to commit a murder, I think you do need bravery—or perhaps, more often, just conceit. Yes, conceit."

"But I would hardly say that Walter Hudd had a sufficient motive."

"Wouldn't you?" said Miss Marple. "He hates it here. He wants to get away. He wants to get Gina away. And if it's really money he wants, it would be important for Gina to get all the money before she—er—definitely forms an attachment to someone else."

"An attachment to someone else," said Lewis, in an astonished voice.

Miss Marple wondered at the blindness of enthusiastic social reformers.

"That's what I said. Both the Restaricks are in love with her, you know."

"Oh I don't think so," said Lewis absently.

He went on:

"Stephen's invaluable to us—quite invaluable. The way he's got those lads coming along—keen—interested. They gave a splendid show last month. Scenery, costumes, everything. It just shows, as I've always said to Maverick, that it's lack of drama in their lives that leads these boys to crime. To dramatise yourself is a child's natural instinct. Maverick says —ah yes, Maverick—"

Lewis broke off.

"I want Maverick to see Inspector Curry about Edgar. The whole thing is so ridiculous really."

"What do you really know about Edgar Lawson, Mr. Serrocold?"

"Everything," said Lewis positively. "Everything, that is, that one needs to know. His background, upbringing—his deep-seated lack of confidence in himself—"

Miss Marple interrupted.

"Couldn't Edgar Lawson have poisoned Mrs. Serrocold?" she asked.

"Hardly. He's only been here a few weeks. And anyway, it's ridiculous! Why should Edgar want to poison my wife? What could he possibly gain by doing so?"

"Nothing material, I know. But he might have—some *odd* reason. He *is* odd, you know."

"You mean unbalanced?"

"I suppose so. No, I don't—not quite. What I mean is he's all *wrong.*"

It was not a very lucid exposition of what she felt. Lewis Serrocold accepted the words at their face value.

"Yes," he said with a sigh. "He's all wrong, poor lad. And he was showing such marked improvement. I can't really understand why he had this sudden setback . . ."

Miss Marple leaned forward eagerly.

"Yes, that's what I wondered. If—"

She broke off as Inspector Curry came into the room.

12

LEWIS SERROCOLD went away and Inspector Curry sat down and gave Miss Marple a rather peculiar smile.

"So Mr. Serrocold has been asking you to act as watch dog," he said.

"Well, yes," she added apologetically. "I hope you don't mind—"

"*I* don't mind. I think it's a very good idea. Does Mr. Serrocold know just how well qualified you are for the post?"

"I don't quite understand, Inspector."

"I see. He thinks you're just a very nice elderly lady who was at school with his wife." He shook his head at her. "We know you're a bit more than that, Miss Marple, aren't you? Crime is right down your street. Mr. Serrocold only knows one aspect of crime—the promising beginners. Makes me a bit sick, sometimes. Daresay I'm wrong and old-fashioned. But there are plenty of good decent lads about, lads who could do with a start in life. But there, honesty has to be its own reward—millionaires don't leave trust funds to help the worth while. Well—well, don't pay any attention to me. I'm old-fashioned. I've seen boys—and girls—with everything against them, bad homes, bad luck, every disadvantage, and they've had the grit to win through. That's the kind I shall leave my packet to, if I ever have one. But then, of course, that's what I never shall have. Just my pension and a nice bit of garden."

He nodded his head at Miss Marple.

"Superintendent Blacker told me about you last night. Said you'd had a lot of experience of the seamy side of human nature. Well now, let's have your point of view. Who's the nigger in the woodpile? The G.I. husband?"

"That," said Miss Marple, "would be very convenient for everybody."

Inspector Curry smiled softly to himself.

"A G.I. pinched my best girl," he said reminiscently. "Naturally, I'm prejudiced. His manner doesn't help. Let's have the amateur point of view. Who's been secretly and systematically poisoning Mrs. Serrocold?"

"Well," said Miss Marple judicially, "one is always inclined, human nature being what it is, to think of the *husband.* Or if it's the other way round, the wife. That's the first assumption, don't you think, in a poisoning case?"

"I agree with you every time," said Inspector Curry.

"But really—in this case—" Miss Marple shook her head. "No, frankly—I can *not* seriously consider Mr. Serrocold. Because you see, Inspector, he really *is* devoted to his wife. Naturally he would make a parade of being so—but it isn't a parade. It's very quiet, but it's genuine. He loves his wife, and I'm quite certain he wouldn't poison her."

"To say nothing of the fact that he wouldn't have any motive for doing so. She's made over her money to him already."

"Of course," said Miss Marple primly, "there are other reasons for a gentleman wanting his wife out of the way. An attachment to a young woman, for instance. But I really don't see any signs of it in this case. Mr. Serrocold does not act as though he had any romantic preoccupation. I'm really afraid," she sounded quite regretful about it, "we shall have to wash him out."

"Regrettable, isn't it?" said the Inspector. He grinned. "And anyway, he couldn't have killed Gulbrandsen. It seems to me that there's no doubt that the one thing hinges on the other. Whoever is poisoning Mrs. Serrocold killed Gulbrandsen to prevent him spilling the beans. What we've got to get at now is who had an opportunity to kill Gulbrandsen last night. And our prize suspect—there's no doubt about it—is young Walter Hudd. It was he who switched on a reading lamp which resulted in a fuse going, thereby giving him the opportunity to leave the Hall and go to the fuse box. The fuse box is in the kitchen passage which opens off from the main corridor. It was during his absence from the Great Hall that the shot was heard. So that's suspect No. 1 perfectly placed for committing the crime."

"And suspect No. 2?" asked Miss Marple.

"Suspect 2 is Alex Restarick who was alone in his car between the lodge and the house and took too long getting there."

"Anybody else?" Miss Marple leaned forward eagerly—remembering to add: "It's very kind of you to tell me all this."

"It's not kindness," said Inspector Curry. "I've got to have your help. You put your finger on the spot when you said 'Anybody else?' Because there I've got to depend on *you*. You were there, in the Hall last night, and you can tell me *who left it*. . . ."

"Yes—yes, I ought to be able to tell you . . . But can I? You see—the circumstances—"

"You mean that you were all listening to the argument going on behind the door of Mr. Serrocold's study."

Miss Marple nodded vehemently.

"Yes, you see we were all really very frightened. Mr. Lawson looked—he really did—quite demented. Apart from Mrs. Serrocold who seemed quite unaffected, we all feared that he would do a mischief to Mr. Serrocold. He was shouting, you know, and saying the most terrible things —we could hear them quite plainly—and what with that and with most of the lights being out—I didn't really notice anything else."

"You mean that whilst that scene was going on, anybody could have slipped out of the Hall, gone along the corridor, shot Mr. Gulbrandsen and slipped back again?"

"I think it would have been possible . . ."

"Could you say definitely that anybody was in the Great Hall the whole time?"

Miss Marple considered.

"I could say that Mrs. Serrocold was—because I was watching her. She was sitting quite close to the study door, and she never moved from her seat. It surprised me, you know, that she was able to remain so calm."

"And the others?"

"Miss Bellever went out—but I think—I am almost sure—that that was *after* the shot. Mrs. Strete? I really don't know. She was sitting behind me, you see. Gina was over by the far window. I *think* she remained there the whole time but of course I cannot be sure. Stephen was at the piano. He stopped playing when the quarrel began to get heated—"

"We mustn't be misled by the time you heard the shot," said Inspector Curry. "That's a trick that's been done before now, you know. Fake up a shot so as to fix the time of a crime, and fix it wrong. *If* Miss Bellever had cooked up something of that kind (far fetched—but you never know) then she'd leave as she did, openly, after the shot was heard. No, we can't go by the shot. The limits are between when Christian Gulbrandsen left the Hall to the moment when Miss Bellever found him dead, and we can only eliminate those people who were known not to have had opportunity. That gives us Lewis Serrocold and young Edgar Lawson in the study, and Mrs. Serrocold in the Hall. It's very unfortunate, of course, that Gulbrandsen should be shot on the same evening that this schemozzle happened between Serrocold and this young Lawson."

"Just unfortunate, you think?" murmured Miss Marple.

"Oh? What do you think?"

"It occurred to me," murmured Miss Marple, "that it might have been *contrived.*"

"So that's your idea?"

"Well, everybody seems to think it very odd that Edgar Lawson should quite suddenly have a relapse, so to speak. He'd got this curious complex, or whatever the term is, about his unknown father. Winston Churchill and Viscount Montgomery—all quite likely in his state of mind. Just any famous man he happened to think of. But suppose somebody puts it into his head that it's Lewis Serrocold who is really his father, that it's Lewis Serrocold who has been persecuting him—that he ought by rights to be the Crown Prince as it were of Stonygates. In his weak mental state he'll accept the idea—work himself up into a frenzy, and sooner or later will make the kind of scene he did make. And what a wonderful cover *that* will be! Everybody will have their attention fixed on the dangerous situation that is developing—especially if somebody has thoughtfully supplied him with a revolver."

"Hm, yes. Walter Hudd's revolver."

"Oh yes," said Miss Marple, "I'd thought of that. But you know, Walter is uncommunicative and he's certainly sullen and ungracious, but I don't really think he's *stupid.*"

"So you don't think it's Walter?"

"I think everybody would be very relieved if it *was* Walter. That sounds very unkind, but it's because he is an outsider."

"What about his wife?" asked Inspector Curry. "Would she be relieved?"

Miss Marple did not answer. She was thinking of Gina and Stephen Restarick standing together as she had seen them on her first day. And she thought of the way Alex Restarick's eyes had gone straight to Gina as he had entered the Hall last night. What was Gina's own attitude?

2

Two hours later Inspector Curry tilted back his chair, stretched himself and sighed.

"Well," he said, "We've cleared a good deal of ground."

Sergeant Lake agreed.

"The servants are out," he said. "They were together all through the critical period—those that sleep here. The ones that don't live in had gone home."

Curry nodded. He was suffering from mental fatigue.

He had interviewed physiotherapists, members of the teaching staff, and what he called to himself the "two young lags" whose turn it had been to dine with the family that night. All their stories dovetailed and checked. He could write them off. Their activities and habits were communal. There were no lonely souls among them. Which was useful for the purpose of alibis. Curry had kept Dr. Maverick who was, as far as he could judge, the chief person in charge of the Institute, to the end.

"But we'll have him in now, Lake."

So the young doctor bustled in, neat and spruce and rather inhuman looking behind his pince nez.

Maverick confirmed the statements of his staff, and agreed with Curry's findings. There had been no slackness, no loophole in the College impregnability. Christian Gulbrandsen's death could not be laid to the account of the "young patients" as Curry almost called them—so hypnotized had he become by the fervent medical atmosphere.

"But patients is exactly what they are, Inspector," said Dr. Maverick with a little smile.

It was a superior smile, and Inspector Curry would not have been human if he had not resented it just a little.

He said professionally:

"Now as regards your own movements, Dr. Maverick? Can you give me an account of them?"

"Certainly. I have jotted them down for you with the approximate times."

Dr. Maverick had left the Great Hall at fifteen minutes after nine with Mr. Lacy and Dr. Baumgarten. They had gone to Dr. Baumgarten's rooms where they had all three remained discussing certain courses of treatment until Miss Bellever had come hurrying in and asked Dr. Maverick to go to the Great Hall. That was at approximately half past nine. He had gone at once to the Hall and had found Edgar Lawson in a state of collapse.

Inspector Curry stirred a little.

"Just a minute, Dr. Maverick. Is this young man, in your opinion, definitely a mental case?"

Dr. Maverick smiled the superior smile again.

"We are all mental cases, Inspector Curry."

Tomfool answer, thought the Inspector. He knew quite well *he* wasn't a mental case, whatever Dr. Maverick might be!

"Is he responsible for his actions? He knows what he is doing, I suppose?"

"Perfectly."

"Then when he fired that revolver at Mr. Serrocold it was definitely attempted murder."

"No, no, Inspector Curry. Nothing of *that* kind."

"Come now, Dr. Maverick. I've seen the two bullet holes in the wall. They must have gone dangerously near to Mr. Serrocold's head."

"Perhaps. But Lawson had no intention of killing Mr. Serrocold or even of wounding him. He is very fond of Mr. Serrocold."

"It seems a curious way of showing it."

Dr. Maverick smiled again. Inspector Curry found that smile very trying.

"Everything one does is intentional. Every time you, Inspector, forget a name or a face it is because, unconsciously, you *wish* to forget it."

Inspector Curry looked unbelieving.

"Every time you make a slip of the tongue, that slip has a meaning. Edgar Lawson was standing a few feet away from Mr. Serrocold. He could easily have shot him dead. Instead, he missed him. Why did he miss him? Because he *wanted* to miss him. It is as simple as that. Mr. Serrocold was never in any danger—and Mr. Serrocold himself was quite aware of that fact. He understood Edgar's gesture for exactly what it was —a gesture of defiance and resentment against a universe that has denied him the simple necessities of a child's life—security and affection."

"I think I'd like to see this young man."

"Certainly if you wish. His outburst last night has had a cathartic effect. There is a great improvement today. Mr. Serrocold will be very pleased."

Inspector Curry stared hard at him, but Dr. Maverick was serious as always.

Curry sighed.

"Do you have any arsenic?" he asked.

"Arsenic?" The question took Dr. Maverick by surprise. It was clearly unexpected. "What a very curious question. Why arsenic?"

"Just answer the question, please."

"No, I have no arsenic of any kind in my possession."

"But you have some drugs?"

"Oh certainly. Sedatives. Morphia—the barbiturates. The usual things."

"Do you attend Mrs. Serrocold?"

"No. Dr. Gunter of Market Kimble is the family physician. I hold a medical degree, of course, but I practice purely as a psychiatrist."

"I see. Well, thank you very much, Dr. Maverick."

As Dr. Maverick went out, Inspector Curry murmured to Lake that psychiatrists gave him a pain in the neck.

"We'll get on to the family now," he said. "I'll see young Walter Hudd first."

Walter Hudd's attitude was cautious. He seemed to be studying the police officer with a slightly wary expression. But he was quite cooperative.

There was a good deal of defective wiring in Stonygates—the whole electric system was very old fashioned. They wouldn't stand for a system like that in the States.

"It was installed, I believe, by the late Mr. Gulbrandsen when electric light was a novelty," said Inspector Curry with a faint smile.

"I'll say that's so! Sweet old feudal English and never been brought up to date."

The fuse which controlled most of the lights in the Great Hall had gone and he had gone out to the fuse box to see about it. In due course he got it repaired and came back.

"How long were you away?"

"Why that I couldn't say for sure. The fuse box is in an awkward place. I had to get steps and a candle. I was maybe ten minutes—perhaps a quarter of an hour."

"Did you hear a shot?"

"Why no, I didn't hear anything like that. There are double doors through to the kitchen quarters and one of them is lined with a kind of felt."

"I see. And when you came back into the Hall, what did you see?"

"They were all crowded round the door into Mr. Serrocold's study. Mrs. Strete said that Mr. Serrocold had been shot—but actually that wasn't so. Mr. Serrocold was quite all right. The boob had missed him."

"You recognised the revolver?"

"Sure I recognised it! It was mine."

"When did you see it last?"

"Two or three days ago."

"Where did you keep it?"

"In the drawer in my room."

"Who knew that you kept it there?"

"I wouldn't know who knows what in this house."

"What do you mean by that, Mr. Hudd?"

"Aw, they're all nuts!"

"When you came into the Hall, was everybody else there?"

"What d'you mean by everybody?"

"The same people who were there when you went to repair the fuse."

"Gina was there . . . and the old lady with white hair—and Miss Bellever. . . . I didn't notice particularly—but I should say so."

"Mr. Gulbrandsen arrived quite unexpectedly the day before yesterday, did he not!"

"I guess so. It wasn't his usual routine, I understand."

"Did anyone seem upset by his arrival?"

Walter Hudd took a moment or two before he answered:

"Why no, I wouldn't say so."

Once more there was a touch of caution in his manner.

"Have you any idea why he came?"

"Their precious Gulbrandsen Trust I suppose. The whole setup here is crazy."

"You have these 'setups' as you call it, in the States."

"It's one thing to endow a scheme, and another to give it the personal touch as they do here. I had enough of psychiatrists in the Army. This place is stiff with them. Teaching young thugs to make raffia baskets and carve pipe racks. Kids' games! It's sissy!"

Inspector Curry did not comment on this criticism. Possibly he agreed with it.

He said, eyeing Walter carefully:

"So you have no idea who could have killed Mr. Gulbrandsen?"

"One of the bright boys from the College practising his technique, I'd say."

"No, Mr. Hudd, that's out. The College, in spite of its carefully produced atmosphere of freedom, is none the less a place of detention and is run on those lines. Nobody can run in and out of it after dark and commit murders."

"I wouldn't put it past them! Well—if you want to fix it nearer home, I'd say your best bet was Alex Restarick."

"Why do you say that?"

"He had the opportunity. He drove up through the grounds alone in his car."

"And why should he kill Christian Gulbrandsen?"

Walter shrugged his shoulders.

"I'm a stranger. I don't know the family setups. Maybe the old boy had heard something about Alex and was going to spill the beans to the Serrocolds."

"With what result?"

"They might cut off the dough. He can use dough—uses a good deal of it by all accounts."

"You mean—in theatrical enterprises?"

"That's what he calls it?"

"Do you suggest it was otherwise?"

Again Walter Hudd shrugged his shoulders.

"I wouldn't know," he said.

13

ALEX RESTARICK was voluble. He also gestured with his hands.

"I know, I know! I'm the ideal suspect. I drive down here alone and on the way to the house, I get a creative fit. I can't expect you to understand. How should you?"

"I might," Curry put in drily, but Alex Restarick swept on.

"It's just one of those things! They come upon you there's no knowing when or how. An effect—an idea—and everything else goes to the winds. I'm producing *Limehouse Nights* next month. Suddenly—last night—the setup was wonderful . . . *The* perfect lighting. Fog—and the headlights cutting through the fog and being thrown back—and reflecting dimly a tall pile of buildings. Everything helped! The shots—the running footsteps—and the chug chugging of the electric power engine—could have been a launch on the Thames. And I thought—that's it—but what am I going to use to get just these effects?—and—"

Inspector Curry broke in.

"You heard shots? Where?"

"Out of the fog, Inspector." Alex waved his hands in the air—plump well kept hands. "Out of the fog. That was the wonderful part about it."

"It didn't occur to you that anything was wrong?"

"Wrong? Why should it?"

"Are shots such a usual occurrence?"

"Ah, I knew you wouldn't understand! The shots fitted into the scene I was creating. I *wanted* shots. Danger—opium—crazy business. What did I care what they were really? Backfires from a lorry on the road? A poacher after rabbits?"

"They snare rabbits mostly round here."

Alex swept on:

"A child letting off fireworks? I didn't even think about them *as*—shots. I was in Limehouse—or rather at the back of the stalls—looking at Limehouse."

"How many shots?"

"I don't know," said Alex petulantly. "Two or three. Two close together, I do remember that."

Inspector Curry nodded.

"And the sound of running footsteps, I think you said? Where were they?"

"They came to me out of the fog. Somewhere near the house."

Inspector Curry said gently:

"That would suggest that the murderer of Christian Gulbrandsen came from *outside.*"

"Of course. Why not? You don't really suggest, do you, that he came from inside the house?"

Still very gently, Inspector Curry said:

"We have to think of everything."

"I suppose so," said Alex Restarick generously. "What a soul destroying job yours must be, Inspector! The details, the times and places, the petifogging *pettiness* of it. And in the end—what good is it all? Does it bring the wretched Christian Gulbrandsen back to life?"

"There's quite a satisfaction in getting your man, Mr. Restarick."

"The Wild Western touch!"

"Did you know Mr. Gulbrandsen well?"

"Not well enough to murder him, Inspector. I had met him, off and on, since I lived here as a boy. He made brief appearances from time to time. One of our captains of industry. The type does not interest me. He has quite a collection, I believe, of Thorwaldsen's statuary—" Alex shuddered. "That speaks for itself, does it not? My God, these rich men!"

Inspector Curry eyed him meditatively. Then he said: "Do you take any interest in poisons, Mr. Restarick?"

"In poisons? My dear man, he was surely not poisoned first and shot afterwards. That would be too madly detective story."

"He was not poisoned. But you haven't answered my question."

"Poison has a certain appeal . . . It has not the crudeness of the revolver bullet or the blunt weapon. I have no special knowledge of the subject, if that is what you mean."

"Have you ever had arsenic in your possession?"

"In sandwiches—after the show? The idea has its allurements. You don't know Rose Glidon? These actresses who think they have a name! No, I have never thought of arsenic. One extracts it from weed killers or flypapers, I believe."

"How often are you down here, Mr. Restarick?"

"It varies, Inspector. Sometimes not for several weeks. But I try to get down for week ends whenever I can. I always regard Stonygates as my true home."

"Mrs. Serrocold has encouraged you to do so?"

"What I owe Mrs. Serrocold can never be repaid. Sympathy, under-standing, affection—"

"And quite a lot of solid cash as well, I believe?"

Alex looked faintly disgusted.

"She treats me as a son, and she has belief in my work."

"Has she ever spoken to you about her will?"

"Certainly. But may I ask what is the point of all these questions, Inspector? There is nothing wrong with Mrs. Serrocold."

"There had better not be," said Inspector Curry grimly.

"Now what can you possibly mean by that?"

"If you don't know, so much the better," said Inspector Curry. "And if you do—I'm warning you."

When Alex had gone Sergeant Lake said:

"Pretty bogus, would you say?"

Curry shook his head.

"Difficult to say. He may have genuine creative talent. He may just like living soft and talking big. One doesn't know. Heard running footsteps, did he? I'd be prepared to bet he made that up."

"For any particular reason?"

"Definitely for a particular reason. We haven't come to it yet, but we will."

"After all, sir, one of those smart lads may have got out of the College buildings unbeknownst. Probably a few cat burglars amongst them, and if so—"

"That's what we're meant to think. Very convenient. But if that's so, Lake, I'll eat my new soft hat."

2

"I was at the piano," said Stephen Restarick. "I'd been strumming softly when the row blew up. Between Lewis and Edgar."

"What did you think of it?"

"Well—to tell the truth I didn't really take it seriously. The poor beg-gar has these fits of venom. He's not really loopy, you know. All this nonsense is a kind of blowing off steam. The truth is, we all get under his skin—particularly Gina, of course."

"Gina? You mean Mrs. Hudd? Why does she get under his skin?"

"Because she's a woman—and a beautiful woman, and because she thinks he's funny! She's half Italian, you know, and the Italians have that unconscious vein of cruelty. They've no compassion for anyone who's old or ugly, or peculiar in any way. They point with their fingers and jeer. That's what Gina did, metaphorically speaking. She'd no use for young Edgar. He was ridiculous, pompous, and at bottom fundamentally unsure of himself. He wanted to impress, and he only succeeded in looking silly. It wouldn't mean anything to her that the poor fellow suffered a lot."

"Are you suggesting that Edgar Lawson is in love with Mrs. Hudd?" asked Inspector Curry.

Stephen replied cheerfully:

"Oh yes. As a matter of fact we all are, more or less! She likes us that way."

"Does her husband like it?"

"He takes a dim view. He suffers, too, poor fellow. The thing can't last, you know. Their marriage, I mean. It will break up before long. It was just one of these war affairs."

"This is all very interesting," said the Inspector. "But we're getting away from our subject which is the murder of Christian Gulbrandsen."

"Quite," said Stephen. "But I can't tell you anything about it. I sat at the piano, and I didn't leave the piano until dear Jolly came in with some rusty old keys and tried to fit one to the lock of the study door."

"You stayed at the piano. Did you continue to play the piano?"

"A gentle obbligato to the life and death struggle in Lewis's study? No, I stopped playing when the tempo rose. Not that I had any doubts as to the outcome. Lewis has what I can only describe as a dynamic eye. He could easily break up Edgar just by looking at him."

"Yet Edgar Lawson fired two shots at him."

Stephen shook his head gently.

"Just putting on an act, that was. Enjoying himself. My dear mother used to do it. She died or ran away with someone when I was four but I remember her blazing off with a pistol if anything upset her. She did it at a night club once. Made a pattern on the wall. She was an excellent shot. Quite a bit of trouble she caused. She was a Russian dancer, you know."

"Indeed. Can you tell me, Mr. Restarick, who left the Hall yesterday evening whilst you were there—during the relevant time?"

"Wally—to fix the lights. Juliet Bellever to find a key to fit the study door. Nobody else, as far as I know."

"Would you have noticed if somebody did?"

Stephen considered.

"Probably not. That is if they just tiptoed out and back again. It was so dark in the Hall—and there was the fight to which we were all listening avidly."

"Is there anyone you are sure *was* there the whole time?"

"Mrs. Serrocold—yes, and Gina. I'd swear to them."

"Thank you, Mr. Restarick."

Stephen went towards the door. Then he hesitated and came back.

"What's all this," he said, "about arsenic?"

"Who mentioned arsenic to you?"

"My brother."

"Ah—yes."

Stephen said:

"Has somebody been giving Mrs. Serrocold arsenic?"

"Why should you mention Mrs. Serrocold?"

"I've read of the symptoms of arsenical poisoning. Peripheral neuritis, isn't it? It would square more or less with what she's been suffering from lately. And then Lewis snatching away her tonic last night. Is *that* what's been going on here?"

"The matter is under investigation," said Inspector Curry in his most official manner.

"Does she know about it herself?"

"Mr. Serrocold was particularly anxious that she should not be— alarmed."

"Alarmed isn't the right word, Inspector. Mrs. Serrocold is never alarmed . . . Is that what lies behind Christian Gulbrandsen's death? Did he find out she was being poisoned—but how could he find out? Anyway, the whole thing seems most improbable. It doesn't make sense."

"It surprises you very much, does it, Mr. Restarick?"

"Yes, indeed. When Alex spoke to me I could hardly believe it."

"Who, in your opinion, would be likely to administer arsenic to Mrs. Serrocold?"

For a moment a grin appeared upon Stephen Restarick's handsome face.

"Not the usual person. You can wash out the husband. Lewis Serrocold's got nothing to gain. And also he worships that woman. He can't bear her to have an ache in her little finger."

"Who then? Have you any idea?"

"Oh yes. I'd say it was a certainty."

"Explain please."

Stephen shook his head.

"It's a certainty psychologically speaking. Not in any other way. No evidence of any kind. And you probably wouldn't agree."

Stephen Restarick went out nonchalantly, and Inspector Curry drew cats on the sheet of paper in front of him.

He was thinking three things. A, that Stephen Restarick thought a good deal of himself, B, that Stephen Restarick and his brother presented a united front, and C, that Stephen Restarick was a handsome man where Walter Hudd was a plain one.

He wondered about two other things—what Stephen meant by "psychologically speaking" and whether Stephen could possibly have seen Gina from his seat at the piano. He rather thought not.

3

Into the Gothic gloom of the library, Gina brought an exotic glow. Even Inspector Curry blinked a little at the radiant young woman who sat down, leaned forward over the table and said expectantly, "Well?"

Inspector Curry, observing her scarlet shirt and dark green slacks said drily:

"I see you're not wearing mourning, Mrs. Hudd?"

"I haven't got any," said Gina. "I know everyone is supposed to have a little black number and wear it with pearls. But I don't. I hate black. I think it's hideous, and only receptionists and housekeepers and people like that ought to wear it. Anyway Christian Gulbrandsen wasn't really a relation. He's my grandmother's stepson."

"And I suppose you didn't know him very well?"

Gina shook her head.

"He came here three or four times when I was a child, but then in the war I went to America, and I only came back here to live about six months ago."

"You have definitely come back here to live? You're not just on a visit?"

"I haven't really thought," said Gina.

"You were in the Great Hall last night, when Mr. Gulbrandsen went to his room?"

"Yes. He said good night and went away. Grandam asked if he had everything he wanted and he said yes—that Jolly had fixed him up fine. Not those words, but that kind of thing. He said he had letters to write."

"And then?"

Gina described the scene between Lewis and Edgar Lawson. It was the same story as Inspector Curry had by now heard many times, but it took an added colour, a new gusto, under Gina's handling. It became drama.

"It was Wally's revolver," she said. "Fancy Edgar's having the guts to go and pinch it out of his room. I'd never have believed he'd have the guts."

"Were you alarmed when they went into the study and Edgar Lawson locked the door?"

"Oh no," said Gina, opening her enormous brown eyes very wide. "I loved it. It was so ham, you know, and so madly theatrical. Everything Edgar does is always ridiculous. One can't take him seriously for a moment."

"He did fire the revolver, though?"

"Yes. We all thought then that he'd shot Lewis after all."

"And did you enjoy that?" Inspector Curry could not refrain from asking.

"Oh no, I was terrified, then. Everyone was, except Grandam. She never turned a hair."

"That seems rather remarkable."

"Not really. She's that kind of person. Not quite in this world. She's the sort of person who never believes *anything* bad can happen. She's sweet."

"During all this scene, who was in the Hall?"

"Oh we were all there. Except Uncle Christian, of course."

"Not *all,* Mrs. Hudd. People went in and out."

"Did they?" asked Gina vaguely.

"Your husband, for instance, went out to fix the lights."

"Yes. Wally's great at fixing things."

"During his absence, a shot was heard, I understand. A shot that you all thought came from the Park?"

"I don't remember that . . . Oh yes, it was just after the lights had come on again and Wally had come back."

"Did anyone else leave the Hall?"

"I don't think so. I don't remember."

"Where were you sitting, Mrs. Hudd?"

"Over by the window."

"Near the door to the library?"

"Yes."

"Did you yourself leave the Hall at all?"

"Leave? With all the excitement? Of course not."

Gina sounded scandalised by the idea.

"Where were the others sitting?"

"Mostly round the fireplace, I think. Aunt Mildred was knitting and so was Aunt Jane—Miss Marple, I mean—Grandam was just sitting."

"And Mr. Stephen Restarick?"

"Stephen? He was playing the piano to begin with. I don't know where he went later."

"And Miss Bellever?"

"Fussing about, as usual. She practically never sits down. She was looking for keys or something."

She said suddenly:

"What's all this about Grandam's tonic? Did the chemist make a mistake in making it up or something?"

"Why should you think that?"

"Because the bottle's disappeared and Jolly's been fussing round madly looking for it, in no end of a stew. Alex told her the police had taken it away. Did you?"

Instead of replying to the question, Inspector Curry said:

"Miss Bellever was upset, you say?"

"Oh! Jolly always fusses," said Gina carelessly. "She likes fussing. Sometimes I wonder how Grandam can stand it."

"Just one last question, Mrs. Hudd. You've no ideas yourself as to who killed Christian Gulbrandsen and why?"

"One of the queers did it, I should think. The thug ones are really quite sensible. I mean they only cosh people so as to rob a till or get money or jewellery—not just for fun. But one of the queers—you know, what they call mentally maladjusted—might do it for fun, don't you think? Because I can't see what other reason there could be for killing Uncle Christian except fun, do you? At least I don't mean fun, exactly—but—"

"You can't think of a motive?"

"Yes, that's what I mean," said Gina gratefully. "He wasn't robbed or anything, was he?"

"But you know, Mrs. Hudd, the College buildings were locked and barred. Nobody could get out from there without a pass."

"Don't you believe it," Gina laughed merrily. "Those boys could get out from anywhere! They've taught me a lot of tricks."

"She's a lively one," said Lake when Gina had departed. "First time I've seen her close up. Lovely figure, hasn't she. Sort of a foreign figure, if you know what I mean."

Inspector Curry threw him a cold glance. Sergeant Lake said hastily that she was a merry one. "Seems to have enjoyed it all, as you might say."

"Whether Stephen Restarick is right or not about her marriage breaking up, I notice that she went out of her way to mention that Walter Hudd was back in the Great Hall, before that shot was heard."

"Which according to everyone else, isn't so?"

"Exactly."

"She didn't mention Miss Bellever leaving the Hall to look for keys, either."

"No," said the Inspector thoughtfully, "she didn't. . . ."

14

MRS. STRETE fitted into the library very much better than Gina Hudd had done. There was nothing exotic about Mrs. Strete. She wore black with onyx beads, and she wore a hairnet over carefully arranged grey hair.

She looked, Inspector Curry reflected, exactly as the relict of a Canon of the Established Church should look—which was almost odd, because so few people ever did look like what they really were.

Even the tight line of her lips had an ascetic Ecclesiastical flavour. She expressed Christian Endurance, and possibly Christian Fortitude. But not, Curry thought, Christian Charity.

Moreover it was clear that Mrs. Strete was offended.

"I should have thought that you could have given me *some* idea of when you would want me, Inspector. I have been forced to sit around waiting all the morning."

It was, Curry judged, her sense of importance that was hurt. He hastened to pour oil on the troubled waters.

"I'm very sorry, Mrs. Strete. Perhaps you don't quite know how we set about these things. We start, you know, with the less important evidence —get it out of the way, so to speak. It's valuable to keep to the last a person on whose judgement we can rely—a good observer—by whom we can check what has been told us up to date."

Mrs. Strete softened visibly.

"Oh I see. I hadn't quite realised . . ."

"Now you're a woman of mature judgement, Mrs. Strete. A woman of the world. And then this is your home—you're the daughter of the house, and you can tell me all about the people who are in it."

"I can certainly do that," said Mildred Strete.

"So you see that when we come to the question of who killed Christian Gulbrandsen, you can help us a great deal."

"But is there any question? Isn't it perfectly obvious who killed my brother?"

Inspector Curry leant back in his chair. His hand stroked his small neat moustache.

"Well—we have to be careful," he said. "You think it's obvious?"

"Of course. That dreadful American husband of poor Gina's. He's the only stranger here. We know absolutely nothing about him. He's probably one of these dreadful American gangsters."

"But that wouldn't quite account for his killing Christian Gulbrandsen, would it? Why should he?"

"Because Christian had found out something about him. That's what he came here for so soon after his last visit."

"Are you sure of that, Mrs. Strete?"

"Again it seems to me quite obvious. He let it be thought his visit was in connection with the Trust—but that's nonsense. He was here for that only a month ago. And nothing of importance has arisen since. So he must have come on some private business. He saw Walter on his last visit, and he may have recognised him—or perhaps made inquiries about him in the States—naturally he has agents all over the world—and found out something really damaging. Gina is a very silly girl. She always has been. It is just like her to marry a man she knows nothing about—she's always been man mad! A man wanted by the police, perhaps, or a man who's already married, or some bad character in the underworld. But my brother Christian wasn't an easy man to deceive. He came here, I'm sure, to settle the whole business. Expose Walter and show him up for what he is. And so, naturally, Walter shot him."

Inspector Curry, adding some out-sized whiskers to one of the cats on his blotting pad, said:

"Ye—es."

"Don't you agree with me that that's what *must* have happened?"

"It could be—yes," admitted the Inspector.

"What other solution could there be? Christian had no enemies. What I can't understand is why you haven't already arrested Walter?"

"Well, you see, Mrs. Strete, we have to have evidence."

"You could probably get that easily enough. If you wired to America—"

"Oh yes, we shall check up on Mr. Walter Hudd. You can be sure of that. But until we can prove motive, there's not very much to go upon. There's opportunity, of course—"

"He went out just after Christian, pretending the lights had fused—"

"They did fuse."

"He could easily arrange that."

"True."

"That gave him his excuse. He followed Christian to his room, shot him and then repaired the fuse and came back to the Hall."

"His wife says he came back before you heard the shots from outside."

"Not a bit of it! Gina would say anything. The Italians are never truthful. And she's a Roman Catholic, of course."

Inspector Curry sidestepped the ecclesiastical angle.

"You think his wife was in it with him?"

Mildred Strete hesitated for a moment.

"No—no, I don't think that." She seemed rather disappointed not to think so. She went on: "That must have been partly the motive—to prevent Gina's learning the truth about him. After all, Gina is his bread and butter."

"And a very beautiful girl."

"Oh yes. I've always said Gina is good-looking. A very common type in Italy, of course. But if you ask me, it's *money* that Walter Hudd is after. That's why he came over here and has settled down living on the Serrocolds."

"Mrs. Hudd is very well off, I understand?"

"Not at present. My father settled the same sum on Gina's mother, as he did on me. But of course she took her husband's nationality (I believe the law is altered now) and what with the war and his being a Fascist, Gina has very little of her own. My mother spoils her, and her American aunt, Mrs. Van Rydock, spent fabulous sums on her and bought her everything she wanted during the war years. Nevertheless, from Walter's point of view, he can't lay his hands on much until my mother's death when a very large fortune will come to Gina."

"And to you, Mrs. Strete."

A faint colour came into Mildred Strete's cheek.

"And to me, as you say. My husband and myself always lived quietly. He spent very little money except on books—he was a great scholar. My own money has almost doubled itself. It is more than enough for my simple needs. Still one can always use money for benefit of others. Any money that comes to me, I shall regard as a sacred trust."

"But it won't be in a Trust, will it?" said Curry wilfully misunderstanding. "It will come to you absolutely."

"Oh yes—in that sense. Yes, it will be mine absolutely."

Something in the ring of that last word made Inspector Curry raise his head sharply. Mrs. Strete was not looking at him. Her eyes were shining and her long thin mouth was curved in a triumphant smile.

Inspector Curry said in a considering voice:

"So in your view—and of course you've had ample opportunities of judging—Master Walter Hudd wants the money that will come to his wife when Mrs. Serrocold dies. By the way, she's not very strong is she, Mrs. Strete?"

"My mother has always been delicate."

"Quite so. But delicate people often live as long or longer than people who have robust health."

"Yes, I suppose they do."

"You haven't noticed your mother's health failing just lately?"

"She suffers from rheumatism. But then one must have something as one grows older. I've no sympathy with people who make a fuss over inevitable aches and pains."

"Does Mrs. Serrocold make a fuss?"

Mildred Strete was silent for a moment. She said at last:

"She does not make a fuss herself, but she is used to being made a fuss of. My stepfather is far too solicitous. And as for Miss Bellever, she makes herself positively ridiculous. In any case, Miss Bellever has had a very bad influence in this house. She came here many years ago, and her devotion to my mother, though admirable in itself, has really become somewhat of an infliction. She literally tyrannises over my mother. She runs the whole house and takes far too much upon herself. I think it annoys Lewis sometimes. I should never be surprised if he told her to go. She has no tact—no tact whatever, and it is trying for a man to find his wife completely dominated by a bossy woman."

Inspector Curry nodded his head gently.

"I see . . . I see . . ."

He watched her speculatively.

"There's one thing I don't quite get, Mrs. Strete. The position of the two Restarick brothers?"

"More foolish sentiment. Their father married my poor mother for her money. Two years afterwards he ran away with a Yugoslavian singer of the lowest morals. He was a very unworthy person. My mother was soft-hearted enough to be sorry for these two boys. Since it was out of the question for them to spend their holidays with a woman of such notorious morals, she more or less adopted them. They have been hangers on here ever since. Oh yes, we've plenty of spongers in this house, I can tell you that."

"Alex Restarick had an opportunity of killing Christian Gulbrandsen. He was in his car alone—driving from the Lodge to the house—what about Stephen?"

"Stephen was in the Hall with us. I don't approve of Alex Restarick—he is getting to look very coarse and I imagine he leads an irregular life—but I don't really see him as a murderer. Besides, why should he kill my brother?"

"That's what we always come back to, isn't it?" said Inspector Curry genially. "What did Christian Gulbrandsen know—about someone—that made it necessary for that someone to kill him?"

"Exactly," said Mrs. Strete triumphantly. "It *must* be Walter Hudd."

"Unless it's someone nearer home."

Mildred said sharply,

"What did you mean by that?"

Inspector Curry said slowly:

"Mr. Gulbrandsen seemed very concerned about Mrs. Serrocold's health whilst he was here."

Mrs. Strete frowned.

"Men always fuss over Mother because she looks fragile. I think she likes them to! Or else Christian had been listening to Juliet Bellever."

"You're not worried about your mother's health yourself, Mrs. Strete?"

"No. I hope I'm sensible. Naturally Mother is not young—"

"And death comes to all of us," said Inspector Curry. "But not ahead of its appointed time. That's what we have to prevent."

He spoke meaningly. Mildred Strete flared into sudden animation.

"Oh it's wicked—wicked. No one else here really seems to care. Why should they? I'm the only person who was a blood relation to Christian. To Mother, he was only a grown-up stepson. To Gina, he isn't really any relation at all. But he was my own brother."

"Half brother," suggested Inspector Curry.

"Half brother, yes. But we were both Gulbrandsens in spite of the difference in age."

Curry said gently,

"Yes—yes, I see your point . . ."

Tears in her eyes, Mildred Strete marched out. Curry looked at Lake.

"So she's quite certain it's Walter Hudd," he said. "Won't entertain for a moment the idea of its being anybody else."

"And she may be right."

"She certainly may. Wally fits. Opportunity—and motive. Because if he wants money quick, his wife's grandmother would have to die. So Wally tampers with her tonic, and Christian Gulbrandsen sees him do it —or hears about it in some way. Yes, it fits very nicely."

He paused and said:

"By the way, Mildred Strete likes money. . . . She mayn't spend it, but she likes it. I'm not sure why . . . She may be a miser—with a miser's passion. Or she may like the power that money gives. Money for benevolence, perhaps? She's a Gulbrandsen. She may want to emulate Father."

"Complex, isn't it?" said Sergeant Lake, and scratched his head.

Inspector Curry said,

"We'd better see this screwy young man Lawson and after that we'll go to the Great Hall and work out who was where—and if and why—and when . . . We've heard one or two rather interesting things this morning."

2

It was very difficult, Inspector Curry thought, to get a true estimate of someone from what other people said.

Edgar Lawson had been described by a good many different people that morning but looking at him now, Curry's own impressions were almost ludicrously different.

Edgar did not impress him as "queer" or "dangerous," or "arrogant" or even as "abnormal." He seemed a very ordinary young man, very much cast down and in a state of humility approaching that of Uriah Heep's. He looked young and slightly common and rather pathetic.

He was only too anxious to talk and to apologize.

"I know I've done very wrong. I don't know what came over me— really I don't. Making that scene and kicking up such a row. And actually shooting off a pistol. At Mr. Serrocold, too, who's been so good to me and so patient, too."

He twisted his hands nervously. They were rather pathetic hands, with bony wrists.

"If I've got to be had up for it, I'll come with you at once. I deserve it. I'll plead guilty."

"No charge has been made against you," said Inspector Curry crisply. "So we've no evidence on which to act. According to Mr. Serrocold, letting off the pistol was an accident."

"That's because he's so good. There never was a man as good as Mr. Serrocold! He's done everything for me. And I go and repay him by acting like this."

"What made you act as you did?"

Edgar looked embarrassed.

"I made a fool of myself."

Inspector Curry said drily,

"So it seems. You told Mr. Serrocold in the presence of witnesses that you had discovered that he was your father. Was that true?"

"No, it wasn't."

"What put that idea into your head? Did someone suggest it to you?"

"Well, it's a bit hard to explain."

Inspector Curry looked at him thoughtfully, then said in a kindly voice:

"Suppose you try. *We* don't want to make things hard for you."

"Well, you see, I had rather a hard time of it as a kid. The other boys jeered at me. Because I hadn't got a father. Said I was a little bastard— which I was, of course. Mum was usually drunk and she had men coming in all the time. My father was a foreign seaman, I believe. The house was always filthy and it was all pretty fair Hell. And then I got to thinking suppose my Dad had been not just some foreign sailor, but someone important—and I used to make up a thing or two. Kid stuff first— changed at birth—really the rightful heir—that sort of thing. And then I went to a new school and I tried it on once or twice hinting things. Said my father was really an Admiral in the Navy. I got to believing it myself. I didn't feel so bad then."

He paused and then went on.

"And then—later—I thought up some other ideas. I used to stay at hotels and told a lot of silly stories about being a fighter pilot—or about being in Military Intelligence. I got all sort of mixed up. I didn't seem able to stop telling lies.

"Only I didn't really try to get money by it. It was just swank so as to make people think a bit more of me. I didn't want to be dishonest. Mr. Serrocold will tell you—and Dr. Maverick—they've got all the stuff about it."

Inspector Curry nodded. He had already studied Edgar's case history and his police record.

"Mr. Serrocold got me clear in the end and brought me down here. He said he needed a secretary to help him—and I did help him! I really did. Only the others laughed at me. They were always laughing at me."

"What others? Mrs. Serrocold?"

"No, not Mrs. Serrocold. She's a lady—she's always gentle and kind. No, but Gina treated me like dirt. And Stephen Restarick. And Mrs. Strete looked down on me for not being a gentleman. So did Miss Bellever—and what's she? She's a paid companion, isn't she?"

Curry noted the signs of rising excitement.

"So you didn't find them very sympathetic?"

Edgar said passionately:

"It was because of me being a bastard. If I'd had a proper father they wouldn't have gone on like that."

"So you appropriated a couple of famous fathers?"

Edgar blushed.

"I always seem to get to telling lies," he muttered.

"And finally you said Mr. Serrocold was your father. Why?"

"Because that would stop them once for all, wouldn't it? If *he* was my father they couldn't do anything to me!"

"Yes. But you accused him of being your enemy—of persecuting you."

"I know—" He rubbed his forehead. "I got things all wrong. There are times when I don't—when I don't get things quite right. I get muddled."

"And you took the revolver from Mr. Walter Hudd's room?"

Edgar looked puzzled.

"Did I? Is that where I got it?"

"Don't you remember where you got it?"

Edgar said:

"I meant to threaten Mr. Serrocold with it. I meant to frighten him. It was kid stuff all over again."

Inspector Curry said patiently:

"How did you get the revolver?"

"You just said—out of Walter's room."

"You remember doing that now?"

"I must have got it from his room. I couldn't have got hold of it any other way, could I?"

"I don't know," said Inspector Curry. "Somebody—might have given it to you?"

Edgar was silent—his face a blank.

"Is that how it happened?"

Edgar said passionately:

"I don't remember. I was so worked up. I walked about the garden in a red mist of rage. I thought people were spying on me, watching me, trying to hound me down. Even that nice white haired old lady . . . I can't understand it all now. I feel I must have been mad. I don't remember where I was and what I was doing half of the time!"

"Surely you remember who told you Mr. Serrocold was your father?"

Edgar gave the same blank stare.

"Nobody told me," he said sullenly. "It just came to me."

Inspector Curry sighed. He was not satisfied. But he judged he could make no further progress at present.

"Well, watch your step in future," he said.

"Yes, sir. Yes, indeed I will."

As Edgar went Inspector Curry slowly shook his head.

"These pathological cases are the devil!"

"D'you think he's mad, sir?"

"Much less mad than I'd imagined. Weak headed, boastful, a liar—yet a certain pleasant simplicity about him. Highly suggestible I should imagine . . ."

"You think someone did suggest things to him?"

"Oh yes, old Miss Marple was right there. She's a shrewd old bird. But I wish I knew who it was. He won't tell. If we only knew that. . . . Come on, Lake, let's have a thorough reconstruction of the scene in the Hall."

3

"That fixes it pretty well."

Inspector Curry was sitting at the piano. Sergeant Lake was in a chair by the window overlooking the lake.

Curry went on.

"If I'm half turned on the piano stool, watching the study door I can't see you."

Sergeant Lake rose softly and edged quietly through the door to the library.

"All this side of the room was dark. The only lights that were on were the ones beside the study door. No, Lake, I didn't see you go. Once in the library, you could go out through the other door to the corridor—two minutes to run along to the Oak Suite, shoot Gulbrandsen and come back through the library to your chair by the window.

"The women by the fire have their backs to you. Mrs. Serrocold was sitting *here*— on the right of the fireplace, near the study door. Everyone agrees she didn't move and she's the only one who's in the line of direct vision. Miss Marple was here. She was looking past Mrs. Serrocold to the study. Mrs. Strete was on the left of the fireplace—close to the door out of the Hall to the lobby, and it's a very dark corner. She *could* have gone and come back. Yes, it's possible."

Curry grinned suddenly.

"And I could go." He slipped off the music stool and sidled along the wall and out through the door. "The only person who might notice I wasn't still at the piano would be Gina Hudd. And you remember what Gina said: 'Stephen was at the piano to begin with. *I don't know where he was later.*'"

"So you think it's Stephen?"

"I don't know who it is," said Curry. "It wasn't Edgar Lawson or Lewis Serrocold or Mrs. Serrocold or Miss Jane Marple. But for the rest—" He sighed. "It's probably the American. Those fused lights were a bit too convenient—a coincidence. And yet, you know, I rather like the chap. Still, that isn't evidence."

He peered thoughtfully at some music on the side of the piano. "Hindemith? Who's he? Never heard of him. Shostakovitch! What names these people have." He got up and then looked down at the old-fashioned music stool. He lifted the top of it.

"Here's the old-fashioned stuff. Handel's Largo. Czerny's Exercises. Dates back to old Gulbrandsen, most of this: 'I know a lovely Garden'— Vicar's wife used to sing that when I was a boy—"

He stopped—the yellow pages of the song in his hand. Beneath them, reposing on Chopin's Preludes, was a small automatic pistol.

"Stephen Restarick," exclaimed Sergeant Lake joyfully.

"Now don't jump to conclusions," Inspector Curry warned him. "Ten to one that's what we're meant to think."

15

MISS MARPLE climbed the stairs and tapped on the door of Mrs. Serrocold's bedroom.

"May I come in, Carrie Louise?"

"Of course, Jane dear."

Carrie Louise was sitting in front of the dressing table, brushing her silvery hair. She turned her head over her shoulder.

"Is it the police? I'll be ready in a few minutes."

"Are you all right?"

"Yes, of course. Jolly insisted on my having my breakfast in bed. And Gina came into the room with it on tiptoe as though I might be at death's door! I don't think people realise that tragedies like Christian's death are much less shock to someone old. Because one knows by then how anything may happen—and how little anything really matters that happens in this world."

"Ye—es," said Miss Marple dubiously.

"Don't you feel the same, Jane? I should have thought you would."

Miss Marple said slowly:

"Christian was murdered."

"Yes . . . I see what you mean. You think that *does* matter?"

"Don't you?"

"Not to Christian," said Carrie Louise simply. "It matters, of course, to whoever murdered him."

"Have you any idea who murdered him?"

Mrs. Serrocold shook her head in a bewildered fashion.

"No, I've absolutely no idea. I can't even think of a reason. It must have been something to do with his being here before—just over a month ago. Because otherwise I don't think he would have come here suddenly again for no particular reason. Whatever it was must have started off then. I've thought and I've thought, but I can't remember anything unusual."

"Who was here in the house?"

"Oh! the same people who are here now—yes, Alex was done from London about then. And—oh yes, Ruth was here."

"Ruth?"

"Her usual flying visit."

"Ruth," said Miss Marple again. Her mind was active. Christian Gulbrandsen and Ruth? Ruth had come away worried and apprehensive, but had not known why. Something was wrong was all that Ruth could say. Christian Gulbrandsen had also been worried and apprehensive, but Christian Gulbrandsen had known or suspected something that Ruth did not. He had known or suspected that someone was trying to poison Carrie Louise. How had Christian Gulbrandsen come to entertain those suspicions? What had he seen or heard? Was it something that Ruth also had seen or heard but which she had failed to appreciate at its rightful significance? Miss Marple wished that she knew what it could possibly have been. Her own vague hunch that it (whatever it was) had to do with Edgar Lawson seemed unlikely since Ruth had not even mentioned him.

She sighed.

"You're all keeping something from me, aren't you?" asked Carrie Louise.

Miss Marple jumped a little as the quiet voice spoke.

"Why do you say that?"

"Because you are. Not Jolly. But everyone else. Even Lewis. He came in while I was having my breakfast, and he acted very oddly. He drank some of my coffee and even had a bit of toast and marmalade. That's so unlike him, because he always has tea and he doesn't like marmalade, so he must have been thinking of something else—and I suppose he must have forgotten to have his own breakfast. He does forget things like meals, and he looked so concerned and preoccupied."

"Murder—" began Miss Marple.

Carrie Louise said quickly:

"Oh I know. It's a terrible thing. I've never been mixed up in it before. You have, haven't you, Jane?"

"Well—yes, actually I have," Miss Marple admitted.

"So Ruth told me."

"Did she tell you that last time she was down here?" asked Miss Marple curiously.

"No, I don't think it was then. I can't really remember."

Carrie Louise spoke vaguely, almost absentmindedly.

"What are you thinking about, Carrie Louise?"

Mrs. Serrocold smiled and seemed to come back from a long way away.

"I was thinking of Gina," she said. "And of what you said about Stephen Restarick. Gina's a dear girl, you Know, and she does really love Wally. I'm sure she does."

Miss Marple said nothing.

"Girls like Gina like to kick up their heels a bit." Mrs. Serrocold spoke in an almost pleading voice. "They're young and they like to feel their power. It's natural, really. I know Wally Hudd isn't the sort of man we imagined Gina marrying. Normally she'd never have met him. But she did meet him, and fell in love with him—and presumably she knows her own business best."

"Probably she does," said Miss Marple.

"But it's so very important that Gina should be happy."

Miss Marple looked curiously at her friend.

"It's important, I suppose, that everyone should be happy."

"Oh yes. But Gina's a very special case. When we took her mother—when we took Pippa—we felt that it was an experiment that had simply got to succeed. You see, Pippa's mother—"

Carrie Louise paused.

Miss Marple said:

"Who was Pippa's mother?"

Carrie Louise said: "Eric and I agreed that we would never tell anybody that. She never knew herself."

"I'd like to know," said Miss Marple.

Mrs. Serrocold looked at her doubtfully.

"It isn't just curiosity," said Miss Marple. "I really—well—*need* to know. I can hold my tongue, you know."

"You could always keep a secret, Jane," said Carrie Louise with a reminiscent smile. "Dr. Galbraith—he's the Bishop of Cromer now—he knows. But no one else. Pippa's mother was Katherine Elsworth."

"Elsworth? Wasn't that the woman who administered arsenic to her husband? Rather a celebrated case."

"Yes."

"She was hanged?"

"Yes. But you know it's not at all sure that she did it. The husband was an arsenic eater—they didn't understand so much about those things then."

"She soaked flypapers."

"The maid's evidence, we always thought, was definitely malicious."

"And Pippa was her daughter?"

"Yes. Eric and I determined to give the child a fresh start in life—with love and care and all the things a child needs. We succeeded. Pippa was—herself. The sweetest happiest creature imaginable."

Miss Marple was silent a long time.

Carrie Louise turned away from the dressing table.

"I'm ready now. Perhaps you'll ask the Inspector or whatever he is to come up to my sitting room. He won't mind, I'm sure."

2

Inspector Curry did not mind. In fact he rather welcomed the chance of seeing Mrs. Serrocold on her own territory.

As he stood there waiting for her, he looked round him curiously. It was not his idea of what he termed to himself "a rich woman's boudoir."

It had an old-fashioned couch and some rather uncomfortable looking Victorian chairs with twisted woodwork backs. The chintzes were old and faded but of an attractive pattern displaying the Crystal Palace. It was one of the smaller rooms, though even then it was larger than the drawing room of most modern houses. But it had a cosy rather crowded appearance with its little tables, its bric-a-brac, and its photographs. Curry looked at an old snapshot of two little girls, one dark and lively, the other plain and staring out sulkily on the world from under a heavy fringe. He had seen that same expression that morning. "Pippa and Mildred" was written on the photograph. There was a photograph of Eric Gulbrandsen hanging on the wall, with a gold mount and a heavy ebony frame. Curry had just found a photograph of a good looking man with eyes crinkling with laughter, whom he presumed was John Restarick when the door opened and Mrs. Serrocold came in.

She wore black, a floating and diaphanous black. Her little pink and white face looked unusually small under its crown of silvery hair, and there was a frailness about her that caught sharply at Inspector Curry's heart. He understood at that moment a good deal that had perplexed him earlier in the morning. He understood why people were so anxious to spare Caroline Louise Serrocold everything that could be spared her.

And yet, he thought, she isn't the kind that would ever make a fuss. . . .

She greeted him, asked him to sit down, and took a chair near him. It was less he who put her at her ease than she who put him at his. He started to ask his questions and she answered them readily and without hesitation. The failure of the lights, the quarrel between Edgar Lawson and her husband, the shot they had heard. . . .

"It did not seem to you that the shot was in the house?"

"No, I thought it came from outside. I thought it might have been the backfire of a car."

"During the quarrel between your husband and this young fellow Lawson in the study, did you notice anybody leaving the Hall?"

"Wally had already gone to see about the lights. Miss Bellever went out shortly afterwards—to get something, but I can't remember what."

"Who else left the Hall?"

"Nobody, so far as I know."

"Would you know, Mrs. Serrocold?"

She reflected a moment.

"No, I don't think I should."

"You were completely absorbed in what you could hear going on in the study?"

"Yes."

"And you were apprehensive as to what might happen there?"

"No—no, I wouldn't say that. I didn't think anything would really happen."

"But Lawson had a revolver?"

"Yes."

"And was threatening your husband with it?"

"Yes. But he didn't mean it."

Inspector Curry felt his usual slight exasperation at this statement. So she was another of them!

"You can't possibly have been sure of that, Mrs. Serrocold."

"Well, but I was sure. In my own mind, I mean. What is it the young people say—putting on an act? That's what I felt it was. Edgar's only a boy. He was being melodramatic and silly and fancying himself as a bold desperate character. Seeing himself as the wronged hero in a romantic story. I was quite sure he would never fire that revolver."

"But he did fire it, Mrs. Serrocold."

Carrie Louise smiled.

"I expect it went off by accident."

Again exasperation mounted in Inspector Curry.

"It was not accident. Lawson fired that revolver twice—and fired it at your husband. The bullets only just missed him."

Carrie Louise looked startled and then grave.

"I can't really believe that. Oh yes—" she hurried on to forestall the Inspector's protest. "Of course I have to believe it if you tell me so. But I still feel there must be a simple explanation. Perhaps Dr. Maverick can explain it to me."

"Oh yes, Dr. Maverick will explain it all right," said Curry grimly. "Dr. Maverick can explain anything. I'm sure of that."

Unexpectedly Mrs. Serrocold said:

"I know that a lot of what we do here seems to you foolish and point-less, and psychiatrists can be very irritating sometimes. But we *do* achieve results, you know. We have our failures, but we have successes too. And what we try to do is *worth* doing. And though you probably won't believe it, Edgar is really devoted to my husband. He started this silly business about Lewis's being his father because he wants so much to have a father like Lewis. But what I can't understand is why he should suddenly get *violent*. He had been so very much better—really practically normal. Indeed he has always seemed normal to me."

The Inspector did not argue the point.

He said: "The revolver that Edgar Lawson had was one belonging to your granddaughter's husband. Presumably Lawson took it from Walter Hudd's room. Now tell me, have you ever seen *this* weapon before?"

On the palm of his hand he held out the small black automatic.

Carrie Louise looked at it.

"No, I don't think so."

"I found it in the piano stool. It has recently been fired. We haven't had time to check on it fully yet, but I should say that it is almost certainly the weapon with which Mr. Gulbrandsen was shot."

She frowned.

"And you found it in the piano stool?"

"Under some very old music. Music that I should say had not been played for years."

"Hidden, then?"

"Yes. You remember who was at the piano last night?"

"Stephen Restarick."

"He was playing?"

"Yes. Just softly. A funny melancholy little tune."

"When did he stop playing, Mrs. Serrocold?"

"When did he stop? I don't know."

"But he did stop? He didn't go on playing all through the quarrel?"

"No. The music just died down."

"Did he get up from the piano stool?"

"I don't know. I've no idea what he did until he came over to the study door to try and fit a key to it."

"Can you think of any reason why Stephen Restarick should shoot Mr. Gulbrandsen?"

"None whatever," she added thoughtfully: "I don't believe he did."

"Gulbrandsen might have found something discreditable about him."

"That seems to me very unlikely."

Inspector Curry had a wild wish to reply:

"Pigs may fly but they're very unlikely birds." It had been a saying of his grandmother's. Miss Marple, he thought, was sure to know it.

3

Carrie Louise came down the broad stairway and three people converged upon her from different directions, Gina from the long corridor, Miss Marple from the library, and Juliet Bellever from the Great Hall.

Gina spoke first.

"Darling!" she exclaimed passionately. "Are you all right? They haven't bullied you or given you third degree or anything?"

"Of course not, Gina. What odd ideas you have! Inspector Curry was charming and most considerate."

"So he ought to be," said Miss Bellever. "Now, Cara, I've got all your letters here and a parcel. I was going to bring them up to you."

"Bring them into the library," said Carrie Louise.

All four of them went into the library.

Carrie Louise sat down and began opening her letters. There were about twenty or thirty of them.

As she opened them, she handed them to Miss Bellever who sorted them into heaps, explaining to Miss Marple as she did so:

"Three main categories. One—from relations of the boys. Those I hand over to Dr. Maverick. Begging letters I deal with myself. And the rest are personal—and Cara gives me notes on how to deal with them."

The correspondence once disposed of, Mrs. Serrocold turned her attention to the parcel, cutting the string with scissors.

Out of the neat wrappings, there appeared an attractive box of chocolates tied up with a gold ribbon.

"Someone must think it's my birthday," said Mrs. Serrocold with a smile.

She slipped off the ribbon and opened the box. Inside was a visiting card. Carrie Louise looked at it with slight surprise. *"With love from Alex,"* she said. "How odd of him to send me a box of chocolates by post on the same day he was coming down here."

Uneasiness stirred in Miss Marple's mind.

She said quickly.

"Wait a minute, Carrie Louise. Don't eat one yet."

Mrs. Serrocold looked faintly surprised.

"I was going to hand them round."

"Well, don't. Wait while I ask— Is Alex about the house, do you know, Gina?"

Gina said quickly: "Alex was in the Hall just now, I think."

She went across, opened the door, and called him.

Alex Restarick appeared in the doorway a moment later.

"Madonna darling! So you're up. None the worse?"

He came across to Mrs. Serrocold and kissed her gently on both cheeks.

Miss Marple said:

"Carrie Louise wants to thank you for the chocolates."

Alex looked surprised.

"What chocolates?"

"These chocolates," said Carrie Louise.

"But I never sent you any chocolates, darling."

"The box has got your card in," said Miss Bellever.

Alex peered down.

"So it has. How odd. How very odd . . . I certainly didn't send them."

"What a very extraordinary thing," said Miss Bellever.

"They look absolutely scrumptious," said Gina, peering into the box. "Look, Grandam, there are your favourite Kirsch ones in the middle."

Miss Marple gently but firmly took the box away from her. Without a word she took it out of the room and went to find Lewis Serrocold. It took her some time because he had gone over to the College—she found him in Dr. Maverick's room there. She put the box on the table in front of him. He listened to her brief account of the circumstances. His face grew suddenly stern and hard.

Carefully, he and the doctor lifted out chocolate after chocolate and examined them.

"I think," said Dr. Maverick, "that these ones I have put aside have almost certainly been tampered with. You see the unevenness of the chocolate coating underneath? The next thing to do is to get them analysed."

"But it seems incredible," said Miss Marple. "Why, everyone in the house might have been poisoned!"

Lewis nodded. His face was still white and hard.

"Yes. There is a ruthlessness—a disregard—" he broke off. "Actually, I think all these particular chocolates are Kirsch flavouring. That is Caroline's favourite. So, you see, there is knowledge behind this."

Miss Marple said quietly:

"If it is as you suspect—if there is—*poison*—in these chocolates, then

I'm afraid Carrie Louise will have to know what is going on. She must be put upon her guard."

Lewis Serrocold said heavily:

"Yes. She will have to know that someone wants to kill her. I think that she will find it almost impossible to believe."

16

" 'ERE, MISS. It is true as there's an 'ideous poisoner at work?"

Gina pushed the hair back from her forehead, and jumped as the hoarse whisper reached her. There was paint on her cheek and paint on her slacks. She and her selected helpers had been busy on the backcloth of the Nile at Sunset for their next theatrical production.

It was one of these helpers who was now asking the question. Ernie, the boy who had given her such valuable lessons in the manipulations of locks. Ernie's fingers were equally dextrous at stage carpentry and he was one of the most enthusiastic theatrical assistants.

His eyes now were bright and beady with pleasurable anticipation.

"Where on earth did you get that idea?" asked Gina indignantly.

Ernie shut one eye.

"It's all round the dorms," he said. "But look 'ere, Miss, it wasn't one of *us*. Not a thing like that. And nobody wouldn't do a thing to Mrs. Serrocold. Even Jenkins wouldn't cosh *her*. 'Tisn't as though it was the old bitch. Wouldn't 'alf like to poison 'er, I wouldn't."

"Don't talk like that about Miss Bellever."

"Sorry, Miss. It slipped out. What poison was it, Miss? Strickline, was it? Makes you arch your back and die in agonies, that does. Or was it Prussian acid?"

"I don't know what you're talking about, Ernie."

Ernie winked again.

"Not 'alf you don't. Mr. Alex it was done it, so they say. Brought them chocs down from London. But that's a lie. Mr. Alex wouldn't do a thing like that, would he, Miss?"

"Of course he wouldn't," said Gina.

"Much more likely to be Mr. Birnbaum. When he's giving us P.T. he makes the most awful faces and Don and I think as he's batty."

"Just move that turpentine out of the way."

Ernie obeyed, murmuring to himself:

"Don't 'arf see life 'ere! Old Gulbrandsen done in yesterday and now a secret poisoner. D'you think it's the same person doing both? What ud you say, Miss, if I told you as I know oo it was done 'im in?"

"You can't possibly know anything about it."

"Coo, carn't I neither? Supposin' I was outside last night and saw something."

"How could you have been out? The College is locked up after roll call at seven."

"Roll call . . . I can get out whenever I likes, Miss. Locks don't mean nothing to me. Get out and walk around the grounds just for the fun of it, I do."

Gina said:

"I wish you'd stop telling lies, Ernie."

"Who's telling lies?"

"You are. You tell lies and you boast about things that you've never done at all."

"That's what you say, Miss. You wait till the coppers come round and arsk me all about what I saw last night."

"Well, what did you see?"

"Ah," said Ernie, "wouldn't you like to know?"

Gina made a rush at him and he beat a strategic retreat. Stephen came over from the other side of the theatre and joined Gina. They discussed various technical matters and then, side by side, they walked back towards the house.

"They all seem to know about Grandam and the chocs," said Gina. "The boys, I mean. How do they get to know?"

"Local grapevine of some kind."

"And they knew about Alex's card. Stephen, surely it was very stupid to put Alex's card in the box when he was actually coming down here."

"Yes, but who knew he was coming down here? He decided to come on the spur of the moment and sent a telegram. Probably the box was posted by then. And if he hadn't come down, putting his card in would have been quite a good idea. Because he does send Caroline chocolates sometimes."

He went on slowly:

"What I simply can't understand is—"

"Is why anyone should want to poison Grandam," Gina cut in. "I know. It's *inconceivable!* She's so adorable—and absolutely everyone *does* adore her."

Stephen did not answer. Gina looked at him sharply.

"I know what you're thinking, Steve!"

"I wonder."

"You're thinking that Wally—doesn't adore her. But Wally would never poison anyone. The idea's laughable."

"The loyal wife!"

"Don't say that in that sneering tone of voice."

"I didn't mean to sneer. I think you *are* loyal. I admire you for it. But darling Gina, you can't keep it up, you know."

"What do you mean, Steve?"

"You know quite well what I mean. You and Wally don't belong together. It's just one of those things that doesn't work. He knows it too. The split is going to come any day now. And you'll both be much happier when it has come."

Gina said:

"Don't be idiotic."

Stephen laughed.

"Come now, you can't pretend that you're suited to each other or that Wally's happy here."

"Oh, I don't know what's the matter with him," cried Gina. "He sulks the whole time. He hardly speaks. I—I don't know what to do about him. Why can't he enjoy himself here? We had such fun together once—everything was fun—and now he might be a different person. Why do people have to change so?"

"Do I change?"

"No, Steve darling. You're always Steve. Do you remember how I used to tag round after you in the holidays?"

"And what a nuisance I used to think you—that miserable little kid Gina. Well, the tables are turned now. You've got me where you want me, haven't you, Gina?"

Gina said quickly:

"Idiot." She went on hurriedly, "Do you think Ernie was lying? He was pretending he was roaming about in the fog last night, and hinting that he could tell things about the murder. Do you think that might be true?"

"True? Of course not. You know how he boasts. Anything to make himself important."

"Oh I know. I only wondered—"

They walked along side by side without speaking.

2

The setting sun illuminated the west façade of the house. Inspector Curry looked towards it.

"Is this about the place where you stopped your car last night?" he asked.

Alex Restarick stood back a little as though considering.

"Near enough," he said. "It's difficult to tell exactly because of the fog. Yes, I should say this was the place."

Inspector Curry stood looking round with an appraising eye.

The gravelled sweep of the drive swept round in a slow curve, and at this point, emerging from a screen of rhododendrons, the west façade of the house came suddenly into view with its terrace and yew hedges and steps leading down to the lawns. Thereafter the drive continued in its curving progress, sweeping through a belt of trees and round between the lake and the house until it ended in the big gravel sweep at the east side of the house.

"Dodgett," said Inspector Curry.

Police Constable Dodgett, who had been holding himself at the ready, started spasmodically into motion. He hurled himself across the intervening space of lawn in a diagonal line towards the house, reached the terrace, went in by the side door. A few moments later the curtains of one of the windows were violently agitated. Then Constable Dodgett reappeared out of the garden door, and ran back to rejoin them, breathing like a steam engine.

"Two minutes and forty-two seconds," said Inspector Curry, clicking the stop watch with which he had been timing him. "They don't take long, these things, do they?"

His tone was pleasantly conversational.

"I don't run as fast as your constable," said Alex. "I presume it *is* my supposed movements you have been timing?"

"I'm just pointing out that you had the opportunity to do murder. That's all, Mr. Restarick. I'm not making any accusations—as yet."

Alex Restarick said kindly to Constable Dodgett who was still panting:

"I can't run as fast as you can, but I believe I'm in better training."

"It's since 'aving the bronchitis last winter," said Dodgett.

Alex turned back to the Inspector.

"Seriously, though, in spite of trying to make me uncomfortable and observing my reactions—and you must remember that we artistic folk are oh! so sensitive, such tender plants!—" his voice took on a mocking note— "you can't really believe I had anything to do with all this? I'd hardly send a box of poisoned chocolates to Mrs. Serrocold and put my card inside, would I?"

"That might be what we are meant to think. There's such a thing as a double bluff, Mr. Restarick."

"Oh, I see. How ingenious you are. By the way, those chocolates *were* poisoned?"

"The six chocolates containing Kirsch flavouring in the top layer were poisoned, yes. They contained aconitine."

"Not one of my favourite poisons, Inspector. Personally, I have a weakness for curare."

"Curare has to be introduced into the bloodstream, Mr. Restarick, not into the stomach."

"How wonderfully knowledgeable the police force are," said Alex admiringly.

Inspector Curry cast a quiet sideways glance at the young man. He noted the slightly pointed ears, the unEnglish Mongolian type of face. The eyes that danced with mischievous mockery. It would have been hard at any time to know what Alex Restarick was thinking. A satyr—or did he mean a faun? An overfed faun, Inspector Curry thought suddenly, and somehow there was an unpleasantness about that idea.

A twister with brains—that's how he would sum up Alex Restarick. Cleverer than his brother. Mother had been a Russian or so he had heard. "Russians" to Inspector Curry were what "Bony" had been in the early days of the nineteenth century and what "the Huns" had been in the early twentieth century. Anything to do with Russia was bad in Inspector Curry's opinion, and if Alex Restarick had murdered Gulbrandsen he would be a very satisfactory criminal. But unfortunately Curry was by no means convinced that he had.

Constable Dodgett, having recovered his breath, now spoke.

"I moved the curtains as you told me, sir," he said. "And counted thirty. I noticed that the curtains have a hook torn off at the top. Means that there's a gap. You'd see the light in the room from outside."

Inspector Curry said to Alex:

"Did you notice light streaming out from that window last night?"

"I couldn't see the house at all because of the fog. I told you so."

"Fog's patchy, though. Sometimes it clears for a minute here and there."

"It never cleared so that I could see the house—the main part, that is. The gymnasium building close at hand loomed up out of the mist in a deliciously unsubstantial way. It gave a perfect illusion of dock warehouses. As I told you, I am putting on a Limehouse Ballet and—"

"You told me," agreed Inspector Curry.

"One gets in the habit, you know, of looking at things from the point of view of a stage set, rather than from the point of view of reality."

"I daresay. And yet a stage set's real enough, isn't it, Mr. Restarick?"

"I don't see exactly what you mean, Inspector."

"Well, it's made of real materials—canvas and wood and paint and cardboard. The illusion is in the eye of the beholder not in the set itself. That, as I say, is real enough, as real behind the scenes as it is in front."

Alex stared at him.

"Now that, you know, is a *very* penetrating remark, Inspector. It's given me an idea."

"For another ballet?"

"No, not for another ballet . . . Dear me, I wonder if we've all been rather stupid?"

3

The Inspector and Dodgett went back to the house across the lawn. (Looking for footprints, Alex said to himself. But here he was wrong. They had looked for footprints very early that morning and had been unsuccessful because it had rained heavily at 2 A.M.) Alex walked slowly up the drive, turning over in his mind the possibilities of his new idea.

He was diverted from this however by the sight of Gina walking on the path by the lake. The house was on a slight eminence and the ground sloped gently down from the front sweeps of gravel to the lake which was bordered by rhododendrons and other shrubs. Alex ran down the gravel and found Gina.

"If you could black out the absurd Victorian monstrosity," he said, screwing up his eyes, "this would make a very good Swan Lake, with you, Gina, as the Swan Maiden. You are more like the Snow Queen though, when I come to think of it. Ruthless, determined to have your own way, quite without pity or kindliness or the rudiments of compassion. You are very *very* feminine, Gina dear."

"How malicious you are, Alex dear!"

"Because I refuse to be taken in by you? You're very pleased with yourself, aren't you, Gina? You've got us all where you want us. Myself, Stephen, and that large simple husband of yours."

"You're talking nonsense."

"Oh no, I'm not. Stephen's in love with you, I'm in love with you, and Wally's desperately miserable. What more could a woman want?"

Gina looked at him and laughed.

Alex nodded his head vigorously.

"You have the rudiments of honesty, I'm glad to see. That's the Latin in you. You don't go to the trouble of pretending that you're not attractive to men—and that you're terribly sorry about it if they are attracted to you. You like having men in love with you, don't you, cruel Gina? Even miserable little Edgar Lawson!"

Gina looked at him steadily.

She said in a quiet serious tone:

"It doesn't last very long, you know. Women have a much worse time of it in the world than men do. They're more vulnerable. They have children, and they mind—terribly—about their children. As soon as they lose their looks, the men they love don't love them anymore. They're betrayed and deserted and pushed aside. I don't blame men. I'd be the same myself. I don't like people who are old or ugly or ill or who whine about their troubles or who are ridiculous like Edgar, strutting about and pretending he's important and worthwhile. You say I'm cruel? It's a cruel world! Sooner or later it will be cruel to *me!* But now I'm young and I'm nice looking and people find me attractive." Her teeth flashed out in her peculiar warm sunny smile. "Yes, I enjoy it, Alex. Why shouldn't I?"

"Why indeed?" said Alex. "What I want to know is what you are going to do about it. Are you going to marry Stephen or are you going to marry me?"

"I'm married to Wally."

"Temporarily. Every woman should make one mistake matrimonially —but there's no need to dwell on it. Having tried out the show in the provinces, the time has come to bring it to the West End."

"And you're the West End?"

"Indubitably."

"Do you really want to marry me? I can't imagine you married."

"I insist on marriage. *Affaires,* I always think, are so very old-fashioned. Difficulties with passports and hotels and all that. I shall *never* have a mistress unless I can't get her any other way!"

Gina's laugh rang out fresh and clear.

"You do amuse me, Alex."

"It is my principal asset. Stephen is much better looking than I am. He's extremely handsome and very intense which, of course, women adore. But intensity is fatiguing in the home. With me, Gina, you will find life entertaining."

"Aren't you going to say you love me madly?"

"However true that may be, I shall certainly not say it. It would be one up to you and one down to me if I did. No, all I am prepared to do is to make you a businesslike offer of marriage."

"I shall have to think about it," said Gina, smiling.

"Naturally. Besides, you've got to put Wally out of his misery first. I've a lot of sympathy with Wally. It must be absolute hell for him to be married to you and trailed along at your chariot wheels into this heavy family atmosphere of philanthropy."

"What a beast you are, Alex!"

"A perceptive beast."

"Sometimes," said Gina, "I don't think Wally cares for me one little bit. He just doesn't notice me any more."

"You've stirred him up with a stick and he doesn't respond? Most annoying."

Like a flash Gina swung her palm and delivered a ringing slap on Alex's smooth cheek.

"Touché!" cried Alex.

With a quick deft movement he gathered her into his arms and before she could resist, his lips fastened on hers in a long ardent kiss. She struggled a moment and then relaxed . . .

"Gina!"

They sprang apart. Mildred Strete, her face red, her lips quivering, glared at them balefully. For a moment the eagerness of her words choked their utterance.

"Disgusting . . . disgusting . . . you abandoned beastly girl . . . you're like your mother. . . . You're a bad lot . . . I always knew you were a bad lot . . . utterly depraved . . . and you're not only an adulteress—you're a murderess too. Oh yes, you are. I know what I know!"

"And what do you know? Don't be ridiculous, Aunt Mildred."

"I'm no aunt of yours, thank goodness. No blood relation to you. Why you don't even know who your mother was or where she came from! But you know well enough what my father was like and my mother. What sort of a child do you think they would adopt? A criminal's child or a prostitute's probably! That's the sort of people they were. They ought to have remembered that bad blood will tell. Though I daresay that it's the Italian in you that makes you turn to *poison.*"

"How dare you say that?"

"I shall say what I like. You can't deny now, can you, that somebody tried to poison Mother? And who's the most likely person to do that? Who comes into an enormous fortune if Mother dies? You do, Gina, and you may be sure that the police have not overlooked that fact."

Still trembling, Mildred moved rapidly away.

"Pathological," said Alex. "Definitely pathological. Really *most* interesting. It makes one wonder about the late Canon Strete . . . religious scruples, perhaps? . . . Or would you say impotent?"

"Don't be disgusting, Alex. Oh I hate her, I hate her, I hate her."

Gina clenched her hands and shook with fury.

"Lucky you hadn't got a knife in your stocking," said Alex. "If you had, dear Mrs. Strete might have known something about murder from the point of view of the victim. Calm down, Gina. Don't look so melodramatic and like Italian Opera."

"How dare she say I tried to poison Grandam?"

"Well, darling, *somebody* tried to poison her. And from the point of view of motive you're well in the picture, aren't you?"

"Alex!" Gina stared at him, dismayed. "Do the police think so?"

"It's extremely difficult to know what the police think. . . . They keep their own counsel remarkably well. They're by no means fools, you know. That reminds me—"

"Where are you going?"

"To work out an idea of mine."

17

"You SAY somebody has been trying to *poison* me?"

Carrie Louise's voice held bewilderment and disbelief.

"You know," she said, "I can't really believe it . . ."

She waited a few moments, her eyes half closed.

Lewis said gently, "I wish I could have spared you this, dearest."

Almost absently she stretched out a hand to him and he took it.

Miss Marple, sitting close by, shook her head sympathetically.

Carrie Louise opened her eyes.

"Is it really true, Jane?" she asked.

"I'm afraid so, my dear."

"Then everything—" Carrie Louise broke off.

She went on:

"I've always thought I knew what was real and what wasn't. . . . *This* doesn't seem real—but it is . . . So I may be wrong everywhere . . . But who could want to do such a thing to me? Nobody in this house could want to—*kill* me?"

Her voice still held incredulity.

"That's what I would have thought," said Lewis. "I was wrong."

"And Christian knew about it? That explains it."

"Explains what?" asked Lewis.

"His manner," said Carrie Louise. "It was very odd, you know. Not at all his usual self. He seemed—upset about me—and as though he was wanting to say something to me—and then not saying it. And he asked me if my heart was strong. And if I'd been well lately. Trying to hint to me, perhaps. But why not say something straight out? It's so much simpler just to say straight out."

"He didn't want to—cause you pain, Caroline."

"Pain? But why— Oh I see . . ." Her eyes widened. "So *that's* what you believe. But you're wrong, Lewis, quite wrong. I can assure you of that."

Her husband avoided her eyes.

"I'm sorry," said Mrs. Serrocold after a moment or two. "But I can't believe anything of what has happened lately is true. Edgar shooting at you. Gina and Stephen. That ridiculous box of chocolates. It just isn't *true.*"

Nobody spoke.

Caroline Louise Serrocold sighed.

"I suppose," she said, "that I must have lived outside reality for a long time. . . . Please, both of you, I think I would like to be alone. . . . I've got to try and understand . . ."

2

Miss Marple came down the stairs and into the Great Hall to find Alex Restarick standing near the large arched entrance door with his hand flung out in a somewhat flamboyant gesture.

"Come in, come in," said Alex happily and as though he were the owner of the Great Hall. "I'm just thinking about last night."

Lewis Serrocold who had followed Miss Marple down from Carrie Louise's sitting room, crossed the Great Hall to his study and went in and shut the door.

"Are you trying to reconstruct the crime?" asked Miss Marple with subdued eagerness.

"Eh?" Alex looked at her with a frown. Then his brow cleared.

"Oh *that,*" he said. "Not exactly. I was looking at the whole thing from an entirely different point of view. I was thinking of this place in the terms of the theatre. Not reality, but artificiality! Just come over here. Think of it in the terms of a stage set. Lighting, entrances, exits. Dramatis Personae. Noises off. All very interesting. Not all my own idea. The Inspector gave it to me. I think he's rather a cruel man. He did his best to frighten me this morning."

"And did he frighten you?"

"I'm not sure."

Alex described the Inspector's experiment and the timing of the performance of the puffing Constable Dodgett.

"Time," he said, "is so very misleading. One thinks things take such a long time, but really, of course, they don't."

"No," said Miss Marple.

Representing the audience, she moved to a different position. The stage set now consisted of a vast tapestry covered wall going up to dimness, with a grand piano up L. and a window and window seat up R. Very near the window seat was the door into the library. The piano stool was only about eight feet from the door into the square lobby which led to the corridor. Two very convenient exits! The audience, of course, had an excellent view of both of them. . . .

But last night, there had been no audience. Nobody, that is to say, had been facing the stage set that Miss Marple was now facing. The audience, last night, had been sitting with their backs to that particular stage.

How long, Miss Marple wondered, would it have taken to slip out of the room, run along the corridor, shoot Gulbrandsen and come back? Not nearly so long as one would think. Measured in minutes and seconds a very short time indeed. . . .

What had Carrie Louise meant when she had said to her husband: "So *that's* what you believe—but you're wrong, Lewis!"

"I must say that that was a very penetrating remark of the Inspector's," Alex's voice cut in on her meditations. "About a stage set being real. Made of wood and cardboard and stuck together with glue and as real on the unpainted as on the painted side. 'The illusion,' he pointed out, 'is in the eyes of the audience.' "

"Like conjurers," Miss Marple murmured vaguely. *"They do it with mirrors* is, I believe, the slang phrase."

Stephen Restarick came in, slightly out of breath.

"Hullo, Alex," he said. "That little rat, Ernie Gregg—I don't know if you remember him?"

"The one who played Feste when you did *Twelfth Night?* Quite a bit of talent there I thought."

"Yes, he's got talent of a sort. Very good with his hands too. Does a lot of our carpentry. However, that's neither here nor there. He's been boasting to Gina that he gets out at night and wanders about the grounds. Says he was wandering round last night and boasts he saw something."

Alex spun round.

"Saw what?"

"Says he's not going to tell! Actually I'm pretty certain he's only trying to show off and get into the limelight. He's an awful liar, but I thought perhaps he ought to be questioned."

Alex said sharply: "I should leave him for a bit. Don't let him think we're too interested."

"Perhaps—yes I think you may be right there. This evening, perhaps."

Stephen went on into the library.

Miss Marple, moving gently round the Hall in her character of mobile audience, collided with Alex Restarick as he stepped back suddenly.

Miss Marple said, "I'm so sorry."

Alex frowned at her, said in an absent sort of way,

"I beg your pardon," and then added in a surprised voice: "Oh, it's *you.*"

It seemed to Miss Marple an odd remark for someone with whom she had been conversing for some considerable time.

"I was thinking of something else," said Alex Restarick. "That boy Ernie—" He made vague motions with both hands.

Then, with a sudden change of manner, he crossed the Hall and went through the library door shutting it behind him.

The murmur of voices came from behind the closed door, but Miss Marple hardly noticed them. She was uninterested in the versatile Ernie and what he had seen or pretended to see. She had a shrewd suspicion that Ernie had seen nothing at all. She did not believe for a moment that on a cold raw foggy night like last night, Ernie would have troubled to use his picklocking activities and wander about in the Park. In all probability he never *had* got out at night. Boasting, that was all it had been.

"Like Johnnie Backhouse," thought Miss Marple who always had a good storehouse of parallels to draw upon selected from inhabitants of St. Mary Mead.

"I seen you last night," had been Johnnie Backhouse's unpleasant taunt to all he thought it might affect.

It had been a surprisingly successful remark. So many people, Miss Marple reflected, have been in places where they are anxious not to be seen!

She dismissed Johnnie from her mind and concentrated on a vague something which Alex's account of Inspector Curry's remarks had stirred to life. Those remarks had given Alex an idea. She was not sure that they had not given her an idea, too. The same idea? Or a different one?

She stood where Alex Restarick had stood. She thought to herself, "This is not a real hall. This is only cardboard and canvas and wood. This is a stage scene . . ." Scrappy phrases flashed across her mind. "Illusion—" "In the eyes of the audience." *"They do it with mirrors . . ."* Bowls of goldfish . . . yards of coloured ribbon . . . vanishing ladies . . . All the panoply and misdirection of the conjurer's art . . .

Something stirred in her consciousness—a picture—something that Alex had said . . . something that he had described to her . . . Constable Dodgett puffing and panting . . . Panting . . . Something shifted in her mind—came into sudden focus . . .

"Why of *course!*" said Miss Marple. *"That must be it . . ."*

18

"OH WALLY, how you startled me!"

Gina, emerging from the shadows by the theatre, jumped back a little, as the figure of Wally Hudd materialised out of the gloom. It was not yet quite dark, but had that eerie half light when objects lose their reality and take on the fantastic shapes of nightmare.

"What are you doing down here? You never come near the theatre as a rule."

"Maybe I was looking for you, Gina. It's usually the best place to find you, isn't it?"

Wally's soft, faintly drawling voice held no special insinuation and yet Gina flinched a little.

"It's a job and I'm keen on it. I like the atmosphere of paint and canvas, and back stage generally."

"Yes. It means a lot to you. I've seen that. Tell me, Gina, how long do you think it will be before this business is all cleared up?"

"The inquest's tomorrow. It will just be adjourned for a fortnight or something like that. At least, that's what Inspector Curry gave us to understand."

"A fortnight," said Wally thoughtfully. "I see. Say three weeks, perhaps. And after that—we're free. I'm going back to the States then."

"Oh! but I can't rush off like that," cried Gina. "I couldn't leave Grandam. And we've got these two new productions we're working on—"

"I didn't say we. I said I was going."

Gina stopped and looked up at her husband. Something in the effect of the shadows made him seem very big. A big quiet figure—and in some way, or so it seemed to her, faintly menacing . . . Standing over her. Threatening—what?

"Do you mean"—she hesitated—"you don't want me to come?"

"Why, no—I didn't say that."

"You don't care if I come or not? Is that it?"

She was suddenly angry.

"See here, Gina. This is where we've got to have a showdown. We didn't know much about each other when we got married—not much about each other's backgrounds, not much about the other one's folks.

We thought it didn't matter. We thought nothing mattered except having a swell time together. Well, stage one is over. Your folks didn't—and don't—think much of me. Maybe they're right. I'm not their kind. But if you think I'm staying on here, kicking my heels, and doing odd jobs in what I consider is just a crazy setup—well, think again! I want to live in my own country, doing the kind of job I want to do, and can do. My idea of a wife is the kind of wife who used to go along with the old pioneers, ready for anything, hardship, unfamiliar country, danger, strange surroundings . . . Perhaps that's too much to ask of you, but it's that or nothing! Maybe I hustled you into marriage. If so, you'd better get free of me and start again. It's up to you. If you prefer one of these arty boys—it's your life and you've got to choose. But I'm going home."

"I think you're an absolute *pig,"* said Gina. "I'm enjoying myself here."

"Is that so? Well, I'm not. You even enjoy murder, I suppose?"

Gina drew in her breath sharply.

"That's a cruel wicked thing to say. I was very fond of Uncle Christian. And don't you realise that someone has been quietly poisoning Grandam for months? It's horrible!"

"I told you I didn't like it here. I don't like the kind of things that go on. I'm quitting."

"If you're allowed to! Don't you realise you'll probably be arrested for Uncle Christian's murder? I hate the way Inspector Curry looks at you. He's just like a cat watching a mouse with a nasty sharp-clawed paw all ready to pounce. Just because you were out of the Hall fixing those lights, and because you're not English, I'm sure they'll go fastening it on you."

"They'll need some evidence first."

Gina wailed:

"I'm frightened for you, Wally. I've been frightened all along."

"No good being scared. I tell you they've got nothing on me!"

They walked in silence towards the house.

Gina said:

"I don't believe you really want me to come back to America with you. . . ."

Walter Hudd did not answer.

Gina turned on him and stamped her foot.

"I hate you. I hate you. You are horrible—a beast—a cruel unfeeling beast. After all I've tried to do for you! You want to be rid of me. You don't care if you never see me again. Well, I don't care if *I* never see *you* again! *I* was a stupid little fool ever to marry you and I shall get a divorce as soon as possible and I shall marry Stephen or Alexis and be much happier than I ever could be with you. And I hope you go back to the States and marry some horrible girl who makes you really miserable!"

"Fine!" said Wally. "Now we know where we are!"

2

Miss Marple saw Gina and Wally go into the house together.

She was standing at the spot where Inspector Curry had made his experiment with Constable Dodgett earlier in the afternoon.

Miss Bellever's voice behind her made her jump.

"You'll get a chill, Miss Marple, standing about like that after the sun's gone down."

Miss Marple fell meekly into step with her and they walked briskly through the house.

"I was thinking about conjuring tricks," said Miss Marple. "So difficult when you're watching them to see how they're done, and yet, once they are explained, so absurdly simple. (Although, even now, I can't imagine how conjurers produce bowls of goldfish!) Did you ever see the Lady who is Sawn in Half—*such* a thrilling trick. It fascinated me when I was eleven years old, I remember. And I never *could* think how it was done. But the other day there was an article in some paper giving the whole thing away. I don't think a newspaper should do that, do you? It seems it's not one girl—but *two*. The head of the one and the feet of the other. You think it's one girl and it's really two—and the other way round would work equally well, wouldn't it?"

Miss Bellever looked at her with faint surprise. Miss Marple was not often so fluffy and incoherent as this. "It's been too much for the old lady, all this," she thought.

"When you only look at one side of a thing, you only see one side," continued Miss Marple. "But everything fits in perfectly well if you can only make up your mind what is reality and what is illusion." She added abruptly, "Is Carrie Louise—all right?"

"Yes," said Miss Bellever. "She's all right. But it must have been a shock, you know—finding out that someone wanted to kill her. I mean particularly a shock to *her*, because she doesn't understand violence."

"Carrie Louise understands some things that we don't," said Miss Marple thoughtfully. "She always has."

"I know what you mean—but she doesn't live in the real world."

"Doesn't she?"

Miss Bellever looked at her in surprise.

"There never was a more unworldly person than Cara—"

"You don't think that perhaps—" Miss Marple broke off, as Edgar Lawson passed them, swinging along at a great pace. He gave a kind of shamefaced nod, but averted his face as he passed.

"I've remembered now who he reminds me of," said Miss Marple. "It came to me suddenly just a few moments ago. He reminds me of a young man called Leonard Wylie. His father was a dentist but he got old and blind and his hand used to shake, and so people preferred to go to the son. But the old man was very miserable about it, and moped, said he was no good for anything any more, and Leonard, who was very soft-hearted and rather foolish, began to pretend he drank more than he should. He always smelt of whisky and he used to sham being rather fuddled when his patients came. His idea was that they'd go back to the father again and say the younger man was no good."

"And did they?"

"Of course not," said Miss Marple. "What happened was what anybody with any sense could have told him would happen! The patients went to Mr. Reilly, the rival dentist. So many people with good hearts have no sense. Besides, Leonard Wylie was so unconvincing. . . . His idea of drunkenness wasn't in the least like real drunkenness, and he overdid the whisky—spilling it on his clothes, you know, to a perfectly impossible extent."

They went into the house by the side door.

19

INSIDE THE house, they found the family assembled in the library. Lewis was walking up and down and there was an air of general tension in the atmosphere.

"Is anything the matter?" asked Miss Bellever.

Lewis said shortly: "Ernie Gregg is missing from roll call tonight."

"Has he run away?"

"We don't know. Maverick and some of the staff are searching the grounds. If we cannot find him we must communicate with the police."

"Grandam!" Gina ran over to Carrie Louise, startled by the whiteness of her face. "You look ill."

"I am unhappy. The poor boy . . ."

Lewis said: "I was going to question him this evening as to whether he had seen anything noteworthy last night. I have the offer of a good post for him and I thought that after discussing that, I would bring up the other topic. Now—" he broke off.

Miss Marple murmured softly:

"Foolish boy . . . Poor foolish boy . . ."

She shook her head, and Mrs. Serrocold said gently:

"So *you* think so too, Jane . . . ?"

Stephen Restarick came in. He said, "I missed you at the theatre, Gina. I thought you said you would—Hullo, what's up?"

Lewis repeated his information, and as he finished speaking Dr. Maverick came in with a fair-haired boy with pink cheeks and a suspiciously angelic expression. Miss Marple remembered his being at dinner on the night she had arrived at Stonygates.

"I've brought Arthur Jenkins along," said Dr. Maverick. "He seems to have been the last person to talk to Ernie."

"Now, Arthur," said Lewis Serrocold, "please help us if you can. Where has Ernie gone? Is this just a prank?"

"I dunno, sir. Straight, I don't. Didn't say nothing to me, he didn't. All full of the play at the theatre he was, that's all. Said as how he'd had a smashing idea for the scenery, what Mrs. Hudd and Mr. Stephen thought was first class."

"There's another thing, Arthur. Ernie claims he was prowling about the grounds after lock-up last night. Was that true?"

" 'Course it ain't. Just boasting, that's all. Perishing liar, Ernie. *He* never got out at night. Used to boast he could, but he wasn't that good with locks! He couldn't do anything with a lock as *was* a lock. Anyway 'e was in larst night, that I do know."

"You're not saying that just to satisfy us, Arthur?"

"Cross my heart," said Arthur virtuously.

Lewis did not look quite satisfied.

"Listen," said Dr. Maverick. "What's that?"

A murmur of voices was approaching. The door was flung open and looking very pale and ill, the spectacled Mr. Birnbaum staggered in.

He gasped out: "We've found him—*them*. It's horrible . . ."

He sank down on a chair and mopped his forehead.

Mildred Strete said sharply:

"What do you mean—found—*them?*"

Birnbaum was shaking all over.

"Down at the theatre," he said. "Their heads crushed in—the big counterweight must have fallen on them. Alexis Restarick and that boy Ernie Gregg. They're both dead. . . ."

20

"I've Brought you a cup of strong soup, Carrie Louise," said Miss Marple. "Now please drink it."

Mrs. Serrocold sat up in the big carved oak four poster bed. She looked very small and childlike. Her cheeks had lost their rose pink flush, and her eyes had a curiously absent look. She took the soup obediently from Miss Marple. As she sipped it, Miss Marple sat down in a chair beside the bed.

"First, Christian," said Carrie Louise, "and now Alex—and poor sharp silly little Ernie. Did he really—know anything?"

"I don't think so," said Miss Marple. "He was just telling lies—making himself important by hinting that he had seen or knew something. The tragedy is that somebody believed his lies . . ."

Carrie Louise shivered. Her eyes went back to their faraway look.

"We meant to do so much for these boys . . . We did do something. Some of them have done wonderfully well. Several of them are in really responsible positions. A few slid back—that can't be helped. Modern civilised conditions are so complex—too complex for some simple and undeveloped natures. You know Lewis's great scheme? He always felt that transportation was a thing that had saved many a potential criminal in the past. They were shipped overseas—and they made new lives in simpler surroundings. He wants to start a modern scheme on that basis. To buy up a great tract of territory—or a group of islands. Finance it for some years, make it a cooperative self supporting community—with everyone having a stake in it. But cut off so that the early temptation to go back to cities and the bad old ways can be neutralised. It's his dream. But it will take a lot of money, of course, and there aren't many philanthropists with vision now. We want another Eric. Eric would have been enthusiastic."

Miss Marple picked up a little pair of scissors and looked at them curiously.

"What an odd pair of scissors," she said. "They've got two finger holes on one side and one on the other."

Carrie Louise's eyes came back from that frightening far distance.

"Alex gave them to me this morning," she said. "They're supposed to make it easier to cut your right hand nails. Dear boy, he was so enthusiastic. He made me try them then and there."

"And I suppose he gathered up the nail clippings and took them tidily away," said Miss Marple.

"Yes," said Carrie Louise. "He—" she broke off. "Why did you say that?"

"I was thinking about Alex. He had brains. Yes, he had brains."

"You mean—that's why he died?"

"I think so—yes."

"He and Ernie—it doesn't bear thinking about. When do they think it happened?"

"Late this evening. Between six and seven o'clock probably . . ."

"After they'd knocked off work for the day?"

"Yes."

Gina had been down there that evening—and Wally Hudd. Stephen, too, said he had been down to look for Gina . . .

But as far as that went, anybody could have—

Miss Marple's train of thought was interrupted.

Carrie Louise said quietly and unexpectedly:

"How much do you know, Jane?"

Miss Marple looked up sharply. The eyes of the two women met.

Miss Marple said slowly: "If I was quite sure . . ."

"I think you are sure, Jane."

Jane Marple said slowly, "What do you want me to do?"

Carrie leaned back against her pillows.

"It is in your hands, Jane— You'll do what you think right."

She closed her eyes.

"Tomorrow"—Miss Marple hesitated—"I shall have to try and talk to Inspector Curry—if he'll listen. . . ."

21

INSPECTOR CURRY said rather impatiently:

"Yes, Miss Marple?"

"Could we, do you think, go into the Great Hall?"

Inspector Curry looked faintly surprised.

"Is that your idea of privacy? Surely in here—" He looked round the study.

"It's not privacy I'm thinking of so much. It's something I want to show you. Something Alex Restarick made me see."

Inspector Curry, stifling a sigh, got up and followed Miss Marple.

"Somebody has been talking to you?" he suggested hopefully.

"No," said Miss Marple. "It's not a question of what people have said. It's really a question of conjuring tricks. They do it with mirrors, you know—that sort of thing—if you understand me."

Inspector Curry did not understand. He stared and wondered if Miss Marple was quite right in the head.

Miss Marple took up her stand and beckoned the Inspector to stand beside her.

"I want you to think of this place as a stage set, Inspector. As it was on the night Christian Gulbrandsen was killed. You're here in the audience looking at the people on the stage. Mrs. Serrocold and myself and Mrs. Strete, and Gina and Stephen—and just like on the stage there are entrances and exits and the characters go out to different places. Only you don't think when you're in the audience where they are *really* going to. They go out 'to the front door' or 'to the kitchen' and when the door opens you see a little bit of painted backcloth. But *really* of course they go out to the wings—or the back of the stage with carpenters and electricians, and other characters waiting to come on—they go out—to a different world."

"I don't quite see, Miss Marple—"

"Oh, I know—I daresay it sounds very silly—but if you think of this as a play and the scene is 'the Great Hall of Stonygates'—what exactly is *behind* the scene?—I mean—what is back stage? The terrace—isn't it?— the terrace *and a lot of windows opening onto it.*

"And that, you see, is how the conjuring trick was done. It was the trick of the Lady Sawn in Half that made me think of it."

"The Lady Sawn in Half?" Inspector Curry was now quite sure that Miss Marple was a mental case.

"A most thrilling conjuring trick. You must have seen it—only not really one girl but two girls. The head of one and the feet of the other. It looks like one person and is really two. And so I thought it could just as well be *the other way about. Two* people could be really one person."

"Two people really one?" Inspector Curry looked desperate.

"Yes. Not for long. How long did your constable take in the Park to run to this house and back? Two minutes and forty-five seconds, wasn't it? This would be less than that. Well under two minutes."

"What was under two minutes?"

"The conjuring trick. The trick when it wasn't two people but one person. In there—in the study. We're only looking at the visible part of the stage. Behind the scenes there is the terrace and a *row of windows.* So easy when there are two people in the study to open the study window, get out, run along the terrace (those footsteps Alex heard) in at the side door, shoot Christian Gulbrandsen and run back, and during that time, the other person in the study does both voices so that we're all quite sure there are *two* people in there. And so there were most of the time, but not for that little period of under—two minutes."

Inspector Curry found his breath and his voice.

"Do you mean that it was *Edgar Lawson* who ran along the terrace and shot Gulbrandsen? Edgar Lawson who poisoned Mrs. Serrocold?"

"But you see, Inspector, *no one has been poisoning Mrs. Serrocold at all.* That's where the misdirection comes in. Someone very cleverly used the fact that Mrs. Serrocold's sufferings from arthritis were not unlike the symptoms of arsenical poisoning. It's the old conjurer's trick of forcing a card on you. Quite easy to add arsenic to a bottle of tonic—quite easy to add a few lines to a typewritten letter. But the *real* reason for Mr. Gulbrandsen's coming here was the most likely reason—something to do with the Gulbrandsen Trust. Money, in fact. Suppose that there had been embezzlement—embezzlement on a very big scale—you see where that points? To just one person—"

"Lewis Serrocold?"

"Lewis Serrocold . . ."

22

letter from Gina Hudd to her aunt Mrs. Van Rydock.

—and so you see, darling Aunt Ruth, the whole thing has been just like a nightmare—especially the end of it. I've told you all about this funny young man Edgar Lawson. He always was a complete rabbit—and when the Inspector began questioning him and breaking him down, he lost his nerve completely and scuttled like a rabbit. Just lost his nerve and ran— literally ran. Jumped out of the window and round the house and down the drive and then there was a policeman coming to head him off, and he swerved and ran full tilt for the Lake. He leaped into a rotten old punt that's mouldered there for years and pushed off. Quite a mad senseless thing to do, of course, but as I say he was just a panic stricken rabbit. And then Lewis gave a great shout and said "That punt's rotten" and raced off to the Lake too. The punt went down and there was Edgar struggling in the water. He couldn't swim. Lewis jumped in and swam out to him. He got to him but they were both in difficulty because they'd got among the reeds. One of the Inspector's men went in with a rope round him but he got entangled too and they had to pull him in. Aunt Mildred said "They'll drown—they'll drown—they'll both drown . . ." in a silly sort of way, and Grandam just said "Yes." I can't describe to you just how she made that one word sound. Just "yes" and it went through you like—like a sword.

Am I being just silly and melodramatic? I suppose I am. But it did sound like that . . .

And then—when it was all over, and they'd got them out and tried artificial respiration (but it was no good), the Inspector came to us and said to Grandam:

"I'm afraid, Mrs. Serrocold, there's no hope."

Grandam said very quietly:

"Thank you, Inspector."

Then she looked at us all. Me longing to help but not knowing how, and Jolly, looking grim and tender and ready to minister as usual, and Stephen stretching out his hands, and funny old Miss Marple looking so sad, and tired, and even Wally looking upset. All so fond of her and wanting to do something.

But Grandam just said "Mildred." And Aunt Mildred said "Mother." And they went away together into the house, Grandam looking so small and frail and leaning on Aunt Mildred. I never realised, until then, how fond of each other they were. It didn't show much, you know.

Gina paused and sucked the end of her fountain pen. She resumed:

About me and Wally—we're coming back to the States as soon as we can. . . .

23

"WHAT MADE you guess, Jane?"

Miss Marple took her time about replying. She looked thoughtfully at the other two—Carrie Louise thinner and frailer and yet curiously untouched—and the old man with the sweet smile and the thick white hair. Dr. Galbraith, Bishop of Cromer.

The Bishop took Carrie Louise's hand in his.

"This has been a great sorrow to you, my poor child, and a great shock."

"A sorrow, yes, but not really a shock."

"No," said Miss Marple. "That's what I discovered, you know. Everyone kept saying how Carrie Louise lived in another world from this and was out of touch with reality. But actually, Carrie Louise, it was reality you were in touch with, and not the illusion. You are never deceived by illusion like most of us are. When I suddenly realised that, I saw that I must go by what *you* thought and felt. You were quite sure that no one would try to poison you, you couldn't believe it—and you were quite right *not* to believe it, because it wasn't so! You never believed that Edgar would harm Lewis—and again you were right. He never *would* have harmed Lewis. You were sure that Gina did not love anyone but her husband—and that again was quite true.

"So therefore, if I was to go by you, all the things that *seemed* to be true were only illusions. Illusions created for a definite purpose—in the same ways that conjurers create illusions, to deceive an audience. We were the audience.

"Alex Restarick got an inkling of the truth first because he had the chance of seeing things from a different angle—from the outside angle. He was with the Inspector in the drive and he looked at the house and realised the possibilities of the windows—and he remembered the sound of running feet he had heard that night, and then the timing of the constable showed him what a very short time things take to what we should imagine they would take. The constable panted a lot, and later, thinking of a puffing constable, I remembered that Lewis Serrocold was out of breath that night when he opened the study door. He'd just been running hard, you see . . .

"But it was Edgar Lawson that was the pivot of it all to me. There was always something wrong to me about Edgar Lawson. All the things he said and did were exactly right for what he was supposed to be, but he himself wasn't right. Because he was actually a normal young man playing the part of a schizophrenic—and he was always, as it were, a little larger than life. He was always theatrical.

"It must have all been very carefully planned and thought out. Lewis must have realised on the occasion of Christian's last visit that something had aroused his suspicions. And he knew Christian well enough to know that if he suspected he would not rest until he had satisfied himself that his suspicions were either justified or unfounded."

Carrie Louise stirred.

"Yes," she said. "Christian was like that. Slow and painstaking, but actually very shrewd. I don't know what it was aroused his suspicions but he started investigating—and he found out the truth."

The Bishop said: "I blame myself for not having been a more conscientious trustee."

"It was never expected of you to understand finance," said Carrie Louise. "That was originally Mr. Gilfoy's province. Then, when he died, Lewis's great experience put him in what amounted to complete control. And that, of course, was what went to his head."

The pink colour came up in her cheeks.

"Lewis was a great man," she said. "A man of great vision, and a passionate believer in what could be accomplished—with money. He didn't want it for himself—or at least not in the greedy vulgar sense—he did want the power of it—he wanted the power to do great good with it—"

"He wanted," said the Bishop, "to be God." His voice was suddenly stern. "He forgot that man is only the humble instrument of God's will."

"And so he embezzled the Trust funds?" said Miss Marple.

Dr. Galbraith hesitated.

"It wasn't only that . . ."

"Tell her," said Carrie Louise. "She is my oldest friend."

The Bishop said:

"Lewis Serrocold was what one might call a financial wizard. In his years of highly technical accountancy, he had amused himself by working out various methods of swindling which were practically foolproof. This had been merely an Academic study, but when he once began to envisage the possibilities that a vast sum of money could encompass, he put these methods into practice. You see, he had at his disposal some first class material. Amongst the boys who passed through here, he chose out a small select band. They were boys whose bent was naturally criminal, who loved excitement and who had a very high order of intelligence. We've not got nearly to the bottom of it all, but it seems clear that this esoteric circle was secret and specially trained and by and by were placed in key positions, where, by carrying out Lewis's directions, books were falsified in such a way that large sums of money were converted without any suspicion being aroused. I gather that the operations and the ramifications are so complicated that it will be months before the auditors can unravel it all. But the net result seems to be that under various names and banking accounts and companies Lewis Serrocold would have been able to dispose of a colossal sum with which he intended to establish an overseas colony for a cooperative experiment in which juvenile delinquents should eventually own this territory and administer it. It may have been a fantastic dream—"

"It was a dream that might have come true," said Carrie Louise.

"Yes, it might have come true. But the means Lewis Serrocold adopted were dishonest means, and Christian Gulbrandsen discovered that. He was very upset, particularly by the realisation of what the discovery and the probable prosecution of Lewis would mean to you, Carrie Louise."

"That's why he asked me if my heart was strong, and seemed so worried about my health," said Carrie Louise. "I couldn't understand it."

"Then Lewis Serrocold arrived back from the North and Christian met him outside the house and told him that he knew what was going on. Lewis took it calmly, I think. Both men agreed they must do all they could to spare you. Christian said he would write to me and ask me to come here, as a co-trustee, to discuss the position."

"But of course," said Miss Marple. "Lewis Serrocold had already prepared for this emergency. It was all planned. He had brought the young man who was to play the part of Edgar Lawson to the house. There was a real Edgar Lawson—of course—in case the police looked up his record. This false Edgar knew exactly what he had to do—act the part of a schizophrenic victim of persecution—and give Lewis Serrocold an alibi for a few vital minutes.

"The next step had been thought out too. Lewis's story that you, Carrie Louise, were being slowly poisoned—when one actually came to think of it there was only Lewis's story of what Christian had told *him*—that, and a few lines added on the typewriter whilst he was waiting for the police. It was easy to add arsenic to the tonic. No danger for you there—since he was on the spot to prevent you drinking it. The chocolates were just an added touch—and of course the original chocolates weren't poisoned—only those he substituted before turning them over to Inspector Curry."

"And Alex guessed," said Carrie Louise.

"Yes—that's why he collected your nail parings. They would show if arsenic actually had been administered over a long period."

"Poor Alex—poor Ernie."

There was a moment's silence as the other two thought of Christian Gulbrandsen, of Alexis Restarick, and of the boy Ernie—and of how quickly the act of murder could distort and deform.

"But surely," said the Bishop, "Lewis was taking a big risk in persuading Edgar to be his accomplice—even if he had some hold over him—"

Carrie shook her head.

"It wasn't exactly a hold over him. Edgar was devoted to Lewis."

"Yes," said Miss Marple. "Like Leonard Wylie and his father. I wonder perhaps if—"

She paused delicately.

"You saw the likeness, I suppose?" said Carrie Louise.

"So you knew that all along?"

"I guessed. I knew Lewis had once had a short infatuation for an actress, before he met me. He told me about it. It wasn't serious, she was a golddigging type of woman and she didn't care for him, but I've no doubt at all that Edgar was actually Lewis's son. . . ."

"Yes," said Miss Marple. "That explains everything . . ."

"And he gave his life for him in the end," said Carrie Louise. She looked pleadingly at the Bishop. "He did, you know."

There was a silence and then Carrie Louise said:

"I'm glad it ended that way . . . with his life given in the hope of saving the boy . . . People who can be very good can be very bad, too. I always knew that was true about Lewis. . . . But—he loved me very much—and I loved him."

"Did you—ever suspect him?" asked Miss Marple.

"No," said Carrie Louise. "Because I was puzzled by the poisoning. I knew Lewis would never poison me and yet that letter of Christian's said definitely that someone *was* poisoning me—so I thought that everything I thought I knew about people must be wrong. . . ."

Miss Marple said: "But when Alex and Ernie were found killed. You suspected then?"

"Yes," said Carrie Louise. "Because I didn't think anyone else but Lewis would have dared. And I began to be afraid of what he might do next . . ."

She shivered slightly.

"I admired Lewis. I admired his—what shall I call it—his goodness? But I do see that if you're—good, you have to be humble as well."

Dr. Galbraith said gently:

"That, Carrie Louise, is what I have always admired in you—your humility."

The lovely blue eyes opened wide in surprise.

"But *I'm* not clever—and not particularly good. I can only admire goodness in other people."

"Dear Carrie Louise," said Miss Marple.

Epilogue

"I THINK Grandam will be quite all right with Aunt Mildred," said Gina. "Aunt Mildred seems much nicer now—not so peculiar, if you know what I mean?"

"I know what you mean," said Miss Marple.

"So Wally and I will go back to the States in a fortnight's time."

Gina cast a look sideways at her husband.

"I shall forget all about Stonygates and Italy and all my girlish past and become a hundred percent American. Our son will be always addressed as Junior. I can't say fairer than that, can I, Wally?"

"You certainly cannot, Kate," said Miss Marple.

Wally, smiling indulgently at an old lady who got names wrong, corrected her gently:

"Gina, not Kate."

But Gina laughed.

"She knows what she's saying! You see—she'll call *you* Petruchio in a moment!"

"I just think," said Miss Marple to Walter, "that you have acted very wisely, my boy."

"She thinks you're just the right husband for me," said Gina.

Miss Marple looked from one to the other. It was very nice, she thought, to see two young people so much in love, and Walter Hudd was completely transformed from the sulky young man she had first encountered, into a good-humoured smiling giant. . . .

"You two remind me," she said, "of—"

Gina rushed forward and placed a hand firmly over Miss Marple's mouth.

"No, darling," she exclaimed. "Don't say it. I'm suspicious of these village parallels. They've always got a sting in the tail. You really are a wicked old woman, you know."

Her eyes went misty.

"When I think of you, and Aunt Ruth and Grandam all being young together . . . How I wonder what you were all like! I can't imagine it somehow. . . ."

"I don't suppose you can," said Miss Marple. "It was all a long time ago. . . ."